WINGS OF FIRE

Also Edited by Jonathan Strahan

Best Short Novels (2004 through 2007)
Fantasy: The Very Best of 2005
Science Fiction: The Very Best of 2005
The Best Science Fiction and Fantasy of the Year: Volumes 1 – 4
Eclipse One: New Science Fiction and Fantasy
Eclipse Two: New Science Fiction and Fantasy
Eclipse Three: New Science Fiction and Fantasy
The Starry Rift: Tales of New Tomorrows
Engineering Infinity (forthcoming)
Life on Mars: Tales of New Tomorrows (forthcoming)
Under My Hat: Tales from the Cauldron (forthcoming)
Godlike Machines (forthcoming)

With Lou Anders
Swords and Dark Magic: The New Sword and Sorcery (forthcoming)

With Charles N. Brown
The Locus Awards: Thirty Years of the Best in Fantasy and Science Fiction
Fritz Leiber: Selected Stories

With Jeremy G. Byrne
The Year's Best Australian Science Fiction and Fantasy: Volume 1
The Year's Best Australian Science Fiction and Fantasy: Volume 2
Eidolon 1

With Terry Dowling
The Jack Vance Treasury
The Jack Vance Reader
Wild Thyme, Green Magic
Hard Luck Diggings: The Early Jack Vance

With Gardner Dozois
The New Space Opera
The New Space Opera 2

With Karen Haber
Science Fiction: Best of 2003
Science Fiction: Best of 2004
Fantasy: Best of 2004

WINGS OF FIRE

Edited by
Jonathan Strahan
and Marianne S. Jablon

NIGHT SHADE BOOKS
SAN FRANCISCO

First Edition

Printed in Canada

ISBN: 978-1-59780-187-4

Night Shade Books
Please visit us on the web at
http://www.nightshadebooks.com

Dedication

On the afternoon of August 2, 2008 over too much drink and too many laughs, this book and several others were inspired by Jeremy Lassen and the late Charles N. Brown. This book is dedicated to those two friends and to the memory of that long, fine afternoon.

Acknowledgments

This book grew out of a conversation with the late Charles N. Brown and Jeremy Lassen of Night Shade Books, and we would like to thank them both for their involvement in the genesis this book. We'd also like to acknowledge the efforts of Howard Morhaim and Katie Menick of the Howard Morhaim Literary Agency; Jason Williams, Ross E. Lockhart and everyone at Night Shade Books (the best posse ever!); Todd Lockwood, who provided an incredible piece of cover art; Robert Silverberg, who went well above and beyond the call of duty; and Peter S. Beagle, Kathleen Bellamy, Holly Black, Ginjer Buchanan, Connor Cochran, Vaughne Hansen, David G. Hartwell, John Helfers, Margo Lanagan, Todd McCaffrey, Kay McCauley, Garth Nix, Diana Tyler, Anna J. Webman, and Dave Wix, each of whom went above and beyond the call of duty in some way while we were compiling this book. Our sincere thanks to you all.

We would also like to thank the following people who made story recommendations for the book through the Wings of Fire database: John Joseph Adams, Richard J. Arndt, Ron Brinkmann, David Cake, John Harmon, Nik Hawkins, Rich Horton, David Barr Kirtley, Susan Loyal, Simon Petrie, Tansy Rayner Roberts, Paul Strain, Charles A. Tan, Jason Tyler, Jason M. Waltz, Desmond Warzel, Tehani Wessely, and the members of the Fictionmags mailing list.

CONTENTS

INTRODUCTION

Quick. What does a dragon look like? Think about it for a moment. Picture it in your mind. Imagine it as a real three-dimensional creature. We suspect that if you asked almost any reader, and certainly any reader of fantastic or speculative fiction, they would come up with *something*. It might be large and scaly, fiercesome and fiery, wispy and windswept, or even, oddly, small and cute, but that reader would know the answer to the question you were asking. He or she would know *what* a dragon is, what it is supposed to *look like*, and what it is supposed to be able to *do*. Depending on whether that reader came from a European background or an Oriental one, the dragon would be either large, bat-winged, with a four legs and a snake-like body cover in scales, or it would be more lizard-like, possibly wouldn't fly at all, and would be strongly associated with water.

And yet, there is no such thing as a dragon, is there? How did a creature that is no more substantial than a pixie or a pouka become more familiar to us than a platypus or a potoroo? There are reports of "dragons" in as diverse texts as *The Iliad* and the *King James Bible*, Marco Polo mentioned encountering them on his visits to China, and dragons appear in differing forms in myth, legends and historical reports throughout Europe and Asia.

Often these reports were because witnesses misunderstood the evidence they encountered. There's at least one report, for example, that the bones of a dragon had been discovered in Wucheng, Sichuan, China in 300 BC. Later analysis found them to be dinosaur remains. In fact, although the notion has been discredited, it has even been suggested that the widespread depiction of dragons is connected to some kind of unconscious inherited memory of dinosaurs.

The late Avram Davidson in his fine "Adventure in Unhistory" article "An Abundance of Dragons" suggests many more rational, and some simply more attractive, explanations for why dragons are so ubiquitous. Personally we're greatly attracted to his idea that the airborne Oriental dragons associated with rain and storms are simply based on lightning seen during storms. It seems elegant and appropriate, which is almost as important as the truth, where dragons are concerned.

Modern dragons, the dragons which appear in *Wings of Fire*, are sometimes

I

elegant, sometimes fierce, but always captivating. The first dragon Jonathan recalls encountering was in the pages of J.R.R. Tolkien's *The Hobbit*. Smaug, fierce and terrible, was the archetypal Western dragon, using his strength to protect his enormous hoard, the one weakness that would ultimately lead to his destruction. He was followed soon after—Jonathan was a precocious reader—by Anne McCaffrey's intelligent, telepathic firebreathers from Pern and Ursula K. Le Guin's beautiful and wise dragons from Earthsea. There have been many, many others. Wise dragons, cruel dragons, funny dragons, cozy dragons, enormous dragons, and tiny dragons. Dragons as a metaphor for the devil and temptation, and dragons as faithful friends and true allies.

There's no end, it seems to what a dragon can be, and we had that on our collective editorial mind when we sat down to collect the stories that make up *Wings of Fire*. We had a fairly simple brief from our publisher. Collect dragon stories and make them the best dragon stories we could find. We expanded that slightly, deciding that we wouldn't attempt to define what a dragon was beyond that it should be real within the confines of the story (at least most of the time) and that it should be described as a dragon. We knew we wanted to focus on modern fantasy, but wanted to be open to stories from any era and any genre. We also considered whether we should focus on lesser known tales, and avoid those that had been widely collected in previous volumes. After much discussion we decided that it was more important to compile a book filled with the best and most widely loved stories that we could find, even if there was a risk that they might be happily familiar to some of our readers. By way of compensation for that, we also invited two writers to contribute original stories for the book. In the end Holly Black and Margo Lanagan both delivered fine stories that stand with the best dragon tales that we could find.

In the end we have the twenty-seven stories collected here. There are famous dragons from Earthsea and Pern, wise dragons, wicked dragons, dragons as large as mountain ranges and dragons that can fit on a bookshelf. They all have one thing in common, though. They're magical. One dictionary defines as dragon as being "a fabulous monster variously represented as a huge, winged reptile, often spouting fire." The late Ogden Nash famously said that "When there are monsters there are miracles." We think that's what you'll find in the pages to follow: monsters and miracles.

Jonathan Strahan & Marianne S. Jablon
Perth, Western Australia
March 2010

STABLE OF DRAGONS

Peter S. Beagle

Peter S. Beagle was born in 1939 in New York City. A poem he wrote in his senior year of high school won him a scholarship to the University of Pittsburgh, where he earned a creative writing degree and made his first professional sale. His first novel, *A Fine and Private Place*, was published when he was nineteen. It was followed by non-fiction travelogue *I See By My Outfit* in 1965 and by his best known work, modern fantasy classic *The Last Unicorn*, in 1968. Beagle's other books include novels *The Folk of the Air*, *The Innkeeper's Song* and *Tamsin*, and a number of story collections, non-fiction books, screenplays and teleplays. His two most recent story collections are *We Never Talk about My Brother* and *Mirror Kingdoms: The Best of Peter S. Beagle*. His writing career spans fifty years, the last few of which have seen a great number of remarkable short stories, including "Two Hearts," winner of the both the Hugo and Nebula awards. He has also received two Mythopoeic awards as well as Locus, WSFA Small Press and Grand Prix de l'Imaginaire awards for his work.

I keep nine dragons in an old cow barn,
And sometimes I go down to look at them.
I didn't build the barn—I bought it
From a little old lady from Pasadena,
Who was arrested, the last I heard,
For selling the North Star
To a blind man.
    I bred the dragons.
I fed them on sorrowful meat and marmalade
And lighter fluid and an occasional postadolescent
Chicken. And then I built a house
Far away from the stable, because things burn down
Where dragons are.
    Outside the barn
Are fallen birds, their wings scorched

To fluff. The earth is livid, broken veined and rashed,
Pimpled with crimson ash—and dragon droppings,
Big enough to fertilize the whole frigid world.
Within are dragons.

    The roof beams are low.
They are crowded and it makes them short-tempered.
They smell of marshes and the lowland sea,
Starfish and seaweed and smashed clams dying in the sun.
They have small ears and their eyes are octagonal;
Their teeth are urine-yellow as contempt, and the hairs of their
    manes
Are like chains.

    The barn is lanced
With the raucous fire of their laughter, for they do
Breathe fire. Or perhaps the fire breathes them.
Dragon-scented fire it is, and it casts their shadows
On the mud-plastered walls.

    The males are coin scaled and sluggish.
Their wings are short and weak, useless
As an idea to a general. They cannot fly.
They will not walk. Therefore they lie amid applauding ashes
And breathe irrelevant damnation.

    But the females!
They are the purple of outdoor claustrophobia,
And they move like dusk. They have winter-colored wings,
As wide as cathedral doors. They pace the floors
Of their stalls, and their claws make an impatient sound,
As if they were scratching at the earth
To be let in.

    It is a waking sound.
I hear it in my high bed at night, and I cannot sleep
Until they do. And they never sleep
Unless they are satisfied. And they are never all satisfied
At once. There is always someone awake.
When I come in, their heads turn on their crested necks,
And they look at me out of their stained-glass eyes.
They know my name.

    I have mated with them.
I'm not the first. I never was an innovator. Knights used to do it.
They killed them later, when the angled eyes were dark with sleep,
And the knights were ashamed. So they killed them
And some were made saints for it. But I think
They were a little lonely in bed with their wives
For a while.

I have embraced dragons in my time.
I have held my mouth on white-toothed fire, and been drawn
Down the whirlpool gullet that seared me to wakefulness.
I have felt claws sunk in my back,
Straining me against silver-dollar scales, and heard a strange heart
Exploding in my ears like a drunken grandfather clock.
And I have left my seed to care for itself
In a new and bitter cave.
    Then I have crawled away
And lain in the fields, my flaking skin crackling like wrapping
 paper, reddening the well-meaning air
With my blood. And from the stable
Through the scarred, shut door, there comes no sound
Of querulous claws.
    A dragon is sleeping.
I think that I shall have a son someday.
He will be handsome, with sharp teeth.

THE RULE OF NAMES
Ursula K. Le Guin

Ursula K. Le Guin is one of the most important and respected writers in the history of science fiction. Born in 1929, she graduated from Columbia University in 1951 and married historian Alfred L. Kroeber in 1953. Her first work appeared in the early 1960s and was followed by numerous novels, short story collections, poetry collections, books for children, essays, books in translation, and anthologies. She is the author of the classic Earthsea series of fantasy novels and stories, and the Hainish series of science fiction novels and stories, including landmark novels *The Left Hand of Darkness* and *The Dispossessed*. Her twenty-one novels, eleven volumes of short stories, three collections of essays, twelve books for children, six volumes of poetry and four of translation have been recognised with the Hugo, Nebula, World Fantasy, Theodore Sturgeon Memorial, Tiptree, Locus, Ditmar, Endeavour, Prometheus, Rhysling, Gandalf, Jupiter and SFRA Pilgrim Awards. Le Guin is an SF Hall of Fame Living Inductee, a recipient of the World Fantasy Award for Lifetime Achievement, and is a recipient of the PEN/Malamud Award for Short Fiction. Seemingly unaware that she's supposed to be entering the later stages of her career and an appropriately respectable dotage, Le Guin has published a remarkable series of novels and stories in the past five years, most recently including the YA Western Shore trilogy and historical novel, *Lavinia*.

Mr. Underhill came out from under his hill, smiling and breathing hard. Each breath shot out of his nostrils as a double puff of steam, snow-white in the morning sunshine. Mr. Underhill looked up at the bright December sky and smiled wider than ever, showing snow-white teeth. Then he went down to the village.

"Morning, Mr. Underhill," said the villagers as he passed them in the narrow street between houses with conical, overhanging roofs like the fat red caps of toadstools. "Morning, morning!" he replied to each. (It was of course bad luck to wish anyone a *good* morning; a simple statement of the time of day was quite enough, in a place so permeated with Influences as Sattins Island, where a careless adjective might change the weather for a week.) All of them spoke to him, some with affection, some with affectionate disdain. He was all the little island had in the way of a wizard, and so deserved respect—but how could you respect a little fat man of fifty who waddled along with his toes turned in, breathing steam and smiling? He was no great shakes as a workman either. His fireworks were fairly elaborate but his elixirs were weak. Warts he charmed off frequently reappeared after three days; tomatoes he enchanted grew no bigger than cantaloupes; and those rare times when a strange ship stopped at Sattins Harbor, Mr. Underhill always stayed under his hill—for fear, he explained, of the evil eye. He was, in other words, a wizard the way wall-eyed Gan was a carpenter: by default. The villagers made do with badly hung doors and inefficient spells, for this generation, and relieved their annoyance by treating Mr. Underhill quite familiarly, as a mere fellow-villager. They even asked him to dinner. Once he asked some of them to dinner, and served a splendid repast, with silver, crystal, damask, roast goose, sparkling Andrades '639, and plum pudding with hard sauce; but he was so nervous all through the meal that it took the joy out of it, and besides, everybody was hungry again half an hour afterwards. He did not like anyone to visit his cave, not even the anteroom, beyond which in fact nobody had ever got. When he saw people approaching the hill he always came trotting to meet them. "Let's sit out here under the pine trees!" he would say, smiling and waving towards the fir-grove, or if it was raining, "Let's go and have a drink at the inn, eh?" though everybody knew he drank nothing stronger than well-water.

Some of the village children, teased by that locked cave, poked and pried and made raids while Mr. Underhill was away; but the small door that led into the inner chamber was spell-shut, and it seemed for once to be an effective spell. Once a couple of boys, thinking the wizard was over on the West Shore curing Mrs. Ruuna's sick donkey, brought a crowbar and a hatchet up there, but at the first whack of the hatchet on the door there came a roar of wrath from inside, and a cloud of purple steam. Mr. Underhill had got home early. The boys fled. He did not come out, and the boys came to no harm, though they said you couldn't believe what a huge hooting howling hissing horrible bellow that little fat man could make unless you'd heard it.

His business in town this day was three dozen fresh eggs and a pound of liver; also a stop at Seacaptain Fogeno's cottage to renew the seeing-charm on the old man's eyes (quite useless when applied to a case of detached retina, but Mr. Underhill kept trying), and finally a chat with old Goody Guld the concertina-maker's widow. Mr. Underhill's friends were mostly old people. He was timid with the strong young men of the village, and the girls were shy of him. "He makes me nervous, he smiles so much," they all said, pouting, twisting silky ringlets round a finger. "Nervous" was a newfangled word, and their mothers all replied grimly, "Nervous my foot, silliness is the word for it. Mr. Underhill is a very respectable wizard!"

After leaving Goody Guld, Mr. Underhill passed by the school, which was being held this day out on the common. Since no one on Sattins Island was literate, there were no books to learn to read from and no desks to carve initials on and no blackboards to erase, and in fact no schoolhouse. On rainy days the children met in the loft of the Communal Barn, and got hay in their pants; on sunny days the schoolteacher, Palani, took them anywhere she felt like. Today, surrounded by thirty interested children under twelve and forty uninterested sheep under five, she was teaching an important item on the curriculum: the Rules of Names. Mr. Underhill, smiling shyly, paused to listen and watch. Palani, a plump, pretty girl of twenty, made a charming picture there in the wintry sunlight, sheep and children around her, a leafless oak above her, and behind her the dunes and sea and clear, pale sky. She spoke earnestly, her face flushed pink by wind and words. "Now you know the Rules of Names already, children. There are two, and they're the same on every island in the world. What's one of them?"

"It ain't polite to ask anybody what his name is," shouted a fat, quick boy, interrupted by a little girl shrieking, "You can't never tell your own name to nobody my ma says!"

"Yes, Suba. Yes, Popi dear, don't screech. That's right. You never ask anybody his name. You never tell your own. Now think about that a minute and then tell me why we call our wizard Mr. Underhill." She smiled across the curly heads and the woolly backs at Mr. Underhill, who beamed, and nervously clutched his sack of eggs.

"'Cause he lives under a hill!" said half the children.

"But is it his truename?"

"No!" said the fat boy, echoed by little Popi shrieking, "No!"

"How do you know it's not?"

"'Cause he came here all alone and so there wasn't anybody knew his truename so they could not tell us, and *he* couldn't—"

"Very good, Suba. Popi, don't shout. That's right. Even a wizard can't tell his truename. When you children are through school and go through the Passage, you'll leave your child-names behind and keep only your truenames, which you must never ask for and never give away. Why is that the rule?"

The children were silent. The sheep bleated gently. Mr. Underhill answered the question: "Because the name is the thing," he said in his shy, soft, husky voice, "and the truename is the true thing. To speak the name is to control the thing. Am I right, Schoolmistress?"

She smiled and curtseyed, evidently a little embarrassed by his participation. And he trotted off towards his hill, clutching the eggs to his bosom. Somehow the minute spent watching Palani and the children had made him very hungry. He locked his inner door behind him with a hasty incantation, but there must have been a leak or two in the spell, for soon the bare anteroom of the cave was rich with the smell of frying eggs and sizzling liver.

The wind that day was light and fresh out of the west, and on it at noon a little boat came skimming the bright waves into Sattins harbour. Even as it rounded the point a sharp-eyed boy spotted it, and knowing, like every child on the island, every sail and spar of the forty boats of the fishing fleet, he ran down the street calling out, "A foreign boat, a foreign boat!" Very seldom was the lonely isle visited by a boat from some equally lonely isle of the East Reach, or an adventurous trader from the Archipelago. By the time the boat was at the pier half the village was there to greet it, and fishermen were following it homewards, and cowherds and clamdiggers and herb-hunters were puffing up and down all the rocky hills, heading towards the harbour.

But Mr. Underhill's door stayed shut.

There was only one man aboard the boat. Old Seacaptain Fogeno, when they told him that, drew down a bristle of white brows over his unseeing eyes. "There's only one kind of man," he said, "that sails the Outer Reach alone. A wizard, or a warlock, or a Mage…"

So the villagers were breathless hoping to see for once in their lives a Mage, one of the mighty White Magicians of the rich, towered, crowded inner islands of the Archipelago. They were disappointed, for the voyager was quite young, a handsome black-bearded fellow who hailed them cheerfully from his boat, and leaped ashore like any sailor glad to have made port. He introduced himself at once as a sea-pedlar. But when they told Seacaptain Fogeno that he carried an oaken walking-stick around with him, the old man nodded. "Two wizards in one town," he said. "Bad!" And his mouth snapped shut like an old carp's.

As the stranger could not give them his name, they gave him one right away: Blackbeard. And they gave him plenty of attention. He had a small mixed cargo of cloth and sandals and *piswi* feathers for trimming cloaks and cheap incense and levity stones and fine herbs and great glass beads from Venway—the usual pedlar's lot. Everyone on Sattins Island came to look, to chat with the voyager, and perhaps to buy something—"Just to remember him by!" cackled Goody Guld, who like all the women and girls of the village was smitten with Blackbeard's bold good looks. All the boys hung round him too, to hear him tell of his voyages to far, strange islands of the Reach or describe the great rich islands of the Archipelago, the Inner Lanes, the roadsteads white with ships, and the golden roofs of Havnor. The men willingly listened to his tales; but some of them wondered why a trader should sail alone, and kept their eyes thoughtfully upon his oaken staff.

But all this time Mr. Underhill stayed under his hill.

"This is the first island I've ever seen that had no wizard," said Blackbeard one evening to Goody Guld, who had invited him and her nephew and Palani in for a cup of rushwash tea. "What do you do when you get a toothache, or the cow goes dry?"

"Why, we've got Mr. Underhill!" said the old woman.

"For what that's worth," muttered her nephew Birt, and then blushed purple and spilled his tea. Birt was a fisherman, a large, brave, wordless young man. He loved the schoolmistress, but the nearest he had come to telling her of his love was to give baskets of fresh mackerel to her father's cook.

"Oh, you do have a wizard?" Blackbeard asked. "Is he invisible?"

"No, he's just very shy," said Palani. "You've only been here a week, you know, and we see so few strangers here…" She also blushed a little, but did not spill her tea.

Blackbeard smiled at her. "He's a good Sattinsman, then, eh?"

"No," said Goody Guld, "no more than you are. Another cup, nevvy? Keep it in the cup this time. No, my dear, he came in a little bit of a boat, four years ago was it? just a day after the end of the shad run, I recall, for they was taking up the nets over in East Creek, and Pondi Cowherd broke his leg that very morning—five years ago it must be. No, four. No, five it is, 'twas the year the garlic didn't sprout. So he sails in on a bit of a sloop loaded full up with great chests and boxes and says to Seacaptain Fogeno, who wasn't blind then, though old enough goodness knows to be blind twice over, "I hear tell," he says, "you've got no wizard nor warlock at all, might you be wanting one?"—"Indeed, if the magic's white!" says the Captain, and before you could say cuttlefish Mr. Underhill had settled down in the cave under the hill and was charming the mange off Goody Beltow's cat. Though the fur grew in grey, and 'twas an orange cat. Queer-looking thing it was after that. It died last winter in the cold spell. Goody Beltow took on so at that cat's death, poor thing, worse than when her man was drowned on the Long Banks, the year of the long herring-runs, when nevvy Birt here was but a babe in petticoats." Here Birt spilled his tea again, and Blackbeard grinned, but Goody Guld proceeded undismayed, and talked on till nightfall.

Next day Blackbeard was down at the pier, seeing after the sprung board in his boat which he seemed to take a long time fixing, and as usual drawing the taciturn Sattinsmen into talk. "Now which of these is your wizard's craft?" he asked. "Or has he got one of those the Mages fold up into a walnut shell when they're not using it?"

"Nay," said a stolid fisherman. "She's oop in his cave, under hill."

"He carried the boat he came in up to his cave?"

"Aye. Clear oop. I helped. Heavier as lead she was. Full oop with great boxes, and they full oop with books o' spells, he says. Heavier as lead she was." And the solid fisherman turned his back, sighing stolidly. Goody Guld's nephew, mending a net nearby, looked up from his work and asked with equal stolidity, "Would ye like to meet Mr. Underhill, maybe?"

Blackbeard returned Birt's look. Clever black eyes met candid blue ones for a long moment; then Blackbeard smiled and said, "Yes. Will you take me up to the hill, Birt?"

"Aye, when I'm done with this," said the fisherman. And when the net was mended, he and the Archipelagan set off up the village street towards the high green hill above it. But as they crossed the common Blackbeard said, "Hold on a while, friend Birt. I have a tale to tell you, before we meet your wizard."

"Tell away," says Birt, sitting down in the shade of a live-oak.

"It's a story that started a hundred years ago, and isn't finished yet—though it soon will be, very soon… In the very heart of the Archipelago, where the islands crowd thick as flies on honey, there's a little isle called Pendor. The sealords of Pendor were mighty men, in the old days of war before the League. Loot and ransom and tribute came pouring into Pendor, and they gathered a great treasure there, long ago. Then from somewhere away out in the West Reach, where dragons breed on the lava isles, came one day a very mighty dragon. Not one of those overgrown lizards most of you Outer Reach folk call dragons, but a big, black, winged, wise, cunning monster, full of strength and subtlety, and like all dragons loving gold and precious stones above all things. He killed the Sealord and his soldiers, and the people of Pendor fled in their ships by night. They all fled away and left the dragon coiled up in Pendor Towers. And there he stayed for a hundred years, dragging his scaly belly over the emeralds and sapphires and coins of gold, coming forth only once in a year or two when he must eat. He'd raid nearby islands for his food. You know what dragons eat?"

Birt nodded and said in a whisper, "Maidens."

"Right," said Blackbeard. "Well, that couldn't be endured forever, nor the thought of him sitting on all that treasure. So after the League grew strong, and the Archipelago wasn't so busy with wars and piracy, it was decided to attack Pendor, drive out the dragon, and get the gold and jewels for the treasury of the League. They're forever wanting money, the League is. So a huge fleet gathered from fifty islands, and seven Mages stood in the prows of the seven strongest ships, and they sailed towards Pendor…They got there. They landed. Nothing stirred. The houses all stood empty, the dishes on the tables full of a hundred years' dust. The bones of the old Sealord and his men lay about in the castle courts and on the stairs. And the Tower rooms reeked of dragon. But there was no dragon. And no treasure, not a diamond the size of a poppy seed, not a single silver bead… Knowing that he couldn't stand up to seven Mages, the dragon had skipped out. They tracked him, and found he'd flown to a deserted island up north called Udrath; they followed his trail there, and what did they find? Bones again. His bones—the dragon's. But no treasure. A wizard, some unknown wizard from somewhere, must have met him singlehanded, and defeated him—and then made off with the treasure, right under the League's nose!"

The fisherman listened, attentive and expressionless.

"Now that must have been a powerful wizard and a clever one, first to kill a dragon, and second to get off without leaving a trace. The lords and Mages of the Archipelago couldn't track him at all, neither where he'd come from nor where he'd made off to. They were about to give up. That was last spring; I'd been off on a three-year voyage up in the North Reach, and got back about that time. And they asked me to help them find the unknown wizard. That was clever of them. Because I'm not only a wizard myself, as I think some of the oafs here have guessed, but I am also a descendant of the Lords of Pendor. That treasure is mine. It's mine, and knows that it's mine. Those fools of the League couldn't find it, because it's not theirs. It belongs to the House of Pendor, and the great emerald, the star of the hoard, Inalkil the Greenstone, knows its master. Behold!" Blackbeard raised his oaken staff and cried aloud, "Inalkil!" The tip of the staff began to glow green, a fiery green radiance, a dazzling haze the color of April grass, and at the same moment the staff tipped in the wizard's hand, leaning, slanting till it pointed straight at the side of the hill above them.

"It wasn't so bright a glow, far away in Havnor," Blackbeard murmured, "but the staff pointed true. Inalkil answered when I called. The jewel knows its master. And I know the thief, and I shall conquer him. He's a mighty wizard, who could overcome a dragon. But I am mightier. Do you want to know why, oaf? Because I know his name!"

As Blackbeard's tone got more arrogant, Birt had looked duller and duller, blanker and blanker; but at this he gave a twitch, shut his mouth, and stared at the Archipelagan. "How did you... learn it?" he asked very slowly.

Blackbeard grinned, and did not answer.

"Black magic?"

"How else?"

Birt looked pale, and said nothing.

"I am the Sealord of Pendor, oaf, and I will have the gold my fathers won, and the jewels my mothers wore, and the Greenstone! For they are mine—Now, you can tell your village boobies the whole story after I have defeated this wizard and gone. Wait here. Or you can come and watch, if you're not afraid. You'll never get the chance again to see a great wizard in all his power." Blackbeard turned, and without a backward glance strode off up the hill towards the entrance to the cave.

Very slowly, Birt followed. A good distance from the cave he stopped, sat down under a hawthorn tree, and watched. The Archipelagan had stopped; a stiff, dark figure alone on the green swell of the hill before the gaping cave-mouth, he stood perfectly still. All at once he swung his staff up over his head, and the emerald radiance shone about him as he shouted, "Thief, thief of the Hoard of Pendor, come forth!"

There was a crash, as of dropped crockery, from inside the cave, and a lot of dust came spewing out. Scared, Birt ducked. When he looked again he saw Blackbeard still standing motionless, and at the mouth of the cave, dusty and dishevelled, stood Mr. Underhill. He looked small and pitiful, with his toes turned in as usual, and his little bowlegs in black tights, and no staff—he never had had one, Birt suddenly thought. Mr. Underhill spoke. "Who are you?" he said in his husky little voice.

"I am the Sealord of Pendor, thief, come to claim my treasure!"

At that, Mr. Underhill slowly turned pink, as he always did when people were rude to him. But he then turned something else. He turned yellow. His hair bristled out, he gave a coughing roar—and was a yellow lion leaping down the hill at Blackbeard, white fangs gleaming.

But Blackbeard no longer stood there. A gigantic tiger, color of night and lightning, bounded to meet the lion…

The lion was gone. Below the cave all of a sudden stood a high grove of trees, black in the winter sunshine. The tiger, checking himself in mid-leap just before he entered the shadow of the trees, caught fire in the air, became a tongue of flame lashing out at the dry black branches…

But where the trees had stood a sudden cataract leaped from the hillside, an arch of silvery crashing water, thundering down upon the fire. But the fire was gone…

For just a moment before the fisherman's staring eyes two hills rose—the green one he knew, and a new one, a bare, brown hillock ready to drink up the rushing waterfall. That passed so quickly it made Birt blink, and after blinking he blinked again, and moaned, for what he saw now was a great deal worse. Where the cataract had been there hovered a dragon. Black wings darkened all the hill, steel claws reached groping, and from the dark, scaly, gaping lips fire and steam shot out.

Beneath the monstrous creature stood Blackbeard, laughing.

"Take any shape you please, little Mr. Underhill!" he taunted. "I can match you. But the game grows tiresome. I want to look upon my treasure, upon Inalkil. Now, big dragon, little wizard, take your true shape. I command you by the power of your truename—Yevaud!"

Birt could not move at all, not even to blink. He cowered staring whether he would or not. He saw the black dragon hang there in the air above Blackbeard. He saw the fire lick like many tongues from the scaly mouth, the steam jet from the red nostrils. He saw Blackbeard's face grow white, white as chalk, and the beard-fringed lips trembling.

"Your name is Yevaud!"

"Yes," said a great, husky, hissing voice. "My truename is Yevaud, and my true shape is this shape."

"But the dragon was killed—they found dragon-bones on Udrath Island—"

"That was another dragon," said the dragon, and then stooped like a hawk, talons outstretched. And Birt shut his eyes.

When he opened them the sky was clear, the hillside empty, except for a reddish-blackish, trampled spot, and a few talon-marks in the grass.

Birt the fisherman got to his feet and ran. He ran across the common, scattering sheep to right and left, and straight down the village street to Palani's father's house. Palani was out in the garden weeding the nasturtiums. "Come with me!" Birt gasped. She stared. He grabbed her wrist and dragged her with him. She screeched a little, but did not resist. He ran with her straight to the pier, pushed her into his fishing-sloop the *Queenie*, untied the painter, took up the oars and set off rowing like a demon. The last that Sattins Island saw of him and Palani was the *Queenie*'s sail vanishing in the direction of the nearest island westward.

The villagers thought they would never stop talking about it, how Goody Guld's nephew Birt had lost his mind and sailed off with the schoolmistress on the very same day that the pedlar Blackbeard disappeared without a trace, leaving all his feathers and beads behind. But they did stop talking about it, three days later. They had other things to talk about, when Mr. Underhill finally came out of his cave.

Mr. Underhill had decided that since his truename was no longer a secret, he might as well drop his disguise. Walking was a lot harder than flying, and besides, it was a long, long time since he had had a real meal.

THE ICE DRAGON
George R. R. Martin

George R.R. Martin was born in Bayonne, New Jersey in 1948 and received a B.S. in Journalism from Northwestern University in 1970. A comic book fan and collector in high school, Martin began to write fiction for comic fanzines and made his first professional sale to *Galaxy* in February 1971. This was followed by major novella "A Song for Lya", which won the Hugo Award. His stories have won the Nebula Award twice, the Bram Stoker Award, and the World Fantasy Award and have been collected in ten volumes to date, including most recently *GRRM: A RRetrospective*.

Martin's first science fiction novel, *Dying of the Light*, published in the same year *Star Wars* hit the screens, was a powerful romance about a huge festival on a dying world. It was followed by seven more novels, including vampire novel *Fevre Dream* and rock 'n' roll novel *The Armageddon Rag*. Martin is best known for his epic fantasy series A Song of Ice and Fire, which to date includes *A Game of Thrones*, *A Clash of Kings*, *A Storm of Swords*, and *A Feast for Crows*. Upcoming is a fifth volume, *A Dance for Dragons,* which will be finished when it's finished. In the meantime, A Song of Ice and Fire is to be adapted by HBO for television. Martin's most recent books are the anthologies *Songs of the Dying Earth* and *Warriors*, both co-edited with Gardner Dozois, and several new volumes in the continuing Wild Cards shared world series.

Adara liked the winter best of all, for when the world grew cold the ice dragon came.

She was never quite sure whether it was the cold that brought the ice dragon or the ice dragon that brought the cold. That was the sort of question that often troubled her brother Geoff, who was two years older than her and insatiably curious, but Adara did not care about such things. So long as the cold and the snow and the ice dragon all arrived on schedule, she was happy.

She always knew when they were due because of her birthday. Adara was a winter child, born during the worst freeze that anyone could remember, even

Old Laura, who lived on the next farm and remembered things that had happened before anyone else was born. People still talked about that freeze. Adara often heard them.

They talked about other things as well. They said it was the chill of that terrible freeze that had killed her mother, stealing in during her long night of labor past the great fire that Adara's father had built, and creeping under the layers of blankets that covered the birthing bed. And they said that the cold had entered Adara in the womb, that her skin had been pale blue and icy to the touch when she came forth, and that she had never warmed in all the years since. The winter had touched her, left its mark upon her, and made her its own.

It was true that Adara was always a child apart. She was a very serious little girl who seldom cared to play with the others. She was beautiful, people said, but in a strange, distant sort of way, with her pale skin and blond hair and wide clear blue eyes. She smiled, but not often. No one had ever seen her cry. Once when she was five she had stepped upon a nail imbedded in a board that lay concealed beneath a snow-bank, and it had gone clear through her foot, but Adara had not wept or screamed even then. She had pulled her foot loose and walked back to the house, leaving a trail of blood in the snow, and when she had gotten there she had said only, "Father, I hurt myself." The sulks and tempers and tears of ordinary childhood were not for her.

Even her family knew that Adara was different. Her father was a huge, gruff bear of a man who had little use for people in general, but a smile always broke across his face when Geoff pestered him with questions, and he was full of hugs and laughter for Teri, Adara's older sister, who was golden and freckled, and flirted shamelessly with all the local boys. Every so often he would hug Adara as well, especially when he was drunk, which was frequent during the long winters. But there would be no smiles then. He would only wrap his arms around her, and pull her small body tight against him with all his massive strength, sob deep in his chest, and fat wet tears would run down his ruddy cheeks. He never hugged her at all during the summers. During the summers he was too busy.

Everyone was busy during the summers except for Adara. Geoff would work with his father in the fields and ask endless questions about this and that, learning everything a farmer had to know. When he was not working he would run with his friends to the river, and have adventures. Teri ran the house and did the cooking, and worked a bit at the inn by the crossroads during the busy season. The innkeeper's daughter was her friend, and his youngest son was more than a friend, and she would always come back giggly and full of gossip and news from travellers and soldiers and king's messengers. For Teri and Geoff the summers were the best time, and both of them were too busy for Adara.

Their father was the busiest of all. A thousand things needed to be done each day, and he did them, and found a thousand more. He worked from dawn to dusk. His muscles grew hard and lean in summer, and he stank from sweat each night when he came in from the fields, but he always came in smiling. After supper he would sit with Geoff and tell him stories and answer his questions, or teach Teri things she did not know about cooking, or stroll down to the inn. He was a summer man, truly.

He never drank in summer, except for a cup of wine now and again to celebrate his brother's visits.

That was another reason why Teri and Geoff loved the summers, when the world was green and hot and bursting with life. It was only in summer that Uncle Hal, their father's younger brother, came to call. Hal was a dragonrider in service to the king, a tall slender man with a face like a noble. Dragons cannot stand the cold, so when winter fell Hal and his wing would fly south. But each summer he returned, brilliant in the king's green-and-gold uniform, en route to the battlegrounds to the north and west of them. The war had been going on for all of Adara's life.

Whenever Hal came north, he would bring presents; toys from the king's city, crystal and gold jewelry, candies, and always a bottle of some expensive wine that he and his brother could share. He would grin at Teri and make her blush with his compliments, and entertain Geoff with tales of war and castles and dragons. As for Adara, he often tried to coax a smile out of her, with gifts and jests and hugs. He seldom succeeded.

For all his good nature, Adara did not like Hal; when Hal was there, it meant that winter was far away.

Besides, there had been a night when she was only four, and they thought her long asleep, that she overheard them talking over wine. "A solemn little thing," Hal said. "You ought to be kinder to her, John. You cannot blame *her* for what happened."

"Can't I?" her father replied, his voice thick with wine. "No, I suppose not. But it is hard. She looks like Beth, but she has none of Beth's warmth. The winter is in her, you know. Whenever I touch her I feel the chill, and I remember that it was for her that Beth had to die."

"You are cold to her. You do not love her as you do the others."

Adara remembered the way her father laughed then. "Love her? Ah, Hal. I loved her best of all, my little winter child. But she has never loved back. There is nothing in her for me, or you, any of us. She is such a cold little girl." And then he began to weep, even though it was summer and Hal was with him. In her bed, Adara listened and wished that Hal would fly away. She did not quite understand all that she had heard, not then, but she remembered it, and the understanding came later.

She did not cry; not at four, when she heard, or six, when she finally understood. Hal left a few days later, and Geoff and Teri waved to him excitedly when his wing passed overhead, thirty great dragons in proud formation against the summer sky. Adara watched with her small hands by her sides.

There were other visits in other summers, but Hal never made her smile, no matter what he brought her.

Adara's smiles were a secret store, and she spent of them only in winter. She could hardly wait for her birthday to come, and with it the cold. For in winter she was a special child.

She had known it since she was very little, playing with the others in the snow. The cold had never bothered her the way it did Geoff and Teri and their friends. Often Adara stayed outside alone for hours after the others had fled in search of warmth, or run off to Old Laura's to eat the hot vegetable soup she liked to make for the children. Adara would find a secret place in the far corner of the fields, a different place each winter, and there she would build a tall white castle, patting the snow in place with small bare hands, shaping it into towers and battlements like those Hal often talked about on the king's castle in the city. She would snap icicles off from the lower branches of trees, and use them for spires and spikes and guardposts, ranging them all about her castle. And often in the dead of winter would come a brief thaw and a sudden freeze, and overnight her snow castle would turn to ice, as hard and strong as she imagined real castles to be. All through the winters she would build on her castle, and no one ever knew. But always the spring would come, and a thaw not followed by a freeze; then all the ramparts and walls would melt away, and Adara would begin to count the days until her birthday came again.

Her winter castles were seldom empty. At the first frost each year, the ice lizards would come wriggling out of their burrows, and the fields would be overrun with the tiny blue creatures, darting this way and that, hardly seeming to touch the snow as they skimmed across it. All the children played with the ice lizards. But the others were clumsy and cruel, and they would snap the fragile little animals in two, breaking them between their fingers as they might break an icicle hanging from a roof. Even Geoff, who was too kind ever to do something like that, sometimes grew curious, and held the lizards too long in his efforts to examine them, and the heat of his hands would make them melt and burn and finally die.

Adara's hands were cool and gentle, and she could hold the lizards as long as she liked without harming them, which always made Geoff pout and ask angry questions. Sometimes she would lie in the cold, damp snow and let the lizards crawl all over her, delighting in the light touch of their feet as they skittered across her face. Sometimes she would wear ice lizards hidden in her hair as she went about her chores, though she took care never to take them inside where the heat of the fire would kill them. Always she would gather up scraps after the family ate, and bring them to the secret place where her castle was a-building, and there she would scatter them. So the castles she erected were full of kings and courtiers every winter; small furry creatures that snuck out from the woods, winter birds with pale white plumage, and hundreds and hundreds of squirming, struggling ice lizards, cold and quick and fat. Adara liked the ice lizards better than any of the pets the family had kept over the years.

But it was the ice dragon that she loved.

She did not know when she had first seen it. It seemed to her that it had always been a part of her life, a vision glimpsed during the deep of winter, sweeping across the frigid sky on wings serene and blue. Ice dragons were rare, even in those days, and whenever it was seen the children would all point and wonder, while the old folks muttered and shook their heads. It was a sign of a long and bitter winter when ice dragons were abroad in the land. An ice dragon had been seen flying across the face of the moon on the night Adara had been born, people said, and each winter since it had been seen again, and those winters had been very bad indeed, the spring coming later each year. So the people would set fires and pray and hope to keep the ice dragon away, and Adara would fill with fear.

But it never worked. Every year the ice dragon returned. Adara knew it came for her.

The ice dragon was large, half again the size of the scaled green war dragons that Hal and his fellows flew. Adara had heard legends of wild dragons larger than mountains, but she had never seen any. Hal's dragon was big enough, to be sure, five times the size of a horse, but it was small compared to the ice dragon, and ugly besides.

The ice dragon was a crystalline white, that shade of white that is so hard and cold that it is almost blue. It was covered with hoarfrost, so when it moved its skin broke and crackled as the crust on the snow crackles beneath a man's boots, and flakes of rime fell off.

Its eyes were clear and deep and icy.

Its wings were vast and batlike, colored all a faint translucent blue. Adara could see the clouds through them, and oftentimes the moon and stars, when the beast wheeled in frozen circles through the skies.

Its teeth were icicles, a triple row of them, jagged spears of unequal length, white against its deep blue maw.

When the ice dragon beat its wings, the cold winds blew and the snow swirled and scurried and the world seemed to shrink and shiver. Sometimes when a door flew open in the cold of winter, driven by a sudden gust of wind, the householder would run to bolt it and say, "An ice dragon flies nearby."

And when the ice dragon opened its great mouth, and exhaled, it was not fire that came streaming out, the burning sulfurous stink of lesser dragons.

The ice dragon breathed cold.

Ice formed when it breathed. Warmth fled. Fires guttered and went out, shriven by the chill. Trees froze through to their slow secret souls, and their limbs turned brittle and cracked from their own weight. Animals turned blue and whimpered and died, their eyes bulging and their skin covered over with frost.

The ice dragon breathed death into the world; death and quiet and *cold*. But Adara was not afraid. She was a winter child, and the ice dragon was her secret.

She had seen it in the sky a thousand times. When she was four, she saw it on the ground.

She was out building on her snow castle, and it came and landed close to her, in the emptiness of the snow-covered fields. All the ice lizards ran away. Adara simply stood. The ice dragon looked at her for ten long heartbeats, before it took to the air again. The wind shrieked around her and through her as it beat its wings to rise, but Adara felt strangely exalted.

Later that winter it returned, and Adara touched it. Its skin was very cold. She took off her glove nonetheless. It would not be right otherwise. She was half afraid it would burn and melt at her touch, but it did not. It was much more sensitive to heat than even the ice lizards, Adara knew somehow. But she was special, the winter child, cool. She stroked it, and finally gave its wing a kiss that hurt her lips. That was the winter of her fourth birthday, the year she touched the ice dragon.

The winter of her fifth birthday was the year she rode upon it for the first time.

It found her again, working on a different castle at a different place in the fields, alone as ever. She watched it come, and ran to it when it landed, and pressed herself against it. That had been the summer when she had heard her father talking to Hal.

They stood together for long minutes until finally Adara, remembering Hal, reached out and tugged at the dragon's wing with a small hand. And the dragon beat its great wings once, and then extended them flat against the snow, and Adara scrambled up to wrap her arms about its cold white neck.

Together, for the first time, they flew.

She had no harness or whip, as the king's dragonriders use. At times the beating of the wings threatened to shake her loose from where she clung, and the coldness of the dragon's flesh crept through her clothing and bit and numbed her child's flesh. But Adara was not afraid.

They flew over her father's farm, and she saw Geoff looking very small below, startled and afraid, and knew he could not see her. It made her laugh an icy, tinkling laugh, a laugh as bright and crisp as the winter air.

They flew over the crossroads inn, where crowds of people came out to watch them pass.

They flew above the forest, all white and green and silent.

They flew high into the sky, so high that Adara could not even see the ground below, and she thought she glimpsed another ice dragon, way off in the distance, but it was not half so grand as hers.

They flew for most of the day, and finally the dragon swept around in a great circle, and spiraled down, gliding on its stiff and glittering wings. It let her off in the field where it had found her, just after dusk.

Her father found her there, and wept to see her, and hugged her savagely. Adara did not understand that, nor why he beat her after he had gotten her back to the house. But when she and Geoff had been put to sleep, she heard him slide out of his own bed and come padding over to hers. "You missed it all," he said. "There was an ice dragon, and it scared everybody. Father was afraid it had eaten you."

Adara smiled to herself in the darkness, but said nothing.

She flew on the ice dragon four more times that winter, and every winter after that. Each year she flew farther and more often than the year before, and the ice dragon was seen more frequently in the skies above their farm.

Each winter was longer and colder than the one before.

Each year the thaw came later.

And sometimes there were patches of land, where the ice dragon had lain to rest, that never seemed to thaw properly at all.

There was much talk in the village during her sixth year, and a message was sent to the king. No answer ever came.

"A bad business, ice dragons," Hal said that summer when he visited the farm. "They're not like real dragons, you know. You can't break them or train them. We have tales of those that tried, found frozen with their whip and harness in hand. I've heard about people that have lost hands or fingers just by touching one of them. Frostbite. Yes, a bad business."

"Then why doesn't the king do something?" her father demanded. "We sent a message. Unless we can kill the beast or drive it away, in a year or two we won't have any planting season at all."

Hal smiled grimly. "The king has other concerns. The war is going badly, you know. They advance every summer, and they have twice as many dragonriders as we do. I tell you, John, it's hell up there. Some year I'm not going to come back. The king can hardly spare men to go chasing an ice dragon." He laughed. "Besides, I don't think anybody's ever killed one of the things. Maybe we should just let the enemy take this whole province. Then it'd be *his* ice dragon."

But it wouldn't be, Adara thought as she listened. No matter what king ruled the land, it would always be *her* ice dragon.

Hal departed and summer waxed and waned. Adara counted the days until her birthday. Hal passed through again before the first chill, taking his ugly dragon south for the winter. His wing seemed smaller when it came flying over the forest that fall, though, and his visit was briefer than usual, and ended with a loud quarrel between him and her father.

"They won't move during the winter," Hal said. "The winter terrain is too treacherous, and they won't risk an advance without dragonriders to cover them from above. But come spring, we aren't going to be able to hold them. The king may not even try. Sell the farm now, while you can still get a good price. You can buy another piece of land in the south."

"This is my land," her father said. "I was born here. You too, though you seem to have forgotten it. Our parents are buried here. And Beth too. I want to lie beside her when I go."

"You'll go a lot sooner than you'd like if you don't listen to me," Hal said angrily. "Don't be stupid, John. I know what the land means to you, but it isn't worth your life." He went on and on, but her father would not be moved. They ended the evening swearing at each other, and Hal left in the dead of the night, slamming the door behind him as he went.

Adara, listening, had made a decision. It did not matter what her father did or did not do. She would stay. If she moved, the ice dragon would not know where to find her when winter came, and if she went too far south it would never be able to come to her at all.

It did come to her, though, just after her seventh birthday. That winter was the coldest one of all. She flew so often and so far that she scarcely had time to work on her ice castle.

Hal came again in the spring. There were only a dozen dragons in his wing, and he brought no presents that year. He and her father argued once again. Hal raged and pleaded and threatened, but her father was stone. Finally Hal left, off to the battlefields.

That was the year the king's line broke, up north near some town with a long name that Adara could not pronounce.

Teri heard about it first. She returned from the inn one night flushed and excited. "A messenger came through, on his way to the king," she told them. "The enemy won some big battle, and he's to ask for reinforcements. He said our army is retreating."

Their father frowned, and worry lines creased his brow. "Did he say anything of the king's dragonriders?" Arguments or no, Hal was family.

"I asked," Teri said. "He said the dragonriders are the rear guard. They're supposed to raid and burn, delay the enemy while our army pulls back safely. Oh, I hope Uncle Hal is safe!"

"Hal will show them," Geoff said. "Him and Brimstone will burn 'em up."

Their father smiled. "Hal could always take care of himself. At any rate, there is nothing we can do. Teri, if any more messengers come through, ask them how it goes."

She nodded, her concern not quite covering her excitement. It was all quite thrilling.

In the weeks that followed, the thrill wore off, as the people of the area began to comprehend the magnitude of the disaster. The king's highway grew busier and busier, and all the traffic flowed from north to south, and all the travellers wore green-and-gold: At first the soldiers marched in disciplined columns, led by officers wearing plumed golden helmets, but even then they were less than stirring. The columns marched wearily, and the uniforms were filthy and torn, and the swords and pikes and axes the soldiers carried were nicked and ofttimes stained. Some men had lost their weapons; they limped along blindly, empty-handed. And the trains of wounded that followed the columns were often longer than the columns themselves. Adara stood in the grass by the side of the road and watched them pass. She saw a man with no eyes supporting a man with only one leg, as the two of them walked together. She saw men with no legs, or no arms, or both. She saw a man with his head split open by an axe, and many men covered with caked blood and filth, men who moaned low in their throats as they walked. She *smelled* men with bodies that were horribly greenish and puffed-up. One of them died and was left abandoned by the side of the road. Adara told her father and he and some of the men from the village came out and buried him.

Most of all, Adara saw the burned men. There were dozens of them in every column that passed, men whose skin was black and seared and falling off, who had lost an arm or a leg or half of a face to the hot breath of a dragon. Teri told them what the officers said, when they stopped at the inn to drink or rest; the enemy had many, many dragons.

For almost a month the columns flowed past, more every day. Even Old Laura admitted that she had never seen so much traffic on the road. From time to time a lone messenger on horseback rode against the tide, galloping toward the north, but always alone. After a time everyone knew there would be no reinforcements.

An officer in one of the last columns advised the people of the area to pack up whatever they could carry, and move south. "They are coming," he warned. A few listened to him, and indeed for a week the road was full of refugees from towns farther north. Some of them told frightful stories. When they left, more of the local people went with them.

But most stayed. They were people like her father, and the land was in their blood.

The last organized force to come down the road was a ragged troop of cavalry, men as gaunt as skeletons riding horses with skin pulled tight around their ribs. They thundered past in the night, their mounts heaving and foaming, and the only one to pause was a pale young officer, who reigned his mount up briefly and shouted, "Go, go. They are burning everything!" Then he was off after his men.

The few soldiers who came after were alone or in small groups. They did not always use the road, and they did not pay for the things they took. One swordsman killed a farmer on the other side of town, raped his wife, stole his money, and ran. His rags were green-and-gold.

Then no one came at all. The road was deserted.

The innkeeper claimed he could smell ashes when the wind blew from the north. He packed up his family and went south. Teri was distraught. Geoff was wide-eyed and anxious and only a bit frightened. He asked a thousand questions about the enemy, and practiced at being a warrior. Their father went about his labors, busy as ever. War or no war, he had crops in the field. He smiled less than usual, however, and he began to drink, and Adara often saw him glancing up at the sky while he worked.

Adara wandered the fields alone, played by herself in the damp summer heat, and tried to think of where she would hide if her father tried to take them away.

Last of all, the king's dragonriders came, and with them Hal.

There were only four of them. Adara saw the first one, and went and told her father, and he put his hand on her shoulder and together they watched it pass, a solitary green dragon with a vaguely tattered look. It did not pause for them.

Two days later, three dragons flying together came into view, and one of them detached itself from the others and circled down to their farm while the other two headed south.

Uncle Hal was thin and grim and sallow-looking. His dragon looked sick. Its eyes ran, and one of its wings had been partially burned, so it flew in an awkward, heavy manner, with much difficulty. "Now will you go?" Hal said to his brother, in front of all the children.

"No. Nothing has changed."

Hal swore. "They will be here within three days," he said. "Their dragonriders may be here even sooner."

"Father, I am scared," Teri said.

He looked at her, saw her fear, hesitated, and finally turned back to his brother. "I am staying. But if you would, I would have you take the children."

Now it was Hal's turn to pause. He thought for a moment, and finally shook his head. "I can't, John. I would, willingly, joyfully, if it were possible. But it isn't. Brimstone is wounded. He can barely carry me. If I took on any extra weight, we might never make it."

Teri began to weep.

"I'm sorry, love," Hal said to her. "Truly I am." His fists clenched helplessly.

"Teri is almost full-grown," their father said. "If her weight is too much, then take one of the others."

Brother looked at brother, with despair in their eyes. Hal trembled. "Adara," he said finally. "She's small and light." He forced a laugh. "She hardly weighs anything at all. I'll take Adara. The rest of you take horses, or a wagon, or go on foot. But go, damn you, go."

"We will see," their father said noncommittally. "You take Adara, and keep her safe for us."

"Yes," Hal agreed. He turned and smiled at her. "Come, child. Uncle Hal is going to take you for a ride on Brimstone."

Adara looked at him very seriously. "No," she said. She turned and slipped through the door and began to run.

They came after her, of course, Hal and her father and even Geoff. But her father wasted time standing in the door, shouting at her to come back, and when he began to run he was ponderous and clumsy, while Adara was indeed small and light and fleet of foot. Hal and Geoff stayed with her longer, but Hal was weak, and Geoff soon winded himself, though he sprinted hard at her heels for a few moments. By the time Adara reached the nearest wheat field, the three of them were well behind her. She quickly lost herself amid the grain, and they searched for hours in vain while she made her way carefully toward the woods.

When dusk fell, they brought out lanterns and torches and continued their search. From time to time she heard her father swearing, or Hal calling out her name. She stayed high in the branches of the oak she had climbed, and smiled down at their lights as they combed back and forth through the fields. Finally she drifted off to sleep, dreaming about the coming of winter and wondering how she would live until her birthday. It was still a long time away.

Dawn woke her; dawn and a noise in the sky.

Adara yawned and blinked, and heard it again. She shinnied to the uppermost limb of the tree, as high as it would bear her, and pushed aside the leaves.

There were dragons in the sky.

She had never seen beasts quite like these. Their scales were dark and sooty, not green like the dragon Hal rode. One was a rust color and one was the shade of dried blood and one was black as coal. All of them had eyes like glowing embers, and steam rose from their nostrils, and their tails flicked back and forth as their dark, leathery wings beat the air. The rust-colored one opened its mouth and roared, and the forest shook to its challenge, and even the branch that held Adara trembled just a little. The black one made a noise too, and when it opened its maw a spear of flame lanced out, all orange and blue, and touched the trees below. Leaves withered and blackened, and smoke began to rise from where the dragon's breath had fallen. The one the color of blood flew close overhead, its wings creaking and straining, its mouth half-open. Between its yellowed teeth Adara saw soot and cinders, and the wind stirred by its passage was fire and sandpaper, raw and chafing against her skin. She cringed.

On the backs of the dragons rode men with whip and lance, in uniforms of black-and-orange, their faces hidden behind dark helmets. The one on the rust dragon gestured with his lance, pointing at the farm buildings across the fields. Adara looked.

Hal came up to meet them.

His green dragon was as large as their own, but somehow it seemed small to Adara as she watched it climb upward from the farm. With its wings fully extended, it was plain to see how badly injured it was; the right wing tip was charred, and it leaned heavily to one side as it flew. On its back, Hal looked like one of the tiny toy soldiers he had brought them as a present years before.

The enemy dragonriders split up and came at him from three sides. Hal saw what they were doing. He tried to turn, to throw himself at the black dragon head-on, and flee the other two. His whip flailed angrily, desperately. His green dragon opened its mouth, and roared a weak challenge, but its flame was pale and short and did not reach the oncoming enemy.

The others held their fire. Then, on a signal, their dragons all breathed as one. Hal was wreathed in flames.

His dragon made a high wailing noise, and Adara saw that it was burning, *he* was burning, they were all burning, beast and master both. They fell heavily to the ground, and lay smoking amidst her father's wheat.

The air was full of ashes.

Adara craned her head around in the other direction, and saw a column of smoke rising from beyond the forest and the river. That was the farm where Old Laura lived with her grandchildren and *their* children.

When she looked back, the three dark dragons were circling lower and lower above her own farm. One by one they landed. She watched the first of the riders dismount and saunter toward their door.

She was frightened and confused and only seven, after all. And the heavy air of summer was a weight upon her, and it filled her with a helplessness and thickened all her fears. So Adara did the only thing she knew, without thinking, a thing that came naturally to her. She climbed down from her tree and ran. She ran across the fields and through the woods, away from the farm and her family and the dragons, away from all of it. She ran until her legs throbbed with pain, down in the direction of the river. She ran to the coldest place she knew, to the deep caves underneath the river bluffs, to chill shelter and darkness and safety.

And there in the cold she hid. Adara was a winter child, and cold did not bother her. But still, as she hid, she trembled.

Day turned into night. Adara did not leave her cave.

She tried to sleep, but her dreams were full of burning dragons.

She made herself very small as she lay in the darkness, and tried to count how many days remained until her birthday. The caves were nicely cool; Adara could almost imagine that it was not summer after all, that it was winter, or near to winter. Soon her ice dragon would come for her, and she would ride on its back to the land of always-winter, where great ice castles and cathedrals of snow stood eternally in endless fields of white, and the stillness and silence were all.

It almost felt like winter as she lay there. The cave grew colder and colder, it seemed. It made her feel safe. She napped briefly. When she woke, it was colder still. A white coating of frost covered the cave walls, and she was sitting on a bed of ice. Adara jumped to her feet and looked up toward the mouth of the cave, filled with a wan dawn light. A cold wind caressed her. But it was coming from outside, from the world of summer, not from the depths of the cave at all.

She gave a small shout of joy, and climbed and scrambled up the ice-covered rocks.

Outside, the ice dragon was waiting for her.

It had breathed upon the water, and now the river was frozen, or at least a part of it was, although she could see that the ice was fast melting as the summer sun rose. It had breathed upon the green grass that grew along the banks, grass as high as Adara, and now the tall blades were white and brittle, and when the ice dragon moved its wings the grass cracked in half and tumbled, sheared as clean as if it had been cut down with a scythe.

The dragon's icy eyes met Adara's, and she ran to it and up its wing, and threw her arms about it. She knew she had to hurry. The ice dragon looked smaller than she had ever seen it, and she understood what the heat of summer was doing to it.

"Hurry, dragon," she whispered. "Take me away, take me to the land of always-winter. We'll never come back here, never. I'll build you the best castle of all, and take care of you, and ride you every day. Just take me away, dragon, take me home with you."

The ice dragon heard and understood. Its wide translucent wings unfolded and beat the air, and bitter arctic winds howled through the fields of summer. They rose. Away from the cave. Away from the river. Above the forest. Up and up. The ice dragon swung around to the north. Adara caught a glimpse of her father's farm, but it was very small and growing smaller. They turned their back to it, and soared.

Then a sound came to Adara's ears. An impossible sound, a sound that was too small and too far away for her to ever have heard it, especially above the beating of the ice dragon's wings. But she heard it nonetheless. She heard her father scream.

Hot tears ran down her cheeks, and where they fell upon the ice dragon's back they burned small pockmarks in the frost. Suddenly the cold beneath her hands was biting, and when she pulled one hand away Adara saw the mark that it had made upon the dragon's neck. She was scared, but still she clung. "Turn back," she whispered. "Oh, *please*, dragon. Take me back."

She could not see the ice dragon's eyes, but she knew what they would look like. Its mouth opened and a blue-white plume issued, a long cold streamer that hung in the air. It made no noise; ice dragons are silent. But in her mind Adara heard the wild keening of its grief.

"Please," she whispered once again. "Help me." Her voice was thin and small.

The ice dragon turned.

The three dragons were outside of the barn when Adara returned, feasting on the burned and blackened carcasses of her father's stock. One of the dragonriders was standing near them, leaning on his lance and prodding his dragon from time to time.

He looked up when the cold gust of wind came shrieking across the fields, and shouted something, and sprinted for the black dragon. The beast tore a last hunk of meat from her father's horse, swallowed, and rose reluctantly into the air. The rider flailed his whip.

Adara saw the door of the farmhouse burst open. The other two riders rushed out, and ran for their dragons. One of them was struggling into his pants as he ran. He was bare-chested.

The black dragon roared, and its fire came blazing up at them. Adara felt the searing blast of heat, and a shudder went through the ice dragon as the flame played along its belly. Then it craned its long neck around, and fixed its baleful empty eyes upon the enemy, and opened its frost-rimed jaws. Out from among its icy teeth its breath came streaming, and that breath was pale and cold.

It touched the left wing of the coal-black dragon beneath them, and the dark beast gave a shrill cry of pain, and when it beat its wings again, the frost-covered wing broke in two. Dragon and dragonrider began to fall.

The ice dragon breathed again.

They were frozen and dead before they hit the ground.

The rust-colored dragon was flying at them, and the dragon the color of blood with its bare-chested rider. Adara's ears were filled with their angry roaring, and she could feel their hot breath around her, and see the air shimmering with heat, and smell the stink of sulfur.

Two long swords of fire crossed in midair, but neither touched the ice dragon, though it shriveled in the heat, and water flew from it like rain whenever it beat its wings.

The blood-colored dragon flew too close, and the breath of the ice dragon blasted the rider. His bare chest turned blue before Adara's eyes, and moisture condensed on him in an instant, covering him with frost. He screamed, and died, and fell from his mount, though his harness hand remained behind, frozen to the neck of his dragon. The ice dragon closed on it, wings screaming the secret song of winter, and a blast of flame met a blast of cold. The ice dragon shuddered once again, and twisted away, dripping. The other dragon died.

But the last dragonrider was behind them now, the enemy in full armor on the dragon whose scales were the brown of rust. Adara screamed, and even as she did the fire enveloped the ice dragon's wing. It was gone in less than an instant, but the wing was gone with it, melted, destroyed.

The ice dragon's remaining wing beat wildly to slow its plunge, but it came to earth with an awful crash. Its legs shattered beneath it, and its wing snapped in two places, and the impact of the landing threw Adara from its back. She tumbled to the soft earth of the field, and rolled, and struggled up, bruised but whole.

The ice dragon seemed very small now, and very broken. Its long neck sank wearily to the ground, and its head rested amid the wheat.

The enemy dragonrider came swooping in, roaring with triumph. The dragon's eyes burned. The man flourished his lance and shouted.

The ice dragon painfully raised its head once more, and made the only sound that Adara ever heard it make: a terrible thin cry full of melancholy, like the sound the north wind makes when it moves around the towers and battlements of the white castles that stand empty in the land of always-winter.

When the cry had faded, the ice dragon sent cold into the world one final time: a long smoking blue-white stream of cold that was full of snow and stillness and the end of all living things. The dragonrider flew right into it, still brandishing whip and lance. Adara watched him crash.

Then she was running, away from the fields, back to the house and her family within, running as fast as she could, running and panting and crying all the while like a seven year old.

Her father had been nailed to the bedroom wall. They had wanted him to watch while they took their turns with Teri. Adara did not know what to do, but she untied Teri, whose tears had dried by then, and they freed Geoff, and then they got their father down. Teri nursed him and cleaned out his wounds. When his eyes opened and he saw Adara, he smiled. She hugged him very hard, and cried for him.

By night he said he was fit enough to travel. They crept away under cover of darkness, and took the king's road south.

Her family asked no questions then, in those hours of darkness and fear. But later, when they were safe in the south, there were questions endlessly. Adara gave them the best answers she could. But none of them ever believed her, except for Geoff, and he grew out of it when he got older. She was only seven, after all, and she did not understand that ice dragons are never seen in summer, and cannot be tamed nor ridden.

Besides, when they left the house that night, there was no ice dragon to be seen. Only the huge corpses of three war dragons, and the smaller bodies of three dragonriders in black-and-orange. And a pond that had never been there before, a small quiet pool where the water was very cold. They had walked around it carefully, headed toward the road.

Their father worked for another farmer for three years in the south. His hands were never as strong as they had been, before the nails had been pounded through them, but he made up for that with the strength of his back and his arms, and his determination. He saved whatever he could, and he seemed happy. "Hal is gone, and my land," he would tell Adara, "and I am sad for that. But it is all right. I have my daughter back." For the winter was gone from her now, and she smiled and laughed and even wept like other little girls.

Three years after they had fled, the king's army routed the enemy in a great battle, and the king's dragons burned the foreign capital. In the peace that followed, the northern provinces changed hands once more. Teri had recaptured her spirit and married a young trader, and she remained in the south. Geoff and Adara returned with their father to the farm.

When the first frost came, all the ice lizards came out, just as they had always done. Adara watched them with a smile on her face, remembering the way it had been. But she did not try to touch them. They were cold and fragile little things, and the warmth of her hands would hurt them.

SOBEK

Holly Black

Holly Black was born in New Jersey, married her high school sweetheart and nearly got a degree in library science from Rutgers before her first book tour interrupted her studies. She is the author of the bestselling The Spiderwick Chronicles, which was made into a feature film released in 2008. Her first story appeared in 1997, but she first got attention with her debut novel, *Tithe: A Modern Faerie Tale*. She has written eleven Spiderwick books and three novels in the Modern Faerie Tale sequence, including Andre Norton Award winner *Valiant: A Modern Tale of Faerie*. Black's most recent books are her first short story collection, *The Poison Eaters and Others*, and *White Cat*, the first novel in her new Curse Worker series. She was nominated for an Eisner Award for graphic novel series, The Good Neighbors, and recently co-edited anthology *Zombies vs. Unicorns* with Justine Larbalestier.

Mom had always been a little off, so I figured if she wanted to be high priestess of a cult made up of three people, then *whatever*. It seemed harmless. Besides, I thought it would help her get over getting fired from the superstore. Maybe even distract her from thinking about Hank, the stock guy that she talked about all the time.

Even though Mom worked mostly at the checkout counter and he was in the back, they met for lunch. Hank. At first I thought that he was the one that put the ideas in her head about Sobek the Destroyer and the no-souls, because he was at the center of most of her fantasies. She told me Hank was "born into many bodies," whatever that means. I just figured he was trying to get in her pants with some metaphysical bullshit.

I found out later that Hank was happily married with three kids. After Mom lost her job, she took me to the superstore with her—to buy milk, eggs and toilet paper, *she'd said*—then slipped into the back. I followed her.

Hank was a tall, gaunt guy with big glasses. Those glasses made his eyes look big, but when Mom came in, his eyes got even bigger.

"It was the no-souls," she said. "You know how they are, always talking. It was

33

a no-soul conspiracy that got me fired."

He looked puzzled. "I don't think that it was anybody's—"

"You *know* it was the no-souls. You *know*! Did they get to you too? Does that mean you're not going to help me, Hank?"

"That's not what I'm saying." You could hear the fear in his voice. It suddenly occurred to me that they weren't *meeting* for lunch, she was cornering him during lunch to preach all this stuff.

Now, I kind of think it was the firing that really sent her over the edge. Before that she'd had some wacky beliefs and maybe sometimes they slipped over into real life, but without the superstore it was all Sobek all the time.

She made a shrine to him in the corner of our apartment, buying plastic alligators and gluing plastic gems to their backs or painting their tails with gold. One night I looked through her books and realized what Sobek was. A demon crocodile, worshipped in Egypt. Some old myth.

"I've seen him," she told me. "In the sewers."

"Mom, he's a *crocodile* god," I said. "It's *alligators* that live in the sewers. *And* it's an urban legend." She'd taken to drawing black lines around her eyes so that she looked more like an Egyptian priestess. I thought she just looked like an old goth.

"Amaya, you should pray to him. He's trying to take the evil out of the world, but his power comes from our prayers."

"Okay," I said. When she was like this, you just had to go along with her.

Just like I went along with her when she kept me out of school for two weeks because she was afraid to be alone. Or how she told me that one of my friends, Lydia, was some kind of monstrous no-soul person. Mom would scream and chant when Lydia came over. That sucked, but I went along with it and never brought her by. It wasn't like I liked having people over anyway.

Even without Mom's job, we were mostly okay. Dad, an engineer so rational that metaphors annoyed him, paid his alimony and child support exactly on time every month—enough to cover the rent, utilities and food if we were careful. Looking back, I almost wish that we hadn't had enough money. Maybe then she would have had a reason to try and hold it together.

"I've worked since I was younger than you," she would say. "I deserve a break."

I thought maybe she was right. Maybe she could burn this out of her system like she'd burned through a bunch of other obsessions. Like when she said that she was a reincarnation of someone my father had killed in a past life and kept calling him and shouting "murderer" over the phone until my stepmother reportedly pulled the cord out of the wall.

But hanging around the house, she met Miranda and her boyfriend, Paulo. Miranda was the super's niece, so they lived in an apartment for free. Paulo used to walk dogs for people, but one of them had gotten away and there was some kind of legal thing going on with the owners that I never really understood. I think they were suing him, but what they hoped to get out of it, I have no idea.

Anyway, Miranda and Paulo seemed to spend most of their time sitting on the front stoop, smoking unfiltered cigarettes. Sometimes Miranda cadged money out of one of her relatives.

They got way into Sobek.

To Miranda, Sobek was going to change her fortunes and show all her sisters and brothers who called her lazy that she was just different. Special. Destined for glorious things they would never understand.

To Paulo, Sobek was a warrior-god who swept enemies out of the path of his followers. To hear Paulo talk, there were a lot of enemies in need of sweeping. He was the one that changed the sobriquet from Sobek the Repairer to Rager, although it never really caught on.

Somewhere along the way, Mom decided that Paulo *was* Hank—that Paulo was another one of the bodies that Hank's soul had been born into. Miranda probably wasn't too happy about that.

But their favorite activity was talking about the no-souls. No-souls look like people, but they're rotten on the inside. And they control everything. No-souls are the reason things are so screwed up in the world. Mom and Miranda and Paulo loved naming people they knew who were probably no-souls. It was their favorite thing.

Paulo and Miranda started calling our apartment building Arsinoe, after a town that Sobek was really fond of, but after a while they forgot that and just started calling the place Crocodopolis. I called it that too, because it made me laugh.

Look, I didn't know that this is how these things start. They don't warn you in school and I guess didn't watch the right kind of television. Even the fact that I was nervous most of the time—scared of the way they were acting, scared of how quickly my mother got angry—didn't tip me off.

After Mom and Paulo and Miranda filled the whole place with glittery, adorned plastic alligators and nothing happened, they started looking for Sobek. First they went back to the place where Mom said she'd seen him in a grate. The manhole was impossible to pry up, but they would throw strips of bacon down into the darkness.

Then, somehow, Paulo bought a manhole cover removal tool off of craigslist and they were wading around in the shallow water, making their devotions. Most of the time they came back defeated and dirty, but once or twice they claimed to have seen a tail or something.

My mother was always the one that saw him and soon he started talking to her. Visiting her. Slinking into her bedroom when she was alone at night. Demanding that Miranda and Paulo prove their loyalty.

She had scratches all over her body in the morning, long and dark, like some kind of claws scraped over her soft flesh. Holy scars to mark a priestess.

I wondered how she faked them. I knew *why*, even if she didn't. She was afraid of losing her disciples. I guess it was just a matter of time before they stepped up their game and decided that they needed to *give* Sobek something in order to *get* something. A sacrifice. Me.

They had lots of reasons. For one thing, I was in the way. I cost money to feed. Plus, I made fun of them. When my best friend Shana came over, we would look through their notebooks and laugh so hard that we were in serious danger of peeing our pants. They would make up prayers like, "Sobek, whose sweat became the Nile, let this lottery ticket drenched in *our* sweat bring us enough cash to venerate you properly."

I think it bothered them that I could tell there was some sexual tension bound up in all this praying. They closed the door to the living room to finish their rituals and came out sweaty and half-dressed. I knew it bothered Paulo and Miranda to look me in the face afterward. So they didn't like me. And having a kid around made my mom seem too ordinary to be a prophet.

But the last reason is the reason I hate the most, even if it is true. They took me because I was the only one dumb enough and trusting enough to go down into the sewer with them.

I was afraid of them, sometimes, when they got really weird. But I wasn't afraid enough. I thought that if I kept going along with things, they'd get better. My mother was slipping into some other reality from which I had no idea how to get her back, so my plan was to wait it out. When they told me to pray to Sobek, I prayed. When they told me that soon everything would be different and they would be rewarded, I nodded. Mostly, the results of going along with things were just boring.

"You go on down this time with your Mom," Paulo said, once he'd removed the manhole cover. "I'll look out for the cops."

"It looks dark." I could just see the glint of ripples of water moving many feet below where I stood.

I'd always been the one to watch for cops when they went into the sewers. I would stand in the mouth of the alley, looking down at the shine of the street-lights on the murky water and then back toward traffic. Sometimes I would stare down the manhole for so long that my mind would get occupied with thoughts of other things—school and friends and plans for how I could maybe someday make it to college and from there to engineering school—and my eyes would play tricks on me. Once I thought I saw a tail dragging through the water. Another time I thought there was a flash of golden eyes the size of tennis balls. I nearly shouted for my mother, but by the time I opened my mouth, whatever trick of the light that messed with my vision was gone.

Either way, I was pretty sure I didn't want to go down there.

"I'm good," I told Paulo. "I don't mind watching for the cops. I don't get bored."

My mother laughed and kissed me on the forehead. "That's right. Only boring people get bored." It was one of her favorite sayings.

Paulo put his hand over his stomach. "I don't feel good, Amaya. Go on with your mother and Miranda this time. Maybe you'll have more luck than us. You've got young eyes."

"No way," I said. "This is your thing. I'm just here to help."

"Just take a quick look around and you can come right up if you don't like it," Mom said. "You don't have to even get off the ladder."

That filled me with so much relief that I did it. Gingerly, I got down on my hands and knees on the asphalt and slipped one sneakered foot onto whatever rung it reached. The metal felt slippery and I hesitated before I grabbed the first rung and started climbing down. The air was hot with decomposition and smelled rancidly sweet.

"We know why we can't see him, Amaya," said my mom. Gold-toned bracelets jangled on her wrists. "He needs a virgin."

Miranda leaned down and stroked my hair back from my face. "You are a virgin, aren't you?"

I pulled away from her the only way I could, stepping down several more rungs. "Don't be so gross," I said.

There was a heavy clank and darkness. I screamed, really screamed, so hard that my throat hurt.

"Shhhhh, my mother called from the grate. "Wait for your eyes to adjust."

I blinked a few times and could only see a vague light making the walls glisten. My hands hurt where I was holding on to the bar.

"Open it," I yelled. "I want to come up. I don't like it down here."

"Just look around," Miranda said. "Do you see anything? Is he down there?"

I started thinking fast. Would they be mad if I went down there and didn't see anything? They were going to make me wait for a while unless I saw something. So, the sooner the better, right? But if I said something right away, they might suspect I was lying.

"I can't see," I said, finally. "Maybe if you took off the cover again, I'd do better?"

"We don't know if Sobek likes light," Paulo said. His voice sounded strained, weird.

"Sobek is supposed to be a god. You think he's afraid of *sunlight*?"

"It might not be Sobek," Miranda said. "Your mother's visions hint that it may be one of his sacred crocodiles. One that's still growing."

"Honey, we're going to leave you alone now," Mom said. She sounded just like a concerned mother should sound, except she wasn't. "We'll come back tomorrow and you can tell us what you saw. You're going to meet a god, baby. You're so lucky."

Cold terror knotted my stomach. I shouted and begged and threatened, but no one said anything else to me and finally I realized I was alone. They'd gone and my only hope was that they really would come back tomorrow.

By then my hands were cramped so badly from gripping the metal bar that I was afraid they wouldn't hold anything else. I took an unsteady step down, slid my shaking hand onto the next rung. Then, I put my left foot wrong and my hold wasn't nearly good enough to keep me on the ladder.

I fell into the wet, stinking refuse. The breath was knocked out of me. My knees pulsed with pain and my hands felt scraped raw.

In the darkness, something moved, sounding like the scrape of claws along the walls. The water rippled.

Sobek the Destroyer. He didn't seem so funny now.

I scrambled to my feet and started on a stumbling run, hands in front of me. I ran and ran, my heartbeat sounding like footsteps behind me, until the passageway curved and I had to stop long enough to figure out where to go next. I leaned against a slimy wall and realized that I was being silly.

There were no alligators in this sewer. What I'd heard were probably rats. Or, like, a billion cockroaches.

I shook my head and pressed my fingers to my eyes. Then I told myself—out loud—there was no crocodile god.

"Sobek isn't real," I said. "He's like Santa Claus. He's like the closet monster."

I waited a long moment, to hear if blasphemy got me struck down, but nothing happened. I let out my breath.

I had to find a dry place—or at least a less disgusting place—to wait out the night. There was no way to tell time—my watch didn't glow or anything—but morning would come eventually. Then Mom would let me out and I would never, ever trust any of them again.

That started me shuffling again, trying to discern if the waterline rose or fell and feeling along the disgusting walls for some kind of ridge or ramp. If I could just find a place to hole up until then, I'd be fine. Cold and scraped up and totally covered in grossness, but fine.

Then I thought about what my mother and Miranda said about me before they shoved me in the hole. That whole weird thing about me being a virgin. There's only one thing I could think of that you did with virgins in ceremonies—sacrifice them.

My heart started beating as fast as when I was running, so fast that my hand automatically went to my chest, like I could stop my heart from leaping out of my skin.

My mother might not be coming back. She might have dropped me down here to die.

The more I thought about it, the more scared I got, because even if she came back, she really might not let me out of here.

The thing about living with my Mom is that I knew there was a rational, calculating part of her. A part that knew she'd get in trouble for locking her underage daughter in a sewer overnight and that my not being around to tell anyone was her best chance of making it seem like she did nothing wrong.

So I figured that if she did come tomorrow, she'd ask me if Sobek spoke to me. No answer would be the right one. If I said I saw Sobek, she'd send me back to give him another message. If I said I didn't, she'd say I just needed more time.

I'm never getting out of here.

The thought sunk into me like the filthy water seeped into my clothes. I tried to shake it off, to tell myself that there had to be other ways out, but it was hard as I moved deeper and deeper into the tunnels. Hard as my legs ached with the strain of moving through water. Each step made my muscles burn. My sneakers were soaked and heavy with mud, my socks swollen with it.

I kept going, walking for what felt like miles.

My fingers finally brushed the edge of a wide pipe halfway up the wall. It seemed dry inside. If I could get up there, then I could at least rest for a little while.

It took me three tries, leaping up and trying to brace my stomach on the edge like it was a balance beam, then scrabbling with my fingers. On my second try, I fell, knocking my jaw against the metal and falling on my ass in the water. For a moment, I thought I would just start sobbing.

The third try landed me on my belly in the pipe. I heard an echo of my thump down the metal and then the sound of scrabbling claws. *Rats*, I told myself. I was too tired to care. It wasn't wet or covered in foulness. For right then, I didn't have to move. Leaning my head against the curve of the pipe I closed my eyes.

I thought I would just rest for a moment, but despite my surroundings I fell asleep. I must have been exhausted.

My dreams were restless. In one, I saw this guy I liked who sat near me in English class. He was standing over a grate, looking down at me. I was flushed, but really pretty. Like Sleeping Beauty.

He spat on me.

I jerked my head, knocking my cheek against the curved side of the pipe. I woke to the reek of rot and with it, the realization of where I was.

I was shaking with chills, even though I remembered the tunnels as being warm.

You have a fever, I told myself. Was I getting sick? It was hard to concentrate. My mind was racing—flitting from imagining I was in my own bed to slipping into another dream of claws and something huge crawling toward me down the tunnel in the dark.

I heard a long hiss.

I jumped in terror. My sneakers squeaked against metal as I tried to climb backward.

"Sobek?" I whispered. My mouth began to move over the words of stupid sweat prayer automatically.

I felt the weight of body, scaled and warm, as though live coals burned within it, against my shoulder. A long tongue pushed at my hair. Alligators don't have tongues like that. Neither do crocodiles.

I thought of all the cuts I'd gotten falling off the metal railing and all the filthy water I'd waded through. I was sure the cuts were infected. I was feverish. Dreaming.

I held as still as I could, shivering with cold and terror as the long body slid over mine, claws digging lightly into my skin, tail dragging behind it. Then it was gone and my relief was so profound that it wore me out.

When I woke up, there was a soft light coming through a grating far above me, too far to hope that if I screamed, I'd be heard. Occasionally a shadow strobed past, in a way that I thought might suggest traffic.

Sweat slicked my face and plastered curls of my damp hair to my skin. The fever must have broken while I slept.

Crazy is hereditary. Everyone knows that. Whatever made my mother the way she was also must be crawling around in my brain, just waiting for the chance to bloom like mold.

Trauma was a good trigger.

That's why I liked engineering. Electronics. Things that worked the way they were supposed to. If they broke, you could fix them again.

I was lying on a collection of burlap bags that smelled pleasantly of coffee beans. All around me were broken things—iron wheels from factory carts, bent candlesticks, dented microwave ovens, glittering shards of cracked Christmas balls piled together in a deflated tire, mannequins missing body parts, stacks of broken televisions. There wasn't enough light for me to see the edges of the room, but I was sure there was even more junk hidden in the dark.

Beside me was a half-eaten bagel on a paper plate. Beside it was a metal thermos. I opened the top and inhaled. It didn't smell like anything, but there seemed to be some liquid inside. My stomach growled.

"You're awake," said a voice from the dark.

I started to get up and realized that under the burlap sacks, I was undressed. I looked around frantically for my clothes.

A boy came out of the dark, moving cautiously toward me like he was afraid I was going to startle. His face was smudged with dirt, his pale hair sticking up at odd angles.

"Are you okay?" he said, voice sounded raspy. He coughed. "You were really sick."

"Where's my stuff?" I shouted. Wrapping one of the coffee bean bags around myself, I started toward the edges of the room that I couldn't see.

He held both his hands up, palms toward me in surrender. "Calm down. You had a fever and you were really scraped up. Your clothes were rubbing dirt into your wounds. I cleaned pus off you, so do not even think of yelling at me."

I took a long look at him. His face was partially shadowed, but he didn't look like he was lying. He was wearing a T-shirt that hung on him, like he'd lost weight. It made him seem even taller than he was.

"What's your name?" I asked. I wished it was even darker right then so that he couldn't see how embarrassed I was. No boy had ever seen me naked before. I felt conscious of myself in a way I wasn't used to—aware of my body, its curves and flaws.

"Hank," he said. "I've been down here two weeks." He laughed a little in an odd manic way. "I was going kind of crazy. When I found you in the tunnels, I thought you were dead. I nearly tripped over you."

"*Two weeks*?" I asked. My voice shook.

He sat down on the remains of a television and pushed back greasy hair with one hand. "This crazy woman who's obsessed with my dad used to come by my house and watch the place from across the street. One night, I'm coming home from a friend's and she and these two other people just grabbed me. I don't know if they planned on it or what, but here I am. I thought they were going to kill me."

"They grabbed me too," I said. His name rang in my head. Hank. Lots of people were named after their dads.

"How come?" he asked.

"That crazy woman? She's my mother."

For a moment, he just stared at me in astonishment. "Oh," he said and frowned as though he was trying to figure something out. "So you know about the dragon?"

I swallowed hard. "Dragon?"

Apparently my own inner crazy isn't the only thing I should be worried about.

"I don't think I heard you right. You mean their crazy made-up religion?"

"No," he said. "I mean the dragon in the tunnels. It's the reason we can't leave—it sleeps near the only way out. Didn't you hear it?"

I thought about the thing sliding over me in the dark. "I guess not."

"It's real," he said.

I nodded, because I knew agreeing was what he wanted me to do. "Okay."

"Look, I know where there's a pipe of fresh water. I'm going to go there and fill up some more bottles for us. And there's a grate outside a deli where trash gets dropped. People are careless with the dumpster or something. That's what I've been eating and that's what I feed to the dragon. I'm going to go and—"

"You *feed* it?"

He nodded. "Yeah, otherwise it might attack. I'm pretty sure that's what we're here for—to be that thing's dinner."

"Ah," I said.

He must have realized how freaked out I was getting, because he suddenly shifted tone. "But we're going to be fine. We're going to find a way out of here. God, you must think I sound totally insane."

I shook my head. "I don't know what to think." I didn't. My mind was going over possibilities. The thing that moved over me had a head too small for an alligator—plus it felt warm. But it had to be something real, something rational.

"Just stay here. I know my way by now—I'll see if I can find us some food. You should rest or something." He stood up and looked at me, like he was trying to decide something. Then he left.

I listened as he rattled down a pipe, waiting for his steps to stop echoing.

As soon as he was gone, I crawled back over to the coffee sacks and stuffed the bagel in my mouth, chewing it greedily. I washed it down with gulps of water from the thermos. Then I ripped arm holes in one of the sacks so I could wear it like a dress.

After tripping over some tin cans and sliding on some boxes, I discovered that, as far as I could tell, we were in a nexus of pipes. They snaked off downward in several directions.

Looking around at the room, I wondered where all the stuff in it had come from. I doubted he'd had time to collect all of it. Had there been someone here before us? Had there been other sacrifices? The thought chilled me.

I needed to see better.

After my parents' divorce, the judge said that I was supposed to spend weekends with my dad. At first that was what happened, before my mom stopped being able to handle the scheduling and dad stopped demanding visits. But back when I did see my dad, he'd take me to science museums and we'd buy kits for home.

That's where I learned how to make a flashlight out of regular household items.

First you need batteries. I found those after pulling apart a couple of ancient tape decks. I had no idea whether the batteries had any charge left, but I kept hoping. You're supposed to tape them together, but the best I could do was tie them together tightly with one of the strings from the coffee sack—luckily Dad and I had also gone to a special exhibit on sailing knots.

Then there's supposed to be aluminum foil, to stabilize. I skipped that part, since I couldn't find any. But I did manage to get the batteries attached to two long pieces of wood before I heard a movement in one of the pipes.

"Hank?" I called, climbing back on my nest of burlap and tucking my makeshift part of a flashlight under one side.

He limped in, tripping over several of the boxes, and fell. I jumped up. Blood was running down his leg.

"What happened?"

He looked up at me from the floor. His voice was steady, but slow. Distant. "You never told me your name."

"I'm Amaya," I said as I leaned over him.

"Amaya," he repeated. He was sweating and his eyes looked weird.

"You're in shock," I said. I wasn't sure or anything, but that's what people said on cop shows.

"I fell," he said. "I went to feed the dragon and it wasn't by the grate. I thought maybe I could climb up high enough to stick my fingers through. Maybe someone would notice. But I saw it unwinding from the dark and I panicked." He laughed. "I forgot I was still holding food. The dragon must have smelled it."

"Come on, let me look at your leg," I said. All I knew about was fixing machines; I had no idea what to do with people.

I pushed up the cuff of his jeans and tried to wash out a shallow scrape with what was left of the water in the thermos. His ankle had already swollen up. Just touching it made him flinch. I helped him get over to the burlap sacks.

"I think I twisted it," he said faintly. "I'm going to die down here. I'm glad at least one person will know what happened to me, but it sucks. It really sucks. I don't want to—"

"We're getting out," I said. "Honest. I promise."

He snorted. "You *promise*? Like I promised you things were going to be fine? Before you got here I was thinking of just going down and letting that thing eat me. What was the point of delaying it? But then you're here and I want to show off. Look at me, I can get us out. And I wind up like this."

"I think we should elevate your leg," I told him, purposefully ignoring everything he'd said.

"Okay," he said, defeated, his words slurred. I had no idea if that was part of shock or if he was just tired. "Do you know how to splint a leg?"

I shook my head.

"I was in boy scouts and I got a badge for first-aid that included splints. Never did one for real though," he said with a wince. "I'll talk you through it."

"Okay," I said.

"Go find me something stiff and long enough to go from my knee to my ankle. That and rope." He was talking oddly.

I hunted among the junk. There wasn't any rope, but I found enough long strips of string, parts of bags, and cloth to braid together into something pretty tough. He kept nodding off while I worked, though.

"Amaya," he called muzzily.

"Yeah?" I said, pulling a plank of wood off a piece of fencing.

"What are you going to do when you get out of here? The very first thing?"

"When *we* get out of here," I said.

"Sure," Hank said. "We."

"A burger," I said. "A big fat one with cheese and mustard and pickles. Then a whole bag of Doritos. How about you?"

"Pizza," said Hank. "With every topping from anchovies to pineapple. Heaped. And a gallon of orange soda."

I made a face, but he couldn't see me. Too bad, I'm sure it would have made him laugh. "Okay, other than food?"

"A hot bath," he laughed. "When my mom died, we never cleaned out her stuff from the bathroom. There's a whole shelf of half-empty bubble baths. I am going to use them *all*."

"I'm sorry about your mother. I didn't know she was dead."

"Yeah," said Hank. "You don't know anything about me."

"You don't know anything about me either," I said, picking up a strip of torn upholstery fabric and braiding it into my makeshift rope.

"I know about your mother. You know if we get out of here, they're going to arrest her, right?"

"Because you'll press charges. I know."

"She tried to kill us," he said.

"*I know!*" I shouted back at him. My voice echoed off the walls.

"Sorry," he said. "I'm just hurting. I'm a jerk when I'm hurting."

I walked over with my rope and board. He explained about making sure his leg was straight, padding the board and putting it under his leg, tying it so he still had circulation. I tried to keep my fingers gentle on his skin.

"Where are you going to go?" he asked.

"You mean because I can't go home?" I shrugged my shoulders. "My dad would probably let me stay with him, although I don't know if he'd like it. He didn't exactly fight Mom for custody. But then, my mom steamrollered over him pretty much all the time. Or I guess I could couch-surf."

There was a long pause. I looked over at him and saw that he was either asleep or unconscious.

Not sure what else to do, I looked around for the rest of the parts to my flashlight. I found two small screws fairly easily and inserted them into cardboard. A paper clip attached to one screw. Then I pulled out two wires from the back of the television and wrapped one around the negative end of the battery and the other around the paper-clip-less screw.

I was almost ready.

The final part needed a working light bulb. I found one broken and two burnt-out ones in the pile of refuse. Luckily, the Science Museum covered fixing those too. It wouldn't have been hard, except for the dim light.

Basically, the filament usually breaks so that there is no longer one clean connection. But the ends are pretty springy and flexible. So you just spin the bulb and wait for them to catch again. Unless the break is really bad, they usually will.

When I put the bulb back into my bootleg flashlight, it burned bright, stinging my eyes. For the first time in what feels like months, I could finally see.

"Wow," Hank said blearily. I hadn't realized he woke up again. "Not a lot of girls know that stuff."

I grinned. "I'm a good person to be trapped in a sewer with."

"Yeah," he said.

In the light, I could see that despite the hollows of his cheekbones and the blue bruises around his eyes, Hank was the kind of guy you looked at twice. He had a nice mouth.

I felt suddenly self-conscious. "Where is it?" I asked Hank. "Can you give me a map to this dragon?"

"You still don't believe me, do you?"

"It doesn't matter," I said. "Maybe it's a dragon. Maybe it's some other kind of animal. It's still got to keep getting fed and obviously you can't go feed it."

He sighs and traces the directions on the dirt of the floor. I roll the remaining bulb to get the filament to attach and shove it in my pocket.

The odd thing about light is how it makes distance different. The sewer looked narrow, navigable now that I could see it. It wasn't a labyrinth full of monsters, just a dirty tunnel.

I carefully picked my way along, according to Hank's scratchy map. In one of my hands, a length of sharpened pipe hung, like a sword.

As the light splashed along the walls, I wondered about my mother. If there really was something in the tunnel that I can't explain, did that mean that her magic was real? Did it mean that my mother, in her crappy apartment, could call down the gods? Even a crocodile—even an alligator—was so unlikely it seemed mystical. Even that would be hard to explain.

That thought lasted until I came to the dragon.

Hank was right; there was no other way to describe it. It had the triangular shaped head of a cat, a long sinuous neck, and a thin black lizard's body. Its eyes reflected gold when the flashlight caught them. It let out a long hiss and something that might have been a curl of smoke escaped from its mouth.

I took a step back, holding up the pipe. The dragon watched me, but didn't advance.

Was this what my mother saw? Was this the thing that pushed her over the edge? I had no idea how I could be looking at this thing, how it could be real, but I understood suddenly the desire to co-opt a mythology that would explain it away.

The dragon sniffed the air and let out a little sound, like a cry. Then it took a few steps toward me.

I realized then what I'd failed to really see before. The dragon wasn't full-grown. I mean, I could see right away that it was smaller than they were in the movies—about the size of a very large horse—but when it moved, it was with kittenish unsteadiness.

Without the flashlight, I would have run. But with it, I stared in fascination as the dragon wobbled up to me, tongue flicking out. I winced and put out my hand. It sniffed, breath hot on my skin. Maybe it really could breathe fire.

"You hungry?" I asked it.

The creature startled and skittered back at the sound of my voice. It was *afraid*. Of *me*. Of us. I wondered where its mother was, whether she might be nearby, a larger and more dangerous monster. But if she wasn't…

Past the creature, I could see the metal steps attached to the tunnel wall. The ones that Hank said would let us get up to the surface. If I made a loud enough sound and was fast enough, if the creature really was a little timid, I might be able to kill it.

Hit it hard enough and then just keep hitting.

The dragon butted its head against my thigh abruptly. It was stronger that it looked and I staggered back from the weight. It bumped me again. I thought of sharks—the way they are supposed to knock into things before taking a bite out of them.

"Hey," I said, gripping the steel rod tighter. "Stop it!"

The creature looked up at me with its strange eyes—unreadably animal. I reached down gingerly to touch its head. Its skin felt warm and slightly damp. As I rubbed my fingers down its neck, its eyes drifted closed and it turned to show me the long length of its vulnerable throat.

Hank went in front, climbed the ladder and banged on the bottom of the manhole. I'd already taken care of the dragon.

It took a while, but Hank's screaming and shouting finally brought three guys out of a nearby pizza place to crowbar up the manhole. They said an ambulance would be on the way, but that was the last thing we wanted.

The sunlight was so bright that it made us shade our eyes. Seeing ourselves reflected in the store window, our cracked lips and wild hair, our dirt-stained skin, I couldn't help thinking that we must look not quite human ourselves.

I wasn't sure I quite felt human, either.

"Ready?" Hank asked.

I nodded.

Poor Sobek totally panicked when Hank and I hauled her up. Good thing I had her wrapped pretty tightly in one of those burlap coffee bags. She'd mostly shredded her way out of it by the time we dumped her on the asphalt, but at least we got her out of the sewer. We'd woven a collar for her out of scraps of cloth and string, so even though she was freaking out, we were able to tug her into the shade.

Like I'd said to Hank in the tunnels, we couldn't leave her there. Her mother was gone. Someone had to be responsible.

"Got any money?" I asked. "I would kill for that cheeseburger."

We pooled our cash and I walked a few blocks to a fast food restaurant that said I had to walk over to the drive-up window, since I was too dirty to be served inside. I didn't care. When I brought back the food, we split it evenly. Three ways.

The dragon gulped down her burger in seconds and started chewing on the wrapper. She seemed pretty adaptable. And she sure was cute.

"What now?" Hank asked.

"You better go home. You need someone to look at that ankle. Besides," I said, "you've got charges to file."

"You could come with me," Hank said gravely.

"Thanks," I said, shaking my head. "But I can take care of myself."

"I know that," he said. "*You idiot*. Do you really think I don't know that?

I shrugged my shoulders.

"But you don't have to face everything alone," he said and grabbed hold of my arm. Even though we were dirty and tired, when he kissed me, everything else kind of faded away for a moment.

A rumbling truck passed, brakes screeching. We pulled apart, not quite looking at one another. Sobek tucked her face against his thigh and shivered.

I grinned. "I'm not alone. I've got Sobek."

"She's not so scary in the daylight, is she?" Hank said, with a laugh. "Certainly not scary enough to live up to that name."

My eyes were starting to adjust to the sun.

I rubbed the bridge of the dragon's nose, where she liked to be petted. "She's going to grow so big that she doesn't have to be afraid of anything."

So are we.

KING DRAGON

Michael Swanwick

Michael Swanwick's first two short stories were published in 1980, and both appeared on the Nebula ballot that year. One of the major writers working in the field today, he has been nominated for at least one of the field's major awards in almost every successive year (he may have been out of the country in 1983 and 1986), and has won the Hugo, Nebula, World Fantasy, Theodore Sturgeon Memorial, and the Locus awards. He has published nine collections of short fiction, seven novels, an appreciation of Hope Mirlees, and a Hugo Award-nominated book-length interview with editor Gardner Dozois. His most recent book is collection *The Best of Michael Swanwick*. He is currently working on a new novel featuring his itinerant duo, Darger and Sir Plus.

Swanwick's 1993 novel *The Iron Dragon's Daughter* features elves in Armani and dragons as jet fighters. A dark, technological and brutal tale, it is an example of what Swanwick labeled "hard fantasy" in his essay "In the Tradition". The story that follows appeared in 2003 and is part of his novel, *The Dragons of Babel*, published by Tor Books. Set during a Vietnam-style war in Faerie, it introduces that novel's protagonist. As Swanwick said in an interview, "He goes off to a much stranger place than his native Faerie, toward adventures I hope will be satisfying to the fantasy reader while at the same time being a subversion of all that is good and decent in fantasy!"

The dragons came at dawn, flying low and in formation, their jets so thunderous they shook the ground like the great throbbing heartbeat of the world. The village elders ran outside, half unbuttoned, waving their staffs in circles and shouting words of power. *Vanish*, they cried to the land, and *sleep* to the skies, though had the dragons' half-elven pilots cared they could have easily seen through such flimsy spells of concealment. But the pilots' thoughts were turned toward the West, where Avalon's industrial strength was based, and where its armies were rumored to be massing.

Will's aunt made a blind grab for him, but he ducked under her arm and ran out into the dirt street. The gun emplacements to the south were speaking now, in booming shouts that filled the sky with bursts of pink smoke and flak.

Half the children in the village were out in the streets, hopping up and down in glee, the winged ones buzzing about in small, excited circles. Then the yage-witch came hobbling out from her barrel and, demonstrating a strength Will had never suspected her of having, swept her arms wide and then slammed together her hoary old hands with a *boom!* that drove the children, all against their will, back into their huts.

All save Will. He had been performing that act which rendered one immune from child-magic every night for three weeks now. Fleeing from the village, he felt the enchantment like a polite hand placed on his shoulder. One weak tug, and then it was gone.

He ran, swift as the wind, up Grannystone Hill. His great-great-great-grand-mother lived there still, alone at its tip, as a grey standing stone. She never said anything. But sometimes, though one never saw her move, she went down to the river at night to drink. Coming back from a night-time fishing trip in his wee coracle, Will would find her standing motionless there and greet her respectfully. If the catch was good, he would gut an eel or a small trout, and smear the blood over her feet. It was the sort of small courtesy elderly relatives appreciated.

"Will, you young fool, turn back!" a cobbley cried from the inside of a junk refrigerator in the garbage dump at the edge of the village. "It's not safe up there!"

But Will didn't want to be safe. He shook his head, long blond hair flying behind him, and put every ounce of his strength into his running. He wanted to see dragons. Dragons! Creatures of almost unimaginable power and magic. He wanted to experience the glory of their flight. He wanted to get as close to them as he could. It was a kind of mania. It was a kind of need.

It was not far to the hill, nor a long way to its bald and grassy summit. Will ran with a wildness he could not understand, lungs pounding and the wind of his own speed whistling in his ears.

And then he was atop the hill, breathing hard, with one hand on his grand-mother stone.

The dragons were still flying overhead in waves. The roar of their jets was astounding. Will lifted his face into the heat of their passage, and felt the wash of their malice and hatred as well. It was like a dark wine that sickened the stomach and made the head throb with pain and bewilderment and wonder. It repulsed him and made him want more.

The last flight of dragons scorched over, twisting his head and spinning his body around, so he could keep on watching them, flying low over farms and fields and the Old Forest that stretched all the way to the horizon and beyond. There was a faint brimstone stench of burnt fuel in the air. Will felt his heart grow so large it seemed impossible his chest could contain it, so large that it threatened to encompass the hill, farms, forest, dragons, and all the world beyond.

Something hideous and black leaped up from the distant forest and into the air, flashing toward the final dragon. Will's eyes felt a painful wrenching *wrongness*, and then a stone hand came down over them.

"*Don't look,*" said an old and calm and stony voice. "*To look upon a basilisk is no way for a child of mine to die.*"

"Grandmother?" Will asked.

"*Yes?*"

"If I promise to keep my eyes closed, will you tell me what's happening?"

There was a brief silence. Then: "*Very well. The dragon has turned. He is fleeing.*"

"Dragons don't flee," Will said scornfully. "Not from anything." Forgetting his promise, he tried to pry the hand from his eyes. But of course it was useless, for his fingers were mere flesh.

"*This one does. And he is wise to do so. His fate has come for him. Out from the halls of coral it has come, and down to the halls of granite will it take him. Even now his pilot is singing his death-song.*"

She fell silent again, while the distant roar of the dragon rose and fell in pitch. Will could tell that momentous things were happening, but the sound gave him not the least clue as to their nature. At last he said, "Grandmother? Now?"

"*He is clever, this one. He fights very well. He is elusive. But he cannot escape a basilisk. Already the creature knows the first two syllables of his true name. At this very moment it is speaking to his heart, and telling it to stop beating.*"

The roar of the dragon grew louder again, and then louder still. From the way it kept on growing, Will was certain the great creature was coming straight toward him. Mingled with its roar was a noise that was like a cross between a scarecrow screaming and the sound of teeth scraping on slate.

"*Now they are almost touching. The basilisk reaches for its prey…*"

There was a deafening explosion directly overhead. For an astonishing instant, Will felt certain he was going to die. Then his grandmother threw her stone cloak over him and, clutching him to her warm breast, knelt down low to the sheltering earth.

When he awoke, it was dark and he lay alone on the cold hillside. Painfully, he stood. A somber orange-and-red sunset limned the western horizon, where the dragons had disappeared. There was no sign of the War anywhere.

"Grandmother?" Will stumbled to the top of the hill, cursing the stones that hindered him. He ached in every joint. There was a constant ringing in his ears, like factory bells tolling the end of a shift. "Grandmother!"

There was no answer.

The hilltop was empty.

But scattered down the hillside, from its top down to where he had awakened, was a stream of broken stones. He had hurried past them without looking on his way up. Now he saw that their exterior surfaces were the familiar and comfortable grey of his stone-mother, and that the freshly-exposed interior surfaces were slick with blood.

One by one, Will carried the stones back to the top of the hill, back to the spot where his great-great-great-grandmother had preferred to stand and watch over the village. It took hours. He piled them one on top of another, and though it felt like more work than he had ever done in his life, when he was finished, the cairn did not rise even so high as his waist. It seemed impossible that this could be all that remained of she who had protected the village for so many generations.

By the time he was done, the stars were bright and heartless in a black, moonless sky. A night-wind ruffled his shirt and made him shiver, and with sudden clarity he wondered at last why he was alone. Where was his aunt? Where were the other villagers?

Belatedly remembering his basic spell-craft, he yanked out his rune-bag from a hip pocket, and spilled its contents into his hand. A crumpled blue-jay's feather, a shard of mirror, two acorns, and a pebble with one side blank and the other marked with an X. He kept the mirror-shard and poured the rest back into the bag. Then he invoked the secret name of the *lux aeterna*, inviting a tiny fraction of its radiance to enter the mundane world.

A gentle foxfire spread itself through the mirror. Holding it at arm's length so he could see his face reflected therein, he asked the oracle glass, "Why did my village not come for me?"

The mirror-boy's mouth moved. "They came." His skin was pallid, like a corpse's.

"Then why didn't they bring me home?" And why did *he* have to build his stone-grandam's cairn and not they? He did not ask that question, but he felt it to the core of his being.

"They didn't find you."

The oracle-glass was maddeningly literal, capable only of answering the question one asked, rather than that which one wanted answered. But Will persisted. "Why didn't they find me?"

"You weren't here."

"Where was I? Where was my Granny?"

"You were nowhere."

"How could we be nowhere?"

Tonelessly, the mirror said, "The basilisk's explosion warped the world and the mesh of time in which it is caught. The sarsen-lady and you were thrown forward, halfway through the day."

It was as clear an explanation as Will as going to get. He muttered a word of unbinding, releasing the invigorating light back to whence it came. Then, fearful that the blood on his hands and clothes would draw night-gaunts, he hurried homeward.

When he got to the village, he discovered that a search party was still scouring the darkness, looking for him. Those who remained had hoisted a straw man upside-down atop a tall pole at the center of the village square, and set it ablaze against the chance he was still alive, to draw him home.

And so it had.

Two days after those events, a crippled dragon crawled out of the Old Forest and into the village. Slowly he pulled himself into the center square. Then he collapsed. He was wingless and there were gaping holes in his fuselage, but still the stench of power clung to him, and a miasma of hatred. A trickle of oil seeped from a gash in his belly and made a spreading stain on the cobbles beneath him.

Will was among those who crowded out to behold this prodigy. The others whispered hurtful remarks among themselves about its ugliness. And truly it was built of cold, black iron, and scorched even darker by the basilisk's explosion, with jagged stumps of metal where its wings had been and ruptured plates here and there along its flanks. But Will could see that, even half-destroyed, the dragon was a beautiful creature. It was built with dwarven skill to high-elven design—how could it *not* be beautiful? It was, he felt certain, that same dragon which he had almost-seen shot down by the basilisk.

Knowing this gave him a strange sense of shameful complicity, as if he were in some way responsible for the dragon's coming to the village.

For a long time no one spoke. Then an engine hummed to life somewhere deep within the dragon's chest, rose in pitch to a clattering whine, and fell again into silence. The dragon slowly opened one eye.

"Bring me your truth-teller," he rumbled.

The truth-teller was a fruit-woman named Bessie Applemere. She was young and yet, out of respect for her office, everybody called her by the honorific Hag. She came, clad in the robes and wide hat of her calling, breasts bare as was traditional, and stood before the mighty engine of war. "Father of Lies." She bowed respectfully.

"I am crippled, and all my missiles are spent," the dragon said. "But still am I dangerous."

Hag Applemere nodded. "It is the truth."

"My tanks are yet half-filled with jet fuel. It would be the easiest thing in the world for me to set them off with an electrical spark. And were I to do so, your village and all who live within it would cease to be. Therefore, since power engenders power, I am now your liege and king."

"It is the truth."

A murmur went up from the assembled villagers.

"However, my reign will be brief. By Samhain, the Armies of the Mighty will be here, and they shall take me back to the great forges of the East to be rebuilt."

"You believe it so."

The dragon's second eye opened. Both focused steadily on the truth-teller. "You do not please me, Hag. I may someday soon find it necessary to break open your body and eat your beating heart."

Hag Applemere nodded. "It is the truth."

Unexpectedly, the dragon laughed. It was cruel and sardonic laughter, as the mirth of such creatures always was, but it was laughter nonetheless. Many of the villagers covered their ears against it. The smaller children burst into tears. "You amuse me," he said. "All of you amuse me. We begin my reign on a gladsome note."

The truth-teller bowed. Watching, Will thought he detected a great sadness in her eyes. But she said nothing.

"Let your lady-mayor come forth, that she might give me obeisance."

Auld Black Agnes shuffled from the crowd. She was scrawny and thrawn and bent almost double from the weight of her responsibilities. They hung in a black leather bag around her neck. From that bag, she brought forth a flat stone from the first hearth of the village, and laid it down before the dragon. Kneeling, she placed her left hand, splayed, upon it.

Then she took out a small silver sickle.

"Your blood and ours. Thy fate and mine. Our joy and your wickedness. Let all be as one." Her voice rose in a warbling keen:

"Black spirits and white, red spirits and grey,
Mingle, mingle, mingle, you that mingle may."

Her right hand trembled with palsy as it raised the sickle up above her left. But her slanting motion downward was swift and sudden. Blood spurted, and her little finger went flying.

She made one small, sharp cry, like a sea-bird's, and no more.

"I am satisfied," the dragon said. Then, without transition: "My pilot is dead and he begins to rot." A hatch hissed open in his side. "Drag him forth."

"Do you wish him buried?" a kobold asked hesitantly.

"Bury him, burn him, cut him up for bait—what do I care? When he was alive, I needed him in order to fly. But he's dead now, and of no use to me."

"Kneel."

Will knelt in the dust beside the dragon. He'd been standing in line for hours, and there were villagers who would be standing in that same line hours from now, waiting to be processed. They went in fearful, and they came out dazed. When a lily-maid stepped down from the dragon, and somebody shouted a question at her, she simply shook her tear-streaked face, and fled. None would speak of what happened within.

The hatch opened.

"Enter."

He did. The hatch closed behind him.

At first he could see nothing. Then small, faint lights swam out of the darkness. Bits of green and white stabilized, became instrument lights, pale luminescent flecks on dials. One groping hand touched leather. It was the pilot's couch. He could smell, faintly, the taint of corruption on it.

"Sit."

Clumsily, he climbed into the seat. The leather creaked under him. His arms naturally lay along the arms of the couch. He might have been made for it. There were handgrips. At the dragon's direction, he closed his hands about them and turned them as far as they would go. A quarter-turn, perhaps.

From beneath, needles slid into his wrists. They stung like blazes, and Will jerked involuntarily. But when he tried, he discovered that he could not let go of the grips. His fingers would no longer obey him.

"Boy," the dragon said suddenly, "what is your true name?"

Will trembled. "I don't have one."

Immediately, he sensed that this was not the right answer. There was a silence. Then the dragon said dispassionately, "I can make you suffer."

"Sir, I am certain you can."

"Then tell me your true name."

His wrists were cold—cold as ice. The sensation that spread up his forearms to his elbows was not numbness, for they ached terribly. It felt as if they were packed in snow. "I don't *know* it!" Will cried in an anguish. "I don't know, I was never told, I don't think I have one!"

Small lights gleamed on the instrument panel, like forest eyes at night.

"Interesting." For the first time, the dragon's voice displayed a faint tinge of emotion. "What family is yours? Tell me everything about them."

Will had no family other than his aunt. His parents had died on the very first day of the War. Theirs was the ill fortune of being in Brocielande Station when the dragons came and dropped golden fire on the rail yards. So Will had been shipped off to the hills to live with his aunt. Everyone agreed he would be safest there. That was several years ago, and there were times now when he could not remember his parents at all. Soon he would have only the memory of remembering.

As for his aunt, Blind Enna was little more to him than a set of rules to be contravened and chores to be evaded. She was a pious old creature, forever killing small animals in honor of the Nameless Ones and burying their corpses under the floor or nailing them above doors or windows. In consequence of which, a faint perpetual stink of conformity and rotting mouse hung about the hut. She mumbled to herself constantly and on those rare occasions when she got drunk—two or three times a year—would run out naked into the night and, mounting a cow backwards, lash its sides bloody with a hickory switch so that it ran wildly uphill and down until finally she tumbled off and fell asleep. At dawn Will would come with a blanket and lead her home. But they were never exactly close.

All this he told in stumbling, awkward words. The dragon listened without comment.

The cold had risen up to Will's armpits by now. He shuddered as it touched his shoulders. "Please…" he said. "Lord Dragon… your ice has reached my chest. If it touches my heart, I fear that I'll die."

"Hmmm? Ah! I was lost in thought." The needles withdrew from Will's arms. They were still numb and lifeless, but at least the cold had stopped its spread.

He could feel a tingle of pins and needles in the center of his fingertips, and so knew that sensation would eventually return.

The door hissed open. "You may leave now."

He stumbled out into the light.

An apprehension hung over the village for the first week or so. But as the dragon remained quiescent and no further alarming events occurred, the timeless patterns of village life more or less resumed. Yet all the windows opening upon the center square remained perpetually shuttered and nobody willingly passed through it anymore, so that it was as if a stern silence had come to dwell within their midst.

Then one day Will and Puck Berrysnatcher were out in the woods, checking their snares for rabbits and camelopards (it had been generations since a pard was caught in Avalon but they still hoped), when the Scissors-Grinder came puffing down the trail. He lugged something bright and gleaming within his two arms.

"Hey, bandy-man!" Will cried. He had just finished tying his rabbits' legs together so he could sling them over his shoulder. "Ho, big-belly! What hast thou?"

"Don't know. Fell from the sky."

"Did *not!*" Puck scoffed. The two boys danced about the fat cobber, grabbing at the golden thing. It was shaped something like a crown and something like a bird-cage. The metal of its ribs and bands was smooth and lustrous. Black runes adorned its sides. They had never seen its like. "I bet it's a roc's egg—or a phoenix's!"

And simultaneously Will asked, "Where are you taking it?"

"To the smithy. Perchance the hammermen can beat it down into something useful." The Scissors-Grinder swatted at Puck with one hand, almost losing his hold on the object. "Perchance they'll pay me a penny or three for it."

Daisy Jenny popped up out of the flowers in the field by the edge of the garbage dump and, seeing the golden thing, ran toward it, pigtails flying, singing, "Gimme-gimme-gimme!" Two hummingirls and one chimney-bounder came swooping down out of nowhere. And the Cauldron Boy dropped an armful of scavenged scrap metal with a crash and came running up as well. So that by the time the Meadows Trail became Mud Street, the Scissors-Grinder was red-faced and cursing, and knee-deep in children.

"Will, you useless creature!"

Turning, Will saw his aunt, Blind Enna, tapping toward him. She had a peeled willow branch in each hand, like long white antennae, that felt the ground before her as she came. The face beneath her bonnet was grim. He knew this mood, and knew better than to try to evade her when she was in it. "Auntie…" he said.

"Don't you Auntie me, you slugabed! There's toads to be buried and stoops to be washed. Why are you never around when it's time for chores?"

She put an arm through his and began dragging him homeward, still feeling ahead of herself with her wands.

Meanwhile, the Scissors-Grinder was so distracted by the children that he let his feet carry him the way they habitually went—through Center Square, rather than around it. For the first time since the coming of the dragon, laughter and children's voices spilled into that silent space. Will stared yearningly over his shoulder after his dwindling friends.

The dragon opened an eye to discover the cause of so much noise. He reared up his head in alarm. In a voice of power he commanded, "*Drop that!*"

Startled, the Scissors-Grinder obeyed.

The device exploded.

Magic in the imagination is a wondrous thing, but magic in practice is terrible beyond imagining. An unending instant's dazzlement and confusion left Will lying on his back in the street. His ears rang horribly, and he felt strangely numb. There were legs everywhere—people running. And somebody was hitting him with a stick. No, with two sticks.

He sat up, and the end of a stick almost got him in the eye. He grabbed hold of it with both hands and yanked at it angrily. "Auntie!" he yelled. Blind Enna went on waving the other stick around, and tugging at the one he had captured, trying to get it back. "Auntie, stop that!" But of course she couldn't hear him; he could barely hear himself through the ringing in his ears.

He got to his feet and put both arms around his aunt. She struggled against him, and Will was astonished to find that she was no taller than he. When had *that* happened? She had been twice his height when first he came to her. "Auntie Enna!" he shouted into her ear. "It's me, Will, I'm right here."

"Will." Her eyes filled with tears. "You shiftless, worthless thing. Where are you when there are chores to be done?"

Over her shoulder, he saw how the square was streaked with black and streaked with red. There were things that looked like they might be bodies. He blinked. The square was filled with villagers, leaning over them. Doing things. Some had their heads thrown back, as if they were wailing. But of course he couldn't hear them, not over the ringing noise.

"I caught two rabbits, Enna," he told his aunt, shouting so he could be heard. He still had them, slung over his shoulder. He couldn't imagine why. "We can have them for supper."

"That's good," she said. "I'll cut them up for stew, while you wash the stoops."

Blind Enna found her refuge in work. She mopped the ceiling and scoured the floor. She had Will polish every piece of silver in the house. Then all the furniture had to be taken apart, and cleaned, and put back together again. The rugs had to be boiled. The little filigreed case containing her heart had to be taken out of the cupboard where she normally kept it and hidden in the very back of the closet.

The list of chores that had to be done was endless. She worked herself, and Will as well, all the way to dusk. Sometimes he cried at the thought of his friends who had died, and Blind Enna hobbled over and hit him to make him stop. Then, when he did stop, he felt nothing. He felt nothing, and he felt like a monster for feeling nothing. Thinking of it made him begin to cry again, so he wrapped his arms tight around his face to muffle the sounds, so his aunt would not hear and hit him again.

It was hard to say which—the feeling or the not—made him more miserable.

The very next day, the summoning bell was rung in the town square and, willing or no, all the villagers once again assembled before their king dragon. "Oh, ye foolish creatures!" the dragon said. "Six children have died and old *Tanarahumra*—he whom you called the Scissors-Grinder—as well, because you have no self-discipline."

Hag Applemere bowed her head sadly. "It is the truth."

"You try my patience," the dragon said. "Worse, you drain my batteries. My reserves grow low, and I can only partially recharge them each day. Yet I see now that I dare not be King Log. You must be governed. Therefore, I require a speaker. Somebody slight of body, to live within me and carry my commands to the outside."

Auld Black Agnes shuffled forward. "That would be me," she said wearily. "I know my duty."

"No!" the dragon said scornfully. "You aged crones are too cunning by half. I'll choose somebody else from this crowd. Someone simple… a child."

Not me, Will thought wildly. *Anybody else but me.*

"Him," the dragon said.

So it was that Will came to live within the dragon king. All that day and late into the night he worked drawing up plans on sheets of parchment, at his lord's careful instructions, for devices very much like stationary bicycles that could be used to recharge the dragon's batteries. In the morning, he went to the blacksmith's forge at the edge of town to command that six of the things be immediately built. Then he went to Auld Black Agnes to tell her that all day and every day six villagers, elected by lot or rotation or however else she chose, were to sit upon the devices pedaling, pedaling, all the way without cease from dawn to sundown, when Will would drag the batteries back inside.

Hurrying through the village with his messages—there were easily a dozen packets of orders, warnings, and advices that first day—Will experienced a strange sense of unreality. Lack of sleep made everything seem impossibly vivid. The green moss on the skulls stuck in the crotches of forked sticks lining the first half-mile of the River Road, the salamanders languidly copulating in the coals of the smithy forge, even the stillness of the carnivorous plants in his auntie's garden as they waited for an unwary frog to hop within striking distance… such homely sights were transformed. Everything was new and strange to him.

By noon, all the dragon's errands were run, so Will went out in search of friends. The square was empty, of course, and silent. But when he wandered out into the lesser streets, his shadow short beneath him, they were empty as well. It was eerie. Then he heard the high sound of a girlish voice and followed it around a corner.

There was a little girl playing at jump-rope and chanting:

"Here-am-I-and
All-a-lone;
What's-my-name?
It's-Jum-ping—"

"Joan!" Will cried, feeling an unexpected relief at the sight of her.

Jumping Joan stopped. In motion, she had a certain kinetic presence. Still, she was hardly there at all. A hundred slim braids exploded from her small, dark head. Her arms and legs were thin as reeds. The only things of any size at all about her were her luminous brown eyes. "I was up to a million!" she said angrily. "Now I'll have to start all over again."

"When you start again, count your first jump as a million-and-one."

"It doesn't work that way and you know it! What do you want?"

"Where is everybody?"

"Some of them are fishing and some are hunting. Others are at work in the fields. The hammermen, the tinker, and the Sullen Man are building bicycles-that-don't-move to place in Tyrant Square. The potter and her 'prentices are digging clay from the riverbank. The healing-women are in the smoke-hutch at the edge of the woods with Puck Berrysnatcher."

"Then that last is where I'll go. My thanks, wee-thing."

Jumping Joan, however, made no answer. She was already skipping rope again, and counting "A-hundred-thousand-one, a-hundred-thousand-two…"

The smoke-hutch was an unpainted shack built so deep in the reeds that whenever it rained it was in danger of sinking down into the muck and never being seen again. Hornets lazily swam to and from a nest beneath its eaves. The door creaked noisily as Will opened it.

As one, the women looked up sharply. Puck Berrysnatcher's body was a pale white blur on the shadowy ground before them. The women's eyes were green and unblinking, like those of jungle animals. They glared at him wordlessly. "I w-wanted to see what you were d-doing," he stammered.

"We are inducing catatonia," one of them said. "Hush now. Watch and learn."

The healing-women were smoking cigars over Puck. They filled their mouths with smoke and then, leaning close, let it pour down over his naked, broken body. By slow degrees the hut filled with bluish smoke, turning the healing-women to ghosts and Puck himself into an indistinct smear on the dirt floor. He sobbed and murmured in pain at first, but by slow degrees his cries grew quieter, and then silent. At last his body shuddered and stiffened, and he ceased breathing.

The healing-women daubed Puck's chest with ocher, and then packed his mouth, nostrils, and anus with a mixture of aloe and white clay. They wrapped his body with a long white strip of linen.

Finally they buried him deep in the black marsh mud by the edge of Hagmere Pond.

When the last shovelful of earth had been tamped down, the women turned as one and silently made their ways home, along five separate paths. Will's stomach rumbled, and he realized he hadn't eaten yet that day. There was a cherry tree not far away whose fruit was freshly come to ripeness, and a pigeon pie that he knew of which would not be well-guarded.

Swift as a thief, he sped into town.

He expected the dragon to be furious with him when he finally returned to it just before sundown, for staying away as long as he could. But when he sat down in the leather couch and the needles slid into his wrists, the dragon's voice was a murmur, almost a purr. "How fearful you are! You tremble. Do not be afraid, small one. I shall protect and cherish you. And you, in turn, shall be my eyes and ears, eh? Yes, you will. Now, let us see what you learned today."

"I—"

"Shussssh," the dragon breathed. "Not a word. I need not your interpretation, but direct access to your memories. Try to relax. This will hurt you, the first time, but with practice it will grow easier. In time, perhaps, you will learn to enjoy it."

Something cold and wet and slippery slid into Will's mind. A coppery foulness filled his mouth. A repulsive stench rose up in his nostrils. Reflexively, he retched and struggled.

"Don't resist. This will go easier if you open yourself to me."

More of that black and oily sensation poured into Will, and more. Coil upon coil, it thrust its way inside him. His body felt distant, like a thing that no longer belonged to him. He could hear it making choking noises.

"Take it all."

It hurt. It hurt more than the worst headache Will had ever had. He thought he heard his skull cracking from the pressure, and still the intrusive presence pushed into him, its pulsing mass permeating his thoughts, his senses, his memories. Swelling them. Engorging them. And then, just as he was certain his head must explode from the pressure, it was done.

The dragon was within him.

Squeezing shut his eyes, Will saw, in the dazzling, pain-laced darkness, the dragon king as he existed in the spirit world: Sinuous, veined with light, humming with power. Here, in the realm of ideal forms, he was not a broken, crippled *thing*, but a sleek being with the beauty of an animal and the perfection of a machine.

"Am I not beautiful?" the dragon asked. "Am I not a delight to behold?"

Will gagged with pain and disgust. And yet—might the Seven forgive him for thinking this!—it was true.

Every morning at dawn Will dragged out batteries weighing almost as much as himself into Tyrant Square for the villagers to recharge—one at first, then more as the remaining six standing bicycles were built. One of the women would be waiting to give him breakfast. As the dragon's agent, he was entitled to go into any hut and feed himself from what he found there, but the dragon deemed this method more dignified. The rest of the day he spent wandering through the village and, increasingly, the woods and fields around the village, observing. At first he did not know what he was looking for. But by comparing the orders he transmitted with what he had seen the previous day, he slowly came to realize that he was scouting out the village's defensive position, discovering its weaknesses, and looking for ways to alleviate them.

The village was, Will saw, simply not defensible from any serious military force. But it could be made more obscure. Thorn-hedges were planted, and poison oak. Footpaths were eradicated. A clearwater pond was breached and drained, lest it be identified as a resource for advancing armies. When the weekly truck came up the River Road with mail and cartons of supplies for the store, Will was loitering nearby, to ensure that nothing unusual caught the driver's eye. When the bee-warden declared a surplus that might be sold down-river for silver, Will relayed the dragon's instructions that half the overage be destroyed, lest the village get a reputation for prosperity.

At dimity, as the sunlight leached from the sky, Will would feel a familiar aching in his wrists and a troubling sense of need, and return to the dragon's cabin to lie in painful communion with him and share what he had seen.

Evenings varied. Sometimes he was too sick from the dragon's entry into him to do anything. Other times, he spent hours scrubbing and cleaning the dragon's interior. Mostly, though, he simply sat in the pilot's couch, listening while the dragon talked in a soft, almost inaudible rumble. Those were, in their way, the worst times of all.

"You don't have cancer," the dragon murmured. It was dark outside, or so Will believed. The hatch was kept closed tight and there were no windows. The only light came from the instruments on the control panel. "No bleeding from the rectum, no loss of energy. Eh, boy?"

"No, dread lord."

"It seems I chose better than I suspected. You have mortal blood in you, sure as moonlight. Your mother was no better than she ought to be."

"Sir?" he said uncomprehendingly.

"I said your mother was a *whore!* Are you feeble-minded? Your mother was a whore, your father a cuckold, you a bastard, grass green, mountains stony, and water wet."

"My mother was a good woman!" Ordinarily, he didn't talk back. But this time the words just slipped out.

"Good women sleep with men other than their husbands all the time, and for more reasons than there are men. Didn't anybody tell you that?" He could hear a note of satisfaction in the dragon's voice. "She could have been bored, or reckless, or blackmailed. She might have wanted money, or adventure, or revenge upon your father. Perchance she bet her virtue upon the turn of a card. Maybe she was overcome by the desire to roll in the gutter and befoul herself. She may even have fallen in love. Unlikelier things have happened."

"I won't listen to this!"

"You have no choice," the dragon said complacently. "The door is locked and you cannot escape. Moreover I am larger and more powerful than you. This is the *Lex Mundi*, from which there is no appeal."

"You lie! You lie! You lie!"

"Believe what you will. But, however got, your mortal blood is your good fortune. Lived you not in the asshole of beyond, but in a more civilized setting, you would surely be conscripted for a pilot. All pilots are half-mortal, you know, for only mortal blood can withstand the taint of cold iron. You would live like a prince, and be trained as a warrior. You would be the death of thousands." The dragon's voice sank musingly. "How shall I mark this discovery? Shall I…? Oho! Yes. I will make you my lieutenant."

"How does that differ from what I am now?"

"Do not despise titles. If nothing else, it will impress your friends."

Will had no friends, and the dragon knew it. Not anymore. All folk avoided him when they could, and were stiff-faced and wary in his presence when they could not. The children fleered and jeered and called him names. Sometimes they flung stones at him or pottery shards or—once—even a cow-pat, dry on the outside but soft and gooey within. Not often, however, for when they did, he would catch them and thrash them for it. This always seemed to catch the little ones by surprise.

The world of children was much simpler than the one he inhabited.

When Little Red Margotty struck him with the cow-pat, he caught her by the ear and marched her to her mother's hut. "See what your brat has done to me!" he cried in indignation, holding his jerkin away from him.

Big Red Margotty turned from the worktable, where she had been canning toads. She stared at him stonily, and yet he thought a glint resided in her eye of suppressed laughter. Then, coldly, she said. "Take it off and I shall wash it for you."

Her expression when she said this was so disdainful, that Will felt an impulse to peel off his trousers as well, throw them in her face for her insolence, and command her to wash them for a penance. But with the thought came also an awareness of Big Red Margotty's firm, pink flesh, of her ample breasts and womanly haunches. He felt his lesser self swelling to fill out his trousers and make them bulge.

This too Big Red Margotty saw, and the look of casual scorn she gave him then made Will burn with humiliation. Worse, all the while her mother washed his jerkin, Little Red Margotty danced around Will at a distance, holding up her skirt and waggling her bare bottom at him, making a mock of his discomfort.

On the way out the door, his damp jerkin draped over one arm, he stopped and said, "Make for me a sark of white damask, with upon its breast a shield: Argent, dragon rouge rampant above a village sable. Bring it to me by dawn-light tomorrow."

Outraged, Big Red Margotty said: "The cheek! You have no right to demand any such thing!"

"I am the dragon's lieutenant, and that is right enough for anything."

He left, knowing that the red bitch would perforce be up all night sewing for him. He was glad for every miserable hour she would suffer.

Three weeks having passed since Puck's burial, the healing-women decided it was time at last to dig him up. They said nothing when Will declared that he would attend—none of the adults said anything to him unless they had no choice—but, tagging along after them, he knew for a fact that he was unwelcome.

Puck's body, when they dug it up, looked like nothing so much as an enormous black root, twisted and formless. Chanting all the while, the women unwrapped the linen swaddling and washed him down with cow's urine. They dug out the life-clay that clogged his openings. They placed the finger-bone of a bat beneath his tongue. An egg was broken by his nose and the white slurped down by one medicine woman and the yellow by another.

Finally, they injected him with 5 cc. of dextroamphetamine sulfate.

Puck's eyes flew open. His skin had been baked black as silt by his long immersion in the soil, and his hair bleached white. His eyes were a vivid and startling leaf-green. In all respects but one, his body was as perfect as ever it had been. But that one exception made the women sigh unhappily for his sake.

One leg was missing, from above the knee down.

"The Earth has taken her tithe," one old woman observed sagely.

"There was not enough left of the leg to save," said another.

"It's a pity," said a third.

They all withdrew from the hut, leaving Will and Puck alone together.

For a long time Puck did nothing but stare wonderingly at his stump of a leg. He sat up and ran careful hands over its surface, as if to prove to himself that the missing flesh was not still there and somehow charmed invisible. Then he stared at Will's clean white shirt, and at the dragon arms upon his chest. At last, his unblinking gaze rose to meet Will's eyes.

"*You* did this!"

"No!" It was an unfair accusation. The land-mine had nothing to do with the dragon. The Scissors-Grinder would have found it and brought it into the village in any case. The two facts were connected only by the War, and the War was not Will's fault. He took his friend's hand in his own. "*Tchortyrion…*" he said in a low voice, careful that no unseen person might overhear.

Puck batted his hand away. "That's not my true name anymore! I have walked in darkness and my spirit has returned from the halls of granite with a new name—one that not even the dragon knows!"

"The dragon will learn it soon enough," Will said sadly.

"You wish!"

"Puck..."

"My old use-name is dead as well," said he who had been Puck Berrysnatcher. Unsteadily pulling himself erect, he wrapped the blanket upon which he had been laid about his thin shoulders. "You may call me No-name, for no name of mine shall ever pass your lips again."

Awkwardly, No-name hopped to the doorway. He steadied himself with a hand upon the jamb, then launched himself out into the wide world.

"Please! Listen to me!" Will cried after him.

Wordlessly, No-name raised one hand, middle finger extended.

Red anger welled up inside Will. "Asshole!" he shouted after his former friend. "Stump-leggity hopper! Johnny-three-limbs!"

He had not cried since that night the dragon first entered him. Now he cried again.

In mid-summer an army recruiter roared into town with a bright green-and-yellow drum lashed to the motorcycle behind him. He wore a smart red uniform with two rows of brass buttons, and he'd come all the way from Brocielande, looking for likely lads to enlist in the service of Avalon. With a screech and a cloud of dust, he pulled up in front of the Scrannel Dogge, heeled down the kickstand, and went inside to rent the common room for the space of the afternoon.

Outside again, he donned his drum harness, attached the drum, and sprinkled a handful of gold coins on its head. *Boom-Boom-de-Boom!* The drumsticks came down like thunder. *Rap-Tap-a-Rap!* The gold coins leaped and danced, like raindrops on a hot griddle. By this time, there was a crowd standing outside the Scrannel Dogge.

The recruiter laughed. "Sergeant Bombast is my name!" *Boom! Doom! Boom!* "Finding heroes is my game!" He struck the sticks together overhead. *Click! Snick! Click!* Then he thrust them in his belt, unharnessed the great drum, and set it down beside him. The gold coins caught the sun and dazzled every eye with avarice. "I'm here to offer certain brave lads the very best career a man ever had. The chance to learn a skill, to become a warrior... and get paid damn well for it, too. Look at me!" He clapped his hands upon his ample girth. "Do I look underfed?"

The crowd laughed. Laughing with them, Sergeant Bombast waded into their number, wandering first this way, then that, addressing first this one, then another. "No, I do not. For the very good reason that the Army feeds me well. It feeds me, and clothes me, and all but wipes me arse when I asks it to. And am I grateful? Am I grateful? I am *not*. No, sirs and maidens, so far from grateful am I that I require that the Army pay me for the privilege! And how much, do you ask? How much am I paid? Keeping in mind that my shoes, my food, my breeches, my snot-rag—" he pulled a lace handkerchief from one sleeve and waved it daintily in the air—"are all free as the air we breathe and the dirt we rub in our hair at Candlemas eve. How much am I *paid?*" His seemingly-random wander had brought him back to the drum again. Now his fist came down on the drum, making it shout and the gold leap up into the air with wonder. "Forty-three copper pennies a month!"

The crowd gasped.

"Payable quarterly in good honest gold! As you see here! *Or* silver, for them as worships the horned matron." He chucked old Lady Favor-Me-Not under the chin, making her blush and simper. "But that's not all—no, not the half of it! I see you've noticed these coins here. Noticed? Pshaw! You've noticed that I *meant* you to notice these coins! And why not? Each one of these little beauties weighs a full Trojan ounce! Each one is of the good red gold, laboriously mined by kobolds in the griffin-haunted Mountains of the Moon. How could you not notice them? How could you not wonder what I meant to do with them? Did I bring them here simply to scoop them up again, when my piece were done, and pour them back into my pockets?

"Not a bit of it! It is my dearest hope that I leave this village penniless. I *intend* to leave this village penniless! Listen careful now, for this is the crux of the matter. This here gold's meant for bonuses. Yes! *Recruitment* bonuses! In just a minute I'm going to stop talking. I'll reckon you're glad to hear that!" He waited for the laugh. "Yes, believe it or not, Sergeant Bombast is going to shut up and walk inside this fine establishment, where I've arranged for exclusive use of the common room, and something more as well. Now, what I want to do is to talk—just talk, mind you!—with lads who are strong enough and old enough to become soldiers. How old is that? Old enough to get your girlfriend in trouble!" Laughter again. "But not too old, neither. How old is that? Old enough that your girlfriend's jumped you over the broom, and you've come to think of it as a good bit of luck!

"So I'm a talkative man, and I want some lads to talk *with*. And if you'll do it, if you're neither too young nor too old and are willing to simply hear me out, with absolutely no strings attached…" He paused. "Well, fair's fair and the beer's on me. Drink as much as you like, and I'll pay the tab." He started to turn away, then swung back, scratching his head and looking puzzled. "Damn me, if there isn't something I've forgot."

"The gold!" squeaked a young dinter.

"The gold! Yes, yes, I'd forget me own head if it weren't nailed on. As I've said, the gold's for bonuses. Right into your hand it goes, the instant you've signed the papers to become a soldier. And how much? One gold coin? Two?" He grinned wolfishly. "Doesn't nobody want to guess? No? Well, hold onto your pizzles… I'm offering *ten gold coins* to the boy who signs up today! And ten more apiece for as many of his friends as wants to go with him!"

To cheers, he retreated into the tavern.

The dragon, who had foreseen his coming from afar, had said, "Now do we repay our people for their subservience. This fellow is a great danger to us all. He must be caught unawares."

"Why not placate him with smiles?" Will had asked. "Hear him out, feed him well, and send him on his way. That seems to me the path of least strife."

"He will win recruits—never doubt it. Such men have tongues of honey, and glamour-stones of great potency."

"So?"

"The War goes ill for Avalon. Not one of three recruited today is like to ever return."

"I don't care. On their heads be the consequences."

"You're learning. Here, then, is our true concern: The first recruit who is administered the Oath of Fealty will tell his superior officers about my presence here. He will betray us all, with never a thought for the welfare of the village, his family, or friends. Such is the puissance of the Army's sorcerers."

So Will and the dragon had conferred, and made plans.

Now the time to put those plans into action was come.

The Scrannel Dogge was bursting with potential recruits. The beer flowed freely, and the tobacco as well. Every tavern pipe was in use, and Sergeant Bombast had sent out for more. Within the fog of tobacco smoke, young men laughed and joked and hooted when the recruiter caught the eye of that lad he deemed most apt to sign, smiled, and crooked a beckoning finger. So Will saw from the doorway.

He let the door slam behind him.

All eyes reflexively turned his way. A complete and utter silence overcame the room.

Then, as he walked forward, there was a scraping of chairs and putting down of mugs. Somebody slipped out the kitchen door, and another after him. Wordlessly, a knot of three lads in green shirts left by the main door. The bodies eddied and flowed. By the time Will reached the recruiter's table, there was nobody in the room but the two of them.

"I'll be buggered," Sergeant Bombast said wonderingly, "if I've ever seen the like."

"It's my fault," Will said. He felt flustered and embarrassed, but luckily those qualities fit perfectly the part he had to play.

"Well, I can *see* that! I can see that, and yet shave a goat and marry me off to it if I know what it means. Sit down, boy, sit! Is there a curse on you? The evil eye? Transmissible elf-pox?"

"No, it's not that. It's…well, I'm half-mortal."

A long silence.

"Seriously?"

"Aye. There is iron in my blood. 'Tis why I have no true name. Why, also, I am shunned by all." He sounded patently false to himself, and yet he could tell from the man's face that the recruiter believed his every word. "There is no place in this village for me anymore."

The recruiter pointed to a rounded black rock that lay atop a stack of indenture parchments. "This is a name-stone. Not much to look at, is it?"

"No, sir."

"But its mate, which I hold under my tongue, is." He took out a small, lozenge-shaped stone and held it up to be admired. It glistered in the light, blood-crimson yet black in its heart. He placed it back in his mouth. "Now, if you were to lay your hand upon the name-stone on the table, your true name would go straight to the one in my mouth, and so to my brain. It's how we enforce the contracts our recruits sign."

"I understand." Will calmly placed his hand upon the black name-stone. He watched the recruiter's face, as nothing happened. There were ways to hide a true name, of course. But they were not likely to be found in a remote river-village in the wilds of the Debatable Hills. Passing the stone's test was proof of nothing. But it was extremely suggestive.

Sergeant Bombast sucked in his breath slowly. Then he opened up the small lockbox on the table before him, and said, "D'ye see this gold, boy?"

"Yes."

"There's eighty ounces of the good red here—none of your white gold nor electrum neither!—closer to you than your one hand is to the other. Yet the bonus you'd get would be worth a dozen of what I have here. *If*, that is, your claim is true. Can you prove it?"

"Yes, sir. I can."

"Now, explain this to me again," Sergeant Bombast said. "You live in a house of *iron?*" They were outside now, walking through the silent village. The recruiter had left his drum behind, but had slipped the name-stone into a pocket and strapped the lockbox to his belt.

"It's where I sleep at night. That should prove my case, shouldn't it? It should prove that I'm… what I say I am."

So saying, Will walked the recruiter into Tyrant Square. It was a sunny, cloudless day, and the square smelled of dust and cinnamon, with just a bitter undertaste of leaked hydraulic fluid and cold iron. It was noon.

When he saw the dragon, Sergeant Bombast's face fell.

"Oh, fuck," he said.

As if that were the signal, Will threw his arms around the man, while doors flew open and hidden ambushers poured into the square, waving rakes, brooms, and hoes. An old hen-wife struck the recruiter across the back of his head with her distaff. He went limp and heavy in Will's arms. Perforce, Will let him fall.

Then the women were all over the fallen soldier, stabbing, clubbing, kicking and cursing. Their passion was beyond all bounds, for these were the mothers of those he had tried to recruit. They had all of them fallen in with the orders the dragon had given with a readier will than they had ever displayed before for any of his purposes. Now they were making sure the fallen recruiter would never rise again to deprive them of their sons.

Wordlessly, they did their work and then, wordlessly, they left.

"Drown his motorcycle in the river," the dragon commanded afterwards. "Smash his drum and burn it, lest it bear witness against us. Bury his body in the midden-heap. There must be no evidence that ever he came here. Did you recover his lockbox?"

"No. It wasn't with his body. One of the women must have stolen it."

The dragon chuckled. "Peasants! Still, it works out well. The coins are well-buried already under basement flagstones, and will stay so indefinitely. And when an investigator come through looking for a lost recruiter, he'll be met by a universal ignorance, canny lies, and a cleverly-planted series of misleading evidence. Out of avarice, they'll serve our cause better than ever we could order it ourselves."

A full moon sat high in the sky, enthroned within the constellation of the Mad Dog and presiding over one of the hottest nights of the summer when the dragon abruptly announced, "There is a resistance."

"Sir?" Will stood in the open doorway, lethargically watching the sweat fall, drop by drop from his bowed head. He would have welcomed a breeze, but at this time of year when those who had built well enough slept naked on their rooftops and those who had not burrowed into the mud of the riverbed, there were no night-breezes cunning enough to thread the maze of huts and so make their way to the square.

"Rebels against my rule. Insurrectionists. Mad, suicidal fools."

A single drop fell. Will jerked his head to move his moon-shadow aside, and saw a large black circle appear in the dirt. "Who?"

"The greenshirties."

"They're just kids," Will said scornfully.

"Do not despise them because they are young. The young make excellent soldiers and better martyrs. They are easily dominated, quickly trained, and as ruthless as you command them to be. They kill without regret, and they go to their deaths readily, because they do not truly understand that death is permanent."

"You give them too much credit. They do no more than sign horns at me, glare, and spit upon my shadow. Everybody does that."

"They are still building up their numbers and their courage. Yet their leader, the No-name one, is shrewd and capable. It worries me that he has made himself invisible to your eye, and thus to mine. Walking about the village, you have oft enough come upon a nest in the fields where he slept, or scented the distinctive tang of his scat. Yet when was the last time you saw him in person?"

"I haven't even seen these nests nor smelt the dung you speak of."

"You've seen and smelled, but not been aware of it. Meanwhile, No-name skillfully eludes your sight. He has made himself a ghost."

"The more ghostly the better. I don't care if I never see him again."

"You will see him again. Remember, when you do, that I warned you so."

The dragon's prophecy came true not a week later. Will was walking his errands and admiring, as he so often did these days, how ugly the village had become in his eyes. Half the huts were wattle-and-daub—little more than sticks and dried mud. Those which had honest planks were left unpainted and grey, to keep down the yearly assessment when the teind-inspector came through from the central government. Pigs wandered the streets, and the occasional scavenger bear as well, looking moth-eaten and shabby. Nothing was clean, nothing was new, nothing was ever mended.

Such were the thoughts he was thinking when somebody thrust a gunnysack over his head, while somebody else punched him in the stomach, and a third person swept his feet out from under him.

It was like a conjuring trick. One moment he was walking down a noisy street, with children playing in the dust and artisans striding by to their workshops and goodwives leaning from windows to gossip or sitting in doorways shucking peas, and the next he was being carried swiftly away, in darkness, by eight strong hands.

He struggled, but could not break free. His cries, muffled by the sack, were ignored. If anybody heard him—and there had been many about on the street a moment before—nobody came to his aid.

After what seemed an enormously long time, he was dumped on the ground. Angrily, he struggled out of the gunnysack. He was lying on the stony and slightly damp floor of the old gravel pit, south of the village. One crumbling wall was overgrown with flowering vines. He could hear birdsong upon birdsong. Standing, he flung the gunnysack to the ground and confronted his kidnappers.

There were twelve of them and they all wore green shirts.

He knew them all, of course, just as he knew everyone else in the village. But, more, they had all been his friends, at one time or another. Were he free of the dragon's bondage, doubtless he would be one of their number. Now, though, he was filled with scorn for them, for he knew exactly how the dragon would deal with them, were they to harm his lieutenant. He would accept them into his body, one at a time, to corrupt their minds and fill their bodies with cancers. He would tell the first in excruciating detail exactly how he was going to die, stage by stage, and he would make sure the eleven others watched as it happened. Death after death, the survivors would watch and anticipate. Last of all would be their leader, No-name.

Will understood how the dragon thought.

"Turn away," he said. "This will do you nor your cause any good whatsoever."

Two of the greenshirties took him by the arms. They thrust him before No-name. His former friend leaned on a crutch of ash-wood. His face was tense with hatred and his eyes did not blink.

"It is good of you to be so concerned for our *cause*," No-name said. "But you do not understand our *cause*, do you? Our *cause* is simply this."

He raised a hand, and brought it down fast, across Will's face. Something sharp cut a long scratch across his forehead and down one cheek.

"*Llandrysos*, I command you to die!" No-name cried. The greenshirties holding Will's arms released them. He staggered back a step. A trickle of something warm went tickling down his face. He touched his hand to it. Blood.

No-name stared at him. In his outstretched hand was an elf-shot, one of those small stone arrowheads found everywhere in the fields after a hard rain. Will did not know if they had been made by ancient civilizations or grew from pebbles by spontaneous generation. Nor had he known, before now, that to scratch somebody with one while crying out his true name would cause that person to die. But the stench of ozone that accompanied death-magic hung in the air, lifting the small hairs on the back of his neck and tickling his nose with its eldritch force, and the knowledge of what had almost happened was inescapable.

The look of absolute astonishment on No-name's face curdled and became rage. He dashed the elf-shot to the ground. "You were *never* my friend!" he cried in a fury. "The night when we exchanged true names and mingled blood, you lied! You were as false then as you are now!"

It was true. Will remembered that long-ago time when he and Puck had rowed their coracles to a distant river-island, and there caught fish which they grilled over coals and a turtle from which they made a soup prepared in its own shell. It had been Puck's idea to swear eternal friendship and Will, desperate for a name-friend and knowing Puck would not believe he had none, had invented a true name for himself. He was careful to let his friend reveal first, and so knew to shiver and roll up his eyes when he spoke the name. But he had felt a terrible guilt then for his deceit, and every time since when he thought of that night.

Even now.

Standing on his one good leg, No-name tossed his crutch upward and seized it near the tip. Then he swung it around and smashed Will in the face.

Will fell.

The greenshirties were all over him then, kicking and hitting him.

Briefly, it came to Will that, if he were included among their number, there were thirteen present and engaged upon a single action. We are a coven, he thought, and I the random sacrifice, who is worshiped with kicks and blows. Then there was nothing but his suffering and the rage that rose up within him, so strong that though it could not weaken the pain, yet it drowned out the fear he should have felt on realizing that he was going to die. He knew only pain and a kind of wonder: a vast, world-encompassing astonishment that so profound a thing as death could happen to *him*, accompanied by a lesser wonder that No-name and his merry thugs had the toughness to take his punishment all the way to death's portal, and that vital step beyond. They were only boys, after all. Where had they learned such discipline?

"I think he's dead," said a voice. He thought it was No-name's, but he couldn't be sure. His ears rang, and the voice was so very, very far away.

One last booted foot connected with already-broken ribs. He gasped, and spasmed. It seemed unfair that he could suffer pain on top of pain like this.

"That is our message to your master dragon," said the distant voice. "If you live, take it to him."

Then silence. Eventually, Will forced himself to open one eye—the other was swollen shut—and saw that he was alone again. It was a gorgeous day, sunny without being at all hot. Birds sang all about him. A sweet breeze ruffled his hair.

He picked himself up, bleeding and weeping with rage, and stumbled back to the dragon.

Because the dragon would not trust any of the healing-women inside him, Will's injuries were treated by a fluffer, who came inside the dragon to suck the injuries from Will's body and accept them as her own. He tried to stop her as soon as he had the strength to do so, but the dragon overruled him. It shamed and sickened him to see how painfully the girl hobbled outside again.

"Tell me who did this," the dragon whispered, "and we shall have revenge."

"No."

There was a long hiss, as a steam valve somewhere deep in the thorax vented pressure. "You toy with me."

Will turned his face to the wall. "It's my problem and not yours."

"You *are* my problem."

There was a constant low-grade mumble and grumble of machines that faded to nothing when one stopped paying attention to it. Some part of it was the ventilation system, for the air never quite went stale, though it often had a flat under-taste. The rest was surely reflexive—meant to keep the dragon alive. Listening to those mechanical voices, fading deeper and deeper within the tyrant's corpus, Will had a vision of an interior that never came to an end, all the night contained within that lightless iron body, expanding inward in an inversion of the natural order, stars twinkling in the vasty reaches of distant condensers and fuel-handling systems and somewhere a crescent moon, perhaps, caught in his gear train. "I won't argue," Will said. "And I will never tell you anything."

"You will."

"*No!*"

The dragon fell silent. The leather of the pilot's couch gleamed weakly in the soft light. Will's wrists ached.

The outcome was never in doubt. Try though he might, Will could not resist the call of the leather couch, of the grips that filled his hand, of the needles that slid into his wrists. The dragon entered him, and had from him all the information he desired, and this time he did not leave.

Will walked through the village streets, leaving footprints of flame behind him. He was filled with wrath and the dragon. "*Come out!*" he roared. "Bring out your greenshirties, every one of them, or I shall come after them, street by street and house by house." He put a hand on the nearest door, and wrenched it from its hinges. Broken fragments of boards fell flaming to the ground. "Spillikin cowers herewithin. Don't make me come in after him!"

Shadowy hands flung Spillikin face-first into the dirt at Will's feet.

Spillikin was a harmless albino stick-figure of a marsh-walker who screamed when Will closed a cauterizing hand about his arm to haul him to his feet.

"Follow me," Will/the dragon said coldly.

So great was Will's twin-spirited fury that none could stand up to him. He burned hot as a bronze idol, and the heat went before him in a great wave, withering plants, charring house-fronts, and setting hair ablaze when somebody did not flee from him quickly enough. "*I am wrath!*" he screamed. "*I am blood-vengeance! I am justice!* Feed me or suffer!"

The greenshirties were, of course, brought out.

No-name was, of course, not among their number.

The greenshirties were lined up before the dragon in Tyrant Square. They knelt in the dirt before him, heads down. Only two were so unwary as to be caught in their green shirts. The others were bare-chested or in mufti. All were terrified, and one of them had pissed himself. Their families and neighbors had followed after them and now filled the square with their wails of lament. Will quelled them with a look.

"Your king knows your true names," he said sternly to the greenshirties, "and can kill you at a word."

"It is true," said Hag Applemere. Her face was stony and impassive. Yet Will knew that one of the greenshirties was her brother.

"More, he can make you suffer such dementia as would make you believe yourselves in Hell, and suffering its torments forever."

"It is true," the hag said.

"Yet he disdains to bend the full weight of his wrath upon you. You are no threat to him. He scorns you as creatures of little or no import."

"It is true."

"One only does he desire vengeance upon. Your leader—he who calls himself No-name. This being so, your most merciful lord has made this offer: Stand." They obeyed, and he gestured toward a burning brand. "Bring No-name to me while this fire yet burns, and you shall all go free. Fail, and you will suffer such torments as the ingenuity of a dragon can devise."

"It is true."

Somebody—not one of the greenshirties—was sobbing softly and steadily. Will ignored it. There was more Dragon within him than Self. It was a strange feeling, not being in control. He liked it. It was like being a small coracle carried helplessly along by a raging current. The river of emotion had its own logic; it knew where it was going. "Go!" he cried. " Now!"

The greenshirties scattered like pigeons.

Not half an hour later, No-name was brought, beaten and struggling, into the square. His former disciples had tied his hands behind his back, and gagged him with a red bandanna. He had been beaten—not so badly as Will had been, but well and thoroughly.

Will walked up and down before him. Those leaf-green eyes glared up out of that silt-black face with a pure and holy hatred. There could be no reasoning with this boy, nor any taming of him. He was a primal force, an anti-Will, the spirit of vengeance made flesh and given a single unswerving purpose.

Behind No-name stood the village elders in a straight, unmoving line. The Sullen Man moved his mouth slowly, like an ancient tortoise having a particularly deep thought. But he did not speak. Nor did Auld Black Agnes, nor the yage-witch whose use-name no living being knew, nor Lady Nightlady, nor Spadefoot, nor Annie Hop-the-Frog, nor Daddy Fingerbones, nor any of the others. There were mutters and whispers among the villagers, assembled into a loose throng behind them, but nothing coherent. Nothing that could be heard or punished. Now and again, the buzzing of wings rose up over the murmurs and died down again like a cicada on a still summer day, but no one lifted up from the ground.

Back and forth Will stalked, restless as a leopard in a cage, while the dragon within him brooded over possible punishments. A whipping would only strengthen No-name in his hatred and resolve. Amputation was no answer—he had lost one limb already, and was still a dangerous and unswerving enemy. There was no gaol in all the village that could hope to hold him forever, save for the dragon himself, and the dragon did not wish to accept so capricious an imp into his own body.

Death seemed the only answer.

But what sort of death? Strangulation was too quick. Fire was good, but Tyrant Square was surrounded by thatch-roofed huts. A drowning would have to be carried out at the river, out of sight of the dragon himself, and he wanted the manna of punishment inextricably linked in his subjects' minds to his own physical self. He could have a wine-barrel brought in and filled with water, but then the victim's struggles would have a comic element to them. Also, as a form of strangulation, it was still too quick.

Unhurriedly, the dragon considered. Then he brought Will to a stop before the crouching No-name. He raised up Will's head, and let a little of the dragon-light shine out through Will's eyes.

"Crucify him."

To Will's horror, the villagers obeyed.

It took hours. But shortly before dawn, the child who had once been Puck Berrysnatcher, who had been Will's best friend and had died and been reborn as Will's Nemesis, breathed his last. His body went limp as he surrendered his name to his revered ancestress, Mother Night, and the exhausted villagers could finally turn away and go home and sleep.

Later, after he had departed Will's body at last, the dragon said, "You have done well."

Will lay motionless on the pilot's couch and said nothing.

"I shall reward you."

"No, lord," Will said. "You have done too much already."

"Haummn. Do you know the first sign that a toady has come to accept the rightness of his lickspittle station?"

"No, sir."

"It is insolence. For which reason, you will not be punished but rather, as I said, rewarded. You have grown somewhat in my service. Your tastes have matured. You want something better than your hand. You shall have it. Go into any woman's house and tell her what she must do. You have my permission."

"This is a gift I do not desire."

"Says you! Big Red Margotty has three holes. She will refuse none of them to you. Enter them in whatever order you wish. Do what you like with her tits. Tell her to look glad when she sees you. Tell her to wag her tail and bark like a dog. As long as she has a daughter, she has no choice but to obey. Much the same goes for any of my beloved subjects, of whatever gender or age."

"They hate you," Will said.

"And thou as well, my love and my delight. And thou as well."

"But you with reason."

A long silence. Then, "I know your mind as you do not. I know what things you wish to do with Red Margotty and what things you wish to do *to* her. I tell you, there are cruelties within you greater than anything I know. It is the birthright of flesh."

"You lie!"

"Do I? Tell me something, dearest victim. When you told the elders to crucify No-name, the command came from me, with my breath and in my voice. But the form... did not the *choice* of the punishment come from you?"

Will had been lying listlessly on the couch staring up at the featureless metal ceiling. Now he sat upright, his face white with shock. All in a single movement he stood, and turned toward the door.

Which seeing, the dragon sneered, "Do you think to leave me? Do you honestly think you *can*? Then try!" The dragon slammed his door open. The cool and pitiless light of earliest morning flooded the cabin. A fresh breeze swept in, carrying with it scents from the fields and woods. It made Will painfully aware of how his own sour stench permeated the dragon's interior. "You need me more than I ever needed you—I have seen to that! You cannot run away, and if you could, your hunger would bring you back, wrists foremost. You *desire* me. You are empty without me. Go! Try to run! See where it gets you."

Will trembled.

He bolted out the door and ran.

The first sunset away from the dragon, Will threw up violently as the sun went down, and then suffered spasms of diarrhea. Cramping, and aching and foul, he hid in the depths of the Old Forest all through the night, sometimes howling and sometimes rolling about the forest floor in pain. A thousand times he thought he must return. A thousand times he told himself: Not yet. Just a little longer and you can surrender. But not yet.

The craving came in waves. When it abated, Will would think: If I can hold out for one day, the second will be easier, and the third easier yet. Then the sick yearning would return, a black need in the tissues of his flesh and an aching in his bones, and he would think again: Not yet. Hold off for just a few more minutes. Then you can give up. Soon. Just a little longer.

By morning, the worst of it was over. He washed his clothes in a stream, and hung them up to dry in the wan predawn light. To keep himself warm, he marched back and forth singing the *Chansons Amoreuses de Merlin Sylvanus*, as many of its five hundred verses as he could remember. Finally, when the clothes were only slightly damp, he sought out a great climbing oak he knew of old, and from a hollow withdrew a length of stolen clothesline. Climbing as close to the tippy-top of the great tree as he dared, he lashed himself to its bole. There, lightly rocked by a gentle wind, he slept at last.

Three days later, Hag Applemere came to see him in his place of hiding. The truth-teller bowed before him. "Lord Dragon bids you return to him," she said formally.

Will did not ask the revered hag how she had found him. Wise-women had their skills; nor did they explain themselves. "I'll come when I'm ready," he said. "My task here is not yet completed." He was busily sewing together leaves of oak, yew, ash, and alder, using a needle laboriously crafted from a thorn, and short threads made from grasses he had pulled apart by hand. It was no easy work.

Hag Applemere frowned. "You place us all in certain danger."

"He will not destroy himself over me alone. Particularly when he is sure that I must inevitably return to him."

"It is true."

Will laughed mirthlessly. "You need not ply your trade here, hallowed lady. Speak to me as you would to any other. I am no longer of the dragon's party." Looking at her, he saw for the first time that she was not so many years older than himself. In a time of peace, he might even have grown fast enough to someday, in two years or five, claim her for his own, by the ancient rites of the greensward and the midnight sun. Only months ago, young as he was, he would have found this an unsettling thought. But now his thinking had been driven to such extremes that it bothered him not.

"Will," she said then, cautiously, "whatever are you up to?"

He held up the garment, complete at last, for her to admire. "I have become a greenshirtie." All the time he had sewn, he was bare chested, for he had torn up his dragon sark and used it for tinder as he needed fire. Now he donned its leafy replacement.

Clad in his fragile new finery, Will looked the truth-teller straight in the eye.

"You *can* lie," he said.

Bessie looked stricken. "Once," she said, and reflexively covered her womb with both hands. "And the price is high, terribly high."

He stood. "Then it must be paid. Let us find a shovel now. It is time for a bit of grave-robbery."

It was evening when Will returned at last to the dragon. Tyrant Square had been ringed about with barbed wire, and a loudspeaker had been set upon a pole with wires leading back into his iron hulk, so that he could speak and be heard in the absence of his lieutenant.

"Go first," Will said to Hag Applemere, "that he may be reassured I mean him no harm."

Breasts bare, clad in the robes and wide hat of her profession, Bessie Applemere passed through a barbed-wire gate (a grimpkin guard opened it before her and closed it after her) and entered the square. "Son of Cruelty." She bowed deeply before the dragon.

Will stood hunched in the shadows, head down, with his hands in his pockets. Tonelessly, he said, "I have been broken to your will, great one. I will be your stump-cow, if that is what you want. I beg you. Make me grovel. Make me crawl. Only let me back in."

Hag Applemere spread her arms and bowed again. "It is true."

"You may approach." The dragon's voice sounded staticky and yet triumphant over the loudspeaker.

The sour-faced old grimpkin opened the gate for him, as it had earlier been opened for the hag. Slowly, like a maltreated dog returning to the only hand that had ever fed him, Will crossed the square. He paused before the loudspeaker, briefly touched its pole with one trembling hand, and then shoved that hand back into his pocket. "You have won. Well and truly, have you won."

It appalled him how easily the words came, and how natural they sounded coming from his mouth. He could feel the desire to surrender to the tyrant, accept what punishments he would impose, and sink gratefully back into his bondage. A little voice within cried: *So easy! So easy!* And so it would be, perilously easy indeed. The realization that a part of him devoutly wished for it made Will burn with humiliation.

The dragon slowly forced one eye half-open. "So, boy…" Was it his imagination, or was the dragon's voice less forceful than it had been three days ago? "You have learned what need feels like. You suffer from your desires, even as I do. I… I… am weakened, admittedly, but I am not all so weak as *that!* You thought to prove that I needed you—you have proved the reverse. Though I have neither wings nor missiles and my electrical reserves are low, though I cannot fire my jets without destroying the village and myself as well, yet am I of the mighty, for I have neither pity nor remorse. Thought you I craved a mere boy? Thought you to make me dance attendance on a soft, unmuscled half-mortal mongrel fey? Pfaugh! I do not need you. Never think that I… that I *need* you!"

"Let me in," Will whimpered. "I will do whatever you say."

"You... you understand that you must be punished for your disobedience?"

"Yes," Will said. "Punish me, please. Abase and degrade me, I beg you."

"As you wish," the dragon's cockpit door hissed open, "so it shall be."

Will took one halting step forward, and then two. Then he began to run, straight at the open hatchway. Straight at it—and then to one side.

He found himself standing before the featureless iron of the dragon's side. Quickly, from one pocket he withdrew Sergeant Bombast's soulstone. Its small blood-red mate was already in his mouth. There was still grave-dirt on the one, and a strange taste to the other, but he did not care. He touched the soulstone to the iron plate, and the dragon's true name flowed effortlessly into his mind.

Simultaneously, he took the elf-shot from his other pocket. Then, with all his strength, he drew the elf-shot down the dragon's iron flank, making a long, bright scratch in the rust.

"What are you doing?" the dragon cried in alarm. "Stop that! The hatch is open, the couch awaits!" His voice dropped seductively. "The needles yearn for your wrists. Even as I yearn for—"

"Baalthazar, of the line of Baalmoloch, of the line of Baalshabat," Will shouted, "I command thee to *die!*"

And that was that.

All in an instant and with no fuss whatever, the dragon king was dead. All his might and malice was become nothing more than inert metal, that might be cut up and carted away to be sold to the scrap-foundries that served their larger brothers with ingots to be re-forged for the War.

Will hit the side of the dragon with all the might of his fist, to show his disdain. Then he spat as hard and fierce as ever he could, and watched the saliva slide slowly down the black metal. Finally, he unbuttoned his trousers and pissed upon his erstwhile oppressor.

So it was that he finally accepted that the tyrant was well and truly dead.

Bessie Applemere—hag no more—stood silent and bereft on the square behind him. Wordlessly, she mourned her sterile womb and sightless eyes. To her, Will went. He took her hand, and led her back to her hut. He opened the door for her. Her sat her down upon her bed. "Do you need anything?" he asked. "Water? Some food?"

She shook her head. "Just go. Leave me to lament our victory in solitude."

He left, quietly closing the door behind him. There was no place to go now but home. It took him a moment to remember where that was.

"I've come back," Will said.

Blind Enna looked stricken. Her face turned slowly toward him, those vacant eyes filled with shadow, that ancient mouth open and despairing. Like a sleepwalker, she stood and stumbled forward and then, when her groping fingers tapped against his chest, she threw her arms around him and burst into tears. "Thank the Seven! Oh, thank the Seven! The blessed, blessed, merciful Seven!"

she sobbed over and over again, and Will realized for the first time that, in her own inarticulate way, his aunt genuinely and truly loved him.

And so, for a season, life in the village returned to normal. In the autumn the Armies of the Mighty came through the land, torching the crops and leveling the buildings. Terror went before them and the villagers were forced to flee, first into the Old Forest, and then to refugee camps across the border. Finally, they were loaded into cattle cars and taken away to far Babylonia in Faerie Minor, where the streets are bricked of gold and the ziggurats touch the sky, and there Will found a stranger destiny than any he might previously have dreamed.

But that is another story, for another day.

THE LAILY WORM

Nina Kiriki Hoffman

Nina Kiriki Hoffman was born in San Gabriel, CA, and grew up in Santa Barbara. Her first story, "A Night Out", appeared in Jessica Amanda Salmonson's *Tales by Moonlight* anthology. The first of her nine novels, *Child of an Ancient City* (with Tad Williams), appeared in 1992 and was followed by Bram Stoker Award winner, *The Thread that Binds the Bones*, Nebula and World Fantasy Award nominee *The Silent Strength of Stones*, *A Red Heart of Memories* and *Past the Size of Dreaming*, *A Stir of Bones*, and Tiptree and Mythopoeic Award nominee *A Fistful of Sky*. Hoffman then turned to SF with Philip K. Dick Award nominee *Catalyst: A Novel of Alien Contact* before returning to fantasy with Mythopoeic and Endeavour Award finalist *Spirits that Walk in Shadow* and her most recent novel *Fall of Light*. Coming up is a new novel, *Thresholds*. Hoffman's more than 250 short stories have been nominated for the World Fantasy and Nebula Awards and are collected in *Legacy of Fire*, *Courting Disasters and Other Strange Affinities*, *Common Threads*, and *Time Travelers, Ghosts, and Other Visitors*.

In addition to writing, Hoffman does production work for *F&SF*, teaches writing at her local community college, and works with teen writers. She lives in Eugene, Oregon.

After our mother died, our father married the worst woman the world did ever see.

My sister Masery and I didn't suspect this at first. Stepmother was nice to us before she had her own child, nice in ways we weren't used to. Most of the things we did with her were never things we had done with my own mother while she lived. Stepmother took us hunting in the forest, taught us to shoot bows and handle knives when my sister was ten and I was eight. "You'll need skills," Stepmother told us. "You can't count on finding the perfect husband, Masery, nor you the perfect wife, Perry, in spite of your royal blood."

Before she transformed us, I had thought Stepmother was teaching us lessons just because we needed them. After, when I had plenty of time to think, I realized she was telling us her own woes. Stepmother had royal blood in her veins; she was born in a foreign court. Our father was royal, too, right enough, as had been our mother, cousins of the king; but Father had quarreled with the queen just after he married Stepmother, and so we were all exiled to Hopelost Keep, a drafty castle in the north, told to watch the wild seas for reivers. Who would rob us here, when the land yielded barely enough for our little settlement to live on? Winters were long and harsh, summers sweet and too soon fled. The growing season was so short we had trouble storing up enough to get us through each freezing winter. Even the animals were skinny and tough. The Norsemen pillaged farther south, where they could find gold and iron, better-stocked cellars and warmer women.

Still, Father took his duties seriously, and led his lean and silent soldiers on patrols up and down the coast, watching, always watching. Always absent.

At first Stepmother pined for court life, but then she warmed to me and Masery. She made no friends among the villagers—they thought her too strange, with her slanting eyes and her accent that changed words into something else. Masery and I were the only ones she talked to, with Father on patrol most of his days and sleeping away from us most nights.

Stepmother taught us foreign witcheries, knots to tie in your hair to keep a lover true, knots to tie in your lover's hair to send him away from you. Herbs she taught us as well, those to send others to sleep or sweeten their tempers, those to brighten the eye and shine the hair. All manner of glamours she taught my sister Masery and since I was there, I learned as well, though many of these things weren't skills suitable for boys or princes to learn. She taught us the art of the needle, and kitchen mysteries.

I believed she loved us. All the things she taught Masery, I believed she thought of Masery as her own daughter. As for me, I knew she thought of me as an afterthought and a tagalong, but still, she ruffled my hair sometimes, dropped careless kisses on my cheek, gave me scraps of praise when I managed a trick well. Especially she liked my gift with light, to make it dance in darkness, to bend it to shine where no light had shone before.

All this changed when, three years after she married my father, Stepmother became pregnant. Instead of coming to our rooms in the morning to dress Masery's hair and help her tend to her clothes, Stepmother stayed away from us. Masery asked me to help her comb and braid her hair and button her buttons, and in return, I sought her help with mending the knees of my trousers and the elbows of my shirts, which tore and frayed often. Stepmother no longer bought me new clothing when I outgrew the old, and I was growing.

We didn't know why Stepmother stopped caring for us until her belly grew. Then I lived in hope of a brother or sister, someone smaller than I on whom I could practice some of the tricks Stepmother had taught me, as Masery had practiced her arts on me.

One day when Stepmother was in her seventh month, she called me and Masery to her and said, "It is time for you children to go to court and foster with the king."

I wondered how we were to go to court when the queen had banished our family. Perhaps Stepmother had corresponded with someone at court, gained us a pardon and positions. Masery and I asked no questions; we had learned not to question Stepmother. She could be kind, but when the mood was on her, she could be cruel too.

"Perry, you will be a page, in training to be a knight, and Masery a lady-in-waiting. Walk with me. Let me give you one last blessing before you go."

We left the castle, walked beyond the battlements out to the road that led to southern settlements and into the forest where people went to cut wood. Though she was heavy with child, Stepmother walked quickly and well. She took the northern fork to the harbor, then branched away from the road on a narrow track that led to the top of a cliff overlooking the sea.

We stood and looked out to sea. Clouds hung low over the long gray distances, but breaks in them flooded the sea with scatters of silvery sunlight. Waves surged, grew whitecaps; wind blew spray up into the sky. The air was damp and smelled salty.

I wondered when I would come home, and thought: I used to be homesick for our house near the king's castle, where life was easy and the food was rich and we had a garden where fruit trees grew, and servants who smiled. And yet, with all that Stepmother had taught me, I had learned to love this harsh land as well. I could hit a flying duck with an arrow if luck was with me, and knock over a hare with a stone. I knew the names of plants, which ones to eat, which to make into tinctures or ointments to cure ills. I knew a few words of the language of fire; I could coax a log to burn even after it had charred. I could translate some of the whispers in the walls of the keep: I had heard stories of others who had lived there ages earlier. In the long dark winter nights, I had learned a little of the language of snow, and heard tales of heaven the snowflakes whispered as they fell. This place, too, was home.

Stepmother brought out the silver wand of transformation. Masery and I held hands and stood before Stepmother. What would she turn us into? Would she make me stronger, and Masery more beautiful, so we would find favor in the eyes of our cousins at court? Could she give me the tongue of a diplomat, or Masery the skill of a musician? Perhaps she would transform our clothing so we would be more worthy of being seen in royal places. Since Stepmother's pregnancy, despite Masery's and my skill with the needle and other arts Stepmother had taught us, we had not been able to keep our clothes from wearing out, nor our hair from tangling.

"Live your natures, my sometime children," whispered Stepmother. She tapped me thrice with the wand.

A horrible, strange thing happened. Inside me something huge awoke, and looked out through my stomach with burning orange eyes. It laughed, and the laugh came out of my throat; and then it crawled up out of my mouth, its head dark silver, spiky and glistening. I didn't know how it happened, but for a brief time I was still myself, staring at this worm as it poured out of my throat and mouth, only how could it come from inside me, when it was larger than I was? And then I looked through other eyes, and the body I had been growing into all my days melted into the scales and spines of the dragon.

Stepmother tapped Masery thrice with her wand.

A great silvery scaled snout stuck out below my eyes. Long whiskery things trailed from it, waving with a life of their own. I opened my mouth, and oh, it opened wider and wider: I felt my own maw, gaping, a cut in my head that sliced back into my throat, reached almost to my spine. The tip of my new tongue flickered out. It was long and black, split at the tip like a snake's.

I tasted a hundred things on the wind: coming snow, sea salt, crushed wet leaves that carpeted the forest floor behind us, wood smoke from the keep below, blood from the fall butchering of pigs, the cinnamon, musk, and amber scent of Stepmother. And something else, something new, an oily, fishy scent. I bent my heavy head and with one eye looked before me. A large fish the size of a human child flopped on the rock, mouth gaping and closing.

Fish—I was hungry; fires lit in my belly—and something more. The scent of Sister.

A hiss poured out of my throat.

Stepmother took two steps back and laughed. "Why, Perry, how fine you are, and how strange. I so expected a mouse!"

Fire roared up my throat. I closed my mouth a moment, gathered fire on my tongue, then opened my mouth to breathe on Stepmother.

She held up the wand. "No!" she cried. "No!" She tapped me thrice with the wand. "Resistance, transform into obedience! Perry, you are mine now, mine! You will do my bidding. You will not hurt me!"

I felt invisible chains drop onto me, lock into my will. I swallowed my own fire.

"You will do this work for me. Guard that tree." She pointed down the coast to where an ancient oak spread its branches. The tree was so old and so long settled that the sea had eaten inland to it; some of its roots stuck out of the low cliff it stood on and dangled toward the small crescent of beach below. "Live there. See that no one approaches it; kill any who dare. That's my good and noble Perry." She stroked my head.

How I longed to burn her hand with my skin! But she was unscathed, though I knew my body hosted heat inside and out.

"As for you, Masery, this form too I didn't expect for you. I thought you might become a cat, and hoped I could take you home with me. But you can't be my pet, so get you gone. Perry, toss her into the sea."

I could hardly understand what I had become, let alone that this giant fish was my sister. I didn't need to understand anything but Stepmother's orders, though. I reached out, saw my own dragon hand for the first time: fingers as long as my arms used to be, tipped with claws of dark jewel; a scaled palm engraved with the lines of folds. I grasped my sister gently, her scales to mine, and lifted her as carefully as I could, for within Stepmother's order there was this much flex, that I could choose my grip. I carried my sister to the edge of the cliff and threw her as far out to sea as I could, hoping and praying she would be able to breathe water now, and would know how to swim.

Then I turned away from Stepmother and walked on my new four feet, dragging my spiky tail, down the cliff path toward the tree she had told me to guard.

Stepmother laughed. "Good boy," she cried. I did not look back.

I wrapped myself around the foot of the tree. The tree sang to me, a soothing, welcoming song whose words I did not yet understand, though I took their tone.

Also, there was a scent from higher up. I could taste it: a cinnamon scent. Somewhere in the tree's crown was something that belonged to Stepmother.

The tree had scattered acorns all around it. As a boy, I had never eaten them, but now I was so hungry, I decided to try. I could tell, when I had licked up a mouthful of gritty little orbs, that my teeth were not shaped to crunch such things, but I bit down on one anyway. Bitter filled my mouth. Fire shot up my throat and roasted the acorns on my tongue, and then, ah, then they fell apart and tasted better, a little like porridge, a little like roasted chestnuts. I roasted and ate many of them, then curled around the tree's foot.

The night was cold, but I did not feel it; I only knew because with every breath I breathed out, steam rose from my nostrils. I slept before the moon rose.

In the morning I felt stiff with cold—not as though I were freezing, more as though my body had begun turning to stone. While I was flexing muscles I did not know from my previous life—how many ribs did I have? The tail moved when I wanted it to, but how could that work? How did I know how to make my tail behave? Did my fingers really have extra joints, and how was it that I had muscles in my nose that could send my new whiskers twitching?—I noticed people across the way, creeping through the forest's fringe.

"Hey," I called. Was that the baker's son Fon? The miller's daughter Kiki?

"Fon, Kiki," I cried "Halloo!"

Only, what erupted from my throat was a fountain of flame, and my voice came out a growl.

Both of them screamed and ran away.

Oh, dear.

And yet, now I was warm again. I stretched, shifted, and flamed. Warmth settled into my belly, and all my muscles moved as though oiled.

My stomach growled, and small flames puffed from my mouth. I searched the ground for acorns and realized I'd eaten all the nearby ones the night before. I cast farther afield.

To one side of my tree was the low cliff that dropped away to the ocean. Waves fretted its base only ten feet below. I peered over the edge but saw only very shallow water, nothing to eat. I turned toward the forest instead.

Some of those trees were oaks. I left my post and ambled over, filled my mouth with acorns, roasted, crunched, and swallowed them. A hare startled as I approached a bush, and I was so surprised I opened my mouth and flamed it. Ah, the scent of charred hare. Delicious. I ran to it and ate it. Caught, killed, cooked in one move. For the first time, I was happy about one of my new abilities. I wanted to hunt again, but the rumbles in my belly had quieted, and the tree called me back.

I made a ring around its base with my body and lay, looking out to sea.

I discovered my new life: the tree called me to lie near it. Only when hunger overpowered me could I leave the tree. The farther I went from it, the worse I felt. Once in a while, when the tide was high, I could lean down into the water and snatch unwary fish; sometimes I steamed them with my breath until they floated to the surface, and then they were easy to catch.

Four days after my transformation, Masery came ashore.

She was a bigger fish than any I'd seen so close to the cliff. At first, when I sensed her, that flickering movement unexplained by water's workings, I was excited; hunger always lay in the back of my throat, and I was ready to eat again. Then I sensed the sister in her, and waited. I had thought of her now and again during my vigil by the tree, wondered if she had survived her transformation and my treatment of her afterward, the far toss into rough waters.

She swam right up until she had beached herself. I watched in alarm, wondering if she was killing herself, wondering whether to reach down and flip her back into the water. Her scent changed, though, and then she also changed. She shapeshifted back into her human self, naked, shivering, her hair a tangled mess. Gasping, she sat up, then stood. She faced me, took a staggering step back. "Brother?" she whispered.

Masery, I thought. I was afraid to speak. I remembered how I had tried to speak to Fon and Kiki, only to flame at them.

"Is it really you?" She crept closer. "Brother?"

I lowered my head and looked away. In the first days of my enchantment I had not thought much about my appearance, only tried out my new body and wondered how I could change back into myself. Did I really want to, now that Stepmother openly hated me? Father had not been home in months. What did I have to go back to? Masery and I had a few friends in the village, the children, whom we had sometimes snuck out to meet when Stepmother was brooding over her spellbooks. I had tried to greet them, and look what had happened. What else was there for me but to guard this tree and hunt?

"Brother," said Masery. She stood at the base of the low cliff and raised her arms. "Lift me up."

How brave, my sister, to face a dragony worm like me. I reached down and wrapped my hands around her waist, lifted her up and set her beside me.

"Oh," she said. "You're warm." She leaned against my flank.

THE LAILY WORM • 83

I turned away. "Masery," I tried to say. A hiss and a small flame.

"You can't speak? How little she's left you! Brother, dearest brother." She stroked my eyebrow whiskers. "I managed at the last a tiny guarding spell while she was tapping your shoulder and before she tapped mine, so I have my own form one day a week. I don't know how to counteract the fortunes she's given us, though." She sat beside me, leaned against me, hugged me, though my spines probably prickled. "Stay here. I'm going home to see what I can steal."

"Masery!" I spoke flames.

She patted my shoulder. "Don't worry. I'll use stealth spells. I just want clothing, and something for your hair. I'll visit the kitchen, too." She ran away, and left me to worry.

She returned when the sun was halfway down the sky. She wore her gardening dress, a soiled mustard shift, and carried two bundles. The greasy one smelled wonderful.

"Here." She opened that one, and brought out three whole roasted chickens. "Poor cook. She couldn't see me, but she saw that they were gone. Such a shriek she raised!" She set them on the ground in front of me. I took each into my mouth, chewed it to shreds, bones and all, roasted it a little further and swallowed with great gulps that wagged my head up and down.

Masery watched me with interest but no fear. I wasn't sure I could have been so calm in her place, watching a dragon bolt his meat.

When I finished eating, Masery opened the other bundle. "Here's your flute, Perry. I know you can't play the way you are now, but I didn't want to leave it for that child Stepmother will have. Here's my favorite necklace, from Mother, and some of my clothes. I don't need them while I'm a fish, but I want to visit you every week when I have my own form, so I'm going to hide them in the tree. You have to guard the tree, yes? A nod I can understand."

I nodded.

"I wonder why," said Masery.

I liked the tree. It whispered stories into my dreams, the deeds of kings and queens and princes and princesses, sorcerers and witless virgin maidens, brave knights and cowardly jesters, talking animals and walking plants. Why did the tree know stories of men? Why did the tree choose to share them with me? I had no idea, but it made the solitude less onerous. I knew that something caught high in the tree's branches smelled of Stepmother, too, but I didn't know how to tell Masery that.

"Maybe she just wanted you away from the house, but I suspect her of different motives. She could have ordered you to go far from our keep. Stepmother always has her reasons. Anyway, at least I know where to find you. And now, for your hair."

I was surprised to learn I even had hair. I had never gotten a good look at my new self, other than my tail and hindquarters, which I could see by curling my long, snaky neck, and my front claws. I could also see my snout, with its bristling, whiskery, scaly things, thicker than hair as I knew it. I could sense things through the whiskers—movement in the air, changes in the weather, a few things I didn't yet understand.

But hair? With these scales?

Masery took a silver comb from her bundle. "Put your head down."

I laid my long, long chin on the backs of my hands and closed my eyes. Masery stroked my head. "Oh, Perry, you have tiny jewels all over you. You're beautiful!"

My ears twitched, and she stroked them. I couldn't tell what they looked like, but they felt quite different from my human ears—longer, more mobile, directional. I could open my ears, angle them, swivel them; I could aim my hearing in a way I hadn't been able to before, and hear noises I had never imagined. Skyward, the zooms and buzzes of even the tiniest bugs flying past; seaward, under the surface of water rushing, the hiss of sand sliding over itself; toward the forest, the slither of leaves touching other leaves. The languages I had started to learn in human form, fire, snow, the past, those I heard better than I had, but I couldn't yet translate new words in fire and snow. My tree: its words were clear. Maybe all trees talked, and my hearing had just been inadequate before. Next time I went hunting, I would—

Masery's comb stroked something at the top of my head, and I fell into bliss, the perfect bliss of having an itch scratched just hard enough and long enough to satisfy its calling. The teeth of the comb stroked across the top of my head. I moaned in delight. Tiny puffs of smoke rose from my mouth.

Masery combed my hair and whispered, "Never forget who we are, Brother. Never forget, no matter how deep you sink into your animal. Never forget who we are."

With each stroke, she woke another memory: our real mother, when we still lived at court, dressing us both for presentation to the king, giving me a peppermint drop to quiet me as she combed some nasty tangles from my hair, Masery standing by, six years old and already groomed, beautiful in dark blue velvet, with tiny pearls around her neck, her hair in curls. Father, taking us each up before him on his horse and riding us around the meadow at home in the south. How the horse bumped between my legs, until Father taught me to rise with its rhythm. He set my hands on the reins, though he still kept hold of them, and I stopped being afraid I would fall and began to learn how to talk to the horse with nudges and tugs. Cook giving us hot biscuits and butter on a cold winter morning.

Masery let down a bucket into the ocean and pulled up water, and she washed my head. It hadn't occurred to me to wash since I gained my new form. Masery's gentle ablutions brought me strange comfort. Perhaps I was worth caring about and keeping clean, even though I had lost my human body. I remembered baths in front of the fire in winter, emptying ewers of steaming water into the copper tub to mix with the cold water already there, how I had to climb in and work my arms and legs to get a true mix of hot and cold so the water would be warm all through.

I didn't need the seawater to be warm; it warmed as it met my hot skin. Masery's touch felt gentle and soothing.

"Perry," Masery said, when I was truly and happily trapped in memories of my human self, "I have to go now. I'll return next week. Guard my things for me." She undressed, closed the comb and my flute and her dress into the bundle, and climbed up the tree to lodge the bundle and the bucket in the lower branches. She kissed my cheek and dived over the cliff. I scuttled forward and watched as she silvered and sleekened and swam away, a fish once more.

Three chickens kept me fed more than a day. I lay under the tree and digested, listening to the tree's whispered tales and watching.

A few days later, a knight rode along the cliff path toward me. He had a lance. I had never seen him before. Who was he, and where was he going? Was he a traveler? Why follow the cliff path? Was he heading for the next village along the coast? Why carry a lance all that way? How useful was it unless you were going to tourney?

"Hail, loathsome worm," he cried when he was still fifty feet away. He held his reins tight, for his horse pranced and sweated beneath him, its nostrils flaring wide. "I have come to slay you!"

I had been dreaming of history lessons with our old tutor before we had to leave court. Masery, the tutor, and I sat before a fire in the nursery at the old house. Our tutor had drawn pictures to illustrate the lessons. His hand was deft, whether he drew griffins, kings, or cats. It took me a moment to shake myself free of memory and realize that this knight was speaking to me.

"Don't," I cried. "Leave me alone. I have never harmed a human."

With those words, I made myself a liar, for instead of sound, flame shot from my mouth, and when the flame touched the horse, it bucked the knight off and fled.

The knight lay on his back on the ground, the lance broken beneath him. Then he struggled to his feet. One of his arms dangled useless at his side. He groaned. I smelled his fear and pain, a sour, bitter scent mixed with blood. He unbuckled his sword so he could draw it with the wrong hand. "Wicked, vile creature," he said. "I will rid the Earth of you."

Then I lost all the human I had ever been, and turned wholly into my dragon self, and I made a liar of the knight. Flame roared out of me, roasted him in his armor, dropped him smoking and screaming to the ground. I ran to him, my scales impervious to my own fire, and stamped on his head, crushing it.

Later, I woke and saw what I had done. I loathed myself and lay, sickened, at the foot of my tree. I had just killed a hero. Every story the tree had told me ended with the hero triumphing over the dragon or the witch or the sorcerer, winning the fair maiden, riding into a happy future. *I* was the wicked dragon, and I had won. This was wrong.

How could I kill someone and stay right with myself? I wanted to die.

The stink of the cooked knight tainted the air until finally I went into the forest, dug a hole—my claws proved strangely suited to such a task—and dropped him in. I buried him deep and covered him over and scratched a cross into the earth above him. Then I slunk back to my tree.

Sleep was a long time coming. My stomach was so soured with disgust that it kept speaking to me in grumbles and small gouts of flame. Finally I calmed enough to listen to my tree, and it told me a different sort of story, of a brave young dragon fighting for its life against a monstrous knight, emerging victorious.

When I woke I was still heartsick, but I felt better. The tree told me more stories where the dragon was the hero, and gradually I let loose of fretting about my evil deed.

Masery came again the next week. I wanted to tell her everything, but I still had no speech but a nod or flame. She dressed and snuck off to the castle and brought me back a slab of beef, which I cooked in my own flame and ate. Then she combed my hair and washed my head, and I remembered all the best things about our life before. She told me nothing of her own life under the water, though I longed to know. She left around sunset.

So the tenor of my days was set. I guarded my tree, waited for Masery's return, and hunted a little farther afield each day. Knights came, one after another, and I forgot I was human, and killed them. I always remembered I was human afterward, and gave them as decent a burial as I could. I wished I could speak to them, though, ask them why they came to kill me, who had sent them here so far from normal routes, who they were.

After I killed the sixth knight, I tried to frame speech with my mouth, tried to wake my throat into voice. The tree listened as I shaped hisses into whispers, searched and found words. The next knight I would challenge with speech before he attacked. The work of calling back words occupied my days.

When Masery came that week, I whispered her name.

"Perry! You can speak! How wonderful!" She hugged my head.

"Masery. I've killed six knights."

She drew back and looked at me. She walked a little ways away. I thought: now I've lost her. She'll never speak to me again. I wondered how I could kill myself. Bash my head into my oak? Leap from a higher cliff to crash to the rocks below? Starve myself?

Masery returned. "What happened?" she asked.

I told her about the first knight, how I spooked his horse, how he came at me with a sword and I roasted him. I told her of the others, who had also refused to run away, though I showed the later ones I could flame things before I actually aimed my flame at them. I tried to frighten them off. I tried to gesture at them to run away. They only drew their swords and came at me, screaming, and then—then I killed them. And was sick afterward.

Masery combed my hair and washed my head, and I remembered being human. The images were smaller, now, dimmer, veiled in a shimmer of flame. She whispered to me: "You only did what you had to, Brother. They came to fight you. You gave them what they desired."

That day, she did not kiss me before she left.

The seventh knight stopped to listen to my challenge. "I don't wish to harm you," I said. "Please go back."

"You speak with the devil's tongue, tempting me to abandon my quest! Have at you!" he cried, and charged me. His horse was better disciplined than the others' had been, and did not bolt at the first touch of flame. I didn't want to hurt a blameless creature. I flamed the horse's feet. When the hair burned on his hide—I smelled the peculiar pungency of singeing hair—he rose up, cast his knight to the ground, and ran away. This knight landed on his feet somehow, perhaps because his armor was lighter than the others', and drew his sword.

"Won't you save me from having to kill you?" I said.

"They call me coward, back home. I'm going to prove them wrong. Don't speak to me again."

"At least tell me your name so I will know what to scratch on your grave."

"Silence, Worm!"

He came at me then, and, as I had learned from past knights, I released my human self and let myself become wholly dragon. The dragon raged with flame, toasted the knight. The knight broke through the first wall of flame and hacked at the dragon's neck, scoring a long, shallow wound, and that threw the dragon into a frenzy. He flamed and flamed.

"Wait," cried the knight at last, reduced to a burned heap on the ground, his sword long fallen from his hand, his shield flaming on the ground a distance away from him, his armor burning him from the heat it had absorbed. "Wait," he said, though he was so badly injured he could not have survived even if given mercy.

The dragon did not listen, though somewhere inside it, I heard and tried to stop us. The dragon breathed out a long stream of flame that burned the features off the knight's face. A last scream, cut off when his throat was no longer whole. The dragon stomped the dead knight, the only one who had actually cut us. There was not much left for me to bury.

The eighth knight was my father.

He dismounted and tied his horse to a tree in the forest's fringe. Perhaps he had learned from all the other horses I had sent running. He approached me, wary of the char marks on the ground. He steeled himself and walked forward to come face to face with me.

"Now I find you here, on my lands, you stinking worm," he cried, "and hear about the devastation you've wreaked in my absence! You pestilence! You blight on a fair country! You killer of the king's champions! Now it's time for you to die." He drew his sword.

"Father," I said.

He staggered back, then righted himself.

I laid my head on my claws. "Father," I whispered. "I never meant to kill the others. They would not stop. They would not listen. At the last I couldn't help myself. Wouldn't you fight back, too, if someone stabbed you?" My voice was full of hisses and smoke, and yet, the words were clear enough to halt my father.

"Who are you, Worm, who claim my paternity?" he cried.

"I'm Perry. Peregrine of Hopelost. Your son. Stepmother enchanted me and Masery while you were gone. She wanted us out of the way once she got with child. Father."

He did not speak for a moment, and then he swayed. He pushed up his helm and rubbed his face with the back of his gloved hand. "Is it the devil who speaks to me?" he asked.

"Father. Please, Father."

"Perry?" He fell to his knees in a clatter of armor before me. "I knew I stayed away from home too long, but after all, there were reivers at Hidden Cove, and we had to fight off the first wave, and guard against the next two, and Genevra sent no word of trouble; we had no reason to hasten our return. I came home yesterday to find you gone. She said she'd sent you to foster at court. And all the village was full of the news of this dragon haunting the coast, and how knights had been sent for, and how all had been vanquished, or so it was thought; only their horses returned. Genevra warned me not to come here. She said you were a puissant dragon and would only kill me. She begged me to send my men instead, and to fight you with spears and arrows tipped with diamonds. But how could I honorably do that? Perry."

I turned to look at him. He stared into my eyes, his brow furrowed. "Are you in truth my son, or is this just another of evil's tricks?"

"Father." I laid my head down again and closed my eyes. "Kill me if you must; I will strive not to fight you. If you can, ask the villagers not to fish in the harbor. Masery was transformed into the mackerel of the sea, save for one afternoon a week, when she visits me as herself. If that will prove anything to you, come back on Saturday and see. But whatever you do, beware of Stepmother. Don't let her know you've spoken with me. She has her own son now, and perhaps she needs you no longer." Masery, during one of her weekly forays to the keep, had heard the news about our little half-brother. A fine boy, they all said.

Father leaned on his sword as he climbed to his feet. "I will think on all these things." He scrubbed his gloved hand over his face once more. "I am so weary of battle." He turned and marched back to his horse, led it to a fallen tree and mounted. He rode away.

The next day a lad from the keep castle rode out on a sturdy pony and tossed a burlap sack in my direction, then rode off in a hurry before I could respond. I crept to the sack, and clawed it open. I knew before I opened it that inside lay something delicious. The smoked haunch of a pig, as fine as anything Masery had brought me. I ate and was content.

The following day the same lad threw me another sack with roasted chickens in it, and the day after that, a beef roast.

The day after that was Saturday. Masery came up out of the water and dressed herself, as she always did, then pulled out her comb and the bucket and set to grooming me. "Perry, Perry," she said. "What was your week like?"

"Father has returned," I said.

She sat up straight, comb in hand. "Has he?"

"He came to kill me, but I spoke and he left. I told him about your visits. Sister, what was your week like?" I had asked her every week since I found words again, and she had always shrugged and said she was as happy as she could be, considering everything.

"Well," she said, "I got married."

I lifted my head and turned so I could see her with both eyes. "Who—whom did you marry, Sister mine?"

"His name is Silverthin, and he is a prince under the waters. I had to tell you, Perry, because I don't know how long I'll be able to visit you anymore. Silverthin has a witch in his court who can make my transformation permanent. Silverthin worries about me because I worry so much about you." She leaned against my side.

"Father has been feeding me," I said. "Perhaps you no longer need to worry about me."

"I worry about you forgetting who you are."

"Maybe it would be better if I did. Maybe it would be better if I lost my human side. Then when some knight comes to kill me and succeeds, I won't even care."

"Don't say that." She combed my hair, combed memories back into my mind, the taste of sap sugar candy at the harvest fair, the day I was allowed to tip wine on the roots of the apple trees in the orchard so they would share our joy at the season and bring us a good harvest next year, the smell of wax as we lit the first candles of the evening, ready to sit at Mother's feet while she read to us after supper. "Never forgot who you are," Masery sang softly to me. "Never forget."

But she was going to forget. She was going to let a witch turn her into her new self and leave her that way. Why should I remember any longer?

I heard clanking, and smell-tasted the scent of smoke and marsh and sweat that was my father. Masery leapt up. I closed a claw around her ankle. "It may be your last chance to speak with him," I said. "Please wait."

Father came into the clearing, bareheaded but otherwise locked into armor. "Masery," he said, and ran to us. "Masery!"

My sister kicked free of my grasp, dropped her comb and bucket, and dived over the cliff into the sea. Father rushed to the cliff and looked for her, and I followed. Her dress floated, empty, on the surge of the tide. Of her, there was only a silver flicker under the surface, beyond where the waves broke. She was gone.

Father dropped beside me, groaning. "Why did she run?" he asked.

"I don't know. She's found a love under the sea. She came to tell me today that she probably won't be back."

He took the comb Masery had used on my hair and held it on both hands, lifted it to his nose and smelled it. Could he smell her on it? More likely me, smoke and the clean dirt I slept in and lay in, bitter oak for the one that spoke stories in my dreams and dropped acorns and leaves on me.

"Perry," he said at last. "I believe you now. I'm going to speak to my wife."

"Take care, Father. Don't let her harm you."

He nodded. "I've been a warrior a long time, my son," he said, "and I am not without powers of my own." He rose, left. I should go with him, I thought. I was stronger as my dragon self than I had been as a boy. Maybe I could protect him.

But then I remembered the further transformation Stepmother had made in me: she had made me obedient to her will. Ordered me to stay with the tree. Suppose I fought off that compulsion and went back with Father. Suppose she ordered me to attack him? Made me kill my own father?

I spent another night under my tree, listening to stories of homecoming heroes. In my drowsy state I did not notice whether they were knights or dragons.

The next morning, Father returned, with Stepmother in his grip. Her hair was disheveled, her gown smudged. "Now, woman," Father said to her, bringing her face to face with me. "Undo what you've done to my boy." He pushed her from him, and she stumbled forward, then caught her balance and stopped.

"Ah, Perry, how fine you've grown. Being a dragon suits you." She smiled at me. Then she straightened and pulled her silver wand out of her sleeve. "But your father wants you back as a boy. I'm sorry. I hope you don't mind." She struck me three times across the forehead with the wand, muttering something under her breath. I shivered and shook, angry and frightened at the change I felt. I opened my mouth, ready to pour forth flame, but what came out of me was a muscle-armed man, his hair glossy and wet. I coughed and choked on him and then it happened again: I melted, all the dragon, jeweled length of me, into this shape that had emerged from me. There was a sense of being two shapes at once, jangling, jarring, wrong, and then an easing as I lost my dragon self. I stood up, clutched my head in my hands.

My father took off his cloak and wrapped me in it. After a moment, my stomach and my vision steadied. I tried to find myself again, but half the sounds and most of the smells had faded. I felt as though I floated in some strange bath of air that had washed away the real world.

"No harm done," said Stepmother. "See how he's grown into a fine young man!"

"Now get me back my daughter," said Father.

"Of course, of course." She went to stand at the cliff's edge, and raised a tiny silver horn to her lips and blew.

I didn't hear a sound, but I felt as though I would have with my dragon ears. My human ears didn't swivel. I felt deprived. Father and I stood beside Stepmother and looked out to sea. Soon, the water turned silver with the arrival of fish, schooling so thickly one could have walked out to sea on their backs and not gotten one's feet wet. "Masery? Where is Masery?" Stepmother asked the fish. We both stared at all the fish, looking for my sister.

"Here," called a fish some distance out.

"Come closer," said Stepmother, "or I won't be able to change you back."

"You shaped me once, Stepmother, but never again will I let you do that. Leave me be."

"Masery, are you sure?" Father called.

"She has cast this grief upon me. Consider me dead to you, and blame her for it, Father," she called, and swam away. All the other fish swam away too.

"I did my best, Kendrick," said Stepmother. "You saw. She is wilfull and won't come home. But you have your son again. Isn't that enough?"

"No, Genevra, it is not enough. You need to suffer the way my children have." He took the wand from her and bound her hands behind her and led her toward the woods.

"Kendrick," she whimpered. "I am your son's mother."

"That's not enough to excuse your crimes. I've raised motherless children before," said Father, and then they had gone so far I didn't hear them any longer.

But you haven't, I thought. We were only motherless a year before you brought Stepmother home.

Everything had changed. I leaned against the oak and looked. My eyes were farther from the ground now, my ears and nose less sensitive. I tried to summon up my internal fire, and coughed. Only noise came out of my mouth. Could I be happy in this shape? Even the oak had gone dumb; the whisper of breeze in its leaves no longer made words for me.

Well, there was one thing I had wanted to do as a dragon that I couldn't manage. I could no longer smell the cinnamon scent that had told me night and day something of Stepmother's was up in the tree, but now I could climb. So I did: I shed Father's cloak and climbed up the tree, higher and higher, until the branches were slender and wouldn't support my weight. I wished again I could smell with the sensitive tip of my tongue, that wash of information from the air into my mouth and then my brain, but I couldn't. I searched through the tree's crown with just my hands, which were soon scratched and bleeding. How could anything be hidden up here? Maybe I had dreamed it.

But then I found it, tucked into a crotch of the tree, the branches almost grown over it: a small wooden box with ivory inlay in the shape of lilies on its top. I tugged at it. At first I thought the tree had grown too tightly around it to release, but then something shivered in the tree; I felt it in the bark against the soles of my feet, in my arms where I leaned against branches, in the air. The tree moved just enough to loose the box into my hand.

Somewhere in the distance the sound of crackling, burning. A shriek, and then a scream. Then another.

I climbed carefully down, the box in one hand. When I reached the ground, I sat on my father's cloak and opened the box. Inside was something black, repellent, and shriveled. I clapped the lid closed again. I couldn't look at the contents of the box without feeling sick to my stomach.

Screams from the forest, the scent of smoke, meat cooking. The same meat I had cooked in its own armor when I defeated the knights. "No, Kendrick, no," screamed Stepmother, and then a howl of anguish.

I flinched, though I had known without knowing what my father must be doing.

He doesn't even know what her real crime is, I thought. I wished I could warm myself with my own fire again, and listen to tree tales through the long winter night. She had given me that and taken it away.

I opened the box that held my stepmother's heart. As long as her heart was safe, she couldn't perish. She must be screaming just for show.

I closed my fist around my stepmother's heart and squeezed.

THE HARROWING OF THE DRAGON OF HOARSBREATH

Patricia A. McKillip

Patricia A. McKillip was born in Salem, Oregon in 1948. Educated at San Jose State University in California, she received a B.A. in 1971 and an M.A. in English in 1973. She published two short children's books, *The Throme of the Erril of Sherill* and *The House on Parchment Street* in 1973. Her first longer novel, the sophisticated young-adult fantasy *The Forgotten Beasts of Eld*, won the 1975 World Fantasy Award. She switched to children's mainstream for *The Night Gift*, but returned to young-adult fantasy in the Riddle of Stars trilogy.

McKillip followed that with *Stepping from the Shadows*, an adult contemporary novel with some magic realist elements, and then YA science fantasy duology *Moon-Flash,* and *The Moon and the Face.* Her adult SF novel *Fool's Run* was followed by YA fantasy *The Changeling Sea*, fantasy duology *The Sorceress and the Cygnet* and *The Cygnet and the Firebird*. In 1995 she published *The Book of Atrix Wolf*, the first in a sequence of remarkable stand-alone fantasies marked by great sophistication and elegance, which include *Winter Rose, Song for the Basilisk, The Tower at Stony Wood*, World Fantasy Award winner *Ombria in Shadow, In the Forests of Serre, Alphabet of Thorn, Od Magic, Solstice Wood* and *The Bell at Sealey Head.* Her short fiction was collected in *Harrowing the Dragon.* Coming up is a new novel *The Bards of Bone Plain.* McKillip was awarded the World Fantasy Award for Lifetime Achievement in 2008.

Once, on the top of a world, there existed the ring of an island named Hoarsbreath, made out of gold and snow. It was all mountain, a grim, briny, yellowing ice-world covered with winter twelve months out of thirteen. For one month, when the twin suns crossed each other at the world's cap, the snow melted from the peak of Hoarsbreath. The hardy trees shrugged the snow off their boughs, and sucked in light and mellow air, pulling themselves toward the suns. Snow and icicles melted off the roofs of the miners' village; the snow-tunnels they had dug from house to tavern to storage barn to mineshaft sagged to the ground; the dead-white river flowing down from the mountain to the sea turned blue and began to move again. Then the miners gathered the gold they had dug by firelight out of the chill, harsh darkness of the deep mountain, and took it downriver, across the sea to the main-land, to trade for food and furs, tools and a liquid fire called worm-spoor, because it was gold and bitter, like the leavings of dragons. After three swallows of it, in a busy city with a harbor frozen only part of the year, with people who wore rich furs, kept horses and sleds to ride in during winter, and who knew the patterns of the winter stars since they weren't buried alive by the snow, the miners swore they would never return to Hoarsbreath. But the gold waiting in the dark, secret places of the mountain-island drew at them in their dreaming, lured them back.

For two hundred years after the naming of Hoarsbreath, winter followed winter, and the miners lived rich isolated, precarious lives on the pinnacle of ice and granite, cursing the cold and loving it, for it kept lesser folk away. They mined, drank, spun tales, raised children who were sent to the mainland when they were half-grown, to receive their education, and find easier, respectable lives. But always a few children found their way back, born with a gnawing in their hearts for fire, ice, stone, and the solitary pursuit of gold in the dark.

Then, two miners' children came back from the great world and destroyed the island.

They had no intention of doing that. The younger of them was Peka Krao. After spending five years on the mainland, boring herself with schooling, she came back to Hoarsbreath to mine. At seventeen, she was good-natured and sturdy, with dark eyes, and dark, braided hair. She loved every part of Hoarsbreath, even its chill, damp shafts at midwinter and the bone-jarring work of hewing through darkness and stone to unbury its gold. Her instincts for gold were uncanny: she seemed to sense it through her fingertips touching bare rock. The miners called her their good luck. She could make wormspoor, too, one of the few useful things she had learned on the mainland. It lost its bitterness, somehow, when she made it: it aged into a rich, smokey gold that made the miners forget their sore muscles, and inspired marvellous tales out of them that whittled away at the endless winter.

She met the Dragon-Harrower one evening at a cross-section of tunnel between her mother's house and the tavern. She knew all the things to fear in her world: a rumble in the mountain, a guttering torch in the mines, a crevice in the snow, a crack of ice underfoot. There was little else she couldn't handle with a soft word or her own right arm. Even when he loomed out of the darkness unexpectedly into her taper-light, she wasn't afraid. But he made her stop instinctively, like an animal might stop, faced with something that puzzled its senses.

His hair was dead-white, with strands bright as wormspoor running through it; his eyes were the light, hard blue of dawn during suns-crossing. Rich colors flashed out of him everywhere in her light: from a gold knife-hilt and a brass pack buckle; from the red ties of his cloak that were weighted with ivory, and the blue and silver threads in his gloves. His heavy fur cloak was closed, but she felt that if he shifted, other colors would escape from it into the cold, dark air.

At first she thought he must be ancient: the taper-fire showed her a face that was shadowed and scarred, remote with strange experience, but no more than a dozen years older than hers.

"Who are you?" she breathed. Nothing on Hoarsbreath glittered like that in midwinter; its colors were few and simple: snow, damp fur and leather, fire, gold.

"I can't find my father," he said. "Lule Yarrow."

She stared at him, amazed that his colors had their beginnings on Hoarsbreath. "He's dead." His eyes widened slightly, losing some of their hardness. "He fell in a crevice. They chipped him out of the ice at suns-crossing, and buried him six years ago."

He looked away from her a moment, down at the icy ridges of tramped snow. "Winter." He broke the word in two, like an icicle. Then he shifted his pack, sighing. "Do they still have wormspoor on this ice-tooth?"

"Of course. Who are you?"

"Ryd Yarrow. Who are you?"

"Peka Krao."

"Peka. I remember. You were squalling in somebody's arms when I left."

"You look a hundred years older than that," she commented, still puzzling, holding him in her light, though she was beginning to feel the cold. "Seventeen years you've been gone. How could you stand it, being away from Hoarsbreath so long? I couldn't stand five years of it. There are so many people whose names you don't know, trying to tell you about things that don't matter, and the flat earth and the blank sky are everywhere. Did you come back to mine?"

He glanced up at the grey-white ceiling of the snow-tunnel, barely an inch above his head. "The sky is full of stars, and the gold wake of dragon-flights," he said softly. "I am a Dragon-Harrower. I am trained and hired to trouble dragons out of their lairs. That's why I came back here."

"Here. There are no dragons on Hoarsbreath."

His smile touched his eyes like a reflection of fire across ice. "Hoarsbreath is a dragon's heart."

She shifted, her own heart suddenly chilled. She said tolerantly. "That sounds like a marvellous tale to me."

"It's no tale. I know. I followed this dragon through centuries, through ancient writings, through legends, through rumors of terror and deaths. It is here, sleeping, coiled around the treasures of Hoarsbreath. If you on Hoarsbreath rouse it, you are dead. If I rouse it, I will end your endless winter."

"I like winter." Her protest sounded very small, muted within the thick snow-walls, but he heard it. He lifted his hand, held it lightly against the low ceiling above his head.

"You might like the sky beyond this. At night it *is* a mine of lights and hidden knowledge."

She shook her head. "I like close places, full of fire and darkness. And faces I know. And tales spun out of wormspoor. If you come with me to the tavern, they'll tell you where your father is buried, and give you lodgings, and then you can leave."

"I'll come to the tavern. With a tale."

Her taper was nearly burned down, and she was beginning to shiver. "A dragon." She turned away from him. "No one will believe you anyway."

"You do."

She listened to him silently, warming herself with wormspoor, as he spoke to the circle of rough, fire-washed faces in the tavern. Even in the light, he bore little resemblance to his father, except for his broad cheekbones and the threads of gold in his hair. Under his bulky cloak, he was dressed as plainly as any miner, but stray bits of color still glinted from him, suggesting wealth and distant places.

"A dragon," he told them, "is creating your winter. Have you ever asked yourselves why winter on this island is nearly twice as long as winter on the mainland twenty miles away? You live in dragon's breath, in the icy mist of its bowels, hoarfrost cold, that grips your land in winter the way another dragon's breath might burn it to flinders. One month out of the year, in the warmth of suns-crossing, it looses its ring-grip on your island, slides into the sea, and goes to mate. Its ice-kingdom begins to melt. It returns, loops its length around its mountain of ice and gold. Its breath freezes the air once more, locks the river into its bed, you into your houses, the gold into its mountain, and you curse the cold and drink until the next dragon-mating." He paused. There was not a sound around him. "I've been to strange places in this world, places even colder than this, where the suns never cross, and I have seen such monsters. They are ancient as rock, white as old ice, and their skin is like iron. They breed winter and they cannot be killed. But they can be driven away, into far corners of the world where they are dangerous to no one. I'm trained for this. I can rid you of your winter. Harrowing is dangerous work, and usually I am highly paid. But I've been looking for this ice-dragon for many years, through its spoor of legend and destruction. I tracked it here, one of the oldest of its kind, to the place where I was born. All I ask from you is a guide."

He stopped, waiting. Peka, her hands frozen around her glass, heard someone swallow. A voice rose and faded from the tavern-kitchen; sap hissed in the fire. A couple of the miners were smiling; the others looked satisfied and vaguely expectant, wanting the tale to continue. When it didn't, Kor Flynt, who had mined Hoarsbreath for fifty years, spat wormspoor into the fire. The flame turned a baleful gold, and then subsided. "Suns-crossing," he said politely, reminding a scholar of a scrap of knowledge children acquired with their first set of teeth, "causes the seasons."

"Not here," Ryd said. "Not on Hoarsbreath. I've seen. I know."

Peka's mother Ambris leaned forward. "Why," she asked curiously, "would a miner's son become a dragon-harrower?" She had a pleasant, craggy face; her dark hair and her slow, musing voice were like Peka's. Peka saw the Dragon-Harrower ride between two answers in his mind. Meeting Ambris' eyes, he made a choice, and his own eyes strayed to the fire.

"I left Hoarsbreath when I was twelve. When I was fifteen, I saw a dragon in the mountains east of the city. Until then, I had intended to come back and mine. I began to learn about dragons. The first one I saw burned red and gold under the suns' fire; it swallowed small hills with its shadow. I wanted to call it, like a hawk. I wanted to fly with it. I kept studying, meeting other people who studied them, seeing other dragons. I saw a night-black dragon in the northern deserts; it scales were dusted with silver, and the flame that came out of it was silver. I saw people die in that flame, and I watched the harrowing of that dragon. It lives now on the underside of the world, in shadow.

"We keep watch on all known dragons. In the green mid-world belt, rich with rivers and mines, forests and farmland, I saw a whole mining town burned to the ground by a dragon so bright I thought at first it was sun-fire arching down to the ground. Someone I loved had the task of tracking that one to its cave, deep beneath the mine-shafts. I watched her die, there. I nearly died. The dragon is sealed into the bottom of the mountain, by stone and by words. That is the dragon which harrowed me." He paused to sip wormspoor. His eyes lifted, not to Ambris, but to Peka. "Now do you understand what danger you live in? What if one year the dragon sleeps through its mating-time, with the soft heat of the suns making it sluggish from dreaming? You don't know it's there, wrapped around your world. It doesn't know you're there, stealing its gold. What if you sail your boats full of gold downriver and find the great white bulk of it sprawled like a wall across your passage? Or worse, you find its eye opening like a third, dead sun to see your hands full of its gold? It would slide its length around the mountain, coil upward and crush you all, then breathe over the whole of the island, and turn it dead-white as its heart, and it would never sleep again."

There was another silence. Peka felt something play along her spine like the thin, quavering, arthritic fingers of wind. "It's getting better," she said, "your tale." She took a deep swallow of wormspoor and added, "I love sitting in a warm, friendly place listening to tales I don't have to believe."

Kor Flynt shrugged. "It rings true, lass."

"It is true," Ryd said.

"Maybe so," she said. "And it may be better if you just let the dragon sleep."

"And if it wakes unexpectedly? The winter killed my father. The dragon at the heart of winter could destroy you all."

"There are other dangers. Rock falls, sudden floods, freezing winds. A dragon is simply one more danger to live with."

He studied her. "I saw a dragon once with wings as softly blue as a spring sky. Have you ever felt spring on Hoarsbreath? It could come."

She drank again. "You love them," she said. "Your voice loves them and hates them, Dragon-Harrower."

"I hate them," he said flatly. "Will you guide me down the mountain?"

"No. I have work to do."

He shifted, and the colors rippled from him again, red, gold, silver, spring-blue. She finished the wormspoor, felt it burn in her like liquid gold. "It's only a tale.

All your dragons are just colors in our heads. Let the dragon sleep. If you wake it, you'll destroy the night."

"No," he said. "You will see the night. That's what you're afraid of."

Kor Flynt shrugged. "There probably is no dragon, anyway."

"Spring, though," Ambris said; her face had softened. "Sometimes I can smell it from the mainland, and, and I always wonder. Still, after a hard day's work, sitting beside a roaring fire sipping dragon-spit, you can believe anything. Especially this." She looked into her glass at the glowering liquid. "Is this some of yours, Peka? What did you put into it?"

"Gold." The expression in Ryd's eyes made her swallow sudden tears of frustration. She refilled her glass. "Fire, stone, dark, wood-smoke, night air smelling like cold tree-bark. You don't care, Ryd Yarrow."

"I do care," he said imperturbably. "It's the best wormspoor I've ever tasted."

"And I put a dragon's heart into it." She saw him start slightly; ice and hoar-frost shimmered from him. "If that's what Hoarsbreath is." A dragon beat into her mind, its wings of rime, its breath smoldering with ice, the guardian of winter. She drew breath, feeling the vast bulk of it looped around them all, dreaming its private dreams. Her bones seemed suddenly fragile as kindling, and the gold wormspoor in her hands a guilty secret. "I don't believe it," she said, lifting her glass. "It's a tale."

"Oh, go with him, lass," her mother said tolerantly. "There may be no dragon, but we can't have him swallowed up in the ice like his father. Besides, it may be a chance for spring."

"Spring is for flatlanders. There are things that shouldn't be wakened. I know."

"How?" Ryd asked.

She groped, wishing for the first time for a flatlander's skill with words. She said finally, "I feel it," and he smiled. She sat back in her chair, irritated and vaguely frightened. "Oh, all right, Ryd Yarrow, since you'll go with or without me. I'll lead you down to the shores in the morning. Maybe by then you'll listen to me."

"You can't see beyond your snow-world," he said implacably. "It is morning."

They followed one of the deepest mine-shafts, and clambered out of it to stand in the snow half-way down the mountain. The sky was lead grey; across the mists ringing the island's shores, they could see the ocean, a swirl of white, motionless ice. The mainland harbor was locked. Peka wondered if the ships were stuck like birds in the ice. The world looked empty and somber.

"At least in the dark mountain there is fire and gold. Here, there isn't even a sun." She took out a skin of wormspoor, sipped it to warm her bones. She held it out to Ryd, but he shook his head.

"I need all my wits. So do you, or we'll both end up preserved in ice at the bottom of a crevice."

"I know. I'll keep you safe." She corked the skin and added, "In case you were wondering."

But he looked at her, startled out of his remoteness. "I wasn't. Do you feel that strongly?"

"Yes."

"So did I, when I was your age. Now I feel very little." He moved again. She stared after him, wondering how he kept her smoldering and on edge. She said abruptly, catching up with him,

"Ryd Yarrow."

"Yes."

"You have two names. Ryd Yarrow, and Dragon-Harrower. One is a plain name this mountain gave you. The other you got from the world, the name that gives you color. One name I can talk to, the other is the tale at the bottom of a bottle of wormspoor. Maybe you could understand me if you hadn't brought your past back to Hoarsbreath."

"I do understand you," he said absently. "You want to sit in the dark all your life and drink wormspoor."

She drew breath and held it. "You talk but you don't listen," she said finally. "Just like all the other flatlanders." He didn't answer. They walked in silence awhile, following the empty bed of an old river. The world looked dead, but she could tell by the air, which was not even freezing spangles of breath on her hood-fur, that the winter was drawing to an end. "Suns-crossing must be only two months away," she commented surprisedly.

"Besides, I'm not a flatlander," he said abruptly, surprising her again. "I do care about the miners, about Hoarsbreath. It's because I care that I want to challenge that ice-dragon with all the skill I possess. Is it better to let you live surrounded by danger, in bitter cold, carving half-lives out of snow and stone, so that you can come fully alive for one month of the year?"

"You could have asked us."

"I did ask you."

She sighed. "Where will it live, if you drive it away from Hoarsbreath?"

He didn't answer for a few paces. In the still day, he loosed no colors, though Peka thought she saw shadows of them around his pack. His head was bowed; his eyes were burning back at a memory. "It will find some strange, remote places where there is no gold, only rock; it can ring itself around emptiness and dream of its past. I came across an ice-dragon unexpectedly once, in a land of ice. The bones of its wings seemed almost translucent. I could have sworn it cast a white shadow."

"Did you want to kill it?"

"No. I loved it."

"Then why do you—" But he turned at her suddenly, almost angrily, waking out of a dream.

"I came here because you've built your lives on top of a terrible danger, and I asked for a guide, not a gad-fly."

"You wanted me," she said flatly. "And you don't care about Hoarsbreath. All you want is that dragon. Your voice is full of it. What's a gad-fly?"

"Go ask a cow. Or a horse. Or anything else that can't live on this forsaken, frostbitten lump of ice."

"Why should you care, anyway? You've got the whole great world to roam in. Why do you care about one dragon wrapped around the tiny island on the top of nowhere?"

"Because it's beautiful and deadly and wrapped around my heartland. And I don't know—I don't know at the end of things which of us will be left on Hoarsbreath." She stared at him. He met her eyes fully. "I'm very skilled. But that is one very powerful dragon."

She whirled, fanning snow. "I'm going back. Find your own way to your harrowing. I hope it swallows you."

His voice stopped her. "You'll always wonder. You'll sit in the dark, drinking wormspoor twelve months out of thirteen, wondering what happened to me. What an ice-dragon looks like, on a winter's day, in full flight."

She hovered between two steps. Then, furiously, she followed him. They climbed deeper into mist, and then into darkness. They camped at night, ate dried meat and drank wormspoor beside a fire in the snow. The night-sky was sullen and starless as the day. They woke to grey mists and travelled on. The cold breathed up around them; walls of ice, yellow as old ivory, loomed over them. They smelled the chill, sweaty smell of the sea. The dead riverbed came to an end over an impassible cliff. They shifted ground, followed a frozen stream downward. The ice-walls broke up into great jewels of ice, blue, green, gold, massed about them like a giant's treasure hoard. Peka stopped to stare at them. Ryd said with soft, bitter satisfaction,

"Wormspoor."

She drew breath. "Wormspoor." Her voice sounded small, absorbed by cold. "Ice-jewels, fallen stars. Down here you could tell me anything and I might believe it. I feel very strange." She uncorked the wormspoor and took a healthy swig. Ryd reached for it, but he only rinsed his mouth and spat. His face was pale; his eyes red-rimmed, tired.

"How far down do you think we are?"

"Close. There's no dragon. Just mist." She shuddered suddenly at the soundlessness. "The air is dead. Like stone. We should reach the ocean soon."

"We'll reach the dragon first."

They descended hillocks of frozen jewels. The stream they followed fanned into a wide, skeletal filigree of ice and rock. The mist poured around them, so painfully cold it burned their lungs. Peka pushed fur over her mouth, breathed through it. The mist or wormspoor she had drunk was forming shadows around her, flickerings of faces and enormous wings. Her heart felt heavy; her feet dragged like boulders when she lifted them. Ryd was coughing mist; he moved doggedly, as if into a hard wind. The stream fanned again, going very wide before it met the sea. They stumbled down into a bone-searing flow of mist. Ryd disappeared; Peka found him again, bumping into him, for he had stopped. The threads of mist untangled above them, and she saw a strange black sun, hooded with a silvery web. As she blinked at it, puzzled, the web rolled up. The dark sun gazed back at her. She became aware then of her own heartbeat, of a rhythm in the mists, of a faint, echoing pulse all around her: the icy heartbeat of Hoarsbreath.

She drew a hiccup of a breath, stunned. There was a mountain-cave ahead of them, from which the mists breathed and eddied. Icicles dropped like bars between its grainy-white surfaces. Within it rose stones or teeth as milky white as quartz. A wall of white stretched beyond the mists, vast, earthworm round, solid as stone. She couldn't tell in the blur and welter of mist, where winter ended and the dragon began.

She made a sound. The vast, silvery eyelid drooped like a parchment unrolled, then lifted again. From the depths of the cave came a faint, rumbling, a vague, drowsy waking question: Who?

She heard Ryd's breath finally. "Look at the scar under its eye," he said softly. She saw a jagged track beneath the black sun. "I can name the Harrower who put that there three hundred years ago. And the broken eyetooth. It razed a marble fortress with its wings and jaws; I know the word that shattered that tooth, then. Look at its wing-scales. Rimed with silver. It's old. Old as the world." He turned finally, to look at her. His white hair, slick with mists, made him seem old as winter. "You can go back now. You won't be safe here."

"I won't be safe up there, either," she whispered. "Let's both go back. Listen to its heart."

"Its blood is gold. Only one Harrower ever saw that and lived."

"Please." She tugged at him, at his pack. Colors shivered into the air: sulphur, malachite, opal. The deep rumble came again; a shadow quickened in the dragon's eye. Ryd moved quickly, caught her hands. "Let it sleep. It belongs here on Hoarsbreath. Why can't you see that? Why can't you see? It's a thing made of gold, snow, darkness—" But he wasn't seeing her; his eyes, remote and alien as the black sun, were full of memories and calculations. Behind him, a single curved claw lay like a crescent moon half-buried in the snow.

Peka stepped back from the Harrower, envisioning a bloody moon through his heart, and the dragon roused to fury, coiling upward around Hoarsbreath, crushing the life out of it. "Ryd Yarrow," she whispered. "Ryd Yarrow. Please." But he did not hear his name.

He began to speak, startling echoes against the solid ice around them. "Dragon of Hoarsbreath, whose wings are of hoarfrost, whose blood is gold—" The backbone of the hoar-dragon rippled slightly, shaking away snow. "I have followed your path of destruction from your beginnings in a land without time and without seasons. You have slept one night too long on this island. Hoarsbreath is not your dragon's dream; it belongs to the living, and I, trained and titled Dragon-Harrower, challenge you for its freedom." More snow shook away from the dragon, baring a rippling of scale, and the glistening of its nostrils. The rhythm of its mist was changing. "I know you," Ryd continued, his voice growing husky, strained against the silence. "You were the white death of the fishing-island Klonos, of ten Harrowers in Ynyme, of the winter palace of the ancient lord of Zuirsh. I have harried nine ice-dragons—perhaps your children—out of the known world. I have been searching for you many years, and I came back to the place where I was born to find you here. I stand before you armed with knowledge, experience, and the dark wisdom of necessity. Leave Hoarsbreath, go back to your birthplace forever, or I will harry you down to the frozen shadow of the world."

The dragon gazed at him motionlessly, an immeasurable ring of ice looped about him. The mist out of its mouth was for a moment suspended. Then its jaws crashed together, spitting splinters of ice. It shuddered, wrenched itself loose from the ice. Its white head reared high, higher, ice booming and cracking around it. Twin black suns stared down at Ryd from the grey mist of the sky. Before it roared, Peka moved.

She found herself on a ledge above Ryd's head, without remembering how she got there. Ryd vanished in a flood of mist. The mist turned fiery; Ryd loomed out of them like a red shadow, dispersing them. Seven crescents lifted out of the snow, slashed down at him scarring the air. A strange voice shouted Ryd's name. He flung back his head and cried a word. Somehow the claw missed him, wedged deep into the ice.

Peka sat back. She was clutching the skin of wormspoor against her heart; she could feel her heartbeat shaking it. Her throat felt raw; the strange voice had been hers. She uncorked the skin, took a deep swallow, and another. Fire licked down her veins. A cloud of ice billowed at Ryd. He said something else, and suddenly he was ten feet away from it, watching a rock where he had stood freeze and snap into pieces.

Peka crouched closer to the wall of ice behind her. From her high point she could see the briny, frozen snarl of the sea. It flickered green, then an eerie orange. Bands of color pinioned the dragon briefly like a rainbow, arching across its wings. A scale caught fire; a small bone the size of Ryd's forearm snapped. Then the cold wind of the dragon's breath froze and shattered the rainbow. A claw slapped at Ryd; he moved a fraction of a moment too slowly. The tip of a talon caught his pack. It burst open with an explosion of glittering colors. The dragon hooded its eyes; Peka hid hers under her hands.

She heard Ryd cry out in pain. Then he was beside her instead of in several pieces, prying the wormspoor out of her hands.

He uncorked it, his hands shaking. One of them was seared silver.

"What are they?" she breathed. He poured wormspoor on his burned hand, then thrust it into the snow. The colors were beginning to die down.

"Flame," he panted. "Dragon-flame. I wasn't prepared to handle it."

"You carry it in your pack?"

"Caught in crystals, in fire-leaves. It will be more difficult than I anticipated."

Peka felt language she had never used before clamor in her throat. "It's all right," she said dourly. "I'll wait."

For a moment, as he looked at her, there was a memory of fear in his eyes. "You can walk across the ice to the mainland from here."

"You can walk to the mainland," she retorted. "This is my home. I have to live with or without that dragon. Right now, there's no living with it. You woke it out of its sleep. You burnt its wing. You broke its bone. You told it there are people on its island. You are going to destroy Hoarsbreath."

"No. This will be my greatest harrowing." He left her suddenly, and appeared flaming like a torch on the dragon's skull, just between its eyes. His hair and his hands spattered silver. Word after word came out of him, smoldering, flashing, melting in the air. The dragon's voice thundered; its skin rippled and shook. Its claw ripped at ice, dug chasms out of it. The air clapped nearby, as if its invisible tail had lifted and slapped at the ground. Then it heaved its head, flung Ryd at the wall of mountain. Peka shut her eyes. But he fell lightly, caught up a crystal as he rose, and sent a shaft of piercing gold light at the upraised scales of its underside, burrowing towards its heart.

Peka got unsteadily to her feet, her throat closing with a sudden whimper. But the dragon's tail, flickering out of the mist behind Ryd, slapped him into a snowdrift twenty feet away. It gave a cold, terrible hiss; mist bubbled over everything, so that for a few minutes Peka could see nothing beyond the lip of the ledge. She drank to stop her shivering. Finally a green fire blazed within the white swirl. She sat down again slowly, waited.

Night rolled in from the sea. But Ryd's fires shot in raw, dazzling streaks across the darkness, illuminating the hoary, scarred bulk of dragon in front of him. Once, he shouted endless poetry at the dragon, lulling it until its mist-breath was faint and slow from its maw. It nearly put Peka to sleep, but Ryd's imperceptible steps closer and closer to the dragon kept her watching. The tale was evidently an old one to the dragon; it didn't wait for an ending. Its head lunged and snapped unexpectedly, but a moment too soon. Ryd leaped for shelter in the dark, while the dragon's teeth ground painfully on nothingness. Later, Ryd sang to it, a whining, eerie song that showered icicles around Peka's head. One of the dragon's teeth cracked, and it made an odd, high-pitched noise. A vast webbed wing shifted free to fly, unfolding endlessly over the sea. But the dragon stayed, sending mist at Ryd to set him coughing. A foul ashy-grey miasma followed it, blurring over them. Peka hid her face in her arms. Sounds like the heaving of boulders and the spattering of fire came from beneath her. She heard the dragon's dry roar, like stones dragged against one another. There was a smack, a musical shower of breaking icicles, and a sharp, anguished curse. Ryd appeared out of the turmoil of light and air, sprawled on the ledge beside Peka.

His face was cut, with ice she supposed, and there was blood in his white hair. He looked at her with vague amazement.

"You're still here."

"Where else would I be? Are you winning or losing?"

He scooped up snow, held it against his face. "I feel as if I've been fighting for a thousand years... Sometimes, I think I tangle in its memories, as it thinks of other harrowers, old dragon-battles, distant places. It doesn't remember what I am, only that I will not let it sleep... Did you see its wingspan? I fought a red dragon once with such a span. Its wings turned to flame in the sunlight. You'll see this one in flight by dawn."

She stared at him numbly, huddled against herself. "Are you so sure?"

"It's old and slow. And it can't bear the gold fire." He paused, then dropped the snow in his hand with a sigh, and leaned his face against the ice-wall. "I'm tired, too. I have one empty crystal, to capture the essence of its mist, its heart's breath. After that's done, the battle will be short." He lifted his head at her silence, as if he could hear her thoughts. "What?"

"You'll go on to other dragons. But all I've ever had is this one."

"You never know—"

"It doesn't matter that I never knew it. I know now. It was coiled all around us in the winter, while we lived in warm darkness and firelight. It kept out the world. Is that such a terrible thing? Is there so much wisdom in the flatlands that we can't live without?"

He was silent again, frowning a little, either in pain or faint confusion. "It's a dangerous thing, a destroyer."

"So is winter. So is the mountain, sometimes. But they're also beautiful. You are full of so much knowledge and experience that you forgot how to see simple things. Ryd Yarrow, miner's son. You must have loved Hoarsbreath once."

"I was a child, then."

She sighed. "I'm sorry I brought you down here. I wish I were up there with the miners, in the last peaceful night."

"There will be peace again," he said, but she shook her head wearily.

"I don't feel it." She expected him to smile, but his frown deepened. He touched her face suddenly with his burned hand.

"Sometimes I almost hear what you're trying to tell me. And then it fades against all my knowledge and experience. I'm glad you stayed. If I die, I'll leave you facing one maddened dragon. But still, I'm glad."

A black moon rose high over his shoulder and she jumped. Ryd rolled off the ledge, into the mists. Peka hid her face from the peering black glare. Blue lights smouldered through the mist, the moon rolled suddenly out of the sky and she could breathe again.

Streaks of dispersing gold lit the dawn-sky like the sunrises she saw one month out of the year. Peka, in a cold daze on the ledge, saw Ryd for the first time in an hour. He was facing the dragon, his silver hand outstretched. In his palm lay a crystal so cold and deathly white that Peka, blinking at it, felt its icy stare into her heart.

She shuddered. Her bones turned to ice; mist seemed to flow through her veins. She breathed bitter, frozen air as heavy as water. She reached for the wormspoor; her arm moved sluggishly, and her fingers unfolded with brittle movements. The dragon was breathing in short, harsh spurts. The silvery hoods were over its eyes. Its unfolded wing lay across the ice like a limp sail. Its jaws were open, hissing faintly, but its head was reared back, away from Ryd's hand. Its heartbeat, in the silence, was slow, slow.

Peka dragged herself up, icicle by icicle. In the clear wintry dawn, she saw the beginning and the end of the enormous ring around Hoarsbreath. The dragon's tail lifted wearily behind Ryd, then fell again, barely making a sound. Ryd stood still; his eyes, relentless, spring-blue, were his only color. As Peka watched, swaying on the edge, the world fragmented into simple things: the edges of silver on the dragon's scales, Ryd's silver fingers, his old-man's hair, the pure white of the dragon's hide. They face one another, two powerful creatures born out of the same winter, harrowing one another. The dragon rippled along its bulk; its head reared farther back, giving Peka a dizzying glimpse of its open jaws. She saw the cracked tooth, crumbled like a jewel she might have battered inadvertently with her pick, and winced. Seeing her, it hissed, a tired, angry sigh.

She stared down at it; her eyes seemed numb, incapable of sorrow. The wing on the ice was beginning to stir. Ryd's head lifted. He looked bone-pale, his face expressionless with exhaustion. But the faint, icy smile of triumph in his eyes struck her as deeply as the stare from the death-eye in his palm.

She drew in mist like the dragon, knowing that Ryd was not harrowing an old, tired ice-dragon, but one out of his memories who never seemed to yield. "You bone-brained dragon," she shouted, "how can you give up Hoarsbreath so easily? And to a Dragon-Harrower whose winter is colder and more terrible than yours." Her heart seemed trapped in the weary, sluggish pace of its heart. She knelt down, wondering if it could understand her words, or only feel them. "Think of Hoarsbreath," she pleaded, and searched for words to warm them both. "Fire. Gold. Night. Warm dreams, winter tales, silence—" Mist billowed at her and she coughed until tears froze on her cheeks. She heard Ryd call her name on a curious, inflexible note that panicked her. She uncorked the wormspoor with trembling fingers, took a great gulp, and coughed again as the blood shocked through her. "Don't you have any fire at all in you? Any winter flame?" Then a vision of gold shook her: the gold within the dragon's heart, the warm gold of wormspoor, the bitter gold of dragon's blood. Ryd said her name again, his voice clear as breaking ice. She shut her eyes against him, her hands rising through a chill, dark dream. As he called the third time, she dropped the wormspoor down the dragon's throat.

The hoods over its eyes rose; they grew wide, white-rimmed. She heard a convulsive swallow. Its head snapped down; it made a sound between a bellow and a whimper. Then its jaws opened again and it raked the air with gold flame.

Ryd, his hair and eyebrows scored suddenly with gold, dove into the snow. The dragon hissed at him again. The stream beyond him turned fiery, ran towards the sea. The great tail pounded furiously; dark cracks tore through the ice. The frozen cliffs began to sweat under the fire; pillars of ice sagged down, broke against the ground. The ledge Peka stood on crumbled at a wave of gold. She fell with it in a small avalanche of ice-rubble. The enormous white ring of dragon began to move, blurring endlessly past her eyes as the dragon gathered itself. A wing arched up toward the sky, then another. The dragon hissed at the mountain, then roared desperately, but only flame came out of its bowels, where once it had secreted winter. The chasms and walls of ice began breaking apart. Peka, struggling out of the snow, felt a lurch under her feet. A wind sucked at her her hair, pulled at her heavy coat. Then it drove down at her, thundering, and she sat in the snow. The dragon, aloft, its wingspan the span of half the island, breathed fire at the ocean, and its husk of ice began to melt.

Ryd pulled her out of the snow. The ground was breaking up under their feet. He said nothing; she thought he was scowling, though he looked strange with singed eyebrows. He pushed at her, flung her toward the sea. Fire sputtered around them. Ice slid under her; she slipped and clutched at the jagged rim of it. Brine splashed in her face. The ice whirled, as chunks of the mountain fell into the sea around them. The dragon was circling the mountain, melting huge peaks and cliffs. They struck the water hard, heaving the ice-floes farther from the island. The mountain itself began to break up, as ice tore away from it, leaving only a bare peak riddled with mine-shafts.

Peka began to cry. "Look what I've done. Look at it." Ryd only grunted. She thought she could see figures high on the top of the peak, staring down at the vanishing island. The ocean, churning, spun the ice-floe toward the mainland. The river was flowing again, a blue-white streak spiralling down from the peak. The dragon was over the mainland now, billowing fire at the harbor, and ships without crews or cargo were floating free.

"Wormspoor," Ryd muttered. A wave ten feet high caught up with them, spilled, and shoved them into the middle of the channel. Peka saw the first of the boats taking the swift, swollen current down from the top of the island. Ryd spat out seawater, and took a firmer grip of the ice. "I lost every crystal, every dragon's fire I possessed. They're at the bottom of the sea. Thanks to you. Do you realize how much work, how many years—"

"Look at the sky." It spun above her, a pale, impossible mass of nothing. "How can I live under that? Where will I ever find dark, quiet places full of gold?"

"I held that dragon. It was just about to leave quietly, without taking half of Hoarsbreath with it."

"How will we live on the island again? All its secrets are gone."

"For fourteen years I studied dragons, their lore, their flights, their fires, the patterns of their lives and their destructions. I had all the knowledge I thought possible for me to acquire. No one—"

"Look at all that dreary flatland—"

"No one," he said, his voice rising, "ever told me you could harrow a dragon by pouring wormspoor down its throat!"

"Well, no one told me, either!" She slumped beside him, too despondent for anger. She watched more boats carrying miners, young children, her mother, down to the mainland. Then the dragon caught her eye, pale against the winter sky, somehow fragile, beautifully crafted, flying into the wake of its own flame.

It touched her mourning heart with the fire she had given it. Beside her, she felt Ryd grow quiet. His face, tired and battered, held a young, forgotten wonder, as he watched the dragon blaze across the world's cap like a star, searching for its winter. He drew a soft, incredulous breath.

"What did you put into that wormspoor?"

"Everything."

He looked at her, then turned his face toward Hoarsbreath. The sight made him wince. "I don't think we left even my father's bones at peace," he said hollowly, looking for a moment less Dragon-Harrower than a harrowed miner's son.

"I know," she whispered.

"No, you don't," he sighed. "You feel. The dragon's heart. My heart. It's not a lack of knowledge or experiences that destroyed Hoarsbreath, but something else I lost sight of: you told me that. The dark necessity of wisdom."

She gazed at him, suddenly uneasy for he was seeing her. "I'm not wise. Just lucky—or unlucky."

"Wisdom is a flatlander's word for your kind of feeling. You put your heart into everything—wormspoor, dragons, gold—and they become a kind of magic."

"I do not. I don't understand what you're talking about, Ryd Yarrow. I'm a miner; I'm going to find another mine—"

"You have a gold-mine in your heart. There are other things you can do with yourself. Not harrow dragons, but become a Watcher. You love the same things they love."

"Yes. Peace and quiet and private places—"

"I could show you dragons in their beautiful, private places all over the world. You could speak their language."

"I can't even speak my own. And I hate the flatland." She gripped the ice, watching it come.

"The world is only another tiny island, ringed with a great dragon of stars and night."

She shook her head, not daring to meet his eyes. "No. I'm not listening to you anymore. Look what happened the last time I listened to your tales."

"It's always yourself you are listening to," he said. The grey ocean swirled the ice under them, casting her back to the bewildering shores of the world. She was still trying to argue when the ice moored itself against the scorched pilings of the harbor.

THE BULLY AND THE BEAST

Orson Scott Card

Orson Scott Card was born in Richland, Washington in 1951, and grew up in California, Arizona, and Utah. In addition to writing he teaches classes and workshops, directs plays and is a professor of English at Southern Virginia University. Winner of four Hugos, two Nebulas, one World Fantasy Award and eight Locus Awards, Card has written more than forty novels and over sixty-five short stories. He is best known for his science fiction novels *Ender's Game*, *Ender's Shadow* and *Speaker for the Dead* and for his American frontier fantasy series The Tales of Alvin Maker, beginning with *Seventh Son*. He also writes contemporary fantasy, biblical novels, non-fiction, poetry, plays and scripts. His short fiction has appeared in a number of collections, among them career retrospectives *Maps in a Mirror* and *Keeper of Dreams*. In the early '80s he edited two dragon anthologies—*Dragons of Light* and *Dragons of Darkness*. His most recent novel is *Hidden Empire*. Forthcoming is young adult novel *Bully and the Beast*, based on the short story below.

The page entered the Count's chamber at a dead run. He had long ago given up sauntering—when the Count called, he expected a page to appear immediately, and any delay at all made the Count irritable and likely to assign a page to stable duty.

"My lord," said the page.

"My lord indeed," said the Count. "What kept you?" The Count stood at the window, his back to the boy. In his arms he held a velvet gown, incredibly embroidered with gold and silver thread. "I think I need to call a council," said the Count. "On the other hand, I haven't the slightest desire to submit myself to a gaggle of jabbering knights. They'll be quite angry. What do you think?"

No one had ever asked the page for advice before, and he wasn't quite sure what was expected of him. "Why should they be angry, my lord?"

"Do you see this gown?" the Count asked, turning around and holding it up.

"Yes, my lord."

"What do you think of it?"

"Depends, doesn't it, my lord, on who wears it."

"It cost eleven pounds of silver."

The page smiled sickly. Eleven pounds of silver would keep the average knight in arms, food, women, clothing, and shelter for a year with six pounds left over for spending money.

"There are more," said the Count. "Many more."

"But who are they for? Are you going to marry?"

"None of your business!" roared the Count. "If there's anything I hate, it's a meddler!" The Count turned again to the window and looked out. He was shaded by a huge oak tree that grew forty feet the castle walls. "What's today?" asked the Count.

"Thursday, my lord."

"The day, the day!"

"Eleventh past Easter Feast."

"The tribute's due today," said the Count. "Due on Easter, in fact, but today the Duke will be certain I'm not paying."

"Not paying the tribute, my lord?"

"How? Turn me upside down and shake me, but I haven't a farthing. The tribute money's gone. The money for new arms is gone. The travel money is gone. The money for new horses is gone. Haven't got any money at all. But gad, boy, what a wardrobe." The Count sat on the sill of the window. "The Duke will be here very quickly, I'm afraid. And he has the latest in debt collection equipment."

"What's that?"

"An army." The Count sighed. "Call a council, boy. My knights may jabber and scream, but they'll fight. I know they will."

The page wasn't sure. "They'll be very angry, my lord. Are you sure they'll fight?"

"Oh, yes," said the Count. "If they don't, the Duke will kill them."

"Why?"

"For not honoring their oath to me. Do go now, boy, and call a council."

The page nodded. Kind of felt sorry for the old boy. Not much of a Count, as things went, but he could have been worse, and it was pretty plain the castle would be sacked and the Count imprisoned and the women raped and the page sent off home to his parents. "A council!" he cried as he left the Count's chamber. "A council!"

In the cold cavern of the pantry under the kitchen, Bork pulled a huge keg of ale from its resting place and lifted it, not easily, but without much strain, and rested it on his shoulders. Head bowed, he walked slowly up the stairs. Before Bork worked in the kitchen, it used to take two men most of an afternoon to move the huge kegs. But Bork was a giant, or what passed for a giant in those days. The Count himself was of average height, barely past five feet. Bork was nearly seven feet tall, with muscles like an ox. People stepped aside for him.

"Put it there," said the cook, hardly looking up. "And don't drop it."

Bork didn't drop the keg. Nor did he resent the cook's expecting him to be clumsy. He had been told he was clumsy all his life, ever since it became plain at the age of three that he was going to be immense. Everyone knew that big people were clumsy. And it was true enough. Bork was so strong he kept doing things he never meant to do, accidentally. Like the time the swordmaster, admiring his strength, had invited him to learn to use the heavy battleswords. Bork hefted them easily enough, of course, though at the time he was only twelve and hadn't reached his full strength.

"Hit me," the swordmaster said.

"But the blade's sharp," Bork told him.

"Don't worry. You won't come near me." The swordmaster had taught a hundred knights to fight. None of them had come near him. And, in fact, when Bork swung the heavy sword the swordmaster had his shield up in plenty of time. He just hadn't counted on the terrible force of the blow. The shield was battered aside easily, and the blow threw the sword upward, so it cut off the swordmaster's left arm just below the shoulder, and only narrowly missed slicing deeply into his chest.

Clumsy, that was all Bork was. But it was the end of any hope of his becoming a knight. When the swordmaster finally recovered, he consigned Bork to the kitchen and the blacksmith's shop, where they needed someone with enough strength to skewer a cow end to end and carry it to the fire, where it was convenient to have a man who, with a double-sized ax, could chop down a large tree in half an hour, cut it into logs, and carry a month's supply of firewood into the castle in an afternoon.

A page came into the kitchen. "There's a council, cook. The Count wants ale, and plenty of it."

The cook swore profusely and threw a carrot at the page. "Always changing the schedule! Always making me do extra work." As soon as the page had escaped, the cook turned on Bork. "All right, carry the ale out there, and be quick about it. Try not to drop it."

"I won't," Bork said.

"He won't," the cook muttered. "Clever as an ox, he is."

Bork manhandled the cask into the great hall. It was cold, though outside the sun was shining. Little light and little warmth reached the inside of the castle. And since it was spring, the huge logpile in the pit in the middle of the room lay cold and damp.

The knights were beginning to wander into the great hall and sit on the benches that lined the long, pock-marked slab of a table. They knew enough to carry their mugs—councils were always well-oiled with ale. Bork had spent years as a child watching the knights practice the arts of war, but the knights seemed more natural carrying their cups than holding their swords at the ready. They were more dedicated to their drinking than to war.

"Ho, Bork the Bully," one of the knights greeted him. Bork managed a half-smile. He had learned long since not to take offense.

"How's Sam the stableman?" asked another, tauntingly.

Bork blushed and turned away, heading for the door to the kitchen.

The knights were laughing at their cleverness. "Twice the body, half the brain," one of them said to the others. "Probably hung like a horse," another speculated, then quipped, "Which probably accounts for those mysterious deaths among the sheep this winter." A roar of laughter, and cups beating on the table. Bork stood in the kitchen trembling. He could not escape the sound—the stones carried it echoing to him wherever he went.

The cook turned and looked at him. "Don't be angry, boy," he said. "It's all in fun."

Bork nodded and smiled at the cook. That's what it was. All in fun. And besides, Bork deserved it, he knew. It was only fair that he be treated cruelly. For he had earned the title Bork the Bully, hadn't he? When he was three, and already massive as a ram, his only friend, a beautiful young village boy named Winkle, had hit upon the idea of becoming a knight. Winkle had dressed himself in odds and ends of leather and tin, and made a makeshift lance from a hog prod.

"You're my destrier," Winkle cried as he mounted Bork and rode him for hours. Bork thought it was a fine thing to be a knight's horse. It became the height of his ambition, and he wondered how one got started in the trade. But one day Sam, the stableman's son, had taunted Winkle for his make-believe armor, and it had turned into a fist fight, and Sam had thoroughly bloodied Winkle's nose. Winkle screamed as if he were dying, and Bork sprang to his friend's defense, walloping Sam, who was three years older, along the side of his head.

Ever since then Sam spoke with a thickness in his voice, and often lost his balance; his jaw, broken in several places, never healed properly, and he had problems with his ear.

It horrified Bork to have caused so much pain, but Winkle assured him that Sam deserved it. "After all, Bork, he was twice my size, and he was picking on me. He's a bully. He had it coming."

For several years Winkle and Bork were the terror of the village. Winkle would constantly get into fights, and soon the village children learned not to resist him. If Winkle lost a fight, he would scream for Bork, and though Bork was never again so harsh as he was with Sam, his blows still hurt terribly. Winkle loved it. Then one day he tired of being a knight, dismissed his destrier, and became fast friends with the other children. It was only then that Bork began to hear himself called Bork the Bully; it was Winkle who convinced the other children that the only villain in the fighting had been Bork. "After all," Bork overheard Winkle say one day, "he's twice as strong as anyone else. Isn't fair for him to fight. It's a cowardly thing for him to do, and we mustn't have anything to do with him. Bullies must be punished."

Bork knew Winkle was right, and ever after that he bore the burden of shame. He remembered the frightened looks in the other children's eyes when he approached them, the way they pleaded for mercy. But Winkle was always screaming and writhing in agony, and Bork always hit the child despite his terror, and for that bullying Bork was still paying. He paid in the ridicule he accepted from the knights; he paid in the solitude of all his days and nights; he paid by working as hard as he could, using his strength to serve instead of hurt.

But just because he knew he deserved the punishment did not mean he enjoyed it. There were tears in his eyes as he went about his work in the kitchen. He tried to hide them from the cook, but to no avail. "Oh, no, you're not going to cry, are you?" the cook said. "You'll only make your nose run and then you'll get snot in the soup. Get out of the kitchen for a while!"

Which is why Bork was standing in the doorway of the great hall watching the council that would completely change his life.

"Well, where's the tribute money gone to?" demanded one of the knights. "The harvest was large enough last year!"

It was an ugly thing, to see the knights so angry. But the Count knew they had a right to be upset—it was they who would have to fight the Duke's men, and they had a right to know why.

"My friends," the Count said. "My friends, some things are more important than money. I invested the money in something more important than tribute, more important than peace, more important than long life. I invested the money in beauty. Not to create beauty, but to perfect it." The knights were listening now. For all their violent preoccupations, they all had a soft spot in their hearts for true beauty. It was one of the requirements for knighthood. "I have been entrusted with a jewel, more perfect than any diamond. It was my duty to place that jewel in the best setting money could buy. I can't explain. I can only show you." He rang a small bell, and behind him one of the better-known secret doors in the castle opened, and a wizened old woman emerged. The Count whispered in her ear, and the woman scurried back into the secret passage.

"Who's she?" asked one of the knights.

"She is the woman who nursed my children after my wife died. My wife died in childbirth, you remember. But what you don't know is that the child lived. My two sons you know well. But I have a third child, my last child, whom you know not at all, and this one is not a son."

The Count was not surprised that several of the knights seemed to puzzle over this riddle. Too many jousts, too much practice in full armor in the heat of the afternoon.

"My child is a daughter."

"Ah," said the knights.

"At first, I kept her hidden away because I could not bear to see her—after all, my most beloved wife had died in bearing her. But after a few years I overcame my grief, and went to see the child in the room where she was hidden, and lo! She was the most beautiful child I had ever seen. I named her Brunhilda, and from that moment on I loved her. I was the most devoted father you could imagine. But I did not let her leave the secret room. Why, you may ask?"

"Yes, why!" demanded several of the knights.

"Because she was so beautiful I was afraid she would be stolen from me. I was terrified that I would lose her. Yet I saw her every day, and talked to her, and the older she got, the more beautiful she became, and for the last several years I could no longer bear to see her in her mother's cast-off clothing. Her beauty is such that only the finest cloths and gowns and jewels of Flanders, of Venice, of Florence would do for her. You'll see! The money was not ill spent."

And the door opened again, and the old woman emerged, leading forth Brunhilda.

In the doorway, Bork gasped. But no one heard him, for all the knights gasped, too.

She was the most perfect woman in the world. Her hair was a dark red, flowing behind her like an auburn stream as she walked. Her face was white from being indoors all of her life, and when she smiled it was like the sun breaking out on a stormy day. And none of the knights dared look at her body for very long, because the longer they looked the more they wanted to touch her, and the Count said, "I warn you. Any man who lays a hand on her will have to answer to me. She is a virgin, and when she marries she shall be a virgin, and a king will pay half his kingdom to have her, and still I'll feel cheated to have to give her up."

"Good morning, my lords," she said, smiling. Her voice was like the song of leaves dancing in the summer wind, and the knights fell to their knees before her.

None of them was more moved by her beauty than Bork, however. When she entered the room he forgot himself; there was no room in his mind for anything but the great beauty he had seen for the first time in his life. Bork knew nothing of courtesy. He only knew that, for the first time in his life, he had seen something so perfect that he could not rest until it was his. Not his to own, but his to be owned by. He longed to serve her in the most degrading ways he could think of, if only she would smile upon him; longed to die for her, if only the last moment of his life were filled with her voice saying, "You may love me."

If he had been a knight, he might have thought of a poetic way to say such things. But he was not a knight, and so his words came out of his heart before his mind could find a way to make them clever. He strode blindly from the kitchen door, his huge body casting a shadow that seemed to the knights like the shadow of death passing over them. They watched with uneasiness that soon turned to outrage as he came to the girl, reached out, and took her small white hands in his.

"I love you," Bork said to her, and tears came unbidden to his eyes. "Let me marry you."

At that moment several of the knights found their courage. They seized Bork roughly by the arms, meaning to pull him away and punish him for his effrontery. But Bork effortlessly tossed them away. They fell to the ground yards from him. He never saw them fall; his gaze never left the lady's face.

She looked wonderingly into his eyes. Not because she thought him attractive, because he was ugly and she knew it. Not because of the words he had said, because she had been taught that many men would say those words, and she was to pay no attention to them. What startled her, what amazed her, was the deep truth in Bork's face. That was something she had never seen, and though she did not recognize it for what it was, it fascinated her.

The Count was furious. Seeing the clumsy giant holding his daughter's small white hands in his was outrageous. He would not endure it. But the giant had such great strength that to tear him away would mean a full-scale battle, and in such a battle Brunhilda might be injured. No, the giant had to be handled delicately, for the moment.

"My dear fellow," said the Count, affecting a joviality he did not feel. "You've only just met."

Bork ignored him. "I will never let you come to harm," he said to the girl.

"What's his name?" the Count whispered to a knight. "I can't remember his name."

"Bork," the knight answered.

"My dear Bork," said the Count. "All due respect and everything, but my daughter has noble blood, and you're not even a knight."

"Then I'll become one," Bork said.

"It's not that easy, Bork, old fellow. You must do something exceptionally brave, and then I can knight you and we can talk about this other matter. But in the meantime, it isn't proper for you to be holding my daughter's hands. Why don't you go back to the kitchen like a good fellow?"

Bork gave no sign that he heard. He only continued looking into the lady's eyes. And finally it was she who was able to end the dilemma.

"Bork," she said, "I will count on you. But in the meantime, my father will be angry with you if you don't return to the kitchen."

Of course, Bork thought. Of course, she is truly concerned for me, doesn't want me to come to harm on her account. "For your sake," he said, the madness of love still on him. Then he turned and left the room.

The Count sat down, sighing audibly. "Should have got rid of him years ago. Gentle as a lamb, and then all of a sudden goes crazy. Get rid of him—somebody take care of that tonight, would you? Best to do it in his sleep. Don't want any casualties when we're likely to have a battle at any moment."

The reminder of the battle was enough to sober even those who were on their fifth mug of ale. The wizened old woman led Brunhilda away again. "But not to the secret room, now. To the chamber next to mine. And post a double guard outside the door, and keep the key yourself," said the Count.

When she was gone, the Count looked around at the knights. "The treasury has been emptied in a vain attempt to find clothing to do her justice. I had no other choice."

And there was not a knight who would say the money had been badly spent.

The Duke came late that afternoon, much sooner than he was expected. He demanded the tribute. The Count refused, of course. There was the usual challenge to come out of the castle and fight, but the Count, outnumbered ten to one, merely replied, rather saucily, that the Duke should come in and get him. The messenger who delivered the sarcastic message came back with his tongue in a bag around his neck. The battle was thus begun grimly; and grimly it continued.

The guard watching on the south side of the castle was slacking. He paid for it. The Duke's archers managed to creep up to the huge oak tree and climb it without any alarm being given, and the first notice any of them had was when the guard fell from the battlements with an arrow in his throat.

The archers—there must have been a dozen of them—kept up a deadly rain of arrows. They wasted no shots. The squires dropped dead in alarming numbers until the Count gave orders for them to come inside. And when the human targets were all under cover, the archers set to work on the cattle and sheep milling in the open pens. There was no way to protect the animals. By sunset, all of them were dead.

"Dammit," said the cook. "How can I cook all this before it spoils?"

"Find a way," said the Count. "That's our food supply. I refuse to let them starve us out."

So all night Bork worked, carrying the cattle and sheep inside, one by one. At first the villagers who had taken refuge in the castle tried to help him, but he could carry three animals inside the kitchen in the time it took them to drag one, and they soon gave it up.

The Count saw who was saving the meat. "Don't get rid of him tonight," he told the knights. "We'll punish him for his effrontery in the morning."

Bork only rested twice in the night, taking naps for an hour before the cook woke him again. And when dawn came, and the arrows began coming again, all the cattle were inside, and all but twenty sheep.

"That's all we can save," the cook told the Count.

"Save them all."

"But if Bork tries to go out there, he'll be killed!"

The Count looked the cook in the eyes. "Bring in the sheep or have him die trying."

The cook was not aware of the fact that Bork was under sentence of death. So he did his best to save Bork. A kettle lined with cloth and strapped onto the giant's head; a huge kettle lid for a shield. "It's the best we can do," the cook said.

"But I can't carry sheep if I'm holding a shield," Bork said.

"What can I do? The Count commanded it. It's worth your life to refuse."

Bork stood and thought for a few moments, trying to find a way out of his dilemma. He saw only one possibility. "If I can't stop them from hitting me, I'll have to stop them from shooting at all."

"How!" the cook demanded, and then followed Bork to the blacksmith's shop, where Bork found his huge ax leaning against the wall.

"Now's not the time to cut firewood," said the blacksmith.

"Yes it is," Bork answered.

Carrying the ax and holding the kettle lid between his body and the archers,

Bork made his way across the courtyard. The arrows pinged harmlessly off the metal. Bork got to the drawbridge. "Open up!" he shouted, and the drawbridge fell away and dropped across the moat. Bork walked across, then made his way along the moat toward the oak tree.

In the distance the Duke, standing in front of his dazzling white tent with his emblem of yellow on it, saw Bork emerge from the castle. "Is that a man or a bear?" he asked. No one was sure.

The archers shot at Bork steadily, but the closer he got to the tree, the worse their angle of fire and the larger the shadow of safety the kettle lid cast over his body. Finally, holding the lid high over his head, Bork began hacking one-handed at the trunk. Chips of wood flew with each blow; with his right hand alone he could cut deeper and faster than a normal man with both hands free.

But he was concentrating on cutting wood, and his left arm grew tired holding his makeshift shield, and an archer was able to get off a shot that slipped past the shield and plunged into his left arm, in the thick muscle at the back.

He nearly dropped the shield. Instead, he had the presence of mind to let go of the ax and drop to his knees, quickly balancing the kettle lid between the trunk, his head, and the top of the ax handle. Gently he pulled at the arrow shaft. It would not come backward. So he broke the arrow and pushed the stub the rest of the way through his arm until it was out the other side. It was excruciatingly painful, but he knew he could not quit now. He took hold of the shield with his left arm again, and despite the pain held it high as he began to cut again, girdling the tree with a deep white gouge. The blood dripped steadily down his arm, but he ignored it, and soon enough the bleeding stopped and slowed.

On the castle battlements, the Count's men began to realize that there was a hope of Bork's succeeding. To protect him, they began to shoot their arrows into the tree. The archers were well hidden, but the rain of arrows, however badly aimed, began to have its effect. A few of them dropped to the ground, where the castle archers could easily finish them off; the others were forced to concentrate on finding cover.

The tree trembled more and more with each blow, until finally Bork stepped back and the tree creaked and swayed. He had learned from his lumbering work in the forest how to make the tree fall where he wanted it; the oak fell parallel to the castle walls, so it neither bridged the moat nor let the Duke's archers scramble from the tree too far from the castle. So when the archers tried to flee to the safety of the Duke's lines, the castle bowmen were able to kill them all.

One of them, however, despaired of escape. Instead, though he already had an arrow in him, he drew a knife and charged at Bork, in a mad attempt to avenge his own death on the man who had caused it. Bork had no choice. He swung his ax through the air and discovered that men are nowhere near as sturdy as a tree.

In the distance, the Duke watched with horror as the giant cut a man in half with a single blow. "What have they got!" he said. "What is this monster?"

Covered with the blood that had spurted from the dying man, Bork walked back toward the drawbridge, which opened again as he approached. But he did not get to enter. Instead the Count and fifty mounted knights came from the gate on horseback, their armor shining in the sunlight.

"I've decided to fight them in the open," the Count said. "And you, Bork, must fight with us. If you live through this, I'll make you a knight!"

Bork knelt. "Thank you, my Lord Count," he said.

The Count glanced around in embarrassment. "Well, then. Let's get to it. Charge!" he bellowed.

Bork did not realize that the knights were not even formed in a line yet. He simply followed that command and charged, alone, toward the Duke's lines. The Count watched him go, and smiled.

"My Lord Count," said the nearest knight. "Aren't we going to attack with him?"

"Let the Duke take care of him," the Count said.

"But he cut down the oak and saved the castle, my lord."

"Yes," said the Count. "An exceptionally brave act. Do you want him to try to claim my daughter's hand?"

"But my lord," said the knight, "if he fights beside us, we might have a chance of winning. But if he's gone, the Duke will destroy us."

"Some things," said the Count, with finality, "are more important than victory. Would you want to go on living in a world where perfection like Brunhilda's was possessed by such a man as that?"

The knights were silent, then, as they watched Bork approach the Duke's army, alone.

Bork did not realize he was alone until he stood a few feet away from the Duke's lines. He had felt strange as he walked across the fields, believing he was marching into battle with the knights he had long admired in their bright armor and deft instruments of war. Now the exhilaration was gone. Where were the others? Bork was afraid.

He could not understand why the Duke's men had not shot any arrows at him. Actually, it was a misunderstanding. If the Duke had known that Bork was a commoner and not a knight at all, Bork would have had a hundred arrows bristling from his corpse. As it was, however, one of the Duke's men called out, "You, sir! Do you challenge us in single combat?"

Of course. That was it—the Count did not intend Bork to face an army, he intended him to face a single warrior. The whole outcome of the battle would depend on him alone! It was a tremendous honor, and Bork wondered if he could carry it off.

"Yes! Single combat!" he answered. "Your strongest, bravest man!"

"But you're a giant!" cried the Duke's man.

"But I'm wearing no armor." And to prove his sincerity, Bork took off his helmet, which was uncomfortable anyway, and stepped forward. The Duke's knights backed away, making an opening for him, with men in armor watching him pass from both sides. Bork walked steadily on, until he came to a cleared circle where he faced the Duke himself.

"Are you the champion?" asked Bork.

"I'm the Duke," he answered. "But I don't see any of my knights stepping forward to fight you."

"Do you refuse the challenge, then?" Bork asked, trying to sound as brave and scornful as he imagined a true knight would sound.

The Duke looked around at his men, who, if the armor had allowed, would have been shuffling uncomfortably in the morning sunlight. As it was, none of them looked at him.

"No," said the Duke. "I accept your challenge myself." The thought of fighting the giant terrified him. But he was a knight, and known to be a brave man; he had become Duke in the prime of his youth, and if he backed down before a giant now, his duchy would be taken from him in only a few years; his honor would be lost long before. So he drew his sword and advanced upon the giant.

Bork saw the determination in the Duke's eyes, and marvelled at a man who would go himself into a most dangerous battle instead of sending his men. Briefly Bork wondered why the Count had not shown such courage; he determined at that moment that if he could help it the Duke would not die. The blood of the archer was more than he had ever wanted to shed. Nobility was in every movement of the Duke, and Bork wondered at the ill chance that had made them enemies.

The Duke lunged at Bork with his sword flashing. Bork hit him with the flat of the ax, knocking him to the ground. The Duke cried out in pain. His armor was dented deeply; there had to be ribs broken under the dent.

"Why don't you surrender?" asked Bork.

"Kill me now!"

"If you surrender, I won't kill you at all."

The Duke was surprised. There was a murmur from his men.

"I have your word?"

"Of course. I swear it."

It was too startling an idea.

"What do you plan to do, hold me for ransom?"

Bork thought about it. "I don't think so."

"Well, what then? Why not kill me and have done with it?" The pain in his chest now dominated the Duke's voice, but he did not spit blood, and so he began to have some hope.

"All the Count wants you to do is go away and stop collecting tribute. If you promise to do that, I'll promise that not one of you will be harmed."

The Duke and his men considered in silence. It was too good to believe. So good it was almost dishonorable even to consider it. Still—there was Bork, who had broken the Duke's body with one blow, right through the armor. If he chose to let them walk away from the battle, why argue?

"I give my word that I'll cease collecting tribute from the Count, and my men and I will go in peace."

"Well, then, that's good news," Bork said. "I've got to tell the Count." And Bork turned away and walked into the fields, heading for where the Count's tiny army waited.

"I can't believe it," said the Duke. "A knight like that, and he turns out to be generous. The Count could have his way with the King, with a knight like that."

They stripped the armor off him, carefully, and began wrapping his chest with bandages.

"If he were mine," the Duke said, "I'd use him to conquer the whole land."

The Count watched, incredulous, as Bork crossed the field.

"He's still alive," he said, and he began to wonder what Bork would have to say about the fact that none of the knights had joined his gallant charge.

"My Lord Count!" cried Bork, when he was within range. He would have waved, but both his arms were exhausted now. "They surrender!"

"What?" the Count asked the knights near him. "Did he say they surrender?"

"Apparently," a knight answered. "Apparently he won."

"Damn!" cried the Count. "I won't have it!"

The knights were puzzled. "If anybody's going to defeat the Duke, *I* am! Not a damnable commoner! Not a giant with the brains of a cockroach! Charge!"

"What?" several of the knights asked.

"I said charge!" And the Count moved forward, his warhorse plodding carefully through the field, building up momentum.

Bork saw the knights start forward. He had watched enough mock battles to recognize a charge. He could only assume that the Count hadn't heard him. But the charge had to be stopped—he had given his word, hadn't he? So he planted himself in the path of the Count's horse.

"Out of the way, you damned fool!" cried the Count. But Bork stood his ground. The Count was determined not to be thwarted. He prepared to ride Bork down.

"You can't charge!" Bork yelled. "They surrendered!"

The Count gritted his teeth and urged his horse forward, his lance prepared to cast Bork out of the way.

A moment later the Count found himself in midair, hanging to the lance for his life. Bork held it over his head, and the knights laboriously halted their charge and wheeled to see what was going on with Bork and the Count.

"My Lord Count," Bork said respectfully. "I guess you didn't hear me. They surrendered. I promised them they could go in peace if they stopped collecting tribute."

From his precarious hold on the lance, fifteen feet off the ground, the Count said, "I didn't hear you."

"I didn't think so. But you *will* let them go, won't you?"

"Of course. Could you give a thought to letting me down, old boy?"

And so Bork let the Count down, and there was a peace treaty between the

Duke and the Count, and the Duke's men rode away in peace, talking about the generosity of the giant knight.

"But he isn't a knight," said a servant to the Duke.

"What? Not a knight?"

"No. Just a villager. One of the peasants told me, when I was stealing his chickens."

"Not a knight," said the Duke, and for a moment his face began to turn a shade of red that made his knights want to ride a few feet further from him—they knew his rage too well already.

"We were tricked, then," said a knight, trying to fend off his lord's anger by anticipating it.

The Duke said nothing for a moment. Then he smiled. "Well, if he's not a knight, he should be. He has the strength. He has the courtesy. Hasn't he?"

The knights agreed that he had.

"He's the moral equivalent of a knight," said the Duke. Pride assuaged, for the moment, he led his men back to his castle. Underneath, however, even deeper than the pain in his ribs, was the image of the Count perched on the end of a lance held high in the air by the giant, Bork, and he pondered what it might have meant, and what, more to the point, it might mean in the future.

Things were getting out of hand, the Count decided. First of all, the victory celebration had not been his idea, and yet here they were, riotously drunken in the great hall, and even villagers were making free with the ale, laughing and cheering among the knights. That was bad enough, but worse was the fact that the knights were making no pretense about it—the party was in honor of Bork.

The Count drummed his fingers on the table. No one paid any attention. They were too busy—Sir Alwishard trying to keep two village wenches occupied near the fire, Sir Silwiss pissing in the wine and laughing so loud that the Count could hardly hear Sir Braig and Sir Umlaut as they sang and danced along the table, kicking plates off with their toes in time with the music. It was the best party the Count had ever seen. And it wasn't for him, it was for that damnable giant who had made an ass of him in front of all his men and all the Duke's men and, worst of all, the Duke. He heard a strange growling sound, like a savage wolf getting ready to spring. In a lull in the bedlam he suddenly realized that the sound was coming from his own throat.

Get control of yourself, he thought. The real gains, the solid gains were not Bork's—they were mine. The Duke is gone, and instead of paying him tribute from now on, he'll be paying me. Word would get around, too, that the Count had won a battle with the Duke. After all, that was the basis of power—who could beat whom in battle. A duke was just a man who could beat a count, a count someone who could beat a baron, a baron someone who could beat a knight.

But what was a person who could beat a duke?

"You should be king," said a tall, slender young man standing near the throne. The Count looked at him, making a vague motion with his hidden hand. How had the boy read his thoughts?

"I'll pretend I didn't hear that."

"You heard it," said the young man.

"It's treason."

"Only if the king beats you in battle. If *you* win, it's treason *not* to say so."

The Count looked the boy over. Dark hair that looked a bit too carefully combed for a villager. A straight nose, a pleasant smile, a winning grace when he walked. But something about his eyes gave the lie to the smile. The boy was vicious somehow. The boy was dangerous.

"I like you," said the Count.

"I'm glad." He did not sound glad. He sounded bored.

"If I'm smart, I'll have you strangled immediately."

The boy only smiled more.

"Who are you?"

"My name is Winkle. And I'm Bork's best friend."

Bork. There he was again, that giant sticking his immense shadow into everything tonight. "Didn't know Bork the Bully had any friends."

"He has one. Me. Ask him."

"I wonder if a friend of Bork's is really a friend of mine," the Count said.

"I said I was his best friend. I didn't say I was a good friend." And Winkle smiled.

A thoroughgoing bastard, the Count decided, but he waved to Bork and beckoned for him to come. In a moment the giant knelt before the Count, who was irritated to discover that when Bork knelt and the Count sat, Bork still looked down on him.

"This man," said the Count, "claims to be your friend."

Bork looked up and recognized Winkle, who was beaming down at him, his eyes filled with love, mostly. A hungry kind of love, but Bork wasn't discriminating. He had the admiration and grudging respect of the knights, but he hardly knew them. This was his childhood friend, and at the thought that Winkle claimed to be his friend Bork immediately forgave all past slights and smiled back. "Winkle," he said. "Of course we're friends. He's my *best* friend."

The Count made the mistake of looking in Bork's eyes and seeing the complete sincerity of his love for Winkle. It embarrassed him, for he knew Winkle all too well already, from just the moments of conversation they had had. Winkle was nobody's friend. But Bork was obviously blind to that. For a moment the Count almost pitied the giant, had a glimpse of what his life must be like, if the predatory young villager was his best friend.

"Your majesty," said Winkle.

"Don't call me that."

"I only anticipate what the world will know in a matter of months."

Winkle sounded so confident, so sure of it. A chill went up the Count's spine. He shook it off. "I won one battle, Winkle. I still have a huge budget deficit and a pretty small army of fairly lousy knights."

"Think of your daughter, even if *you* aren't ambitious. Despite her beauty she'll be lucky to marry a duke. But if she were the daughter of a king, she could marry anyone in all the world. And her own lovely self would be a dowry—no prince would think to ask for more."

The Count thought of his daughter, the beautiful Brunhilda, and smiled.

Bork also smiled, for he was also thinking of the same thing.

"Your majesty," Winkle urged, "with Bork as your right-hand man and me as your counselor, there's nothing to stop you from being king within a year or two. Who would be willing to stand against an army with the three of us marching at the head?"

"Why three?" asked the Count.

"You mean, why me. I thought you would already understand that—but then, that's what you need me for. You see, your majesty, you're a good man, a godly man, a paragon of virtue. You would never think of seeking power and conniving against your enemies and spying and doing repulsive things to people you don't like. But kings *have* to do those things or they quickly cease to be kings."

Vaguely the Count remembered behaving in just that way many times, but Winkle's words were seductive—they *should* be true.

"Your majesty, where you are pure, I am polluted. Where you are fresh, I am rotten. I'd sell my mother into slavery if I had a mother and I'd cheat the devil at poker and win hell from him before he caught on. And I'd stab any of your enemies in the back if I got the chance."

"But what if my enemies aren't your enemies?" the Count asked.

"Your enemies are *always* my enemies. I'll be loyal to you through thick and thin."

"How can I trust you, if you're so rotten?"

"Because you're going to pay me a lot of money." Winkle bowed deeply.

"Done," said the Count.

"Excellent," said Winkle, and they shook hands. The Count noticed that Winkle's hands were smooth—he had neither the hard horny palms of a village workingman nor the slick calluses of a man trained to warfare.

"How have you made a living, up to now?" the Count asked.

"I steal," Winkle said, with a smile that said I'm joking and a glint in his eye that said I'm not.

"What about me?" asked Bork.

"Oh, you're in it, too," said Winkle. "You're the king's strong right arm."

"I've never met the king," said Bork.

"Yes you have," Winkle retorted. "That is the king."

"No he's not," said the giant. "He's only a count."

The words stabbed the Count deeply. *Only* a count. Well, that would end. "Today I'm only a count," he said patiently. "Who knows what tomorrow will bring? But Bork—I shall knight you. As a knight you must swear absolute loyalty to me and do whatever I say. Will you do that?"

"Of course I will," said Bork. "Thank you, my Lord Count." Bork arose and called to his new friends throughout the hall in a voice that could not be ignored. "My Lord Count has decided I will be made a knight!" There were cheers and applause and stamping of feet. "And the best thing is," Bork said, "that now I can marry the Lady Brunhilda."

There was no applause. Just a murmur of alarm. Of course. If he became a knight, he was eligible for Brunhilda's hand. It was unthinkable—but the Count himself had said so.

The Count was having second thoughts, of course, but he knew no way to back out of it, not without looking like a word-breaker. He made a false start at speaking, but couldn't finish. Bork waited expectantly. Clearly he believed the Count would confirm what Bork had said.

It was Winkle, however, who took the situation in hand. "Oh, Bork," he said sadly—but loudly, so that everyone could hear. "Don't you understand? His majesty is making you a knight out of gratitude. But unless you're a king or the son of a king, you have to do something exceptionally brave to earn Brunhilda's hand."

"But, wasn't I brave today?" Bork asked. After all, the arrow wound in his arm still hurt, and only the ale kept him from aching unmercifully all over from the exertion of the night and the day just past.

"You were brave. But since you're twice the size and ten times the strength of an ordinary man, it's hardly fair for you to win Brunhilda's hand with ordinary bravery. No, Bork—it's just the way things work. It's just the way things are done. Before you're worthy of Brunhilda, you have to do something ten times as brave as what you did today."

Bork couldn't think of something ten times as brave. Hadn't he gone almost unprotected to chop down the oak tree? Hadn't he attacked a whole army all by himself, and won the surrender of the enemy? What could be ten times as brave?

"Don't despair," the Count said. "Surely in all battles ahead of us there'll be *something* ten times as brave. And in the meantime, you're a knight, my friend, a great knight, and you shall dine at my table every night! And when we march into battle, there you'll be, right beside me—"

"A few steps ahead," Winkle whispered discreetly.

"A few steps ahead of me, to defend the honor of my country—"

"Don't be shy," whispered Winkle.

"No, not my country. My kingdom. For from today, you men no longer serve a count! You serve a king!"

It was a shocking declaration, and might have caused sober reflection if there had been a sober man in the room. But through the haze of alcohol and torch-light and fatigue, the knights looked at the Count and he did indeed seem kingly. And they thought of the battles ahead and were not afraid, for they had won a glorious victory today and not one of them had shed a drop of blood. Except, of course, Bork. But in some corner of their collected opinions was a viewpoint they would not have admitted to holding, if anyone brought the subject out in the open. The opinion so well hidden from themselves and each other was simple: Bork is not like me. Bork is not one of us. Therefore, Bork is expendable.

The blood that still stained his sleeve was cheap. Plenty more where that came from.

And so they plied him with more ale until he fell asleep, snoring hugely on the table, forgetting that he had been cheated out of the woman he loved; it was easy to forget, for the moment, because he was a knight, and a hero, and at last he had friends.

It took two years for the Count to become King. He began close to home, with other counts, but soon progressed to the great dukes and earls of the kingdom. Wherever he went, the pattern was the same. The Count and his fifty knights would ride their horses, only lightly armored so they could travel with reasonable speed. Bork would walk, but his long legs easily kept up with the rest of them. They would arrive at their victim's castle, and three squires would hand Bork his new steel-handled ax. Bork, covered with impenetrable armor, would wade the moat, if there was one, or simply walk up to the gates, swing the ax, and begin chopping through the wood. When the gates collapsed, Bork would take a huge steel rod and use it as a crow, prying at the portcullis, bending the heavy iron like pretzels until there was a gap wide enough for a mounted knight to ride through.

Then he would go back to the Count and Winkle.

Throughout this operation, not a word would have been said; the only activity from the Count's other men would be enough archery that no one would be able to pour boiling oil or hot tar on Bork while he was working. It was a precaution, and nothing more—even if they set the oil on the fire the moment the Count's little army approached, it would scarcely be hot enough to make water steam by the time Bork was through.

"Do you surrender to his Majesty the King?" Winkle would cry.

And the defenders of the castle, their gate hopelessly breached and terrified of the giant who had so easily made a joke of their defences, would usually surrender. Occasionally there was some token resistance—when that happened, at Winkle's insistence, the town was brutally sacked and the noble's family was held in prison until a huge ransom was paid.

At the end of two years, the Count and Bork and Winkle and their army marched on Winchester. The King—the real king—fled before them and took up his exile in Anjou, where it was warmer anyway. The Count had himself crowned king, accepted the fealty of every noble in the country, and introduced his daughter Brunhilda all around. Then, finding Winchester not to his liking, he returned to his castle and ruled from there. Suitors for his daughter's hand made a constant traffic on the roads leading into the country; would-be courtiers and nobles vying for positions filled the new hostelries that sprang up on the other side of the village. All left much poorer than they had arrived. And while much of that money found its way into the King's coffers, much more of it went to Winkle, who believed that skimming off the cream meant leaving at least a quarter of it for the King.

And now that the wars were done, Bork hung up his armor and went back to normal life. Not quite normal life, actually. He slept in a good room in the castle, better than most of the knights. Some of the knights had even come to enjoy his company, and sought him out for ale in the evenings or hunting in the daytime—Bork could always be counted on to carry home two deer himself, and was much more convenient than a packhorse. All in all, Bork was happier than he had ever thought he would be.

Which is how things were going when the dragon came and changed it all forever.

Winkle was in Brunhilda's room, a place he had learned many routes to get to, so that he went unobserved every time. Brunhilda, after many gifts and more flattery, was on the verge of giving in to the handsome young advisor to the King when strange screams and cries began coming from the fields below. Brunhilda pulled away from Winkle's exploring hands and, clutching her half-open gown around her, rushed to the window to see what was the matter.

She looked down, to where the screams were coming from, and it wasn't until the dragon's shadow fell across her that she looked up. Winkle, waiting on the bed, only saw the claws reach in and, gently but firmly, take hold of Brunhilda and pull her from the room. Brunhilda fainted immediately, and by the time Winkle got to where he could see her, the dragon had backed away from the window and on great flapping wings was carrying her limp body off toward the north whence he had come.

Winkle was horrified. It was so sudden, something he could not have foreseen or planned against. Yet still he cursed himself and bitterly realized that his plans might be ended forever. A dragon had taken Brunhilda who was to be his means of legitimately becoming king; now the plot of seduction, marriage, and inheritance was ruined.

Ever practical, Winkle did not let himself lament for long. He dressed himself quickly and used a secret passage out of Brunhilda's room, only to reappear in the corridor outside it a moment later. "Brunhilda!" he cried, beating on the door. "Are you all right?"

The first of the knights reached him, and then the King, weeping and wailing and smashing anything that got in his way. Brunhilda's door was down in a moment, and the King ran to the window and cried out after his daughter, now a pinpoint speck in the sky many miles away. "Brunhilda! Brunhilda! Come back!" She did not come back. "Now," cried the King, as he turned back into the room and sank to the floor, his face twisted and wet with grief, "Now I have nothing, and all is in vain!"

My thoughts precisely, Winkle thought, but I'm not weeping about it. To hide his contempt he walked to the window and looked out. He saw, not the dragon, but Bork, emerging from the forest carrying two huge logs.

"Sir Bork," said Winkle.

The King heard a tone of decision in Winkle's voice. He had learned to listen to whatever Winkle said in that tone of voice. "What about him?"

"Sir Bork could defeat the dragon," Winkle said, "if any man could."

"That's true," the King said, gathering back some of the hope he had lost. "Of course that's true."

"But will he?" asked Winkle.

"Of course he will. He loves Brunhilda, doesn't he?"

"He said he did. But Your Majesty, is he really loyal to you? After all, why wasn't he here when the dragon came? Why didn't he save Brunhilda in the first place?"

"He was cutting wood for the winter."

"Cutting wood? When Brunhilda's life was at stake?"

The King was outraged. The illogic of it escaped him—he was not in a logical mood. So he was furious when he met Bork at the gate of the castle.

"You've betrayed me!" the King cried.

"I have?" Bork was smitten with guilt. And he hadn't even meant to.

"You weren't here when we needed you. When *Brunhilda* needed you!"

"I'm sorry," Bork said.

"Sorry, sorry, sorry. A lot of good it does to say you're sorry. You swore to protect Brunhilda from any enemy, and when a really dangerous enemy comes along, how do you repay me for everything I've done for you? You hide out in the forest!"

"What enemy?"

"A dragon," said the King, "as if you didn't see it coming and run out into the woods."

"Cross my heart, Your Majesty, I didn't know there was a dragon coming." And then he made the connection in his mind. "The dragon—it took Brunhilda?"

"It took her. Took her half-naked from her bedroom when she leaped to the window to call to you for help."

Bork felt the weight of guilt, and it was a terrible burden. His face grew hard and angry, and he walked into the castle, his harsh footfalls setting the earth to trembling. "My armor!" he cried. "My sword!"

In minutes he was in the middle of the courtyard, holding out his arms as the heavy mail was draped over him and the breastplate and helmet were strapped and screwed into place. The sword was not enough—he also carried his huge ax and a shield so massive two ordinary men could have hidden behind it.

"Which way did he go?" Bork asked.

"North," the King answered.

"I'll bring back your daughter, Your Majesty, or die in the attempt."

"Damn well better. It's all your fault."

The words stung, but the sting only impelled Bork further. He took the huge sack of food the cook had prepared for him and fastened it to his belt, and without a backward glance strode from the castle and took the road north.

"I almost feel sorry for the dragon," said the King.

But Winkle wondered. He had seen how large the claws were as they grasped Brunhilda—she had been like a tiny doll in a large man's fingers. The claws were razor sharp. Even if she were still alive, could Bork really best the dragon? Bork the Bully, after all, had made his reputation picking on men smaller than he, as Winkle had ample reason to know. How would he do facing a dragon at least five times his size? Wouldn't he turn coward? Wouldn't he run as other men had run from *him*?

He might. But Sir Bork the Bully was Winkle's only hope of getting Brunhilda and the kingdom. If he could do anything to ensure that the giant at least *tried* to fight the dragon, he would do it. And so, taking only his rapier and a sack of food, Winkle left the castle by another way, and followed the giant along the road toward the north.

And then he had a terrible thought.

Fighting the dragon was surely ten times as brave as anything Bork had done before. If he won, wouldn't he have a claim on Brunhilda's hand himself?

It was not something Winkle wished to think about. Something would come to him, some way around the problem when the time came. Plenty of opportunity to plan something—*after* Bork wins and rescues her.

Bork had not rounded the second turn in the road when he came across the old woman, waiting by the side of the road. It was the same old woman who had cared for Brunhilda all those years that she was kept in a secret room in the castle. She looked wizened and weak, but there was a sharp look in her eyes that many had mistaken for great wisdom. It was not great wisdom. But she did know a few things about dragons.

"Going after the dragon, are you?" she asked in a squeaky voice. "Going to get Brunhilda back, are you?" She giggled darkly behind her hand.

"I am if anyone can," Bork said.

"Well, anyone can't," she answered.

"*I* can."

"Not a prayer, you big bag of wind!"

Bork ignored her and started to walk past.

"Wait!" she said, her voice harsh as a dull file taking rust from armor. "Which way will you go?"

"North," he said. "That's the way the dragon took her."

"A quarter of the world is north, Sir Bork the Bully, and a dragon is small compared to all the mountains of the earth. But I know a way you can find the dragon, if you're really a knight.

"Light a torch, man. Light a torch, and whenever you come to a fork in the way, the light of the torch will leap the way you ought to go. Wind or no wind, fire seeks fire, and there is a flame at the heart of every dragon."

"They *do* breathe fire, then?" he asked. He did not know how to fight fire.

"Fire is light, not wind, and so it doesn't come from the dragon's mouth or the dragon's nostrils. If he burns you, it won't be with his breath." The old woman cackled like a mad hen. "No one knows the truth about dragons anymore!"

"Except you."

"I'm an old wife," she said. "And I know. They don't eat human beings, either. They're strict vegetarians. But they kill. From time to time they kill."

"Why, if they aren't hungry for meat?"

"You'll see," she said. She started to walk away, back into the forest.

"Wait!" Bork called. "How far will the dragon be?"

"Not far," she said. "Not far, Sir Bork. He's waiting for you. He's waiting for you and all the fools who come to try to free the virgin." Then she melted away into the darkness.

Bork lit a torch and followed it all night, turning when the flame turned, unwilling to waste time in sleep when Brunhilda might be suffering unspeakable degradation at the monster's hands. And behind him, Winkle forced himself to stay awake, determined not to let Bork lose him in the darkness.

All night, and all day, and all night again Bork followed the light of the torch, through crooked paths long unused, until he came to the foot of a dry, tall hill, with rocks and crags along the top. He stopped, for here the flame leaped high, as if to say, "Upward from here." And in the silence he heard a sound that chilled him to the bone. It was Brunhilda, screaming as if she were being tortured in the cruelest imaginable way. And the screams were followed by a terrible roar. Bork cast aside the remnant of his food and made his way to the top of the hill. On the way he called out, to stop the dragon from whatever it was doing.

"Dragon! Are you there!"

The voice rumbled back to him with a power that made the dirt shift under Bork's feet. "Yes indeed."

"Do you have Brunhilda?"

"You mean the little virgin with the heart of an adder and the brain of a gnat?"

In the forest at the bottom of the hill, Winkle ground his teeth in fury, for despite his designs on the kingdom, he loved Brunhilda as much as he was capable of loving anyone.

"Dragon!" Bork bellowed at the top of his voice. "Dragon! Prepare to die!"

"Oh dear! Oh dear!" cried out the dragon. "Whatever shall I do?"

And then Bork reached the top of the hill, just as the sun topped the distant mountains and it became morning. In the light Bork immediately saw Brunhilda tied to a tree, her auburn hair glistening. All around her was the immense pile of gold that the dragon, according to custom, kept. And all around the gold was the dragon's tail.

Bork looked at the tail and followed it until finally he came to the dragon, who was leaning on a rock chewing on a tree trunk and smirking. The dragon's wings were clad with feathers, but the rest of him was covered with tough gray hide the color of weathered granite. His teeth, when he smiled, were ragged, long, and pointed. His claws were three feet long and sharp as a rapier from tip to base. But in spite of all this armament, the most dangerous thing about him was his eyes. They were large and soft and brown, with long lashes and gently arching brows. But at the center each eye held a sharp point of light, and when Bork looked at the eyes that light stabbed deep into him, seeing his heart and laughing at what it found there.

For a moment, looking at the dragon's eyes, Bork stood transfixed. Then the dragon reached over one wing toward Brunhilda, and with a great growling noise he began to tickle her ear.

Brunhilda was unbearably ticklish, and she let off a bloodcurdling scream.

"Touch her not!" Bork cried.

"Touch her what?" asked the dragon, with a chuckle. "I will not."

"Beast!" bellowed Bork. "I am Sir Bork the Big! I have never been defeated in battle! No man dares stand before me, and the beasts of the forest step aside when I pass!"

"You must be awfully clumsy," said the dragon.

Bork resolutely went on. He had seen the challenges and jousts—it was obligatory to recite and embellish your achievements in order to strike terror into the heart of the enemy. "I can cut down trees with one blow of my ax! I can cleave an ox from head to tail, I can skewer a running deer, I can break down walls of stone and doors of wood!"

"Why can't I ever get a handy servant like that?" murmured the dragon. "Ah, well, you probably expect too large a salary."

The dragon's sardonic tone might have infuriated other knights; Bork was only confused, wondering if this matter was less serious than he had thought. "I've come to free Brunhilda, dragon. Will you give her up to me, or must I slay you?"

At that the dragon laughed long and loud. Then it cocked its head and looked at Bork. In that moment Bork knew that he had lost the battle. For deep in the dragon's eyes he saw the truth.

Bork saw himself knocking down gates and cutting down trees, but the deeds no longer looked heroic. Instead he realized that the knights who always rode behind him in these battles were laughing at him, that the King was a weak and vicious man, that Winkle's ambition was the only emotion he had room for; he saw that all of them were using him for their own cards, and cared nothing for him at all.

Bork saw himself asking for Brunhilda's hand in marriage, and he was ridiculous, an ugly, unkempt, and awkward giant in contrast to the slight and graceful girl. He saw that the King's hints of the possibility of their marriage were merely a trick, to blind him. More, he saw what no one else had been able to see—that Brunhilda loved Winkle, and Winkle wanted her.

And at last Bork saw himself as a warrior, and realized that in all the years of his great reputation and in all his many victories, he had fought only one man—an archer who ran at him with a knife. He had terrorized the weak and the small, but never until now had he faced a creature larger than himself. Bork looked in the dragon's eyes and saw his own death.

"Your eyes are deep," said Bork softly.

"Deep as a well, and you are drowning."

"Your sight is clear." Bork's palms were cold with sweat.

"Clear as ice, and you will freeze."

"Your eyes," Bork began. Then his mouth was suddenly so dry that he could barely speak. He swallowed. "Your eyes are filled with light."

"Bright and tiny as a star," the dragon whispered. "And see; your heart is afire."

Slowly the dragon stepped away from the rock, even as the tip of his tail reached behind Bork to push him into the dragon's waiting jaws. But Bork was not in so deep a trance that he could not see.

"I see that you mean to kill me," Bork said. "But you won't have me as easily as that." Bork whirled around to hack at the tip of the dragon's tail with his ax. But he was too large and slow, and the tail flicked away before the ax was fairly swung.

The battle lasted all day. Bork fought exhaustion as much as he fought the dragon, and it seemed the dragon only toyed with him. Bork would lurch toward the tail or a wing or the dragon's belly, but when the ax or sword fell where the dragon had been, it only sang in the air and touched nothing.

Finally Bork fell to his knees and wept. He wanted to go on with the fight, but his body could not do it. And the dragon looked as fresh as it had in the morning.

"What?" asked the dragon. "Finished already?"

Then Bork felt the tip of the dragon's tail touch his back, and the sharp points of the claws pressed gently on either side. He could not bear to look up at what he knew he would see. Yet neither could he bear to wait, not knowing when the blow would come. So he opened his eyes, and lifted his head, and saw.

The dragon's teeth were nearly touching him, poised to tear his head from his shoulders.

Bork screamed. And screamed again when the teeth touched him, when they pushed into his armor, when the dragon lifted him with teeth and tail and talons until he was twenty feet above the ground. He screamed again when he looked into the dragon's eyes and saw, not hunger, not hatred, but merely amusement.

And then he found his silence again, and listened as the dragon spoke through clenched teeth, watching the tongue move massively in the mouth only inches from his head.

"Well, little man. Are you afraid?"

Bork tried to think of some heroic message of defiance to hurl at the dragon, some poetic words that might be remembered forever so that his death would be sung in a thousand songs. But Bork's mind was not quick at such things; he was not accustomed to speech, and had no ear for gallantry. Instead he began to think it would be somehow cheap and silly to die with a lie on his lips.

"Dragon," Bork whispered. "I'm frightened."

To Bork's surprise, the teeth did not pierce him then. Instead, he felt himself being lowered to the ground, heard a grating sound as the teeth and claws let go of his armor. He raised his visor, and saw that the dragon was now lying on the ground, laughing, rolling back and forth, slapping its tail against the rocks, and clapping its claws together. "Oh, my dear tiny friend," said the dragon. "I thought the day would never dawn."

"What day?"

"Today," answered the dragon. It had stopped laughing, and it once again drew near to Bork and looked him in the eye. "I'm going to let you live."

"Thank you," Bork said, trying to be polite.

"Thank me? Oh no, my midget warrior. You won't thank me. Did you think my teeth were sharp? Not half so pointed as the barbs of your jealous, disappointed friends."

"I can go?"

"You can go, you can fly, you can dwell in your castle for all I care. Do you want to know why?"

"Yes."

"Because you were afraid. In all my life, I have only killed brave knights who knew no fear. You're the first, the very first, who was afraid in that final moment. Now go." And the dragon gave Bork a push and sent him down the hill.

Brunhilda, who had watched the whole battle in curious silence, now called after him. "Some kind of knight you are! Coward! I hate you! Don't leave me!" The shouts went on until Bork was out of earshot.

Bork was ashamed.

Bork went down the hill and, as soon as he entered the cool of the forest, he lay down and fell asleep.

Hidden in the rocks, Winkle watched him go, watched as the dragon again began to tickle Brunhilda, whose gown was still open as it had been when she was taken by the dragon. Winkle could not stop thinking of how close he had come to having her. But now, if even Bork could not save her, her cause was hopeless, and Winkle immediately began planning other ways to profit from the situation.

All the plans depended on his reaching the castle before Bork. Since Winkle had dozed off and on during the day's battle, he was able to go farther—to a village, where he stole an ass and rode clumsily, half-asleep, all night and half the next day and reached the castle before Bork awoke.

The King raged. The King swore. The King vowed that Bork would die.

"But Your Majesty," said Winkle, "you can't forget that it is Bork who inspires fear in the hearts of your loyal subjects. You can't kill him—if he were dead, how long would you be king?"

That calmed the man down. "Then I'll let him live. But he won't have a place in this castle, that's certain. I won't have him around here, the coward. Afraid!

Told that dragon he was afraid! Pathetic. The man has no gratitude." And the King stalked from the court.

When Bork got home, weary and sick at heart, he found the gate of the castle closed to him. There was no explanation—he needed none. He had failed the one time it mattered most. He was no longer worthy to be a knight.

And now it was as it had been before. Bork was ignored, despised, feared, he was completely alone. But still, when it was time for great strength, there he was, doing the work of ten men, and not thanked for it. Who would thank a man for doing what he must to earn his bread.

In the evenings he would sit in his hut, staring at the fire that pushed a column of smoke up through the hole in the roof. He remembered how it had been to have friends, but the memory was not happy, for it was always poisoned by the knowledge that the friendship did not outlast Bork's first failure. Now the knights spat when they passed him on the road or in the fields.

The flames did not let Bork blame his troubles on them, however. The flames constantly reminded him of the dragon's eyes, and in their dance he saw himself, a buffoon who dared to dream of loving a princess, who believed that he was truly a knight. Not so, not so. I was never a knight, he thought. I was never worthy. Only now am I receiving what I deserve. And all his bitterness turned inward, and he hated himself far more than any of the knights could hate him.

He had made the wrong choice. When the dragon chose to let him go, he should have refused. He should have stayed and fought to the death. He should have died.

Stories kept filtering through the village, stories of the many heroic and famous knights who accepted the challenge of freeing Brunhilda from the dragon. All of them went as heroes. All of them died as heroes. Only Bork had returned alive from the dragon, and with every knight who died Bork's shame grew. Until he decided that he would go back. Better to join the knights in death than to live his life staring into the flames and seeing the visions of the dragon's eyes.

Next time, however, he would have to be better prepared. So after the spring plowing and planting and lambing and calving, where Bork's help was indispensable to the villagers, the giant went to the castle again. This time no one barred his way, but he was wise enough to stay as much out of sight as possible. He went to the one-armed swordmaster's room. Bork hadn't seen him since he accidentally cut off his arm in sword practice years before.

"Come for the other arm, coward?" asked the swordmaster.

"I'm sorry," Bork said. "I was younger then."

"You weren't any smaller. Go away."

But Bork stayed, and begged the swordmaster to help him. They worked out an arrangement. Bork would be the swordmaster's personal servant all summer, and in exchange the swordmaster would try to teach Bork how to fight.

They went out into the fields every day, and under the swordmaster's watchful eye he practiced sword-fighting with bushes, trees, rocks—anything but the swordmaster, who refused to let Bork near him. Then they would return to the swordmaster's rooms, and Bork would clean the floor and sharpen swords and burnish shields and repair broken practice equipment. And always the swordmaster said, "Bork, you're too stupid to do anything right!" Bork agreed. In a summer of practice, he never got any better, and at the end of the summer, when it was time for Bork to go out in the fields and help with the harvest and the preparations for winter, the swordmaster said, "It's hopeless, Bork. You're too slow. Even the bushes are more agile than you. Don't come back. I still hate you, you know."

"I know," Bork said, and he went out into the fields, where the peasants waited impatiently for the giant to come carry sheaves of grain to the wagons.

Another winter looking at the fire, and Bork began to realize that no matter how good he got with the sword, it would make no difference. The dragon was not to be defeated that way. If excellent swordplay could kill the dragon, the dragon would be dead by now—the finest knights in the kingdom had already died trying.

He had to find another way. And the snow was still heavy on the ground when he again entered the castle and climbed the long and narrow stairway to the tower room where the wizard lived.

"Go away," said the wizard, when Bork knocked at his door. "I'm busy."

"I'll wait," Bork answered.

"Suit yourself."

And Bork waited. It was late at night when the wizard finally opened the door. Bork had fallen asleep leaning on it—he nearly knocked the magician over when he fell inside.

"What the devil are you—you waited!"

"Yes," said Bork, rubbing his head where it had hit the stone floor.

"Well, I'll be back in a moment." The wizard made his way along a narrow ledge until he reached the place where the wall bulged and a hole opened onto the outside of the castle wall. In wartime, such holes were used to pour boiling oil on attackers. In peacetime, they were even more heavily used. "Go on inside and wait," the wizard said.

Bork looked around the room. It was spotlessly clean, the walls were lined with books, and here and there a fascinating artifact hinted at hidden knowledge and arcane powers—a sphere with the world on it, a skull, an abacus, beakers and tubes, a clay pot from which smoke rose, though there was no fire under it. Bork marvelled until the wizard returned.

"Nice little place, isn't it?" the wizard asked. "You're Bork, the bully, aren't you?"

Bork nodded.

"What can I do for you?"

"I don't know," Bork asked. "I want to learn magic. I want to learn magic powerful enough that I can use it to fight the dragon."

The wizard coughed profusely.

"What's wrong?" Bork asked

"It's the dust," the wizard said.

Bork looked around and saw no dust. But when he sniffed the air, it felt thick in his nose, and a tickling in his chest made him cough, too.

"Dust?" asked Bork. "Can I have a drink?"

"Drink," said the wizard. "Downstairs—"

"But there's a pail of water right here. It looks perfectly clean—"

"Please don't—"

But Bork put the dipper in the pail and drank. The water sloshed into his mouth, and he swallowed, but it felt dry going down, and his thirst was unslaked. "What's wrong with the water?" Bork asked.

The wizard sighed and sat down. "It's the problem with magic, Bork old boy. Why do you think the King doesn't call on me to help him in wars? He knows it, and now you'll know it, and the whole world probably will know it by Thursday."

"You don't know any magic?"

"Don't be a fool! I know all the magic there is! I can conjure up monsters that would make your dragon look tame! I can snap my fingers and have a table set with food to make the cook die of envy. I can take an empty bucket and fill it with water, with wine, with gold—whatever you want. But try spending the gold, and they'll hunt you down and kill you. Try drinking the water and you'll die of thirst."

"It isn't real."

"An illusion. Handy, sometimes. But that's all. Can't create anything in your head. That pail, for instance—" And the wizard snapped his fingers. Bork looked, and the pail was filled, not with water, but with dust and spider webs. That wasn't all. He looked around the room, and was startled to see that the bookshelves were gone, as were the other trappings of great wisdom. Just a few books on a table in a corner, some counters covered with dust and papers and half-decayed food, and the floor inches deep in garbage.

"The place is horrible," the wizard said. "I can't bear to look at it." He snapped his fingers, and the old illusion came back. "Much nicer, isn't it?"

"Yes."

"I have excellent taste, haven't I? Now, you wanted me to help you fight the dragon, didn't you? Well, I'm afraid it's out of the question. You see, my illusions only work on human beings, and occasionally on horses. A dragon wouldn't be fooled for a moment. You understand?"

Bork understood, and despaired. He returned to his hut and stared again at the flames. His resolution to return and fight the dragon again was undimmed. But now he knew that he would go as badly prepared as he had before, and his death and defeat would be certain. Well, he thought, better death than life as Bork the coward, Bork the bully who only has courage when he fights people smaller than himself.

The winter was unusually cold, and the snow was remarkably deep. The firewood ran out in February, and there was no sign of an easing in the weather.

The villagers went to the castle and asked for help, but the King was chilly himself, and the knights were all sleeping together in the great hall because there wasn't enough firewood for their barracks and the castle, too. "Can't help you," the King said.

So it was Bork who led the villagers—the ten strongest men, dressed as warmly as they could, yet still cold to the bone in the wind—and they followed in the path his body cut in the snow. With his huge ax cut down tree after tree; the villagers set the wedges and Bork split the huge logs; the men carried what they could but it was Bork who made seven trips and carried most of the wood home. The village had enough to last until spring—more than enough, for, as Bork had expected, as soon as the stacks of firewood were deep in the village, the King's men came and took their tax of it.

And Bork, exhausted and frozen from the expedition, was carefully nursed back to health by the villagers. As he lay coughing and they feared he might die, it occurred to them how much they owed to the giant. Not just the firewood, but the hard labor in the farming work, and the fact that Bork had kept the armies far from their village, and they felt what no one in the castle had let himself feel for more than a few moments—gratitude. And so it was that when he had mostly recovered, Bork began to find gifts outside his door from time to time. A rabbit, freshly killed and dressed; a few eggs; a vast pair of hose that fit him very comfortably; a knife specially made to fit his large grip and to ride with comfortable weight on his hip. The villagers did not converse with him much. But then, they were not talkative people. The gifts said it all.

Throughout the spring, as Bork helped in the plowing and planting, with the villagers working alongside, he realized that this was where he belonged—with the villagers, not with the knights. They weren't rollicking good company, but there was something about sharing a task that must be done that made for stronger bonds between them than any of the rough camaraderie of the castle. The loneliness was gone.

Yet when Bork returned home and stared into the flames in the center of his hut, the call of the dragon's eyes became even stronger, if that were possible. It was not loneliness that drove him to seek death with the dragon. It was something else, and Bork could not think what. Pride? He had none—he accepted the verdict of the castle people that he was a coward. The only guess he could make was that he loved Brunhilda and felt a need to rescue her. The more he tried to convince himself, however, the less he believed it.

He had to return to the dragon because, in his own mind, he knew he should have died in the dragon's teeth, back when he fought the dragon before. The common folk might love him for what he did for them, but he hated himself for what he was.

He was nearly ready to head back for the dragon's mountain when the army came.

"How many men are there?" the King asked Winkle.

"I can't get my spies to agree," Winkle said. "But the lowest estimate was two thousand men."

"And we have a hundred and fifty here in the castle. Well, I'll have to call on my dukes and counts for support."

"You don't understand, Your Majesty. These *are* your dukes and counts. This isn't an invasion. This is a rebellion."

The King paled. "How do they dare?"

"They dare because they heard a rumor, which at first they didn't believe was true. A rumor that your giant knight had quit, that he wasn't in your army anymore. And when they found out for sure that the rumor was true, they came to cast you out and return the old King to his place."

"Treason!" the King shouted. "Is there no loyalty?"

"I'm loyal," Winkle said, though of course he had already made contact with the other side in case things didn't go well. "But it seems to me that your only hope is to prove the rumors wrong. Show them that Bork is still fighting for you."

"But he isn't. I threw him out two years ago. The coward was even rejected by the dragon."

"Then I suggest you find a way to get him back into the army. If you don't, I doubt you'll have much luck against that crowd out there. My spies tell me they're placing wagers about how many pieces you can be cut into before you die."

The King turned slowly and stared at Winkle, glared at him, gazed intently in his eyes. "Winkle, after all we've done to Bork over the years, persuading him to help us now is a despicable thing to do."

"True."

"And so it's your sort of work, Winkle. Not mine. *You* get him back in the army."

"I can't do it. He hates me worse than anyone, I'm sure. After all, I've betrayed him more often."

"You get him back in the army within the next six hours, Winkle, or I'll send pieces of you to each of the men in that traitorous group that you've made friends with in order to betray me."

Winkle managed not to look startled. But he *was* surprised. The King had somehow known about it. The King was not quite the fool he had seemed to be.

"I'm sending four knights with you to make sure you do it right."

"You misjudge me, Your Majesty," Winkle said.

"I hope so, Winkle. Persuade Bork for me, and you live to eat another breakfast."

The knights came, and Winkle walked with them to Bork's hut. They waited outside.

"Bork, old friend," Winkle said. Bork was sitting by the fire, staring in the flames. "Bork, you aren't the sort to hold grudges, are you?"

Bork spat into the flames.

"Can't say I blame you," Winkle said. "We've treated you ungratefully. We've been downright cruel. But you rather brought it on yourself, you know. It isn't *our* fault you turned coward in your fight with the dragon, is it?"

Bork shook his head. "My fault, Winkle. But it isn't my fault the army has come, either. I've lost my battle. You lose yours."

"Bork, we've been friends since we were three—"

Bork looked up suddenly, his face so sharp and lit with the glow of the fire, that Winkle could not go on.

"I've looked in the dragon's eyes," Bork said, "and I know who you are."

Winkle wondered if it was true, and was afraid. But he had courage of a kind, a selfish courage that allowed him to dare anything if he thought he would gain by it.

"Who I am? No one knows anything as it is, because as soon as it's known it changes. You looked in the dragon's eyes years ago, Bork. Today I am not who I was then. Today you are not who you were then. And today the King needs you."

"The King is a petty count who rode to greatness on my shoulders. He can rot in hell."

"The other knights need you, then. Do you want them to die?"

"I've fought enough battles for them. Let them fight on their own."

And Winkle stood helplessly, wondering how he could possibly persuade this man, who would not be persuaded.

It was then that a village child came. The knights caught him lurking near Bork's hut; they roughly shoved him inside. "He might be a spy," a knight said.

For the first time since Winkle came, Bork laughed. "A spy? Don't you know your own village, here? Come to me, Laggy." And the boy came to him, and stood near him as if seeking the giant's protection. "Laggy's a friend of mine," Bork said. "Why did you come, Laggy?"

The boy wordlessly held out a fish. It wasn't large, but it was still wet from the river.

"Did you catch this?" Bork said.

The boy nodded.

"How many did you catch today?"

The boy pointed at the fish.

"Just the one? Oh, then I can't take this, if it's all you caught."

But as Bork handed the fish back, the boy retreated, refused to take it. He finally opened his mouth and spoke. "For you," he said, and then he scurried out of the hut and into the bright morning sunlight.

And Winkle knew he had his way to get Bork into the battle.

"The villagers," Winkle said.

Bork looked at him quizzically.

And Winkle *almost* said, "If you don't join the army, we'll come out here and burn the village and kill all the children and sell the adults into slavery in Germany." But something stopped him; a memory, perhaps, of the fact that he was once a village child himself. No, not that. Winkle was honest enough with himself to know that what stopped him from making the threat was a mental picture of Sir Bork striding into battle, not in front of the King's army, but at the head of the rebels. A mental picture of Bork's ax biting deep into the gate of the castle, his huge crow prying the portcullis free. This was not the time to threaten Bork.

So Winkle took the other tack. "Bork, if they win this battle, which they surely will if you aren't with us, do you think they'll be kind to this village? They'll burn and rape and kill and capture these people for slaves. They hate us, and to them these villagers are part of us, part of their hatred. If you don't help us, you're killing them."

"I'll protect them," Bork said.

"No, my friend. No, if you don't fight with us, as a knight, they won't treat you chivalrously. They'll fill you full of arrows before you get within twenty feet of their lines. You fight with us, or you might as well not fight at all."

Winkle knew he had won. Bork thought for several minutes, but it was inevitable. He got up and returned to the castle, strapped on his old armor, took his huge ax and his shield, and, with his sword belted at his waist, walked into the courtyard of the castle. The other knights cheered, and called out to him as if he were their dearest friend. But the words were hollow and they knew it, and when Bork didn't answer they soon fell silent.

The gate opened and Bork walked out, the knights on horseback behind him.

And in the rebel camp, they knew that the rumors were a lie—the giant still fought with the King, and they were doomed. Most of the men slipped away into the woods. But the others, particularly the leaders who would die if they surrendered as surely as they would die if they fought, stayed. Better to die valiantly than as a coward, they each thought, and so as Bork approached he still faced an army—only a few hundred men, but still an army.

They came out to meet Bork one by one, as the knights came to the dragon on his hill. And one by one, as they made their first cut or thrust, Bork's ax struck, and their heads flew from their bodies, or their chests were cloven nearly in half, or the ax reamed them end to end, and Bork was bright red with blood and a dozen men were dead and not one had touched him.

So they came by threes and fours, and fought like demons, but still Bork took them, and when even more than four tried to fight him at once they got in each other's way and he killed them more easily.

And at last those who still lived despaired. There was no honor in dying so pointlessly. And with fifty men dead, the battle ended, and the rebels laid down their arms in submission.

Then the King emerged from the castle and rode to the battleground, and paraded triumphantly in front of the defeated men.

"You are all sentenced to death at once," the King declared.

But suddenly he found himself pulled from his horse, and Bork's great hands held him. The King gasped at the smell of gore; Bork rubbed his bloody hands on the King's tunic, and took the King's face between his sticky palms.

"No one dies now. No one dies tomorrow. These men will all live, and you'll send them home to their lands, and you'll lower their tribute and let them dwell in peace forever."

The King imagined his own blood mingling with that which already covered Bork, and he nodded. Bork let him go. The King mounted his horse again, and spoke loudly, so all could hear. "I forgive you all. I pardon you all. You may return to your homes. I confirm you in your lands. And your tribute is cut in half from this day forward. Go in peace. If any man harms you, I'll have his life."

The rebels stood in silence.

Winkle shouted at them "Go! You heard the King! You're free! Go home!"

And they cheered, and long-lived-the-King, and then bellowed their praise to Bork.

But Bork, if he heard them, gave no sign. He stripped off his armor and let it lie in the field. He carried his great ax to the stream, and let the water run over the metal until it was clean. Then he lay in the stream himself, and the water carried off the last of the blood, and when he came out he was clean.

Then he walked away, to the north road, ignoring the calls of the King and his knights, ignoring everything except the dragon who waited for him on the mountain. For this was the last of the acts Bork would perform in his life for which he would feel shame. He would not kill again. He would only die, bravely, in the dragon's claws and teeth.

The old woman waited for him on the road.

"Off to kill the dragon, are you?" she asked in a voice that the years had tortured into gravel. "Didn't learn enough the first time?" She giggled behind her hand.

"Old woman, I learned everything before. Now I'm going to die."

"Why? So the fools in the castle will think better of you?"

Bork shook his head.

"The villagers already love you. For your deeds today, you'll already be a legend. If it isn't for love or fame, why are you going?"

Bork shrugged. "I don't know. I think he calls to me. I'm through with my life, and all I can see ahead of me are his eyes."

The old woman nodded. "Well, well, Bork. I think you're the first knight that the dragon won't be happy to see. We old wives know, Bork. Just tell him the truth, Bork."

"I've never known the truth to stop a sword," he said.

"But the dragon doesn't carry a sword."

"He might as well."

"No, Bork, no," she said, clucking impatiently. "You know better than that. Of all the dragon's weapons, which cut you the deepest?"

Bork tried to remember. The truth was, he realized, that the dragon had never cut him at all. Not with his teeth nor his claws. Only the armor had been pierced. Yet there had been a wound, a deep one that hadn't healed, and it had been cut in him, not by teeth or talons, but by the bright fires in the dragon's eyes.

"The truth," the old woman said. "Tell the dragon the truth. Tell him the truth, and you'll live!"

Bork shook his head. "I'm not going there to live," he said. He pushed past her, and walked on up the road.

But her words rang in his ears long after he stopped hearing her call after him. The truth, she had said. Well, then, why not? Let the dragon have the truth. Much good may it do him.

This time Bork was in no hurry. He slept every night, and paused to hunt for berries and fruit to eat in the woods. It was four days before he reached the dragon's hill, and he came in the morning, after a good night's sleep. He was afraid, of course; but still there was a pleasant feeling about the morning, a tingling of excitement about the meeting with the dragon. He felt the end coming near, and he relished it.

Nothing had changed. The dragon roared; Brunhilda screamed. And when he reached the top of the hill, he saw the dragon tickling her with his wing. He was not surprised to see that she hadn't changed at all—the two years had not aged her, and though her gown still was open and her breasts were open to the sun and the wind, she wasn't even freckled or tanned. It could have been yesterday that Bork fought with the dragon the first time. And Bork was smiling as he stepped into the flat space where the battle would take place.

Brunhilda saw him first. "Help me! You're the four hundred and thirtieth knight to try! Surely that's a lucky number!" Then she recognized him. "Oh, no. You again. Oh well, at least while he's fighting you I won't have to put up with his tickling."

Bork ignored her. He had come for the dragon, not Brunhilda.

The dragon regarded him calmly. "You are disturbing my nap time."

"I'm glad," Bork said. "You've disturbed me, sleeping and waking, since I left you. Do you remember me?"

"Ah yes. You're the only knight who was ever afraid of me."

"Do you really believe that?" Bork asked.

"It hardly matters what I believe. Are you going to kill me today?"

"I don't think so," said Bork. "You're much stronger than I am, and I'm terrible at battle. I've never defeated anyone who was more than half my strength."

The lights in the dragon's eyes suddenly grew brighter, and the dragon squinted to look at Bork. "Is that so?" asked the dragon.

"And I'm not very clever. You'll be able to figure out my next move before I know what it is myself."

The dragon squinted more, and the eyes grew even brighter.

"Don't you want to rescue this beautiful woman?" the dragon asked.

"I don't much care," he said. "I loved her once. But I'm through with that. I came for you."

"You don't love her anymore?" asked the dragon.

Bork almost said, "Not a bit." But then he stopped. The truth, the old woman had said. And he looked into himself and saw that no matter how much he hated himself for it, the old feelings died hard. "I love her, dragon. But it doesn't do me any good. She doesn't love me. And so even though I desire her, I don't want her."

Brunhilda was a little miffed. "That's the stupidest thing I've ever heard," she said. But Bork was watching the dragon, whose eyes were dazzlingly bright. The monster was squinting so badly that Bork began to wonder if he could see at all.

"Are you having trouble with your eyes?" Bork asked.

"Do you think *you* ask the questions here? I ask the questions."

"Then ask."

"What in the world do I want to know from you?"

"I can't think of anything," Bork answered. "I know almost nothing. What little I do know, you taught me."

"Did I? What was it that you learned?"

"You taught me that I was not loved by those I thought had loved me. I learned from you that deep within my large body is a very small soul."

The dragon blinked, and its eyes seemed to dim a little.

"Ah," said the dragon.

"What do you mean, 'Ah'?" asked Bork.

"Just 'Ah,'" the dragon answered. "Does every *ah* have to mean something?"

Brunhilda sighed impatiently. "How long does this go on? Everybody else who comes up here is wonderful and brave. You just stand around talking about how miserable you are. Why don't you fight?"

"Like the others?" asked Bork.

"They're so brave," she said.

"They're all dead."

"Only a coward would think of that," she said scornfully.

"It hardly comes as a surprise to you," Bork said. "Everyone knows I'm a coward. Why do you think I came? I'm of no use to anyone, except as a machine to kill people at the command of a King I despise."

"That's my father you're talking about!"

"I'm nothing, and the world will be better without me in it."

"I can't say I disagree," Brunhilda said.

But Bork did not hear her, for he felt the touch of the dragon's tail on his back, and when he looked at the dragon's eyes they had stopped glowing so brightly. They were almost back to normal, in fact, and the dragon was beginning to reach out its claws.

So Bork swung his ax, and the dragon dodged, and the battle was on, just as before.

And just as before, at sundown Bork stood pinned between tail and claws and teeth.

"Are you afraid to die?" asked the dragon, as it had before.

Bork almost answered *yes* again, because that would keep him alive. But then

THE BULLY AND THE BEAST • 143

he remembered that he had come in order to die, and as he looked in his heart he still realized that however much he might fear death, he feared life more.

"I came here to die," he said. "I still want to."

And the dragon's eyes leaped bright with light. Bork imagined that the pressure of the claws lessened.

"Well, then, Sir Bork, I can hardly do you such a favor as to kill you." And the dragon let him go.

That was when Bork became angry.

"You can't do this to me!" he shouted.

"Why not?" asked the dragon, who was now trying to ignore Bork and occupied itself by crushing boulders with its claws.

"Because I insist on my right to die at your hands."

"It's not a right, it's a privilege," said the dragon.

"If you don't kill me, then I'll kill you!"

The dragon sighed in boredom, but Bork would not be put off. He began swinging the ax, and the dragon dodged, and in the pink light of sunset the battle was on again. This time, though, the dragon only fell back and twisted and turned to avoid Bork's blows. It made no effort to attack. Finally Bork was too tired and frustrated to go on.

"Why don't you fight!" he shouted. Then he wheezed from the exhaustion of the chase.

The dragon was panting, too. "Come on now, little man, why don't you give it up and go home. I'll give you a signed certificate testifying that I asked you to go, so that no one thinks you're a coward. Just leave me alone."

The dragon began crushing rocks and dribbling them over its head. It lay down and began to bury itself in gravel.

"Dragon," said Bork, "a moment ago you had me in your teeth. You were about to kill me. The old woman told me that truth was my only defense. So I must have lied before, I must have said something false. What was it? Tell me!"

The dragon looked annoyed. "She had no business telling you that. It's privileged information."

"All I ever said to you was the truth."

"Was it?"

"Did I lie to you? Answer—yes or no!"

The dragon only looked away, its eyes still bright. It lay on its back and poured gravel over its belly.

"I did then. I lied. Just the kind of fool I am to tell the truth and still get caught in a lie."

Had the dragon's eyes dimmed? Was there a lie in what he had just said?

"Dragon," Bork insisted, "if you don't kill me or I don't kill you, then I might as well throw myself from the cliff. There's no meaning to my life, if I can't die at your hands!"

Yes, the dragon's eyes were dimming, and the dragon rolled over onto its belly, and began to gaze thoughtfully at Bork.

"Where is the lie in that?"

"Lie? Who said anything about a lie?" But the dragon's tail was beginning to creep around so it could get behind Bork.

And then it occurred to Bork that the dragon might not even know. That the dragon might be as much a prisoner of the fires of truth inside him as Bork was, and that the dragon wasn't deliberately toying with him at all. Didn't matter, of course. "Never mind what the lie is, then," Bork said. "Kill me now, and the world will be a better place!"

The dragon's eyes dimmed, and a claw made a pass at him, raking the air by his face.

It was maddening, to know there was a lie in what he was saying and not know what it was. "It's the perfect ending for my meaningless life," he said. "I'm so clumsy I even have to stumble into death."

He didn't understand why, but once again he stared into the dragon's mouth, and the claws pressed gently but sharply against his flesh.

The dragon asked the question of Bork for the third time. "Are you afraid, little man, to die?"

This was the moment, Bork knew. If he was to die, he had to lie to the dragon now, for if he told the truth the dragon would set him free again. But to lie, he had to know what the truth was, and now he didn't know at all. He tried to think of where he had gone astray from the truth, and could not. What had he said? It was that he was clumsy; it was true that he was stumbling into death. What else then?

He had said his life was meaningless. Was that the lie? He had said his death would make the world a better place. Was that the lie?

And so he thought of what would happen when he died. What hole would his death make in the world? The only people who might miss him were the villagers. That was the meaning of his life, then—the villagers. So he lied.

"The villagers won't miss me if I die. They'll get along just fine without me."

But the dragon's eyes brightened, and the teeth withdrew, and Bork realized to his grief that his statement had been true after all. The villagers wouldn't miss him if he died. The thought of it broke his heart, the last betrayal in a long line of betrayals.

"Dragon, I can't outguess you! I don't know what's true and what isn't! All I learn from you is that everyone I thought loved me doesn't. Don't ask me questions! Just kill me and end my life. Every pleasure I've had turns to pain when you tell me the truth."

And now, when he had thought he was telling the truth, the claws broke his skin, and the teeth closed over his head, and he screamed. "Dragon! Don't let me die like this! What is the pleasure that your truth won't turn to pain? What do I have left?"

The dragon pulled away, and regarded him carefully. "I told you, little man, that I don't answer questions. I ask them."

"Why are you here?" Bork demanded. "This ground is littered with the bones of men who failed your tests. Why not mine? Why not mine? Why can't I die? Why did you keep sparing my life? I'm just a man, I'm just alive, I'm just trying to do the best I can in a miserable world and I'm sick of trying to figure out what's true and what isn't. End the game, dragon. My life has never been happy, and I want to die."

The dragon's eyes went black, and the jaws opened again, and the teeth approached, and Bork knew he had told his last lie, that this lie would be enough. But with the teeth inches from him Bork finally realized what the lie was, and the realization was enough to change his mind. "No," he said, and he reached out and seized the teeth, though they cut his fingers. "No," he said, and he wept. "I have been happy. I have." And, gripping the sharp teeth, the memories raced through his mind. The many nights of comradeship with the knights in the castle. The pleasures of weariness from working in the forest and the fields. The joy he felt when alone he won a victory from the Duke, the rush of warmth when the boy brought him the single fish he had caught; and the solitary pleasures, of waking and going to sleep, of walking and running, of feeling the wind on a hot day and standing near a fire in the deep of winter. They were all good, and they had all happened. What did it matter if later the knights despised him? What did it matter of the villagers' love was only a fleeting thing, to be forgotten after he died? The reality of the pain did not destroy the reality of the pleasure; grief did not obliterate joy. They each happened in their time, and because some of them were dark it did not mean that none of them were light.

"I have been happy," Bork said. "And if you let me live, I'll be happy again. That's what my life means, doesn't it? That's the truth, isn't it, dragon? My life matters because I'm alive, joy or pain, whatever comes, I'm alive and that's meaning enough. It's true, isn't it, dragon! I'm not here to fight you. I'm not here for you to kill me. I'm here to make myself alive!"

But the dragon did not answer. Bork was gently lowered to the ground. The dragon withdrew its talons and tail, pulled its head away, and curled up on the ground, covering its eyes with its claws.

"Dragon, did you hear me?"

The dragon said nothing.

"Dragon, look at me!"

The dragon sighed. "Man, I cannot look at you."

"Why not?"

"I am blind," the dragon answered. It pulled its claws away from its eyes. Bork covered his face with his hands. The dragon's eyes were brighter than the sun.

"I feared you, Bork," the dragon whispered. "From the day you told me you were afraid, I feared you. I knew you would be back. And I knew this moment would come."

"What moment?" Bork asked.

"The moment of my death."

"Are you dying?"

"No," said the dragon. "Not yet. You must kill me."

As Bork looked at the dragon lying before him, he felt no desire for blood. "I don't want you to die."

"Don't you know that a dragon cannot live when it has met a truly honest man? It's the only way we ever die, and most dragons live forever."

But Bork refused to kill him.

The dragon cried out in anguish. "I am filled with all the truth that was discarded by men when they chose their lies and died for them. I am in constant pain, and now that I have met a man who does not add to my treasury of falsehood, you are the cruelest of them all."

And the dragon wept, and its eyes flashed and sparkled in every hot tear that fell, and finally Bork could not bear it. He took his ax and hacked off the dragon's head, and the light in its eyes went out. The eyes shriveled in their sockets until they turned into small, bright diamonds with a thousand facets each. Bork took the diamonds and put them in his pocket.

"You killed him," Brunhilda said wonderingly.

Bork did not answer. He just untied her, and looked away while she finally fastened her gown. Then he shouldered the dragon's head and carried it back to the castle, Brunhilda running to keep up with him. He only stopped to rest at night because she begged him to. And when she tried to thank him for freeing her, he only turned away and refused to hear. He had killed the dragon because it wanted to die. Not for Brunhilda. Never for her.

At the castle they were received with rejoicing, but Bork would not go in. He only laid the dragon's head beside the moat and went to his hut, fingering the diamonds in his pocket, holding them in front of him in the pitch blackness of his hut to see that they shone with their own light, and did not need the sun or any other fire but themselves.

The King and Winkle and Brunhilda and a dozen knights came to Bork's hut. "I have come to thank you," the King said, his cheeks wet with tears of joy.

"You're welcome," Bork said. He said it as if to dismiss them.

"Bork," the King said. "Slaying the dragon was ten times as brave as the bravest thing any man has done before. You can have my daughter's hand in marriage."

Bork looked up in surprise.

"I thought you never meant to keep your promise, Your Majesty."

The King looked down, then at Winkle, then back at Bork. "Occasionally," he said, "I keep my word. So here she is, and thank you."

But Bork only smiled, fingering the diamonds in his pocket. "It's enough that you offered, Your Majesty. I don't want her. Marry her to a man she loves."

The King was puzzled. Brunhilda's beauty had not waned in her years of captivity. She had the sort of beauty that started wars. "Don't you want *any* reward?" asked the King.

Bork thought for a moment. "Yes," he said. "I want to be given a plot of ground far away from here. I don't want there to be any count, or any duke, or any king over me. And any man or woman or child who comes to me will be free, and no one can pursue them. And I will never see you again, and you will never see me again."

"That's all you want?"

"That's all."

"Then you shall have it," the King said.

Bork lived all the rest of his life on his little plot of ground. People did come to him. Not many, but five or ten a year all his life, and a village grew up where no one came to take a king's tithe or a duke's fifth or a count's fourth. Children grew up who knew nothing of the art of war and never saw a knight or a battle or the terrible fear on the face of a man who knows his wounds are too deep to heal. It was everything Bork could have wanted, and he was happy all his years there.

Winkle, too, achieved everything he wanted. He married Brunhilda, and soon enough the King's sons had accidents and died, and the King died after dinner one night, and Winkle became King. He was at war all his life, and never went to sleep at night without fear of an assassin coming upon him in the darkness. He governed ruthlessly and thoroughly and was hated all his life; later generations, however, remembered him as a great King. But he was dead then, and didn't know it.

Later generations never heard of Bork.

He had only been out on his little plot of ground for a few months when the old wife came to him. "Your hut is much bigger than you need," she said. "Move over."

So Bork moved over, and she moved in.

She did not magically turn into a beautiful princess. She was foul-mouthed and nagged Bork unmercifully. But he was devoted to her, and when she died a few years later he realized that she had given him more happiness than pain, and he missed her. But the grief of her dying did not taint any of the joys of his memory of her; he just fingered the diamonds, and remembered that grief and joy were not weighed in the same scale, one making the other seem less substantial.

And at last he realized that Death was near; that Death was reaping him like wheat, eating him like bread. He imagined Death to be a dragon, devouring him bit by bit, and one night in a dream he asked Death, "Is my flavor sweet?"

Death, the old dragon, looked at him with bright and understanding eyes, and said, "Salty and sour, bitter and sweet. You sting and you soothe."

"Ah," Bork said, and was satisfied.

Death poised itself to take the last bite. "Thank you," it said.

"You're welcome," Bork answered, and he meant it.

CONCERTO ACCADEMICO
Barry N. Malzberg

Barry N. Malzberg started his career as an agent for the Scott Meredith Literary Agency in New York in 1965, and he has seen the field from many angles, as reader, writer, editor, agent, and critic. He began publishing short stories in 1967, novels in 1970, and became known as a prolific writer of fiction that took a sardonic view of the meaning—or lack thereof—in individuals' lives and undertakings, to the point of occasionally being labeled anti-SF in his outlook. Notable novels include *Beyond Apollo*, winner of the first John W. Campbell Award; *Herovit's World*; *Guernica Night*; *Galaxies*; and *The Remaking of Sigmund Freud*. His eleven short story collections include *The Passage of the Light: The Recursive Science Fiction of Barry N. Malzberg* and *In the Stone House*. His collection of critical essays *The Engines of the Night* won a Locus Award. An expansion of that book, *Breakfast in the Ruins*, won the Locus Award again in 2007, and was nominated for the Hugo Award the same year. Malzberg lives with his wife Joyce in Teaneck, New Jersey.

The first dragon entered orchestra hall and moved gracelessly, a three ton package, toward the podium just as the Tarrytown Symphony was beginning the third movement of the Vaughan Williams Ninth Symphony. Glassop, in the third chair of the seconds, on the outside thanks to the oldstyle antiphonal seating that gave the seconds their own arch opposite the firsts, was among the first to see it but he kept very calm, bowing only slightly disturbed by the entrance of the green beast, slithering now down the aisle. Fulkes, the conductor was, of course, unaware of the dragon at this point and Glassop did not see fit to enlighten him. In the dim light the auditorium, no artificial illumination being turned on for a day rehearsal; the beast looked like a floating, cleaned-up crocodile. Glassop had seen pictures in the children's books, knew at least what he was looking at. He was no dummy. The beast was definitely a dragon and it looked most determined, as if it had a mission. Glassop hit the pizzicatos, listening to the theme crawling from the bassoons, tried to concentrate upon the notes. You had to stay calm in this business, if you got caught up in the moment by moment stuff, you could be destroyed like Nikisch throwing the baton on his toe and dying of septicemia in the days before antibiotics. And Toscanini, of course, taking out a violist's eye with a flung baton. "Excuse me," Schmitt, his seatmate said, "but is that a reptile coming down the aisle?" Schmitt had played in the Oslo Philharmonic, second stand firsts he had complained to Glassop, before he had decided to join his daughter and spend his pension in America. He was a dour Scandinavian and not such a good violinist, but Glassop knew that he was observant.

"It's a dragon," Glassop said. "Like in the forest or maybe with the queen."

"I know what it is, dummy," Schmitt said. "But where does it come from?"

Glassop shrugged. Sometimes no answer was the best answer. The dragon paused midway between the back doors and the podium and seemed to paw the ground, fixed the woodwinds on risers of the Tarrytown Symphony with a dim and preoccupied pair of eyes. Fulkes banged the baton on the empty music stand, said "Woodwinds, woodwinds!" until all of them stopped. Glassop rested his violin on his knee, looked at the middle-aged conductor whose life was edged in disappointment, Glassop supposed, married to an heiress and conducting a semi-professional orchestra in Westchester when his real ambitions lay somewhat to the south. Once as an assistant conductor of the New York Philharmonic he had filled in for Boulez at a children's concert, but that was a long time ago.

"*Woodwinds,*" Fulkes said, "that is not the way that this very sinister passage is played. You must make legato, must lead the way toward the flugelhorn!"

"Dragons," Schmitt said. "They were rumored to be in the forests of Riga when I was a young man. Of course I am not a young man now, my friend. Do you smell that beast?"

Glassop inhaled delicate draughts of air, thinking of his grandson, Zeke, and what he would make of a dragon in the orchestra hall. Probably the boy would be as matter of fact as Schmitt or perhaps as oblivious as Wilkes. Children nowadays were exposed to too much sensation, murders on the MTV, dragons were nothing to them. The one at issue pawed the tiled floors and then sat gracelessly on its haunches, fixing Fulkes' back with an insistent and compelling expression. It might have been holding an oboe for the degree of attention it now showed.

"This is a most sinister symphony," Fulkes said. "Vaughan Williams composed it in 1958, in the last year of his life. He was eighty-six years old and not feeling very well and he looked, in the words of Colin Davis, like a sack of bricks. We must acquaint ourselves with a man who thought of himself as being on friendly terms with death, who saw death, so to speak, as a disheveled guest in his own home, perhaps an elderly acquaintance who himself looked like a sack of bricks. Later on it is time for the middle strings to plumb the nature of the north region, but now the woodwinds must gracefully usher the old fellow in. Do you understand?"

Glassop shrugged, and stared over at the fourth stand firsts where, on the inside, sat Gertrude whom he loved. Gertrude had come to the Tarrytown Symphony only as a means, she said, of filling up the hours while her children slowly dismantled her life but Glassop thought that he knew better, that he could look deeply into her very soul. Thirty years younger than he and most of the string section of this orchestra of refugees from Communism or decadence or retirees from capitalism, she had she said a mature and loving heart and no prejudice at all against second violinists or older men. If her husband and children were only to die, she had told Glassop once in the sacramental confines of the rear booth at the college coffee shop, she would genuinely consider his offer, his aching need. Of course this was not likely at any time in the foreseeable, but then again you did not know.

Gertrude looked over at him, said something. *Dra-gon,* Glassop lip-read expertly. Do *you see the dra-gon?* She made a circle of her right thumb and forefinger, gripped the bow, raised it, pointed to the far aisle. *Am I cra-zy?* Glassop lip-read. *Is that a dra-gon?*

No, Glassop motioned with his head, then nodded yes. No, you are not crazy. Yes, that is a dragon. He did this twice to make sure that the message could not be confused. Gertrude sighed, shrugged, raised the bow again. Are *we the only ones?* she said. *To see it? To see the dra-gon?* Glassop shrugged. Who knew? It was enough to manage your own perceptions, let alone account for those of others. *I don't* know, he mouthed back to her. Now it was her turn to shrug, and then turn a page of the score as if in dismissal. Well, that was what the emotion of pure love got you at sixty-seven. If he were lucky he would, with the Greek philosopher, have the beast taken from him soon enough. In the meantime, he had the assurance from Gertrude who was the recipient of his earnest if unavailing passion that he was not mad, that he had indeed glimpsed a dragon in the aisle. Perhaps others had, too. Perhaps the entire orchestra had grasped the situation but was remaining very calm. That was the nature of the Tarrytown Symphony. These were people who had, most of them, been through a great deal, much displacement, the fulcrum of dispossession had had its way with two out of three of them and a dragon in orchestra hall was at this time among the lesser of their concerns.

"That is good enough," Fulkes said. "We try again now. From the beginning of the movement, please. Remember, should we get that far that the last movement is *attaca,* you must make the audience feel the transition rather than see it. Vaughan Williams died just three weeks after the premiere and the night before Boult made the recording. We will endeavor now not to do the same."

Glassop put the fiddle under his chin, listened to Bamett's snare drum, watched Leonard Zeller put the clarinet through the opening phrases. What was it like for Vaughan Williams in that last year? Glassop wondered. Eighty-six years old, still writing symphonies, did *he* see dragons? English music was full of moats, castles, knights and unicorns, surely there must have been room for a dragon there. The Czechs had goblins and water sprites, dour Scandinavians like Schmitt were concerned largely with dwarfs. But dragons were kind of hard to place, not really nationalized in the way that most myths were. Glassop followed Fulkes' baton, was cued in, played his way through the grim answering theme.

The dragon rose suddenly to all fours and bellowed, then raised its front legs to rear to a surprising height, perhaps half the distance to the roof of the orchestra hall. The sound was surprisingly high, fluted, not what one would associate with a menacing beast. However, it stopped the woodwinds cold and broke down Solomon before he could raise the flugelhorn. There was no question now of the visibility of the dragon or the attention of the Tarrytown Symphony. The players were indeed fixated upon the situation. Fulkes turned, stared into the auditorium, then whirled back and faced them. "Oh, my," he said, "oh, my, it is very large." He grasped his chest, pounded it in an odd rhythm, then dropped the baton, "I think I am going to faint," Fulkes said. "It is a great, a surprising strain."

The dragon wandered toward the edge of the stage, perched on the floor then right under the second violins, closest to Glassop. At the fourth stand on the outside, Glassop had the most privileged of vantage points, he could stare the animal down eye to eye and at the same time maintain some perspective. "Oh, my," Fulkes said, lunging to the right, then the left. "I have never seen anything like this." He fell to his knees, crept around the podium, found the baton and lurching into a half-crouch fled the podium, lunging through the firsts at hobbling speed and exiting behind the curtain. There were sounds of consternation among the bassi and two of the firsts at the rear stand rose to follow Fulkes, possibly to check upon his health, but otherwise all remained calm. Glassop stared at the dragon, an elongated and amiable crocodile with large, fixed eyes and a peculiarly generous expression around the mouth. The beast exhaled and the smell of flowers wafted its way to Glassop, filling his nostrils with sweet and ancient odors.

"Oh, what a grand circumstance," Schmitt said, entranced, holding his violin with two hands against his belly and looking at the engaging beast beneath them. "Magic," Schmitt said as if having returned from the land of the fiords that very morning. "It is magic."

Glassop put his violin slowly, firmly on the floor. Magic, he thought, Schmitt was right. The quality was of magic. Seen from this angle the beast was enormous yet somehow accessible. Peacefully it exuded its floral scent and then Glassop extended his hand to touch a scale, the dragon licked Glassop's hand with the greatest and gentlest of attention. Glassop felt a strange and wondrous peace filling him.

He stood carefully, making sure that he did not bump his violin, a simulated machine-made Amati worth perhaps twelve hundred dollars but of some sentimental meaning and went to the podium, mounted it slowly and stiffly. The Tarrytown Symphony—old men, older men, middle-aged women, a few people of indeterminate age and of course his beloved, harried Gertrude—stared at him. The rear stand first violinists had followed Fulkes and there were a few gaps in the woodwinds and bassi but the body of the seventy-three member orchestra remained on stage. Glassop found himself filled with an odd and persuasive joy, something unlike anything he had felt in these many years. He looked at the dragon—which was now submitting to Schmitt's scratchings and whispered confidences—for courage and then he looked at Gertrude who gave him her most attentive and dedicated coffee-shop smile and then he addressed the orchestra.

"At eighty-six," Glassop said, "Ralph Vaughan Williams, the great British composer who Colin Davis described as looking in his dotage like a sack of bricks experienced wonders, knew wonders, composed in that eighty-seventh year of his the greatest of his nine symphonies and lived to hear its premiere. He heard wonders, saw dragons, saw lovely and mythical beasts against the screen of his consciousness, wrote a fierce and humorous commentary. Can we do less? In our own near-dotage can we ask less of ourselves than did Ralph Vaughan Williams?

"Come," Glassop said, feeling massive, solid, feeling the full *locality* of himself and basking in the sudden and expanded breath of the dragon, "We will make music together. In E minor we will make such sounds as Ralph Vaughan Williams heard from the fen, as he moved toward the far region. Gertrude," Gloss said, "I truly love you, wreckage that I am, I confer upon you the benison of my understanding and my simple, unadorned, insubstantial passion." He raised the baton. "From the beginning," Glassop said, "we will start the E Minor symphony from the beginning with its earnest, descending theme and we will move on and on through its thirty-seven minutes of steady grandeur. Celli, prepare to lead."

Glassop, no longer a refugee, raised his hands. The music sighed from the celli. Behind him Glassop could hear the sound of the dragon's heart as it opened its joyous mouth to emit fire, the pure fire ascending from its living breath and in the arch of Gertrude's bow Glassop dreamed that he could see the mysterious fen, the walking stick of Ralph Vaughan Williams, the splendid old man himself as riding the fire of the dragon he sped toward eternity.

—in memory of Sir Adrian Boult

THE DRAGON'S BOY

Jane Yolen

Jane Yolen is the award-winning author of more than 300 books, mostly written for children. Known as the "Hans Christian Andersen of America", she is a professional storyteller on the stage, has been an editor, and is the mother of three grown children, and the grandmother of six. Her best-known work, the critically acclaimed *Owl Moon* won the prestigious Caldecott Medal in 1988. Her fiction has won the Christopher Medal (twice) the Nebula (twice), World Fantasy Award, Society of Children's Book Writers (twice), Mythopoeic Society's Aslan (three times), Boys' Clubs of America Junior Book Award, and she had a National Book Award finalist. Six colleges have given her honorary doctorates. Her works for adults include the powerful holocaust fantasy *Briar Rose*, and the Great Alta trilogy. Some of her short fiction has been collected in *Once upon a Time (She Said)*. Her three children all work in the book business. She's waiting to see if any of her six grandchildren will follow.

It was on a day in early spring with the clouds scudding across a gray sky that the boy found the cave. He had been chasing after Lord Ector's brachet hound, the one who always slipped her chain to go after hare. She had slipped him as well, leaving him lost in the boggy wasteland north of the castle walls. He had crossed and recrossed a small, meandering stream, following her, wading thigh-deep in water that—he was painfully aware of it—would only come up to the other boys' knees. The reminder of his height only made him crankier.

The sun was high, his stomach empty, and the brachet had quit baying an hour earlier. She was no doubt back at the kennel yard, slopping up her food. But she was his responsibility, and he had to stay out until he was sure. Besides, he was lost. Well, not exactly lost but *bothered* a bit, which was a phrase he had picked up from the master of hounds, a whey-colored man for all that he was out of doors most of the day.

The boy looked around for a place to get out of the noon sun, for the low, hummocky swamp with its brown pools and quaking mosses offered little shelter. And then he saw a small tor mounding up over the bog. He decided to climb it a bit to see if he could find a place where he might shelter, maybe even survey the land. He'd never been quite this far from the castle on his own before and certainly had never come out into the northern fens where the peat-hags

155

reigned, and he needed time to think about the way home. And the brachet. If the mound had been higher, he wouldn't have attempted it. The High Tor, the really large mound northwest of the manor, had somewhat of an evil reputation. But this hillock was hardly that. He needed to get his bearings and sight the castle walls or at least a tower.

He was halfway up the tor when he saw the cave.

It was only an unprepossessing black hole in the rock, as round as if it had been carved and then smoothed by a master hand. He stepped in, being careful of the long, spearlike hanging rocks, and let his eyes get used to the dark. Only then did he hear the breathing. It was not very loud, but it was steady and rumbling, with an occasional pop! that served as punctuation.

He held his breath and began to back out of the cave, hit his head on something that rang in twenty different tones, and said a minor curse under his breath.

"Staaaaaaaaaay," came a low command.

He stopped. And so, for a stuttering moment, did his heart. "Whooooooooooo are you?" It was less an echo bouncing off cave walls than an elongated sigh.

The boy bit his lip and answered in a voice that broke several times in odd places. "I am nobody. Just Artos. A fosterling from the castle." Then he added hastily, "Sir."

A low rumbling sound, more like a snore than a sentence, was all that was returned to him. It was that homey sound that freed him of his terror long enough to ask, "And who are you?" He hesitated. "Sir."

Something creaked. There was a strange clanking. Then the voice, augmented almost tenfold, boomed at him, "I am the Great Riddler. I am the Master of Wisdoms. I am the Word and I am the Light. I Was and Am and Will Be."

Artos nearly fainted from the noise. He put his right hand before him as if to hold back the sound. When the echoes had ended, he said in a quiet little voice, "Are you a hermit, sir? An anchorite? Are you a druid? A penitent knight?"

The great whisper that answered him came in a rush of wind. "I am The Dragon."

"Oh," said Artos.

"Is that all you can say?" asked the dragon. "I tell you I am The Dragon and all you can answer is *oh*?"

The boy was silent.

The great breathy voice sighed. "Sit down, boy. It has been a long time since I have had company in my cave. A long time and a lonely time."

"But... but... but." It was not a good beginning.

"No *buts*," said the dragon.

"But..." Artos began again, needing greatly to uphold his end of the conversation.

"Shush, boy, and listen. I will pay for your visit."

The boy sat. It was not greed that stayed him. Rather, he was comforted by the thought that he was not to be eaten.

"So, Artos, how would you like your payment? In gold, in jewels, or in wisdom?"

A sudden flame from the center of the cave lit up the interior and, for the first time, Artos could see that there were jewels scattered about the floor as thick as pebbles. But dragons were known to be great game players. Cunning, like an old habit, claimed the boy. Like most small people, he had a genius for escape. "Wisdom, sir," he said.

Another bright flame spouted from the cave center. "An excellent choice," said the dragon. "I've been needing a boy just your age to pass my wisdom on to. So listen well."

Artos did not move and hoped that the dragon would see by his attitude that he was listening.

"My word of wisdom for the day is this: Old dragons, like old thorns, can still prick. And I am a very old dragon. Take care."

"Yes, sir," said Artos, thinking but not saying that that was a bit of wit often spoken on the streets of the village nestled inside the castle walls. But the warning by the villagers was of priests and thorns, not dragons. Aloud he said, "I will remember. Sir."

"Go now," said the dragon. "And as a reward for being such a good listener, you may take that small jewel. There." The strange clanking that Artos had heard before accompanied the extension of a gigantic foot with four enormous toes, three in the front and one in the back. It scrabbled along the cave floor, then stopped not far from Artos. Then the nail from the center toe extended peculiarly and tapped on a red jewel the size of a leek bulb.

Artos moved cautiously toward the jewel and the claw. Hesitating a moment, he suddenly leaned over and grabbed up the jewel. Then he scuttered back to the cave entrance.

"I will expect you tomorrow," said the dragon. "You will come during your time off."

"How did you know I had time off?" asked Artos.

"When you have become as wise as a dragon, you will know these things." Artos sighed.

"There is a quick path from the back bridge. Discover it. And you will bring me stew. With *meat*!" The nail was suddenly sheathed and, quite rapidly, the foot was withdrawn into the dark center of the cave.

"To-tomorrow," promised the boy, not meaning a word of it.

The next morning at the smithy, caught in the middle of a quarrel between Old Linn the apothecary and Magnus Pieter the swordmaker, Artos was reminded of his promise. He had not forgotten the dragon—indeed the memory of the great clanking scales, the giant claw, the shaft of searing breath, the horrendous whisper had haunted his dreams. But he had quite conveniently forgotten his promise, or shunted it aside, or buried it behind layers of caution, until the argument had broken out.

"But there is never any *meat* in my gravy," whined Old Linn.

"Nor any meat in your manner," replied the brawny smith. "Nor were you mete for battle." The smith rather fancied himself a words-man as well as a swordsman. And until Old Linn had had a fit, falling face first into his soup in the middle of entertaining the visiting high king, the smith had been spitted regularly by Old Linn's quick tongue. Now Linn was too slow for such ragging and he never told tales after meals anymore. It was said he had lost the heart for it after his teeth had left prints on the table. But he was kept on at the castle because Lord Ector had a soft heart and a long memory. And because—so backstair gossip had it—Linn had a cupboard full of strange herbs locked up behind doors covered with deep-carved runes.

Artos, who had been at the smithy to try and purchase a sword with his red jewel, was caught with his bargaining only just begun. He had not even had time to show the gem to Magnus Pieter when Old Linn had shambled in and, without any prelude, started his whining litany. His complaints were always laid at the smith's door. No one else in the castle was as old as the pair of them. Not even Lord Ector. They were best of friends by their long and rancorous association.

"My straw is ne'er changed but once a se'nnight," Linn complained. "My slops are ne'er emptied. I am given the dregs of the wine to drink. And now I must sit, if I am to be welcomed at all, well below the salt."

The smith smiled and returned to tapping on his piece of steel. He had stopped when Artos had begun his inquiries. In time to the beat of the hammer, he said, "But you have straw, though you no longer earn it. And a pot for your slops, which you can empty yourself. You have wine, even though you ne'er pay for it. And even below the salt, there is gravy in your bowl."

That was when Old Linn had whined piteously, "But there is never any meat in my gravy."

It was the word meat and Magnus Pieter's seven or eight variations on it that rung like a knell in Artos's head. For meat had been the dragon's final word.

He slunk off without even the promise of a sword, that shining piece of steel that might make him an equal in the eyes of the other boys, the gem still burning brightly in his tightly clenched hand.

He brought a small pot of gravy with three pieces of meat with him. Strolling casually out the back gate as if he had all the time in the world, nodding slightly at the guards over the portcullis, Artos could feel his heartbeat quicken. He had walked rather more quickly over the moat bridge, glancing at the gray-green water where the old moat tortoise lazed atop the rusted crown of a battle helm. Once he was across, however, he began to run.

It was difficult not to spill the stew, but he managed. The path was a worn thread through a wilderness of peat mosses and tangled brush. He even clambered over two rock outcroppings in the path that were studded with stones that looked rather like lumps of meat themselves. And, actually, climbing over the rocks was easier than wheedling the pot of stew had been. He only had it because Mag the scullion was sweet on him and he had allowed her to kiss him full on the lips.

She hadn't noticed how he had held his breath, hoping to avoid the stink of her garlic, and closed his eyes not to see her bristly mustache. And she sighed so much after the kiss she hadn't had time to ask what he needed the stew for. But what if the dragon wanted gravy every day and he had to give Mag more kisses? It didn't bear thinking about, so Artos thought instead about the path. The dragon had been right. There was a quicker route back to the mound. Its only disadvantages were the two large rocks and the old thorny briar bushes. But they, at least, were safer than the peat pools which held bones enough way far down.

He got to the cave rather more quickly than he had bargained. Breathless, he squinted into the dark hole. This time he heard no heavy dragon breathing.

"Maybe," he said aloud to himself, his own voice lending him badly needed courage, "there's no one home. So I can just leave the gravy—and go."

"Staaaaaaaaay," came the sudden rumbling.

Artos almost dropped the pot.

"I have the gravy," he shouted quickly. He hadn't meant to be so loud, but fear always made him either too quiet or too loud. He was never sure which it was to be.

"Then give it meeeeeeeee," said the voice, followed by the clanking as the great claw extended halfway into the cave.

Artos could tell it was the foot by its long shadow. This time there was no stream of fire, only a hazy smoldering light from the back of the cave. Feeling a little braver then, he said, "I shall need to take the pot back with me. Sir."

"You shall take a bit of wisdom instead," came the voice.

Artos wondered if it would make him wise enough to avoid Mag's sweaty embrace. Somehow he doubted it.

"Tomorrow you shall have the pot. When you bring me more."

"*More?*" This time Artos's voice squeaked.

"Mooooooooore," said the dragon. "With meat!" The nail extended, just as it had the day before, and caught under the pot handle. There was a horrible screeching as the pot was lifted several inches into the air, then slowly withdrawn into the recesses of the cave. There were strange scrabbling noises as if the dragon were sorting through its possessions, and then the clanking resumed. The claw returned and dropped something at Artos's feet.

He looked down. It was a book, rather tatty around the edges, he thought, though in the cave light it was hard to be sure. "Wisssssssssdom," said the dragon.

Artos shrugged. "It's just a book. I know my letters. Father Bertram taught me."

"Letterssssssss turn matter into sssssssspirit," hissed the dragon.

"You mean it's a book of magic?"

"All booksssssss are magic, boy." The dragon sounded just a bit cranky.

"Well, I can read," said Artos, stooping to pick up the book. He added a quick, "Thank you," thinking he should seem grateful. *Old thorns and old dragons…* he reminded himself.

"You can read *letters*, my boy, which is more than I can say for your castle contemporaries. And you can read *words*. But you must learn to read *inter linea,* between the lines."

Edging backward to the cave's mouth, Artos opened the book and scanned the first page. His fingers underlined each word, his mouth formed them. He turned the page. Then he looked up puzzled. "There is nothing written between the lines. Sir."

Something rather like a chuckle crossed with a cough echoed from the cave. "There is always something written between the lines. But it takes great wisdom to read it."

"Then why me, sir? I have little wisdom."

"Because… because you are here."

"Here?"

"Today. And not back at Ector's feeding his brachet or cleaning out the mews or sweating in the smithy or fighting with that pack of unruly boys. Here. For the getting of wisdom." The dragon made stretching noises.

"Oh."

There was a sudden tremendous wheezing and clanking and a strange, "Oh-oh," from the dragon.

Artos peered into the back of the cave nervously. It was all darkness and shadow and an occasional finger of firelight. "Are you all right? Sir?"

A long silence followed during which Artos wondered whether he should go to the dragon. He wondered if he had even the smallest amount of wisdom needed to help out. Then, just as he was about to make the plunge, the dragon's voice came hissing back. "Yessssss, boy."

"Yes what, sir?"

"Yessssss I am all right."

"Well, then," said Artos, putting one foot quietly behind the other, "thank you for my wisdom."

A furious flame spat across the cave, leaping through the darkness to lick Artos's feet. He jumped back, startled at the dragon's accuracy and suddenly hideously afraid. Had it just been preparation for the dragon's dinner after all? He suddenly wished for the sword he had not yet purchased, turned, and ran out of the cave.

The dragon's voice followed him. "Ssssssssilly child. That was not the wisdom."

From a safe place alongside the outside wall of the cave, Artos peeked in. "There's more?" he asked.

"By the time I am through with you, Artos Pendragon, Arthur son of the dragon, you will read *inter linea* in people as well." There was a loud moan and another round of furious clanking, and then total silence.

Taking it as a dismissal and holding the book hard against his chest, Artos ran down the hill. Whatever else he thought about as he neared the castle walls, topmost in his mind was what he would tell Mag about the loss of the gravy pot. It might mean another kiss. That was the fell thought that occupied him all the way home.

Artos could not read the book without help, he knew it at once. The sentences were much too long and interspersed with Latin and other languages. Perhaps that was the between the lines the dragon had meant. The only help available was Old Linn, and he did not appear until well after dinner. Unfortunately, that was the time that Artos was the busiest, feeding the dogs, checking the jesses on the hawks, cleaning the smithy. Father Bertram might have helped had he still been alive, though somehow Artos doubted it. The dragon's book was neither Testament nor commentary, that much he *could* read, and the good father had been fierce about what he had considered proper fare. The castle bonfires had often burned texts of which he disapproved. Even Lady Marion's *Book of Hours*, which had taken four scribes the full part of a year to set down, had gone up in Father Bertram's righteous flames because Adam and Eve had no fig leaves. This Artos had on good authority, though he had never seen it himself, for Lady Marion had complained to Lady Sylvia who had tittered about it to her serving girls who passed the news along with the gravy to young Cai who had mentioned it as a joke to his friends in the cow shed when Artos, who had been napping in the haymow, overheard them.

No, the good Father Bertram would never have helped. Old Linn, though, was different. He could read four tongues well: English, Latin, Greek, and bardic runes. It was said his room was full of books. He could recite the "Conception of Pyrderi," a tale Artos loved for the sheer sound of it, and the stories about the children of Llyr and the Cauldron and the Iron House and the horse made for Bran. Or at least Linn used to be able to tell them all. Before he had been taken ill so suddenly and dramatically, his best piece had always been the "Battle of the Trees." Artos could not remember a time when dinners of great importance at the castle had not ended with Linn's declaiming of it. In fact, Lord Ector's Irish retainers called Linn *shanachie*, which, as far as Artos could tell from their garbled and endless explanations, simply meant "storyteller." But they said the word with awe when coupling it to Old Linn's name.

The problem, Artos thought, was that the old man hated him. Well, perhaps *hate* was too strong a word, but he seemed to prefer the young gentlemen of the house, not the impoverished fosterling. Linn especially lavished attention on Sir Cai who, as far as Artos was concerned, long ago let his muscles o'ertake his head. And Sir Bedvere, slack-jawed and hardhanded. And Sir Lancot, the pretty boy. Once Artos, too, had tried to curry favor with the trio of lordlings, fetching and carrying and helping them with their schoolwork. But then they all grew up, and the three grew up faster and taller and louder. And once Sir Lancot as a joke had pulled Artos's pants down around his ankles in the courtyard and the other two called out the serving maids to gawk. And that led to Mag's getting sweet on him, which was why he had grown to despise Mag and pity the boys, even though they were older and bigger and better placed than he.

Still, there was a time for putting aside such feelings, thought Artos. The getting of wisdom was surely such a time. He would need help in reading the dragon's book. None of the others, Cai or Bedvere or Lancot, could read half as well as he. They could only just make out the prayers in their psalters. Sir Ector could not read at all. So it would have to be Old Linn.

But to his despair, the apothecary could not be found after dinner. In desperation, he went to talk to the old man's best friend, the smith.

"Come now, young Art," called out Magnus Pieter as Artos approached the smith. "Did we not have words just yesterday? Something about a sword and a stone?"

Artos tried to think of a way to get the conversation around to Linn's whereabouts, but the conversation would not move at his direction. The smith willed it where he would. At last there was nothing left to do but remove the leathern bag around his neck and take out the jewel. He dropped it onto the anvil. It made a funny little pinging sound.

Magnus sucked on his lower lip and snorted through his nose. "By God, boy, and where'd you get that stone?"

To tell the truth meant getting swat for a liar. He suddenly realized it would be the same if he showed the book to Linn. So he lied. "I was left it by... Father Bertram," he said. "And I've..." The lies came slowly. He was by inclination an honest boy. He preferred silence to an untruth.

"Kept it till now, have you?" asked the smith. "Well, well, and of course you have. After all, there's not much in that village of ours to spend such a jewel on."

Artos nodded silently, thankful to have Magnus Pieter do the lying for him.

"And what would you be wanting for such a jewel?" asked the smith with the heavy-handed jocularity he always confused with cunning.

Knowing that he must play the innocent in order to get the better bargain, Artos said simply, "Why, a sword, of course."

"Of course!" Magnus Pieter laughed, hands on hips, throwing his head way back.

Since the other two smiths he had met laughed in just that way, Artos assumed it was something taught.

The smith stopped laughing and cocked his head to one side. "Well?"

"I am old enough to have a sword of my own," said Artos. "And now I can pay for a good one."

"How good?" asked the smith in his heavy manner.

Artos knelt before the anvil and the red jewel was at the level of his eyes. As if he were addressing the stone and not the smith, he chanted a bit from a song Old Linn used to sing:

And aye their swordes soe sore can byte,
Throughe help of gramarye...

From behind him the smith sighed. "Aye," the old man said, "and a good sword it shall be. A fine blade, a steel of power. And while I make it for you, young poet, you must think of a good name for your sword from this stone." He reached across Artos's shoulder and plucked up the jewel, holding it high over both their heads.

Artos stood slowly, never once taking his eyes from the jewel. For a moment he thought he saw dragon fire leaping and crackling there. Then he remembered the glowing coals of the forge. The stone reflected that, nothing more.

"Perhaps," he said, thinking out loud, "perhaps I shall call it Inter Linea."

The smith smiled. "Fine name, that. Makes me think of foreign climes." He pocketed the stone and began to work. Artos turned and left, for he had chores to do in the mews.

Each day that followed meant another slobbery kiss from Mag and another pot of stew. It seemed to Artos a rather messy prelude to wisdom. But after a week of it, he found the conversations with the dragon worth the mess.

The dragon spoke knowingly of other lands where men walked on their heads instead of feet. Of lands down beneath the sea where the bells rang in underwater churches with each passing wave. It taught Artos riddles and their answers, like

As round as an apple, as deep as a cup,
And all the king's horses can't pull it up,

which was a *well*, of course.

And it sang him ballads from the prickly, gorse-covered land of the Scots who ran naked and screaming into battle. And songs from the cold, icy Norsemen who prowled in their dragon ships. And love songs from the silk-and-honey lands of Araby.

And once the dragon taught him a trick with pots and jewels, clanking and creaking noisily all the while, its huge foot mixing up the pots till Artos's head fair ached to know under which one lay the emerald as big as an egg. And that game he had used later with Lancot and Bedvere and Cai and won from them a number of gold coins till they threatened him. With his promised new sword he might have beaten them, but not with his bare hands. So he used a small man's wiles to trick them once again, picked up the winnings, and left them grumbling over the cups and peas he had used for the game.

And so day by day, week by week, month by month, Artos gained wisdom.

It took three tries and seven months before Artos had his sword. Each new steel had something unacceptable about it. The first had a hilt that did not sit comfortably in his hand. Bedvere claimed it instead, and Magnus Pieter was so pleased with the coins Sir Bedvere paid it was weeks before he was ready to work another. Instead he shoed horses, made latches, and built a gigantic candelabrum for the dining room to Lady Marion's specifications.

The second sword had a strange crossbar that the smith swore would help protect the hand. Artos thought the sword unbalanced but Cai, who prized newness over all things, insisted that he wanted that blade. Again Magnus Pieter was pleased enough to spend the weeks following making farm implements like plowshares and hoes.

The third sword was still bright with its tempering when Lancot claimed it.

"Cai and Bedvere have new swords," Lancot said, his handsome face drawn down with longing. He reached his hand out.

Artos, who had been standing in the shadows of the smithy, was about to say something when Old Linn hobbled in. His mouth and hair spoke of a lingering illness, both being yellowed and lifeless. But his voice was strong.

"You were always a man true to his word," he reminded the smith.

"And true to my swords," said Magnus Pieter, pleased with the play.

Artos stepped from the shadows then and held out his hand. The smith put the sword in it and Artos turned it this way and that to catch the light. The watering on the blade made a strange pattern that looked like the flame from a dragon's mouth. It sat well and balanced in his hand.

"He likes the blade," said Old Linn.

Magnus Pieter shrugged, smiling.

Artos turned to thank the apothecary but he was gone and so was Lancot. When he peered out the smithy door, there were the two of them walking arm in arm up the winding path toward the castle.

"So you've got your Inter Linea now," said the smith. "And about time you took one. Nothing wrong with the other two."

"*And* you got a fine price for them," Artos said.

The smith returned to his anvil, and the clang of hammer on new steel ended their conversation.

Artos ran out of the castle grounds, hallooing so loudly even the tortoise dozing on the rusted helm lifted its sleepy head. He fairly leaped over the two rocks in the path. They seemed to have gotten smaller with each trip to the dragon's lair. He was calling still when he approached the entrance to the cave.

"Ho, old flametongue," he cried out, the sword allowing him his first attempt at familiarity. "Furnace-lung, look what I have. My sword. From the stone you gave me. It is a rare beauty."

There was no answer.

Suddenly afraid that he had overstepped the bounds and that the dragon lay sulking within, Artos peered inside.

The cave was dark, cold, silent.

Slowly Artos walked in and stopped about halfway. He felt surrounded by the icy silence. But that was all. There was no sense of dragon there. No presence.

"Sir? Father dragon? Are you home?" He put a hand up to one of the hanging stones to steady himself. In the complete dark he had little sense of what was up and what was down.

Then he laughed. "Oh, I know, you have gone out on a flight." It was the only answer that came to him, though the dragon had never once mentioned flying. But everyone knows dragons have wings. And wings mean flight. Artos laughed again, a hollow little chuckle. Then he turned toward the small light of the cave entrance. "I'll come back tomorrow. At my regular time," he called over his shoulder. He said it out loud just in case the dragon's magic extended to retrieving words left in the still cave air. "Tomorrow," Artos promised.

But the pattern had been altered subtly and, like a weaving gone awry, could not be changed back to the way it had been without a weakness in the cloth.

The next day Artos did not go to the cave. Instead he practiced swordplay with willow wands in the main courtyard, beating Cai soundly and being beaten in turn by both Bedvere and Lancot.

The following morn, he and the three older boys were sent by Lady Marion on a fortnight's journey to gather gifts of jewels and silks from the market towns for the coming holy days. Some at Ector's castle celebrated the solstice with the druids, some kept the holy day for the Christ child's birth, and a few of the old soldiers still drank bull's blood and spoke of Mithras in secret meetings under the castle, for there was a vast warren of halls and rooms there. But they all gave gifts to one another at the year's turning, whichever gods they knelt to.

It was Artos's first such trip. The other boys had gone the year before under Linn's guidance. This year the four of them were given leave to go alone. Cai was so pleased he forgave Artos for the beating. Suddenly, they were the best of friends. And Bedvere and Lancot, who had beaten him, loved Artos now as well, for even when he had been on the ground with the wand at his throat and his face and arms red from the lashings, he had not cried "Hold." There had been not even the hint of tears in his eyes. They admired him for that.

With his bright new sword belted at his side, brand-new leggings from the castle stores, and the new-sworn friends riding next to him, it was no wonder Artos forgot the dragon and the dark cave. Or, if he did not exactly forget, what he remembered was that the dragon hadn't been there when he wanted it the most. So, for a few days, for a fortnight, Artos felt he could, like Cai, glory in the new.

He did not glory in the dragon. It was old, old past counting the years, old past helping him, old and forgetful.

They came home with red rosy cheeks polished by the winter wind and bags packed with treasure. An extra two horses carried the overflow.

Cai, who had lain with his first girl, a serving wench of little beauty and great reputation, was full of new boasts. Bedvere and Lancot had won a junior tourney for boys under sixteen, Bedvere with his sword and Lancot his lance. And though Artos had been a favorite on the outbound trip, full of wonderful stories, riddles, and songs, as they turned toward home he had lapsed into long silences. By the time they were but a day's hard ride away, it was as if his mouth were bewitched.

The boys teased him, thinking it was Mag who worried him. "Afraid of Old Garlic, then?" asked Cai. "At least Rosemary's breath was sweet." (Rosemary being the serving wench's name.)

"Or are you afraid of my sword?" said Bedvere.

"Or my lance?" Lancot added brightly.

When he kept silent, they tried to wheedle the cause of his set lips by reciting castle gossip. Every maiden, every alewife, every false nurse was named. Then they turned their attention to the men. They never mentioned dragons, though, for they did not know one lived by the castle walls. Artos had never told them of it.

But it was the dragon, of course, that concerned him. With each mile he remembered the darkness, the complete silence of the cave. At night he dreamed of it, the cave opening staring down from the hill like the empty eye socket of a long-dead beast.

They unpacked the presents carefully and carried them up to Lady Marion's quarters. She, in turn, fed them wine and cakes in her apartments, a rare treat. Her minstrel, a handsome boy except for his wandering left eye, sang a number of songs while they ate, even one in a Norman dialect. Artos drank only a single mouthful of the sweet wine. He ate nothing. He had heard all the songs before.

Thus it was well past sundown before Lady Marion let them go.

Artos would not join the others who were going to report to Lord Ector. He pushed past Cai and ran down the stairs. The other boys called after him, but he ignored them. Only the startled ends of their voices followed him.

He hammered on the gate until the guards lifted the iron portcullis, then he ran across the moat bridge. Dark muddy lumps in the mushy ice were the only signs of life.

As he ran, he held his hand over his heart, cradling the two pieces of cake he had slipped into his tunic. Since he had had no time to beg stew from Mag, he hoped seed cakes would do instead. He did not, for a moment, believe the dragon had starved to death without his poor offering of stew. The dragon had existed many years before Artos had found the cave. It was not the *size* of the stew, but the fact of it.

He stubbed his toe on the second outcropping hard enough to force a small mewing sound between his lips. The tor was icy and that made climbing it difficult. Foolishly he'd forgotten his gloves with his saddle gear. And he'd neglected to bring a light.

When he got to the mouth of the cave and stepped in, he was relieved to hear heavy breathing echoing off the cave wall, until he realized it was the sound of his own ragged breath.

"*Dragon!*" he cried out, his voice a misery.

Suddenly there was a small moan and an even smaller glow, like dying embers that have been breathed upon one last time.

"Is that you, my son?" The voice was scarcely a whisper, so quiet the walls could not find enough to echo.

"Yes, dragon," said Artos. "It is I."

"Did you bring me any stew?"

"Only two seed cakes."

"I like seed cakes."

"Then I'll bring them to you."

"Noooooooo." The sound held only the faintest memory of the powerful voice of before.

But Artos had already started toward the back of the cave, one hand in front to guide himself around the overhanging rocks. He was halfway there when he stumbled against something and fell heavily to his knees. Feeling around, he touched a long, metallic curved blade.

"Has someone been here? Has someone tried to slay you?" he cried. Then, before the dragon could answer, Artos's hand traveled farther along the blade to its strange metallic base.

His hands told him what his eyes could not, his mouth spoke what his heart did not want to hear. "It is the dragon's foot."

He leaped over the metal construct and scrambled over a small rocky wall. Behind it, in the dying glow of a small fire, lay an old man on a straw bed. Near him were tables containing beakers full of colored liquids—amber, rose, green, and gold. On the wall were strange toothed wheels with handles.

The old man raised himself on one arm. "Pendragon," he said and tried to set his lips into a welcoming smile. "Son."

"Old Linn," replied Artos angrily, "I am no son of yours."

"There was once," the old man began quickly, settling into a story before Artos's anger had time to gel, "a man who would know Truth. And he traveled all over the land looking."

Without willing it, Artos was pulled into the tale.

"He looked along the seacoasts and in the quiet farm dales. He went into the country of lakes and across vast deserts seeking Truth. At last, one dark night in a small cave atop a hill, he found her. Truth was a wizened old woman with but a single tooth left in her head. Her eyes were rheumy. Her hair greasy strands. But when she called him into her cave, her voice was low and lyric and pure and that was how he knew he had found Truth."

Artos stirred uneasily.

The old man went on. "He stayed a year and a day by her side and learned all she had to teach. And when his time was done, he said, 'My Lady Truth, I must go back to my own home now. But I would do something for you in exchange.'" Linn stopped. The silence between them grew until it was almost a wall.

"Well, what did she say?" Artos asked at last.

"She told him, 'When you speak of me, tell your people that I am young and beautiful.'"

For a moment Artos said nothing. Then he barked out a short, quick laugh.

"So much for Truth."

Linn sat up and patted the mattress beside him, an invitation that Artos ignored. "Would you have listened these seven months to an old apothecary who had a tendency to fits?"

"You did not tell me the truth."

"I did not lie. You *are* the dragon's son."

Artos set his mouth and turned his back on the old man. His voice came out low and strained. "*I… am… not… your… son.*"

"It is true that you did not spring from my loins," said the old man. "But I carried you here to Ector's castle and waited and hoped you would seek out my wisdom. But you longed for the truth of lance and sword. I did not have that to give." His voice was weak and seemed to end in a terrible sigh.

Artos did not turn around. "I believed in the dragon."

Linn did not answer.

"I *loved* the dragon."

The silence behind him was so loud that at last Artos turned around. The old man had fallen onto his side and lay still. Artos felt something warm on his cheeks and realized it was tears. He ran to Linn and knelt down, pulling the old man onto his lap. As he cradled him, Linn opened his eyes.

"Did you bring me any stew?" he asked.

"I…" The tears were falling unchecked now. "I brought you seed cakes."

"I like seed cakes," Linn said. "But couldn't you get any stew from Old Garlic?"

Artos felt his mouth drop open. "How did you know about her?"

The old man smiled, showing terrible teeth. He whispered, "I am the Great Riddler. I am the Master of Wisdoms. I am the Word and I am the Light. I Was and Am and Will Be." He hesitated. "I am The Dragon."

Artos smiled back and then carefully stood with the old man in his arms. He was amazed at how frail Linn was. His bones, Artos thought, must be as hollow as the wing bones of a bird.

There was a door in the cave wall and Linn signaled him toward it. Carrying the old apothecary through the doorway, Artos marveled at the runes carved in the lintel. Past the door was a warren of hallways and rooms. From somewhere ahead he could hear the chanting of many men.

Artos looked down at the old man and whispered to him. "Yes. I understand. You *are* the dragon, indeed. And I am the dragon's boy. But I will not let you die just yet. I have not finished getting my wisdom."

Smiling broadly, the old man turned toward him like a baby rooting at its mother's breast, found the seed cakes, ate one of them and then, with a gesture both imperious and fond, stuffed the other in Artos's mouth.

THE MIRACLE AQUILINA
Margo Lanagan

Margo Lanagan was born in Newcastle, New South Wales, Australia, and has a BA in History from Sydney University. She spent ten years as a freelance book editor and currently makes a living as a technical writer. Lanagan has published junior and teenage fiction novels, including fantasies *WildGame*, *The Tankermen*, and *Walking Through Albert*. She has also written instalments in two shared-world fantasy series for junior readers, and has published three acclaimed original story collections: *White Time*, double World Fantasy Award winner *Black Juice*, and *Red Spikes*. Her latest book is a fantasy novel, *Tender Morsels*, a World Fantasy Award winner and Printz Award Honor book. Lanagan is working on a new novel, *The Brides of Rollrock Island*, and collection *Yellowcake*. Lanagan lives in Sydney, Australia.

You'd have thought the bread-dough was the Captain's head, the way I went at it, squashing any mouth or eye that opened. *Bringing shame upon us*—smush, I smeared that mouth shut. *No daughter of mine*—punch, that one too. Daughter of his? I was my own self; he did not own me. If I was anyone else's I was Klepper's; he owned more parts of me than Father did, than father wanted to *know* about. I was *married* to Klepper in all but name; part of him floated in me, growing slowly into a bigger shame—

Thump, squash—I shook the thought out of my head. Reddy was spinning one of her stories—of a fisher-girl and a kingmaker, this one—to keep Amber and Roper quiet at their needlework, and I began to listen too, to stop from thinking more, from caring, from fearing. And I was almost lost in the poor girl's story—how insolent she was to the king, and how lucky he did not have her hanged for it!—when the Captain strode in, all leathered-plate and rage. He had his helmet on, even; he was only indoors for a moment.

"Here," he said. "I'll show you." He came for me, and so swiftly I didn't even flinch away. He grasped my arm; he tore me off the dough and pushed me to the door, my hands all floury claws. "I'll show you how girls end up, that don't do as they're told."

Reddy was half up, and Amber and Roper turned in their seats, a matched pair, but they would do nothing, only gape there. They would never defy him, or question; they would never save me. Then we were out on the bright street, and me all apronned and floury. I shook him off, but he caught my elbow again, hard, that everyone should see he was in command of me.

"This woman." He muttered it as if woman-ness itself were an evil. "She worships wooden saints—you've seen them. She prostrates herself before those foolish things. Which would be bad enough."

There was a law, that those people be left at peace in their beliefs. Even if our Aquilin gods were richer and more clearly seen—for their stories and families were all written down strand for strand, and painted on walls for those of us who couldn't read, and taught in church and school—still we were to indulge the saint-followers, allow them their shrines and mutterings, only jeer among ourselves.

"She was one of ours, from a faithful family, but her nurse impressed her to the saints-belief, corrupted her." Ah, that was the cause of his bitterness, was it?

"She's to be punished for that?" I said, because I was not sure what the law was, for our people gone over to the saints' ways, but I did not think we could call it exactly a *crime*.

"No!" He pushed me to the right, through the council portico, along the colonnade there, people glancing at us but too important about their own business to accost us. "She refused the King himself, is her offence!"

"Refused him what?" I struggled as much as I could without making a scene. "Let go of me! I will walk with you!"

"You will," he said, "you will." And did not let go. "Refused him herself. Her hand, or failing that her body. Wife or concubine he offered her. Wife! Out in the fields with her sheep, she was! Who knows what vermin were on her; who knows what lads had been at her willy-nilly? And our King says *I will have you, I will save you, you are beautiful enough to be queen or mistress to me*! And *No!*, she says! She would rather turn to leather out there on the hillside, making her signs on herself, chattering to her pixies. A madwoman, or at the least imprudent! You will see, though." He shook me, and I staggered. "You will see how imprudence is dealt with, and wilfulness."

We were going down the backs now, where it was unpaved, and smelt, and was narrow. He pushed me ahead of him. There was the barracks, with soldiers smoking at the upper windows, grinning down, and the woman-houses, the crones at the doors watching us shrewdly as we passed. Then we turned the corner, and there was the prison, blind of windows, its wall-tops all spikes and potsherds.

The guard at the entry-way saluted my father, staring hard at nothing. For a moment I felt the bitterness of belonging to a Captain. This guard's respect was for my father's rank only; the Captain the man was as nothing to him. *I* was as nothing, a parcel or a document the Captain brought with him to his place of work.

In we went, and along in the blind stony darkness, farther in and along again, until we were deep in the place. He was imprisoning me? He was placing me in a cell, to teach me this lesson? I would not learn it, no matter what weight of stone and military he put about me, no matter how long he kept me from the world.

Finally we came to a door that stood open; here the guard gave me a look of alarm, even as he sharpened his stance for my father. From inside came the sound of a whip through the air, like a little outraged shout, and a slap on something wet.

The chamber was vast, yet not airy. Evils were done here, it was easy to tell; their equipments reared and languished in the shadows, away from the men grouped torchlit in the middle of the room.

The woman was in a cleared space at their centre, as straight as if she stood on a hilltop stretching to glimpse a distant beacon. Her back was to us; her dress-cloth was shredded into her flesh from the whipping; her blood ran freely down.

"Her legs," said the King. You could tell him by his seatedness and stillness; if a gathering can have two centres, he was the other.

Two soldiers hoisted up her skirts, from bare dirty heels, from white calves. The backs of her knees made my insides shrink, the vulnerable creases of them, the fine skin.

"Her buttocks, too," said His Majesty.

Something gave, in the crowd of men—a kind of relief, or excitement. The soldiers pulled the skirts up above her thighs and buttocks—all I could think was how soft, how that flesh would sting to the whip. My own buttocks clenched at the sight, my own thighs expected that sting. But the woman herself, she stood straight and trembled not at all, as if there were no indignity in what they did, let alone any pain to come.

They made her hold her own skirts aside; the first strokes striped, then diamonded her flesh. She did not wince, or cry out. Her back glittered crimson in the torches' light, and black with the wet threads; now the stripes on her thighs and calves began to join together red; now the first gleam of blood showed there.

"The arrogance of her!" growled the Captain to himself, and this seemed to remind him that he had a voice, and he took my arm harder, and shook it. "You see? This is what's done to girls who will not be bid!"

He met my eye and he was all hot rage, that this demonstrating to me was even necessary. He could not turn me by the power of his words. He could raise his voice as loud and long as he liked, but he could not control me by the raising, as once he'd used to. *I will see whom I please,* I'd said. *I will marry whom I please. It is Klepper I want, not some rock-headed legionnaire you owe a favour to.*

"Cease," said the King's cold voice onto the congested air, and there was no sound but the breathing of the soldiers who had been taking turns to beat the woman. "Let me see her," he said.

She did not wait for them to turn her, but dropped her skirts, and spun on the wetness of her own spilt blood, to face him. The soldiers moved to take her arms, much as the Captain had mine, but the King waved them aside, a casual movement, but involving many weighty rings, from which red light flashed, and a shard of kingfisher blue.

They stepped back from her; she stood, tall and full of joy, and truly my breath stopped in my throat for several moments, for it was clear what drove the King to want to marry her. She was the model of an Aquilina: broad-browed, straight-nosed, full-lipped, strong-jawed, all strength and delicacy combined. Her eyes were clear, green, open; they gazed down at the King, almost in amusement, I thought. I loved her in an instant myself, for what they had done to her, and for why. But he is the *King!*, I thought. What does she have, that she can dismiss the King's wishes? That she is not dazzled by him, that she holds her own ground? I wanted to know, and I wanted it for myself.

"What have you to say, shepherdess?" There was steel in the King's voice, for he saw, as all of us could see, that she had defeated him with her carriage and beauty.

"I have nothing to say, sir," she said happily.

"Are you mad, girl?" said a courtier at the King's side. I had seen that man before. I didn't like him; he was all bones and brains. "Have your pains driven you mad, that you affect such cheer, such insolence?"

She glanced at him bemused, then returned her gaze to His Majesty. "I assure you, I have all my senses at my own command."

"You will marry me, then," he said, his voice momentarily softer, fuller, with something in it that would have been pleading, had this not been the Aquilin king, who pled with no one, not prelate or general or sultan or sent prince from foreign parts of anywhere in the world.

"I will not," she said. "As I have told you, I belong body and soul—"

"To your lord," said Mr. Bones-and-brains disgustedly. "Yes, girl, we have heard all that." He waved her to turn her back on us again. "Bite deeper, lads! Scatter the floor with her flesh!"

Willingly she turned. But a gasp went up, from me and from all around me. For though her blood had stained all the back of her skirt, though she stood in a puddle and her feet were red with it, her flesh within the torn dress-back was white, was clean, as if no whip had touched it. And when they lifted her skirts, her calves there, and then her thighs and buttocks, were unwelted and unbled, restored entirely to wholeness, to perfection.

Astonishment stilled them all, the soldiers agape, the nobles hands to mouths. Then gradually all turned from the marvel of the woman's recovery to His Majesty. He gazed on her grimly, up and down, his eyes a-glisten with moving thought. What would he do? What power was being shown him, that undid this work of his upon this woman's body? Whom did she have behind her, and how would he conquer them?

"Put her in the pot," he said very softly—you see, Father, how much power a *soft* voice can carry? "We will make a soup of her."

There, again, the air changed; the excitement pitched itself a little higher, into a kind of gaiety. All was business and haste to obey him, our King our church our god and saints. I had never seen it so direct, how his will drove us, how he sat at the centre and played us all like game-pieces, or as a spinner's foot sets the pedal, then the wheel, in motion.

Pale-faced, the Captain pulled me back against the wall. "She is some kind of monster!" He watched the summoned servants run for kindling.

"She is one of us," I said. Her Aquilin hair gleamed motionless, smooth black around her head, caught away forward over one shoulder so as not to snarl with the blood-wetted whip. "And she is a miracle. If truly it is her Lord—"

He slapped my cheek, hard.

I regarded him, half my face burning from the blow, my eyes drinking back the tears that had sprung from the shock of it. His fear and weakness were written strong as his rage in his face. *Don't think I cannot force you,* he had said to me. But I did think it; I knew it. My sisters would bow their heads and do what he told them, but I—he had this weakness in him, when it came to me. He had this softness. I would have my way.

"We should worship her as a miracle," I said evenly, coldly, straight into his eyes.

"We should kill her, and smartly! She is a demon! The longer she lives, the longer she dazzles such fools as you! You will see," he hissed close to my face, "how pretty she is, all red-boiled and bursting. You will see what insolence will bring you, and thinking you can please yourself!"

It took some while to ready the pot, though boiling water was brought down from the council-house kitchens. It was a large pot, big enough to boil several people at once, I would have thought. They built the fire so high that the walkway around the top of the pot began to scorch, and a man was sent up there, to keep it wettened, and not catch fire himself. Every face about me, except for the King's and the more important of the courtiers' imitating him, was alive with surprise and curiosity, or with a kind of greed—whether for more suffering by the Aquilina or more embarrassment of the King I could not tell—and some with suppressed mirth. Whatever his state of mind, every man here, at this moment, contained very little more than the vitality of his interest in what would befall them next, this woman and this king, what damage would be done by each upon the other. I was glad the maid had her back to us still and did not see any of this, how eagerly men wished her ill, and the lengths they were going to, to see her harmed and to have that harm endure.

They led the woman to a spread net of rope, such as is used to tangle and tie a mad bull in, and subdue it. They made her stand in the middle of it; they threw the corner-ties over a ceiling-beam and the net rose around her and lifted her, and up it carried her to the railing of the pot-platform, where a hook held it aside from the rising steam. Up went the King and his nearest; one of these turned and beckoned for more to climb the wooden steps, and my father was high-ranked enough that he could bustle me up there, and press me to the front of the crowd, where a second railing kept us from pitching forward ourselves into the bubbles, into the cauldron full of torch-flash and darkness.

"You see what fate awaits you, girl," said the King, stilling the murmur around him that the sight of the water had started.

Silence from the net.

"Answer His Majesty!" snapped some official.

"His Majesty did not ask a question," she said coolly; I could not see her face for stripes of rope-shadow. But her voice was clear enough, fine and light among these rumblers and roarers. "Yes," she said, "I see my fate there in that water, in that fire—is that the answer you wish for?" A green eye, only, looking sharpish out.

"You know the answer I want, girl," said the King, and truly he did look most handsome and noble, regarding her fiercely and gently both, as if he could not quite believe what he had come to, as if he might take pity on her at any moment, did she show any sign of distress, or of indecision. "Marry me and you live. Refuse me and I lower you to boiling."

"Then lower me, Your Majesty, if those are my only choices. For my body and soul are not mine to give to you." And her fingers, strong and lean and sun-browned, sprang through the netting and grasped it in preparation.

Soldiers unhooked her, and let her out to swing in the steam, in the silence but for the fire-noise, but for the water bursting and rolling. Within the ropes, she looked up and listened, as if she were a child hiding, waiting for the seeker to find her, for her amusement to begin.

The King gave a sign. Some other behind him passed it on, and the men below began to let out the rope.

It would have been most unsatisfactory for His Majesty, for the drowning woman let out not a whimper, let alone a scream or a begging for mercy, but went down into the water silent as a turnip or herbouquet, and the water closed over her head, and her dark hair lifted and snaked on the bubbled water a moment among the ropes. Then, only the weighted corner ropes stood stiff out of the turmoiling water, and the steam buffeted all our faces, without cease.

"There," said the King. His be-ringed hand gestured for the bringing up of her body. Little sighs of accomplishment sounded around us, murmurs of excitement at the prospect of seeing what had been done on her, but my father the Captain only leaned, with his wrists on the rail and his hands fisted, looking down, watching the woman boil.

Up they hoisted her, but we could not see her immediately for the steam pouring up and the water pouring down, and then she was only a slumped thing in the net there. The man with the hook-stick caught and pulled the net towards the platform, and a space was made, several people having to move down the steps to make room.

But not us; we were only one layer of watchers from where she was brought to land. Her small foot hung white below.

"You said she would be boiled red," I whispered to the Captain.

The foot touched the wooden platform and dragged as if it were dead—but then the touch woke it, and it braced itself against the boards, and in the moment that the net was loosed from above and fell open about her, up rose the shepherdess, the miracle girl, to standing. The steam of the boiled rope, of her boiled self, rushed up, rushed out. "Praise my Lord and Lady and all the Saints for their works and wonders!" came her clear, happy voice out of the cloud, and there she was, not a mark upon her, no worse for her wetting, or for being wrapped in boiling-wet cloth and cloaked in boiling-wet hair.

All fell back from her—in horror, in wonder, in both—and the Captain pulled me back too, so it should appear I did the right thing, instead of standing forward and laughing and clapping my hands with delight, as I was tempted to do.

The King? I saw a flash in his eyes, just a moment there and then gone, of the rage I had seen in the Captain's face, hissing and pressed close to mine. Then the handsome man was dead-pan again.

"Bring my robe and mask," he said, and on the word *mask* his voice broke to a growl. "Bring me a flask of spirit. Bring reeds, bring knives—you know what I need." He did not look at those he commanded; his gaze was fixed on the steaming, smiling woman.

The courtiers looked to Bones-and-brains, who was a little forward of them, startled-faced and on the point of speaking. But the King was motionless, watching the shepherdess like a hunter keeping a faun in sight as he fits an arrow to the string. Mr. Bones stepped back into the servants' doubtful silence, not taking his eyes from his master. "You heard His Majesty," he said sharply over his shoulder.

The whole platform about us was glances like knives or darts thrown hither and thither, the very air dangerous with them. The Captain kept his grim face so steady that I could watch in his eyes the last of the steam rising off the lady, but the rest of the court and chamber were too nervous to speak or stay still. "Where should we be?" hissed someone. "Is it safe for us?"

The King stepped towards the outer railing, men scattering like shooed flies before him. He looked down on the great room; there was standing-room for many watchers around the rack, and the wheel, and on either side of the cat-pit. "Along the wall there," he said with a large gesture.

"All along, sir?" said Mr. Bones, with doubt in his voice, then, "Very well," he added most obediently.

"What is he doing? What is he planning?" I hissed under the turn and shuffle of people around us, the quiet exclamations around the King's iron silence.

"He does it in battle," said the Captain, his voice dead of opinion or feeling. "Only a King has this power; the priests awaken it when they invest him."

"Power to what?" I knew a dozen outlandish stories: that the King could fly, or call down thunderbolts, or conjure great winds to flatten the enemy like a field of grain stalks.

The Captain only watched. No one seemed ready to climb down from our platform here. Men ran about below, and castle-servants came with arms full of *reeds*, of all things, green harmless reeds, and were told where and how to lay them on the flags. Mr. Bones directed them very quietly and calmly, perhaps hoping to be halted in this work by his king, and not wanting to miss hearing that command.

They laid out a wide shape with the reeds lengthwise up and down it, something like a very fat, very flattened scorpion, legged and tailed. Then bags and bags, they brought, of tiny knives with nubby handles smooth as finger-bones, and the blades also short like fish-fins, with one vicious edge. I had seen someone draw the shape in the dust somewhere, whispering, and sweep the shape away when I asked what it was. Dozens of these knife-lets they laid out in a kind of crown around the shape's head, and in a double line fanning inward down its middle, then flaring outward and edging its tail. All while they worked the King watched closed-mouthed from the platform, and the shepherdess behind him at the centre of her net and her strangeness stood sodden and proud-backed, clasping her hands before her, her face neither raised in arrogance nor lowered in humiliation. She met no one's gaze and spoke not a word, but only was fully engaged with her own thoughts and her own will. Around her grew a fear and a thickening silence, pricked by knife-clinks on the flagstones, underlined by Bones-and-brains's soft voice.

The shape was complete upon the floor; now a priest approached the platform, a pile of darkness in his arms. He was an older priest, not frail—no Aquilin priest lacks bodily strength—but honed almost to a skeleton by his life of privations and the cruel torchlight.

"Wait, I will come down," said the King, and a sigh of terror and doubt sounded around my father and me, a tiny wind, quick-suppressed. The King turned at the top of the stairs: 'Bring her!' he cried, and with a shock I thought he meant bring *me*, but of course he spoke of the woman there. "Come, men." He glanced at the assembly, and I took care to put my face behind a man's shoulder, so that he would not see and dismiss me. "Stand like men behind your god and king."

The Captain held me back, while others with many doubtful glances at one another shuffled stairwards and down. Soldiers took the woman in hand. She came awake at their touch, but did not resist it, and allowed herself to be taken as if this were a favour being done her, not a punishment being administered. And as the guard passed with her, she saw me, unshielded now by any man but only in my floury apron, with still my sleeves rolled up for the baking and my hands half-wiped of the makings, and the strings of my house-cap dangling down.

I stifled a curtsey; she saw that. She saw, I was sure, all my thoughts and words caught in my throat, too many of them to say. It surprised her greatly to see me here so domestic, so unbelonging—she paused, and the guard allowed it, and she held her mouth on the point of its blossoming into a smile. Her gaze touched my Captain's hand upon my arm, the tightness of his grip. She gave the tiniest, tiniest tilt of her head and a nod to me, in the fleet moment in which we met, and she went on, her wet skirt drawing a train of water across the boards of the platform. I felt myself to have been blessed. Every moment rang and swelled with meanings now, death had been so close, and the wonders so great by which she had evaded it.

"We stay here," said the Captain. He drew me to the corner of the platform and penned me there, standing behind me. I felt very vulnerable, with my clear view, vulnerable to dismissal, vulnerable to whatever evil might happen below. I shielded my own father, who had called himself my protector once, who had stood to my defence in tiny battles I had had, against my sisters, my mother, my fellows. Now he had sworn himself my enemy over this matter with Klepper; he wanted me to feel the full brunt of the world, as punishment for having gone against him.

All eyes were on the priest. His face was haughty as only a priest's can be and not be laughed at. He accepted the empty spirit-flask from the King, and laid it in a wooden box made perfectly to its size. He unravelled the dark stuff from his arms and draped it upon His Majesty with great care. What was it made from? It seemed not more than shadow or gauze, but sometimes great clots and knots came out of the pile, to be loosened or left in their mass, like the clothing of beggars, or indeed of whipped people's garments, cut to threads and then re-matted by the beatings. Was it black, was it purple?

Then out of the last armful of cloth-stuff, a head-dress of uncertain design but suggesting once having been plumed, and a ragged mask, skull-like and dog-like and altogether repellent—these emerged and finally covered our king's handsomeness, so that all I could recognise him by was his bearing within the threads and tatters, by his stillness when all about were leaning to each other, and whispering, and shifting from foot to foot. His stillness seemed to me an actual substance, like a smoke or smell, that spread out among his followers and froze them too in their places, turned the guard to stone who had just ushered the house servants out of the chamber.

It had no need to still the Captain and me, for we were already motionless, all but unbreathing above the gathering. My eyes took in the last tiniest movements: the settling of reeds on the flags, the wagging shaft of light from a knife-blade as it rocked to a halt. The woman herself, positioned at the scorpion's head where the knives were laid densest, moved not a hair or a finger, but against the king's fearsome stillness—I felt it, I almost *saw* it—she poured out her own, which was of a different make, radiant and graceful, and careless of all the fear that infected the air around.

Several moments of perfect stillness passed. Then His Majesty drew a mighty breath; it whistled in through the mask's apertures; it swelled the chest of his webbed and ragged drapery.

When he spoke, it was with a voice not his own. Monstrously deep, was this voice, and breathy with the breath of different lungs, not a king's, not any kind of man's. Vast hollows full of smoke and stone were these caves of lungs, and the chamber rang enlarged with the breath and voice of them, and the air stung with the burning, with the danger introduced to the place.

The woman regarded him, uncowed by the wordless noise spilling from the mask, or by the force with which its sounding filled and tested the limits of the room.

And then I did not see what she did, or how the king-monster next moved, for the reeds on the floor began to hiss together and to rattle and to rise, and the knives to glint and stand, some on their handles, some on the tips of their blades.

Then they leaped up, and I gasped—but they did not come at us. At the scorpion's head they fitted their blades together, and grew and worked against each other; along its spine they danced up in an arch and bobbed there, winking. The reeds flew out, to make a fine weaving, to indicate an outline: a long sketchy crocodile-head, muscled shoulders, strong haunches, between them a bulky belly flattened as yet to the floor. The tail went from wisps to cable at the foot of the platform, and the knifelets busied and tinkled along its length, then firmed in their places, and even the reedy parts began to smoothen out, and their green-ness to gleam, and when I looked up to the rest it was bulked there clearly alive, trembling with a pulse from some big magicked heart inside it, swelling and shrinking and swelling with its ongoing breath. And eager, it was, restrained—only just—by the king's voice pouring through the mask.

Completed, the creature described a great hunched curve, nearly to my eye-level on the high platform; all men were dolls beside it, and the shepherdess was the smallest doll of all. Spiked head to tail-tip, was the beast, with knife-blades become spines, and its claws were of the same sharpness. Its mouth could not contain all its mass of teeth, but two of them must needle upward and another two down, outside its lips of glinting mail. From its nostrils puffed an air choking in its heat and smell, and the thing did not care that we could not breathe it, we courtiers, we watchers. All its attention, as a cat's is with a sparrow, was directed from the limits of its poised body, its bunched muscles, through its dazzle-yellow eyes, upon the woman before it, standing in my view like a priest between candles, between the two gleaming uprights of its projecting teeth.

As the King spoke, it huffed a breath at her. She blinked, but no more than that; her clothing sizzled dry at the front, and a lock of her hair glowed and fell to white ash on her bodice. She gazed at the teeth massed before her—we all did, for they were like lanterns in the dark chamber—at the tongue, golden, curved and crackled on the surface, and within the cracks red, bright as blown-upon coals.

The King ceased his awful ventriloquy. The great lizard grinned, or perhaps only prepared its mouth. It did not pounce like a cat, or like a cat toy with its prey; in a bite it had taken the woman in down to the thighs; in a second one, she was gone, and the thing was reared-headed, tossing her back into its throat as a bird must do a beakful of water, swallowing her down a neck that it stretched out as if purposely to show her travelling down its length and narrowness. The fire-tongue flailed against the scaly lips and the skin stretched and winked, and I will never forget the sound of the lizard gulping—relishless, only mechanical, the kiss and slide of searing flesh within its throat.

The Captain hissed so hard, I felt his spittle on my cheek. "Is what happens when you do not marry as you are told!"

He shook with fear, though, and I did not. Nonsense, I thought. As if the King himself would go through such a business for only me, a captain's daughter of his vast military. Still it did speak to me, this horror before me and my father's spittle cool on my skin. It told me the size of his rage; it showed me the enormity of refusing a king's, or a father's, demands. I could not deny that it impressed itself upon me as a lesson: however enraged the Captain was with my refusal of that foolish soldier, his wrath when he learned the rest of it would be something else again to witness.

Then there was no more space or time or breath for learning, for the creature sprang and bucked as if speared. Flame spouted from its mouth, shrivelling the flesh and igniting the clothing of a guard, and throwing him back so that he fell, and rolled, and tumbled into the cat-pit. Forgotten, he was, immediately, by me and all the company, because the lizard folded, flopped open again and contorted, hugely, dangerously above and below us. It leaped and whipped, growling gasps in its throat, fire and fumes sputtering at its lips. It flung itself to the floor, coiled and writhed there; its tail broke the wheel in a single swipe, and set the pieces burning; it coughed forth a fire-ball that flew against a wall and burst, leaving a vast black star-shape on the stone.

And then, the belly-skin of the beast opened, like a dreadful flower, like a house-fire bursting up through thatch and timbers. Think of any bird you have gutted, any fish or four-legged thing; add fire and magic and stupendous size to the wonders of those internals, and then picture from the glare, from the garden of flame, from the welter of dragon-juices, through the smoke of its dying gasps, a small, cool woman climbing towards you.

The sight of her froze the Captain faster in his fear than had any of the lizard's cavorting. "No!" he whispered at my ear, as I leaned out elated, all but cheering.

She stepped down free of the dying ruin of the creature, to stand on a dagger-shape of flayed skin like some weird cindered carpet, the beast's last breaths heaving behind her. "Sir!" she said, to the King and to the power within and beyond him. "You see you are matched and bettered! I tell you!" She laughed, which in that chamber full of fear, the courtiers piled wide-eyed on the steps where they had scrambled to escape the monster's flailing, was the clearest, refreshingest sound, like water filling a cup when you are thirsty. "I tell you, sir: my Lord's and my Lady's powers are greater than myself, and longer than my life. To kill me, foolish man, makes no mark upon Them. And should you succeed, further I tell you this: Does anyone tell my life, or pen it onto skin, or rush-paper, or read it off again, or even only hear it said, at nurse's knee or among the gossips in the marketplace, they will be blessed, and the women of their family kept strong and fruitful and safe in childbed. My faith is pure and powerful, here and beyond the grave; it is only the very hem of the mantle of the King and Queen who work the world, from the depths of the seas to the heights of the stars, and every continent and creature in between."

The Captain was gone from behind me; others had taken his place, pressing forward, staring down, marvelling at the beast's remains, the straight-backed woman defying the King, the smouldering rack, the flaming wheel, the burnt guard dead in the pit.

And then there he was, my father at the foot of the steps, pushing free of the crowd, drawing his sword.

"I will rid you of her, Your Majesty!" he cried.

He strode to her; she watched him come, unmoved, unafraid, a woman indulging a child. I so strongly expected his humiliation, his defeat, her continuing, that I waited in utter calm as he slashed her throat through to the spine-bones, as she fell, as she bled, her heart living on, unaware that the head was gone, flinging and spreading the bright blood on the charred dragon-skin, slowing, slowing, stopping. My father stood over her the while; we all stood over her, attentive, as closely as the dragon had attended in the moments before it ate her.

But she only died, the shepherdess, and was dead; there were no more miracles to her.

I cried out, loud and high in the huge room under the smoking roof-beams. They held me back from clambering over the railing, from crawling underneath it and smashing my own life away on the flags before my father. "She is maddened," someone said. "She should never have been allowed to see—it has unhinged her." But I was clear in my own mind, afflicted indeed by a terrible sanity, a terrible seeing of this moment as it truly was, with the miracle woman gone from the world and me still prisoned in it, with my lover and my baby and my punishments awaiting, with my angry father—while she was free, dissolved into her faith, glorifying her gods among all the saints there. Such a stab of jealousy I suffered! Such rage did I try to loose, at her and my father both, such grief that a soul so freshly known, so marvellous, was so quickly snatched from my sight.

They tried to help me down; I would not be helped. They had to bind and carry me, and quickly, for the roof was fully afire now, and the King and his closest had been hurried away. My father met us at the foot of the stairs, took me up and slung me like a carcass over his shoulder. I banged away my tears against his back, and strained, as we passed the swollen smouldering corse of the dragon, its juices running out black, to see the body and the skewed head of the saint who had burst him open with her holiness. She lay there uncovered; she would not even be buried with her own rites and customs, but roof slates would rain upon her as she stewed and shrank in the lizard-blood. Beams would crush her bones; fire would consume them.

My father carried me out, through the long halls of the prison and into the day. The courtiers and councillors and soldiers flowed out with us, exclaiming, into the crowd, into the clamour of the town; my noise went unheard among them, and the tears ran unnoticed through my eyebrows, down my forehead, and onto the leather of the Captain's back-plate, drawing long dark lines there.

ORM THE BEAUTIFUL
Elizabeth Bear

Elizabeth Bear was born in Hartford, Connecticut in 1971, on the same day (but a different year) as Frodo and Bilbo Baggins. Her first short fiction appeared in 1996, and was followed after a nearly decade-long gap by fifteen novels, two short story collections, and more than fifty short stories. Bear's "Jenny Casey" trilogy won the Locus Award for Best First Novel, and she won the John W. Campbell Award for Best New Writer in 2005. Her short story "Tideline" won the 2008 Hugo and Sturgeon awards, and "Shoggoths in Bloom" won a Hugo for best novelette in 2009. Her most recent books are novels *Chill, By the Mountain Bound*, and novella *Bone & Jewel Creatures*.

Orm the Beautiful sang in his sleep, to his brothers and sisters, as the sea sings to itself. He would never die. But neither could he live much longer.

Dreaming on jewels, hearing their ancestor-song, he did not think that he would mind. The men were coming; Orm the Beautiful knew it with the wisdom of his bones. He thought he would not fight them. He thought he would close the mountain and let them scratch outside.

He would die there in the mother-cave, and so stay with the Chord. There was no-one after him to take his place as warden, and Orm the Beautiful was old.

Because he was the last warden of the mother-cave, his hoard was enormous, chromatic in hue and harmony. There was jade and lapis—the bequests of Orm the Exquisite and Orm the Luminous, respectively—and chrysoprase and turquoise and the semiprecious feldspars. There were three cracked sections of an amethyst pipe as massive as a fallen tree, and Orm the Beautiful was careful never to breathe fire upon them; the stones would jaundice to smoke color in the heat.

He lay closest by the jagged heap of beryls—green as emerald, green as poison, green as grass—that were the mortal remains of his sister, Orm the Radiant. And just beyond her was the legacy of her mate, Orm the Magnificent, charcoal-and-silver labradorite overshot with an absinthe shimmer. The Magnificent's song, in death, was high and sweet, utterly at odds with the aged slithering hulk he had become before he changed.

Orm the Beautiful stretched his long neck among the glorious rubble of his kin and dozed to their songs. Soon he would be with them, returned to their harmony, their many-threaded round. Only his radiance illuminated them now. Only his eye remembered their sheen. And he too would lose the power to shine with more than reflected light before long, and all in the mother-cave would be dark and full of music.

He was pale, palest of his kin, blue-white as skimmed milk and just as translucent. The flash that ran across his scales when he crawled into the light, however, was spectral: green-electric and blue-actinic, and a vermilion so sharp it could burn an afterimage in a human eye.

It had been a long time since he climbed into the light. Perhaps he'd seal the cave now, to be ready.

Yes.

When he was done, he lay down among his treasures, his beloveds, under the mountain, and his thoughts were dragonish.

But when the men came they came not single spies but in battalions, with dragons of their own. Iron dragons, yellow metal monsters that creaked and hissed as they gnawed the rocks. And they brought, with the dragons, channeled fire.

There was a thump, a tremble, and sifting dust followed. Cold winter air trickling down the shaft woke Orm the Beautiful from his chorale slumber.

He blinked lambent eyes, raising his head from the petrified, singing flank of Orm the Perspicacious. He heard the crunch of stone like the splintering of masticated bones and cocked his head, his ears and tendrils straining forward.

And all the Chord sang astonishment and alarm.

It had happened to others. Slain, captured, taken. Broken apart and carried off, their memories and their dreams lost forever, their songs stripped to exiled fragments to adorn a wrist, a throat, a crown. But it had always been that men could be turned back with stone.

And now they were here at the mother-cave, and undaunted to find it sealed.

This would not do. This threatened them all.

Orm the Beautiful burst from the mountain wreathed in white-yellow flames. The yellow steel dragon was not too much larger than he. It blocked the tunnel mouth; its toothed hand raked and lifted shattered stone. Orm the Beautiful struck it with his claws extended, his wings snapping wide as he cleared the destroyed entrance to the mother-cave.

The cold cut through scale to bone. When fire did not jet from flaring nostrils, his breath swirled mist and froze to rime. Snow lay blackened on the mountainside, rutted and filthy. His wings, far whiter, caught chill carmine sparks from the sun. Fragile steel squealed and rent under his claws.

There was a man in the cage inside the mechanical dragon. He made terrible unharmonious noises as he burned. Orm the Beautiful seized him and ate him quickly, out of pity, head jerking like a stork snatching down a frog.

His throat distended, squeezed, smoothed, contracted. There was no time to eat the contraption, and metal could not suffer in the flames. Orm the Beautiful tore it in half, claw and claw, and soared between the discarded pieces.

Other men screamed and ran. Their machines were potent, but no iron could sting him. Neither their bullets nor the hammer-headed drill on the second steel dragon gave him pause. He stalked them, pounced, gorged on the snap-shaken dead.

He pursued the living as they fled, and what he reached he slew.

When he slithered down the ruined tunnel to the others, they were singing, gathered, worried. He settled among their entwined song, added his notes to the chords, offered harmony. Orm the Beautiful was old; what he brought to the song was rich and layered, subtle and soft.

They will come again, sang Orm the Radiant.

They have found the mother-cave, and they have machines to unearth us, like a badger from its sett, sang Orm the Terrible from his column of black and lavender jade.

We are not safe here anymore, sang Orm the Luminous. *We will be scattered and lost. The song will end, will end.*

His verse almost silenced them all. Their harmony guttered like a fire when the wind slicks across it, and for a moment Orm the Beautiful felt the quiet like a wire around his throat. It was broken by the discord of voices, a rising dissonance like a tuning orchestra, the Chord all frightened and in argument.

But Orm the Courtly raised her voice, and all listened. She was old in life and old in death, and wise beyond both in her singing. *Let the warden decide.*

Another agreed, another, voice after voice scaling into harmony.

And Orm the Beautiful sat back on his haunches, his tail flicked across his toes, his belly aching, and tried to pretend he had any idea at all how to protect the Chord from being unearthed and carted to the four corners of the world.

"I'll think about it when I've digested," he said, and lay down on his side with a sigh.

Around him the Chord sang agreement. They had not forgotten in death the essentialities of life.

With the men and their machines came memory. Orm the Beautiful, belly distended with iron and flesh, nevertheless slept with one eye open. His opalescence lit the mother-cave in hollow violets and crawling greens. The Chord sang around him, thinking while he dreamed. The dead did not rest, or dream.

They only sang and remembered.

The Chord was in harmony when he awoke. They had listened to his song while he slept, and while he stretched—sleek again, and the best part of a yard longer—he heard theirs as well, and learned from them what they had learned from his dinner.

More men would follow. The miners Orm the Beautiful had dined on knew they would not go unavenged. There would be more men, men like ants, with their weapons and their implements. And Orm the Beautiful was strong.

But he was old, and he was only one. And someone, surely, would soon recall that though steel had no power to harm Orm the Beautiful's race, knapped flint or obsidian could slice him opal hide from opal bone.

The mother-cave was full of the corpses of dragons, a chain of song and memory stretching aeons. The Chord was rich in voices.

Orm the Beautiful had no way to move them all.

Orm the Numinous, who was eldest, was chosen to speak the evil news they all knew already. *You must give us away, Orm the Beautiful.*

Dragons are not specifically disallowed in the airspace over Washington, D.C., but it must be said that Orm the Beautiful's presence there was heartily discouraged. Nevertheless, he persevered, holding his flame and the lash of his wings, and succeeded in landing on the National Mall without destroying any of the attacking aircraft.

He touched down lightly in a clear space before the National Museum of Natural History, a helicopter hovering over his head and blowing his tendrils this way and that. There were men all over the grass and pavements. They scattered, screaming, nigh-irresistible prey. Orm the Beautiful's tail-tip twitched with frustrated instinct, and he was obliged to stand on three legs and elaborately clean his off-side fore talons for several moments before he regained enough self-possession to settle his wings and ignore the scurrying morsels.

It was unlikely that he would set a conducive tone with the museum's staff by eating a few as a prelude to conversation.

He stood quietly, inspecting his talons foot by foot and, incidentally, admiring the flashes of color that struck off his milk-pale hide in the glaring sun. When he had been still five minutes, he looked up to find a ring of men surrounding him, males and a few females, with bright metal in their hands and flashing on the chests of uniforms that were a black-blue dark as sodalite.

"Hello," Orm the Beautiful said, in the language of his dinner, raising his voice to be heard over the clatter of the helicopter. "My name is Orm the Beautiful. I should like to speak to the curator, please."

The helicopter withdrew to circle, and the curator eventually produced was a female man. Orm the Beautiful wondered if that was due to some half-remembered legend about his folk's preferences. Sopranos, in particular, had been popular among his kin in the days when they associated more freely with men.

She minced from the white-columned entry, down broad shallow steps between exhibits of petrified wood, and paused beyond the barricade of yellow tape and wooden sawhorses the blue-uniformed men had strung around Orm the Beautiful.

He had greatly enjoyed watching them evacuate the Mall.

The curator wore a dull suit and shoes that clicked, and her hair was twisted back on her neck. Little stones glinted in her earlobes: diamonds, cold and common and without song.

"I'm Katherine Samson," she said, and hesitantly extended her tiny soft hand, half-retracted it, then doggedly thrust it forward again. "You wished to speak to me?"

"I am Orm the Beautiful," Orm the Beautiful replied, and laid a cautious talon-tip against her palm. "I am here to beg your aid."

She squinted up and he realized that the sun was behind him. If its own brilliance didn't blind her pale man's eyes, surely the light shattering on his scales would do the deed. He spread his wings to shade her, and the ring of blue-clad men flinched back as one—as if they were a Chord, though Orm the Beautiful knew they were not.

The curator, however, stood her ground.

His blue-white wings were translucent, and there was a hole in the leather of the left one, an ancient scar. It cast a ragged bright patch on the curator's shoe, but the shade covered her face, and she lowered her eye-shading hand.

"Thank you," she said. And then, contemplating him, she pushed the sawhorses apart. One of the blue men reached for her, but before he caught her arm, the curator was through the gap and standing in Orm the Beautiful's shadow, her head craned back, her hair pulling free around her temples in soft wisps that reminded Orm the Beautiful of Orm the Radiant's tawny tendrils. "You need *my* help? Uh, sir?"

Carefully, he lowered himself to his elbows, keeping the wings high. The curator was close enough to touch him now, and when he tilted his head to see her plainly, he found her staring up at him with the tip of her tongue protruding. He flicked his tongue in answer, tasting her scent.

She *was* frightened. But far more curious.

"Let me explain," he said. And told her about the mother-cave, and the precious bones of his Chord, and the men who had come to steal them. He told her that they were dead, but they remembered, and if they were torn apart, carted off, their song and their memories would be shattered.

"It would be the end of my culture," he said, and then he told her he was dying.

As he was speaking, his head had dipped lower, until he was almost murmuring in her ear. At some point, she'd laid one hand on his skull behind the horns and leaned close, and she seemed startled now to realize that she was touching him. She drew her hand back slowly, and stood staring at the tips of her fingers. "What is that singing?"

She heard it, then, the wreath of music that hung on him, thin and thready though it was in the absence of his Chord. That was well. "It is I."

"Do all—all your people—does that always happen?"

"I have no people," he said. "But yes. Even in death we sing. It is why the Chord must be kept together."

"So when you said it's only you...."

"I am the last," said Orm the Beautiful.

She looked down, and he gave her time to think.

"It would be very expensive," she said, cautiously, rubbing the fingertips together as if they'd lost sensation. "We would have to move quickly, if poachers have already found your... mother-cave. And you're talking about a huge engineering problem, to move them without taking them apart. I don't know where the money would come from."

"If the expense were not at issue, would the museum accept the bequest?"

"Without a question." She touched his eye-ridge again, quickly, furtively. "Dragons," she said, and shook her head and breathed a laugh. "*Dragons.*"

"Money is no object," he said. "Does your institution employ a solicitor?"

The document was two days in drafting. Orm the Beautiful spent the time fretting and fussed, though he kept his aspect as nearly serene as possible. Katherine—the curator—did not leave his side. Indeed, she brought him within the building—the tall doors and vast lobby could have accommodated a far larger dragon—and had a cot fetched so she could remain near. He could not stay in the lobby itself, because it was a point of man-pride that the museum was open every day, and free to all comers. But they cleared a small exhibit hall, and he stayed there in fair comfort, although silent and alone.

Outside, reporters and soldiers made camp, but within the halls of the Museum of Natural History, it was bright and still, except for the lonely shadow of Orm the Beautiful's song.

Already, he mourned his Chord. But if his sacrifice meant their salvation, it was a very small thing to give.

When the contracts were written, when the papers were signed, Katherine sat down on the edge of her cot and said, "The personal bequest," she began. "The one the Museum is meant to sell, to fund the retrieval of your Chord."

"Yes," Orm the Beautiful said.

"May I know what it is now, and where we may find it?"

"It is here before you," said Orm the Beautiful, and tore his heart from his breast with his claws.

He fell with a crash like a breaking bell, an avalanche of skim-milk-white opal threaded with azure and absinthe and vermilion flash. Chunks rolled against Katherine's legs, bruised her feet and ankles, broke some of her toes in her clicking shoes.

She was too stunned to feel pain. Through his solitary singing, Orm the Beautiful heard her refrain: "Oh, no, oh, no, oh, no."

Those who came to investigate the crash found Katherine Samson on her knees, hands raking the rubble. Salt water streaked opal powder white as bone dust down her cheeks. She kissed the broken rocks, and the blood on her fingertips was no brighter than the shocked veins of carnelian flash that shot through them.

Orm the Beautiful was broken up and sold, as he had arranged. The paperwork was quite unforgiving; dragons, it seems, may serve as their own attorneys with great dexterity.

The stones went for outrageous prices. When you wore them on your skin, you could hear the dragonsong. Institutions and the insanely wealthy fought over the relics. No price could ever be too high.

Katherine Samson was bequeathed a few chips for her own. She had them polished and drilled and threaded on a chain she wore about her throat, where her blood could warm them as they pressed upon her pulse. The mother-cave was located with the aid of Orm the Beautiful's maps and directions. Poachers were in the process of excavating it when the team from the Smithsonian arrived.

But the Museum had brought the National Guard. And the poachers were dealt with, though perhaps not with such finality as Orm the Beautiful might have wished.

Each and each, his Chord were brought back to the Museum.

Katherine, stumping on her walking cast, spent long hours in the exhibit hall. She hovered and guarded and warded, and stroked and petted and adjusted Orm the Beautiful's hoard like a nesting falcon turning her eggs. His song sustained her, his warm bones worn against her skin, his voice half-heard in her ear.

He was broken and scattered. He was not a part of his Chord. He was lost to them, as other dragons had been lost before, and as those others his song would eventually fail, and flicker, and go unremembered.

After a few months, she stopped weeping.

She also stopped eating, sleeping, dreaming.

Going home.

They came as stragglers, footsore and rain-draggled, noses peeled by the sun. They came alone, in party dresses, in business suits, in outrageously costly T-shirts and jeans. They came draped in opals and platinum, opals and gold. They came with the song of Orm the Beautiful warm against their skin.

They came to see the dragons, to hear their threaded music. When the Museum closed at night, they waited patiently by the steps until morning. They did not freeze. They did not starve.

Eventually, through the sheer wearing force of attrition, the passage of decades, the Museum accepted them. And there they worked, and lived, for all time.

And Orm the Beautiful?

He had been shattered. He died alone.

The Chord could not reclaim him. He was lost in the mortal warders, the warders who had been men.

But as he sang in their ears, so they recalled him, like a seashell remembers the sea.

WEYR SEARCH

Anne McCaffrey

Anne McCaffrey was born in Cambridge, MA in 1926 and began writing at the age of eight. She graduated from Radcliffe, performed in or directed stage productions, worked as an advertising copywriter and in the 1950s married and had three children. After a divorce in 1970, she and the children moved to Ireland, where she has run stables and raised horses ever since.

Her first story was published in 1953, her first novel, *Restoree*, in 1966. She was the first woman to win both the Hugo and Nebula Awards, in 1968 and 1969, for stories that were incorporated into her second novel, *Dragonflight*, first in the hugely popular Dragonriders of Pern series now totalling twenty-two books, among them *The White Dragon*, the first hardcover SF novel to make the *New York Times* bestseller list.

McCaffrey's seventy-six novels include the Freedom, Doona, Dinosaur Planet, Crystal Singer, Brain & Brawn Ship, Petaybee, Talent, Tower & Hive, Acorna, and Coelura series of novels, all written with various collaborators. Her short fiction is collected in *Get Off the Unicorn* and *The Girl Who Heard Dragons*, and she has edited three anthologies. McCaffrey was awarded the SFWA Grand Master for lifetime achievement in 2005. She lives in a house she designed herself called Dragonhold-Underhill in Wicklow County, Ireland.

When is a legend legend? Why is a myth a myth? How old and disused must a fact be for it to be relegated to the category: Fairy tale? And why do certain facts remain incontrovertible, while others lose their validity to assume a shabby, unstable character?

Rukbat, in the Sagittarian sector, was a golden G-type star. It had five planets, plus one stray it had attracted and held in recent millennia. Its third planet was enveloped by air man could breathe, boasted water he could drink, and possessed a gravity which permitted man to walk confidently erect. Men discovered it, and promptly colonized it, as they did every habitable planet they came to and then…whether callously or through collapse of empire, the colonists never discovered, and eventually forgot to ask…left the colonies to fend for themselves.

When men first settled on Rukbat's third world, and named it Pern, they had taken little notice of the stranger-planet, swinging around its primary in a wildly erratic elliptical orbit. Within a few generations they had forgotten its existence. The desperate path the wanderer pursued brought it close to its stepsister every two hundred [Terran] years at perihelion.

When the aspects were harmonious and the conjunction with its sister-planet close enough, as it often was, the indigenous life of the wanderer sought to bridge the space gap to the more temperate and hospitable planet.

It was during the frantic struggle to combat this menace dropping through Pern's skies like silver threads that Pern's contact with the mother-planet weakened and broke. Recollections of Earth receded further from Pernese history with each successive generation until memory of their origins degenerated past legend or myth, into oblivion.

To forestall the incursions of the dreaded Threads, the Pernese, with the ingenuity of their forgotten Yankee forebears and between first onslaught and return, developed a highly specialized variety of a life form indigenous to their adopted planet…the winged, tailed, and fire-breathing dragons, named for the Earth legend they resembled. Such humans as had a high empathy rating and some innate telepathic ability were trained to make use of and preserve this unusual animal whose ability to teleport was of immense value in the fierce struggle to keep Pern bare of Threads.

The dragons and their dragonmen, a breed apart, and the shortly renewed menace they battled, created a whole new group of legends and myths.

As the menace was conquered the populace in the Holds of Pern settled into a more comfortable way of life. Most of the dragon Weyrs eventually were abandoned, and the descendants of heroes fell into disfavor, as the legends fell into disrepute.

This, then, is a tale of legends disbelieved and their restoration. Yet—how goes a legend? When is myth?

> Drummer, beat, and piper, blow,
> Harper, strike, and soldier, go.
> Free the flame and sear the grasses
> Till the dawning Red Star passes.

Lessa woke, cold. Cold with more than the chill of the everlastingly clammy stone walls. Cold with the prescience of a danger greater than when, ten full Turns ago, she had run, whimpering, to hide in the watch-wher's odorous lair.

Rigid with concentration, Lessa lay in the straw of the redolent cheese room, sleeping quarters shared with the other kitchen drudges. There was an urgency in the ominous portent unlike any other forewarning. She touched the awareness of the watch-wher, slithering on its rounds in the courtyard. It circled at the choke-limit of its chain. It was restless, but oblivious to anything unusual in the predawn darkness.

The danger was definitely not within the walls of Hold Ruath. Nor approaching the paved perimeter without the Hold where relentless grass had forced new growth through the ancient mortar, green witness to the deterioration of the once stone-clean Hold. The danger was not advancing up the now little used causeway from the valley, nor lurking in the craftsmen's stony holdings at the foot of the Hold's cliff. It did not scent the wind that blew from Tillek's cold shores. But still it twanged sharply through her senses, vibrating every nerve in Lessa's slender frame. Fully roused, she sought to identify it before the prescient mood dissolved. She cast outward, toward the Pass, farther than she had ever pressed. Whatever threatened was not in Ruatha... yet. Nor did it have a familiar flavor. It was not, then, Fax.

Lessa had been cautiously pleased that Fax had not shown himself at Hold Ruath in three full Turns. The apathy of the craftsmen, the decaying farmholds, even the green-etched stones of the Hold infuriated Fax, self-styled Lord of the High Reaches, to the point where he preferred to forget the reason why he had subjugated the once proud and profitable Hold.

Lessa picked her way among the sleeping drudges, huddled together for warmth, and glided up the worn steps to the kitchen-proper. She slipped across the cavernous kitchen to the stable-yard door. The cobbles of the yard were icy through the thin soles of her sandals and she shivered as the predawn air penetrated her patched garment.

The watch-wher slithered across the yard to greet her, pleading, as it always did, for release. Glancing fondly down at the awesome head, she promised it a good rub presently. It crouched, groaning, at the end of its chain as she continued to the grooved steps that led to the rampart over the Hold's massive gate. Atop the tower, Lessa stated toward the east where the stony breasts of the Pass rose in black relief against the gathering day.

Indecisively she swung to her left, for the sense of danger issued from that direction as well. She glanced upward, her eyes drawn to the red star which had recently begun to dominate the dawn sky. As she stared, the star radiated a final ruby pulsation before its magnificence was lost in the brightness of Pern's rising sun.

For the first time in many Turns, Lessa gave thought to matters beyond Pern, beyond her dedication to vengeance on the murderer Fax for the annihilation of her family. Let him but come within Ruath Hold now and he would never leave.

But the brilliant ruby sparkle of the Red Star recalled the Disaster Ballads... grim narratives of the heroism of the dragonriders as they braved the dangers of *between* to breathe fiery death on the silver Threads that dropped through Pern's skies. Not one Thread must fall to the rich soil, to burrow deep and multiply, leaching the earth of minerals and fertility. Straining her eyes as if vision would bridge the gap between periol and person, she stared intently eastward. The watch-whet's thin, whistled question reached her just as the prescience waned.

Dawnlight illumined the tumbled landscape, the unplowed fields in the valley below. Dawnlight fell on twisted orchards, where the sparse herds of milchbeasts hunted stray blades of spring grass. Grass in Ruatha grew where it should not, died where it should flourish. An odd brooding smile curved Lessa's lips. Fax realized no profit from his conquest of Ruatha... nor would he, while she, Lessa, lived. And he had not the slightest suspicion of the source of this undoing.

Or had he? Lessa wondered, her mind still reverberating from the savage prescience of danger. East lay Fax's ancestral and only legitimate Hold. Northeast lay little but bare and stony mountains and Benden, the remaining Weyr, which protected Pern.

Lessa stretched, arching her back, inhaling the sweet, untainted wind of morning.

A cock crowed in the stableyard. Lessa whirled, her face alert, eyes darting around the outer Hold lest she be observed in such an uncharacteristic pose. She unbound her hair, letting it fall about her face concealingly. Her body drooped into the sloppy posture she affected. Quickly she thudded down the stairs, crossing to the watch-wher. It lurred piteously, its great eyes blinking against the growing daylight. Oblivious to the stench of its rank breath, she hugged the scaly head to her, scratching its ears and eye ridges. The watch-wher was ecstatic with pleasure, its long body trembling, its clipped wings rustling. It alone knew who she was or cared. And it was the only creature in all Pern she trusted since the day she had blindly sought refuge in its dark stinking lair to escape Fax's thirsty swords that had drunk so deeply of Ruathan blood.

Slowly she rose, cautioning it to remember to be as vicious to her as to all should anyone be near. It promised to obey her, swaying back and forth to emphasize its reluctance.

The first rays of the sun glanced over the Hold's outer wall. Crying out, the watch-wher darted into its dark nest. Lessa crept back to the kitchen and into the cheese room.

> From the Weyr and from the Bowl
> Bronze and brown and blue and green
> Rise the dragonmen of Pern,
> Aloft, on wing, seen, then unseen.

F'lar on bronze Mnementh's great neck appeared first in the skies above the chief Hold of Fax, so-called Lord of the High Reaches. Behind him, in proper wedge formation, the wingmen came into sight. F'lar checked the formation automatically; as precise as at the moment of entry to *between*.

As Mnementh curved in an arc that would bring them to the perimeter of the Hold, consonant with the friendly nature of this visitation, F'lar surveyed with mounting aversion the disrepair of the ridge defences. The firestone pits were empty and the rock-cut gutters radiating from the pits were green-tinged with a mossy growth.

Was there even one lord in Pern who maintained his Hold rocky in observance of the ancient Laws? F'lar's lips tightened to a thinner line. When this Search was over and the Impression made, there would have to be a solemn, punitive Council held at the Weyr. And by the golden shell of the queen, he, F'lar, meant to be its moderator. He would replace lethargy with industry. He would scour the green and dangerous scum from the heights of Pern, the grass blades from its stoneworks. No verdant skirt would be condoned in any farmhold. And the tithings which had been so miserly, so grudgingly presented would, under pain of firestoning, flow with decent generosity into the Dragon weyr.

Mnementh rumbled approvingly as he vaned his pinions to land lightly on the grass-etched flagstones of Fax's Hold. The bronze dragon furled his great wings, and F'lar heard the warning claxon in the Hold's Great Tower. Mnementh dropped to his knees as F'lar indicated he wished to dismount. The bronze rider stood by Mnementh's huge wedgeshaped head, politely awaiting the arrival of the Hold lord. F'lar idly gazed down the valley, hazy with warm spring sunlight. He ignored the furtive heads that peered at the dragonman from the parapet slits and the cliff windows.

F'lar did not turn as a rush of air announced the arrival of the rest of the wing. He knew, however, when F'nor, the brown rider, his half-brother, took the customary position on his left, a dragon-length to the rear. F'lar caught a glimpse of F'nor's boot-heel twisting to death the grass crowding up between the stones.

An order, muffled to an intense whisper, issued from within the great court, beyond the open gates. Almost immediately a group of men marched into sight, led by a heavy-set man of medium height.

Mnementh arched his neck, angling his head so that his chin rested on the ground. Mnementh's many faceted eyes, on a level with F'lar's head, fastened with disconcerting interest on the approaching party. The dragons could never understand why they generated such abject fear in common folk. At only one point in his life span would a dragon attack a human and that could be excused on the grounds of simple ignorance. F'lar could not explain to the dragon the politics behind the necessity of inspiring awe in the holders, lord and craftsman alike. He could only observe that the fear and apprehension showing in the faces of the advancing squad which troubled Mnementh was oddly pleasing to him, F'lar.

"Welcome, Bronze Rider, to the Hold of Fax, Lord of the High Reaches. He is at your service," and the man made an adequately respectful salute.

The use of the third person pronoun could be construed, by the meticulous, to be a veiled insult. This fit in with the information F'lar had on Fax; so he ignored it. His information was also correct in describing Fax as a greedy man. It showed in the restless eyes which flicked at every detail of F'lar's clothing, at the slight frown when the intricately etched sword-hilt was noticed.

F'lar noticed, in his own turn, the several rich rings which flashed on Fax's left hand. The overlord's right hand remained slightly cocked after the habit of the professional swordsman. His tunic, of rich fabric, was stained and none too fresh. The man's feet, in heavy wher-hide boots, were solidly planted, weight balanced forward on his toes. A man to be treated cautiously, F'lar decided, as one should the conqueror of five neighboring Holds. Such greedy audacity was in itself a revelation. Fax had married into a sixth... and had legally inherited, however unusual the circumstances, the seventh. He was a lecherous man by reputation.

Within these seven Holds, F'lar anticipated a profitable Search. Let R'gul go southerly to pursue Search among the indolent, if lovely, women there. The Weyr needed a strong woman this time; Jora had been worse than useless with Nemorth. Adversity, uncertainty: those were the conditions that bred the qualities F'lar wanted in a weyrwoman.

"We ride in Search," F'lar drawled softly, "and request the hospitality of your Hold, Lord Fax."

Fax's eyes widened imperceptibly at mention of Search.

"I had heard Jora was dead," Fax replied, dropping the third person abruptly as if F'lar had passed some sort of test by ignoring it. "So Nemorth has a new queen, hm-m-m?" he continued, his eyes darting across the rank of the ring, noting the disciplined stance of the riders, the healthy color of the dragons.

F'lar did not dignify the obvious with an answer.

"And, my Lord..." Fax hesitated, expectantly inclining his head slightly toward the dragonman.

For a pulse beat, F'lar wondered if the man were deliberately provoking him with such subtle insults. The name of bronze riders should be as well known throughout Pern as the name of the Dragonqueen and her Weyrwoman. F'lar kept his face composed, his eyes on Fax's.

Leisurely, with the proper touch of arrogance, F'nor stepped forward, stopping slightly behind Mnementh's head, one hand negligently touching the jaw hinge of the huge beast.

"The Bronze Rider of Mnementh, Lord F'lar, will require quarters for himself. I, F'nor, brown rider, prefer to be lodged with the wingmen. We are, in number, twelve."

F'lar liked that touch of F'nor's, totting up the wing strength, as if Fax were incapable of counting. F'nor had phrased it so adroitly as to make it impossible for Fax to protest the insult.

"Lord F'lar," Fax said through teeth fixed in a smile, "the High Reaches are honored with your Search."

"It will be to the credit of the High Reaches," F'lar replied smoothly, "if one of its own supplies the Weyr."

"To our everlasting credit," Fax replied as suavely. "In the old days, many notable weyrwomen came from my Holds."

"Your Holds?" asked F'lar, politely smiling as he emphasized the plural. "Ah, yes, you are now overlord of Ruatha, are you not? There have been many from that Hold."

A strange tense look crossed Fax's face. "Nothing good comes from Ruath Hold." Then he stepped aside, gesturing F'lar to enter the Hold.

Fax's troop leader barked a hasty order and the men formed two lines, their metal-edged boots flicking sparks from the stones.

At unspoken orders, all the dragons rose with a great churning of air and dust. F'lar strode nonchalantly past the welcoming files. The men were rolling their eyes in alarm as the beasts glided above to the inner courts. Someone on the high tower uttered a frightened yelp as Mnementh took his position on that vantage point. His great wings drove phosphoric-scented air across the inner court as he maneuvered his great frame onto the inadequate landing space.

Outwardly oblivious to the consternation, fear and awe the dragons inspired, F'lar was secretly amused and rather pleased by the effect. Lords of the Holds needed this reminder that they must deal with dragons, not just with riders, who were men, mortal and murderable. The ancient respect for dragonmen as well as dragonkind must be rein-stilled in modem breasts.

"The Hold has just risen from the table, Lord F'lar, if…" Fax suggested. His voice trailed off at F'lar's smiling refusal.

"Convey my duty to your lady, Lord Fax," F'lar rejoined, noticing with inward satisfaction the tightening of Fax's jaw muscles at the ceremonial request.

"You would prefer to see your quarters first?" Fax countered.

F'lar flicked an imaginary speck from his soft wher-hide sleeve and shook his head. Was the man buying time to sequester his ladies as the old time lords had?

"Duty first," he said with a rueful shrug.

"Of course," Fax all but snapped and strode smartly ahead, his heels pounding out the anger he could not express otherwise. F'lar decided he had guessed correctly.

F'lar and F'nor followed at a slower pace through the double-doored entry with its massive metal panels, into the great hall, carved into the cliffside.

"They eat not badly," F'nor remarked casually to F'lar, appraising the remnants still on the table.

"Better than the Weyr, it would seem," F'lar replied dryly.

"Young roasts and tender," F'nor said in a bitter undertone, "while the stringy, barren beasts are delivered up to us."

"The change is overdue," F'lar murmured, then raised his voice to conversational level. "A well-favored hall," he was saying amiably as they reached Fax. Their reluctant host stood in the portal to the inner Hold, which, like all such Holds, burrowed deep into stone, traditional refuge of all in time of peril.

Deliberately, F'lar turned back to the banner-hung Hall. "Tell me, Lord Fax, do you adhere to the old practices and mount a dawn guard?"

Fax frowned, trying to grasp F'lar's meaning.

"There is always a guard at the Tower."

"An easterly guard?"

Fax's eyes jerked toward F'lar, then to F'nor.

"There are always guards," he answered sharply, "on all the approaches."

"Oh, just the approaches," and F'lar nodded wisely to F'nor.

"Where else?" demanded Fax, concerned, glancing from one dragonman to the other.

"I must ask that of your harper. You do keep a trained harper in your Hold?"

"Of course. I have several trained harpers," and Fax jerked his shoulders straighter.

F'lar affected not to understand.

"Lord Fax is the overlord of six other Holds," F'nor reminded his wing-leader.

"Of course," F'lar assented, with exactly the same inflection Fax had used a moment before.

The mimicry did not go unnoticed by Fax but as he was unable to construe deliberate insult out of an innocent affirmative, he stalked into the glow-lit corridors. The dragonmen followed.

The women's quarters in Fax's Hold had been moved from the traditional innermost corridors to those at cliff-face. Sunlight poured down from three double-shuttered, deep-casement windows in the outside wall. F'lar noted that the bronze hinges were well oiled, and the sills regulation spearlength. Fax had not, at least, diminished the protective wall.

The chamber was richly hung with appropriately gentle scenes of women occupied in all manner of feminine tasks. Doors gave off the main chamber on both sides into smaller sleeping alcoves and from these, at Fax's bidding, his women hesitantly emerged. Fax sternly gestured to a blue-gowned woman, her hair white-streaked, her face lined with disappointments and bitterness, her body swollen with pregnancy. She advanced awkwardly, stopping several feet from her lord. From her attitude, F'lar deduced that she came no closer to Fax than was absolutely necessary.

"The Lady of Crom, mother of my heirs," Fax said without pride or cordiality.

"My Lady..." F'lar hesitated, waiting for her name to be supplied.

She glanced warily at her lord.

"Gemma," Fax snapped curtly.

F'lar bowed deeply. "My Lady Gemma, the Weyr is on Search and requests the Hold's hospitality."

"My Lord F'lar," the Lady Gemma replied in a low voice, "you are most welcome."

F'lar did not miss the slight slur on the adverb nor the fact that Gemma had no trouble naming him. His smile was warmer than courtesy demanded, warm with gratitude and sympathy. Looking at the number of women in these quarters, F'lar thought there might be one or two Lady Gemma could bid farewell without regret.

Fax preferred his women plump and small. There wasn't a saucy one in the lot. If there once had been, the spirit had been beaten out of her. Fax, no doubt, was stud, not lover. Some of the covey had not all winter long made much use of water, judging by the amount of sweet oil gone rancid in their hair. Of them all, if these were all, the Lady Gemma was the only willful one; and she, too old.

The amenities over, Fax ushered his unwelcome guests outside, and led the way to the quarters he had assigned the bronze rider.

"A pleasant room," F'lar acknowledged, stripping off gloves and wher-hide tunic, throwing them carelessly to the table. "I shall see to my men and the beasts. They have been fed recently," he commented, pointing up Fax's omission in inquiring. "I request liberty to wander through the crafthold."

Fax sourly granted what was a dragonman's traditional privilege.

"I shall not further disrupt your routine, Lord Fax, for you must have many demands on you, with seven Holds to supervise." F'lar inclined his body slightly to the overlord, turning away as a gesture of dismissal. He could imagine the infuriated expression on Fax's face from the stamping retreat.

F'nor and the men had settled themselves in a hastily vacated barrackroom. The dragons were perched comfortably on the rocky ridges above the Hold. Each rider kept his dragon in light, but alert, charge. There were to be no incidents on a Search.

As a group, the dragonmen rose at F'lar's entrance.

"No tricks, no troubles, but look around closely," he said laconically. "Return by sundown with the names of any likely prospects." He caught F'nor's grin, remembering how Fax had slurred over some names. "Descriptions are in order and craft affiliation."

The men nodded, their eyes glinting with understanding. They were flatteringly confident of a successful Search even as F'lar's doubts grew now that he had seen Fax's women. By all logic, the pick of the High Reaches should be in Fax's chief Hold… but they were not. Still, there were many large craftholds not to mention the six other High Holds to visit. All the same…

In unspoken accord F'lar and F'nor left the barracks. The men would follow, unobtrusively, in pairs or singly, to reconnoiter the crafthold and the nearer farmholds. The men were as overtly eager to be abroad as F'lar was privately. There had been a time when dragonmen were frequent and favored guests in all the great Holds throughout Pern, from southern Fo'rt to high north Igen. This pleasant custom, too, had died along with other observances, evidence of the low regard in which the Weyr was presently held. F'lar vowed to correct this.

He forced himself to trace in memory the insidious changes. The Records, which each Weyrwoman kept, were proof of the gradual, but perceptible, decline, traceable through the past two hundred full Turns. Knowing the facts did not alleviate the condition. And F'lar was of that scant handful in the Weyr itself who did credit Records and Ballad alike. The situation might shortly reverse itself radically if the old tales were to be believed.

There was a reason, an explanation, a purpose, F'lar felt, for every one of the Weyr laws from First Impression to the Firestone: from the grass-free heights to ridge-running gutters. For elements as minor as controlling the appetite of a dragon to limiting the inhabitants of the Weyr. Although why the other five Weyrs had been abandoned, F'lar did not know. Idly he wondered if there were records, dusty and crumbling, lodged in the disused Weyrs. He must contrive to check when next his wings flew patrol. Certainly there was no explanation in Benden Weyr.

"There is industry but no enthusiasm," F'nor was saying, drawing F'lar's attention back to their tour of the crafthold.

They had descended the guttered ramp from the Hold into the crafthold proper, the broad roadway lined with cottages up to the imposing stone crafthalls. Silently F'lar noted moss-clogged gutters on the roofs, the vines clasping the walls. It was painful for one of his calling to witness the flagrant disregard of simple safety precautions. Growing things were forbidden near the habitations of mankind.

"News travels fast," F'nor chuckled, nodding at a hurrying craftsman, in the smock of a baker, who gave them a mumbled good day. "Not a female in sight."

His observation was accurate. Women should be abroad at this hour, bringing in supplies from the storehouses, washing in the river on such a bright warm day, or going out to the farmholds to help with planting. Not a gowned figure in sight.

"We used to be preferred mates," F'nor remarked caustically.

"We'll visit the Clothmen's Hall first. If my memory serves me right…"

"As it always does…" F'nor interjected wryly. He took no advantage of their blood relationship but he was more at ease with the bronze rider than most of the dragonmen, the other bronze riders included. F'lar was reserved in a close-knit society of easy equality. He flew a tightly disciplined wing but men maneuvered to serve under him. His wing always excelled in the Games. None ever floundered in *between* to disappear forever and no beast in his wing sickened, leaving a man in dragonless exile from the Weyr, a part of him numb forever.

"L'tol came this way and settled in one of the High Reaches," F'lar continued.

"L'tol?"

"Yes, a green rider from S'lel's wing. You remember."

An ill-timed swerve during the Spring Games had brought L'tol and his beast into the full blast of a phosphene emission from S'lel's bronze Tuenth. L'tol had been thrown from his beast's neck as the dragon tried to evade the blast. Another wingmate had swooped to catch the rider but the green dragon, his left wing crisped, his body scorched, had died of shock and phosphene poisoning.

"L'tol would aid our Search," F'nor agreed as the two dragonmen walked up to the bronze doors of the Clothmen's Hall. They paused on the threshold, adjusting their eyes to the dimmer light within. Glows punctuated the wall recesses and hung in clusters above the larger looms where the finer tapestries and fabrics were woven by master craftsmen. The pervading mood was one of quiet, purposeful industry.

Before their eyes had adapted, however, a figure glided to them, with a polite, if curt, request for them to follow him.

They were led to the right of the entrance, to a small office, curtained from the main hall. Their guide turned to them, his face visible in the wallglows. There was that air about him that marked him indefinably as a dragonman. But his face was lined deeply, one side seamed with old burn marks. His eyes, sick with a hungry yearning, dominated his face. He blinked constantly.

"I am now Lytol," he said in a harsh voice.

F'lar nodded acknowledgment.

"You would be F'lar," Lytol said, "and you, F'nor. You've both the look of your sire."

F'lar nodded again.

Lytol swallowed convulsively, the muscles in his face twitching as the presence of dragonmen revived his awareness of exile. He essayed a smile.

"Dragons in the sky! The news spread faster than Threads."

"Nemorth has a new queen."

"Jora dead?" Lytol asked concernedly, his face cleared of its nervous movement for a second.

F'lar nodded.

Lytol grimaced bitterly. "R'gul again, huh." He stared off in the middle distance, his eyelids quiet but the muscles along his jaw took up the constant movement. "You've the High Reaches? All of them?" Lytol asked, turning back to the dragonman, a slight emphasis on "all."

F'lar gave an affirmative nod again.

"You've seen the women." Lytol's disgust showed through the words. It was a statement, not a question, for he hurried on. "Well, there are no better in all the High Reaches," and his tone expressed utmost disdain.

"Fax likes his women comfortably fleshed and docile," Lytol rattled on. "Even the Lady Gemma has learned. It'd be different if he didn't need her family's support. Ah, it would be different indeed. So he keeps her pregnant, hoping to kill her in childbed one day. And he will. He will."

Lytol drew himself up, squaring his shoulders, turning full to the two dragonmen. His expression was vindictive, his voice low and tense.

"Kill that tyrant, for the sake and safety of Pern. Of the Weyr. Of the queen. He only bides his time. He spreads discontent among the other lords. He"…Lytol's laughter had an hysterical edge to it now… "he fancies himself as good as dragonmen."

"There are no candidates then in this Hold?" F'lar said, his voice sharp enough to cut through the man's preoccupation with his curious theory.

Lytol stared at the bronze rider. "Did I not say it?"

"What of Ruath Hold?"

Lytol stopped shaking his head and looked sharply at F'lar, his lips curling in a cunning smile. He laughed mirthlessly.

"You think to find a Torene, or a Moreta, hidden at Ruath Hold in these times? Well, all of that Blood are dead. Fax's blade was thirsty that day. He knew the truth of those harpers' tales, that Ruathan lords gave full measure of hospitality to dragonmen and the Ruathan were a breed apart. There were, you know," Lytol's voice dropped to a confiding whisper, "exiled Weyrmen like myself in that Line."

F'lar nodded gravely, unable to contradict the man's pitiful attempt at self-esteem.

"No," and Lytol chuckled softly. "Fax gets nothing from that Hold but trouble. And the women Fax used to take…" his laugh turned nasty in tone. "It is rumored he was impotent for months afterward."

"Any families in the holdings with Weyr blood?"

Lytol frowned, glanced surprised at F'lar. He rubbed the scarred side of his face thoughtfully.

"There were," he admitted slowly. "There were. But I doubt if any live on." He thought a moment longer, then shook his head emphatically.

F'lar shrugged.

"I wish I had better news for you," Lytol murmured.

"No matter," F'lar reassured him, one hand poised to part the hanging in the doorway.

Lytol came up to him swiftly, his voice urgent.

"Heed what I say, Fax is ambitious. Force R'gul, or whoever is Weyrleader next, to keep watch on the High Reaches."

Lytol jabbed a finger in the direction of the Hold. "He scoffs openly at tales of the Threads. He taunts the harpers for the stupid nonsense of the old ballads and has banned from their repertoire all dragonlore. The new generation will grow up totally ignorant of duty, tradition and precaution."

F'lar was surprised to hear that on top of Lytol's other disclosures. Yet the Red Star pulsed in the sky and the time was drawing near when they would hysterically reavow the old allegiances in fear for their very lives.

"Have you been abroad in the early morning of late?" asked F'nor, grinning maliciously.

"I have," Lytol breathed out in a hushed, choked whisper. "I have…" A groan was wrenched from his guts and he whirled away from the dragonmen, his head bowed between hunched shoulders. "Go," he said, gritting his teeth. And, as they hesitated, he pleaded, "Go!"

F'lar walked quickly from the room, followed by F'nor. The bronze rider crossed the quiet dim Hall with long strides and exploded into the startling sunlight. His momentum took him into the center of the square. There he stopped so abruptly that F'nor, hard on his heels, nearly collided with him.

"We will spend exactly the same time within the other Halls," he announced in a tight voice, his face averted from F'nor's eyes. F'lar's throat was constricted. It was difficult, suddenly, for him to speak. He swallowed hard, several times.

"To be dragonless…" murmured F'nor, pityingly. The encounter with Lytol had roiled his depths in a mournful way to which he was unaccustomed. That F'lar appeared equally shaken went far to dispel F'nor's private opinion that his half-brother was incapable of emotion.

"There is no other way once First Impression has been made. You know that," F'lar roused himself to say curtly. He strode off to the Hall bearing the Leathermen's device.

> The Hold is barred
> The Hall is bare.
> And men vanish.
> The soil is barren,
> The rock is bald.
> All hope banish.

Lessa was shoveling ashes from the hearth when the agitated messenger staggered into the Great Hall. She made herself as inconspicuous as possible so the Warder would not dismiss her. She had contrived to be sent to the Great Hall that morning, knowing that the Warder intended to brutalize the Head Clothman for the shoddy quality of the goods readied for shipment to Fax.

"Fax is coming! With dragonmen!" the man gasped out as he plunged into the dim Great Hall.

The Warder, who had been about to lash the Head Clothman, turned, stunned, from his victim. The courier, a farmholder from the edge of Ruatha, stumbled up to the Warder, so excited with his message that he grabbed the Warder's arm.

"How dare you leave your Hold?" and the Warder aimed his lash at the astonished holder. The force of the first blow knocked the man from his feet. Yelping, he scrambled out of reach of a second lashing. "Dragonmen indeed! Fax? Ha! He shuns Ruatha. There!" The Warder punctuated each denial with another blow, kicking the helpless wretch for good measure, before he turned breathless to glare at the clothman and the two underwarders. "How did he get in here with such a threadbare lie?" The Warder stalked to the great door. It was flung open just as he reached out for the iron handle. The ashenfaced guard officer rushed in, nearly toppling the Warder.

"Dragonmen! Dragons! All over Ruatha!" the man gibbered, arms flailing wildly. He, too, pulled at the Warder's arm, dragging the stupefied official toward the outer courtyard, to bear out the truth of his statement.

Lessa scooped up the last pile of ashes. Picking up her equipment, she slipped out of the Great Hall. There was a very pleased smile on her face under the screen of matted hair.

A dragonman at Ruatha! She must somehow contrive to get Fax so humiliated, or so infuriated, that he would renounce his claim to the Hold, in the presence of a dragonman. Then she could claim her birthright.

But she would have to be extraordinarily wary. Dragonriders were men apart. Anger did not cloud their intelligence. Greed did not sully their judgment. Fear did not dull their reactions. Let the dense-witted believe human sacrifice, unnatural lusts, insane revel. She was not so gullible. And those stories went against her grain. Dragonmen were still human and there was Weyr blood in her veins. It was the same color as that of anyone else; enough of hers had been spilled to prove that.

She halted for a moment, catching a sudden shallow breath. Was this the danger she had sensed four days ago at dawn? The final encounter in her struggle to regain the Hold? No... there had been more to that portent than revenge.

The ash bucket banged against her shins as she shuffled down the low-ceilinged corridor to the stable door. Fax would find a cold welcome. She had laid no new fire on the hearth. Her laugh echoed back unpleasantly from the damp walls. She rested her bucket and propped her broom and shovel as she wrestled with the heavy bronze door that gave into the new stables.

They had been built outside the cliff of Ruatha by Fax's first Warder, a subtler man than all eight of his successors. He had achieved more than all others and Lessa had honestly regretted the necessity of his death. But he would have made her revenge impossible. He would have caught her out before she had learned how to camouflage herself and her little interferences. What had his name been? She could not recall. Well, she regretted his death.

The second man had been properly greedy and it had been easy to set up a pattern of misunderstanding between Warder and craftsmen. That one had been determined to squeeze all profit from Ruathan goods so that some of it would drop into his pocket before Fax suspected a shortage. The craftsmen who had begun to accept the skillful diplomacy of the first Warder bitterly resented the second's grasping, high-handed ways. They resented the passing of the Old Line and, even more so, the way of its passing. They were unforgiving of insult to Ruatha, its now secondary position in the High Reaches, and they resented the individual indignities that holders, craftsmen and farmers alike suffered under the second Warder. It took little manipulation to arrange for matters at Ruatha to go from bad to worse.

The second was replaced and his successor fared no better. He was caught diverting goods, the best of the goods at that. Fax had had him executed. His bony head still hung in the main firepit above the great Tower.

The present incumbent had not been able to maintain the Hold in even the sorry condition in which he had assumed its management. Seemingly simple matters developed rapidly into disasters. Like the production of cloth... Contrary to his boasts to Fax, the quality had not improved, and the quantity had fallen off.

Now Fax was here. And with dragonmen! Why dragonmen? The import of the question froze Lessa, and the heavy door closing behind her barked her heels painfully. Dragonmen used to be frequent visitors at Ruatha, that she knew, and even vaguely remembered. Those memories were like a harper's tale, told of someone else, not something within her own experience. She had limited her fierce attention to Ruatha only. She could not even recall the name of Queen or Weyrwoman from the instructions of her childhood, nor could she recall hearing mention of any queen or weyrwoman by anyone in the Hold these past ten Turns.

Perhaps the dragonmen were finally going to call the lords of the Holds to task for the disgraceful show of greenery about the Holds. Well, Lessa was to blame for much of that in Ruatha but she defied even a dragonman to confront her with her guilt. Did all Ruatha fall to the Threads it would be better than remaining dependent to Fax! The heresy shocked Lessa even as she thought it.

Wishing she could as easily unburden her conscience of such blasphemy, she ditched the ashes on the stable midden. There was a sudden change in air pressure around her. Then a fleeting shadow caused her to glance up.

From behind the cliff above glided a dragon, its enormous wings spread to their fullest as he caught the morning updraft. Turning effortlessly, he descended. A second, a third, a full wing of dragons followed in soundless flight and patterned descent, graceful and awesome. The claxon rang belatedly from the Tower and from within the kitchens there issued the screams and shrieks of the terrified drudges.

Lessa took cover. She ducked into the kitchen where she was instantly seized by the assistant cook and thrust with a buffet and a kick toward the sinks. There she was put to scrubbing grease-encrusted serving bowls with cleansing sand.

The yelping canines were already lashed to the spitrun, turning a scrawny herdbeast that had been set to roast. The cook was ladling seasonings on the carcass, swearing at having to offer so poor a meal to so many guests, and some of them high-rank. Winter-dried fruits from the last scanty harvest had been set to soak and two of the oldest drudges were scraping roots.

An apprentice cook was kneading bread; another, carefully spicing a sauce. Looking fixedly at him, she diverted his hand from one spice box to a less appropriate one as he gave a final shake to the concoction. She added too much wood to the wall oven, insuring ruin for the breads. She controlled the canines deftly, slowing one and speeding the other so that the meat would be underdone on one side, burned on the other. That the feast should be a fast, the food presented found inedible, was her whole intention.

Above in the Hold, she had no doubt that certain other measures, undertaken at different times for this exact contingency, were being discovered.

Her fingers bloodied from a beating, one of the Warder's women came shrieking into the kitchen, hopeful of refuge there.

"Insects have eaten the best blankets to shreds! And a canine who had littered on the best linens snarled at me as she gave suck! And the rushes are noxious, the best chambers full of debris driven in by the winter wind. Somebody left the shutters ajar. Just a tiny bit, but it was enough…" the woman wailed, clutching her hand to her breast and rocking back and forth.

Lessa bent with great industry to shine the plates.

> Watch-wher, watch-wher,
> In your lair,
> Watch well, watch-wher!
> Who goes there?

"The watch-wher is hiding something," F'lar told F'nor as they consulted in the hastily cleaned Great Hall. The room delighted to hold the wintry chill although a generous fire now burned on the hearth.

"It was but gibbering when Canth spoke to it," F'nor remarked. He was leaning against the mantel, turning slightly from side to side to gather some warmth. He watched his wingleader's impatient pacing.

"Mnementh is calming it down," F'lar replied. "He may be able to sort out the nightmare. The creature may be more senile than aware, but…"

"I doubt it," F'nor concurred helpfully. He glanced with apprehension up at the webhung ceiling. He was certain he'd found most of the crawlers, but he didn't fancy their sting. Not on top of the discomforts already experienced in this forsaken Hold. If the night stayed mild, he intended curling up with Canth on the heights. "That would be more reasonable than anything Fax or his Warder have suggested."

"Hm-m-m," F'lar muttered, frowning at the brown rider.

"Well, it's unbelievable that Ruatha could have fallen to such disrepair in ten short Turns. Every dragon caught the feeling of power and it's obvious the watch-wher had been tampered with. That takes a good deal of control."

"From someone of the Blood," F'lar reminded him.

F'nor shot his wingleader a quick look, wondering if he could possibly be serious in the light of all information to the contrary.

"I grant you there is power here, F'lar," F'nor conceded. "It could easily be a hidden male of the old Blood. But we need a female. And Fax made it plain, in his inimitable fashion, that he left none of the old Blood alive in the Hold the day he took it. No, no." The brown rider shook his head, as if he could dispel the lack of faith in his wingleader's curious insistence that the Search would end in Ruath with Ruathan blood.

"That watch-wher is hiding something and only someone of the Blood of its Hold can arrange that," F'lar said emphatically. He gestured around the Hall and toward the walls, bare of hangings. "Ruatha has been overcome. But she resists… subtly. I say it points to the old Blood, *and* power. Not power alone."

The obstinate expression in F'lar's eyes, the set of his jaw, suggested that F'nor seek another topic.

"The pattern was well-flown today," F'nor suggested tentatively. "Does a dragonman good to ride a flaming beast. Does the beast good, too. Keeps the digestive process in order."

F'lar nodded sober agreement. "Let R'gul temporize as he chooses. It is fitting and proper to ride a firespouting beast and these holders need to be reminded of Weyr power."

"Right now, anything would help our prestige," F'nor commented sourly. "What had Fax to say when he hailed you in the Pass?" F'nor knew his question was almost impertinent but if it were, F'lar would ignore it.

F'lar's slight smile was unpleasant and there was an ominous glint in his amber eyes.

"We talked of rule and resistance."

"Did he not also draw on you?" F'nor asked.

F'lar's smile deepened. "Until he remembered I was dragon-mounted."

"He's considered a vicious fighter," F'nor said.

"I am at some disadvantage?" F'lar asked, turning sharply on his brown rider, his face too controlled.

"To my knowledge, no," F'nor reassured his leader quickly. F'lar had tumbled every man in the Weyr, efficiently and easily. "But Fax kills often and without cause."

"And because we dragonmen do not seek blood, we are not to be feared as fighters?" snapped F'lar. "Are you ashamed of your heritage?"

"I? No!" F'nor sucked in his breath. "Nor any of our wing!" he added proudly. "But there is that in the attitude of the men in this progression of Fax's that… that makes me wish some excuse to fight."

"As you observed today, Fax seeks some excuse. And," F'lar added thoughtfully, "there is something here in Ruatha that unnerves our noble overlord."

He caught sight of Lady Tela, whom Fax had so courteously assigned him for comfort during the progression, waving to him from the inner Hold portal.

"A case in point. Fax's Lady Tela is some three months gone."

F'nor frowned at the insult to his leader.

"She giggles incessantly and appears so addlepated that one cannot decide whether she babbles out of ignorance or at Fax's suggestion. As she has apparently not bathed all winter, and is not, in any case, my ideal, I have…" F'lar grinned maliciously "…deprived myself of her kind offices."

F'nor hastily cleared his throat and his expression as Lady Tela approached them. He caught the unappealing odor from the scarf or handkerchief she waved constantly. Dragonmen endured a great deal for the Weyr. He moved away, with apparent courtesy, to join the rest of the dragonmen entering the Hall.

F'lar turned with equal courtesy to Lady Tela as she jabbered away about the terrible condition of the rooms which Lady Gemma and the other ladies had been assigned.

"The shutters, both sets, were ajar all winter long and you should have seen the trash on the floors. We finally got two of the drudges to sweep it all into the fireplace. And then that smoked something fearful 'till a man was sent up." Lady

Tela giggled. "He found the access blocked by a chimney stone fallen aslant. The rest of the chimney, for a wonder, was in good repair."

She waved her handkerchief. F'lar held his breath as the gesture wafted an unappealing odor in his direction.

He glanced up the Hall toward the inner Hold door and saw Lady Gemma descending, her steps slow and awkward. Some subtle difference about her gait attracted him and he stared at her, trying to identify it.

"Oh, yes, poor Lady Gemma," Lady Tela babbled, sighing deeply. "We are so concerned. Why Lord Fax insisted on her coming, I do not know. She is not near her time and yet..." The lighthead's concern sounded sincere.

F'lar's incipient hatred for Fax and his brutality matured abruptly. He left his partner chattering to thin air and courteously extended his arm to Lady Gemma to support her down the steps and to the table. Only the brief tightening of her fingers on his forearm betrayed her gratitude. Her face was very white and drawn, the lines deeply etched around mouth and eyes, showing the effort she was expending.

"Some attempt has been made, I see, to restore order to the Hall," she remarked in a conversational tone.

"Some," F'lar admitted dryly, glancing around the grandly proportioned Hall, its rafter festooned with the webs of many Turns. The inhabitants of those gossamer nests dropped from time to time, with ripe splats, to the floor, onto the table and into the serving platters. Nothing replaced the old banners of the Ruathan Blood, which had been removed from the stark brown stone walls. Fresh rushes did obscure the greasy flagstones. The trestle tables appeared recently sanded and scraped, and the platters gleamed dully in the refreshed glows. Unfortunately, the brighter light was a mistake for it was much too unflattering.

"This was such a graceful Hall," Lady Gemma murmured for F'lar's ears alone.

"You were a friend?" he asked, politely.

"Yes, in my youth." Her voice dropped expressively on the last word, evoking for F'lar a happier girlhood. "It was a noble line!"

"Think you *one* might have escaped the sword?"

Lady Gemma flashed him a startled look, then quickly composed her features, lest the exchange be noted. She gave a barely perceptible shake of her head and then shifted her awkward weight to take her place at the table. Graciously she inclined her head toward F'lar, both dismissing and thanking him.

F'lar returned to his own partner and placed her at the table on his left. As the only person of rank who would dine that night at Ruath Hold, Lady Gemma was seated on his right; Fax would be beyond her. The dragonmen and Fax's upper soldiery would sit at the lower tables. No guildmen had been invited to Ruatha. Fax arrived just then with his current lady and two underleaders, the Warder bowing them effusively into the Hall. The man, F'lar noticed, kept a good distance from his overlord... as well as a Warder might whose responsibility was in this sorry condition. F'lar flicked a crawler away. Out of the corner of his eye, he saw Lady Gemma wince and shudder.

Fax stamped up to the raised table, his face black with suppressed rage. He pulled back his chair roughly, slamming it into Lady Gemma's before he seated himself. He pulled the chair to the table with a force that threatened to rock the none too stable trestle-top from its supporting legs. Scowling, he inspected his goblet and plate, fingering the surface, ready to throw them aside if they displeased him.

"A roast and fresh bread, Lord Fax, and such fruits and roots as are left. Had I but known of your arrival, I could have sent to Crom for…"

"Sent to Crom?" roared Fax, slamming the plate he was inspecting into the table so forcefully the rim bent under his hands. The Warder winced again as if he himself had been maimed.

"The day one of my Holds cannot support itself *or* the visit of its rightful overlord, I shall renounce it."

Lady Gemma gasped. Simultaneously the dragons roared. F'lar felt the unmistakable surge of power. His eyes instinctively sought F'nor at the lower table. The brown rider… all the dragonmen… had experienced that inexplicable shaft of exultation.

"What's wrong, Dragonman?" snapped Fax.

F'lar, affecting unconcern, stretched his legs under the table and assumed an indolent posture in the heavy chair.

"Wrong?"

"The dragons!"

"Oh, nothing. They often roar… at the sunset, at a flock of passing wherries, at mealtimes," and F'lar smiled amiably at the Lord of the High Reaches. Beside him his tablemate gave a squeak.

"Mealtimes! Have they not been fed?"

"Oh, yes. Five days ago."

"Oh. Five… days ago? And are they hungry… now?" Her voice trailed into a whisper of fear, her eyes grew round.

"In a few days," F'lar assured her. Under cover of his detached amusement, F'lar scanned the Hall. That surge had come from nearby. Either in the Hall or just outside. It must have been from within. It came so soon upon Fax's speech that his words must have triggered it. And the power had had an indefinably feminine touch to it.

One of Fax's women? F'lar found that hard to credit. Mnementh had been close to all of them and none had shown a vestige of power. Much less, with the exception of Lady Gemma, any intelligence.

One of the Hall women? So far he had seen only the sorry drudges and the aging females the Warder had as housekeepers. The Warder's personal woman? He must discover if that man had one. One of the Hold guards' women? F'lar suppressed an intense desire to rise and search.

"You mount a guard?" he asked Fax casually.

"Double at Ruath Hold!" he was told in a tight, hard voice, ground out from somewhere deep in Fax's chest.

"Here?" F'lar all but laughed out loud, gesturing around the sadly appointed chamber.

"Here! Food!" Fax changed the subject with a roar.

Five drudges, two of them women in brown-gray rags such that F'lar hoped they had had nothing to do with the preparation of the meal, staggered in under the emplattered herdbeast. No one with so much as a trace of power would sink to such depths, unless...

The aroma that reached him as the platter was placed on the serving table distracted him. It reeked of singed bone and charred meat. The Warder frantically sharpened his tools as if a keen edge could somehow slice acceptable portions from this unlikely carcass.

Lady Gemma caught her breath again and F'lar saw her hands curl tightly around the armrests. He saw the convulsive movement of her throat as she swallowed. He, too, did not look forward to this repast.

The drudges reappeared with wooden trays of bread. Burnt crusts had been scraped and cut, in some places, from the loaves before serving. As other trays were borne in, F'lar tried to catch sight of the faces of the servitors. Matted hair obscured the face of the one who presented a dish of legumes swimming in greasy liquid. Revolted, F'lar poked through the legumes to find properly cooked portions to offer Lady Gemma. She waved them aside, her face ill-concealing her discomfort.

As F'lar was about to turn and serve Lady Tela, he saw Lady Gemma's hand clutch convulsively at the chair arms. He realized that she was not merely nauseated by the unappetizing food. She was seized with labor contractions.

F'lar glanced in Fax's direction. The overlord was scowling blackly at the attempts of the Warder to find edible portions of meat to serve.

F'lar touched Lady Gemma's arm with light fingers. She turned just enough to look at F'lar from the corner of her eye. She managed a socially correct half-smile.

"I dare not leave just now, Lord F'lar. He is always dangerous at Ruatha. And it may only be false pangs."

F'lar was dubious as he saw another shudder pass through her frame. The woman would have been a fine weyrwoman, he thought ruefully, were she but younger.

The Warder, his hands shaking, presented Fax the sliced meats. There were slivers of overdone flesh and portions of almost edible meats, but not much of either.

One furious wave of Fax's broad fist and the Warder had the plate, meats and juice, square in the face. Despite himself, F'lar sighed, for those undoubtedly constituted the only edible portions of the entire beast.

"You call this food? *You call this food?*" Fax bellowed. His voice boomed back from the bare vault of the ceiling, shaking crawlers from their webs as the sound shattered the fragile strands. "Slop! Slop!"

F'lar rapidly brushed crawlers from Lady Gemma who was helpless in the throes of a very strong contraction.

"It's all we had on such short notice," the Warder squealed, juices streaking down his cheeks. Fax threw the goblet at him and the wine went streaming down the man's chest. The steaming dish of roots followed and the man yelped as the hot liquid splashed over him.

"My lord, my lord, had I but known!"

"Obviously, Ruatha cannot support the visit of its Lord. You must renounce it," F'lar heard himself saying.

His shock at such words issuing from his mouth was as great as that of everyone else in the Hall. Silence fell, broken by the splat of falling crawlers and the drip of root liquid from the Warder's shoulders to the rushes. The grating of Fax's boot-heel was clearly audible as he swung slowly around to face the bronze rider.

As F'lar conquered his own amazement and rapidly tried to predict what to do next to mend matters, he saw F'nor rise slowly to his feet, hand on dagger hilt.

"I did not hear you correctly?" Fax asked, his face blank of all expression, his eyes snapping.

Unable to comprehend how he could have uttered such an arrant challenge, F'lar managed to assume a languid pose.

"You did mention," he drawled, "that if any of your Holds could not support itself and the visit of its rightful overlord, you would renounce it."

Fax stared back at F'lar, his face a study of swiftly suppressed emotions, the glint of triumph dominant. F'lar, his face stiff with the forced expression of indifference, was casting swiftly about in his mind. In the name of the Egg, had he lost all sense of discretion?

Pretending utter unconcern, he stabbed some vegetables onto his knife and began to munch on them. As he did so, he noticed F'nor glancing slowly around the Hall, scrutinizing everyone. Abruptly F'lar realized what had happened. Somehow, in making that statement, he, a dragonman, had responded to a covert use of the power. F'lar, the bronze rider, was being put into a position where he would *have* to fight Fax. Why? For what end? To get Fax to renounce the Hold? Incredible! But, there could be only one possible reason for such a turn of events. An exultation as sharp as pain swelled within F'lar. It was all he could do to maintain his pose of bored indifference, all he could do to turn his attention to thwarting Fax, should he press for a duel. A duel would serve no purpose. He, F'lar, had no time to waste on it.

A groan escaped Lady Gemma and broke the eye-locked stance of the two antagonists. Irritated, Fax looked down at her, fist clenched and half-raised to strike her for her temerity in interrupting her lord and master. The contraction that contorted the swollen belly was as obvious as the woman's pain. F'lar dared not look toward her but he wondered if she had deliberately groaned aloud to break the tension.

Incredibly, Fax began to laugh. He threw back his head, showing big, stained teeth, and roared.

"Aye, renounce it, in favor of her issue, if it is male… and lives!" he crowed, laughing raucously.

"Heard and witnessed!" F'lar snapped, jumping to his feet and pointing to the riders. They were on their feet in the instant. "Heard, and witnessed!" they averred in the traditional manner.

With that movement, everyone began to babble at once in nervous relief. The other women, each reacting in her way to the imminence of birth, called orders to the servants and advice to each other. They converged toward Lady Gemma, hovering undecidedly out of Fax's range, like silly wherries disturbed from their roosts. It was obvious they were torn between their fear of the lord and their desire to reach the laboring woman.

He gathered their intentions as well as their reluctance and, still stridently laughing, knocked back his chair. He stepped over it, strode down to the meat-stand and stood hacking off pieces with his knife, stuffing them, juice dripping, into his mouth without ceasing his guffawing.

As F'lar bent toward Lady Gemma to assist her out of her chair, she grabbed his arm urgently. Their eyes met, hers clouded with pain. She pulled him closer.

"He means to kill you, Bronze Rider. He loves to kill," she whispered.

"Dragonmen are not easily killed, but I am grateful to you."

"I do not want you killed," she said, softly, biting at her lip. "We have so few bronze riders."

F'lar stated at her, startled. Did she, Fax's lady, actually believe in the Old Laws?

F'lar beckoned to two of the Warder's men to carry her up into the Hold. He caught Lady Tela by the arm as she fluttered past him.

"What do you need?"

"Oh, oh," she exclaimed, her face twisted with panic; she was distractedly wringing her hands. "Water, hot. Clean cloths. And a birthing-woman. Oh, yes, we must have a birthing-woman."

F'lar looked about for one of the Hold women, his glance sliding over the first disreputable figure who had started to mop up the spilled food. He signaled instead for the Warder and peremptorily ordered him to send for the woman. The Warder kicked at the drudge on the floor.

"You… you! Whatever your name is, go get her from the crafthold. You must know who she is."

The drudge evaded the parting kick the Warder aimed in her direction with a nimbleness at odds with her appearance of extreme age and decrepitude. She scurried across the Hall and out the kitchen door.

Fax sliced and speared meat, occasionally bursting out with a louder bark of laughter as his inner thoughts amused him. F'lar sauntered down to the carcass and, without waiting for invitation from his host, began to carve neat slices also, beckoning his men over. Fax's soldiers, however, waited until their lord had eaten his fill.

> Lord of the Hold, your charge is sure
> In thick walls, metal doors and no verdure.

Lessa sped from the Hall to summon the birthing-woman, seething with frustration. So close! So close! How could she come so close and yet fail? Fax should have challenged the dragonman. And the dragonman was strong and young, his face that of a fighter, stern and controlled. He should not have temporized. Was all honor dead in Pern, smothered by green grass?

And why, oh why, had Lady Gemma chosen that precious moment to go into labor? If her groan hadn't distracted Fax, the fight would have begun and not even Fax, for all his vaunted prowess as a vicious fighter, would have prevailed against a dragonman who had her... Lessa's... support! The Hold must be secured to its rightful Blood again. Fax must not leave Ruatha, alive, again!

Above her, on the High Tower, the great bronze dragon gave forth a weird croon; his many-faceted eyes sparkling in the gathering darkness.

Unconsciously she silenced him as she would have done the watch-wher. Ah, that watch-wher. He had not come out of his den at her passing. She knew the dragons had been at him. She could hear him gibbering in panic.

The slant of the road toward the crafthold lent impetus to her flying feet and she had to brace herself to a sliding stop at the birthing-woman's stone threshold. She banged on the closed door and heard the frightened exclamation within.

"A birth. A birth at the Hold," Lessa cried.

"A birth?" came the muffled cry and the latches were thrown up on the door. "At the Hold?"

"Fax's lady and, as you love life, hurry! For if it is male, it will be Ruatha's own lord."

That ought to fetch her, thought Lessa, and in that instant, the door was flung open by the man of the house. Lessa could see the birthing-woman gathering up her things in haste, piling them into her shawl. Lessa hurried the woman out, up the steep road to the Hold, under the Tower gate, grabbing the woman as she tried to run at the sight of a dragon peering down at her. Lessa drew her into the Court and pushed her, resisting, into the Hall.

The woman clutched at the inner door, balking at the sight of the gathering there. Lord Fax, his feet up on the trestle table, was paring his fingernails with his knife blade, still chuckling. The dragonmen in their wher-hide tunics were eating quietly at one table while the soldiers were having their turn at the meat.

The bronze rider noticed their entrance and pointed urgently toward the inner Hold. The birthing-woman seemed frozen to the spot. Lessa tugged futilely at her arm, urging her to cross the Hall. To her surprise, the bronze rider strode to them.

"Go quickly, woman, Lady Gemma is before her time," he said, frowning with concern, gesturing imperatively toward the Hold entrance. He caught her by the shoulder and led her, all unwilling, Lessa tugging away at her other arm.

When they reached the stairs, he relinquished his grip, nodding to Lessa to escort her the rest of the way. Just as they reached the massive inner door, Lessa noticed how sharply the dragonman was looking at them… at her hand, on the birthing-woman's arm. Warily, she glanced at her hand and saw it, as if it belonged to a stranger: the long fingers, shapely despite dirt and broken nails; her small hand, delicately boned, gracefully placed despite the urgency of the grip. She blurred it and hurried on.

> Honor those the dragons heed,
> In thought and favor, word and deed.
> Worlds are lost or worlds are saved
> By those dangers dragonbraved.
>
> Dragonman, avoid excess;
> Greed will bring the Weyr distress;
> To the ancient Laws adhere,
> Prospers thus the Dragon weyr.

An unintelligible ululation raised the waiting, men to their feet, startled from private meditations and diversion of Bonethrows. Only Fax remained unmoved at the alarm, save that the slight sneer, which had settled on his face hours past, deepened to smug satisfaction.

"Dead-ed-ed," the tidings reverberated down the rocky corridors of the Hold. The weeping lady seemed to erupt out of the passage from the inner Hold, flying down the steps to sink into an hysterical heap at Fax's feet. "She's dead. Lady Gemma is dead. There was too much blood. It was too soon. She was too old to bear more children."

F'lar couldn't decide whether the woman was apologizing for, or exulting in, the woman's death. She certainly couldn't be criticizing her Lord for placing Lady Gemma in such peril. F'lar, however, was sincerely sorry at Gemma's passing. She had been a brave, fine woman.

And now, what would be Fax's next move? F'lar caught F'nor's identically quizzical glance and shrugged expressively.

"The child lives!" a curiously distorted voice announced, penetrating the rising noise in the Great Hall. The words electrified the atmosphere. Every head slewed round sharply toward the portal to the inner Hold where the drudge, a totally unexpected messenger, stood poised on the top step.

"It is male!" This announcement rang triumphantly in the still Hall.

Fax jerked himself to his feet, kicking aside the wailer at his feet, scowling ominously at the drudge. "What did you say, woman?"

"The child lives. It is male," the creature repeated, descending the stairs.

Incredulity and rage suffused Fax's face. His body seemed to coil up.

"Ruatha has a new lord!" Staring intently at the overlord, she advanced, her mien purposeful, almost menacing.

The tentative cheers of the Warder's men were drowned by the roaring of the dragons.

Fax erupted into action. He leaped across the intervening space, bellowing. Before Lessa could dodge, his fist crashed down across her face. She fell heavily to the stone floor, where she lay motionless, a bundle of dirty rags.

"Hold, Fax!" F'lar's voice broke the silence as the Lord of the High Reaches flexed his leg to kick her.

Fax whirled, his hand automatically closing on his knife hilt.

"It was heard and witnessed, Fax," F'lar cautioned him, one hand outstretched in warning, "by dragonmen. Stand by your sworn and witnessed oath!"

"Witnessed? By dragonmen?" cried Fax with a derisive laugh. "Dragonwomen, you mean," he sneered, his eyes blazing with contempt, as he made one sweeping gesture of scorn.

He was momentarily taken aback by the speed with which the bronze rider's knife appeared in his hand.

"Dragonwomen?" F'lar queried, his lips curling back over his teeth, his voice dangerously soft. Glowlight flickered off his circling knife as he advanced on Fax.

"Women! Parasites on Pern. The Weyr power is over. Over!" Fax roared, leaping forward to land in a combat crouch.

The two antagonists were dimly aware of the scurry behind them, of tables pulled roughly aside to give the duelists space. F'lat could spare no glance at the crumpled form of the drudge. Yet he was sure, through and beyond instinct sure, that she was the source of power. He had felt it as she entered the room. The dragons' roaring confirmed it. If that fall had killed her... He advanced on Fax, leaping high to avoid the slashing blade as Fax unwound from the crouch with a powerful lunge.

F'lar evaded the attack easily, noticing his opponent's reach, deciding he had a slight advantage there. But not much. Fax had had much more actual hand-to-hand killing experience than had he whose duels had always ended at first blood on the practice floor. F'lar made due note to avoid closing with the burly lord. The man was heavy-chested, dangerous from sheer mass. F'lar must use agility as his weapon, not brute strength.

Fax feinted, testing F'lar for weakness, or indiscretion. The two crouched, facing each other across six feet of space, knife hands weaving, their free hands, spread-fingered, ready to grab.

Again Fax pressed the attack. F'lar allowed him to close, just near enough to dodge away with a backhanded swipe. Fabric ripped under the tip of his knife. He heard Fax snarl. The overlord was faster on his feet than his bulk suggested and F'lar had to dodge a second time, feeling Fax's knife score his wher-hide jerkin.

Grimly the two circled, each looking for an opening in the other's defense.

Fax plowed in, trying to corner the lighter, faster man between raised platform and wall.

F'lar countered, ducking low under Fax's flailing arm, slashing obliquely across Fax's side. The overlord caught at him, yanking savagely, and F'lar was trapped against the other man's side, straining desperately with his left hand to keep the knife arm up. F'lar brought up his knee, and ducked away as Fax gasped and buckled from the pain in his groin, but Fax struck in passing. Sudden fire laced F'lar's left shoulder.

Fax's face was red with anger and he wheezed from pain and shock. But the infuriated lord straightened up and charged. F'lar was forced to sidestep quickly before Fax could close with him. F'lar put the meat table between them, circling warily, flexing his shoulder to assess the extent of the knife's slash. It was painful, but the arm could be used.

Suddenly Fax scooped up some fatty scraps from the meat tray and hurled them at F'lar. The dragonman ducked and Fax came around the table with a rush. F'lar leaped sideways. Fax's flashing blade came within inches of his abdomen, as his own knife sliced down the outside of Fax's arm. Instantly the two pivoted to face each other again, but Fax's left arm hung limply at his side.

F'lar darted in, pressing his luck as the Lord of the High Reaches staggered. But F'lar misjudged the man's condition and suffered a terrific kick in the side as he tried to dodge under the feinting knife. Doubled with pain, F'lar rolled frantically away from his charging adversary. Fax was lurching forward, trying to fall on him, to pin the lighter dragonman down for a final thrust Somehow F'lar got to his feet, attempting to straighten to meet Fax's stumbling charge. His very position saved him. Fax over-reached his mark and staggered off balance. F'lar brought his right hand over with as much strength as he could muster and his blade plunged through Fax's unprotected back until he felt the point stick in the chest plate.

The defeated lord fell flat to the flagstones. The force of his descent dislodged the dagger from his chestbone and an inch of bloody blade re-emerged.

F'lar stared down at the dead man. There was no pleasure in killing, he realized, only relief that he himself was still alive. He wiped his forehead on his sleeve and forced himself erect, his side throbbing with the pain of that last kick and his left shoulder burning. He half-stumbled to the drudge, still sprawled where she had fallen.

He gently turned her over, noting the terrible bruise spreading across her cheek under the dirty skin. He heard F'nor take command of the tumult in the Hall.

The dragonman laid a hand, trembling in spite of an effort to control himself, on the woman's breast to feel for a heartbeat… It was there, slow but strong.

A deep sigh escaped him for either blow or fall could have proved fatal. Fatal, perhaps, for Pern as well.

Relief was colored with disgust. There was no telling under the filth how old this creature might be. He raised her in his arms, her light body no burden even to his battle-weary strength. Knowing F'nor would handle any trouble efficiently,

F'lar carried the drudge to his own chamber.

Putting the body on the high bed, he stirred up the fire and added more glows to the bedside bracket. His gorge rose at the thought of touching the filthy mat of hair but nonetheless and gently, he pushed it back from the face, turning the head this way and that. The features were small, regular. One arm, clear of rags, was reasonably clean above the elbow but marred by bruises and old scars. The skin was firm and unwrinkled. The hands, when he took them in his, were filthy but well-shaped and delicately boned.

F'lar began to smile. Yes, she had blurred that hand so skillfully that he had actually doubted what he had first seen. And yes, beneath grime and grease, she was young. Young enough for the Weyr. And no born drab. There was no taint of common blood here. It was pure, no matter whose the line, and he rather thought she was indeed Ruathan. One who had by some unknown agency escaped the massacre ten Turns ago and bided her time for revenge. Why else force Fax to renounce the Hold?

Delighted and fascinated by this unexpected luck, F'lar reached out to tear the dress from the unconscious body and found himself constrained not to. The girl had roused. Her great, hungry eyes fastened on his, not fearful or expectant; wary.

A subtle change occurred in her face, F'lar watched, his smile deepening, as she shifted her regular features into an illusion of disagreeable ugliness and great age.

"Trying to confuse a dragonman, girl?" he chuckled. He made no further move to touch her but settled against the great carved post of the bed. He crossed his arms sternly on his chest, thought better of it immediately, and eased his sore arm. "Your name, girl, and rank, too."

She drew herself upright slowly against the headboard, her features no longer blurred. They faced each other across the high bed.

"Fax?"

"Dead. Your name!"

A look of exulting triumph flooded her face. She slipped from the bed, standing unexpectedly tall. "Then I reclaim my own. I am of the Ruathan Blood. I claim Ruath," she announced in a ringing voice.

F'lar stared at her a moment, delighted with her proud bearing. Then he threw back his head and laughed.

"This? This crumbling heap?" He could not help but mock the disparity between her manner and her dress. "Oh, no. Besides, Lady, we dragonmen heard and witnessed Fax's oath renouncing the Hold in favor of his heir. Shall I challenge the babe, too, for you? And choke him with his swaddling cloth?"

Her eyes flashed, her lips parted in a terrible smile.

"There is no heir. Gemma died, the babe unborn. I lied."

"Lied?" F'lar demanded, angry.

"Yes," she taunted him with a toss of her chin. "I lied. There was no babe born. I merely wanted to be sure you challenged Fax."

He grabbed her wrist, stung that he had twice fallen to her prodding.

"You provoked a dragonman to fight? To kill? *When he is on Search?*"

"Search? Why should I care about a Search? I've Ruatha as my Hold again. For ten Turns, I have worked and waited, schemed and suffered for that. What could your Search mean to me?"

F'lar wanted to strike that look of haughty contempt from her face. He twisted her arm savagely, bringing her to her knees before he released his grip. She laughed at him, and scuttled to one side. She was on her feet and out the door before he could give chase.

Swearing to himself, he raced down the rocky corridors, knowing she would have to make for the Hall to get out of the Hold. However, when he reached the Hall, there was no sign of her fleeing figure among those still loitering.

"Has that creature come this way?" he called to F'nor who was, by chance, standing by the door to the Court.

"No. Is she the source of power after all?"

"Yes, she is," F'lar answered, galled all the more. "And Ruathan Blood at that!"

"Oh ho! Does she depose the babe, then?" F'nor asked, gesturing toward the birthing-woman who occupied a seat close to the now blazing hearth.

F'lar paused, about to return to search the Hold's myriad passages. He stared, momentarily confused, at this brown rider.

"Babe? What babe?"

"The male child Lady Gemma bore," F'nor replied, surprised by F'lar's uncomprehending look.

"It lives?"

"Yes. A strong babe, the woman says, for all that he was premature and taken forcibly from his dead dame's belly."

F'lar threw back his head with a shout of laughter. For all her scheming, she had been outdone by truth.

At that moment, he heard Mnementh roar in unmistakable elation and the curious warble of other dragons.

"Mnementh has caught her," F'lar cried, grinning with jubilation. He strode down the steps, past the body of the former Lord of the High Reaches and out into the main court.

He saw that the bronze dragon was gone from his Tower perch and called him. An agitation drew his eyes upward. He saw Mnementh spiraling down into the Court, his front paws clasping something. Mnementh informed F'lar that he had seen her climbing from one of the high windows and had simply plucked her from the ledge, knowing the dragonman sought her. The bronze dragon settled awkwardly onto his hind legs, his wings working to keep him balanced. Carefully he set the girl on her feet and formed a precise cage around her with his huge talons. She stood motionless within that circle, her face toward the wedge-shaped head that swayed above her.

The watch-wher, shrieking terror, anger and hatred, was lunging violently to the end of its chain, trying to come to Lessa's aid. It grabbed at F'lar as he strode to the two.

"You've courage enough, girl," he admitted, resting one hand casually on Mnementh's upper claw. Mnementh was enormously pleased with himself and swiveled his head down for his eye ridges to be scratched.

"You did not lie, you know," F'lar said, unable to resist taunting the girl.

Slowly she turned toward him, her face impassive. She was not afraid of dragons, F'lar realized with approval.

"The babe lives. And it is male."

She could not control her dismay and her shoulders sagged briefly before she pulled herself erect.

"Ruatha is mine," she insisted in a tense low voice.

"Aye, and it would have been, had you approached me directly when the wing arrived here."

Her eyes widened. "What do you mean?"

"A dragonman may champion anyone whose grievance is just. By the time we reached Ruath Hold, I was quite ready to challenge Fax given any reasonable cause, despite the Search." This was not the whole truth but F'lar must teach this girl the folly of trying to control dragonmen. "Had you paid any attention to your harper's songs, you'd know your rights. And," F'lar's voice held a vindictive edge that surprised him, "Lady Gemma might not now lie dead. She suffered far more at that tyrant's hand than you."

Something in his manner told him that she regretted Lady Gemma's death, that it had affected her deeply.

"What good is Ruatha to you now?" he demanded, a broad sweep of his arm taking in the ruined court yard and the Hold, the entire unproductive valley of Ruatha. "You have indeed accomplished your ends; a profitless conquest and its conqueror's death." F'lar snorted; "All seven Holds will revert to their legitimate Blood, and time they did. One Hold, one lord. Of course, you might have to fight others, infected with Fax's greed. Could you hold Ruatha against attack... now... in her decline?"

"Ruatha is mine!"

"Ruatha?" F'lar's laugh was derisive. "When you could be Weyrwoman?"

"Weyrwoman?" she breathed, staring at him.

"Yes, little fool. I said I rode in Search... it's about time you attended to more than Ruatha. And the object of my Search is... you!"

She stared at the finger he pointed at her as if it were dangerous.

"By the First Egg, girl, you've power in you to spate when you can turn a dragonman, all unwitting, to do your bidding. Ah, but never again, for now I am on guard against you."

Mnementh crooned approvingly, the sound a soft rumble in his throat. He arched his neck so that one eye was turned directly on the girl, gleaming in the darkness of the court.

F'lar noticed with detached pride that she neither flinched nor blanched at the proximity of an eye greater than her own head.

"He likes to have his eye ridges scratched," F'lar remarked in a friendly tone, changing tactics.

"I know," she said softly and reached out a hand to do that service.

"Nemorth's queen," F'lar continued, "is close to death. This time we must have a strong Weyrwoman."

"This time... the Red Star?" the girl gasped, turning frightened eyes to F'lar.

"You understand what it means?"

"There is danger..." she began in a bare whisper, glancing apprehensive eastward.

F'lar did not question by what miracle she appreciated the imminence of danger. He had every intention of taking her to the Weyr by sheer force if necessary. But something within him wanted very much for her to accept the challenge voluntarily. A rebellious Weyrwoman would be even more dangerous than a stupid one. This girl had too much power and was too used to guile and strategy. It would be a calamity to antagonize her with injudicious handling.

"There is danger for all Pern. Not just Ruatha," he said, allowing a note of entreaty to creep into his voice. "And *you* are needed. Not by Ruatha," a wave of his hand dismissed that consideration as a negligible one compared to the total picture. "We are doomed without a strong Weyrwoman. Without you."

"Gemma kept saying *all* the bronze riders were needed," she murmured in a dazed whisper.

What did she mean by that statement? F'lar frowned. Had she heard a word he had said? He pressed his argument, certain only that he had already struck one responsive chord.

"You've won here. Let the babe," he saw her startled rejection of that idea and ruthlessly qualified it, "...Gemma's babe... be reared at Ruatha. You have command of all the Holds as Weyrwoman, not ruined Ruatha alone. You've accomplished Fax's death. Leave off vengeance."

She stared at F'lar with wonder, absorbing his words.

"I never thought beyond Fax's death," she admitted slowly. "I never thought what should happen then."

Her confusion was almost childlike and struck F'lar forcibly. He had had no time, or desire, to consider her prodigious accomplishment. Now he realized some measure of her indomitable character. She could not have been much over ten Turns of age herself when Fax had murdered her family. Yet somehow, so young, she had set herself a goal and managed to survive both brutality and detection long enough to secure the usurper's death. What a Weyrwoman she would be! In the tradition of those of Ruathan blood. The light of the paler moon made her look young and vulnerable and almost pretty.

"You can be Weyrwoman," he insisted gently.

"Weyrwoman," she breathed incredulous, and gazed round the inner court bathed in soft moonlight. He thought she wavered.

"Or perhaps you enjoy rags?" he said, making his voice harsh, mocking. "And matted hair, dirty feet and cracked hands? Sleeping in straw, eating rinds? You are young... that is, I assume you are young," and his voice was frankly skeptical. She glared at him, her lips firmly pressed together. "Is this the be-all and end-all of your ambition? What are you that this little corner of the great world is *all* you want?" He paused and with utter contempt added, "The blood of Ruatha has thinned, I see. You're afraid!"

"I am Lessa, daughter of the Lord of Ruath," she countered, stung. She drew herself erect. Her eyes flashed. "I am afraid of nothing!"

F'lar contented himself with a slight smile.

Mnementh, however, threw up his head, and stretched out his sinuous neck to its whole length. His full-throated peal rang out down the valley. The bronze dragon communicated his awareness to F'lar that Lessa had accepted the challenge. The other dragons answered back, their warbles shriller than Mnementh's bellow. The watch-wher which had cowered at the end of its chain lifted its voice in a thin, unnerving screech until the Hold emptied of its startled occupants.

"F'nor," the bronze rider called, waving his wingleader to him. "Leave half the flight to guard the Hold. Some nearby lord might think to emulate Fax's example. Send one rider to the High Reaches with the glad news. You go directly to the Cloth Hall and speak to L'tol... Lytol." F'lar grinned. "I think he would make an exemplary Warder and Lord Surrogate for this Hold in the name of the Weyr and the babe."

The brown rider's face expressed enthusiasm for his mission as he began to comprehend his leader's intentions. With Fax dead and Ruatha under the protection of dragonmen, particularly that same one who had dispatched Fax, the Hold would have wise management.

"She caused Ruatha's deterioration?" he asked.

"And nearly ours with her machinations," F'lar replied but having found the admirable object of his Search, he could not be magnanimous. "Suppress your exultation, brother," he advised quickly as he took note of F'nor's expression. "The new queen must also be Impressed."

"I'll settle arrangements here. Lytol is an excellent choice," F'nor said.

"Who is this Lytol?" demanded Lessa pointedly. She had twisted the mass of filthy hair back from her face. In the moonlight the dirt was less noticeable. F'lar caught F'nor looking at her with an all too easily read expression. He signaled F'nor, with a peremptory gesture, to carry out his orders without delay.

"Lytol is a dragonless man," F'lar told the girl, "no friend to Fax. He will ward the Hold well and it will prosper." He added persuasively with a quelling stare full on her, "Won't it?"

She regarded him somberly, without answering, until he chuckled softly at her discomfiture.

"We'll return to the Weyr," he announced, proffering a hand to guide her to Mnementh's side.

The bronze one had extended his head toward the watch-wher who now lay panting on the ground, its chain limp in the dust.

"Oh," Lessa sighed, and dropped beside the grotesque beast. It raised its head slowly, lurring piteously.

"Mnementh says it is very old and soon will sleep itself to death."

Lessa cradled the bestial head in her arms, scratching it behind the ears.

"Come, Lessa of Pern," F'lar said, impatient to be up and away.

She rose slowly but obediently. "It saved me. It knew me."

"It knows it did well," F'lar assured her, brusquely, wondering at such an uncharacteristic show of sentiment in her.

He took her hand again, to help her to her feet and lead her back to Mnementh. As they turned, he glimpsed the watch-wher, launching itself at a dead run after Lessa. The chain, however, held fast. The beast's neck broke, with a sickening audible snap.

Lessa was on her knees in an instant, cradling the repulsive head in her arms.

"Why, you foolish thing, why?" she asked in a stunned whisper as the light in the beast's green-gold eyes dimmed and died out.

Mnementh informed F'lar that the creature had lived this long only to preserve the Ruathan line. At Lessa's imminent departure, it had welcomed death.

A convulsive shudder went through Lessa's slim body. F'lar watched as she undid the heavy buckle that fastened the metal collar about the watch-wher's neck. She threw the tether away with a violent motion. Tenderly she laid the watch-wher on the cobbles. With one last caress to the clipped wings, she rose in a fluid movement and walked resolutely to Mnementh without a single backward glance. She stepped calmly to the dragon's raised leg and seated herself, as F'lar directed, on the great neck.

F'lar glanced around the courtyard at the remainder of his wing which had reformed there. The Hold folk had retreated back into the safety of the Great Hall. When his wingmen were all astride, he vaulted to Mnementh's neck, behind the girl.

"Hold tightly to my arms," he ordered her as he took hold of the smallest neck ridge and gave the command to fly.

Her fingers closed spasmodically around his forearm as the great bronze dragon took off, the enormous wings working to achieve height from the vertical takeoff. Mnementh preferred to fall into flight from a cliff or tower. Like all dragons, he tended to indolence. F'lar glanced behind him, saw the other dragonmen form the flight line, spread out to cover those still on guard at Ruatha Hold.

When they had reached a sufficient altitude, he told Mnementh to transfer, going *between* to the Weyr.

Only a gasp indicated the girl's astonishment as they hung *between*. Accustomed as he was to the sting of the profound cold, to the awesome utter lack of light and sound, F'lar still found the sensations unnerving. Yet the uncommon transfer spanned no more time than it took to cough thrice.

Mnementh rumbled approval of this candidate's calm reaction as they flicked out of the eerie *between*.

And then they were above the Weyr, Mnementh setting his wings to glide in the bright daylight, half a world away from night-time Ruatha.

As they circled above the great stony trough of the Weyr, F'lar peered at Lessa's face; pleased with the delight mirrored there; she showed no trace of fear as they hung a thousand lengths above the high Benden mountain range. Then, as the seven dragons roared their incoming cry, an incredulous smile lit her face.

The other wingmen dropped into a wide spiral, down, down while Mnementh elected to descend in lazy circles. The dragonmen peeled off smartly and dropped, each to his own tier in the caves of the Weyr. Mnementh finally completed his leisurely approach to their quarters, whistling shrilly to himself as he braked his forward speed with a twist of his wings, dropping lightly at last to the ledge. He crouched as F'lar swung the girl to the rough rock, scored from thousands of clawed landings.

"This leads only to our quarters," he told her as they entered the corridor, vaulted and wide for the easy passage of great bronze dragons.

As they reached the huge natural cavern that had been his since Mnementh achieved maturity, F'lar looked about him with eyes fresh from his first prolonged absence from the Weyr. The huge chamber was unquestionably big, certainly larger than most of the halls he had visited in Fax's procession. Those halls were intended as gathering places for men, not the habitations of dragons. But suddenly he saw his own quarters were nearly as shabby as all Ruatha. Benden was, of a certainty, one of the oldest dragon weyrs, as Ruatha was one of the oldest Holds, but that excused nothing. How many dragons had bedded in that hollow to make solid rock conform to dragon proportions! How many feet had worn the path past the dragon's weyr into the sleeping chamber, to the bathing room beyond where the natural warm spring provided ever-fresh water! But the wall hangings were faded and unraveling and there were grease stains on lintel and floor that should be sanded away.

He noticed the wary expression on Lessa's face as he paused in the sleeping room.

"I must feed Mnementh immediately. So you may bathe first," he said, rummaging in a chest and finding clean clothes for her, discards of other previous occupants of his quarters, but far more presentable than her present covering. He carefully laid back in the chest the white wool robe that was traditional Impression garb. She would wear that later. He tossed several garments at her feet and a bag of sweetsand, gesturing to the hanging that obscured the way to the bath.

He left her, then, the clothes in a heap at her feet, for she made no effort to catch anything.

Mnementh informed him that F'nor was feeding Canth and that he, Mnementh, was hungry, too. *She* didn't trust F'lar but she wasn't afraid of himself.

"Why should she be afraid of you?" F'lar asked. "You're cousin to the watch-wher who was her only friend."

Mnementh informed F'lar that he, a fully matured bronze dragon, was no relation to any scrawny, crawling, chained, and wing-clipped watch-wher.

F'lar, pleased at having been able to tease the bronze one, chuckled to himself. With great dignity, Mnementh curved down to the feeding ground.

> By the Golden Egg of Faranth
> By the Weyrwoman, wise and true,
> Breed a flight of bronze and brown wings,
> Breed a flight of green and blue.
> Breed riders, strong and daring,
> Dragon-loving, born as hatched,
> Flight of hundreds soaring skyward,
> Man and dragon fully matched.

Lessa waited until the sound of the dragonman's footsteps proved he had really gone away. She rushed quickly through the big cavern, heard the scrape of claw and the *whoosh* of the mighty wings. She raced down the short passageway, right to the edge of the yawning entrance. There was the bronze dragon circling down to the wider end of the mile-long barren oval was the Benden Weyr. She had heard of the Weyrs, as any Pernese had, but to be in one was quite a different matter.

She peered up, around, down that sheer rock face. There was no way off but by dragon wing. The nearest cave mouths were an unhandy distance above her; to one side, below her on the other. She was neatly secluded here.

Weyrwoman, he had told her. His woman? In his weyr? Was that what he had meant? No, that was not the impression she got from the dragon. It occurred to her, suddenly, that it was odd she had understood the dragon. Were common folk able to? Or was it the dragonman blood in her line? At all events, Mnementh had inferred something greater, some special rank. She remembered vaguely that, when dragonmen went on Search, they looked for certain women. Ah, certain women. She was one, then, of several contenders. Yet the bronze rider had offered her the position as if she and she, alone, qualified. He had his own generous portion of conceit, that one, Lessa decided. Arrogant he was, though not a bully like Fax.

She could see the bronze dragon swoop down to the running herdbeasts, saw the strike, saw the dragon wheel up to settle on a far ledge to feed. Instinctively she drew back from the opening, back into the dark and relative safety of the corridor.

The feeding dragon evoked scores of horrid tales. Tales at which she had scoffed but now... Was it true, then, that dragons did eat human flesh? Did... Lessa halted that trend of thought. Dragonkind was no less cruel than mankind. The dragon, at least, acted from bestial need rather than bestial greed.

Assured that the dragonman would be occupied a while, she crossed the larger cave into the sleeping room. She scooped up the clothing and the bag of cleansing sand and proceeded to the bathing room.

To be clean! To be completely clean and to be able to stay that way. With distaste, she stripped off the remains of the rags, kicking them to one side. She made a soft mud with the sweetsand and scrubbed her entire body until she drew blood from various half-healed cuts. Then she jumped into the pool, gasping as the warm water made the sweetsand foam in the lacerations.

It was a ritual cleansing of more than surface soil. The luxury of cleanliness was ecstasy.

Finally satisfied she was as clean as one long soaking could make her, she left the pool, reluctantly. Wringing out her hair she tucked it up on her head as she dried herself. She shook out the clothing and held one garment against her experimentally. The fabric, a soft green, felt smooth under her water-shrunken fingers, although the nap caught on her roughened hands. She pulled it over her head. It was loose but the darker-green over-tunic had a sash which she pulled in tight at the waist. The unusual sensation of softness against her bare skin made her wriggle with voluptuous pleasure. The skirt, no longer a ragged hem of tatters, swirled heavily around her, ankles. She smiled. She took up a fresh drying cloth and began to work on her hair.

A muted sound came to her ears and she stopped, hands poised, head bent to one side. Straining, she listened. Yes, there were sounds without. The dragon-man and his beast must have returned. She grimaced to herself with annoyance at this untimely interruption and rubbed harder at her hair. She ran fingers through the half-dry tangles, the motions arrested as she encountered snarls. Vexed, she rummaged on the shelves until she found, as she had hoped to, a coarse-toothed metal comb.

Dry, her hair had a life of its own suddenly, crackling about her hands and clinging to face and comb and dress. It was difficult to get the silky stuff under control. And her hair was longer than she had thought, for, clean and unmatted, it fell to her waist… when it did not cling to her hands.

She paused, listening, and heard no sound at all. Apprehensively, she stepped to the curtain and glanced warily into the sleeping room. It was empty. She listened and caught the perceptible thoughts of the sleepy dragon. Well, she would rather meet the man in the presence of a sleepy dragon than in a sleeping room. She started across the floor and, out of the corner of her eye, caught sight of a strange woman as she passed a polished piece of metal hanging on the wall.

Amazed, she stopped short, staring, incredulous, at the face the metal reflected. Only when she put her hands to her prominent cheekbones in a gesture of involuntary surprise and the reflection imitated the gesture, did she realize she looked at herself.

Why, that girl in the reflector was prettier than Lady Tela, than the clothman's daughter! But so thin. Her hands of their own volition dropped to her neck, to the protruding collarbones, to her breasts which did not entirely accord with the gauntness of the rest of her. The dress was too large for her frame, she noted with an unexpected emergence of conceit born in that instant of delighted appraisal.

And her hair… it stood out around her head like an aureole. It wouldn't lie contained. She smoothed it down with impatient fingers, automatically bringing locks forward to hang around her face. As she irritably pushed them back, dismissing a need for disguise, the hair drifted up again.

A slight sound, the scrape of a boot against stone, caught her back from her bemusement. She waited, momentarily expecting him to appear. She was suddenly timid. With her face bare to the world, her hair behind her ears, her body outlined by a clinging fabric, she was stripped of her accustomed anonymity and was, therefore, in her estimation, vulnerable.

She controlled the desire to run away… the irrational fear. Observing herself in the looking metal, she drew her shoulders back, tilted her head high, chin up; the movement caused her hair to crackle and cling and shift about her head. She was Lessa of Ruatha, of a fine old Blood. She no longer needed artifice to preserve herself; she must stand proudly bare-faced before the world… and that dragonman.

Resolutely she crossed the room, pushing aside the hanging on the doorway to the great cavern.

He was there, beside the head of the dragon, scratching its eye ridges, a curiously tender expression on his face. The tableau was at variance with all she had heard of dragonmen.

She had, of course, heard of the strange affinity between rider and dragon but this was the first time she realized that love was part of that bond. Or that this reserved, cold man was capable of such deep emotion.

He turned slowly, as if loath to leave the bronze beast. He caught sight of her and pivoted completely round, his eyes intense as he took note of her altered appearance. With quick, light steps, he closed the distance between them and ushered her back into the sleeping room, one strong hand holding her by the elbow.

"Mnementh has fed lightly and will need quiet to rest," he said in a low voice. He pulled the heavy hanging into place across the opening.

Then he held her away from him, turning her this way and that, scrutinizing her closely, curious and slightly surprised.

"You wash up… pretty, yes, almost pretty," he said, amused condescension in his voice. She pulled roughly away from him, piqued. His low laugh mocked her. "After all, how could one guess what was under the grime of… ten full Turns?"

At length he said, "No matter. We must eat and I shall require your services." At her startled exclamation, he turned, grinning maliciously now as his movement revealed the caked blood on his left sleeve. "The least you can do is bathe wounds honorably received fighting your battle."

He pushed aside a portion of the drape that curtained the inner wall. "Food for two!" he roared down a black gap in the sheer stone.

She heard a subterranean echo far below as his voice resounded down what must be a long shaft.

"Nemorth is nearly rigid," he was saying as he took supplies from another drape-hidden shelf, "and the Hatching will soon begin anyhow."

A coldness settled in Lessa's stomach at the mention of a Hatching. The mildest tales she had heard about that part of dragonlore were chilling, the worst dismayingly macabre. She took the things he handed her numbly.

"What? Frightened?" the dragonman taunted, pausing as he stripped off his torn and bloodied shirt.

With a shake of her head, Lessa turned her attention to the wide-shouldered, well-muscled back he presented her, the paler skin of his body decorated with random bloody streaks. Fresh blood welled from the point of his shoulder for the removal of his shirt had broken the tender scabs.

"I will need water," she said and saw she had a flat pan among the items he had given her. She went swiftly to the pool for water, wondering how she had come to agree to venture so far from Ruatha. Ruined though it was, it had been hers and was familiar to her from Tower to deep cellar. At the moment the idea had been proposed and insidiously prosecuted by the dragonman, she had felt capable of anything, having achieved, at last, Fax's death. Now, it was all she could do to keep the water from slopping out of the pan that shook unaccountably in her hands.

She forced herself to deal only with the wound. It was a nasty gash, deep where the point had entered and torn downward in a gradually shallower slice. His skin felt smooth under her fingers as she cleansed the wound. In spite of herself, she noticed the masculine odor of him, compounded not unpleasantly of sweat, leather, and an unusual muskiness which must be from close association with dragons.

She stood back when she had finished her ministration. He flexed his arm experimentally in the constricting bandage and the motion set the muscles rippling along side and back.

When he faced her, his eyes were dark and thoughtful.

"Gently done. My thanks." His smile was ironic.

She backed away as he rose but he only went to the chest to take out a clean, white shirt.

A muted rumble sounded, growing quickly louder.

Dragons roaring? Lessa wondered, trying to conquer the ridiculous fear that rose within her. Had the Hatching started? There was no watch-wher's lair to secrete herself in, here.

As if he understood her confusion, the dragonman laughed good-humoredly and, his eyes on hers, drew aside the wall covering just as some noisy mechanism inside the shaft propelled a tray of food into sight.

Ashamed of her unbased fright and furious that he had witnessed it Lessa sat rebelliously down on the fur-covered wall seat, heartily wishing him a variety of serious and painful injuries which she could dress with inconsiderate hands. She would not waste future opportunities.

He placed the tray on the low table in front of her, throwing down a heap of furs for his own seat. There was meat, bread, a tempting yellow cheese and even a few pieces of winter fruit. He made no move to eat nor did she, though the thought of a piece of fruit that was ripe, instead of rotten, set her mouth to watering. He glanced up at her, and frowned.

"Even in the Weyr, the lady breaks bread first," he said, and inclined his head politely to her.

Lessa flushed, unused to any courtesy and certainly unused to being first to eat. She broke off a chunk of bread. It was nothing she remembered having tasted before. For one thing, it was fresh baked. The flour had been finely sifted, without trace of sand or hull. She took the slice of cheese he proffered her and it, too, had an uncommonly delicious sharpness. Made bold by this indication of her changed status, Lessa reached for the plumpest piece of fruit.

"Now," the dragonman began, his hand touching hers to get her attention.

Guiltily she dropped the fruit, thinking she had erred. She stared at him, wondering at her fault. He retrieved the fruit and placed it back in her hand as he continued to speak. Wide-eyed, disarmed, she nibbled, and gave him her full attention.

"Listen to me. You must not show a moment's fear, whatever happens on the Hatching Ground. And you must not let her overeat." A wry expression crossed his face. "One of our main functions is to keep a dragon from excessive eating."

Lessa lost interest in the taste of the fruit. She placed it carefully back in the bowl and tried to sort out not what he had said, but what his tone of voice implied. She looked at the dragonman's face, seeing him as a person, not a symbol, for the first time.

There was a blackness about him that was not malevolent; it was a brooding sort of patience. Heavy black hair, heavy black brows; his eyes, a brown light enough to seem golden, were all too expressive of cynical emotions, or cold hauteur. His lips were thin but well-shaped and in repose almost gentle. Why must he always pull his mouth to one side in disapproval or in one of those sardonic smiles? At this moment, he was completely unaffected.

He meant what he was saying. He did not want her to be afraid. There was no reason for her, Lessa, to fear.

He very much wanted her to succeed. In keeping whom from overeating what? Herd animals? A newly hatched dragon certainly wasn't capable of eating a full beast. That seemed a simple enough task to Lessa... Main function? *Our* main function?

The dragonman was looking at her expectantly.

"Our main function?" she repeated, an unspoken request for more information inherent in her inflection.

"More of that later, first things first." he said, impatiently waving off other questions.

"But what happens?" she insisted.

"As I was told so I tell you. No more, no less. Remember these two points. No fear, and no overeating."

"But…"

"You, however, need to eat. Here." He speared a piece of meat on his knife and thrust it at her, frowning until she managed to choke it down. He was about to force more on her but she grabbed up her half-eaten fruit and bit down into the firm sweet sphere instead. She had already eaten more at this one meal than she was accustomed to having all day at the Hold.

"We shall soon eat better at the Weyr," he remarked, regarding the tray with a jaundiced eye.

Lessa was surprised. This was a feast, in her opinion.

"More than you're used to? Yes, I forgot you left Ruatha with bare bones indeed."

She stiffened.

"You did well at Ruatha. I mean no criticism," he added, smiling at her reaction. "But look at you," and he gestured at her body, that curious expression crossing his face, half-amused, half-contemplative. "I should not have guessed you'd clean up pretty," he remarked. "Nor with such hair." This time his expression was frankly admiring.

Involuntarily she put one hand to her head, the hair crackling over her fingers. But what reply she might have made him, indignant as she was, died aborning. An unearthly keening filled the chamber.

The sounds set up a vibration that ran down the bones behind her ear to her spine. She clapped both hands to her ears. The noise rang through her skull despite her defending hands. As abruptly as it started, it ceased.

Before she knew what he was about, the dragonman had grabbed her by the wrist and pulled her over to the chest.

"Take those off," he ordered, indicating dress and tunic. While she stared at him stupidly, he held up a loose white robe, sleeveless and beltless, a matter of two lengths of fine cloth fastened at shoulder and side seams. "Take it off, or do I assist you?" he asked, with no patience at all.

The wild, sound was repeated and its unnerving tone made her fingers fly faster. She had no sooner loosened the garments she wore, letting them slide to her feet, than he had thrown the other over her head. She managed to get her arms in the proper places before he grabbed her wrist again and was speeding with her out of the room, her hair whipping out behind her, alive with static.

As they reached the outer chamber, the bronze dragon was standing in the center of the cavern, his head turned to watch the sleeping room door. He seemed impatient to Lessa; his great eyes, which fascinated her so, sparkled iridescently. His manner breathed an inner excitement of great proportions and from his throat a high-pitched croon issued, several octaves below the unnerving cry that had roused them all.

With a yank that rocked her head on her neck, the dragonman pulled her along the passage. The dragon padded beside them at such speed that Lessa fully expected they would all catapult off the ledge. Somehow, at the crucial stride, she was a-perch the bronze neck, the dragonman holding her firmly about the waist. In the same fluid movement, they were gliding across the great bowl of the Weyr to the higher wall opposite. The air was full of wings and dragon tails, rent with a chorus of sounds, echoing and re-echoing across the stony valley.

Mnementh set what Lessa was certain would be a collision course with other dragons, straight for a huge round blackness in the cliff-face, high up. Magically, the beasts filed in, the greater wingspread of Mnementh just clearing the sides of the entrance.

The passageway reverberated with the thunder of wings. The air compressed around her thickly. Then they broke out into a gigantic cavern.

Why, the entire mountain must be hollow, thought Lessa, incredulous. Around the enormous cavern, dragons perched in serried ranks blues, greens, browns and only two great bronze beasts like Mnementh, on ledges meant to accommodate hundreds. Lessa gripped the bronze neck scales before her, instinctively aware of the imminence of a great event.

Mnementh wheeled downward, disregarding the ledge of the bronze ones. Then all Lessa could see was what lay on the sandy floor of the great cavern: dragon eggs. A clutch of ten monstrous, mottled eggs, their shells moving spasmodically as the fledglings within tapped their way out. To one side, on a raised portion of the floor, was a golden egg, larger by half again the size of the mottled ones. Just beyond the golden egg lay the motionless ochre hulk of the old queen.

Just as she realized Mnementh was hovering over the floor in the vicinity of that egg, Lessa felt the dragonman's hands on her, lifting her from Mnementh's neck.

Apprehensively, she grabbed at him. His hands tightened and inexorably swung her down. His eyes, fierce and gray, locked with hers.

"Remember, Lessa!"

Mnementh added an encouragement, one great compound eye turned on her. Then he rose from the floor. Lessa half-raised one hand in entreaty, bereft of all support, even that of the sure inner compulsion which had sustained her in her struggle for revenge on Fax. She saw the bronze dragon settle on the first ledge, at some distance from the other two bronze beasts. The dragonman dismounted and Mnementh curved his sinuous neck until his head was beside his rider. The man reached up absently, it seemed to Lessa, and caressed his mount.

Loud screams and wailings diverted Lessa and she saw more dragons descend to hover just above the cavern floor, each rider depositing a young woman until there were twelve girls, including Lessa. She remained a little apart from them as they clung to each other. She regarded them curiously. The girls were not injured in any way she could see, so why such weeping? She took a deep breath against the coldness within her. Let *them* be afraid. She was Lessa of Ruatha and did not need to be afraid.

Just then, the golden egg moved convulsively. Gasping as one, the girls edged away from it, back against the rocky wall. One, a lovely blonde, her heavy plait of golden hair swinging just above the ground, started to step off the raised floor and stopped, shrieking, backing fearfully toward the scant comfort of her peers.

Lessa wheeled to see what cause there might be for the look of horror on the girl's face. She stepped back involuntarily herself.

In the main section of the sandy arena, several of the handful of eggs had already cracked wide open. The fledglings, crowing weakly, were moving toward... and Lessa gulped... the young boys standing stolidly in a semi-circle. Some of them were no older than she had been when Fax's army had swooped down on Ruath Hold.

The shrieking of the women subsided to muffled gasps. A fledgling reached out with claw and beak to grab a boy.

Lessa forced herself to watch as the young dragon mauled the youth, throwing him roughly aside as if unsatisfied in some way. The boy did not move and Lessa could see blood seeping onto the sand from dragon-inflicted wounds.

A second fledgling lurched against another boy and halted, flapping its damp wings impotently, raising its scrawny neck and croaking a parody of the encouraging croon Mnementh often gave. The boy uncertainly lifted a hand and began to scratch the eye ridge. Incredulous, Lessa watched as the fledgling, its crooning increasingly more mellow, ducked its head, pushing at the boy. The child's face broke into an unbelieving smile of elation.

Tearing her eyes from this astounding sight, Lessa saw that another fledgling was beginning the same performance with another boy; Two more dragons had emerged in the interim. One had knocked a boy down and was walking over him, oblivious to the fact that its claws were raking great gashes. The fledgling who followed its hatch-mate stopped by the wounded child, ducking its head to the boy's face; crooning anxiously. As Lessa watched, the boy managed to struggle to his feet, tears of pain streaming down his cheeks. She could hear him pleading with the dragon not to worry, that he was only scratched a little.

It was over very soon. The young dragons paired off with boys? Green riders dropped down to carry off the unacceptable. Blue riders settled to the floor with their beasts and led the couples out of the cavern, the young dragons squealing, crooning, flapping wet wings as they staggered off, encouraged by their newly acquired weyrmates.

Lessa turned resolutely back to the rocking golden egg, knowing what to expect and trying to divine what the successful boys had, or had not done, that caused the baby dragons to single them out.

A crack appeared in the golden shell and was greeted by the terrified screams of the girls. Some had fallen into little heaps of white fabric, others embraced tightly in their mutual fear. The crack widened and the wedge-head broke through, followed quickly by the neck, gleaming gold. Lessa wondered with unexpected detachment how long it would take the beast to mature, considering its by no means small size at birth. For the head was larger than that of the male dragons and they had been large enough to overwhelm sturdy boys of ten full Turns.

Lessa was aware of a loud hum within the Hall. Glancing up at the audience, she realized it emanated from the watching bronze dragons, for this was the birth of their mate, their queen. The hum increased in volume as the shell shattered into fragments and the golden, glistening body of the new female emerged. It staggered out, dipping its sharp beak into the soft sand, momentarily trapped. Flapping its wet wings, it righted itself, ludicrous in its weak awkwardness. With sudden and unexpected swiftness, it dashed toward the terror-stricken girls.

Before Lessa could blink, it shook the first girl with such violence, her head snapped audibly and she fell limply to the sand. Disregarding her, the dragon leaped toward the second girl but misjudged the distance and fell, grabbing out with one claw for support and raking the girl's body from shoulder to thigh. The screaming of the mortally injured girl distracted the dragon and released the others from their horrified trance. They scattered in panicky confusion, racing, running, tripping, stumbling, falling across the sand toward the exit the boys had used.

As the golden beast, crying piteously, lurched down from the raised arena toward the scattered women, Lessa moved. Why hadn't that silly clunk-headed girl stepped side, Lessa thought, grabbing for the wedge-head, at birth not much larger than her own torso. The dragon's so clumsy and weak she's her own worst enemy.

Lessa swung the head round so that the many-faceted eyes were forced to look at her... and found herself lost in that rainbow regard.

A feeling of joy suffused Lessa, a feeling of warmth, tenderness, unalloyed affection and instant respect and admiration flooded mind and heart and soul. Never again would Lessa lack an advocate, a defender, an intimate, aware instantly of the temper of her mind and heart, of her desires. How wonderful was Lessa, the thought intruded into Lessa's reflections, how pretty, how kind, how thoughtful, how brave and clever!

Mechanically, Lessa reached out to scratch the exact spot on the soft eye ridge.

The dragon blinked at her wistfully, extremely sad that she had distressed Lessa. Lessa reassuringly patted the slightly damp, soft neck that curved trustingly toward her. The dragon reeled to one side and one wing fouled on the hind claw. It hurt. Carefully, Lessa lifted the erring foot, freed the wing, folding it back across the dorsal ridge with a pat.

The dragon began to croon in her throat, her eyes following Lessa's every move. She nudged at Lessa and Lessa obediently attended the other eye ridge.

The dragon let it be known she was hungry.

"We'll get you something to eat directly," Lessa assured her briskly and blinked back at the dragon in amazement. How could she be so callous? It was a fact that this little menace had just now seriously injured, if not killed, two women.

She wouldn't have believed her sympathies could swing so alarmingly toward the beast. Yet it was the most natural thing in the world for her to wish to protect this fledgling.

The dragon arched her neck to look Lessa squarely in the eyes. Ramoth repeated wistfully how exceedingly hungry she was, confined so long in that shell without nourishment.

Lessa wondered how she knew the golden dragon's name and Ramoth replied: Why shouldn't she know her own name since it was her and no one else's? And then Lessa was lost again in the wonder of those expressive eyes.

Oblivious to the descending bronze dragons, uncaring of the presence of their riders, Lessa stood caressing the head of the most wonderful creature on all Pern, fully prescient of troubles and glories, but most immediately aware that Lessa of Pern was Weyrwoman to Ramoth the Golden, for now and forever.

PAPER DRAGONS

James P. Blaylock

James P. Blaylock was born in Long Beach, California in 1950. He has been a professional writer and teacher for twenty-five years. He started teaching at Fullerton Community College in 1976, the same year his first short story appeared in print. Currently he is Assistant Professor of English at Chapman University in Orange County, California, and director of the Creative Writing Conservatory at the Orange County High School of the Arts. Blaylock, along with Tim Powers and K.W. Jeter, is considered a pioneer of steampunk. He won the World Fantasy Award for "Thirteen Phantasms" and for the story that follows. His novel *Homunculus* won the Philip K. Dick Award. Some of his other books include *The Last Coin*, *The Paper Grail*, *Lord Kelvin's Machine*, *All the Bells of Earth* and *The Rainy Season*. His most recent books are novel *The Knights of the Cornerstone*, novella "The Ebb Tide" and collection *The Shadow on the Doorstep*.

Strange things are said to have happened in this world—some are said to be happening still—but half of them, if I'm any judge, are lies. There's no way to tell sometimes. The sky above the north coast has been flat gray for weeks—clouds thick overhead like carded wool not fifty feet above the ground, impaled on the treetops, on redwoods and alders and hemlocks. The air is heavy with mist that lies out over the harbor and the open ocean, drifting across the tip of the pier and breakwater now and again, both of them vanishing into the gray so that there's not a nickel's worth of difference between the sky and the sea. And when the tide drops, and the reefs running out toward the point appear through the fog, covered in the brown bladders and rubber leaves of kelp, the pink lace of algae, and the slippery sheets of sea lettuce and eel grass, it's a simple thing to imagine the dark bulk of the fish that lie in deep-water gardens and angle up toward the pale green of shallows to feed at dawn.

There's the possibility, of course, that winged things, their counterparts if you will, inhabit dens in the clouds, that in the valleys and caverns of the heavy, low skies live unguessed beasts. It occurs to me sometimes that if without warning a man could draw back that veil of cloud that obscures the heavens, snatch it back in an instant, he'd startle a world of oddities aloft in the skies: balloon things with hovering little wings like the fins of pufferfish, and spiny, leathery creatures, nothing but bones and teeth and with beaks half again as long as their ribby bodies.

There have been nights when I was certain I heard them, when the clouds hung in the treetops and foghorns moaned off the point and water dripped from the needles of hemlocks beyond the window onto the tin roof of Filby's garage. There were muffled shrieks and the airy flapping of distant wings. On one such night when I was out walking along the bluffs, the clouds parted for an instant and a spray of stars like a reeling carnival shone beyond, until, like a curtain slowly drawing shut, the clouds drifted up against each other and parted no more. I'm certain I glimpsed something—a shadow, the promise of a shadow—dimming the stars. It was the next morning that the business with the crabs began.

I awoke, late in the day, to the sound of Filby hammering at something in his garage—talons, I think it was, copper talons. Not that it makes much difference. It woke me up. I don't sleep until an hour or so before dawn. There's a certain bird, Lord knows what sort, that sings through the last hour of the night and shuts right up when the sun rises. Don't ask me why. Anyway, there was Filby smashing away some time before noon. I opened my left eye, and there atop the pillow was a blood-red hermit crab with eyes on stalks, giving me a look as if he were proud of himself, waving pincers like that. I leaped up. There was another, creeping into my shoe, and two more making away with my pocket watch, dragging it along on its fob toward the bedroom door.

The window was open and the screen was torn. The beasts were clambering up onto the woodpile and hoisting themselves in through the open window to rummage through my personal effects while I slept. I pitched them out, but that evening there were more—dozens of them, bent beneath the weight of seashells, dragging toward the house with an eye to my pocket watch.

It was a migration. Once every hundred years, Dr. Jensen tells me, every hermit crab in creation gets the wanderlust and hurries ashore. Jensen camped on the beach in the cove to study the things. They were all heading south like migratory birds. By the end of the week there was a tiresome lot of them afoot—millions of them to hear Jensen carry on— but they left my house alone. They dwindled as the next week wore out, and seemed to be straggling in from deeper water and were bigger and bigger: The size of a man's fist at first, then of his head, and then a giant, vast as a pig, chased Jensen into the lower branches of an oak. On Friday there were only two crabs, both of them bigger than cars. Jensen went home gibbering and drank himself into a stupor. He was there on Saturday though; you've got to give him credit for that. But nothing appeared. He speculates that somewhere off the coast, in a deep-water chasm a hundred fathoms below the last faded colors is a monumental beast, blind and gnarled from spectacular pressures and wearing a seashell overcoat, feeling his way toward shore.

At night sometimes I hear the random echoes of far-off clacking, just the misty and muted suggestion of it, and I brace myself and stare into the pages of an open book, firelight glinting off the cut crystal of my glass, countless noises out in the foggy night among which is the occasional clack clack clack of what might be Jensen's impossible crab, creeping up to cast a shadow in the front porch lamplight, to demand my pocket watch. It was the night after the sighting of the pig-sized crabs that one got into Filby's garage—forced the door apparently—and made a hash out of his dragon. I know what you're thinking. I thought it was a lie too. But things have since fallen out that make me suppose otherwise. He did, apparently, know Augustus Silver. Filby was an acolyte; Silver was his master. But the dragon business, they tell me, isn't merely a matter of mechanics. It's a matter of perspective. That was Filby's downfall.

There was a gypsy who came round in a cart last year. He couldn't speak, apparently. For a dollar he'd do the most amazing feats. He tore out his tongue, when he first arrived, and tossed it onto the road. Then he danced on it and shoved it back into his mouth, good as new. Then he pulled out his entrails—yards and yards of them like sausage out of a machine—then jammed them all back in and nipped shut the hole he'd torn in his abdomen. It made half the town sick, mind you, but they paid to see it. That's pretty much how I've always felt about dragons. I don't half believe in them, but I'd give a bit to see one fly, even if it were no more than a clever illusion.

But Filby's dragon, the one he was keeping for Silver, was a ruin. The crab—I suppose it was a crab—had shredded it, knocked the wadding out of it. It reminded me of one of those stuffed alligators that turns up in curiosity shops, all eaten to bits by bugs and looking sad and tired, with its tail bent sidewise and a clump of cotton stuffing shoved through a tear in its neck.

Filby was beside himself. It's not good for a grown man to carry on so. He picked up the shredded remnant of a dissected wing and flagellated himself with it. He scourged himself, called himself names. I didn't know him well at the time, and so watched the whole weird scene from my kitchen window: His garage door banging open and shut in the wind, Filby weeping and howling, through the open door, storming back and forth, starting and stopping theatrically, the door slamming shut and slicing off the whole embarrassing business for thirty seconds or so and then sweeping open to betray a wailing Filby scrabbling among the debris on the garage floor—the remnants of what had once been a flesh-and-blood dragon, as it were, built by the ubiquitous Augustus Silver years before. Of course I had no idea at the time. Augustus *Silver*, after all. It almost justifies Filby's carrying on. And I've done a bit of carrying on myself since, although as I said, most of what prompted the whole business has begun to seem suspiciously like lies, and the whispers in the foggy night, the clacking and whirring and rush of wings, has begun to sound like thinly disguised laughter, growing fainter by the months and emanating from nowhere, from the clouds, from the wind and fog. Even the occasional letters from Silver himself have become suspect.

Filby is an eccentric. I could see that straightaway. How he finances his endeavors is beyond me. Little odd jobs, I don't doubt—repairs and such. He has the hands of an archetypal mechanic: spatulate fingers, grime under the nails, nicks and cuts and scrapes that he can't identify. He has only to touch a heap of parts, wave his hands over them, and the faint rhythmic stirrings of order and pattern seem to shudder through the cross-members of his workbench. And here an enormous crab had gotten in, and in a single night had clipped apart a masterpiece, a wonder, a thing that couldn't be tacked back together. Even Silver would have pitched it out. The cat wouldn't want it.

Filby was morose for days, but I knew he'd come out of it. He'd be mooning around the house in a slump, poking at yesterday's newspapers, and a glint of light off a copper wire would catch his eye. The wire would suggest something. That's how it works. He not only has the irritating ability to coexist with mechanical refuse; it speaks to him too, whispers possibilities.

He'd be hammering away some morning soon—damn all crabs—piecing together the ten thousand silver scales of a wing, assembling the jeweled bits of a faceted eye, peering through a glass at a spray of fine wire spun into a braid that would run up along the spinal column of a creature which, when released some misty night, might disappear within moments into the clouds and be gone. Or so Filby dreamed. And I'll admit it: I had complete faith in him, in the dragon that he dreamed of building.

In the early spring, such as it is, some few weeks after the hermit crab business, I was hoeing along out in the garden. Another frost was unlikely. My tomatoes had been in for a week, and an enormous green worm with spines had eaten the leaves off the plants. There was nothing left but stems, and they were smeared up with a sort of slime. Once when I was a child I was digging in the dirt a few days after a rain, and I unearthed a finger-sized worm with the face of a human being. I buried it. But this tomato worm had no such face. He was pleasant, in fact, with little piggy eyes and a smashed-in sort of nose, as worm noses go. So I pitched him over the fence into Filby's yard. He'd climb back over—there was no doubting it. But he'd creep back from anywhere, from the moon. And since that was the case—if it was inevitable—then there seemed to be no reason to put him too far out of his way, if you follow me. But the plants were a wreck. I yanked them out by the roots and threw them into Filby's yard too, which is up in weeds anyway, but Filby himself had wandered up to the fence like a grinning gargoyle, and the clump of a half-dozen gnawed vines flew into his face like a squid. That's not the sort of thing to bother Filby though. He didn't mind. He had a letter from Silver mailed a month before from points south.

I was barely acquainted with the man's reputation then. I'd heard of him—who hasn't? And I could barely remember seeing photographs of a big, bearded man with wild hair and a look of passion in his eye, taken when Silver was involved in the mechano-vivisectionist's league in the days when they first learned the truth about the mutability of matter. He and three others at the university were responsible for the brief spate of unicorns, some few of which are said to roam the hills hereabouts, interesting mutants, certainly, but not the sort of wonder that would satisfy Augustus Silver. He appeared in the photograph to be the sort who would leap headlong into a cold pool at dawn and eat bulgur wheat and honey with a spoon.

And here was Filby, ridding himself of the remains of ravaged tomato plants, holding a letter in his hand, transported. A letter from the master! He'd been years in the tropics and had seen a thing or two. In the hills of the eastern jungles he'd sighted a dragon with what was quite apparently a bamboo rib cage. It flew with the xylophone clacking of wind chimes, and had the head of an enormous lizard, the pronged tail of a devilfish, and clockwork wings built of silver and string and the skins of carp. It had given him certain ideas. The best dragons, he was sure, would come from the sea. He was setting sail for San Francisco. Things could be purchased in Chinatown—certain "necessaries," as he put it in his letter to Filby. There was mention of perpetual motion, of the building of an immortal creature knitted together from parts of a dozen beasts.

I was still waiting for the issuance of that last crab, and so was Jensen. He wrote a monograph, a paper of grave scientific accuracy in which he postulated the correlation between the dwindling number of the creatures and the enormity of their size. He camped on the cliffs above the sea with his son Bumby, squinting through the fog, his eye screwed to the lens of a special telescope—one that saw things, as he put it, particularly clearly— and waiting for the first quivering claw of the behemoth to thrust up out of the gray swells, cascading water, draped with weeds, and the bearded face of the crab to follow, drawn along south by a sort of migratory magnet toward heaven alone knows what. Either the crab passed away down the coast hidden by mists, or Jensen was wrong—there hasn't been any last crab.

The letter from Augustus Silver gave Filby wings, as they say, and he flew into the construction of his dragon, sending off a letter east in which he enclosed forty dollars, his unpaid dues in the Dragon Society. The tomato worm, itself a wingless dragon, crept back into the garden four days later and had a go at a half-dozen fresh plants, nibbling lacy arabesques across the leaves. Hinging it back into Filby's yard would accomplish nothing. It was a worm of monumental determination. I put him into a jar—a big, gallon pickle jar, empty of pickles, of course—and I screwed onto it a lid with holes punched in. He lived happily in a little garden of leaves and dirt and sticks and polished stones, nibbling on the occasional tomato leaf.

I spent more and more time with Filby, watching, in those days after the arrival of the first letter, the mechanical bones and joints and organs of the dragon drawing together. Unlike his mentor, Filby had almost no knowledge of vivisection. He had an aversion to it, I believe, and as a consequence his creations were almost wholly mechanical—and almost wholly unlikely. But he had such an aura of certainty about him, such utter and uncompromising conviction that even the most unlikely project seemed inexplicably credible.

I remember one Saturday afternoon with particular clarity. The sun had shone for the first time in weeks. The grass hadn't been alive with slugs and snails the previous night—a sign, I supposed, that the weather was changing for the drier.

But I was only half right. Saturday dawned clear. The sky was invisibly blue, dotted with the dark specks of what might have been sparrows or crows flying just above the treetops, or just as easily something else, something more vast—dragons, let's say, or the peculiar denizens of some very distant cloud world. Sunlight poured through the diamond panes of my bedroom window, and I swear I could hear the tomato plants and onions and snow peas in my garden unfurling, hastening skyward. But around noon great dark clouds roiled in over the Coast Range, their shadows creeping across the meadows and redwoods, picket fences, and chaparral. A spray of rain sailed on the freshening offshore breeze, and the sweet smell of ozone rose from the pavement of Filby's driveway, carrying on its first thin ghost an unidentifiable sort of promise and regret: the promise of wonders pending, regret for the bits and pieces of lost time that go trooping away like migratory hermit crabs, inexorably, irretrievably into the mists.

So it was a Saturday afternoon of rainbows and umbrellas, and Filby, still animate at the thought of Silver's approach, showed me some of his things. Filby's house was a marvel, given over entirely to his collections. Carven heads whittled of soapstone and ivory and ironwood populated the rooms, the strange souvenirs of distant travel. Aquaria bubbled away, thick with water plants and odd, mottled creatures: spotted eels and leaf fish, gobies buried to their noses in sand, flatfish with both eyes on the same side of their heads, and darting anableps that had the wonderful capacity to see above and below the surface of the water simultaneously and so, unlike the mundane fish that swam beneath, were inclined toward philosophy. I suggested as much to Filby, but I'm not certain he understood. Books and pipes and curios filled a half-dozen cases, and star charts hung on the walls. There were working drawings of some of Silver's earliest accomplishments, intricate swirling sketches covered over with what were to me utterly meaningless calculations and commentary.

On Monday another letter arrived from Silver. He'd gone along east on the promise of something very rare in the serpent line—an elephant trunk snake, he said, the lungs of which ran the length of its body. But he was coming to the west coast, that much was sure, to San Francisco. He'd be here in a week, a month, he couldn't be entirely sure. A message would come. Who could say when? We agreed that I would drive the five hours south on the coast road into the city to pick him up: I owned a car.

Filby was in a sweat to have his creature built before Silver's arrival. He wanted so badly to hear the master's approval, to see in Silver's eyes the brief electricity of surprise and excitement. And I wouldn't doubt for a moment that there was an element of envy involved. Filby, after all, had languished for years at the university in Silver's shadow, and now he was on the ragged edge of becoming a master himself.

So there in Filby's garage, tilted against a wall of rough-cut fir studs and redwood shiplap, the shoulders, neck, and right wing of the beast sat in silent repose, its head a mass of faceted pastel crystals, piano wire, and bone clutched in the soft rubber grip of a bench vise. It was on Friday, the morning of the third letter, that Filby touched the bare ends of two microscopically thin copper rods, and the eyes of the dragon rotated on their axis, very slowly, blinking twice, survey-ing the cramped and dimly lit garage with an ancient, knowing look before the rods parted and life flickered out.

Filby was triumphant. He danced around the garage, shouting for joy, cutting little capers. But my suggestion that we take the afternoon off, perhaps drive up to Fort Bragg for lunch and a beer, was met with stolid refusal. Silver, it seemed, was on the horizon. I was to leave in the morning. I might, quite conceivably, have to spend a few nights waiting. One couldn't press Augustus Silver, of course. Filby himself would work on the dragon. It would be a night and day business, to be sure. I determined to take the tomato worm along for company, as it were, but the beast had dug himself into the dirt for a nap.

This business of my being an emissary of Filby struck me as dubious when I awoke on Saturday morning. I was a neighbor who had been ensnared in a web of peculiar enthusiasm. Here I was pulling on heavy socks and stumbling around the kitchen, tendrils of fog creeping in over the sill, the hemlocks ghostly beyond dripping panes, while Augustus Silver tossed on the dark Pacific swell somewhere off the Golden Gate, his hold full of dragon bones. What was I to say to him beyond, "Filby sent me." Or something more cryptic: "Greetings from Filby." Perhaps in these circles one merely winked or made a sign or wore a peculiar sort of cap with a foot-long visor and a pyramid-encased eye embroidered across the front. I felt like a fool, but I had promised Filby. His garage was alight at dawn, and I had been awakened once in the night by a shrill screech, cut off sharply and followed by Filby's cackling laughter and a short snatch of song.

I was to speak to an old Chinese named Wun Lo in a restaurant off Washington. Filby referred to him as "the connection." I was to introduce myself as a friend of Captain Augustus Silver and wait for orders. Orders—what in the devil sort of talk was that? In the dim glow of lamplight the preceding midnight such secret talk seemed sensible, even satisfactory; in the chilly dawn it was risible.

It was close to six hours into the city, winding along the tortuous road, bits and pieces of it having fallen into the sea on the back of winter rains. The fog rose out of rocky coves and clung to the hillsides, throwing a gray veil over dew-fed wildflowers and shore grasses. Silver fencepickets loomed out of the murk with here and there the skull of a cow or a goat impaled atop, and then the quick passing of a half-score of mailboxes on posts, rusted and canted over toward the cliffs along with twisted cypresses that seemed on the verge of fling-ing themselves into the sea.

Now and again, without the least notice, the fog would disappear in a twin-kling, and a clear mile of highway would appear, weirdly sharp and crystalline in contrast to its previous muted state. Or an avenue into the sky would suddenly appear, the remote end of which was dipped in opalescent blue and which seemed as distant and unattainable as the end of a rainbow. Across one such avenue, springing into clarity for perhaps three seconds, flapped the ungainly bulk of what might have been a great bird, laboring as if against a stiff, tumultuous wind just above the low-lying fog. It might as easily have been something else, much higher. A dragon? One of Silver's creations that nested in the dense emerald fog forests of the Coast Range? It was impossible to tell, but it seemed, as I said, to be struggling—perhaps it was old—and a bit of something, a fragment of a wing, fell clear of it and spun dizzily into the sea. Maybe what fell was just a stick being carried back to the nest of an ambitious heron. In an instant the fog closed, or rather the car sped out of the momentary clearing, and any opportunity to identify the beast, really to study it, was gone. For a moment I considered turning around, going back, but it was doubtful that I'd find that same bit of clarity, or that if I did, the creature would still be visible. So I drove on, rounding bends between redwood-covered hills that might have been clever paintings draped along the ghostly edge of Highway One, the hooks that secured them hidden just out of view in the mists above. Then almost without warning the damp asphalt issued out onto a broad highway and shortly thereafter onto the humming expanse of the Golden Gate Bridge.

Some few silent boats struggled against the tide below. Was one of them the ship of Augustus Silver, slanting in toward the Embarcadero? Probably not. They were fishing boats from the look of them, full of shrimp and squid and bug-eyed rock cod. I drove to the outskirts of Chinatown and parked, leaving the car and plunging into the crowd that swarmed down Grant and Jackson and into Portsmouth Square.

It was Chinese New Year. The streets were heavy with the smell of almond cookies and fog, barbecued duck and gunpowder, garlic and seaweed. Rockets burst overhead in showers of barely visible sparks, and one, teetering over onto the street as the fuse burned, sailed straightaway up Washington, whirling and glowing and fizzing into the wall of a curio shop, then dropping lifeless onto the sidewalk as if embarrassed at its own antics. The smoke and pop of firecrackers, the milling throng, and the nagging senselessness of my mission drove me along down Washington until I stumbled into the smoky open door of a narrow, three-story restaurant. Sam Wo it was called.

An assortment of white-garmented chefs chopped away at vegetables. Woks hissed. Preposterous bowls of white rice steamed on the counter. A fish head the size of a melon blinked at me out of a pan. And there, at a small table made of chromed steel and rubbed formica, sat my contact. It had to be him. Filby had been wonderfully accurate in his description. The man had a gray beard that wagged on the tabletop and a suit of similar color that was several sizes too large, and he spooned up clear broth in such a mechanical, purposeful manner that his eating was almost ceremonial. I approached him. There was nothing to do but brass it out. "I'm a friend of Captain Silver," I said, smiling and holding out a hand. He bowed, touched my hand with one limp finger, and rose. I followed him into the back of the restaurant.

It took only a scattering of moments for me to see quite clearly that my trip had been entirely in vain. Who could say where Augustus Silver was? Singapore? Ceylon? Bombay? He'd had certain herbs mailed east just two days earlier. I was struck at once with the foolishness of my position. What in the world was I doing in San Francisco? I had the uneasy feeling that the five chefs just outside the door were having a laugh at my expense, and that old Wun Lo, gazing out toward the street, was about to ask for money—a fiver, just until payday. I was a friend of Augustus Silver, wasn't I?

My worries were temporarily arrested by an old photograph that hung above a tile-faced hearth. It depicted a sort of weird shantytown somewhere on the north coast. There was a thin fog, just enough to veil the surrounding countryside, and the photograph had clearly been taken at dusk, for the long, deep shadows thrown by strange hovels slanted away landward into the trees. The tip of a lighthouse was just visible on the edge of the dark Pacific, and a scattering of small boats lay at anchor beneath. It was puzzling, to be sure—doubly so, because the lighthouse, the spit of land that swerved round toward it, the green bay amid cypress and eucalyptus was, I was certain, Point Reyes. But the shanty town, I was equally certain, didn't exist, couldn't exist.

The collection of hovels tumbled down to the edge of the bay, a long row of them that descended the hillside like a strange gothic stairway, and all of them, I swear it, were built in part of the ruins of dragons, of enormous winged reptiles—tin and copper, leather and bone. Some were stacked on end, tilted against each other like card houses. Some were perched atop oil drums or upended wooden pallets. Here was nothing but a broken wing throwing a sliver of shade; there was what appeared to be a tolerably complete creature, lacking, I suppose, whatever essential parts had once served to animate it. And standing alongside a cooking pot with a man who could quite possibly have been Wun Lo himself was Augustus Silver.

His beard was immense—the beard of a hill wanderer, of a prospector lately returned from years in unmapped goldfields, and mat beard and broad-brimmed felt hat, his Oriental coat and the sharp glint of arcane knowledge that shone from his eyes, the odd harpoon he held loosely in his right hand, the breadth of his shoulders—all those bits and pieces seemed almost to deify him, as if he were an incarnation of Neptune just out of the bay, or a wandering Odin who had stopped to drink flower-petal tea in a queer shantytown along the coast. The very look of him abolished my indecision. I left Wun Lo nodding in a chair, apparently having forgotten my presence.

Smoke hung in the air of the street. Thousands of sounds—a cacophony of voices, explosions, whirring pinwheels, Oriental music—mingled into a strange sort of harmonious silence. Somewhere to the northwest lay a village built of the skins of dragons. If nothing else—if I discovered nothing of the arrival of Augustus Silver—I would at least have a look at the shantytown in the photograph. I pushed through the crowd down Washington, oblivious to the sparks and explosions. Then almost magically, like the Red Sea, the throng parted and a broad avenue of asphalt opened before me. Along either side of the suddenly clear street were grinning faces, frozen in anticipation. A vast cheering arose, a shouting, a banging on Chinese cymbals and tooting on reedy little horns.

Rounding the corner and rushing along with the maniacal speed of an express train, careered the leering head of a paper dragon, lolling back and forth, a wild rainbow mane streaming behind it. The body of the thing was half a block long, and seemed to be built of a thousand layers of the thinnest sort of pastel-colored rice paper, sheets and sheets of it threatening to fly loose and dissolve in the fog. A dozen people crouched within, racing along the pavement, the whole lot of them yowling and chanting as the crowd closed behind and in a wave pressed along east toward Kearny, the tumult and color muting once again into silence.

The rest of the afternoon had an air of unreality to it, which, strangely, deepened my faith in Augustus Silver and his creations, even though all rational evidence seemed to point squarely in the opposite direction. I drove north out of the city, cutting off at San Rafael toward the coast, toward Point Reyes and Inverness, winding through the green hillsides as the sun traveled down the afternoon sky toward the sea. It was shortly before dark that I stopped for gasoline.

The swerve of shoreline before me was a close cousin of that in the photograph, and the collected bungalows on the hillside could have been the ghosts of the dragon shanties, if one squinted tightly enough to confuse the image through a foliage of eyelashes. Perhaps I've gotten that backward; I can't at all say anymore which of the two worlds had substance and which was the phantom.

A bank of fog had drifted shoreward. But for that, perhaps I could have made out the top of the lighthouse and completed the picture. As it was I could see only the gray veil of mist wisping in on a faint onshore breeze. At the gas station I inquired after a map. Surely, I thought, somewhere close by, perhaps within eyesight if it weren't for the fog, lay my village. The attendant, a tobacco-chewing lump of engine oil and blue paper towels, hadn't heard of it—the dragon village, that is. He glanced sideways at me. A map hung in the window. It cost nothing to look. So I wandered into a steel and glass cubicle, cold with rust and sea air, and studied the map. It told me little. It had been hung recently; the tape holding its corners hadn't yellowed or begun to peel. Through an open doorway to my right was the dim garage where a Chinese mechanic tinkered with the undercarriage of a car on a hoist.

I turned to leave just as the hovering fog swallowed the sun, casting the station into shadow. Over the dark Pacific swell the mists whirled in the sea wind, a trailing wisp arching skyward in a rush, like surge-washed tidepool grasses or the waving tail of an enormous misty dragon, and for a scattering of seconds the last faint rays of the evening sun shone out of the tattered fog, illuminating the old gas pumps, the interior of the weathered office, the dark, tool-strewn garage.

The map in the window seemed to curl at the corners, the tape suddenly brown and dry. The white background tinted into shades of antique ivory and pale ocher, and what had been creases in the paper appeared, briefly, to be hitherto unseen roads winding out of the redwoods toward the sea.

It was the strange combination, I'm sure, of the evening, the dying sun, and the rising fog that for a moment made me unsure whether the mechanic was crouched in his overalls beneath some vast and funny automobile spawned of the peculiar architecture of the early sixties, or instead worked beneath the chrome and iron shell of a tilted dragon, frozen in flight above the greasy concrete floor, and framed by tiers of heater hoses and old dusty tires.

Then the sun was gone. Darkness fell within moments, and all was as it had been. I drove slowly north through the village. There was, of course, no shanty-town built of castaway dragons. There were nothing but warehouses and weedy vacant lots and the weathered concrete and tin of an occasional industrial build-ing. A tangle of small streets comprised of odd, tumbledown shacks, some few of them on stilts as if awaiting a flood of apocalyptic proportions. But the shacks were built of clapboard and asphalt shingles—there wasn't a hint of a dragon anywhere, not even the tip of a rusted wing in the jimsonweed and mustard.

I determined not to spend the night in a motel, although I was tempted to, on the off chance that the fog would dissipate and the watery coastal moonbeams would wash the coastline clean of whatever it was—a trick of sunlight or a trick of fog—that had confused me for an instant at the gas station. But as I say, the day had, for the most part, been unprofitable, and the thought of being twenty dollars out of pocket for a motel room was intolerable.

It was late—almost midnight—when I arrived home, exhausted. My tomato worm slept in his den. The light still burned in Filby's garage, so I wandered out and peeked through the door. Filby sat on a stool, his chin in his hands, staring at the dismantled head of his beast. I suddenly regretted having looked in; he'd demand news of Silver, and I'd have nothing to tell him. The news—or rather the lack of news—seemed to drain the lees of energy from him. He hadn't slept in two days. Jensen had been round hours earlier babbling about an amazingly high tide and of his suspicion that the last of the crabs might yet put in an ap-pearance. Did Filby want to watch on the beach that night? No, Filby didn't. Filby wanted only to assemble his dragon. But there was something not quite right—some wire or another that had gotten crossed, or a gem that had been miscut—and the creature wouldn't respond. It was so much junk.

I commiserated with him. Lock the door against Jensen's crab, I said, and wait until dawn. It sounded overmuch like a platitude, but Filby, I think, was ready to grasp at any reason, no matter how shallow, to leave off his tinkering.

The two of us sat up until the sun rose, drifting in and out of maudlin remi-niscences and debating the merits of a stroll down to the bluffs to see how Jensen was faring. The high tide, apparently, was accompanied by a monumental surf, for in the spaces of meditative silence I could just hear the rush and thunder of long breakers collapsing on the beach. It seemed unlikely to me that there would be giant crabs afoot.

The days that followed saw no break in the weather. It continued dripping and dismal. No new letters arrived from Augustus Silver. Filby's dragon seemed to be in a state of perpetual decline. The trouble that plagued it receded deeper into it with the passing days, as if it were mocking Filby, who groped along in its wake, clutching at it, certain in the morning that he had the problem securely by the tail, morose that same afternoon that it had once again slipped away. The creature was a perfect wonder of separated parts. I'd had no notion of its complexity. Hundreds of those parts, by week's end, were laid out neatly on the garage floor, one after another in the order they'd been dismantled. Concentric circles of them expanded like ripples on a pond, and by Tuesday of the following week masses of them had been swept into coffee cans that sat here and there on the bench and floor. Filby was declining, I could see that. That week he spent less time in the garage than he had been spending there in a single day during the previous weeks, and he slept instead long hours in the afternoon.

I still held out hope for a letter from Silver. He was, after all, out there somewhere. But I was plagued with the suspicion that such a letter might easily contribute to certain of Filby's illusions—or to my own—and so prolong what with each passing day promised to be the final deflation of those same illusions. Better no hope, I thought, than impossible hope, than ruined anticipation.

But late in the afternoon, when from my attic window I could see Jensen picking his way along the bluffs, carrying with him a wood and brass telescope, while the orange glow of a diffused sun radiated through the thinned fog over the sea, I wondered where Silver was, what strange seas he sailed, what rumored wonders were drawing him along jungle paths that very evening.

One day he'd come, I was sure of it. There would be patchy fog illuminated by ivory moonlight. The sound of Eastern music, of Chinese banjos and copper gongs would echo over the darkness of the open ocean. The fog would swirl and part, revealing a universe of stars and planets and the aurora borealis dancing in transparent color like the thin rainbow light of paper lanterns hung in the windswept sky. Then the fog would close, and out of the phantom mists, heaving on the groundswell, his ship would sail into the mouth of the harbor, slowly, cutting the water like a ghost, strange sea creatures visible in the phosphorescent wake, one by one dropping away and returning to sea as if having accompanied the craft across ten thousand miles of shrouded ocean. We'd drink a beer, the three of us, in Filby's garage. We'd summon Jensen from his vigil.

But as I say, no letter came, and all anticipation was so much air. Filby's beast was reduced to parts—a plate of broken meats, as it were. The idea of it reminded me overmuch of the sad bony remains of a Thanksgiving turkey. There was nothing to be done. Filby wouldn't be placated. But the fog, finally, had lifted. The black oak in the yard was leafing out and the tomato plants were knee-high and luxuriant. My worm was still asleep, but I had hopes that the spring weather would revive him. It wasn't, however, doing a thing for Filby. He stared long hours at the salad of debris, and when in one ill-inspired moment I jokingly suggested he send to Detroit for a carburetor, he cast me such a savage look that I slipped out again and left him alone.

On Sunday afternoon a wind blew, slamming Filby's garage door until the noise grew tiresome. I peeked in, aghast. There was nothing in the heaped bits of scrap that suggested a dragon, save one dismantled wing, the silk and silver of which was covered with greasy handprints. Two cats wandered out. I looked for some sign of Jensen's crab, hoping, in fact, that some such rational and concrete explanation could be summoned to explain the ruin. But Filby, alas, had quite simply gone to bits along with his dragon. He'd lost whatever strange inspiration it was that propelled him. His creation lay scattered, not two pieces connected. Wires and fuses were heaped amid unidentifiable crystals, and one twisted bit of elaborate machinery had quite clearly been danced upon and lay now cold and dead, half hidden beneath the bench. Delicate thises and thats sat mired in a puddle of oil that scummed half the floor.

Filby wandered out, adrift, his hair frazzled. He'd received a last letter. There were hints in it of extensive travel, perhaps danger. Silver's visit to the west coast had been delayed again. Filby ran his hand backward through his hair, oblivious to the harrowed result the action effected. He had the look of a nineteenth-century Bedlam lunatic. He muttered something about having a sister in McKinleyville, and seemed almost illuminated when he added, apropos of nothing, that in his sister's town, deeper into the heart of the north coast, stood the tallest totem pole in the world. Two days later he was gone. I locked his garage door for him and made a vow to collect his mail with an eye toward a telling, exotic postmark. But nothing so far has appeared. I've gotten into the habit of spending the evening on the beach with Jensen and his son Bumby, both of whom still hold out hope for the issuance of the last crab. The spring sunsets are unimaginable. Bumby is as fond of them as I am, and can see comparable whorls of color and pattern in the spiral curve of a seashell or in the peculiar green depths of a tidepool.

In fact, when my tomato worm lurched up out of his burrow and unfurled an enormous gauzy pair of mottled brown wings, I took him along to the seaside so that Bumby could watch him set sail, as it were.

The afternoon was cloudless and the ocean sighed on the beach. Perhaps the calm, insisted Jensen, would appeal to the crab. But Bumby by then was indifferent to the fabled crab. He stared into the pickle jar at the half-dozen circles of bright orange dotting the abdomen of the giant sphinx moth that had once crept among my tomato plants in a clever disguise. It was both wonderful and terrible, and held a weird fascination for Bumby, who tapped at the jar, making up and discarding names.

When I unscrewed the lid, the moth fluttered skyward some few feet and looped around in a crazy oval, Bumby charging along in its wake, then racing away in pursuit as the monster hastened south. The picture of it is as clear to me now as rainwater: Bumby running and jumping, kicking up glinting sprays of sand, outlined against the sheer rise of mossy cliffs, and the wonderful moth just out of reach overhead, luring Bumby along the afternoon beach. At last it was impossible to say just what the diminishing speck in the china-blue sky might be—a tiny winged creature silhouetted briefly on the false horizon of our little cove, or some vast flying reptile swooping over the distant ocean where it fell away into the void, off the edge of the flat earth.

DRAGON'S GATE
Pat Murphy

A biologist by training, Pat Murphy spent a number of years writing about fish in a variety of settings, including Scripps Institution, Sea World, and the Inter-American Tropical Tuna Commission. She escaped the fish business in 1982, when she became a writer and editor at The Exploratorium, San Francisco's interactive science museum. In 2007, she left the museum to work at The Crucible, a fire-arts school, and then at Klutz, a publisher of children's books. At Klutz, she authored *Invasion of the Bristlebots* and *Boom! Splat! Kablooey!*

In her fiction, she has little respect for genre boundaries. Her first novel, *The Shadow Hunter* blended science fiction and fantasy. Next came fantasy: *The Falling Woman*, which won the Nebula Award for best novel. That same year she won the Nebula, Sturgeon Memorial, and Locus Awards for her novelette "Rachel in Love". Of her other novels, *The City, Not Long After* is science fiction; *Nadya* is dark fantasy, and her trio of linked books—*There and Back Again*, *Wild Angel*, and *Adventures in Time and Space with Max Merriwell*—are somewhere in between. Her collection *Points of Departure* won a Philip K. Dick Award, and her novelette "Bones" won the World Fantasy Award in 1991. Her latest novel is *The Wild Girls*, a children's book that won the Christopher Award in 2007.

My name is Alita, which means "girl to be trusted." My mother calls me Al. If anyone asks, I tell them it's short for Alonzo, a solid masculine name. At fifteen years of age, I can pass for a boy on the verge of manhood. I dress in men's clothing, preferring tunic and breeches to petticoats and skirts.

My mother plays the harp and sings ballads; I am a storyteller. I know common folk stories (rife with bawdy asides and comic characters), heroic tales favored by the nobility (usually involving handsome princes, beautiful princesses, and courtly love), and morality tales (favored by the clergy, but not by many others). I know how a story should go.

The story that I tell you now is unruly and difficult. It refuses to conform to any of the traditional forms. This story wanders like sheep without a shepherd.

It involves a prince and a dragon, but not until later. There will be magic and wishes and… well, I'll get to all that presently.

I begin my story in the mountain town of Nabakhri, where shepherds and weavers gather each fall. The shepherds come down from the mountains to sell their wool; the weavers come up from the lowlands to buy. My mother and I come to the festival to entertain the lot of them.

Twilight was falling when my mother and I reached the town. We had been traveling for two days, beginning our journey in the warm valley where the Alsi River ran. There, people grew rice and millet and wore bright colorful clothing. In Nabakhri, people grew barley and potatoes, herded goats and sheep, and wore heavy woolen clothing.

The trail that led to town was steep, better suited for goats than for our pony. The evening breeze blew from the great glacier that filled the valley to the west of Nabakhri. Our pony's breath made clouds in the cold, crisp air.

At the edge of town, we waited for a flock of sheep to cross the main path. The sheep bleated in protest as dogs nipped at their heels. One of the shepherds, an older man in a ragged cloak, glanced at us. He smiled as he noted my mother's harp, slung on the side of our pony's pack. "Musicians!" he said. "Are you looking for an inn?"

I nodded. After the long summer alone in the mountains, shepherds are eager for music and good company.

"The inns in the center of the village are full," he said. "Try Sarasri's place. West side of the village, overlooking the glacier. Good food, good drink."

Someone shouted from the direction in which the man's flock was disappearing. The man lifted a hand in farewell and hurried after his sheep.

Sarasri's was a sprawling, ramshackle inn on the edge of town. We hitched the pony by the open door to the tavern, where the air was rich with the scent of lamb stew and fried bread. The barmaid called for Sarasri, the innkeeper.

Sarasri, a stout, round-faced woman, hurried from the kitchen, drying her hands on her apron. In the lowlands, it's unusual for a woman to run an inn, but women from the mountain tribes often go into business for themselves.

"We're looking for a room," I said, but she was shaking her head before the words were out of my mouth.

"Alas, young fellow, there are too many travelers this year," she said. "I don't know that there's a room left anywhere in town."

My mother was not listening. She was looking past Sarasri into the tavern. "What do you think I should play tonight, Al?" she asked me. "It looks like there'll be quite a crowd." She smiled at Sarasri—my mother has a smile that could melt the snow on a mountaintop ten miles distant. "You have such a lovely inn," she said warmly and sincerely.

My mother is warm-hearted and guileless—traits that serve her in good stead. When my father read fortunes with the Tarot cards, my mother was always represented by the Fool, a young man in motley who is about to dance over the edge of a cliff. The Fool is a divine innocent, protected by angels. If he tripped over the cliff's edge, he would fall into a haystack.

Sarasri glanced at my mother. "You are musicians? It would be nice to have music in the tavern tonight." She frowned, thinking hard. "I do have one small room…."

The room was used for storage—burlap sacks of potatoes and baskets filled with wool were stacked against one wall. The remaining space was barely big enough for a bed and a table. The window overlooked the glacier—at least we would not wake in the morning to the clamor of the village.

"Good enough?" I asked my mother.

"This is just wonderful." My mother would be comfortable in a stable stall, as long as she had her harp to play.

My father, a conjurer skilled at illusions and fortune telling, had died three years ago, when I was a girl of twelve. After his death, it fell to me to attend to practical details of life, as my mother was ill-suited to such a task. I did my best to take care of her.

When the weather was warm, we traveled from town to town. Wherever there was a festival, we performed in the taverns, passing the hat for our keep. In the cold months, we stayed in the lowlands, in the small village where my mother was born.

That evening, in Sarasri's tavern, my mother sang for an appreciative (and drunken) crowd of shepherds. Following my mother's performance, I told the tale of King Takla and the ice woman. With the glacier so near, I thought it appropriate to tell a story about the ice women.

Ice women are, of course, cousins of the river women. River women, as every lowlander knows, are magical creatures that take the form of beautiful maidens with green eyes and long hair the color of new leaves. Ice women are just as beautiful, but their eyes are as blue as the ice in the deep glacial caves and their hair is as white as new snow. Just as the river women inhabit the rivers, the ice women live in the high mountain glaciers.

King Takla, the ruler of a small kingdom high in the mountains, was hunting for mountain goats when he found a woman sleeping in a hollow in the glacier. She lay on the bare ice, covered with a white shawl woven of wool as fine and delicate as the first splinters of winter frost on the stones of the mountain. Only her beautiful face was exposed to the cold mountain air.

Takla recognized that she was not an ordinary woman. He knew, as all the hill folks know, that taking an ice woman's shawl gave a man power over her. He snatched up the shawl, revealing the ice woman's naked body. Ah, she was beautiful. Her skin was as smooth and pale as the ice on which she rested. Her face was that of a sleeping child, so innocent and pure.

Takla hid the shawl in his hunting pack. Then, captivated by the woman's beauty, Takla lay beside her on the ice, kissing her pale face, caressing her naked breasts, stroking her thighs.

When she woke and stared at him with cool blue eyes, he spoke to her, saying "You will be my queen, beautiful one." Though she struggled to escape, he grasped her arms and pulled her close to him. Overcome with passion for this pale maiden, he forced himself upon her.

Then Takla wrapped her in his hunting cloak and took her back to his castle to become his queen. He dressed her in fine clothing and adorned her with glittering gems. Her beauty surpassed that of any mortal woman, but she never smiled and she seldom spoke. When she did, her voice was as soft as the sound of wind-blown ice crystals whispering over the snow.

"I must go home," she told Takla. "My mother will miss me. My sisters will miss me."

"You have a husband now," he told her. "Your mother will get over it. And if your sisters are as beautiful as you are, they must come to court and find husbands here." He kissed her pale face.

There are different ways one could tell this tale. In the tavern, I told it from King Takla's point of view, describing the ice woman's beauty, the allure of her naked body. A magical being captivates a man against his will. She is a lovely temptress. Unable to control his passion, the man takes possession of her.

In this version of the story, King Takla is helpless, a strong man stricken by love. In this version, Takla is an honest man in his way—he marries the ice woman, takes her for his queen. What more could any woman want?

I think that the ice woman would tell a very different version of the story. She was sleeping peacefully, bothering no one, when the king raped and abducted her, taking her away from her home and her sisters.

This version of the story would not be as popular in the tavern, but I think about it often, particularly when we perform in a tavern filled with soldiers. I am aware that my mother is a beautiful woman and that the soldiers admire more than her music. Because I dress as a young man, I avoid the soldiers' leers.

Of course, the tale of King Takla does not end with his capture of the ice woman. A man who takes a magical creature to his bed must face the consequences of his action.

After Takla brought the ice woman to his castle, blue-white lights flickered over the ice fields at night. The glacier moaned and creaked as the ice shifted and people said that the ice women were talking among themselves. A year passed and the ice woman bore King Takla a son—a sturdy child with his father's red hair and his mother's piercing blue eyes.

Not long after his son's birth, King Takla went hunting alone in the mountains. While following a path that led beside the glacier, he saw a white mountain goat, standing a hundred yards away on the ice. He shot an arrow, and the beast fell.

Takla made his way across the ice to where the goat had stood. But when he reached the place where the goat had fallen, he found nothing but ice. A trick of the ice women, he thought, and turned to retrace his steps to the rocky mountain slope. A tall woman with white hair blocked his way.

"King Takla," she said. "You must set my daughter free."

Takla studied the woman. This woman was older than his wife, but just as beautiful. The same fair features, the same piercing blue eyes, the same beautiful body.

"Your daughter is my wife and the mother of my son," he said.

"I will reward you handsomely if you let her go," said the woman. She held out a silver hunting horn. "Release my daughter and sound the horn—and I will come and grant you a wish. Three times I will come when the horn is sounded and three wishes I will grant." She held the instrument up so that the king could admire its fine workmanship and contemplate what wishes he might make.

Takla studied the horn and considered the woman's offer. He had, over the passing year, grown weary of his wife's unsmiling silence. Yes, she was beautiful, but he had begun to admire one of his wife's ladies in waiting, a fiery beauty with auburn hair and dark brown eyes. If he accepted the ice woman's offer, his wife would return to her people, leaving him free to marry again. With the ice woman's help, he could become more powerful.

Takla smiled and took the horn from the woman's hand. She stepped aside and he returned to his castle.

He took his wife's white shawl from the trunk where it had been hidden for the past year. When he entered his wife's chambers, she was suckling his infant son. She saw the shawl in his hands and her blue eyes widened. She handed the baby to her lady in waiting, the beauty who had captured the king's attention.

"What have you brought me?" the king's wife asked softly.

"Your mother gave me a gift." The king lifted the horn. "Three wishes will be mine, in exchange for one wish of hers. Her wish is that I set you free."

The king's wife took the shawl from his hands and wrapped it around her shoulders. Without a word, she left the room, running through the corridor, down the stairs, and out to the glacier. She was never seen again.

Takla smiled at the lady in waiting, then kissed his son on the forehead. Since the lady held his son cradled in her arms, bestowing this sign of fatherly affection afforded the king an opportunity to admire her bosom.

Filled with joy and thoughts of continuing power, Takla took the hunting horn and left the castle, climbing to a rock outcropping that overlooked the glacier, the castle, the pass, and the valley.

The Sun was dipping toward the horizon in the west. Takla looked out over his kingdom and thought of his first wish.

He put the horn to his lips and blew. A blue light flickered in the glacier below, then the ice woman stood before him. "What is your wish?" she asked.

"I wish that I may remain above all others as I am now and that my reign will last as long as the stones of the mountain."

The ice woman smiled and lifted her hand. The silver horn fell from the king's hand as a transformation took place. The king became stone, a royal statue gazing over the kingdom.

"As you wish, you will stay here, above all others," the ice woman said. "Your reign will last as long as the stones of the mountain. Until the wind and the weather wear you away, you will reign over this place."

Among the mountain people, there is a saying. "Like a gift of the ice women," they say about presents that end up costing the recipient dearly. It is best not to meddle in magical matters. One must not trust a gift of the ice women.

I had just reached the end of the story when the wind blew the tavern door open. At the time, I thought that was a stroke of good luck; the blast of cold air made my listeners shiver and appreciate the story all the more. "A gift of the ice women," I said, and the crowd laughed.

I passed among the shepherds, gathering coins from those who had enjoyed the tale. When I walked near the kitchen door, I saw that Sarasri was frowning. She spoke to me as I passed. "That's not a good tale to tell so close to the glacier. You'd best keep your shutters closed tonight. The ice women won't like it that you're talking about them."

I was a humble storyteller, far beneath the notice of magical creatures. I didn't think that the ice women would concern themselves with my doings. Still, I followed Sarasri's advice that night. I closed the shutters—not to keep out the ice women, but rather to keep out the cold. Unfortunately the wooden shutters were warped. Though I closed them as tightly as I could, a cold draft blew through the gap between them.

I did not sleep well. I could hear the glacier groaning and creaking as the ice shifted and moved. I was glad when the first light of dawn crept through the gap in the shutters, casting a bright line on my mother, who slept soundly beside me.

Quietly, I dressed and went down to the street. The weather had grown colder and the rocky paths were slick with frost. At a baker's shop I bought sweet buns for our breakfast. The buns were warm against my hands as I carried them back to our room.

When I entered the room, I called to my mother to wake her, but she did not move. I shook her, and still she did not wake. "Mother," I called to her. "Mother?"

She would not wake up. I found Sarasri in the kitchen and she sent a boy to find a healer. I sat by my mother's side, breakfast forgotten.

The healer, an old woman with white hair, sat on the edge of my mother's bed and felt my mother's cheek. She held a silver spoon beneath my mother's nose and watched to see that my mother's breath fogged the silver. She stroked my mother's hand and called to her. Then she shook her head and said, "Ice sickness."

I stared at her. "What do you mean?"

"It comes from the wind off the glacier," Sarasri said. She frowned unhappily. "That's what comes of telling tales about the women of the ice."

"Those who get the ice sickness sleep peacefully until they waste away," the healer said.

I stared at my mother. Her face was so calm and peaceful in sleep. It was hard to believe that anything was amiss. "What can I do?"

"There is one cure," the healer said.

"What is it?" I asked.

"Three drops of dragon's blood. Place them in her mouth and they'll warm her back to life." The healer shrugged. "But we have no dragon's blood and no hero to fetch it for us."

Sarasri shook her head sorrowfully. "As if a hero would help," she said. "How many have journeyed to Dragon's Gate, filled with pride and noble plans? Not a one has returned."

"Do you have to be a hero to fetch dragon's blood?" I asked. "We only need three drops of blood. The dragon doesn't have to die to give up three drops."

Sarasri frowned but the old healer nodded. "That's true," she said. "Slaying the dragon is not necessary, if you can get a bit of blood by some other means." She studied me. Her eyes were a brilliant blue, unfaded by her years. "Do you know anything about dragons?" she asked me.

"Only what I have learned from heroic tales," I said. "And that's not much. The dragon usually dies as soon as the prince shows up."

The old woman nodded. "Those tales are about princes, not about dragons. Those stories describe a dragon as a fire-breathing lizard with wings."

"Is that wrong?" I asked.

"It is not so much wrong as it is incomplete. The essence of a dragon is not in its appearance, but in its nature."

"What is its nature?"

"A dragon is an inferno of anger, blazing with fury, exploding with pain. A dragon is a beast of fire and passion, feeding on fear and hatred." The old woman stood and drew her woolen cloak around her shoulders. "Approached with fear, a dragon responds with fire."

"What if one does not approach with fear?" I asked.

She shrugged. "A difficult task to accomplish," she said. "But if it could be done, you might manage to start a conversation. I have heard that dragons like to talk. But they can smell a liar and that awakens their anger. Never lie to a dragon."

Perhaps this is where the story really begins. With my realization that I had to go to Dragon's Gate and return with three drops of blood from the dragon who had guarded the pass for the past hundred years.

I arranged for Sarasri to care for my mother. I left the pony in Sarasri's stables, since the way ahead was too rough and steep for the animal. Then I followed a footpath that led high into the hills.

Dragon's Gate was once known as Takla's Pass, named after King Takla, who married the ice woman. This mountain pass offered the shortest route from the lowlands to the trading cities on the Northern Sea. Long ago, caravans laden with carpets and spices and gems made their way through the mountains along this road. King Takla—and after him Takla's son, King Rinzen—charged merchants for safe passage.

All that changed a hundred years ago when good King Belen of the lowlands had, at the urging of rich merchants, sought to overthrow King Rinzen and put an end to his tolls. King Belen's army invaded the mountain kingdom. But a dragon released by some black magic drove back his army and closed the pass.

The dragon laid waste to the land. What had once been a thriving kingdom became a barren deserted land. Merchants from the lowlands banded together to offer a reward to any who could slay the dragon and open the road through the pass. But all the heroes who tried to win the reward perished in the attempt: burned by the dragon's fire, slashed by the dragon's claws.

Now merchants sent their goods through the desert and around the mountains to the south, a long and perilous journey. In the desert, bandits preyed on caravans and kidnapped merchants for ransom. But the possibility of being waylaid by bandits was better than the certainty of being killed by the dragon.

The path I took to Dragon's Gate was little better than a goat path. Winter avalanches had covered sections of the old trade route. Prickly shrubs had grown over the old road, and no one had cleared them away.

From Nabakhri, it was three days' hard travel to Dragon's Gate. The villages grew smaller and meaner as I traveled. People along the way asked me where I was going—and shook their heads grimly when they heard of my mission. "Turn back, young man," they said. "You haven't a chance of succeeding."

The last village before the dragon's pass was little better than a collection of grimy huts clinging to the side of the mountain. There a tiny teahouse doubled as an inn. Three shepherds sat by the fire in the common room, dining on lentil stew, fried bread, and tea.

The innkeeper was a stout man with an impressive mustache and a head of hair as thick as the wool on the mountain sheep. "Are you lost?" he asked me. "There is nowhere to go on this trail."

I explained my mission. He served me dinner and sat with me while I ate.

"You say you must approach the dragon without fear," he said. "How can you do that? Only a fool would not fear the dragon."

It was a good question. As I climbed the mountain trails, I had been thinking about how to quell my fear.

"Some of the stories that I tell are very frightening," I told the innkeeper. "But I am not afraid when I tell these tales because I know they will end well. What I am doing now is worthy of a story. If I think of this as a story I am telling, I will not be afraid."

The innkeeper frowned. "But you don't know that there will be a happy ending to this story of yours."

"Of course there will be," I said. "I am telling the story, remember? Why would I tell my own story with an unhappy ending?"

The innkeeper shook his head. "It sounds like you are just fooling yourself."

I nodded. "Indeed I am. What better way to keep away fear?"

The innkeeper shook his head and poured me another cup of tea. He spent the rest of the evening telling me of heroes who went to slay the dragon and never returned.

When I left the village the next morning, I did my best to put this conversation out of my mind. It wasn't easy. Above me loomed the barren crags of Dragon's Gate. Black rocks, like pointed teeth, made sharp silhouettes against the blue sky. One outcropping bore a resemblance to a standing man. That, it was said, was all that remained of King Takla.

Late in the afternoon, I reached the ice field that surrounded the castle where the dragon lived. Over the years, the glacier had flattened the walls that surrounded the castle gardens and had engulfed the outbuildings. The castle's outer walls had collapsed under the pressure of the ice, but the castle keep, the structure's central fortress, still stood. One tall tower rose from the ice field. From where I stood, the tower was as big as my thumb, held at arm's length.

Cautiously I started across the ice fields toward the tower. I used my walking stick to test each patch of ice before trusting my weight to it. Once, the ice collapsed beneath my stick, sending up a spray of snow as it fell. At my feet, where my next step would have taken me, was a crevasse so deep that the bottom was lost in blue light and shadows. The crash of the ice shelf hitting the bottom of the crevasse reverberated through the glacier.

The wind cut through my cloak; I could not stop shivering. At first, my feet ached with the cold. After a time, they became numb. I thought about how it would feel to lie down on the ice, like the ice woman in the story of King Takla. It would be painful at first, but then I would grow numb. I could rest, sleeping as peacefully as my mother slept.

The sky darkened to a deep blue. The light that reflected from cracks deep in the ice was the same beautiful blue. In my weariness, I grew dizzy. Looking up at the sky seemed much the same as gazing down into the ice. My walking stick slipped and I stumbled, falling full length onto the ice. I turned over on my back to look up at the blue sky, grateful to be resting.

I thought about staying there, just for a while. But that would not do. No tavern crowd would pay good money to hear about a hero who gave up and lay down in the snow. So I got up and kept walking on feet that felt like wood.

At last, I reached the tower and circled it, looking for a way in. Halfway around, I discovered a gap in the tower wall. I ducked through the gap and found myself on an ice-slicked stairway. Narrow slits in the walls let in just enough light to reveal the stone steps. Beneath the layers of ice, I could see sconces that had once held torches. The walls were marked with soot where flames had licked the stone.

Though the castle walls blocked the wind, it was even colder in the castle than it had been outside. My teeth chattered; I could not stop shivering. I climbed the stairs slowly, taking care not to slip on the icy steps.

At the top of the stairs was a wide corridor. The walls were clear of ice and the air felt a little warmer. Looking down the corridor, I could see a glimmer of golden light, spilling from an open doorway. I walked toward it.

In the doorway, I stopped and stared, my heart pounding. I could feel fear scratching at the edges of my awareness, but I reminded myself that there would be a happy ending. There had to be a happy ending.

The dragon slept in the center of the great hall. The beast lay on what had once been a fine carpet—now tattered and scorched. The air stank of ashes and smoke. I could feel heat radiating from the beast, like the warmth from a banked fire.

To hold fear at bay, I stared at the dragon and imagined how I might describe the monster when I told this story. The dragon's body was like that of a terrible lizard, a lizard as large as a warhorse. Its wings—great leathery wings—stretched over its back. Its eyes were closed. Its mighty head rested on its front talons. I did not stare for too long at the dragon's jaws and powerful talons. Instead, I considered the rest of the room and decided how best to describe it when I was telling this story in a tavern.

This had once been a magnificent hall. The walls were dark with soot, but I could see paintings beneath the layer of grime. More than a hundred years ago, artists had decorated these walls. On the wall to my left, two men in hunting garb shot arrows at mountain goats, which were bounding away up the mountain. On the far side of the room, the wall was painted with a mountain landscape—the same mountain that lay outside the castle. But the artist had worked in a warmer and happier time. In the painting, wildflowers grew among the gray stones.

In the painting, the stones of the mountain formed a natural cave at the level of the floor. The rocks of the painted cave blended with the very real rocks of a great fireplace, large enough to hold a roasting ox.

Beside that fireplace, a skeleton sat slumped in a carved oak chair. A golden crown rested on the skull. Tatters of rich fabric clung to the bones. They fluttered in the breeze that blew through a large break in the wall to my right.

That wall had been shattered and its painting with it. I tried to imagine the blow that had shattered the wall, sending the stones tumbling inward and leaving a hole big enough to let the dragon pass through. Through the gap, I could see the glacier far below. The first stars of evening were appearing in the darkening sky. I shivered in the cool breeze.

"I smell an enemy," a voice growled.

I looked at the dragon. The beast had not moved, but its eyes were open now. They glowed like the embers of a fire. Colors shifted and flickered in their depths: gold and red and blue. "I know you are an enemy because you stink of the lowlands. You aren't a prince. You aren't a hero. What are you, and why have you come here?"

Be honest, I thought. Dragons can spot a liar. "A humble storyteller," I said.

"A storyteller?" The dragon lifted its head and studied me with glowing eyes. "How unusual. For the past hundred years, all my visitors have come to kill me. They march up the road from the lowlands with their soldiers following behind and their fear wakes me. I feel the shivering in their souls, the hatred in their hearts. I feel it burning and my own fire flares in response. And I shake off sleep and rise to do battle."

The dragon yawned, revealing a terrifying array of teeth. The beast stretched slowly, shaking out its great golden wings with a leathery rustle. Then the monster regarded me once again. "But you're not a hero. You are dressed as a boy, but I know by your smell that you are a girl. You are afraid, but not so very afraid. And you want something from me. What is it you want? Tell me, girl of the lowlands, why I shouldn't roast your bones with a single breath?"

As a storyteller, I have learned that everyone has a story. Not only that, but everyone has a story that they think should be told.

"I have a few reasons for coming here," I said carefully. "As a storyteller, I know many tales in which there are dragons. But those are stories about princes. And in every one of them, the dragon dies at the end of the tale. That doesn't seem right. I thought you might help me to tell a new sort of tale about dragons."

"Very tricky," said the dragon. "You hope to appeal to my vanity. And I notice that you said you had a few reasons and then you told me only one. You hope to intrigue me so that I'll decide you are interesting enough to spare."

When an audience catches you out, I have found it is best to acknowledge that they are right. If you deny it, they'll turn against you. "Have I succeeded?" I asked.

"Perhaps." The dragon continued to study me. "As long as I find you interesting, I will let you live. If I grow bored, I will roast you before I return to sleep. For now, I will spare you because you remind me of a wild girl I once knew." The dragon blinked slowly. "Would you like to hear about that wild girl? She was a lovely princess, until I destroyed her."

Not an entirely promising start. I reminded the dragon of a princess that it had destroyed. But at least the beast was not going to roast me immediately.

Though the heat radiated by the dragon had warmed me, my legs were trembling with weariness. I took a chance and asked, "Might I come in and sit while you tell the tale?"

The dragon stared at me, and for a moment I thought all was lost. Then the monster opened its jaws in a terrible grin. "Of course. I have forgotten the duties of a host. Come in. Sit down. There." The dragon lifted a talon and gestured to a bench beside the chair where the skeleton sat.

I crossed the room and sat on the bench, putting my pack on the stone floor beside me.

"You look cold," the dragon said. "Let me kindle a fire."

The beast opened its mouth and a blast of fire shot into the fireplace beside me. The half-burned logs, remnants of a long-dead fire, blazed.

"Alas, I have no food and drink to offer you," the dragon said. "The kitchens were crushed by the glacier long ago."

I opened my pack and took out a metal flask filled with brandy. "I have a bit of brandy. It's not the best, but I would be happy to share."

The dragon's toothy grin widened. "You drink and I will talk. I will tell the storyteller a story."

I sipped from the flask and felt the warmth of the brandy fill my throat and my chest.

"The wild girl was a princess," the dragon said. "A wild mountain princess more likely to be found hunting bandits than working her embroidery." The beast cocked its head, regarding me thoughtfully. "Tell me, what do you know of this castle, this kingdom?"

I chose my words carefully. "I know of King Takla, who built this castle and captured an ice woman for his queen."

"Very good," the dragon said. "Then you recognize that horn?"

I followed the dragon's gaze and saw a silver hunting horn, lying on the stone floor beside the royal skeleton. "King Takla's horn?" I asked.

"The very same. Blow it and the ice woman will grant your wish. But you must be very careful what you wish for."

I stared at the instrument in amazement. Though I had often told the story of King Takla, I had never thought about what happened to the horn.

"The wild princess of my story was the granddaughter of King Takla. Her father, King Rinzen, was the ruler of this mountain kingdom. He was a good king, noble and wise. Do you know of him?"

"I have heard of him," I admitted. The stories that I knew all emphasized the wealth of King Rinzen and how unfair his tolls had been.

"What have you heard?"

"Far less than I wish to know. Far less than you could tell me."

"An evasive answer," the dragon said, studying me with those great glowing eyes. "You know, I have heard that storytellers are all liars."

"Not necessarily liars," I said. "But careful in choosing the right audience for a tale."

"And I am not the right audience for the lowland tales of King Rinzen," the dragon said.

I nodded.

"Very well. Then I will tell you a tale that you don't hear in the lowlands."

I tipped back my flask and took a swallow of brandy, grateful to have survived this long.

"The men and women of King Rinzen's court hunted in the hills—sometimes for wild goat for the king's table, and sometimes for the bandits who sought to prey on merchant caravans. Decades before, King Takla had driven away the worst of the bandit gangs. But keeping the pass free of robbers and rogues required constant vigilance. You know of all this, of course."

I shook my head. None of the stories told in the lowlands talked about the bandits that King Takla and King Rinzen had driven off. In the lowland tales, these two kings were accounted as no better than bandits themselves.

"I could tell you many fine stories about bandits, about their hidden treasures, their secret caves. But that will have to wait. Just now, I was telling you about King Rinzen's court. The king was fond of musicians and storytellers. Many came to the castle to perform for the court. In this very hall, minstrels played and bards told tales of adventure, while the king listened and rewarded them handsomely for their art."

The dragon paused and I thought the beast might have lost the thread of the story. "What about the princess?" I asked.

The dragon turned its gaze back to me, eyes narrowing. "I suggest that you let me tell this story in my own way," the beast growled.

"Of course," I said hastily. "As you wish. I just wondered about the princess."

"Yes, Princess Tara. One summer evening, Princess Tara came home late from an afternoon of hawking. She knew that a troupe of performers from the lowlands had come to entertain the king. They had come from the court of King Belen, sent by him to King Rinzen. That evening, there was to be a gala performance, but Tara was weary from the hunt. She sent her apologies to her father the king and she did not go to the court that evening. She dined on bread and cheese in her chambers, and went to her bed early.

"That night she woke to the screams of women and the clash of steel." The dragon's eyes were wide open now, glowing more brightly than before. "She pulled on her clothes and ran into the corridor. It was dark except for the glow of smoldering straw. A torch had fallen, igniting the straw that was strewn on the stone floor."

"What did she do?" I asked.

"She listened in the darkness. Someone was running toward her, scattering the burning straw beneath his feet. In the dim light, she recognized a young bard who had come to the castle a week before. His eyes were wild; he was bleeding from a cut over his eye.

"'What is happening?' Tara called to him."

"'Treachery,' he gasped. 'Belen's men are in the castle. There is fighting in the great hall.' Then he ran on, and he was gone.

"Tara rushed through the darkness, hurrying toward the great hall. There, the torches cast a crimson light over a terrible scene. The air was thick with the stench of newly spilled blood. Her father was slumped in the big oak chair by the fire. He had been stabbed in the back. By the door were more dead men—some were castle guards, some were men clad in minstrel garb. The festive cloak of one of the minstrels had been torn by a sword stroke, and Tara could see armor beneath the velvet."

The dragon fell silent. I stared at the skeleton in the chair by the fireplace. King Rinzen, still wearing his crown in death.

"What had happened?" I asked at last.

"Belen's troupe of performers was a troop of assassins. They had killed the king, fought the guard, and opened the gates to the soldiers outside.

"Tara ran to her father's side. She kissed his cold cheek and vowed that she would take revenge for what had happened that night. On the wall above the fireplace hung King Takla's great silver hunting horn, the gift of the ice woman. It had fallen from King Takla's hand when he turned to stone. No one had been bold enough to risk blowing it again. An object of beauty, power, and danger, it hung on the wall above the fireplace.

"Tara could hear the tramping of boots and the rattle of armor in the corridor. Her father was dead and Belen's men had taken the castle. Tara pushed a bench to a spot near the fire and stood on the bench to take down the horn."

I nodded, realizing with a shiver that I was sitting on that very bench.

The dragon continued, its voice low. "Tara put the horn to her lips and blew, sounding a high clear note that echoed from the stone walls. The wall of the tower cracked and crumbled. A wind from the ice fields blew through the breach in the wall. Through the opening, Tara could see the dark sky above and the pale ice below. A blue light rose from the glacier and flew to the tower. A tall woman with flowing white hair appeared before Tara. 'Why have you awakened me?' the woman asked."

"The ice woman," I said.

"Tara's great-grandmother, the mother of the maiden that Takla had stolen," the dragon said. "Tara met the woman's icy gaze. 'I need your aid,' the princess said. 'Belen's men have killed my father.'

"'What do you want of me?' the ice woman said.

"'I want the power to kill my enemies and drive them from our land. I want the strength to avenge my father.'

"'Power and strength and passion,' the woman murmured. 'Death and vengeance. These are dangerous things and you are so young.'

"Tara fell to her knees before the woman. 'You must help me.'

"The woman touched Tara's cheek. Tara could feel her tears freezing at the ice woman's touch.

"'I will grant your wish,' the ice woman said. 'Your heart will become ice; your passion, fire. And then you will have the power you need. But it troubles me to cast this spell on one so young. So I will also tell you how to break the spell and return to yourself. When the tears of your enemy melt the ice of your heart, you will become yourself once again. Until then, you will have your wish.'

"The woman's cold touch moved to Tara's breast, a searing chill that took her breath away. The woman stepped back. 'Now you will take the shape you need. You are filled with fire and passion, anger and pain. Let those dictate your form. You will have the power you seek and I will return to sleep.'

"The sorrow that had filled Tara at her father's death left her when her heart froze at the woman's touch. Rage and the desire for vengeance filled her.

"Transformation came with burning pain—a searing at her shoulders as wings formed; a blazing spasm as her back stretched, the bones creaking as they changed shape. Her jaws lengthened; her teeth grew sharp. Hands became claws." The dragon stretched its wings. Its claws flexed, making new tears in the carpet on which it lay. "Tara became a dragon," the beast said.

I stared at the dragon.

"Her breath was flame," Tara said. "Her scales shone like the coals of a fire, shifting and changing with each passing breeze. Now deep red, brighter than fresh blood; now flickering gold; now shining blue-white, like the heart of a flame." As the dragon spoke, her scales flickered and glowed.

"She spread her wings and flew, swooping low over the soldiers in the road. She opened her terrible jaws and her rage became a blast of fire. The men broke and ran. The horses, mad with fear, trampled the men as they fled. The soldiers died—so many died. In her rage, she did not distinguish between one fleeing figure and another. Belen's men burned in her flames, but so did people of her own castle. Stableboys and chambermaids, peasants and noblemen, fleeing

Belen's men, fleeing the monster in the sky."

The dragon fell silent for a moment, then continued softly. "Now I live here in the castle. For a hundred years, I have lived here. Sometimes, heroes come to slay me—and I kill them instead." The dragon studied me with glowing eyes. I stared back, imagining what it would be like to be imprisoned in the body of a monster.

"Sometimes, my rage dies down, like a fire that is banked. But then someone filled with hate and fear stirs those ashes and the fire returns, as hot as ever.

"Now it is your turn, humble storyteller. Tell me a story and I will decide what to do with you."

I met the dragon's steady gaze. "I will tell you why I am here," I said. "This is not a story I would ordinarily tell, since most audiences favor stories about princes and dragons over stories about storytellers. But I think you will find it interesting. This story begins in a mountain town, one week ago. The town was having its harvest festival, and I traveled there with my mother."

I told her the story that you have already heard—about the inn on the edge of the glacier, about my mother's illness, about the healer who explained that three drops of dragon's blood would cure my mother of the illness inflicted by the ice woman. "Hope is what brings me here," I said. "Hope is what keeps me from fear and hatred."

The dragon's glowing eyes did not waver. "So you hope to slay me and take my blood?" the dragon rumbled.

"Slay you?" I laughed. The dragon stared at me, but it had been a long night. I had finished the flask of brandy and the dragon hadn't killed me yet. The idea that I planned to slay the dragon was so ridiculous that I couldn't help laughing. I pulled my dagger from my belt. The blade was half as long as one of the dragon's talons. "I suppose I planned to chop off your head with this?" I shook my head. "I'm no dragon slayer."

I thought of my mother's warm smile, of her honest heart. If only she could be here instead of me. She would smile and the dragon would know that this was a woman worth helping. "I had hoped that you might help my mother. That was all I hoped."

"Hope," the dragon repeated, her voice softening. "I remember feeling hope when I was human." The dragon's gaze moved from my face to the gap in the wall. "As a lowlander, you are my enemy. But it has been interesting talking with you this long night. It has reminded me of much that I had forgotten, over the passing years."

I glanced through the breach in the wall. A thin crescent Moon had risen over the glacier. The crackling fire in the fireplace beside me had burned to embers. While drinking brandy and talking with the dragon, I had lost track of time. It was nearly dawn.

"You came to me for help," she said. "What more will you do to save your mother? What will you give me in return for three drops of precious blood?"

I spread my hands. "What would you have me do?"

The dragon did not blink. "In memory of the wild girl that I once was, I will give you three drops of blood. But you must return after you take my blood to your mother. You must come back and keep me company for a time. Will you do that?"

"Yes," I said, without hesitation. "It's a bargain. As soon as my mother is well, I will return."

"Very well then," the dragon said, holding out a taloned paw.

I took a small metal vial from my pack. I reached out and took the dragon's talon in my hand. The scales burned against my skin. With my dagger, I pierced the scaly hide and let three drops of blood fall into the vial. They sizzled as they struck the metal.

"You have a long journey ahead of you," the dragon said. "You'd do well to rest before you begin."

As if I could sleep with a dragon at my side. Still, it did not seem wise to argue. I lay down on the carpet between the dragon and the embers of the fire. I pillowed my head on my pack, and closed my eyes. Weary from my long journey, drunk with brandy and success, I slept for a time.

When I woke, the Sun had risen over the glacier. The dragon was sleeping. As quietly as I could, I left the great hall and headed down the mountain.

I will spare you the account of my journey back to my mother's side. Suffice it to say that everyone along the trail was startled to see me, amazed to hear that I had succeeded in my quest.

At last, I reached the inn where my mother slept. Sarasri was astonished to see me. Though she had never believed that I would return, the good woman had been true to her promise. She had taken care of my mother. Pale and thin, my mother slept peacefully in the room where she had been stricken with the ice sickness.

Sarasri summoned the healer, and the old woman came to my mother's chambers. The healer smiled when she saw me.

"Three drops of dragon's blood," I said, holding out the vial.

"Very good," she said.

"Did you slay the dragon?" Sarasri asked, her eyes wide.

I shook my head. "The dragon told me a story and I told the dragon a story. The dragon gave me this blood on the condition that I return to Dragon's Gate when my mother is well."

The healer nodded. "Ah," she said, "you may very well have slain the dragon then."

I stared at the old woman. "I did not. She gave me this blood freely."

"Indeed—she gave it to you as an act of friendship. And that itself may slay the dragon. Dragons feed on hatred and fear. Acting out of love will weaken the beast."

"This act of kindness weakened the dragon?" I said. "That's not fair."

"Hate and fear nourish and strengthen a dragon. Love and friendship erode that strength. Fair or not, it's the way things work." She shrugged. "The next hero may find an easy kill. I have heard that Prince Dexter of Erland will soon be going to Dragon's Gate. But that is no concern of yours."

The old woman took the vial of blood. Her touch was cold on my hand. Gently, she stroked my mother's hair, then wet my mother's lips with the dragon's blood.

As I watched, the color returned to my mother's cheeks. My mother parted her lips, sighed, then opened her eyes and blinked at me. "Al," she murmured. "It must be past breakfast time. I'm ravenous."

Sarasri clapped her hands together and hurried off to fetch food. I held my mother's hands, cold in my grip at first, then warming—and I told her all that had happened. She feasted on scones and fresh milk. And when I thought to look around for the healer, the old woman was gone.

My mother recovered quickly. By the evening, she was out of bed. By the next morning, she was asking what we would do next.

I knew that I had to return to the dragon's castle as soon as possible. The healer's words had left me uneasy. My mother was captivated by the dragon's story, and she said that she would go with me. With some effort, I persuaded her that it was more important that she write a ballad that told Tara's tale.

At last I prevailed. But not before I found out more information about Prince Dexter and his plans.

Erland was a kingdom to the north—a small, cold, barren place. Its population lived by fishing and hunting the great whales that lived in the Northern Seas. Princes were as common as fish heads in Erland. (The king of Erland was a virile man.) Prince Dexter, the youngest of the king's eight sons, had left Erland to seek his fortune.

A group of merchants in the lowlands had offered Dexter a great reward if he would slay the dragon. From the merchants' point of view, it was a very sensible move. If the prince failed, it cost them nothing. If he succeeded, the dragon's death opened an easy route to the trading ports—and Dexter's reward would be nothing compared to the fortunes they would make.

From the prince's point of view—well, I confess, I do not understand the prince's point of view. It seems to me that there are easier ways to make your fortune than attempting to slay a dragon that has killed many heroes. But princes are raised on stories in which the dragon always dies. Like me, the prince believed in a happy ending.

Knowing that the prince would soon be going to Dragon's Gate, I set out on the trail. It was a long, difficult journey—though not as difficult as it had been the first time. It was not as cold as it had been before. As I climbed the pass to reach the castle, I saw a few wildflowers blooming among the gray stones of the mountain. They seemed like a good sign, until I looked down from my high vantagepoint and saw soldiers riding up the trail below me. Their banner was green and white, the colors of Erland.

I climbed the ice-slicked stairs of the castle and made my way to the great hall. The dragon lay where I had seen her last, stretched out on the tattered rug. But her scales were dull and lusterless.

"Tara!" I said. "Wake up!"

The dragon did not move. I threw myself on her great scaly neck. "Wake up!" I shouted again. "There is danger here."

I could feel the barest warmth through the scaly hide. The dragon's breathing was low and shallow.

I could hear the tramping of boots and the rattle of armor in the corridor. Prince Erland and his men had caught up with me. "Can you hear them?" I said. "Can you feel their fear? Can you feel the hatred in their hearts? They have come to kill you. You must wake up."

The dragon did not move.

The prince stepped into the room. His sword was drawn. For a moment I could not help but see the scene as I might have described it in a tale for the tavern crowd. A handsome prince lifted his sword against a terrible monster. But I could see the scene in another way as well: a beast of unearthly beauty, an enchanted princess enslaved and transformed by her own passion, dying for a kindness that had sapped her strength.

I pulled my dagger and stood between the prince and the dragon. The prince looked startled to see me. I could tell by his expression that this was not the way he expected the story to go. I have never heard a story in which anyone tries to protect a dragon.

"You must not kill this dragon," I told him. "She is an enchanted princess. She was weakened because she acted with great kindness. You must not slay her."

"Enchanted princess?" The prince frowned, staring at the sleeping dragon. "I'm not likely to kiss that. A woman capable of laying waste to a kingdom and driving soldiers before her like sheep is no wife for me."

Clearly he had heard too many stories of princes and enchanted princesses. I had suggested neither a kiss nor a royal wedding.

"I think I'd better just kill the beast," the prince was saying. "If you do not step aside, I will have to remove you."

I've told enough stories about princes to know that is what they are trained to do—slay monsters and marry princesses. This prince, like others of his kind, was not a man inclined to change direction quickly.

"I will not step aside," I said, holding out my dagger.

The prince was, however, trained to fight. I was not. With a flick of his sword, the prince struck my dagger aside, stepped in, twisted it from my hands, and tossed it into the corner. Then he lifted his sword.

I fell on the dragon's neck so that the prince could not strike the sleeping dragon without striking me. "Wake up," I murmured to Tara, my eyes filling with tears. It was too much; it was not fair. "You must save yourself." My tears spilled over, dropping onto the beast's neck, trickling over the dull scales.

Where the tears touched, the scales shone with a new brilliance, a blue-white light so bright it dazzled my eyes. The dragon shuddered beneath me. I released my hold on her neck, scrambling away.

The brilliant light—ten times brighter than sunlight on the ice fields—enveloped the dragon. I squinted through my tears at the light. I could see a shadow in the glare, a dark shape that changed as I strained to see what it was.

The light faded, and I blinked, my eyes still dazzled. A woman stood on the tattered rug. Her eyes were as blue as glacial ice. Her hair was the color of flames. She was dressed in an old-fashioned hunting tunic and breeches. Her hand was on the sword at her belt, and I was certain that she knew how to use it. Much experience with bandits, I suspected.

Tara sat by the fire that the soldiers had built, watching the flames.

"Of course, you can claim your reward," I told the prince. "The merchants asked that you do away with the dragon—and you achieved that end. Your men can testify to it: The dragon is gone."

"That's true," the prince agreed.

"It is the way the story had to go," I explained to the prince. "My tears melted the ice in her heart and she returned to her true form."

"And now what happens?" The prince was studying Tara thoughtfully.

Tara turned from contemplating the fire and met his gaze. "Now I return my kingdom to its former glory. With the dragon gone, my people will return." She smiled. "It will take time, but there's no rush."

"You will need help," the prince said. "Such a lovely princess should not rule alone. Perhaps...."

"Perhaps you should remember your own thoughts, as you prepared to slay a dragon," Princess Tara said, still smiling. "A woman capable of laying waste to a kingdom and driving soldiers before her like sheep is no wife for you."

She turned her gaze back to the fire. "My people will return, and so will the bandits. We will hunt the bandits in the hills and the merchants will pay a toll to pass this way."

"Perhaps you'd best not tell the merchants that part just yet," I advised the prince.

Is the story done yet? Not quite. There is still King Takla's horn to account for. That evening, I stood by the glacier and I blew that horn. I saw a flash of blue light over the ice, and then a beautiful woman wrapped in a white shawl stood before me. Her eyes looked familiar—a beautiful, piercing blue. Her hair was white, and she smiled with recognition when she saw me.

"You have called me," the ice woman said. "What do you wish?"

I held out the horn. "Only to return this horn," I said. "Nothing more."

The ice woman studied me. "No other wishes? You do not wish for wealth or fame or glory?"

I smiled and shook my head.

"You dress as a man, yet you are a woman. Would you wish to be a man?"

I thought about Princess Tara, a woman who hunted for bandits and claimed her own kingdom, and shook my head. "I have no wish to make," I said. Then I asked, "How is your daughter?"

"Very well," she said. "She was pleased to return to her home."

I nodded. "Of course she would be."

"How is your mother?" the ice woman asked.

"Doing well. Writing a ballad about Tara."

She took the horn from my extended hand. "You did very well," she said then. "I am glad that you could help my great-granddaughter, Tara."

I bowed to her. "I am grateful to have been of service." When I looked up, she was gone.

I returned to Sarasri's inn in Nabakhri, where my mother waited. I reached the inn early in the afternoon. I went looking for my mother and found her in the kitchen. Sarasri was kneading bread and my mother was playing the harp and keeping her company.

The kitchen was warm. A pot of lamb stew bubbled on the fire. The yeasty scent of bread filled the air. "Al is back!" Sarasri shouted when she saw me. My mother abandoned her music and hugged me. Sarasri heaped lamb stew in a bowl and insisted that I eat it all.

"My wonderful child," my mother said. "You must tell us all that has happened since you left here."

I shook my head, my mouth filled with stew. "Tonight," I said. "I will tell the tale tonight."

The tavern was full that night. People had heard of my mother's illness, of my trip to Dragon's Gate and my return with dragon's blood, of my return to Dragon's Gate to keep my promise.

I smiled at the crowd. Dressed in tunic and breeches, returning in triumph from Dragon's Gate, I knew the story that they expected. It was the story of Al, a heroic young man who confronts a monster.

"My name is Alita," I said. "And that means 'a girl to be trusted.' Some of you know me as Al and think that I am a young man. But the world is filled with illusions—as I learned when I met the dragon. Let me tell you my story."

IN AUTUMN, A WHITE DRAGON LOOKS OVER THE WIDE RIVER

Naomi Novik

Naomi Novik was born in New York in 1973, a first-generation American, and raised on Polish fairy tales, Baba Yaga, and Tolkien. She studied English Literature at Brown University and did graduate work in Computer Science at Columbia University before leaving to participate in the design and development of the computer game *Neverwinter Nights: Shadows of Undrentide*.

Novik's first novel, *His Majesty's Dragon*, was published in 2006 along with *Throne of Jade* and *Black Powder War*, and has been translated into twenty-three languages. She has won the John W. Campbell Award for Best New Writer, the Compton Crook Award for Best First Novel, and the Locus Award for Best First Novel. The fourth volume of the Temeraire series, *Empire of Ivory* was a *New York Times* bestseller. Her most recent books are *Victory of Eagles* and the omnibus *In His Majesty's Service*, and coming up is new Temeraire novel, *Tongues of Serpents*.

Novik lives in New York City with her husband and a multiplying number of computers.

The diplomat, De Guignes, had disappeared somewhere into the palace. Lien remained alone in the courtyard. The pale narrow faces of the foreign servants gawked out at her from the windows of the great house; the soldiers in their blue and white uniforms staring and clutching their long muskets. Other men, more crudely dressed, were stumbling around her; they had come from the stables by their smell, clumsy with sleep and noisy, and they groaned to one another in complaint at the hour as they worked.

The palace, built in square around the courtyard, was not at all of the style she had known at home, and deeply inconvenient. While it possessed in some few places a little pleasing symmetry, it was full of tiny windows arranged on several

267

levels, and the doors were absurdly small—like a peasant's hut or a merchant's home. She could never have gone inside. Some of the laborers were putting up a pavilion on a lawn in the court, made of heavy fabric and sure to be hot and stifling in the warm autumnal weather. Others carried out a wooden trough, such as might be used for feeding pigs, and began to fill it with buckets, water slopping over the sides as they staggered back and forth yawning.

Another handful of men dragged over a pair of lowing cattle, big brown-furred creatures with rolling eyes showing white. They tethered the cows before her and stood back expectantly, as though they meant her to eat them live and unbutchered. The animals stank of manure and terror.

Lien flicked her tail and looked away. Well, she had not come to be comfortable.

De Guignes was coming out of a side door of the house again, and another man with him, a stranger: dressed like the soldiers, but with a plain grey coat over all that at least concealed the rudely tight trousers the others all wore. They approached; the man paused a few paces away to look upon her, not out of fear: there was an eager martial light in his face.

"Sire," De Guignes said, bowing, "permit me to present to you Madame Lien, of China, who has come to make her home with us."

So this was their emperor? Lien regarded him doubtfully. By necessity, over the course of the long overland journey from China in the company of De Guignes and his fellow countrymen, she had grown accustomed to the lack of proper ceremony in their habits; but to go so far as this was almost embarrassing to observe. The serving-men were all watching him without averting their eyes or their faces; there was no sense of distance or respect. The emperor himself clapped De Guignes on the shoulder, as though they had been common soldiers together.

"Madame," the emperor said, looking up at her, "you will tell these men how they may please you. I regret we have only a poor welcome to offer you at present, but there is a better in our hearts, which will soon make amends."

De Guignes murmured something to him, too soft for her to hear, and without waiting for her own answer, the emperor turned away and gestured impatiently, giving orders. The loudly bellowing cows were dragged away again, and a couple of boys came hurrying over to sweep away the stinking pools of urine they had deposited in their fear. In place of the trough, men brought out a great copper basin for her to drink from, bright-polished. The moaning of the cows stopped, somewhere on the other side of the stables, and shortly a roasting scent came: uninteresting, but she was hungry enough, after their long journey, to take her food with no seasoning but appetite.

De Guignes returned to her side after a little more conversation with the emperor. "I hope all meets with your approval?" he said, indicating the pavilion. "His majesty informs me he will give orders that a permanent pavilion be raised for your comfort on the river, and you will be consulted as regards the prospect."

"These things are of little importance," she said. "I am eager, however, to hear more of the emperor's present designs against the nation of Britain."

De Guignes hesitated and said, "I will inquire in the morning for the intelligence you desire, Madame. His majesty may wish to convey his intentions to you himself."

She looked at him and flicked her ruff, which ought to have been to him a warning that he was lamentably transparent, and also that she would not be put off in such a manner for long; but he only looked pleased with himself as he bowed again and went away.

She stayed awake the better part of the night in the pleasant cool upon the lawn before the pavilion, nibbling occasionally at the platter of roasted meat as hunger overcame her distaste; at least it was no more unappetizing for being cold. The rising sun, painful in her eyes and against her skin, drove her at last into the shelter of the pavilion; and she drowsed thickly and uncomfortably in the stifling heat, dreaming of her prince's deep, controlled voice, reciting summer poetry.

In the late afternoon, the sun vanished behind clouds and she could emerge, only to find she had company in the court: three young male dragons of enormous size, all of them dirty, idly gnawing on bloody carcasses, and wearing harnesses like carrying-dragons. They stared at her with rude curiosity; Lien sat back upon her haunches and regarded them icily.

"Good day, madame," one of them said after a moment, daring to break silence first. Lien flattened back her ruff and ignored him entirely, leaning over the copper basin. Several leaves had blown into the water and not been removed; she lifted them out of the way with the tip of her claw and drank.

The three males looked at one another, their tails and wing-tips twitching visibly with uncertainty like hatchlings fresh from the shell. The first one who had spoken—the largest of them, an undistinguished dark brown in color with a belly of mottled cream and grey—tried again. "I am called Fraternité," he offered, and when she made no response, he leaned his head in towards her and said very loudly, "I said, *good day, I am*—"

She blazed her ruff wide and roared at him, a short controlled burst directed at the soft earth before his face, so the dirt sprayed into his face and his nostrils.

He jerked back, coughing and spluttering, making a spectacle of himself and rubbing his face against his side. "What was that for?" he protested, injured; although to her small relief, he and his companions also drew back a little distance, more respectfully.

"If I should desire to make the acquaintance of some person," Lien said, addressing the small tree a few paces away, so as to preserve at least some semblance of a barrier to this sort of familiarity, "I am perfectly capable of inquiring after their name; and if someone is so lost to right behavior as to intrude themselves undesired upon my attention, that person will receive the treatment he deserves."

After a brief silence, the smallest of the three, colored in an unpleasant melange of orange and brown and yellow, ventured, "But how we are to be welcoming if we are not to speak to you?"

Lien paused momentarily, without allowing surprise to show; it required an abrupt and unpleasant adjustment to her new circumstances to realize that these were not some idle gawkers who had carelessly intruded: they had been deliberately sent to her as companions.

She looked them over more closely. Fraternité was perhaps two years out of the shell; he did not yet have his full growth, outrageously disproportionate as his mass already was. The orange-brown male was only a little older, and the last, black with yellow markings, was younger again; he was the only one at all graceful in conformity or coloration, and he stank of a markedly unpleasant odor like lamp-oil.

If she had been at home, or in any civilized part of the world, she would at once have called it a deliberate insult, and she wondered even here; but De Guignes had been so anxious to bring her. The rest of her treatment suggested enough incompetence, she decided, to encompass even this. Perhaps the French even thought it a gracious gesture of welcome; and she could not yet afford to disdain it. She had no way of knowing who might be offended by such a rejection, and what power they might have over other decision-making.

So she resigned herself, and said to the tree, rather grimly, "I am certainly not interested in friendship with anyone who cannot eat in a civilized way, or keep himself in respectable order."

They looked at one another and down at themselves a little doubtfully, and the black and yellow male, who had been eating a raw sheep, turned towards one of the men nearby and said, "Gustav, what does she mean; how am I eating wrong?"

"I don't know, mon brave," the man said. "They said she wanted her food cooked; maybe that is what she means?"

"The content of a stranger's diet, however unhealthful, is scarcely of concern to the disinterested onlooker who may nevertheless object to being approached by one covered in blood and filth and dirty harness, and stinking of carrion," Lien informed the tree, in some exasperation, and closing her eyes put her head down on her forelegs and curled her tail close to signify the conversation was for the moment at an end.

The three males returned some hours later, washed and with their harnesses polished and armor attached, which gave them the dubious distinction of looking like soldiers instead of the lowest sort of city-laborers, although they looked as pleased with themselves as if they had been wearing the emblems of highest rank. Lien kept her sighs to herself and permitted them to introduce themselves: Sûreté was the orange-brown, and Lumière the black and yellow, who took the opportunity to inform her proudly he was a fire-breather, and then for no reason belched a tremendous and smoky torrent of flame into the air.

She regarded him with steady disapproval. After a moment, he let the flame narrow and trail away, his puffed-out chest curving uncertainly back in, and his wings settling back against his body. "I—I heard you do not have fire-breathers, in China," he said.

"Such an unbalanced amount of *yang* makes for unquiet temperament, which is likely why you would do something so peculiar as breathe fire in the middle of a conversation," Lien said, quellingly.

In forcing her to correct this and a thousand other small indelicacies in their behavior, their company soon made her feel a nursemaid to several slightly dim hatchlings, and it was especially tiring to have to correct their manners over the dinner the servants brought. By the end of the meal, however, she could be grateful for their naïvete, because they were as unguarded in their speech as in their behavior, and so proved founts of useful information.

Some of it thoroughly appalling. Their descriptions of their usual meals were enough to put her off from the barely-adequate dinner laid before her, and they counted themselves fortunate for the privilege of spending the evening sleeping directly on the lawn about her pavilion, as compared to their ordinary quarters of bare dirt. Her prince had told her a little of the conditions in the West when he had returned from across the sea, but she had not wholly believed him; it seemed impossible anyone should tolerate such treatment. But she grimly swallowed that indignation along with the coarse vegetables that had been provided in place of rice; she had not come to make these foreign dragons comfortable, either. She had come to complete her prince's work.

The prospects for that were not encouraging. Her companions informed her that the French were presently on the verge of war, and when she sketched a rough map in the earth, they were able to point out the enemy lands: all in the east, away from Britain.

"It is the British, though, who give them money to fight us," Fraternité said, glowering at the small islands; that same money, Lien thought, which they wrung out of the trade which brought the poison of opium into China, in defiance of the Emperor's law, and took silver out.

"When do you go?" she inquired.

"We do not," Lumière said, sulkily, and put his head down on his forelegs. "We must stay back; there isn't enough food."

Lien could well imagine there was not enough food available to sustain these three enormous creatures, when the French insisted on feeding them nothing but cattle, but she did not see how keeping them behind would correct that difficulty. "Well, the army cannot drive enough cattle to feed us all," Fraternité said, bafflingly; it took nearly half an hour of further inquiry until Lien finally realized that the French were supplying their forces entirely from the ground.

She tried to envision the process and shuddered; in her imagination long trains of lowing cattle were marched single-file through the countryside, growing thin and diseased most likely, and probably fed to the dragons only as they fell over dead.

"How many of you go, and how many remain?" she asked, and with a few more questions began to understand the nonsensical arrangement: dragons formed scarcely a thirtieth part of their forces, instead of the fifth share prescribed as ideal since the time of Sun Tzu. The aerial forces, as far as she could tell, seemed nearly incidental to their strategies, which centered instead upon infantry and even cavalry, which should have only served for support. It began to explain their obsession with size, when they could only field such tiny numbers in the air.

She was not certain how it was possible this emperor could have won any battles at all in foreign territory, under these conditions; but the dragons were all delighted to recount for her detailed stories of half a dozen glorious battles and campaigns, which made it plain to her that the enemy was no less inept at managing their aerial strength.

Her companions were less delighted to admit they had been present at none of these thrilling occasions; and indeed had done very little in their lives so far but lie about and practice sluggish and awkward maneuvers.

"Then you may as well begin to learn to write," Lien said, and set them all to scratching lines in the dirt for the first five characters: they were so old they were going to have to practice for a week just to learn those, and it would be years before they could read the simplest text. "And you," she added to Lumière, "are to eat nothing but fish and watercress, and drink a bowlful of mint tea at every meal."

De Guignes returned that afternoon, but was more anxious to see how she had received her companions than to bring her any new intelligence. However wise it might have been, she could not quite bring herself to so much complaisance, and she said to him, "How am I to take it when you send to me companions beyond hope of intelligent conversation on almost any subject, and of such immaturity? That among you war-dragons are of the highest rank, I can accept; but at least you might have sent those of proven experience and wisdom."

De Guignes looked somewhat reluctant, and made some excuse that it had been thought that she might prefer more sprightly company. "These are of the very best stock, I am assured," he said, "and the chief men of his majesty's aerial forces put them forward especially for this duty."

"Heredity alone is no qualification for service, where there is no education," she said. "So far as I can see, these are fit for no duty but eating and the exertion of brute strength; and perhaps—" she stopped, and a cold roiling of indignation formed in her breast as she understood for what duty they were meant.

De Guignes had the decency to look ashamed, and the sense to look anxious; he said, "They were meant to please you, madame, and if they do not, I am sure others—"

"You may tell your emperor," she said, interrupting wrathfully, "that I will oblige him in this when he has gotten an heir to his throne upon the coarsest slattern in the meanest town in his dominion; and not before. You may go."

He retreated before her finality, and she paced a little distance into the court-yard and back, her wings rising and falling from her back to fan her skin against the heat of the sun; it was a little painful, but not more so than the sensation of insult. She scarcely knew how to comport herself properly. She had been used from her hatching to be gawked at sidelong by small and superstitious minds, for her unnatural coloration; and had suffered the pain of knowing that their unease had injured the advancement of her prince. But the stupidest courtier would never have dared to offer her such an offense. Lumière landed before her, returning from a short flight: could he truly think of her in such a way? she wondered, and hissed at him.

"Why are you are bad-tempered again?" he said. "It is a splendid day for flying. Why do we not go see the Seine? There is a nice stretch outside the city, where it is not dirty, and also," he added, with an air of being very pleased with himself, "I have brought you a present, see," and held out to her a large branch covered with leaves of many colors.

"I have been the companion of a prince," Lien said, low and bitterly, "and I have worn rubies and gold; this is your idea of a suitable offering, and yourself a suitable mate?"

Lumière put down the branch, huffily, and snorted. "Well, where are they now, then, if you have all these jewels?" he objected. "And this prince of yours, too—"

She mantled high against the sharp cruelty of the question, her ruff stretched thin and painful to its limits, and her voice trembled with deadly resonance as she said, "You will *never* speak of him again."

Lumière mantled back at her in injured surprise, thin trails of smoke issuing from his nostrils, and then one of his companions, clinging to the harness on his back, called loudly, "Mon brave, she has lost him; lost her captain."

Lumière said, "*Oh*," and dropped his wings at once, staring at her with wide-pupiled eyes. She whirled away from the intrusion of his unwanted sympathy and stalked back across the broad courtyard towards the front of the palace, still trembling with anger, and ignoring the yelled protests of the servants seated herself in the broad, cobblestoned drive directly before the doors, where she could not be evaded.

"I am not here to be a broodmare," she said, when Lumière followed and tried to remonstrate with her, "and if that is all your emperor wants, I will leave at sunset, and find my own way out of this barbaric country. If he desires otherwise, he may so convey to me before then."

She remained there for several hours with no response; enough time, under the painful sun, to consider with cold, brutal calculation the likelihood that she would elsewhere find the means to overthrow a fortified island nation. It was the same calculation that had driven her to these straits in the first place. With her prince dead and his faction scattered, her own reputation tainted beyond all repair, and Prince Mianning given an open road to his false dreams of *modernization*—as though there was anything to be learned from these savages—she was powerless in China.

But she would be equally powerless as a solitary wanderer across this small and uncivilized country. She had considered going to England itself, and raising a rebellion there, but she could see already that the dragons of these nations were so beaten down they could not be roused even in their own service. It could almost have made her pity Temeraire; if there were room in her heart for any emotion at even the thought of his name but hatred.

But unlike her poor, stupid young companions, *he* had chosen his fate even when offered a better one; he had preferred to remain a slave and a slave, further-more, to poison-merchants and soldiers. His destruction was not only desirable but necessary, and that of the British he served; but for that, she required an external weapon, and this emperor was the only one available. If he would not listen to her—

But in the end, he did come out to her again. In the daylight, she could make out a better picture of his appearance, without satisfaction. He was an ugly man, round-faced with thin unkempt hair of muddy color, and he wore the same unflattering and indecent tight-legged garments as his soldiers. He walked with excessive energy and haste, rather than with dignity, and for companion he had only one small slight man carrying a sheaf of paper, who did not even keep up but halted several paces further back, casting pale looks up at her.

"Now, what is this," the emperor said impatiently. "What is wrong with these three we have given you? They do not satisfy you properly?"

Lien flattened her ruff, speechless at this coarseness. One would have thought him a peasant. "I did not come here to *breed* for you," she said. "Even if I were inclined to so lower myself, which I am not, I have more pressing concerns."

"And?" the emperor said. "De Guignes has told me of your preoccupation, and I share it, but Britain cannot simply be attacked from one day to the next. Their navy controls the Channel, and we cannot devote the resources required to achieve a crossing while we have an enemy menacing our eastern flank. A fortified island nation is not so easily—"

"Perhaps you are not aware," Lien said, interrupting him icily, "that I was *zhuang-yuan* in my year; that is, took the first place among the ten thousand scholars who pursued the examinations. It is of course a very small honor, one which is not worthy of much notice; but if you were to keep it in mind, you might consider it unnecessary to explain to me that which should be perfectly obvious to any right-thinking person."

The emperor paused, and then said, "Then if you do not complain that we do not at once invade Britain—"

"I complain that you do nothing which will ever yield their overthrow," Lien said. "De Guignes brings me here with fairy-tales of invasion and an invitation to lend my services to that end, and instead I find you marching uncounted thousands of men away to war in the east, with the best part of what little *real* strength you have left behind, eating unhealthy and expensive quantities of cattle and lying around in wet weather, so exposed there is no use in even trying to make eggs. What is the sense in this absurd behavior?"

He did not answer her at once, but stood in silence a moment, and then turning to his lagging secretary beckoned and said, "You will have General Beaudroit and General Villiers attend me, at once; Madame," he turned back, as the message was sent, "you will explain to me how dragons ought to be fed, if you please; Armand, come nearer, you cannot make notes from there."

The generals arrived an hour later by courier beasts: and at once began to quarrel with her on every point. On the most basic principles of the balance necessary for health, they were completely ignorant and proud to remain so, sneering when she pointed out the utter folly of giving a fire-breather nothing but raw meat. By their lights, dragons could not be fed on anything but animal flesh; and so far as she could tell, they believed the quantity ought to be proportional to a dragon's volume and nothing else.

They refused to consider any means for inuring cavalry to the presence of dragons, nor even the proper function of dragons in the work of supply, which baffled her into a temporary silence, where General Villiers turned to the emperor and said, "Sire, surely we need not waste further time disputing follies with this Chinese beast."

Lien was proud of her self-mastery; she had not given voice to an uncontrolled roar since she had been three months out of the shell. She did not do so now, either, but she put back her ruff, and endured temptation such as she had never known. While Villiers did not even notice; instead he went on, "I must beg you to excuse us: there are a thousand tasks to be accomplished before we march."

She would gladly have torn the creeping vile creature apart with her own bare claws. So far had they lowered her, Lien thought bitterly, in so little time!

And then the emperor looked at Villiers and said, "You have miscounted, monsieur. There are a thousand and two: I must find new generals."

Lien twitched the very end of her tail, a second self-betrayal in as many moments, although she could be grateful that she did not gape and stammer as did the two officials; and in any case her lapse was not observed. The emperor was already turning to his secretary, saying, "Send for Murat: I must have someone who is not a fool," and wheeling back to her for a moment said sharply, "He will attend you tomorrow, and you will describe to him how dragons can be fed on grain, and how the cavalry is to be managed. Armand, take a letter to Berthier—" and walked away from them all.

Like all these Frenchmen, Murat had an appearance which veered between unkempt and unseemly, but he was not, to her satisfaction, a fool. She was cautiously pleased. It would take years, of course, to begin to correct the flaws in the division of their army, and the lamentable deficiencies of their husbandry and agriculture would require a generation or more. But she did not need to be quite so patient, she thought. If the emperor obtained the victory of which he was so certain, in the east, and in the meanwhile she persuaded him to adopt a more rational arrangement of his aerial forces, a force sufficient for invasion might be assembled within the decade, she hoped; or two perhaps.

Three days later, Fraternité woke her in the late afternoon roaring; instinct brought her out of the pavilion straightaway, to see what the matter was, but the three of them were only cavorting about like drunkards.

"We are going to war!" Lumière informed her, mad with delight. "We are not to be left behind, after all; only we will have to eat a lot of gruel and carry things, but that is all right."

She was a little taken aback, and then more when the emperor came to see her that afternoon. "You are coming also," he said, which she was ashamed to find made her chest wish to expand in an undignified manner, although she controlled the impulse. He wanted her opinions on the new arrangements, he informed her; and she was to tell the officers if there were mistakes.

It had not occurred to her that he would attempt in the span of a week to make changes in the organization of his army, and she kept private her first opinion: that he was a madman. In the morning, escorted by her three young companions, she flew to the place of concentration at Mayence, where the dragons were coming in with their first experimental loads of supply. It was, as anyone could have predicted, perfect chaos. The laborers did not know what they were doing, and were clumsy and slow at unloading the dragons, who had been packed incorrectly to begin with; the soldiers did not know how to manage on the carrying harnesses; the cattle were drugged either too much or too little. One could not simply overturn the habits of centuries, however misguided, by giving orders.

She expressed as much in measured terms to the emperor that evening, when he arrived by courier; he listened to her and then said, "Murat says that applying your methods would provide us with a sixfold increase in weight of metal thrown, and tenfold increase in supply for the dragons."

"At the very least," she said, because there was certainly no understating the inefficiency of the present methods. "When done *properly.*"

"For now, I am prepared to settle for doubling my numbers," the emperor said dryly, "so we will tolerate some flaws."

He then dictated a proclamation to his secretary, which was by the hour of the evening meal distributed among the camp and read aloud to the listening soldiers, describing the worst flaws which required correction, and also to her bafflement a lengthy explanation of the reasoning behind the alterations; why he should communicate such information to simple men, likely only to confuse them, she did not understand.

But the next day they did improve a little, and she could not dispute that even fumbling and disorganized, they had bettered the prior state of affairs, although she was still doubtful that it was worth the sacrifice of cohesion and discipline which came when men were following a course in which they had been trained and drilled for years. Of course, the emperor seemed equally willing to sacrifice that discipline in lesser causes. His communications were haphazard at best; while he daily received messages, they came at irregular intervals, and the little couriers cheerfully told her that his army was distributed over hundreds of miles, companies wandering almost independent from one another.

She wondered, and still more at his success, when his couriers were by no means efficient or swift, being bred only for lightness instead of the proper bodily proportions and all far more suitable as skirmishers, and she told him as much that night with even less ceremony. As no one else treated him with the proper degree of awe, she felt it unnecessary to do so herself, and he did not seem to notice any lack of respect. Instead he sent for a chair and sat and asked her questions, endlessly and into the night, while his secretaries and guards drooped around him. His voice at least was pleasant: not so deep as her prince's nor so well-trained, and with a peculiar accent, but clear and strong and carrying.

In the morning, they left for the front, his small courier in the lead; and in the waning hours of the day Lien crested a bank of hills and paused, hovering and silent, while beneath her a vast ant-army of men crawled like small squares of living carpet over the earth, dotting the countryside in either direction as far as her vision could stretch.

It was of course still not rational to make men rather than dragons the center of any military force; still she could not help a strange and disquieting impression of implacable power in the steady marching, as though they might walk on and on across all the world. And in the dusty tracks behind them came on the rattling caravans of black iron, cannons larger than any she had ever seen.

"These throw only sixteen pounds," the emperor said that night, while under his brooding eye Fraternité hefted several of the guns. "Can he take more weight than that?"

"Of course I can," Fraternité said, throwing out his chest.

"No, he cannot," Lien said. "Do not squawk at me," she added, with asperity. "You cannot fly straight through the day with your wing-muscles so constrained."

Fraternité subsided; the emperor however said, "How many hours could he fly with another?"

"No more than two straight," Lien said, and the emperor nodded. The next day, he summoned her and went to gather men from a town called Coblenz, some sixty miles distant. The cannon were loaded on the heaviest dragons, save Lien herself; they were sent two hours on and unloaded; then, having been rested an hour, sent back for other supplies and to carry forward some companies of the infantry. It was an odd and unintuitive back-and-forth, attended with awkwardness and difficulty, but by nightfall the entire company was all reunited, thirty miles nearer to Mayence and not too wretchedly out of order.

The emperor came to her with a gleam of jubilation in his eye that made him handsomer, although she did not think the progress justified as much satisfaction as he displayed, and said so. He laughed and said, "In three days we will see, madame; I bow to you where dragons are concerned, but not men."

The next day, they brought the full company into Mayence before noon, and by that evening had set out again on the wing to Cologne for another, with scarcely a pause in between. Before his three days' time was finished, they had brought in ten thousand men, with their supply, and she had begun to think he was not so much a fool after all: there was that same inevitability in their course which she had felt watching the small marching companies, the momentum of so many men combined; and a spirit of joint effort which animated his countless hordes of tiny soldiers.

"I am satisfied," the emperor told his officers: he had assembled them by Lien's pavilion. "Our next campaign, we will do better; but even at this speed, we will reach Warsaw before winter. Now, gentlemen: I want bigger guns, and I do not see any reason we must send back to France for them."

"There is a fort near Bayreuth," one of the marshals, a young man named Lannes, offered. "They have thirty-two pounders there."

"Will you come?" the emperor asked her, almost like an invitation. He did not mean it so, of course, Lien realized; likely he only wanted her to come and fight, like a soldier-beast.

It made her curt. "It is not fitting for a Celestial to enter into lowly combat."

But he snorted. "I want your opinion on the aerial tactics, not to waste you on the field," he said.

She watched from beside him upon a low rise overlooking the field, while a dozen of his smaller dragons flung themselves in a pell-mell skirmishing rush at the three enormous beasts guarding the fortress. There was nothing of order to the attack, but that meant it required very little training, and she recognized in it all she had described to him of the principles of maximizing maneuverability. The guns fired only infrequently at the little dragons, too small and too close upon the defenders to make good targets, as they nipped and tore at the larger beasts' heads and wings.

The sensation of witnessing her own advice transmuted into acts upon the battlefield was a peculiar one; still more so to watch the defending beasts chased away successfully, and then Lumière diving in, flanked by Fraternité and Sûreté, to blast the ramparts clear with flame while the two others tore up the cannons from their moorings on the wall. They returned triumphantly and lay them at the emperor's feet and hers: great squat wide-mouthed things of pitted iron and scratched wood, ugly and stinking of smoke and oil and blood, and yet also of power, with the enemy's flag lying broken and like a rag half-draped upon them.

She was disquieted by the feeling, and with the sun as her excuse retreated to the shelter of the woods while behind her the enemy general came out of the fortress and knelt down, and through the trees she heard the soldiers crying *Vive la France! Vive l'Empereur! Vive Napoléon!* in a thousand ringing voices. The sound chased her into an uneasy sleep where she spread her jaws wide and roaring brought down the walls of some unnamed fortress, and amid the rubble saw Temeraire broken; but when she turned to show her prince what she had done for him, Napoleon stood there in his place.

She woke wretched and cold all at once, with a light pattering rain beginning to fall upon her skin; she felt a sharp longing for home, for a fragrant bowl of tea and the sight of soft mountains, instead of the sharp angry white-edged peaks lifting themselves out of the trees in the distance. But even as she lifted her head, she smelled the smoke of war, bitter and more acrid than ordinary wood-fire; the smell of victory and of vengeance coming. There were men coming into the clearing to put up a sheltering tent over her, and Napoleon striding in behind them saying, "Come, what are you doing, when you have warned me so of leaving dragons exposed to the weather? We will eat together; and you must have something hot."

ST. DRAGON AND THE GEORGE

Gordon R. Dickson

Gordon R. Dickson was born in 1923 in Edmonton, Canada and moved to Minneapolis, Minnesota as a teenager. Dickson served in the United States Army between 1943 and 1946, and then attended the University of Minnesota, where he received a Bachelor of Arts degree and perhaps more importantly met fellow SF writer Poul Anderson. Dickson's first short story, "Trespass!" (co-written with Anderson), appeared in 1950 and was followed by first novel *Alien from Arcturus* in 1956.

Dickson went on to publish more than sixty novels, 150 short stories and twenty-one short story collections. His stories "Soldier Ask Not", "Lost Dorsai", and "The Cloak and the Staff" all received the Hugo Award, while "Call Him Lord" was awarded the Nebula Award in 1966. Dickson is undoubtedly most famous for the twelve novels that make up the Dorsai military space opera series, the nine science-fantasy novels in the Dragon Knight series, and the four humorous fantasy books in the Hoka! Series (co-written with Poul Anderson). Dickson died in 2001.

I

A trifle diffidently, Jim Eckert rapped with his claw on the blue-painted door.
Silence.

He knocked again. There was the sound of a hasty step inside the small, oddly peak-roofed house and the door was snatched open. A thin-faced old man with a tall pointed cap and a long, rather dingy-looking white beard peered out, irritably.

"Sorry, not my day for dragons!" he snapped. "Come back next Tuesday." He slammed the door.

It was too much. It was the final straw. Jim Eckert sat down on his haunches with a dazed thump. The little forest clearing with its impossible little pool tinkling away like Chinese glass wind chimes in the background, its well-kept greensward with the white gravel path leading to the door before him, and the riotous flower beds of asters, tulips, zinnias, roses and lilies-of-the-valley all

equally impossibly in bloom at the same time about the white finger-post labeled
S. CAROLINUS and pointing at the house—it all whirled about him. It was more
than flesh and blood could bear. At any minute now he would go completely
insane and imagine he was a peanut or a cocker spaniel. Grottwold Hanson had
wrecked them all. Dr. Howells would have to get another teaching assistant for
his English Department. Angie...

Angie!

Jim pounded on the door again. It was snatched open.

"Dragon!" cried S. Carolinus, furiously. "How would you like to be a beetle?"

"But I'm not a dragon," said Jim, desperately.

The magician stared at him for a long minute, then threw up his beard with
both hands in a gesture of despair, caught some of it in his teeth as it fell down
and began to chew on it fiercely.

"Now where," he demanded, "did a dragon acquire the brains to develop the
imagination to entertain the illusion that he is *not* a dragon? Answer me, O Ye
Powers!"

"The information is psychically, though not physiologically correct," replied
a deep bass voice out of thin air beside them and some five feet off the ground.
Jim, who had taken the question to be rhetorical, started convulsively.

"Is that so?" S. Carolinus peered at Jim with new interest. "Hmm." He spat out
a hair or two. "Come in, Anomaly—or whatever you call yourself."

Jim squeezed in through the door and found himself in a large single room. It
was a clutter of mismatched furniture and odd bits of alchemical equipment.

"Hmm," said S. Carolinus, closing the door and walking once around Jim,
thoughtfully. "If you aren't a dragon, what are you?"

"Well, my real name's Jim Eckert," said Jim. "But I seem to be in the body of
a dragon named Gorbash."

"And this disturbs you. So you've come to me. How nice," said the magician,
bitterly. He winced, massaged his stomach and closed his eyes. "Do you know
anything that's good for a perpetual stomach-ache? Of course not. Go on."

"Well, I want to get back to my real body. And take Angie with me. She's my
fiancée and I can send her back but I can't send myself back at the same time. You
see this Grottwold Hanson—well, maybe I better start from the beginning."

"Brilliant suggestion, Gorbash," said Carolinus. "Or whatever your name is,"
he added.

"Well," said Jim. Carolinus winced. Jim hurried on. "I teach at a place called
Riveroak College in the United States—you've never heard of it—"

"Go on, go on," said Carolinus.

"That is, I'm a teaching assistant. Dr. Howells, who heads the English Department, promised me an instructorship over a year ago. But he's never come
through with it; and Angie—Angie Gilman, my fiancée—"

"You mentioned her."

"Yes—well, we were having a little fight. That is, we were arguing about my going to ask Howells whether he was going to give me the instructor's rating for next year or not. I didn't think I should; and she didn't think we could get married—well, anyway, in came Grottwold Hanson."

"In *where* came *who?*"

"Into the Campus Bar and Grille. We were having a drink there. Hanson used to go with Angie. He's a graduate student in psychology. A long, thin geek that's just as crazy as he looks. He's always getting wound up in some new odd-ball organization or other—"

"Dictionary!" interrupted Carolinus, suddenly. He opened his eyes as an enormous volume appeared suddenly poised in the air before him. He massaged his stomach. "Ouch," he said. The pages of the volume began to flip rapidly back and forth before his eyes. "Don't mind me," he said to Jim. "Go on."

"—This time it was the Bridey Murphy craze. Hypnotism. Well—"

"Not so fast," said Carolinus. "*Bridey Murphy... Hypnotism... yes...*"

"Oh, he talked about the ego wandering, planes of reality, on and on like that. He offered to hypnotize one of us and show us how it worked. Angie was mad at me, so she said yes. I went off to the bar. I was mad. When I turned around, Angie was gone. Disappeared."

"Vanished?" said Carolinus.

"Vanished. I blew my top at Hanson. She must have wandered, he said, not merely the ego, but all of her. Bring her back, I said. I can't, he said. It seemed she wanted to go back to the time of St. George and the Dragon. When men were men and would speak up to their bosses about promotions. Hanson'd have to send someone else back to rehypnotize her and send her back home. Like an idiot I said I'd go. Ha! I might've known he'd goof. He couldn't do anything right if he was paid for it. I landed in the body of this dragon."

"And the maiden?"

"Oh, she landed here, too. Centuries off the mark. A place where there actually were such things as dragons—fantastic."

"Why?" said Carolinus.

"Well, I mean—anyway," said Jim, hurriedly. "The point is, they'd already got her—the dragons, I mean. A big brute named Anark had found her wandering around and put her in a cage. They were having a meeting in a cave about deciding what to do with her. Anark wanted to stake her out for a decoy, so they could capture a lot of the local people—only the dragons called people *georges*—"

"They're quite stupid, you know," said Carolinus, severely, looking up from the dictionary. "There's only room for one name in their head at a time. After the Saint made such an impression on them his name stuck."

"Anyway, they were all yelling at once. They've got tremendous voices."

"Yes, you have," said Carolinus, pointedly.

"Oh, sorry," said Jim. He lowered his voice. "I tried to argue that we ought to hold Angie for ransom—" He broke off suddenly. "Say," he said. "I never thought of that. Was I talking dragon, then? What am I talking now? Dragons don't talk English, do they?"

"Why not?" demanded Carolinus, grumpily. "If they're British dragons?"

"But I'm not a dragon—I mean—"

"But you *are* here!" snapped Carolinus. "You and this maiden of yours. Since all the rest of you was translated here, don't you suppose your ability to speak understandably was translated, too? Continue."

"There's not much more," said Jim gloomily. "I was losing the argument and then this very big, old dragon spoke up on my side. Hold Angie for ransom, he said. And they listened to him. It seems he swings a lot of weight among them. He's a great-uncle of me—of this Gorbash who's body I'm in—and I'm his only surviving relative. They penned Angie up in a cave and he sent me off to the Tinkling Water here, to find you and have you open negotiations for ransom. Actually, on the side he told me to tell you to make the terms easy on the georges—I mean humans; he wants the dragons to work toward good relations with them. He's afraid the dragons are in danger of being wiped out. I had a chance to double back and talk to Angie alone. We thought you might be able to send us both back."

He stopped rather out of breath, and looked hopefully at Carolinus. The magician was chewing thoughtfully on his beard.

"Smrgol," he muttered. "Now there's an exception to the rule. Very bright for a dragon. Also experienced. Hmm."

"Can you help us?" demanded Jim. "Look, I can show you—"

Carolinus sighed, closed his eyes, winced and opened them again.

"Let me see if I've got it straight," he said. "You had a dispute with this maiden to whom you're betrothed. To spite you, she turned to this third-rate practitioner, who mistakenly exorcized her from the United States (whenever in the cosmos that is) to here, further compounding his error by sending you back in spirit only to inhabit the body of Gorbash. The maiden is in the hands of the dragons and you have been sent to me by your great-uncle Smrgol."

"That's sort of it," said Jim dubiously, "only—"

"You wouldn't," said Carolinus, "care to change your story to something simpler and more reasonable—like being a prince changed into a dragon by some wicked fairy stepmother? Oh, my poor stomach! No?" He sighed. "All right, that'll be five hundred pounds of gold, or five pounds of rubies, in advance."

"B-but—" Jim goggled at him. "But I don't have any gold—or rubies."

"What? What kind of a dragon are you?" cried Carolinus, glaring at him. "Where's your hoard?"

"I suppose this Gorbash has one," stammered Jim, unhappily. "But I don't know anything about it."

"Another charity patient," muttered Carolinus, furiously. He shook his fist at empty space. "What's wrong with the auditing department? Well?"

"Sorry," said the invisible bass voice.

"That's the third in two weeks. See it doesn't happen again for another ten days." He turned to Jim. "No means of payment?"

"No. Wait—" said Jim. "This stomach-ache of yours. It might be an ulcer. Does it go away between meals?"

"As a matter of fact, it does. Ulcer?"

"High-strung people working under nervous tension get them back where I come from."

"People?" inquired Carolinus suspiciously. "Or dragons?"

"There aren't any dragons where I come from."

"All right, all right, I believe you," said Carolinus, testily. "You don't have to stretch the truth like that. How do you exorcise them?"

"Milk," said Jim. "A glass every hour for a month or two."

"Milk," said Carolinus. He held out his hand to the open air and received a small tankard of it. He drank it off, making a face. After a moment, the face relaxed into a smile.

"By the Powers!" he said. "By the Powers!" He turned to Jim, beaming. "Congratulations, Gorbash, I'm beginning to believe you about that college business after all. The bovine nature of the milk quite smothers the ulcer-demon. Consider me paid."

"Oh, fine. I'll go get Angie and you can hypnotize—"

"What?" cried Carolinus. "Teach your grandmother to suck eggs. Hypnotize! Ha! And what about the First Law of Magic, eh?"

"The what?" said Jim.

"The First Law—the First Law—didn't they teach you anything in that college? Forgotten it already, I see. Oh, this younger generation! The First Law: *for every use of the Art and Science, there is required a corresponding price.* Why do I live by my fees instead of by conjurations? Why does a magic potion have a bad taste? Why did this Hanson-amateur of yours get you all into so much trouble?"

"I don't know," said Jim. "Why?"

"No credit! No credit!" barked Carolinus, flinging his skinny arms wide. "Why, I wouldn't have tried what he did without ten years credit with the auditing department, and *I* am a Master of the Arts. As it was, he couldn't get anything more than your spirit back, after sending the maiden complete. And the fabric of Chance and History is all warped and ready to spring back and cause all kinds of trouble. We'll have to give a little, take a little—"

"GORBASH!" A loud thud outside competed with the dragon-bellow.

"And here we go," said Carolinus dourly. "It's already starting." He led the way outside. Sitting on the greensward just beyond the flower beds was an enormous old dragon Jim recognized as the great-uncle of the body he was in—Smrgol.

"Greetings, Mage!" boomed the old dragon, dropping his head to the ground in salute. "You may not remember me. Name's Smrgol—you remember the business about that ogre I fought at Gormely Keep? I see my grandnephew got to you all right."

"Ah, Smrgol—I remember," said Carolinus. "That was a good job you did."

"He had a habit of dropping his club head after a swing," said Smrgol. "I noticed it along about the fourth hour of battle and the next time he tried it, went in over his guard. Tore up the biceps of his right arm. Then—"

"I remember," Carolinus said. "So this is your nephew."

"Grandnephew," corrected Smrgol. "Little thick-headed and all that," he added apologetically, "but my own flesh and blood, you know."

"You may notice some slight improvement in him," said Carolinus, dryly.

"I hope so," said Smrgol, brightening. "Any change, a change for the better, you know. But I've bad news, Mage. You know that inchworm of an Anark?"

"The one that found the maiden in the first place?"

"That's right. Well, he's stolen her again and run off."

"*What?*" cried Jim.

He had forgotten the capabilities of a dragon's voice. Carolinus tottered, the flowers and grass lay flat, and even Smrgol winced.

"My boy," said the old dragon reproachfully. "How many times must I tell you not to shout. I said, Anark stole the george."

"He means Angie!" cried Jim desperately to Carolinus.

"I know," said Carolinus, with his hands over his ears.

"You're sneezing again," said Smrgol, proudly. He turned to Carolinus. "You wouldn't believe it. A dragon hasn't sneezed in a hundred and ninety years. This boy did it the first moment he set eyes on the george. The others couldn't believe it. Sign of brains, I said. Busy brains make the nose itch. Our side of the family—"

"*Angie!*"

"See there? All right now, boy, you've shown us you can do it. Let's get down to business. How much to locate Anark and the george, Mage?"

They dickered like rug-pedlars for several minutes, finally settling on a price of four pounds of gold, one of silver, and a flawed emerald. Carolinus got a small vial of water from the Tinkling Spring and searched among the grass until he found a small sandy open spot. He bent over it and the two dragons sat down to watch.

"Quiet now," he warned. "I'm going to try a watch-beetle. Don't alarm it."

Jim held his breath. Carolinus tilted the vial in his hand and the crystal water fell in three drops—*Tink! Tink!* And again—*Tink!* The sand darkened with the moisture and began to work as if something was digging from below. A hole widened, black insect legs busily in action flickered, and an odd-looking beetle popped itself halfway out of the hole. Its forelimbs waved in the air and a little squeaky voice, like a cracked phonograph record repeating itself far away over a bad telephone connection, came to Jim's ears.

"*Gone to the Loathly Tower! Gone to the Loathly Tower! Gone to the Loathly Tower!*"

It popped back out of sight. Carolinus straightened up and Jim breathed again.

"The Loathly Tower!" said Smrgol. "Isn't that that ruined tower to the west, in the fens, Mage? Why, that's the place that loosed the blight on the mere-dragons five hundred years ago."

"It's a place of old magic," said Carolinus, grimly. "These places are like ancient sores on the land, scabbed over for a while but always breaking out with new evil when—the twisting of the Fabric by these two must have done it. The evilness there has drawn the evil in Anark to it—lesser to greater, according to the laws of nature. I'll meet you two there. Now, I must go set other forces in motion."

He began to twirl about. His speed increased rapidly until he was nothing but a blur. Then suddenly, he faded away like smoke; and was gone, leaving Jim staring at the spot where he had been.

A poke in the side brought Jim back to the ordinary world.

"Wake up, boy. Don't dally!" the voice of Smrgol bellowed in his ear. "We got flying to do. Come on!"

II

The old dragon's spirit was considerably younger than this body. It turned out to be a four hour flight to the fens on the west seacoast. For the first hour or so Smrgol flew along energetically enough, meanwhile tracing out the genealogy of the mere-dragons and their relationship to himself and Gorbash; but gradually his steady flow of chatter dwindled and became intermittent. He tried to joke about his long-gone battle with the Ogre of Gormely Keep, but even this was too much and he fell silent with labored breath and straining wings. After a short but stubborn argument, Jim got him to admit that he would perhaps be better off taking a short breather and then coming on a little later. Smrgol let out a deep gasping sigh and dropped away from Jim in weary spirals. Jim saw him glide to an exhausted landing amongst the purple gorse of the moors below and lie there, sprawled out.

Jim continued on alone. A couple of hours later the moors dropped down a long land-slope to the green country of the fenland. Jim soared out over its spongy, grass-thick earth, broken into causeways and islands by the blue water, which in shallow bays and inlets was itself thick-choked with reeds and tall marsh grass. Flocks of water fowl rose here and there like eddying smoke from the glassy surface of one mere and drifted over to settle on another a few hundred yards away. Their cries came faintly to his dragon-sensitive ears and a line of heavy clouds was piling up against the sunset in the west.

He looked for some sign of the Loathly Tower, but the fenland stretched away to a faint blue line that was probably the sea, without showing sign of anything not built by nature. Jim was beginning to wonder uneasily if he had not gotten himself lost when his eye was suddenly caught by the sight of a dragon-shape nosing at something on one of the little islands amongst the meres.

Anark! he thought. And Angie!

He did not wait to see more. He nosed over and went into a dive like a jet fighter, sights locked on Target Dragon.

It was a good move. Unfortunately Gorbash-Jim, having about the weight and wingspread of a small flivver airplane, made a comparable amount of noise when he was in a dive, assuming the plane's motor to be shut off. Moreover, the dragon on the ground had evidently had experience with the meaning of such a sound; for, without even looking, he went tumbling head over tail out of the way just as Jim slammed into the spot where, a second before, he had been.

The other dragon rolled over onto his feet, sat up, took one look at Jim, and began to wail.

"It's not fair! It's not fair!" he cried in a (for a dragon) remarkably high-pitched voice. "Just because you're bigger than I am. And I'm all horned up. It's the first good one I've been able to kill in months and you don't need it, not at all. You're big and fat and I'm so weak and thin and hungry—"

Jim blinked and stared. What he had thought to be Angie, lying in the grass, now revealed itself to be an old and rather stringy-looking cow, badly bitten up and with a broken neck.

"It's just my luck!" the other dragon was weeping. He was less than three-quarters Jim's size and so emaciated he appeared on the verge of collapse. "Everytime I get something good, somebody takes it away. All I ever get to eat is fish—"

"Hold on," said Jim.

"Fish, fish, fish. Cold, nasty fi—"

"Hold on, I say! SHUT UP!" bellowed Jim, in Gorbash's best voice.

The other dragon stopped his wailing as suddenly as if his switch had been shut off.

"Yes, sir," he said, timidly.

"What's the matter? I'm not going to take this from you."

The other dragon tittered uncertainly.

"I'm not," said Jim. "It's your cow. All yours."

"He-he-he!" said the other dragon. "You certainly are a card, your honor."

"Blast it, I'm serious!" cried Jim. "What's your name, anyway?"

"Oh, well—" the other squirmed. "Oh well, you know—"

"What's your name?"

"Secoh, your worship!" yelped the dragon, frightenedly. "Just Secoh. Nobody important. Just a little, unimportant mere-dragon, your highness, that's all I am. Really!"

"All right, Secoh, dig in. All I want is some directions."

"Well—if your worship really doesn't..." Secoh had been sidling forward in fawning fashion. "If you'll excuse my table manners, sir. I'm just a mere-dragon—" and he tore into the meat before him in sudden, terrified, starving fashion.

Jim watched. Unexpectedly, his long tongue flickered out to lick his chops. His belly rumbled. He was astounded at himself. Raw meat? Off a dead animal—flesh, bones, hide and all? He took a firm grip on his appetites.

"Er, Secoh," he said. "I'm a stranger around these parts. I suppose you know the territory... Say, how does that cow taste, anyway?"

"Oh, terrubble—mumpf—" replied Secoh, with his mouth full. "Stringy—old. Good enough for a mere-dragon like myself, but not—"

"Well, about these directions—"

"Yes, your highness?"

"I think… you know it's your cow…"

"That's what your honor said," replied Secoh, cautiously.

"But I just wonder… you know I've never tasted a cow like that."

Secoh muttered something despairingly under his breath.

"What?" said Jim.

"I said," said Secoh, resignedly, "wouldn't your worship like to t-taste it—"

"Not if you're going to cry about it," said Jim.

"I bit my tongue."

"Well, in that case…" Jim walked up and sank his teeth in the shoulder of the carcass. Rich juices trickled enticingly over his tongue…

Some little time later he and Secoh sat back polishing bones with the rough uppers of their tongues which were as abrasive as steel files.

"Did you get enough to eat, Secoh?" asked Jim.

"More than enough, sir," replied the mere-dragon, staring at the white skeleton with a wild and famished eye. "Although, if your exaltedness doesn't mind, I've a weakness for marrow…" He picked up a thighbone and began to crunch it like a stick of candy.

"Now," said Jim. "About this Loathly Tower. Where is it?"

"The wh-what?" stammered Secoh, dropping the thighbone.

"The Loathly Tower. It's in the fens. You know of it, don't you?"

"Oh, sir! Yes, sir. But you wouldn't want to go there, sir! Not that I'm presuming to give your lordship advice—" cried Secoh, in a suddenly high and terrified voice.

"No, no," soothed Jim. "What are you so upset about?"

"Well—of course I'm only a timid little mere-dragon. But it's a terrible place, the Loathly Tower, your worship, sir."

"How? Terrible?"

"Well—well, it just is." Secoh cast an unhappy look around him. "It's what spoiled all of us, you know, five hundred years ago. We used to be like other dragons—oh, not so big and handsome as you are, sir. Then, after that, they say it was the Good got the upper hand and the Evil in the Tower was vanquished and the Tower itself ruined. But it didn't help us mere-dragons any, and I wouldn't go there if I was your worship, I really wouldn't."

"But what's so bad? What sort of thing is it?"

"Well, I wouldn't say there was any real *thing* there. Nothing your worship could put a claw on. It's just strange things go to it and strange things come out of it; and lately…"

"Lately what?"

"Nothing—nothing, really, your excellency!" cried Secoh. "You illustriousness shouldn't catch a worthless little mere-dragon up like that. I only meant, lately the Tower's seemed more fearful than ever. That's all."

"Probably your imagination," said Jim, shortly. "Anyway, where is it?"

"You have to go north about five miles." While they had eaten and talked, the sunset had died. It was almost dark now; and Jim had to strain his eyes through the gloom to see the mere-dragon's foreclaw, pointing away across the mere. "To the Great Causeway. It's a wide lane of solid ground running east and west through the fens. You follow it west to the Tower. The Tower stands on a rock overlooking the sea-edge."

"Five miles…" said Jim. He considered the soft grass on which he lay. His armored body seemed undisturbed by the temperature, whatever it was. "I might as well get some sleep. See you in the morning, Secoh." He obeyed a sudden, bird-like instinct and tucked his ferocious head and long neck back under one wing.

"Whatever your excellency desires…" the mere-dragon's muffled voice came distantly to his ear. "Your excellency has only to call and I'll be immediately available…"

The words faded out on Jim's ear, as he sank into sleep like a heavy stone into deep, dark waters.

When he opened his eyes, the sun was up. He sat up himself, yawned, and blinked.

Secoh was gone. So were the leftover bones.

"Blast!" said Jim. But the morning was too nice for annoyance. He smiled at his mental picture of Secoh carefully gathering the bones in fearful silence, and sneaking them away.

The smile did not last long. When he tried to take off in a northerly direction, as determined by reference to the rising sun, he found he had charley horses in both the huge wing-muscles that swelled out under the armor behind his shoulders. The result of course, of yesterday's heavy exercise. Grumbling, he was forced to proceed on foot; and four hours later, very hot, muddy and wet, he pulled his weary body up onto the broad east-and-west-stretching strip of land which must, of necessity, be the Great Causeway. It ran straight as a Roman road through the meres, several feet higher than the rest of the fenland, and was solid enough to support good-sized trees. Jim collapsed in the shade of one with a heartfelt sigh.

He awoke to the sound of someone singing. He blinked and lifted his head. Whatever the earlier verses of the song had been, Jim had missed them; but the approaching baritone voice now caroled the words of the chorus merrily and clearly to his ear:

> "A right good sword, a constant mind
> A trusty spear and true!
> The dragons of the mere shall find
> What Nevile-Smythe can do!"

The tune and words were vaguely familiar. Jim sat up for a better look and a knight in full armor rode into view on a large white horse through the trees. Then everything happened at once. The knight saw him, the visor of his armor came down with a clang, his long spear seemed to jump into his mailed hand and the horse under him leaped into a gallop, heading for Jim. Gorbash's reflexes took over. They hurled Jim straight up into the air, where his punished wing muscles cracked and faltered. He was just able to manage enough of a fluttering flop to throw himself into the upper branches of a small tree nearby.

The knight skidded his horse to a stop below and looked up through the spring-budded branches. He tilted his visor back to reveal a piercing pair of blue eyes, a rather hawk-like nose and a jutting generous chin, all assembled into a clean-shaven young man's face. He looked eagerly up at Jim.

"Come down," he said.

"No thanks," said Jim, hanging firmly to the tree. There was a slight pause as they both digested the situation.

"Dashed caitiff mere-dragon!" said the knight finally, with annoyance.

"I'm not a mere-dragon," said Jim.

"Oh, don't talk rot!" said the knight.

"I'm not," repeated Jim. He thought a minute. "I'll bet you can't guess who I really am."

The knight did not seem interested in guessing who Jim really was. He stood up in his stirrups and probed through the branches with his spear. The point did not quite reach Jim.

"Damn!" Disappointedly, he lowered the spear and became thoughtful. "I can climb the dashed tree," he muttered to himself. "But then what if he flies down and I have to fight him unhorsed, eh?"

"Look," called Jim, peering down—the knight looked up eagerly—"if you'll listen to what I've to say, first."

The knight considered.

"Fair enough," he said, finally. "No pleas for mercy, now!"

"No, no," said Jim.

"Because I shan't grant them, dammit! It's not in my vows. Widows and orphans and honorable enemies on the field of battle. But not dragons."

"No. I just want to convince you who I really am."

"I don't give a blasted farthing who you really are."

"You will," said Jim. "Because I'm not really a dragon at all. I've just been—uh—enchanted into a dragon."

The man on the ground looked skeptical.

"Really," said Jim, slipping a little in the tree. "You know S. Carolinus, the magician? I'm as human as you are."

"Heard of him," grunted the knight. "You'll say *he* put you under?"

"No, he's the one who's going to change me back—as soon as I can find the lady I'm—er—betrothed to. A real dragon ran off with her. I'm after him. Look at me. Do I look like one of these scrawny mere-dragons?"

"Hmm," said the knight. He rubbed his hooked nose thoughtfully.

"Carolinus found she's at the Loathly Tower. I'm on my way there."

The knight stared.

"The Loathly Tower?" he echoed.

"Exactly," said Jim, firmly. "And now you know, your honor as knight and gentleman demands you don't hamper my rescue efforts."

The knight continued to think it over for a long moment or two. He was evidently not the sort to be rushed into things.

"How do I know you're telling the truth?" he said at last.

"Hold your sword up. I'll swear on the cross of its hilt."

"But if you're a dragon, what's the good in that? Dragons don't have souls, dammit!"

"No," said Jim, "but a Christian gentleman has; and if I'm a Christian gentleman, I wouldn't dare forswear myself like that, would I?"

The knight struggled visibly with this logic for several seconds. Finally, he gave up.

"Oh, well..." He held up his sword by the point and let Jim swear on it. Then he put the sword back in its sheath as Jim descended. "Well," he said, still a little doubtfully, "I suppose, under the circumstances, we ought to introduce ourselves. You know my arms?"

Jim looked at the shield which the other swung around for his inspection. It showed a wide X of silver—like a cross lying over sideways—on a red background and above some sort of black animal in profile which seemed to be lying down between the X's bottom legs.

"The gules, a saltire argent, of course," went on the knight, "are the Nevile of Raby arms. My father, as a cadet of the house, differenced with a hart lodged sable—you see it there at the bottom. Naturally, as his heir, I carry the family arms."

"Nevile-Smythe," said Jim, remembering the name from the song.

"Sir Reginald, knight bachelor. And you, sir?"

"Why, uh..." Jim clutched frantically at what he knew of heraldry. "I bear—in my proper body, that is—"

"Quite."

"A...gules, a typewriter argent, on a desk sable. Eckert, Sir James—uh—knight bachelor. Baron of—er—Riveroak."

Nevile-Smythe was knitting his brows.

"Typewriter..." he was muttering, "typewriter..."

"A local beast, rather like a griffin," said Jim, hastily. "We have a lot of them in Riveroak—that's in America, a land over the sea to the west. You may not have heard of it."

"Can't say that I have. Was it there you were enchanted into this dragon-shape?"

"Well, yes and no. I was transported to this land by magic as was the—uh—lady Angela. When I woke here I was bedragoned."

"Were you?" Sir Reginald's blue eyes bulged a little in amazement. "Angela—fair name, that! Like to meet her. Perhaps after we get this muddle cleared up, we might have a bit of a set-to on behalf of our respective ladies."

Jim gulped slightly.

"Oh, you've got one, too?"

"Absolutely. And she's tremendous. The Lady Elinor—" The knight turned about in his saddle and began to fumble about his equipment. Jim, on reaching the ground, had at once started out along the causeway in the direction of the Tower, so that the knight happened to be pacing alongside him on horseback when he suddenly went into these evolutions. It seemed to bother his charger not at all. "Got her favor here someplace—half a moment—"

"Why don't you just tell me what it's like?" said Jim, sympathetically.

"Oh, well," said Nevile-Smythe, giving up his search, "it's a kerchief, you know. Monogrammed. E. d'C. She's a deChauncy. It's rather too bad, though. I'd have liked to show it to you since we're going to the Loathly Tower together."

"We are?" said Jim, startled. "But—I mean, it's my job. I didn't think you'd want—"

"Lord, yes," said Nevile-Smythe, looking somewhat startled himself. "A gentleman of coat-armor like myself—and an outrage like this taking place locally. I'm no knight-errant, dash it, but I *do* have a decent sense of responsibility."

"I mean—I just meant—" stumbled Jim. "What if something happened to you? What would the Lady Elinor say?"

"Why, what could she say?" replied Nevile-Smythe in plain astonishment. "No one but an utter rotter dodges his plain duty. Besides, there may be a chance here for me to gain a little worship. Elinor's keen on that. She wants me to come home safe."

Jim blinked.

"I don't get it," he said.

"Beg pardon?"

Jim explained his confusion.

"Why, how do you people do things, overseas?" said Nevile-Smythe. "After we're married and I have lands of my own, I'll be expected to raise a company and march out at my lord's call. If I've no name as a knight, I'll be able to raise nothing but bumpkins and clodpoles who'll desert at the first sight of steel. On the other hand, if I've a name, I'll have good men coming to serve under my banner; because, you see, they know I'll take good care of them; and by the same token they'll take good care of me—I say, isn't it getting dark rather suddenly?"

Jim glanced at the sky. It was indeed—almost the dimness of twilight although it could, by rights, be no more than early afternoon yet. Glancing ahead up the Causeway, he became aware of a further phenomenon. A line seemed to be cutting across the trees and grass and even extending out over the waters of the meres on both sides. Moreover, it seemed to be moving toward them as if some heavy, invisible fluid was slowly flooding out over the low country of the fenland.

"Why—" he began. A voice wailed suddenly from his left to interrupt him.

"No! No! Turn back, your worship. Turn back! It's death in there!"

They turned their heads sharply. Secoh, the mere-dragon, sat perched on a half-drowned tussock about forty feet out in the mere.

"Come here, Secoh!" called Jim.

"No! No!" The invisible line was almost to the tussock. Secoh lifted heavily into the air and flapped off, crying, "Now it's loose! It's broken loose again. And we're all lost... lost... lost..."

His voice wailed away and was lost in the distance. Jim and Nevile-Smythe looked at each other.

"Now, that's one of our local dragons for you!" said the knight disgustedly. "How can a gentleman of coat armor gain honor by slaying a beast like that? The worst of it is when someone from the Midlands compliments you on being a dragon-slayer and you have to explain—"

At that moment either they both stepped over the line, or the line moved past them—Jim was never sure which; and they both stopped, as by one common, instinctive impulse. Looking at Sir Reginald, Jim could see under the visor how the knight's face had gone pale.

"In manus tuas Domine," said Nevile-Smythe, crossing himself.

About and around them, the serest gray of winter light lay on the fens. The waters of the meres lay thick and oily, still between the shores of dull green grass. A small, cold breeze wandered through the tops of the reeds and they rattled together with a dry and distant sound like old bones cast out into a forgotten courtyard for the wind to play with. The trees stood helpless and still, their new, small leaves now pinched and faded like children aged before their time while all about and over all the heaviness of dead hope and bleak despair lay on all living things.

"Sir James," said the knight, in an odd tone and accents such as Jim had not heard him use before, "wot well that we have this day set our hands to no small task. Wherefore I pray thee that we should push forward, come what may for my heart faileth and I think me that it may well hap that I return not, ne no man know mine end."

Having said this, he immediately reverted to his usual cheerful self and swung down out of his saddle. "Clarivaux won't go another inch, dash it!" he said. "I shall have to lead him—by the bye, did you know that mere-dragon?"

Jim fell into step beside him and they went on again, but a little more slowly, for everything seemed an extra effort under this darkening sky.

"I talked to him yesterday," said Jim. "He's not a bad sort of dragon."

"Oh, I've nothing against the beasts, myself. But one slays them when one finds them, you know."

"An old dragon—in fact he's the granduncle of this body I'm in," said Jim, "thinks that dragons and humans really ought to get together. Be friends, you know."

"Extraordinary thought!" said Nevile-Smythe, staring at Jim in astonishment.

"Well, actually," said Jim, "why not?"

"Well, I don't know. It just seems like it wouldn't do."

"He says men and dragons might find common foes to fight together."

"Oh, that's where he's wrong, though. You couldn't trust dragons to stick by you in a bicker. And what if your enemy had dragons of his own? They wouldn't fight each other. No. No."

They fell silent. They had moved away from the grass onto flat sandy soil. There was a sterile, flinty hardness to it. It crunched under the hooves of Clarivaux, at once unyielding and treacherous.

"Getting darker, isn't it?" said Jim, finally.

The light was, in fact, now down to a grayish twilight through which it was impossible to see more than a dozen feet. And it was dwindling as they watched. They had halted and stood facing each other. The light fled steadily, and faster. The dimness became blacker, and blacker—until finally the last vestige of illumination was lost and blackness, total and complete, overwhelmed them. Jim felt a gauntleted hand touch one of his forelimbs.

"Let's hold together," said the voice of the knight. "Then whatever comes upon us, must come upon us all at once."

"Right," said Jim. But the word sounded cold and dead in his throat.

They stood, in silence and in lightlessness, waiting for they did not know what. And the blankness about them pressed further in on them, now that it had isolated them, nibbling at the very edges of their minds. Out of the nothingness came nothing material, but from within them crept up one by one, like blind white slugs from some bottomless pit, all their inner doubts and fears and unknown weaknesses, all the things of which they had been ashamed and which they had tucked away to forget, all the maggots of their souls.

Jim found himself slowly, stealthily beginning to withdraw his forelimb from under the knight's touch. He no longer trusted Nevile-Smythe—for the evil that must be in the man because of the evil he knew to be in himself. He would move away… off into the darkness alone…

"Look!" Nevile-Smythe's voice cried suddenly to him, distant and eerie, as if from someone already a long way off. "Look back the way we came."

Jim turned about. Far off in the darkness, there was a distant glimmer of light. It rolled toward them, growing as it came. They felt its power against the power of lightlessness that threatened to overwhelm them; and the horse Clarivaux stirred unseen beside them, stamped his hooves on the hard sand, and whinnied.

"This way!" called Jim.

"This way!" shouted Nevile-Smythe

The light shot up suddenly in height. Like a great rod it advanced toward them and the darkness was rolling back, graying, disappearing. They heard a sound of feet close, and a sound of breathing, and then—

It was daylight again.

And S. Carolinus stood before them in tall hat and robes figured with strange images and signs. In his hand upright before him—as if it was blade and buckler, spear and armor all in one—he held a tall carven staff of wood.

"By the Power!" he said. "I was in time. Look there!"

He lifted the staff and drove it point down into the soil. It went in and stood erect like some denuded tree. His long arm pointed past them and they turned around.

The darkness was gone. The fens lay revealed far and wide, stretching back a long way, and up ahead, meeting the thin dark line of the sea. The Causeway had risen until they now stood twenty feet above the mere-waters. Ahead to the west, the sky was ablaze with sunset. It lighted up all the fens and the end of the Causeway leading onto a long and bloody-looking hill, whereon—touched by that same dying light—there loomed above and over all, amongst great tumbled boulders, the ruined, dark and shattered shell of a Tower as black as jet.

III

"—why didn't you wake us earlier, then?" asked Jim.

It was the morning after. They had slept the night within the small circle of protection afforded by Carolinus' staff. They were sitting up now and rubbing their eyes in the light of a sun that had certainly been above the horizon a good two hours.

"Because," said Carolinus. He was sipping at some more milk and he stopped to make a face of distaste. "Because we had to wait for them to catch up with us."

"Who? Catch up?" asked Jim.

"If I knew *who*," snapped Carolinus, handing his empty milk tankard back to the emptier air, "I would have said *who*. All I know is that the present pattern of Chance and History implies that two more will join our party. The same pattern implied the presence of this knight and—oh, so that's who they are."

Jim turned around to follow the magician's gaze. To his surprise, two dragon shapes were emerging from a clump of brush behind them.

"Secoh!" cried Jim. "And—Smrgol! Why—" His voice wavered and died. The old dragon, he suddenly noticed, was limping and one wing hung a little loosely, half-drooping from its shoulder. Also, the eyelid on the same side as the loose wing and stiff leg was sagging more or less at half-mast. "Why, what happened?"

"Oh, a bit stiff from yesterday," huffed Smrgol, bluffly. "Probably pass off in a day or two."

"Stiff nothing!" said Jim, touched in spite of himself. "You've had a stroke."

"Stroke of bad luck, *I'd* say," replied Smrgol, cheerfully, trying to wink his bad eye and not succeeding very well. "No, boy, it's nothing. Look who I've brought along."

"I—I wasn't too keen on coming," said Secoh, shyly, to Jim. "But your grand-uncle can be pretty persuasive, your wo— you know."

"That's right!" boomed Smrgol. "Don't you go calling anybody your worship. Never heard of such stuff!" He turned to Jim. "And letting a george go in where he didn't dare go himself! Boy, I said to him, don't give me this *only a mere-dragon* and *just a mere-dragon*. Mere's got nothing to do with what kind of dragon you are. What kind of a world would it be if we were all like that?" Smrgol mimicked (as well as his dragon-basso would let him) someone talking in a high, simpering voice. "Oh, I'm just a plowland-and-pasture dragon—you'll have to excuse me I'm only a halfway-up-the-hill dragon—*Boy!*" bellowed Smrgol, "I said you're a *dragon!* Remember that. And a dragon acts like a dragon or he doesn't act at all!"

"Hear! Hear!" said Nevile-Smythe, carried away by enthusiasm.

"Hear that, boy? Even the george here knows that. Don't believe I've met you, george," he added, turning to the knight.

"Nevile-Smythe, Sir Reginald. Knight bachelor."

"Smrgol. Dragon."

"Smrgol? You aren't the—but you couldn't be. Over a hundred years ago."

"The dragon who slew the Ogre of Gormely Keep? That's who I am, boy— george, I mean."

"By Jove! Always thought it was a legend, only."

"Legend? Not on your honor, george! I'm old—even for a dragon, but there was a time—well, well, we won't go into that. I've something more important to talk to you about. I've been doing a lot of thinking the last decade or so about us dragons and you georges getting together. Actually, we're really a lot alike—"

"If you don't mind, Smrgol," cut in Carolinus, snappishly, "we aren't out here to hold a parlement. It'll be noon in—when will it be noon, you?"

"Four hours, thirty-seven minutes, twelve seconds at the sound of the gong," replied the invisible bass voice. There was a momentary pause, and then a single mellow, chimed note. "Chime, I mean," the voice corrected itself.

"Oh, go back to bed!" cried Carolinus, furiously.

"I've been up for hours," protested the voice, indignantly.

Carolinus ignored it, herding the party together and starting them off for the Tower. The knight fell in beside Smrgol.

"About this business of men and dragons getting together," said Nevile-Smythe. "Confess I wasn't much impressed until I heard your name. D'you think it's possible?"

"Got to make a start sometime, george." Smrgol rumbled on. Jim, who had moved up to the head of the column to walk beside Carolinus, spoke to the magician.

"What lives in the Tower?"

Carolinus jerked his fierce old bearded face around to look at him.

"What's *living* there?" he snapped. "I don't know. We'll find out soon enough. What *is* there—neither alive nor dead, just in existence at the spot—is the manifestation of pure evil."

"But how can we do anything against that?"

"We can't. We can only contain it. Just as you—if you're essentially a good person—contain the potentialities for evil in yourself, by killing its creatures, your evil impulses and actions."

"Oh?" said Jim.

"Certainly. And since evil opposes good in like manner, its creatures, the ones in the Tower, will try to destroy us."

Jim felt a cold lump in his throat. He swallowed.

"Destroy us?"

"Why no, they'll probably just invite us to tea—" The sarcasm in the old magician's voice broke off suddenly with the voice itself. They had just stepped through a low screen of bushes and instinctively checked to a halt.

Lying on the ground before them was what once had been a man in full armor. Jim heard the sucking intake of breath from Nevile-Smythe behind him.

"A most foul death," said the knight softly, "most foul…" He came forward and dropped clumsily to his armored knees, joining his gauntleted hands in prayer. The dragons were silent. Carolinus poked with his staff at a wide trail of slime that led around and over the body and back toward the Tower. It was the sort of trail a garden slug might have left—if this particular garden slug had been two or more feet wide where it touched the ground.

"A Worm," said Carolinus. "But Worms are mindless. No Worm killed him in such cruel fashion." He lifted his head to the old dragon.

"I didn't say it, Mage," rumbled Smrgol, uneasily.

"Best none of us say it until we know for certain. Come on." Carolinus took up the lead and led them forward again.

They had come up off the Causeway onto the barren plain that sloped up into a hill on which stood the Tower. They could see the wide fens and the tide flats coming to meet them in the arms of a small bay—and beyond that the sea, stretching misty to the horizon.

The sky above was blue and clear. No breeze stirred; but, as they looked at the Tower and the hill that held it, it seemed that the azure above had taken on a metallic cast. The air had a quivering unnaturalness like an atmosphere dancing to heat waves, though the day was chill; and there came on Jim's ears, from where he did not know, a high-pitched dizzy singing like that which accompanies delirium, or high fever.

The Tower itself was distorted by these things. So that although to Jim it seemed only the ancient, ruined shell of a building, yet, between one heartbeat and the next, it seemed to change. Almost, but not quite, he caught glimpses of it unbroken and alive and thronged about with fantastic, half-seen figures. His heart beat stronger with the delusion; and its beating shook the scene before him, all the hill and Tower, going in and out of focus, in and out, *in* and *out*…And there was Angie, in the Tower's doorway, calling him…

"*Stop!*" shouted Carolinus. His voice echoed like a clap of thunder in Jim's ears; and Jim awoke to his senses, to find himself straining against the barrier of Carolinus' staff, that barred his way to the Tower like a rod of iron. "By the Powers!" said the old magician, softly and fiercely. "Will you fall into the first trap set for you?"

"Trap?" echoed Jim, bewilderedly. But he had no time to go further, for at that moment there rose from among the giant boulders at the Tower's base the heavy, wicked head of a dragon as large as Smrgol.

The thunderous bellow of the old dragon beside Jim split the unnatural air.

"*Anark!* Traitor—thief—inchworm! Come down here!"

Booming dragon-laughter rolled back an answer.

"Tell us about Gormely Keep, old bag of bones. Ancient mud-puppy, fat lizard, scare us with words!"

Smrgol lurched forward; and again Carolinus' staff was extended to bar the way.

"Patience," said the magician. But with one wrenching effort, the old dragon had himself until control. He turned, panting, to Carolinus.

"What's hidden, Mage?" he demanded.

"We'll see." Grimly, Carolinus brought his staff, endwise, three times down upon the earth. With each blow the whole hill seemed to shake and shudder.

Up among the rocks, one particularly large boulder tottered and rolled aside. Jim caught his breath and Secoh cried out, suddenly.

In the gap that the boulder revealed, a thick, slug-like head was lifting from the ground. It reared, yellow-brown in the sunlight, its two sets of horns searching and revealing a light external shell, a platelet with a merest hint of spire. It lowered its head and slowly, inexorably, began to flow downhill toward them, leaving its glistening trail behind it.

"Now—" said the knight. But Carolinus shook his head. He struck the ground again.

"Come forth!" he cried, his thin, old voice piping on the quivering air. "By the Powers! Come forth!"

And then they saw it.

From behind the great barricade of boulders, slowly, there reared first a bald and glistening dome of hairless skin. Slowly this rose, revealing two perfectly round eyes below which they saw, as the whole came up, no proper nose, but two air-slits side by side as if the whole of the bare, enormous skull was covered with a simple sheet of thick skin. And rising still further, this unnatural head, as big around as a beach ball, showed itself to possess a wide and idiot-grinning mouth, entirely lipless and revealing two jagged, matching rows of yellow teeth.

Now, with a clumsy, studied motion, the whole creature rose to its feet and stood knee-deep in the boulders and towering above them. It was man-like in shape, but clearly nothing ever spawned by the human race. A good twelve feet high it stood, a rough patchwork kilt of untanned hides wrapped around its thick waist—but this was not the extent of its differences from the race of Man. It had, to begin with, no neck at all. That obscene beachball of a hairless, near-featureless head balanced like an apple on thick, square shoulders of gray, coarse-looking skin. Its torso was one straight trunk, from which its arms and legs sprouted with a disproportionate thickness and roundness, like sections of pipe. Its knees were hidden by its kilt and its further legs by the rocks; but the elbows of its oversize arms had unnatural hinges to them, almost as if they had been doubled, and the lower arms were almost as large as the upper and near-wristless, while the hands themselves were awkward, thick-fingered parodies of the human extremity, with only three digits, of which one was a single, opposed thumb.

The right hand held a club, bound with rusty metal, that surely not even such a monster should have been able to lift. Yet one grotesque hand carried it lightly, as lightly as Carolinus had carried his staff. The monster opened its mouth.

"He!" it went. "He! He!"

The sound was fantastic. It was a bass titter, if such a thing could be imagined. Though the tone of it was as low as the lowest note of a good operatic basso, it clearly came from the creature's upper throat and head. Nor was there any real humor in it. It was an utterance with a nervous, habitual air about it, like a man clearing his throat. Having sounded, it fell silent, watching the advance of the great slug with its round, light blue eyes.

Smrgol exhaled slowly.

"Yes," he rumbled, almost sadly, almost as if to himself. "What I was afraid of. An ogre."

In the silence that followed, Nevile-Smythe got down from his horse and began to tighten the girths of its saddle.

"So, so, Clarivaux," he crooned to the trembling horse. "So ho, boy."

The rest of them were looking all at Carolinus. The magician leaned on his staff, seeming very old indeed, with the deep lines carven in the ancient skin of his face. He had been watching the ogre, but now he turned back to Jim and the other two dragons.

"I had hoped all along," he said, "that it needn't come to this. However," he crackled sourly, and waved his hand at the approaching Worm, the silent Anark and the watching ogre, "as you see… The world goes never the way we want it by itself, but must be haltered and led." He winced, produced his flask and cup, and took a drink of milk. Putting the utensils back, he looked over at Nevile-Smythe, who was now checking his weapons. "I'd suggest, Knight, that you take the Worm. It's a poor chance, but your best. I know you'd prefer that renegade dragon, but the Worm is the greater danger."

"Difficult to slay, I imagine?" queried the knight.

"Its vital organs are hidden deep inside it," said Carolinus, "and being mindless, it will fight on long after being mortally wounded. Cut off those eye-stalks and blind it first, if you can—"

"Wait!" cried Jim, suddenly. He had been listening bewilderedly. Now the word seemed to jump out of his mouth. "What're we going to do?"

"Do?" said Carolinus, looking at him. "Why, fight, of course."

"But," stammered Jim, "wouldn't it be better to go get some help? I mean—"

"Blast it, boy!" boomed Smrgol. "We can't wait for that! Who knows what'll happen if we take time for something like that? Hell's bells, Gorbash, lad, you got to fight your foes when you meet them, not the next day, or the day after that."

"Quite right, Smrgol," said Carolinus, dryly. "Gorbash, you don't understand this situation. Every time you retreat from something like this, it gains and you lose. The next time the odds would be even worse against us."

They were all looking at him. Jim felt the impact of their curious glances. He did not know what to say. He wanted to tell them that he was not a fighter, that he did not know the first thing to do in this sort of battle, that it was none of his business anyway and that he would not be here at all, if it were not for Angie. He was, in fact, quite humanly scared, and floundered desperately for some sort of strength to lean on.

"What—what am I supposed to do?" he said.

"Why, fight the ogre, boy! Fight the ogre!" thundered Smrgol—and the in-human giant up on the slope, hearing him, shifted his gaze suddenly from the Worm to fasten it on Jim. "And I'll take on that louse of an Anark. The george here'll chop up the Worm, the Mage'll hold back the bad influences—and there we are."

"Fight the ogre..." If Jim had still been possessed of his ordinary two legs, they would have buckled underneath him. Luckily his dragon-body knew no such weakness. He looked at the overwhelming bulk of his expected opponent, contrasted the ogre with himself, the armored, ox-heavy body of the Worm with Nevile-Smythe, the deep-chested over-size Anark with the crippled old dragon beside him—and a cry of protest rose from the very depths of his being. "But we can't win!"

He turned furiously on Carolinus, who, however, looked at him calmly. In desperation he turned back to the only normal human he could find in the group.

"Nevile-Smythe," he said. "You don't need to do this."

"Lord, yes," replied the knight, busy with his equipment. "Worms, ogres—one fights them when one runs into them, you know." He considered his spear and put it aside. "Believe I'll face it on foot," he murmured to himself.

"Smrgol!" said Jim. "Don't you see—can't you understand? Anark is a lot younger than you. And you're not well—"

"Er..." said Secoh, hesitantly.

"Speak up, boy!" rumbled Smrgol.

"Well," stammered Secoh, "it's just...what I mean is, I couldn't bring myself to fight that Worm or that ogre—I really couldn't. I just sort of go to pieces when I think of them getting close to me. But I *could*—well, fight another dragon. It wouldn't be quite so bad, if you know what I mean, if that dragon up there breaks my neck—" He broke down and stammered incoherently. "I know I sound awfully silly—"

"Nonsense! Good lad!" bellowed Smrgol. "Glad to have you. I—er—can't quite get into the air myself at the moment—still a bit stiff. But if you could fly over and work him down this way where I can get a grip on him, we'll stretch him out for the buzzards." And he dealt the mere-dragon a tremendous thwack with his tail by way of congratulation, almost knocking Secoh off his feet.

In desperation, Jim turned back to Carolinus.

"There is no retreat," said Carolinus, calmly, before Jim could speak. "This is a game of chess where if one piece withdraws, all fall. Hold back the creatures, and I will hold back the forces—for the creatures will finish me, if you go down, and the forces will finish you if they get me."

"Now, look here, Gorbash!" shouted Smrgol in Jim's ear. "That Worm's almost here. Let me tell you something about how to fight ogres, based on experience. You listening, boy?"

"Yes," said Jim, numbly.

"I know you've heard the other dragons calling me an old windbag when I wasn't around. But I *have* conquered an ogre—the only one in our race to do it in the last eight hundred years—and they haven't. So pay attention, if you want to win your own fight."

Jim gulped.

"All right," he said.

"Now, the first thing to know," boomed Smrgol, glancing at the Worm who was now less than fifty yards distant, "is about the bones in an ogre—"

"Never mind the details!" cried Jim. "What do I do?"

"In a minute," said Smrgol. "Don't get excited, boy. Now, about the bones in an ogre. The thing to remember is that they're big—matter of fact in the arms and legs, they're mainly bone. So there's no use trying to bite clear through, if you get a chance. What you try to do is get at the muscle—that's tough enough as it is—and hamstring. That's point one." He paused to look severely at Jim.

"Now, point two," he continued, "also connected with bones. Notice the elbows on that ogre. They aren't like a george's elbows. They're what you might call double-jointed. I mean, they have two joints where a george has just the one. Why? Simply because with the big bones they got to have and the muscle of them, they'd never be able to bend an arm more than halfway up before the bottom part'd bump the top if they had a george-type joint. Now, the point of all this is that when it swings that club, it can only swing in one way with that elbow. That's up and down. If it wants to swing it side to side, it's got to use its shoulder. Consequently if you can catch it with its club down and to one side of the body, you got an advantage; because it takes two motions to get it back up and in line again—instead of one, like a george."

"Yes, yes," said Jim, impatiently, watching the advance of the Worm.

"Don't get impatient, boy. Keep cool. Keep cool. Now, the knees don't have that kind of joint, so if you can knock it off its feet you got a real advantage. But don't try that, unless you're sure you can do it; because once it gets you pinned, you're a goner. The way to fight it is in-and-out—fast. Wait for a swing, dive in, tear him, get back out again. Got it?"

"Got it," said Jim, numbly.

"Good. Whatever you do, don't let it get a grip on you. Don't pay attention to what's happening to the rest of us, no matter what you hear or see. It's every one for himself. Concentrate on your own foe; and *keep your head*. Don't let your dragon instinct to get in there and slug run away with you. That's why the georges have been winning against us as they have. Just remember you're faster than that ogre and your brains'll win for you if you stay clear, keep your head and don't rush. I tell you, boy—"

He was interrupted by a sudden cry of joy from Nevile-Smythe, who had been rummaging around in Clarivaux's saddle.

"I say!" shouted Nevile-Smythe, running up to them with surprising lightness, considering his armor. "The most marvelous stroke of luck! Look what I found." He waved a wispy stretch of cloth at them.

"What?" demanded Jim, his heart going up in one sudden leap.

"Elinor's favor! And just in time, too. Be a good fellow, will you," went on Nevile-Smythe, turning to Carolinus, "and tie it about my vambrace here on the shield arm. Thank you, Mage."

Carolinus, looking grim, tucked his staff into the crook of his arm and quickly tied the kerchief around the armor of Nevile-Smythe's lower left arm. As he tightened the final knot and let his hands drop away, the knight caught up his shield into position and drew his sword with the other hand. The bright blade flashed like a sudden streak of lightning in the sun, he leaned forward to throw the weight of his armor before him, and with a shout of *"A Nevile-Smythe! Elinor! Elinor!"* he ran forward up the slope toward the approaching Worm.

Jim heard, but did not see, the clash of shell and steel that was their coming together. For just then everything began to happen at once. Up on the hill, Anark screamed suddenly in fury and launched himself down the slope in the air, wings spread like some great bomber gliding in for a crash landing. Behind Jim, there was the frenzied flapping of leathery wings as Secoh took to the air to meet him—but this was drowned by a sudden short, deep-chested cry, like a wordless shout; and, lifting his club, the ogre stirred and stepped clear of the boulders, coming forward and straight down the hill with huge, ground-covering strides.

"Good luck, boy," said Smrgol, in Jim's ear. "And Gorbash—" Something in the old dragon's voice made Jim turn his head to look at Smrgol. The ferocious red mouth-pit and enormous fangs were frighteningly open before him; but behind it Jim read a strange affection and concern in the dark dragon-eyes. "—remember," said the old dragon, almost softly, "that you are a descendant of Ortosh and Agtval, and Gleingul who slew the sea serpent on the tide-banks of the Gray Sands. And be therefore valiant. But remember too, that you are my only living kin and the last of our line…and be careful."

Then Smrgol's head was jerked away, as he swung about to face the coming together of Secoh and Anark in mid-air and bellowed out his own challenge. While Jim, turning back toward the Tower, had only time to take to the air before the rush of the ogre was upon him.

He had lifted on his wings without thinking—evidently this was dragon instinct when attacked. He was aware of the ogre suddenly before him, checking now, with its enormous hairy feet digging deep into the ground. The rust-bound club flashed before Jim's eyes and he felt a heavy blow high on his chest that swept him backward through the air.

He flailed with his wings to regain balance. The over-size idiot face was grinning only a couple of yards off from him. The club swept up for another blow. Panicked, Jim scrambled aside, and saw the ogre sway forward a step. Again the club lashed out—*quick!*—how could something so big and clumsy-looking be so quick with its hands? Jim felt himself smashed down to earth and a sudden lance of bright pain shot through his right shoulder. For a second a gray, thick-skinned forearm loomed over him and his teeth met in it without thought.

He was shaken like a rat by a rat terrier and flung clear. His wings beat for the safety of altitude, and he found himself about twenty feet off the ground, staring down at the ogre, which grunted a wordless sound and shifted the club to strike upwards. Jim cupped air with his wings, to fling himself backward and avoid the blow. The club whistled through the unfeeling air; and, sweeping forward, Jim ripped at one great blocky shoulder and beat clear. The ogre spun to face him, still grinning. But now blood welled and trickled down where Jim's teeth had gripped and torn, high on the shoulder.

—And suddenly, Jim realized something:

He was no longer afraid. He hung in the air, just out of the ogre's reach, poised to take advantage of any opening; and a hot sense of excitement was coursing through him. He was discovering the truth about fights—and about most similar things—that it is only the beginning that is bad. Once the chips are down, several million years of instinct take over and there is no time for thought for anything but confronting the enemy. So it was with Jim—and then the ogre moved in on him again; and that was his last specific intellectual thought of the fight, for everything else was drowned in his overwhelming drive to avoid being killed and, if possible, to kill, himself…

IV

It was a long, blurred time, about which later Jim had no clear memory. The sun marched up the long arc of the heavens and crossed the nooning point and headed down again. On the torn-up sandy soil of the plain he and the ogre turned and feinted, smashed and tore at each other. Sometimes he was in the air, sometimes on the ground. Once he had the ogre down on one knee, but could not press his advantage. At another time they had fought up the long slope of the hill almost to the Tower and the ogre had him pinned in the cleft between two huge boulders and had hefted its club back for the final blow that would smash Jim's skull. And then he had wriggled free between the monster's very legs and the battle was on again.

Now and then throughout the fight he would catch brief kaleidoscopic glimpses of the combats being waged about him: Nevile-Smythe now wrapped about by the blind body of the Worm, its eye-stalks hacked away—and striving in silence to draw free his sword-arm, which was pinned to his side by the Worm's encircling body. Or there would roll briefly into Jim's vision a tangled roaring tumble of flailing leathery wings and serpentine bodies that was Secoh, Anark and old Smrgol. Once or twice he had a momentary view of Carolinus, still standing erect, his staff upright in his hand, his long white beard blowing forward over his blue gown with the cabalistic golden signs upon it, like some old seer in the hour of Armageddon. Then the gross body of the ogre would blot out his vision and he would forget all but the enemy before him.

The day faded. A dank mist came rolling in from the sea and fled in little wisps and tatters across the plain of battle. Jim's body ached and slowed, and his wings felt leaden. But the ever-grinning face and sweeping club of the ogre seemed neither to weaken nor to tire. Jim drew back for a moment to catch his breath; and in that second, he heard a voice cry out.

"Time is short!" it cried, in cracked tones. "We are running out of time. The day is nearly gone!"

It was the voice of Carolinus. Jim had never heard him raise it before with just such a desperate accent. And even as Jim identified the voice, he realized that it came clearly to his ears—and that for sometime now upon the battlefield, except for the ogre and himself, there had been silence.

He shook his head to clear it and risked a quick glance about him. He had been driven back almost to the neck of the Causeway itself, where it entered onto the plain. To one side of him, the snapped strands of Clarivaux's bridle dangled limply where the terrified horse had broken loose from the earth-thrust spear to which Nevile-Smythe had tethered it before advancing against the Worm on foot. A little off from it stood Carolinus, upheld now only by his staff, his old face shrunken and almost mummified in appearance, as if the life had been all but drained from it. There was nowhere else to retreat to; and Jim was alone.

He turned back his gaze to see the ogre almost upon him. The heavy club swung high, looking gray and enormous in the mist. Jim felt in his limbs and wings a weakness that would not let him dodge in time; and, with all his strength, he gathered himself, and sprang instead, up under the monster's guard and inside the grasp of those cannon-thick arms.

The club glanced off Jim's spine. He felt the arms go around him, the double triad of bone-thick fingers searching for his neck. He was caught, but his rush had knocked the ogre off his feet. Together they went over and rolled on the sandy earth, the ogre gnawing with his jagged teeth at Jim's chest and striving to break a spine or twist a neck, while Jim's tail lashed futilely about.

They rolled against the spear and snapped it in half. The ogre found its hold and Jim felt his neck begin to be slowly twisted, as if it were a chicken's neck being wrung in slow motion. A wild despair flooded through him. He had been warned by Smrgol never to let the ogre get him pinned. He had disregarded that advice and now he was lost, the battle was lost. *Stay away*, Smrgol had warned, *use your brains...*

The hope of a wild chance sprang suddenly to life in him. His head was twisted back over his shoulder. He could see only the gray mist above him, but he stopped fighting the ogre and groped about with both forelimbs. For a slow moment of eternity, he felt nothing, and then something hard nudged against his right foreclaw, a glint of bright metal flashed for a second before his eyes. He changed his grip on what he held, clamping down on it as firmly as his clumsy foreclaws would allow—

—and with every ounce of strength that was left to him, he drove the fore-part of the broken spear deep into the middle of the ogre that sprawled above him.

The great body bucked and shuddered. A wild scream burst from the idiot mouth alongside Jim's ear. The ogre let go, staggered back and up, tottering to its feet, looming like the Tower itself above him. Again, the ogre screamed, staggering about like a drunken man, fumbling at the shaft of the spear sticking from him. It jerked at the shaft, screamed again, and, lowering its unnatural head, bit at the wood like a wounded animal. The tough ash splintered between its teeth. It screamed once more and fell to its knees. Then slowly, like a bad actor in an old-fashioned movie, it went over on its side, and drew up its legs like a man with the cramp. A final scream was drowned in bubbling. Black blood trickled from its mouth and it lay still.

Jim crawled slowly to his feet and looked about him.

The mists were drawing back from the plain and the first thin light of late afternoon stretching long across the slope. In its rusty illumination, Jim made out what was to be seen there.

The Worm was dead, literally hacked in two. Nevile-Smythe, in bloody, dinted armor, leaned wearily on a twisted sword not more than a few feet off from Carolinus. A little farther off, Secoh raised a torn neck and head above the intertwined, locked-together bodies of Anark and Smrgol. He stared dazedly at Jim. Jim moved slowly, painfully over to the mere-dragon.

Jim came up and looked down at the two big dragons. Smrgol lay with his eyes closed and his jaws locked in Anark's throat. The neck of the younger dragon had been broken like the stem of a weed.

"Smrgol…" croaked Jim.

"No—" gasped Secoh. "No good. He's gone… I led the other one to him. He got his grip—and then he never let go…" The mere-dragon choked and lowered his head.

"He fought well," creaked a strange harsh voice which Jim did not at first recognize. He turned and saw the Knight standing at his shoulder. Nevile-Smythe's face was white as sea-foam inside his helmet and the flesh of it seemed fallen in to the bones, like an old man's. He swayed as he stood.

"We have won," said Carolinus, solemnly, coming up with the aid of his staff. "Not again in our lifetimes will evil gather enough strength in this spot to break out." He looked at Jim. "And now," he said, "the balance of Chance and History inclines in your favor. It's time to send you back."

"Back?" said Nevile-Smythe.

"Back to his own land, Knight," replied the magician. "Fear not, the dragon left in this body of his will remember all that happened and be your friend."

"Fear!" said Nevile-Smythe, somehow digging up a final spark of energy to expend on hauteur. "I fear no dragon, dammit. Besides, in respect to the old boy here"—he nodded at the dead Smrgol—"I'm going to see what can be done about this dragon-alliance business."

"He was great!" burst out Secoh, suddenly, almost with a sob. "He—he made me strong again. Whatever he wanted, I'll do it." And the mere-dragon bowed his head.

"You come along with me then, to vouch for the dragon end of it," said Nevile-Smythe. "Well," he turned to Jim, "it's goodby, I suppose, Sir James."

"I suppose so," said Jim. "Goodby to you, too. I—" Suddenly he remembered.

"Angie!" he cried out, spinning around. "I've got to go get Angie out of that Tower!"

Carolinus put his staff out to halt Jim.

"Wait," he said. "Listen…"

"Listen?" echoed Jim. But just at that moment, he heard it, a woman's voice calling, high and clear, from the mists that still hid the Tower.

"Jim! Jim, where are you?"

A slight figure emerged from the mist, running down the slope toward them.

"Here I am!" bellowed Jim. And for once he was glad of the capabilities of his dragon-voice. "Here I am, Angie—"

—but Carolinus was chanting in a strange, singing voice, words without meaning, but which seemed to shake the very air about them. The mist swirled, the world rocked and swung. Jim and Angie were caught up, were swirled about, were spun away and away down an echoing corridor of nothingness…

…and then they were back in the Grille, seated together on one side of the table in the booth. Hanson, across from them, was goggling like a bewildered accident victim.

"Where—where am I?" he stammered. His eyes suddenly focused on them across the table and he gave a startled croak. "Help!" he cried, huddling away from them. "Humans!"

"What did you expect?" snapped Jim. "Dragons?"

"No!" shrieked Hanson. "Watch-beetles—like me!" And, turning about, he tried desperately to burrow his way through the wood seat of the booth to safety.

V

It was the next day after that Jim and Angie stood in the third floor corridor of Chumley Hall, outside the door leading to the office of the English Department.

"Well, are you going in or aren't you?" demanded Angie.

"In a second, in a second," said Jim, adjusting his tie with nervous fingers. "Just don't rush me."

"Do you suppose he's heard about Grottwold?" Angie asked.

"I doubt it," said Jim. The Student Health Service says Hanson's already starting to come out of it—except that he'll probably always have a touch of amnesia about the whole afternoon. Angie!" said Jim, turning on her. "Do you suppose, all the time we were there, Hanson was actually being a watch-beetle underground?"

"I don't know, and it doesn't matter," interrupted Angie, firmly. "Honestly,

Jim, now you've finally promised to get an answer out of Dr. Howells about a job, I'd think you'd want to get it over and done with, instead of hesitating like this. I just can't understand a man who can go about consorting with dragons and fighting ogres and then—"

"—still not want to put his boss on the spot for a yes-or-no answer," said Jim. "Hah! Let me tell you something." He waggled a finger in front of her nose. "Do you know what all this dragon-ogre business actually taught me? It wasn't not to be scared, either."

"All right," said Angie, with a sigh. "What was it then?"

"I'll tell you," said Jim. "What I found out…" He paused. "What I found out was not, not to be scared. It was that scared or not doesn't matter; because you just go ahead, anyway."

Angie blinked at him.

"And that," concluded Jim, "is why I agreed to have it out with Howells, after all. Now you know."

He yanked Angie to him, kissed her grimly upon her startled lips, and, letting go of her, turned about. Giving a final jerk to his tie, he turned the knob of the office door, opened it, and strode valiantly within.

THE SILVER DRAGON
Elizabeth A. Lynn

Elizabeth A. Lynn was born in New York in 1946. She published her first story, "We All Have to Go," in 1976. It was followed by a handful of other stories, including World Fantasy Award winner "The Woman Who Loved the Moon," most of which appear in her two short story collections, *The Woman Who Loved the Moon and Other Stories* and *Tales from a Vanished Country*. Lynn's first novel, *A Different Light*, was published in 1978 and her second, fantasy *Watchtower*, was published in 1979. It was the opening volume in her best known work, "The Chronicles of Tornor", and won the World Fantasy Award for Best Novel. It was followed by *The Dancers of Arun* and *The Northern Girl*. Lynn wrote a second SF novel, *The Sardonyx Net*, in 1981 and young adult fantasy *The Silver Horse* in 1984, before stopping writing for a lengthy period. Her first novel in thirteen years, *Dragon's Winter*, was published in 1998. Her latest novel is *Dragon's Treasure*. She lives in the San Francisco Bay area, teaches martial arts, and is at work on a new novel.

This is a story of Iyadur Atani, who was master of Dragon Keep and lord of Dragon's Country a long, long time ago.

At this time, Ryoka was both the same and different than it is today. In Issho, in the west, there was peace, for the mages of Ryoka had built the great wall, the Wizards' Wall, and defended it with spells. Though the wizards were long gone, the power of their magic lingered in the towers and ramparts of the wall. The Isojai feared it, and would not storm it.

In the east, there was no peace. Chuyo was not part of Ryoka, but a separate country. The Chuyokai lords were masters of the sea. They sailed the eastern seas in black-sailed ships, landing to plunder and loot and carry off the young boys and girls to make them slaves. All along the coast of Kameni, men feared the Chuyokai pirates.

In the north, the lords of Ippa prospered. Yet, having no enemies from beyond their borders to fight, they grew bored, and impatient, and quarrelsome. They quarreled with the lords of Issho, with the Talvelai, and the Nyo, and they fought among themselves. Most quarrelsome among them was Martun Hal, lord of Serrenhold. Serrenhold, as all men know, is the smallest and most isolated of the domains of Ippa. For nothing is it praised: not for its tasty beer or its excellence of horseflesh, nor for the beauty of its women, nor the prowess of its men. Indeed, Serrenhold is notable for only one thing: its inhospitable climate. *Bitter as the winds of Serrenhold*, the folk of Ippa say.

No one knew what made Martun Hal so contentious. Perhaps it was the wind, or the will of the gods, or perhaps it was just his nature. In the ten years since he had inherited the lordship from his father Owen, he had killed one brother, exiled another, and picked fights with all his neighbors.

His greatest enmity was reserved for Roderico diCorsini of Derrenhold. There had not always been enmity between them. Indeed, he had once asked Olivia diCorsini, daughter of Roderico diCorsini, lord of Derrenhold, to marry him. But Olivia diCorsini turned him down.

"He is old. Besides, I do not love him," she told her father. "I will not wed a man I do not love."

"Love? What does love have to do with marriage?" Roderico glared at his child. She glared back. They were very alike: stubborn, and proud of it. "Pah. I suppose you *love* someone else."

"I do," said Olivia.

"And who might that be, missy?"

"Jon Torneo of Galva."

"Jon Torneo?" Roderico scowled a formidable scowl. "Jon Torneo? He's a shepherd's son! He smells of sheep fat and hay!" This, as it happened, was not true. Jon Torneo's father, Federico Torneo of Galva, did own sheep. But he could hardly be called a shepherd: he was a wool merchant, and one of the wealthiest men in the domain, who had often come to Derrenhold as Roderico diCorsini's guest.

"I don't care. I love him," Olivia said.

And the very next night she ran away from her father's house, and rode east across the countryside to Galva. To tell you what happened then would be a whole other story. But since the wedding of Olivia diCorsini and Jon Torneo, while of great import to them, is a small part of this story, suffice it to say that Olivia married Jon Torneo, and went to live with him in Galva. Do I need to tell you they were happy? They were. They had four children. The eldest—a boy, called Federico after his grandfather—was a friendly, sturdy, biddable lad. The next two were girls. They were also charming and biddable children, like their brother.

The fourth was Joanna. She was very lovely, having inherited her mother's olive skin and black, thick hair. But she was in no way biddable. She fought with her nurses, and bullied her brother. She preferred trousers to skirts, archery to sewing, and hunting dogs to dolls.

"I want to ride. I want to fight," she said.

"Women do not fight," her sisters said.

"I do," said Joanna.

And her mother, recognizing in her youngest daughter the indomitable stubbornness of her own nature, said, "Let her do as she will."

So Joanna learned to ride, and shoot, and wield a sword. By fourteen she could ride as well as any horseman in her grandfather's army. By fifteen she could outshoot all but his best archers.

"She has not the weight to make a swordsman," her father's arms-master said, "but she'll best anyone her own size in a fair fight."

"She's a hellion. No man will ever want to wed her," Roderico diCorsini said, so gloomily that it made his daughter smile. But Joanna Torneo laughed. She knew very well whom she would marry. She had seen him, shining brighter than the moon, soaring across the sky on his way to his castle in the mountains, and had vowed—this was a fifteen year old girl, remember—that Iyadur Atani, the Silver Dragon, would be her husband. That he was a changeling, older than she by twelve years, and that they had never met disturbed her not a whit.

Despite his age—he was nearly sixty—the rancor of the lord of Serrenhold toward his neighbors did not cool. The year Joanna turned five, his war band attacked and burned Ragnar Castle. The year she turned nine he stormed Voiana, the eyrie of the Red Hawks, hoping for plunder. But he found there only empty chambers, and the rushing of wind through stone.

The autumn Joanna turned fourteen, Roderico diCorsini died: shot through the heart by one of Martun Hal's archers as he led his soldiers along the crest of the western hills. His son, Ege, inherited the domain. Ege diCorsini, though not the warrior his father had been, was a capable man. His first act as lord was to send a large company of troops to patrol his western border. His next act was to invite his neighbors to a council. "For," he said, "it is past time to end this madness." Couriers were sent to Mirrinhold and Ragnar, to Voiana and to far Mako. A courier was even sent to Dragon Keep.

His councilors wondered at this. "Martun Hal has never attacked the Atani," they pointed out. "The Silver Dragon will not join us."

"I hope you are wrong," said Ege diCorsini. "We need him." He penned that invitation with his own hand. And, since Galva lay between Derrenhold and Dragon Keep, and because he loved his sister, he told the courier, whose name was Ullin March, to stop overnight at the home of Jon Torneo.

Ullin March did as he was told. He rode to Galva. He ate dinner that night with the family. After dinner, he spoke quietly with his hosts, apprising them of Ege diCorsini's plan.

"This could mean war," said Jon Torneo.

"It will mean war," Olivia diCorsini Torneo said.

The next day, Ullin March took his leave of the Torneo family, and rode east. At dusk he reached the tall stone pillar that marked the border between the diCorsini's domain and Dragon's Country. He was about to pass the marker, when a slender cloaked form leaped from behind the pillar and seized his horse's bridle.

"Dismount," said a fierce young voice, "or I will kill your horse." Steel glinted against the great artery in grey mare's neck.

Ullin March was no coward. But he valued his horse. He dismounted. The hood fell back from his assailant's face, and he saw that it was a young woman. She was lovely, with olive-colored skin and black hair, tied back behind her neck in a club.

"Who are you?" he said.

"Never mind. The letter you carry. Give it to me."

"No."

The sword tip moved from his horse's neck to his own throat. "I will kill you."

"Then kill me," Ullin March said. Then he dropped, and rolled into her legs. But she had moved. Something hard hit him on the crown of the head.

Dazed and astonished, he drew his sword and lunged at his attacker. She slipped the blow and thrust her blade without hesitation into his arm. He staggered, and slipped to one knee. Again he was hit on the head. The blow stunned him. Blood streamed from his scalp into his eyes. His sword was torn from his grasp. Small hands darted into his shirt, and removed his courier's badge, and the letter.

"I am sorry," the girl said. "I had to do it. I will send someone to help you, I promise." He heard the noise of hoof beats, two sets of them. Cursing, he staggered upright, knowing there was nothing he could do.

Joanna Torneo, granddaughter of Roderico diCorsini, carried her uncle's invitation to Dragon Keep. As it happened, the dragon-lord was at home when she arrived. He was in his hall when a page came running to tell him that a courier from Ege diCorsini was waiting at the gate.

"Put him in the downstairs chamber, and see to his comfort. I will come," said the lord.

"My lord, it's not a him. It's a girl."

"Indeed?" said Iyadur Atani. "See to her comfort, then." The oddity of the event roused his curiosity. In a very short time he was crossing the courtyard to the little chamber where he was wont to receive guests. Within the chamber he found a well-dressed, slightly grubby, very lovely young woman.

"My lord," she said calmly, "I am Joanna Torneo, Ege diCorsini's sister's daughter. I bear you his greetings, and a letter." She took the letter from the pocket of her shirt, and handed it to him.

Iyadur Atani read her uncle's letter.

"Do you know what this letter says?" he asked.

"It invites you to a council."

"And it assures me that the bearer, a man named Ullin March, can be trusted to answer truthfully any questions I might wish to put to him. You are not Ullin March."

"No. I took the letter from him at the border. Perhaps you would be so kind as to send someone to help him? I had to hit him."

"Why?"

"Had I not, he would not have let me take the letter."

"Why did you take the letter?"

"I wanted to meet you."

"Why?" asked Iyadur Atani.

Joanna took a deep breath. "I am going to marry you."

"Are you?" said Iyadur Atani. "Does your father know this?"

"My mother does," said Joanna. She gazed at him. He was a handsome man, fair, and very tall. His clothes, though rich, were simple; his only adornment a golden ring on the third finger of his right hand. It was fashioned in the shape of a sleeping dragon. His gaze was very direct, and his eyes burned with a blue flame. Resolute men, men of uncompromising courage, feared that fiery gaze.

When they emerged, first the girl, radiant despite her mud-stained clothes, and then the lord of the Keep, it was evident to his household that their habitually reserved lord was unusually, remarkably happy.

"This is the lady Joanna Torneo of Galva, soon to be my wife." he said. "Take care of her." He lifted the girl's hand to his lips.

That afternoon he wrote two letters. The first went to Olivia Torneo, assuring her that her beloved daughter was safe in Dragon Keep. The second was to Ege diCorsini. Both letters made their recipients very glad indeed. An exchange of letters followed: from Olivia Torneo to her headstrong daughter, and from Ege diCorsini to the lord of the Keep. Couriers wore ruts in the road from Dragon Keep to Galva, and from Dragon Keep to Derrenhold.

The council was held in the great hall of Derrenhold. Ferris Wulf, lord of Mirrinhold, a doughty warrior, was there, with his captains; so was Aurelio Ragnarin of Ragnar Castle, and Rudolf diMako, whose cavalry was the finest in Ippa. Even Jamis Delamico, matriarch of the Red Hawk clan, had come, accompanied by six dark-haired, dark-eyed women who looked exactly like her. She did not introduce them: no one knew if they were her sisters, or her daughters. Iyadur Atani was not present.

Ege diCorsini spoke first.

"My lords, honored friends," he said, "for nineteen years, since the old lord of Serrenhold died, Martun Hal and his troops have prowled the borders of our territories, snapping and biting like a pack of hungry dogs. His people starve, and groan beneath their taxes. He has attacked Mirrinhold, and Ragnar, and Voiana. Two years ago, my lord of Mirrinhold, his archers killed your son. Last year they killed my father.

"My lords and captains, nineteen years is too long. It is time to muzzle the dogs." The lesser captains shouted. Ege diCorsini went on. "Alone, no one of us has been able to prevail against Martun Hal's aggression. I suggest we unite our forces and attack him."

"How?" said Aurelio Ragnarin. "He hides behind his walls, and only attacks when he is sure of victory."

"We must go to him, and attack him where he lives."

The leaders looked at one another, and then at diCorsini as if he had lost his mind. Ferris Wulf said, "Serrenhold is unassailable."

"How do you know?" Ege diCorsini said. "For nineteen years no one has attacked it."

"You have a plan," said Jamis Delamico.

"I do." He scanned the room. "Forgive me, my lords—I would have the lesser captains leave." Silently, the men left the room. So did the servants.

And Ege diCorsini explained to the lords of Ippa exactly how he planned to defeat Martun Hal.

At the end of his speech, Ferris Wulf said, "You are sure of this?"

"I am."

"I am with you."

"And I," said Aurelio Ragnarin.

"My sisters and my daughters will follow you," Jamis Delamico said.

Rudolf diMako stuck his thumbs in his belt. "Martun Hal has stayed well clear of my domain. But I see that he needs to be taught a lesson. My army is yours to command."

Solitary in his fortress, Martun Hal heard through his spies of his enemies' machinations. He summoned his captains to his side. "Gather the troops," he ordered. "We must prepare to defend our borders. Go," he told his spies. "Watch the highways. Tell me when they come."

Sooner than he expected, the spies returned. "My lord, they come."

"What are their forces?"

"They are a hundred mounted men, and six hundred foot."

"Archers?"

"About a hundred."

"Have they brought a ram?"

"Yes, my lord."

"Ladders? Ropes? Catapults?"

"They have ladders and ropes. No catapults, my lord."

"Pah. They are fools, and over-confident. Their horses will do them no good here. Do they think to leap over Serrenhold's walls? We have three hundred archers, and a thousand foot soldiers," Martun Hal said. His spirits rose. "Let them come. They will lose."

The morning of the battle was clear and cold. Frost hardened the ground. A bitter wind blew across the mountain peaks. The forces of the lords of Ippa advanced steadily upon Serrrenhold Castle. On the ramparts of the castle, archers strung their bows. They were unafraid, for their forces outnumbered the attackers, and besides, no one had ever besieged Serrenhold, and won. Behind the castle gates, the Serrenhold army waited. The swordsmen drew their swords and taunted their foes: "Run, dogs! Run, rabbits! Run, little boys! Go home to your mothers!"

The attackers advanced. Ege diCorsini called to the defenders, "Surrender, and you will live. Fight and you will die."

"We will not surrender," the guard captain said.

"As you wish," diCorsini said. He signaled to his trumpeter. The trumpeter lifted his horn to his lips and blew a sharp trill. Yelling, the attackers charged. Arrows rained from the castle walls. Screaming out of the sky, a flock of hawks flew at the faces of the amazed archers. The rain of arrows faltered.

A valiant band of men from Ragnar Castle scaled the walls, and leaped into the courtyard. Back to back, they fought their way slowly toward the gates. A second group of men smashed its way through a postern gate. They battled in the courtyard with Martun Hal's men.

Ferris Wulf said to Ege diCorsini, "They weaken. But still they outnumber us. We are losing too many men. Call him."

"Not yet," Ege diCorsini said. He signaled. Men brought the ram up. Again and again they hurled it at the gates. But the gates held. The men in the courtyard fought, and died. The hawks attacked the archers again, and the archers turned their bows against the birds, and shot them out of the sky.

A huge red hawk swooped to earth and became Jamis Delamico.

"They are killing my sisters," she said, and her eyes glittered with rage. "Why do you wait? Call him."

"Not yet," said Ege diCorsini. "Look. We are through." The ram broke through the gate. Shouting, men flung themselves at the breach, clawing at the gate with their hands. But there were many more defenders. They drove the diCorsini army back, and closed the gate, and braced it with barrels and wagons and lengths of wood.

"Now," said Ege diCorsini. He signaled the trumpeter. The trumpeter blew again.

Then the dragon came. Huge, silver, deadly, he swooped upon the men of Serrenhold. His silver claws cut the air like scythes. He stooped his head, and his eyes glowed like fire. Fire trickled from his nostrils. He breathed upon the castle walls, and the stone hissed, and melted like snow in the sun. He roared. The sound filled the day, louder and more terrible than thunder. The archers' fingers opened, and their bows clattered to the ground. The swordsmen trembled, and their legs turned to jelly. Shouting, the men of Ippa stormed over the broken gates, and into Serrenhold.

They found the lord of the castle sitting in his hall, with his sword across his lap.

"Come on," he said, rising. "I am an old man. Come and kill me."

He charged them then, hoping to force them to kill him. But though he fought fiercely, killing two of them, and wounding three more, they finally disarmed him. Bruised and bloody, but whole, Martun Hal was bound, and marched at sword's point out of his hall to the courtyard where the lords of Ippa stood.

He bowed mockingly into their unyielding faces.

"Well, my lords. I hope you are pleased with your victory. All of you together, and still it took dragon fire to defeat me."

Ferris Wulf scowled. But Ege diCorsini said, "Why should more men of Ippa die for you? Even your own people are glad the war is over."

"Is it over?"

"It is," diCorsini said firmly.

Martun Hal smiled bleakly. "Yet I live."

"Not for long," someone cried. And Ferris Wulf's chief captain, whose home Martun Hal's men had burned, stepped forward, and set the tip of his sword against the old man's breast.

"No," said Ege diCorsini.

"Why not?" said Ferris Wulf. "He killed your father."

"Whom would you put in his place?" Ege diCorsini said. "He is Serrenhold's rightful lord. His father had three sons, but one is dead, and the other gone, who knows where. He has no children to succeed him. *I* would not reign in Serrenhold. It is a dismal place. Let him keep it. We will set a guard about his border, and restrict the number of soldiers he may have, and watch him."

"And when he dies?" said Aurelio Ragnarin.

"Then we will name his successor."

Glaring, Ferris Wulf fingered the hilt of his sword. "He should die *now*. Then we could appoint a regent, one of our own captains, someone honorable, and deserving of trust."

Ege diCorsini said, "We could do that. But that man would never have a moment's peace. *I* say, let us set a watch upon this land, so that Martun Hal may never trouble our towns and people again, and let him rot in this lifeless place."

"The Red Hawk clan will watch him," Jamis Delamico said.

And so it came to pass. Martun Hal lived. His weapons were destroyed; his war band, all but thirty men, was disbanded and scattered. He was forbidden to travel more than two miles from his castle. The lords of Ippa, feeling reasonably secure in their victory, went home to their castles, to rest and rebuild and prepare for winter.

Ege diCorsini, riding east amid his rejoicing troops, made ready to attend a wedding. He was fond of his niece. His sister had assured him that the girl was absolutely determined to wed Iyadur Atani, and as for the flame-haired, flame-eyed dragon-lord, he seemed equally anxious for the match. Remembering stories he had heard, Ege diCorsini admitted, though only to himself, that Joanna's husband was not the one he would have chosen for her. But no one had asked his opinion.

The wedding was held at Derrenhold, and attended by all the lords of Ippa, except, of course Martun Hal. Rudolf diMako attended, despite the distance, but no one was surprised; there was strong friendship between the diMako and the Atani. Jamis Delamico came. The bride was pronounced to be astonishingly beautiful, and the bride's mother almost as beautiful. The dragon-lord presented the parents of his bride with gifts: a tapestry, a mettlesome stallion and a breeding mare from the Atani stables, a sapphire pendant, and a cup of beaten gold. The couple drank the wine. The priestess said the blessings.

The following morning, Olivia diCorsini Torneo said farewell to her daughter. "I will miss you. Your father will miss you. You must visit often. He is older than he was, you know."

"I will," Joanna promised. Olivia watched the last of her children ride away into the bright autumnal day. The two older girls were both wed, and Federico was not only wed but twice a father.

I don't feel like a grandmother, Olivia Torneo thought. Then she laughed at herself, and went inside to find her husband.

And so there was peace in Ippa. The folk of Derrenhold and Mirrinhold and Ragnar ceased to look over their shoulders. They left their daggers sheathed and hung their battleaxes on the walls. Men who had most of their lives fighting put aside their shields and went home, to towns and farms and wives they barely remembered. More babies were born the following summer than had been born in the previous three years put together. The midwives were run ragged trying to attend the births. Many of the boys, even in Ragnar and Mirrinhold, were named Ege, or Roderico. A few of the girls were even named Joanna.

Martun Hal heard the tidings of his enemies' good fortune, and his hatred of them deepened. Penned in his dreary fortress, he took count of his gold. Discreetly, he let it be known that the lord of Serrenhold, although beaten, was not without resources. Slowly, cautiously, some of those who had served him before his defeat crept across the border to his castle. He paid them, and sent them out again to Derrenhold and Mirrinhold, and even—cautiously—into Iyadur Atani's country.

"Watch," he said, "and when something happens, send me word."

As for Joanna Torneo Atani, she was as happy as she had known she would be. She adored her husband, and was unafraid of his changeling nature. The people of his domain had welcomed her. Her only disappointment, as the year moved from spring to summer and to the crisp cold nights of autumn again, was that she was childless.

"Every other woman in the world is having a baby," she complained to her husband. "Why can't I?"

He smiled, and drew her into the warmth of his arms. "You will."

Nearly three years after the surrender of Martun Hal, with the Hunter's Moon waning in the autumn sky, Joanna Atani received a message from her mother.

Come, it said. Your father needs you. She left the next morning for Galva, accompanied by her maid, and escorted by six of Dragon Keep's most experienced and competent soldiers.

"Send word if you need me," her husband said.

"I will."

The journey took two days. Outside the Galva gates, a beggar warming his hands over a scrap of fire told Joanna what she most wanted to know.

"Your father still lives, my lady. I heard it from Viksa the fruit seller an hour ago."

"Give him gold," Joanna said to her captain as she urged her horse through the gate. Word of her coming hurried before her. By the time Joanna reached her parents' home, the gate was open. Her brother stood before it.

She said, "Is he dead?"

"Not yet." He drew her inside.

Olivia diCorsini Torneo sat at her dying husband's bedside, in the chamber they had shared for twenty-nine years. She still looked young; nearly as young as the day she had left her father's house behind for good. Her dark eyes were clear, and her skin smooth. Only her lustrous thick hair was no longer dark; it was shot through with white, like lace.

She smiled at her youngest daughter, and put up her face to be kissed. "I am glad you could come," she said. "Your sisters are here." She turned back to her husband.

Joanna bent over the bed. "Papa?" she whispered. But the man in the bed, so flat and still, did not respond. A plain white cloth wound around Jon Torneo's head was the only sign of injury: otherwise, he appeared to be asleep.

"What happened?"

"An accident, a week ago. He was bringing the herd down from the high pasture when something frightened the sheep: they ran. He fell among them and was trampled. His head was hurt. He has not woken since. Phylla says there is nothing she can do." Phylla was the Torneo family physician.

Joanna said tremulously, "He always said sheep were stupid. Is he in pain?"

"Phylla says not."

That afternoon, Joanna wrote a letter to her husband, telling him what had happened. She gave it to a courier to take to Dragon Keep.

Do not come, she wrote. *There is nothing you can do. I will stay until he dies.*

One by one his children took their turns at Jon Torneo's bedside. Olivia ate her meals in the chamber, and slept in a pallet laid by the bed. Once each day she walked outside the gates, to talk to the people who thronged day and night outside the house, for Jon Torneo was much beloved. Solemn strangers came up to her weeping. Olivia, despite her own grief, spoke kindly to them all.

Joanna marveled at her mother's strength. She could not match it: she found herself weeping at night, and snapping by day at her sisters. She was even, to her shame, sick one morning.

A week after Joanna's arrival, Jon Torneo died. He was buried, as was proper, within three days. Ege diCorsini was there, as were the husbands of Joanna's sisters, and all of Jon Torneo's family, and half Galva, or so it seemed.

The next morning, in the privacy of the garden, Olivia Torneo said quietly to her youngest daughter, "You should go home."

"Why?" Joanna said. She was dumbstruck. "Have I offended you?" Tears rose to her eyes. "Oh Mother, I'm so sorry…"

"Idiot child," Olivia said, and put her arms around her daughter. "My treasure, you and your sisters have been a great comfort to me. But you should be with your husband at this time." Her gaze narrowed. "Joanna? Do you not know that you are pregnant?"

Joanna blinked. "What makes you—I feel fine," she said.

"Of course you do," said Olivia. "DiCorsini women never have trouble with babies."

Phylla confirmed that Joanna was indeed pregnant.

"You are sure?"

"Yes. Your baby will be born in the spring."

"Is it a boy or a girl?" Joanna asked.

But Phylla could not tell her that.

So Joanna Atani said farewell to her family, and, with her escort about her, departed Galva for the journey to Dragon Keep. As they rode toward the hills, she marked the drifts of leaves on the ground, and the dull color on the hills, and rejoiced. The year was turning. Slipping a hand beneath her clothes, she laid her palm across her belly, hoping to feel the quickening of life in her womb. It seemed strange to be so happy, so soon after her father's untimely death.

Twenty-one days after the departure of his wife from Dragon Keep, Iyadur Atani called one of his men to his side.

"Go to Galva, to the house of Jon Torneo," he said. "Find out what is happening there."

The courier rode to Galva. A light snow fell as he rode through the gates. The steward of the house escorted him to Olivia Torneo's chamber.

"My lady," he said, "I am sent from Dragon Keep to inquire after the well-being of the lady Joanna. May I speak with her?"

Olivia Torneo's face slowly lost its color. She said, "My daughter Joanna left a week ago to return to Dragon Keep. Soldiers from Dragon Keep were with her."

The courier stared. Then he said, "Get me fresh horses."

He burst through the Galva gates as though the demons of hell were on his horse's heels. He rode through the night. He reached Dragon Keep at dawn.

"He's asleep," the page warned.

"Wake him," the courier said. But the page would not. So the courier himself pushed open the door. "My lord? I am back from Galva."

The torches lit in the bedchamber.

"Come," said Iyadur Atani from the curtained bed. He drew back the curtains. The courier knelt on the rug beside the bed. He was shaking with weariness, and hunger, and also with dread.

"My lord, I bear ill news. Your lady left Galva to return home twenty days ago. Since then, no one has seen her."

Fire came into Iyadur Atani's eyes. The courier turned his head. Rising from the bed, the dragon-lord said, "Call my captains."

The captains came. Crisply their lord told them that their lady was missing somewhere between Galva and Dragon Keep, and that it was their task, their only task, to find her. "You *will* find her," he said, and his words seemed to burn the air like flames.

"Aye, my lord," they said.

They searched across the countryside, hunting through hamlet and hut and barn, through valley and cave and ravine. They did not find Joanna Atani.

But midway between Galva and the border between the diCorsini land and Dragon's Country, they found, piled in a ditch and rudely concealed with branches, the bodies of nine men and one woman.

"Six of them we know," Bran, second-in-command of Dragon Keep's archers, reported to his lord. He named them: they were the six men who had comprised Joanna Atani's escort. "The woman is my lady Joanna's maid. My lord, we have found the tracks of many men and horses, riding hard and fast. The trail leads west."

"We shall follow it," Iyadur Atani said. "Four of you shall ride with me. The rest shall return to Dragon Keep, to await my orders."

They followed that trail for nine long days across Ippa, through bleak and stony hills, through the high reaches of Derrenhold, into Serrenhold's wild, wind-swept country. As they crossed the borders, a red-winged hawk swept down upon them. It landed in the snow, and became a dark-haired, dark-eyed woman in a grey cloak.

She said, "I am Madelene of the Red Hawk sisters. I watch this land. Who are you, and what is your business here?"

The dragon-lord said, "I am Iyadur Atani. I am looking for my wife. I believe she came this way, accompanied by many men, perhaps a dozen of them, and their remounts. We have been tracking them for nine days."

"A band of ten men rode across the border from Derrenhold into Serrenhold twelve days ago," the watcher said. "They led ten spare horses. I saw no women among them."

Bran said, "Could she have been disguised? A woman with her hair cropped might look like a boy, and the lady Joanna rides as well as any man."

Madelene shrugged. "I did not see their faces."

"Then you see ill," Bran said angrily. "Is this how the Red Hawk sisters keep watch?" Hawk-changeling and archer glared at one another.

"Enough," Iyadur Atani said. He led them onto the path to the fortress. It wound upward through the rocks. Suddenly they heard the clop of horses' hooves against the stone. Four horsemen appeared on the path ahead of them.

Bran cupped his hands to his lips. "What do you want?" he shouted.

The lead rider shouted back, "It is for us to ask that! You are on our land!"

"Then speak," Bran said.

"Your badges proclaim that you come from Dragon Keep. I bear a message to Iyadur Atani from Martun Hal."

Bran waited for the dragon-lord to declare himself. When he did not, the captain said, "Tell me, and I will carry it to him."

"Tell Iyadur Atani," the lead rider said, "that his wife will be staying in Serrenhold for a time. If any attempt is made to find her, then she will die, slowly and in great pain. That is all." He and his fellows turned their horses, and bolted up the path.

Iyadur Atani said not a word, but the dragon rage burned white-hot upon his face. The men from Dragon Keep looked at him, once. Then they looked away, holding their breath.

Finally he said, "Let us go."

When they reached the border, they found Ege diCorsini, with a large company of well-armed men, waiting for them.

"Olivia sent to me," he said to Iyadur Atani. "Have you found her?"

"Martun Hal has her," the dragon-lord said. "He says he will kill her if we try to get her back." His face was set. "He may kill her anyway."

"He won't kill her," Ege diCorsini said. "He'll use her to bargain with. He will want his weapons and his army back, and freedom to move about his land."

"Give it to him," Iyadur Atani said. "I want my wife."

So Ege diCorsini sent a delegation of his men to Martun Hal, offering to modify the terms of Serrenhold's surrender, if he would release Joanna Atani unharmed.

But Martun Hal did not release Joanna. As diCorsini had said, he used her welfare to bargain with, demanding first the freedom to move about his own country, and then the restoration of his war band, first to one hundred, then to three hundred men.

"We must know where she is. When we know where she is we can rescue her," diCorsini said. And he sent spies into Serrenhold, with instructions to discover where in that bleak and barren country the lady of Ippa was. But Martun Hal, ever crafty, had anticipated this. He sent a message to Iyadur Atani, warning that payment for the trespass of strangers would be exacted upon Joanna's body. He detailed, with blunt and horrific cruelty, what that payment would be.

In truth, despite the threats, he did nothing to hurt his captive. For though years of war had scoured from him almost all human feeling save pride, ambition, and spite, he understood quite well that if Joanna died, and word of that death reached Dragon Keep, no power in or out of Ryoka could protect him.

As for Joanna, she had refused even to speak to him from the day his men had brought her, hair chopped like a boy's, wrapped in a soldier's cloak, into his castle. She did not weep. They put her in an inner chamber, and placed guards on the door, and assigned two women to care for her. They were both named Kate, and since one was large and one not, they were known as Big Kate and Small Kate. She did not rage, either. She ate the meals the women brought her, and slept in the bed they gave her.

Winter came early, as it does in Serrenhold. The wind moaned about the castle walls, and snow covered the mountains. Weeks passed, and Joanna's belly swelled. When it became clear beyond any doubt that she was indeed pregnant, the women who served her went swiftly to tell their lord.

"Are you sure?" he demanded. "If this is a trick, I will have you both flayed!"

"We are sure," they told him. "Send a physician to her, if you question it."

So Martun Hal sent a physician to Joanna's room. But Joanna refused to let him touch her. "I am Iyadur Atani's wife," she said. "I will allow no other man to lay his hands on me."

"Pray that it is a changeling, a dragon-child," Martun Hal said to his captains. And he told the two Kates to give Joanna whatever she needed for her comfort, save freedom.

The women went to Joanna and asked what she wanted.

"I should like a window," Joanna said. The rooms in which they housed her had all been windowless. They moved her to a chamber in a tower. It was smaller than the room in which they had been keeping her, but it had a narrow window, through which she could see sky and clouds, and on clear nights, stars.

When her idleness began to weigh upon her, she said, "Bring me books." They brought her books. But reading soon bored her.

"Bring me a loom."

"A loom? Can you weave?" Big Kate asked.

No," Joanna said. "Can you?"

"Of course."

"Then you can teach me." The women brought her the loom, and with it, a dozen skeins of bright wool. "Show me what to do." Big Kate showed her how to set up the threads, and how to cast the shuttle. The first thing she made was a yellow blanket, a small one.

Small Kate asked, "Who shall that be for?"

"For the babe," Joanna said.

Then she began another: a scarlet cloak, a large one, with a fine gold border.

"Who shall that be for?" Big Kate asked.

"For my lord, when he comes."

One grey afternoon, as Joanna sat at her loom, a red-winged hawk alighted on her windowsill.

"Good day," Joanna said to it. It cocked its head and stared at her sideways out of its left eye. "There is bread on the table." She pointed to the little table where she ate her food. She had left a slice of bread untouched from her midday meal, intending to eat it later. The hawk turned its beak, and stared at her out of its right eye. Hopping to the table, it pecked at the bread.

Then it fluttered to the floor, and became a dark-eyed, dark-haired woman wearing a grey cloak. Crossing swiftly to Joanna's seat, she whispered, "Leave the shutter ajar. I will come again tonight." Before Joanna could answer, she turned into a bird, and was gone.

That evening Joanna could barely eat. Concerned, Big Kate fussed at her. "You have to eat. The babe grows swiftly now; it needs all the nourishment you can give it. Look, here is the cream you wanted, and here is soft ripe cheese, come all the way from Merigny in the south, where they say it snows once every hundred years."

"I don't want it."

Big Kate reached to close the window shutter.

"Leave it!"

"It's freezing."

"I am warm."

"You might be feverish." Small Kate reached to feel her forehead.

"I am not feverish. I'm fine."

They left her. She heard the bar slide across the door. She lay down on her bed. They had left her but a single candle, but light came from the hearth log. The babe moved in her belly.

"Little one, I feel you," she whispered. "Be patient. We shall not always be in this loathsome place." Longingly she gazed at the window.

At last she heard the rustle of wings. A human shadow sprang across the walls of the chamber. A woman's voice said softly, "My lady, do you know me? I am Madelene of the Red Hawk sisters. I was at your wedding."

"I remember." Tears—the first she had shed since the start of her captivity—welled into Joanna's eyes. She knuckled them away. "I am glad to see you."

"And I you," Madelene said. "Since first I knew you were here, I have looked for you. I feared you were in torment, or locked away in some dark dungeon, where I might never find you."

"Can you help me to escape this place?"

Madelene said sadly, "No, my lady. I have not the power to do that."

"I thought not." She reached beneath her pillow, and brought out a golden brooch shaped like a full-blown rose. It had been a gift from her husband on their wedding night. "Never mind. Here. Take this to my husband. Tell him I am unhurt, the babe also. Tell him to come swiftly to bring me home!"

In Dragon Keep, Iyadur Atani's mood grew grimmer, and more remote. Martun Hal's threats obsessed him: he imagined his wife alone, cold, hungry, confined to darkness, perhaps hurt. His appetite vanished; he ceased to eat, or nearly so.

At night he paced the castle corridors, silent as a ghost, cloakless despite the winter cold, his eyes like white flame. His soldiers and his servants began to fear him. One by one, they left the castle.

But some, resolute and loyal, remained. Among them was Bran the archer, now captain of the archery wing, since Jarko, the former captain, had disappeared one moonless December night. When a strange woman appeared among them, claiming to bear a message to Iyadur Atani from his captive wife, it was to Bran the guards brought her.

He recognized her. Leading her to Iyadur Atani's chamber, he pounded on the closed door. It door opened. Iyadur Atani stood framed in the doorway. His face was gaunt.

Madelene held out the golden brooch.

Iyadur Atani knew it at once. The grief and rage and fear that had filled him for four months eased a little. Lifting the brooch from Madelene's palm, he touched it to his lips.

"Be welcome," he said. "Tell me how Joanna is. Is she well?"

"She bade me say that she is, my lord."

"And—the babe?"

"It thrives. It is your child, my lord. Your lady charged me to say that, and to tell you that no matter what rumors you might have heard, neither Martun Hal nor any of his men has touched her. She begs you to please, come quickly to succor her, for she is desperate to be home."

"Can you visit her easily?"

"I can."

"Then return to her, of your kindness. Tell her I love her. Tell her not to despair."

"She will not despair," Madelene said. "Despair is not in her nature. But I have another message for you. This one is from my queen." She meant the matriarch of the Red Hawks, Jamis Delamico. "She said to tell you, where force will not prevail, seek magic. She says; go west, to Lake Urai. Find the sorcerer who lives beside the lake, and ask him how to get your wife back."

Iyadur Atani said, "I did not know there were still sorcerers in the west."

"There is one. The common folk know him as Viksa. But that is not his true name, my queen says."

"And does your queen know the true name of this reclusive wizard?" For everyone knows that unless you know a sorcerer's true name, he or she will not even speak with you.

"She does," said Madelene. She leaned toward the dragon-lord, and whispered in his ear. "And she told me to tell you, be careful when you deal with him. For he is sly, and what he intends he to do, he does not always reveal. But what he says he will do, he will do."

"Thank you," Iyadur Atani said, and he smiled, for the first time in a long time. "Cousin, I am in your debt." He told Bran to see to her comfort, and to provide her with whatever she needed, food, a bath, a place to sleep. Summoning his servants, he asked them to bring him a meal, and wine.

Then he called his officers together. "I am leaving," he said. "You must defend my people, and hold the borders against outlaws and incursions. If you need help, ask for aid from Mako or Derrenhold."

"How long will you be gone, my lord?" they asked him.

"I do not know."

Then he flew to Galva.

"I should have come before," he said. "I am sorry." He assured Olivia that despite her captivity, Joanna was well, and unharmed. "I go now to get her," he said. "When I return, I shall bring her with me."

Issho, the southeastern province of Ryoka, is a rugged place. Though not so grim as Ippa, it has none of the gentle domesticated peace of Nakase. Its plains are colder than those of Nakase, and its rivers are wilder. The greatest of those rivers is the Endor. It starts in the north, beneath that peak which men call the Lookout, Mirrin, and pours ceaselessly south, cutting like a knife through Issho's open spaces to the border where Chuyo and Issho and Nakase meet.

It ends in Lake Urai. Lake Urai is vast, and even on a fair day, the water is not blue, but pewter-grey. In winter, it does not freeze. Contrary winds swirl about it; at dawn and at twilight grey mist obscures its contours, and at all times the chill bright water lies quiescent, untroubled by even the most violent wind. The land about it is sparsely inhabited. Its people are a hardy, silent folk, not particularly friendly to strangers. They respect the lake, and do not willingly discuss its secrets. When the tall, fair-haired stranger appeared among them, having come, so he said, from Ippa, they were happy to prepare his food and take his money, but were inclined to answer his questions evasively, or not at all.

The lake is as you see it. The wizard of the lake? Never heard of him.

But the stranger was persistent. He took a room at The Red Deer in Jen, hired a horse—oddly, he seemed to have arrived without one—and roamed about the lake. The weather did not seem to trouble him. "We have winter in my country." His clothes were plain, but clearly of the highest quality, and beneath his quiet manner there was iron.

"His eyes are different," the innkeeper's wife said. "He's looking for a wizard. Maybe he's one himself, in disguise."

One grey March afternoon, when the lake lay shrouded in mist, Iyadur Atani came upon a figure sitting on a rock beside a small fire. It was dressed in rags, and held what appeared to be a fishing pole.

The dragon-lord dismounted. Tying his horse to a tall reed, he walked toward the fisherman. As he approached, the hunched figure turned. Beneath the ragged hood he glimpsed white hair, and a visage so old and wrinkled that he could not tell if he was facing a man or a woman.

"Good day," he said. The ancient being nodded. "My name is Iyadur Atani. Men call me the Silver Dragon. I am looking for a wizard."

The ancient one shook its head, and gestured, as if to say, Leave me alone. Iyadur Atani crouched.

"Old One, I don't believe you are as you appear," he said in a conversational tone. "I believe you are the one I seek. If you are indeed—" and then he said the name that Madelene of the Red Hawks had whispered in his ear—"I beg you to help me. For I have come a long way to look for you."

An aged hand swept the hood aside. Dark grey eyes stared out of a withered, wrinkled face.

A feeble voice said, "Who told you my name?"

"A friend."

"Huh. Whoever it was is no friend of *mine*. For what does the Silver Dragon need a wizard?"

"If you are truly wise," Iyadur Atani said, "you know."

The sorcerer laughed softly. The hunched figure straightened. The rags became a silken gown with glittering jewels at its hem and throat. Instead of an old man, the dragon-lord faced a man in his prime, of princely bearing, with luminous chestnut hair and eyes the color of a summer storm. The fishing pole became a tall staff. Its crook was carved like a serpent's head. The sorcerer pointed the staff at the ground, and said three words.

A doorway seemed to open in the stony hillside. Joanna Torneo Atani stood within it. She wore furs, and was visibly pregnant.

"Joanna!" The dragon-lord reached for her. But his hands gripped empty air.

"Illusion," said the sorcerer known as Viksa. "A simple spell, but effective, don't you think? You are correct, my lord. I know you lost your wife. I assume you want her back. Tell me, why do you not lead your war band to Serrenhold and rescue her?"

"Martun Hal will kill her if I do that."

"I see."

"Will you help me?"

"Perhaps," said the sorcerer. The serpent in his staff turned its head to stare at the dragon-lord. Its eyes were rubies. "What will you pay me if I help you?"

"I have gold."

Viksa yawned. "I have no interest in gold."

"Jewels," said the dragon-lord, "fine clothing, a horse to bear you wherever you might choose to go, a castle of your own to dwell in..."

"I have no use for those."

"Name your price, and I will pay it," Iyadur Atani said steadily. "I reserve only the life of my wife and my child."

"But not your own?" Viksa cocked his head. "You intrigue me. Indeed, you move me. I accept your offer, my lord. I will help you rescue your wife from Serrenhold. I shall teach you a spell, a very simple spell, I assure you. When you speak it, you will be able to hide within a shadow. In that way you may pass into Serrenhold unseen."

"And its price?"

Viksa smiled. "In payment, I will take—*you*. Not your life, but your service. It has been many years since I had someone to hunt for me, cook for me, build my fire, and launder my clothes. It will amuse me to have a dragon as my servant."

"For how long would I owe you service?"

"As long as I wish it."

"That seems unfair."

The wizard shrugged.

"When would this service start?"

The wizard shrugged again. "It may be next month, or next year. Or it may be twenty years from now. Have we an agreement?"

Iyadur Atani considered. He did not like this wizard. But he could see no other way to get his wife back.

"We have," he said. "Teach me the spell."

So Viksa the sorcerer taught Iyadur Atani the spell which would enable him to hide within a shadow. It was not a difficult spell. Iyadur Atani rode his hired horse back to The Red Deer and paid the innkeeper what remained on his bill. Then he walked into the bare field beside the inn, and became the Silver Dragon. As the innkeeper and his wife watched open-mouthed, he circled the inn once, and then sped north.

"A dragon!" the innkeeper's wife said, with intense satisfaction. "I wonder if he found the sorcerer. See, I told you his eyes were odd." The innkeeper agreed. Then he went up to the room Iyadur Atani had occupied, and searched carefully in every cranny, in case the dragon-lord had chanced to leave some gold behind.

Now it was in Iyadur Atani's mind to fly immediately to Serrenhold Castle. But, remembering Martun Hal's threats, he did not. He flew to a point just south of Serrenhold's southern border. And there, in a nondescript village, he bought a horse, a shaggy brown gelding. From there he proceeded to Serrenhold Castle. It was not so tedious a journey as he had thought it would be. The prickly stunted pine trees that grew along the slopes of the wind-swept hills showed new green along their branches. Birds sang. Foxes loped across the hills, hunting mice and quail and the occasional stray chicken. The journey took six days. At dawn on the seventh day, Iyadur Atani fed the brown gelding and left him in a farmer's yard. It was a fine spring morning. The sky was cloudless; the sun brilliant; the shadows sharp-edged as steel. Thorn-crowned hawthorn bushes lined the road to Serrenhold Castle. Their shadows webbed the ground. A wagon filled with lumber lumbered toward the castle. Its shadow rolled beneath it.

"Wizard," the dragon-lord said to the empty sky, "if you have played me false, I will find you, wherever you try to hide, and eat your heart."

In her prison in the tower, Joanna Torneo Atani walked from one side of her chamber to the other. Her hair had grown long again: it fell around her shoulders. Her belly was round and high under the soft thick drape of her gown. The coming of spring had made her restless. She had asked to be allowed to walk on the ramparts, but this Martun Hal had refused.

Below her window, the castle seethed like a cauldron. The place was never still; the smells and sounds of war continued day and night. The air was thick with soot. Soldiers drilled in the courtyard. Martun Hal was planning an attack on Ege diCorsini. He had told her all about it, including his intention to destroy Galva. *I will burn it to the ground. I will kill your uncle and take your mother prisoner,* he had said. *Or perhaps not. Perhaps I will just have her killed.*

She glanced toward the patch of sky that was her window. If Madelene would only come, she could get word to Galva, or to her uncle in Derrenhold... But Madelene would not come in daylight, it was too dangerous.

She heard a hinge creak. The door to the outer chamber opened. "My lady," Big Kate called. She bustled in, bearing a tray. It held soup, bread, and a dish of thin sour pickles. "I brought your lunch."

"I'm not hungry."

Kate said, troubled, "My lady, you have to eat. For the baby."

"Leave it," Joanna said. "I will eat." Kate set the tray on the table, and left.

Joanna nibbled at a pickle. She rubbed her back, which ached. The baby's heel thudded against the inside of her womb. "My precious, my little one, be still," she said. For it was her greatest fear that her babe, Iyadur Atani's child, might in its haste to be born arrive early, before her husband arrived to rescue them. That he would come, despite Martun Hal's threats, she had no doubt. "Be still."

Silently, Iyadur Atani materialized from the shadows.

"Joanna," he said. He put his arms about her. She reached her hands up. Her fingertips brushed his face. She leaned against him, trembling.

She whispered into his shirt, "How did you...?"

"Magic." He touched the high mound of her belly. "Are you well? Have they mistreated you?"

"I am very well. The babe is well." She seized his hand and pressed his palm over the mound. The baby kicked strongly. "Do you feel?"

"Yes." Iyadur Atani stroked her hair. A scarlet cloak with an ornate gold border hung on a peg. He reached for it, and wrapped it about her. "Now, my love, we go. Shut your eyes, and keep them shut until I tell you to open them." He bent, and lifted her into his arms. Her heart thundered against his chest.

She breathed into his ear, "I am sorry. I am heavy."

"You weigh nothing," he said. His human shape dissolved. The walls of the tower shuddered and burst apart. Blocks of stone and splintered planks of wood toppled into the courtyard. Women screamed. Arching his great neck, the Silver Dragon spread his wings and rose into the sky. The soldiers on the ramparts threw their spears at him, and fled. Joanna heard the screaming and felt the hot wind. The scent of burning filled her nostrils. She knew what must have happened. But the arms about her were her husband's, and human. She did not know how this could be, yet it was. Eyes tight shut, she buried her face against her husband's shoulder.

Martun Hal stood with a courier in the castle hall. The crash of stone and the screaming interrupted him. A violent gust of heat swept through the room. The windows of the hall shattered. Racing from the hall, he looked up, and saw the dragon circling. His men crouched, sobbing in fear. Consumed with rage, he looked about for a bow, a spear, a rock... Finally he drew his sword.

"Damn you!" he shouted impotently at his adversary.

Then the walls of his castle melted beneath a white-hot rain.

In Derrenhold, Ege diCorsini was, wearily, reluctantly, preparing for war.

He did not want to fight Martun Hal, but he would, of course, if troops from Serrenhold took one step across his border. That an attack would be mounted he had no doubt. His spies had told him to expect it. Jamis of the Hawks had sent her daughters to warn him.

Part of his weariness was a fatigue of the spirit. *This is my fault. I should have killed him when I had the opportunity. Ferris was right.* The other part of his weariness was physical. He was tired much of the time, and none of the tonics or herbal concoctions that the physicians prescribed seemed to help. His heart raced oddly. He could not sleep. Sometimes in the night he wondered if the Old One sleeping underground had dreamed of him. When the Old One dreams of you, you die. But he did not want to die and leave his domain and its people in danger, and so he planned a war, knowing all the while that he might die in the middle of it.

"My lord," a servant said, "you have visitors."

"Send them in," Ege diCorsini said. "No, wait." The physicians had said he needed to move about. Rising wearily, he went into the hall.

He found there his niece Joanna, big with child, and with her, her flame-haired, flame-eyed husband. A strong smell of burning hung about their clothes.

Ege diCorsini drew a long breath. He kissed Joanna on both cheeks. "I will let your mother know that you are safe."

"She needs to rest," Iyadur Atani said.

"I do not need to rest. I have been doing absolutely nothing for the last six months. I need to go home," Joanna said astringently. "Only I do not wish to ride. Uncle, would you lend us a litter, and some steady beasts to draw it?"

"You may have anything I have," Ege diCorsini said. And for a moment he was not tired at all.

Couriers galloped throughout Ippa, bearing the news: Martun Hal was dead; Serrenhold Castle was ash, or nearly so. The threat of war was—after twenty years—truly over. Martun Hal's captains—most of them—had died with him. Those still alive hid, hoping to save their skins.

Two weeks after the rescue and the burning of Serrenhold, Ege diCorsini died.

In May, with her mother and sisters at her side, Joanna gave birth to a son. The baby had flame-colored hair and eyes like his father's. He was named Avahir. A year and a half later, a second son was born to Joanna Torneo Atani. He had dark hair, and eyes like his mother's. He was named Jon. Like the man whose name he bore, Jon Atani had a sweet disposition and a loving heart. He adored his brother, and Avahir loved his younger brother fiercely. Their loyalty to each other made their parents very happy.

Thirteen years almost to the day from the burning of Serrenhold, on a bright spring morning, a man dressed richly as a prince, carrying a white birch staff, appeared at the front gate of Atani Castle and requested audience with the dragon-lord. He refused to enter, or even to give his name, saying only, "Tell him the fisherman has come for his catch."

His servants found Iyadur Atani in the great hall of his castle.

"My lord," they said, "a stranger stands at the front gate, who will not give his name. He says, *The fisherman has come for his catch*."

"I know who it is," their lord replied. He walked to the gate of his castle. The sorcerer stood there, leaning on his serpent-headed staff, entirely at ease.

"Good day," he said cheerfully. "Are you ready to travel?"

And so Iyadur Atani left his children and his kingdom to serve Viksa the wizard. I do not know—no one ever asked her, not even their sons—what Iyadur Atani and his wife said to one another that day. Avahir Atani, who at twelve was already full-grown, as changeling children are wont to be, inherited the lordship of Atani Castle. Like his father, he gained the reputation of being fierce, but just.

Jon Atani married a granddaughter of Rudolf diMako, and went to live in that city.

Joanna Atani remained in Dragon Keep. As time passed, and Iyadur Atani did not return, her sisters and her brother, even her sons, urged her to remarry. She told them all not to be fools; she was wife to the Silver Dragon. Her husband was alive, and might return at any time, and how would he feel to find another man warming her bed? She became her son's chief minister, and in that capacity could often be found riding across Dragon's country, and elsewhere in Ippa, to Derrenhold and Mirrinhold and Ragnar, and even to far Voiana, where the Red Hawk sisters, one in particular, always welcomed her. She would not go to Serrenhold.

But always she returned to Dragon Keep.

As for Iyadur Atani: he traveled with the wizard throughout Ryoka, carrying his bags, preparing his oatcakes and his bath water, scraping mud from his boots. Viksa's boots were often muddy, for he was a great traveler, who walked, rather than rode, to his many destinations. In the morning, when Iyadur Atani brought the sorcerer his breakfast, Viksa would say, "Today we go to Rotsa"—or Ruggio, or Rowena. "They have need of magic." He never said how he knew this. And off they would go to Vipurri or Rotsa or Talvela, to Sorvino, Ruggio or Rowena.

Sometimes the need to which he was responding had to do directly with magic, as when a curse needed to be lifted. Often it had to do with common disasters. A river had swollen in its banks and needed to be restrained. A landslide had fallen on a house or barn. Sometimes the one who needed them was noble, or rich. Sometimes not. It did not matter to Viksa. He could enchant a cornerstone, so that the wall it anchored would rise straight and true; he could spell a field, so that its crop would thrust from the soil no matter what the rainfall.

His greatest skill was with water. Some sorcerers draw a portion of their power from an element: wind, water, fire or stone. Viksa could coax a spring out of earth that had known only drought for a hundred years. He could turn stagnant water sweet. He knew the names of every river, stream, brook and waterfall in Issho.

In the first years of his servitude Iyadur Atani thought often of his sons, and especially Avahir, and of Joanna, but after a while his anxiety for them faded.

After a longer while, he found he did not think of them so often—rarely at all, in fact. He even forgot their names. He had already relinquished his own. *Iyadur is too grand a name for a servant*, the sorcerer had remarked. *You need a different name.*

And so the tall, fair-haired man became known as Shadow. He carried the sorcerer's pack, and cooked his food. He rarely spoke.

"Why is he so silent?" women, bolder and more curious than their men, asked the sorcerer.

Sometimes the sorcerer answered, "No reason. It's his nature." And sometimes he told a tale, a long, elaborate fantasy of spells and dragons and sorcerers, a gallant tale in which Shadow had been the hero, but from which he had emerged changed—broken. Shadow, listening, wondered if perhaps this tale was true. It might have been. It explained why his memory was so erratic, and so vague.

His dreams, by contrast, were vivid and intense. He dreamed often of a dark-walled castle flanked by white-capped mountains. Sometimes he dreamed that he was a bird, flying over the castle. The most adventurous of the women, attracted by Shadow's looks, and, sometimes, by his silence, tried to talk with him. But their smiles and allusive glances only made him shy. He thought that he had had a wife, once. Maybe she had left him. He thought perhaps she had. But maybe not. Maybe she had died.

He had no interest in the women they met, though as far as he could tell, his body still worked as it should. He was a powerful man, well-formed. Shadow wondered sometimes what his life had been before he had come to serve the wizard. He had skills: he could hunt and shoot a bow, and use a sword. Perhaps he had served in some noble's war band. He bore a knife now, a good one, with a bone hilt, but no sword. He did not need a sword. Viksa's reputation, and his magic, shielded them both.

Every night, before they slept, wherever they were, in a language Shadow did not know, the sorcerer wove spells of protection about them and their dwelling. The spells were very powerful, and the chant made Shadow's ears hurt. Once, early in their association, he asked the sorcerer what the spell was for.

"Protection," Viksa replied. Shadow had been surprised. He had not realized Viksa had enemies.

But now, having traveled with the sorcerer as long as he had, he knew that even the lightest magic can have consequences, and Viksa's magic was not always light. He could make rain, but he could also make drought. He could lift curses or lay them. He was a man of power, and he had his vanity. He enjoyed being obeyed. Sometimes he enjoyed being feared.

Through spring, summer, and autumn, the wizard traveled wherever he was called to go. But in winter they returned to Lake Urai. He had a house beside the lake, a simple place, furnished with simple things: a pallet, a table, a chair, a shelf for books. But Viksa rarely looked at the books; it seemed he had no real love for study. Indeed, he seemed to have no passion for anything, save sorcery itself—and fishing. All through the Issho winter, despite the bitter winds, he took his little coracle out upon the lake, and sat there with a pole. Sometimes he caught a fish, or two, or half a dozen. Sometimes he caught none.

"Enchant them," Shadow said to him one grey afternoon, when he returned to the house empty-handed. "Call them to your hook with magic."

The wizard shook his head. "I can't."

"Why not?"

"I was one of them once." Shadow looked at him, uncertain. "Before I was a sorcerer, I was a fish."

It was impossible to tell if he was joking or serious. It might have been true. It explained, at least, his affinity for water.

While he fished, Shadow hunted. The country around the lake was rich with game; despite the winter, they did not lack for meat. Shadow hunted deer and badger and beaver. He saw wolves, but did not kill them. Nor would he kill birds, though birds there were; even in winter, geese came often to the lake. Their presence woke in him a wild, formless longing.

One day he saw a white bird, with wings as wide as he was tall, circling over the lake. It had a beak like a raptor. It called to him, an eerie sound. Something about it made his heart beat faster. When Viksa returned from his sojourn at the lake, Shadow described the stranger bird to him, and asked what it was.

"A condor," the wizard said.

"Where does it come from?"

"From the north," the wizard said, frowning.

"It called to me. It looked—noble."

"It is not. It is scavenger, not predator." He continued to frown. That night he spent a long time over his nightly spells.

In spring, the kingfishers and guillemots returned to the lake. And one April morning, when Shadow laid breakfast upon the table, Viksa said, "Today we go to Dale."

"Where is that?"

"In the White Mountains, in Kameni, far to the north." And so they went to Dale, where a petty lordling needed Viksa's help in deciphering the terms and conditions of an ancient prophecy, for within it lay the future of his kingdom.

From Dale they traveled to Secca, where a youthful hedge-witch, hoping to shatter a boulder, had used a spell too complex for her powers, and had managed to summon a stone demon, which promptly ate her. It was an old, powerful demon. It took a day, a night, and another whole day until Viksa, using the strongest spells he knew, was able to send it back into the Void.

They rested that night at a roadside inn, south of Secca. Viksa, exhausted from his battle with the demon, went to bed right after his meal, so worn that he fell asleep without taking the time to make his customary incantations.

Shadow considered waking him to remind him of it, and decided not to. Instead, he, too, slept.

And there, in an inn south of Secca, Iyadur Atani woke.

He was not, he realized, in his bed, or even in his bedroom. He lay on the floor.

The coverlet around his shoulders was rough wool, not the soft quilt he was used to. Also, he was wearing his boots.

He said, "Joanna?" No one answered. A candle sat on a plate at his elbow. He lit it without touching it.

Sitting up soundlessly, he gazed about the chamber, at the bed and its snoring occupant, at the packs he had packed himself, the birchwood staff athwart the doorway… Memory flooded through him. The staff was Viksa's. The man sleeping in the bed was Viksa. And he—*he* was Iyadur Atani, lord of Dragon Keep.

His heart thundered. His skin coursed with heat. The ring on his hand glowed, but he could not feel the burning. Fire coursed beneath his skin. He rose.

How long had Viksa's magic kept him in thrall—five years? Ten years? More?

He took a step toward the bed. The serpent in the wizard's staff opened its eyes. Raising its carved head, it hissed at him.

The sound woke Viksa. Gazing up from his bed at the bright shimmering shape looming over him, he knew immediately what had happened. He had made a mistake. *Fool*, he thought, *O you fool.*

It was too late now.

The guards on the walls of Secca saw a pillar of fire rise into the night. Out of it—so they swore, with such fervor that even the most skeptical did not doubt them—flew a silver dragon. It circled the flames, bellowing with such power and ferocity that all who heard it trembled.

Then it beat the air with its great wings, and leaped north.

In Dragon Keep, a light powdery snow covered the garden. It did not deter the rhubarb shoots breaking through the soil, or the fireweed, or the buds on the birches. A sparrow swung in the birch branches, singing. The clouds that had brought the snow had dissipated; the day was bright and fair, the shadows sharp as the angle of the sparrow's wing against the light.

Joanna Atani walked along the garden path. Her face was lined, and her hair, though still lustrous and thick, was streaked with silver. Her vision, once clear, was cloudy. But her step was vigorous, and her eyes as bright as they had been when first she came to Atani Castle, over thirty years before.

Bending close to the blossoms, she brushed a snowdrop free of snow. A clatter of pans arose in the kitchen. A voice, imperious and young, called from within. It was Hikaru, Avahir's first-born and heir. He was only two, but had the height and grace of a lad twice that age. A woman answered him, her voice soft and firm. That was Geneva Tuolinnen, Hikaru's mother. She was an excellent mother, calm and unexcitable. She was a good seamstress, too, and a superb manager; far better at running the castle than Joanna had ever been. She could scarcely handle a bow, though, and thought swordplay was entirely man's work.

She and Joanna were as friendly as two strong-willed women can be.

Claws scrabbled on stone. A black, floppy-eared puppy bounded across Joanna's feet, nearly knocking her down. Rup the dog-boy scampered after it. They tore through the garden and raced past the kitchen door into the yard. Hikaru called again. A man walked into the garden. Joanna squinted. For a moment she thought it was Avahir, but Avahir was miles away, in Kameni. He was tall. Gabbio the head gardener was short.

The man walked toward her.

"Joanna?" he said.

She knew that voice. For a moment she ceased to breathe. He came to her side. He looked much as he had the morning he had left with the wizard, sixteen years before. His eyes were the same, and his scent, and the heat of his body against hers. She slid her palms beneath his shirt. His skin was warm. Their lips met.

I do not know exactly what Iyadur Atani and his wife first said to one another in the garden that day. Surely there were questions, and answers. Surely there were tears, of sorrow, and of joy.

Later, after those first breathless words of wonder, they sat together on a bench beneath a persimmon tree. He told her of his travels, of his captivity, and of his freedom. She told him of their sons, and particularly of his heir, Avahir, lord of Dragon's Country.

"He is a good lord, respected throughout Ryoka. His people fear him and love him. He is called the Azure Dragon. He married a girl from Issho, a cousin to the Talvela; we are at peace with them, and with the Nyo. Their first-born, Hikaru, is a dragon-child. Jon, too, is wed. He and his wife live in Mako. They have three children, two boys and a girl. You are a grandfather, my love."

He smiled at that. Then he said, "Where is Avahir now?"

"In Kameni, at a council called by Rowan Imorin, the king's war leader, who wishes to lead an army against the Chuyo pirates." She stroked his face. It was not true, as she first thought, that he was unchanged. Still, he looked astonishingly young. She wondered if she seemed old to him.

"Never leave me again," she said.

He lifted her hands to his lips and kissed them, front and back. Then he said, "My love, I would not. But I must. I cannot stay here."

"What are you saying?"

"Avahir is lord of this land now. You know the dragon-nature. We are jealous of power, we dragons. It would go ill were I to stay."

Joanna's blood chilled. She did know. The history of the dragon-folk is filled with tales of rage and rivalry: sons strive against fathers, brothers against brothers, mothers against their children. They are bloody tales. For this reason, among others, the dragon-kindred do not live very long.

She said steadily, "You cannot hurt your son."

"I would not," said Iyadur Atani. "Therefore I must leave."

"Where will you go?"

"I don't know. Will you come with me?"

She locked her fingers through his huge ones, and smiled through tears. "I will go wherever you wish. Only give me time to kiss my grandchild."

And so, Iyadur Atani and Joanna Torneo Atani left Atani Castle. They went quietly, without fuss, accompanied by neither man nor maidservant. They went first to Mako, where Iyadur Atani greeted his younger son, and met his son's wife, and their children.

From there they went to Derrenhold, and from Derrenhold, west, to Voiana, the home of the Red Hawk sisters. And in Voiana, Joanna wrote a letter to Avahir Atani, assuring him, and that she was with her husband, the Silver Dragon, who had returned, and that she was happy and well.

Avahir Atani, who truly loved his mother, flew to Voiana. But he arrived to find them gone. "Where are they?" he asked Jamis Delamico, who was still matriarch of the Red Hawk clan. For the Red Hawk sisters live long.

"They left."

"Where did they go?"

Jamis Delamico shrugged. "They did not tell me where they were going, and I did not ask."

There were no more letters. Over time, word trickled back to Dragon Keep that they had been seen in Rowena, or Sorvino, or Secca, or the mountains north of Dale.

"Where were they going?" Avahir Atani asked, when his servants came to him to tell him these stories. But no one could tell him that.

Time passed; Ippa prospered. In Dragon Keep, a daughter was born to Avanir and Geneva Tuolinnen Atani. They named her Lucia. She was small and dark-haired and feisty. In Derrenhold, and Mako and Mirrinhold, memories of conflict faded. In the windswept west, the folk of Serrenhold rebuilt their lord's tower. In the east, Rowan Imorin, the war leader of Kameni, summoned the lords of all the provinces to unite against the Chuyo pirates. The lords of Ippa, instead of quarreling with each other, joined the lords of Nakase and Kameni. They fought many battles. They gained many victories.

But in one battle, not the greatest, an arrow shot by a Chuyo archer sliced into the throat of Avanir Atani, and killed him. Grimly, his mourning soldiers made a pyre, and burned his body. For the dragon-kindred do not lie in earth.

Hikaru, the Shining Dragon, became lord of Dragon Keep. Like his father and his grandfather before him, he was feared and respected throughout Ippa.

One foggy autumn, a stranger arrived at the gates of Dragon Keep, requesting to see the lord. He was an old man, with silver hair. His back was stooped, but they could see that he had once been powerful. He bore no sword, but only a knife with a bone hilt.

"Who are you?" the servants asked him.

"My name doesn't matter," he answered. "Tell the Shining Dragon that I have a gift for him."

They brought him to Hikaru. Hikaru said, "Old man, I am told you have a gift for me."

"It is so," the old man said. He extended his palm. On it sat a golden brooch, fashioned in the shape of a rose. "It is an heirloom of your house, given by your grandfather, Iyadur, to his wife Joanna, on their wedding night. She is dead now, and so it comes to you. You should give it to your wife, when you wed."

Hikaru said, "How do you come by this thing? Who are you? Are you a sorcerer?"

"I am no one," the old man replied; "a shadow."

"That is not an answer," Hikaru said, and he signaled to his soldiers to seize the stranger.

But the men who stepped forward to hold the old man found their hands passing through empty air. They hunted through the castle for him, but he was gone. They decided that he was a sorcerer, or perhaps the sending of a sorcerer. Eventually they forgot him. When the shadow of the dragon first appeared in Atani Castle, rising like smoke out of the castle walls, few thought of the old man who had vanished into shadow one autumnal morning. Those who did kept it to themselves. But Hikaru Atani remembered. He kept the brooch, and gave it to his wife upon their wedding night. And he told his soldiers to honor the shadow-dragon when it came, and not to speak disrespectfully of it: "For clearly," he said, "it belongs here."

The shadow of the dragon still lives in the walls of Atani Castle. It comes as it chooses, unsummoned. And still, in Dragon's Country, and throughout Ippa and Issho, and even into the east, the singers tell the story of Iyadur Atani, of his wife Joanna, and of the burning of Serrenhold.

THE DRAGONS OF
SUMMER GULCH
Robert Reed

Robert Reed was born in Omaha, Nebraska, that barely-mapped landscape
famous for drought and handguns, in 1956. A boyhood fascination with dinosaurs led to science studies and a degree in biology from Nebraska Wesleyan
University. After a long apprenticeship, he became a full-time writer of science
fiction, and in the last twenty years he has written a dozen novels and nearly 200
shorter stories. Reed's work is often seen in *Asimov's, The Magazine of Fantasy
& Science Fiction, Postscripts,* and other markets. His novella, "A Billion Eves",
won the Hugo in 2007. Recent projects include an enormous alternate-history
novel and a book aimed at young adults. He is married and has one daughter
and today lives in an irrigated, gun-free corner of Lincoln, Nebraska.

1

A hard winter can lift rocks as well as old bones, shoving all that is loose up
through the most stubborn earth. Then snowmelt and flash floods will sweep
across the ground, wiping away the gravel and clay. And later, when a man with
good vision and exceptional luck rides past, all of the world might suddenly
change.

"Would you look at that," the man said to himself in a firm, deep voice. "A claw,
isn't it? From a mature dragon, isn't it? Good Lord, Mr. Barrow. And there's two
more claws set beside that treasure!"

Barrow was a giant fellow with a narrow face and a heavy cap of black hair
that grew from his scalp and the back of his neck and between the blades of his
strong shoulders. Born on one of the Northern Isles, he had left his homeland
as a young man to escape one war, coming to this new country just in time to
be thrown into a massive and prolonged civil conflict. Ten thousand miseries
had abused him over the next years. But he survived the fighting, and upon his
discharge from the Army of the Center, a grateful nation had given him both
his citizenship and a bonus of gold coins. Barrow purchased a one-way ticket on
the Western railroad, aiming to find his fortune in the wilderness. His journey

337

ended in one of the new prairie towns—a place famous for hyrax herds and dragon bones. There he had purchased a pair of quality camels, ample supplies for six months of solitude, and with shovels enough to move a hillside, he had set out into the washlands.

Sliding off the lead camel, he said, "Hold."

The beast gave a low snort, adjusting its hooves to find the most comfortable pose.

Barrow knelt, carefully touching the dragon's middle claw. Ancient as this artifact was, he knew from painful experience that even the most weathered claw was sharp enough to slash. Just as the fossil teeth could puncture the thickest leather gloves, and the edges of the great scales were nastier than any saw blade sharpened on the hardest whetstone.

The claw was a vivid deep purple color—a sure sign of good preservation. With his favorite little pick, Barrow worked loose the mudstone beneath it, exposing its full length and the place where it joined into the front paw. He wasn't an educated man, but Barrow knew his trade: this had been a flying dragon, one of the monsters who once patrolled the skies above a vanished seacoast. The giant paw was meant for gripping. Presumably the dragons used their four feet much as a coon-rascal does, holding their prey and for other simple manipulations. These finger claws were always valuable, but the thick thumb claw—the Claw of God—would be worth even more to buyers. As night fell, Barrow dug by the smoky light of a little fire, picking away at the mudstone until the paw was revealed—a palm-down hand large enough to stand upon and, after ages of being entombed, still displaying the dull red color made by the interlocking scales.

The man didn't sleep ten blinks. Then with first light he followed a hunch, walking half a dozen long strides up the gully and thrusting a shovel into what looked like a mound of ordinary clay.

The shovel was good steel, but a dull *thunk* announced that something beneath was harder by a long ways.

Barrow used the shovel and a big pickax, working fast and sloppy, investing the morning to uncover a long piece of the dragon's back—several daggerlike spines rising from perhaps thirty big plates of ruddy armor.

Exhaustion forced him to take a break, eating his fill and drinking the last of his water. Then, because they were hungry and a little thirsty, he lead both of his loyal camels down the gully, finding a flat plain where sagebrush grew and seepage too foul for a man to drink stood in a shallow alkaline pond.

The happy camels drank and grazed, wandering as far as their long leashes allowed.

Barrow returned to his treasure. Twice he dug into fresh ground, and twice he guessed wrong, finding nothing. The monster's head was almost surely missing. Heads almost always were. But he tried a third time, and his luck held. Not only was the skull entombed along with the rest of the carcass, it was still attached to the body, the long muscular neck having twisted hard to the left as the creature passed from the living.

It had been a quick death, he was certain.

There were larger specimens, but the head was magnificent. What Barrow could see was as long as he was tall, narrow and elegant, a little reminiscent of a pelican's head, but prettier, the giant mouth bristling with a forest of teeth, each tooth bigger than his thumb. The giant dragon eyes had vanished, but the large sockets remained, filled with mudstone and aimed forward like a hawk's eyes. And behind the eyes lay a braincase several times bigger than any man's.

"How did you die?" he asked his new friend.

Back in town, an educated fellow had explained to Barrow what science knew today and what it was guessing. Sometimes the dragons had been buried in mud, on land or underwater, and the mud protected the corpse from its hungry cousins and gnawing rats. If there were no oxygen, then there couldn't be any rot. And that was the best of circumstances. Without rot, and buried inside a stable deep grave, an entire dragon could be kept intact, waiting for the blessed man to ride by on his happy camel.

Barrow was thirsty enough to moan, but he couldn't afford to stop now.

Following the advice of other prospectors, he found the base of the dragon's twin wings—the wings still sporting the leathery flesh strung between the long, long finger bones—and he fashioned a charge with dynamite, setting it against the armored plates of the back and covering his work with a pile of tamped earth to help force the blast downward. Then, with a long fuse, he set off the charge. There was a dull thud followed by a steady rain of dirt and pulverized stone, and he ran to look at what he had accomplished, pulling back the shattered plates—each worth half a good camel when intact—and then using a heavy pick to pull free the shattered insides of the great beast.

If another dragon had made this corpse, attacking this treasure from below, there would be nothing left to find. Many millions of years ago, the precious guts would have been eaten, and lost.

"But still," Barrow told himself. "These claws and scales are enough to pay for my year. If it comes to that."

But it didn't have to come to that.

Inside the fossil lay the reason for all of his suffering and boredom: behind the stone-infected heart was an intricate organ as long as he was tall—a spongelike thing set above the peculiar dragon lungs. The organ was composed of gold and lustrous platinum wrapped around countless voids. In an instant, Barrow had become as wealthy as his dreams had promised he would be. He let out an enormous yell, dancing back and forth across the back of the dead dragon. Then he collapsed beside his treasure, crying out of joy, and when he wiped back the tears one final time, he saw something else.

Eons ago, a fine black mud had infiltrated the dead body, filling the cavities while keeping away the free oxygen.

Without oxygen, there was almost no decay.

Floating in the old mudstone were at least three round bodies, each as large as the largest naval cannon balls. They were not organs, but they belonged inside the dragon. Barrow had heard stories about such things, and the educated man in town had even shown him a shard of something similar. But where the shard was dirty gray, these three balls were white as bone. That was their color in life, he realized, and this was their color now.

With a trembling hand, Barrow touched the nearest egg, and he held his palm against it for a very long while, leaving it a little bit warm.

2

At one point, the whore asked, "Where did you learn all this crap?"

Manmark laughed quietly for a moment. Then he closed the big book and said, "My credentials. Is that what you wish to have?"

"After your money, sure. Your credentials. Yes."

"As a boy, I had tutors. As a young man, I attended several universities. I studied all the sciences and enjoyed the brilliance of a dozen great minds. And then my father died, and I took my inheritance, deciding to apply my wealth and genius in the pursuit of great things."

She was the prettiest woman of her sort in this town, and she was not stupid. Manmark could tell just by staring at her eyes that she had a good, strong mind. But she was just an aboriginal girl, tiny like all of the members of her race, sold by her father for opium or liquor. Her history had to be impoverished and painful. Which was why it didn't bother him too much when she laughed at him, remarking, "With most men, listening is easier than screwing. But with you, I think it's the other way around."

Manmark opened the book again, ignoring any implied insult.

Quietly, he asked the woman, "Can you read?"

"I know which coin is which," she replied. "And my name, when I see it. If it's written out with a simple hand."

"Look at this picture," he told her. "What does it show you?"

"A dragon," she said matter-of-factly.

"Which species of dragon?" Manmark pressed.

She looked at the drawing, blowing air into her cheeks. Then she exhaled, admitting, "I don't know. Is it the flying kind?"

"Hardly."

"Yeah, I guess it isn't. I don't see wings."

He nodded, explaining, "This is a small early dragon. One of the six-legged precursor species, as it happens. It was unearthed on this continent, resting inside some of the oldest rocks from the Age of Dragons." Manmark was a handsome fellow with dreamy golden eyes that stared off into one of the walls of the room. "If you believe in natural selection and in the great depths of time," he continued, "then this might well be the ancestor to the hundred species that we know about, and the thousands we have yet to uncover."

She said, "Huh," and sat back against the piled-up pillows.

"Can I look at the book?" she asked.

"Carefully," he warned, as if speaking to a moody child. "I don't have another copy with me, and it is the best available guide—"

"Just hand it over," she interrupted. "I promise. I won't be rough."

Slowly, and then quickly, the woman flipped through the pages. Meanwhile her client continued to speak about things she could never understand: on this very land, there once stood dragons the size of great buildings—placid and heavily armored vegetarians that consumed entire trees, judging by the fossilized meals discovered in their cavernous bellies. Plus there had been smaller beasts roaming in sprawling herds, much as the black hyraxes grazed on the High Plains. The predatory dragons came in two basic types—the quadrupeds with their saber teeth and the Claws of God on their mighty hands; and later, the winged giants with the same teeth and Claws but also grasping limbs and a brain that might well have been equal to a woman's.

If the girl noticed his insult, she knew better than show it, her face down and nodding while the pages turned. At the back of the book were new kinds of bones and odd sketches. "What is this tiny creature?" she inquired.

Manmark asked, "What does it resemble?"

"Some kind of fowl," she admitted.

"But with teeth," he pointed out. "And where are its wings?"

She looked up, almost smiling. "Didn't it have wings? Or haven't you found them yet?"

"I never work with these little creatures," Manmark reported with a prickly tone. "But no, it and its kind never grew particularly large, and they were never genuinely important. Some in my profession believe they became today's birds. But when their bones were first uncovered, the creatures were mistakenly thought to be a variety of running lizard. Which is why those early fossil hunters dubbed them 'monstrous lizards'…"

She turned the page, paused, and then smiled at a particular drawing. "I know this creature," she said, pushing the book across the rumpled sheets. "I've seen a few shrews in my day."

The tiny mammal huddled beneath a fern frond. Manmark tapped the image with his finger, agreeing, "It does resemble our shrew. As it should, since this long-dead midget is the precursor to them and to us and to every fur-bearing animal in between."

"Really?" she said.

"Without question."

"Without question," she repeated, nodding as if she understood the oceans of time and the slow, remorseless pressures of natural selection.

"Our ancestors, like the ancestors of every bird, were exceptionally tiny," Manmark continued. "The dragons ruled the land and seas, and then they ruled the skies too, while these little creatures scurried about in the shadows, waiting patiently for their turn."

"Their turn?" She closed the book with authority, as if she would never need it again. Then, with a distant gaze, she said, "Now and again, I have wondered.

Why did the dragons vanish from this world?"

Manmark reminded himself that this was an aboriginal girl. Every primitive culture had its stories. Who knew what wild legends and foolish myths she had heard since birth?

"Nobody knows what happened to them," was his first, best answer.

Then, taking back the book, he added, "But we can surmise there was some sort of cataclysm. An abrupt change in climate, a catastrophe from the sky. Something enormous made every large animal extinct, emptying the world for the likes of you and me."

She seemed impressed by the glimpse of the apocalypse. Smiling at him, she set her mouth to say a word or two, perhaps inviting him back over to her side of the great down-filled bed. But then a sudden hard knock shook the room's only door.

Manmark called out, "Who is it?"

"Name's Barrow," said a rough male voice.

Barrow? Did he know that name?

"We spoke some weeks back," the stranger reported, speaking through the heavy oak. "I told you I was going out into the wash country, and you told me to be on the lookout—"

"Yes."

"For something special."

Half-dressed and nearly panicked, Manmark leaped up, unlocking the door while muttering, "Quiet, quiet."

Barrow stood in the hallway, a tall man who hadn't bathed in weeks or perhaps years. He was grimy and tired and poorly fed and mildly embarrassed when he saw the nearly naked woman sitting calmly on the edge of another man's bed. But then he seemed to recall what had brought him here. "You mentioned money," he said to Manmark. "A great deal of money, if a hunter found for you—"

"Yes."

"One or more of them—"

"Quiet," Manmark snapped.

"Eggs," whispered the unwashed fossil hunter.

And with that, Manmark pulled the dullard into the room, clamping a hand over his mouth before he could utter another careless word.

3

Once again, the world was dying.

Zephyr enjoyed that bleak thought while strolling beside the railroad station, passing downwind from the tall stacks of rancid hyrax skins. The skins were waiting for empty cars heading east—the remains of thousands of beasts killed by hunters and then cleaned with a sloppy professional haste. It was a brutal business, and doomed. In just this one year, the nearby herds had been decimated, and soon the northern and southern herds would feel the onslaught of long rifles and malevolent greed. The waste was appalling, what with most of the meat being left behind for the bear-dogs or to rot in the brutal summer sun. But like all great wastes, it would remake the world again. Into this emptiness, new creatures and peoples would come, filling the country overnight, and that new order would persist for a day or a million years before it too would collapse into ruin and despair.

Such were the lessons taught by history.

And science, in its own graceful fashion, reiterated those grand truths.

"Master Zephyr?"

An assistant had emerged from the railroad station, bearing important papers and an expression of weary tension. "Is it arranged?" Zephyr asked. Then, before the man could respond, he added, "I require a suitable car. For a shipment of this importance, my treasures deserve better than to be shoved beneath these bloody skins."

"I have done my best," the assistant promised.

"What is your best?"

"It will arrive in three days," the man replied, pulling a new paper to the top of the stack. "An armored car used to move payroll coins to the Westlands. As you requested, there's room for guards and your dragon scales, and your private car will ride behind it."

"And the dragons' teeth," Zephyr added. "And several dozen Claws of God."

"Yes, sir."

"And four dragon spleens."

"Of course, sir. Yes."

Each of those metallic organs was worth a fortune, even though none were in good condition. Each had already been purchased. Two were owned by important concerns in the Eastlands. The other two were bound for the Great Continent, purchased by wealthy men who lived along the Dragon River: the same crowded green country where, sixty years ago, Zephyr began his life.

The spleens were full of magic, some professed. Others looked on the relics as oddities, beautiful and precious. But a growing number considered them to be worthy of scientific study—which was why one of the Eastland universities was paying Zephyr a considerable sum for a half-crushed spleen, wanting their chance to study its metabolic purpose and its possible uses in the modern world.

Like his father and his grandfather, Zephyr was a trader who dealt exclusively in the remains of dragons. For generations, perhaps since the beginning of civilized life, the occasional scale and rare claws were much in demand, both as objects of veneration as well as tools of war. Even today, modern munitions couldn't punch their way through a quality scale pulled from the back of a large dragon. In the recent wars, soldiers were given suits built of dragon armor—fantastically expensive uniforms intended only for the most elite units—while their enemies had used dragon teeth and claws fired by special guns, trying to kill the dragon men who were marching across the wastelands toward them.

Modern armies were much wealthier than the ancient civilizations. As a consequence, this humble son of a simple trader, by selling to both sides during the long civil war, had made himself into a financial force.

The fighting was finished, at least for today. But every government in the world continued to dream of war, and their stockpiles continued to grow, and as young scientists learned more about these lost times, the intrigue surrounding these beasts could only increase.

"This is good enough," Zephyr told his assistant, handing back the railroad's contract.

"I'll confirm the other details," the man promised, backing away in a pose of total submission. "By telegraph, I'll check on the car's progress, and I will interview the local men, looking for worthy guards."

And Zephyr would do the same. But surreptitiously, just to reassure an old man that every detail was seen to.

Because a successful enterprise had details at its heart, the old man reminded himself. Just as different details, if left unnoticed, would surely bring defeat to the sloppy and the unfortunate.

Zephyr occupied a spacious house built on the edge of the workers' camp—the finest home in this exceptionally young town but relegated to this less desirable ground because, much as everyone who lived in the camp, its owner belonged to a questionable race. Passing through the front door, the white-haired gentleman paused a moment to enjoy the door's etched glass, and in particular the ornate dragons captured in the midst of life, all sporting wings and fanciful breaths of fire. With a light touch, the trader felt the whitish eye of one dragon. Then, with a tense, disapproving voice, the waiting manservant announced, "Sir, you have a visitor."

Zephyr glanced into the parlor, seeing no one.

"I made her wait in the root cellar," the servant replied. "I didn't know where else to place her."

"Who is she?" the old man inquired. And when he heard the name, he said, "Bring her to me. Now."

"A woman like that?" the man muttered in disbelief.

"As your last duty to me, yes. Bring her to the parlor, collect two more weeks of wages, and then pack your belongings and leave my company." With an angry finger, he added, "Your morals should have been left packed and out of sight. Consider this fair warning should you ever find employment again."

Zephyr could sound frightfully angry, if it suited him.

He walked into the parlor, sat on an overstuffed chair, and waited. A few moments later, the young aboriginal woman strolled into the parlor, investing a moment to look at the furnishings and ivory statues. Then she said, "I learned something."

"I assumed as much."

"Like you guessed, it's the barbarian with all the money." She smiled, perhaps thinking of the money. "He's promised huge payoffs to the dragon hunters, and maybe that's why this one hunter brought him word of a big discovery."

"Where is this discovery? Did you hear?"

"No."

"Does this hunter have a name?"

"Barrow."

Unless Barrow was an idiot or a genius, he would have already applied for dig rights, and they would be included in any public record. It would be a simple matter to bribe the clerk—

"There's eggs," she blurted.

Zephyr was not a man easily startled. But it took him a moment to repeat the word, "Eggs." Then he asked, "More than one egg, you mean?"

"Three, and maybe more."

"What sort of dragon is it?"

"Winged."

"A Sky-Demon?" he said with considerable hope.

"From what they said in front of me, I'm sure of it. He has uncovered the complete body of a Sky-Demon, and she died in the final stages of pregnancy." The girl smiled as she spoke, pleased with everything that had happened. "He didn't realize I understood the importance of things, or even that I was listening. That Manmark fellow... he is such a boring, self-important prick—"

"One last question," Zephyr interrupted. "What color were these eggs? Was that mentioned?"

The girl nodded and looked about the room again. Then, picking up a game cube carved from the whitest hyrax ivory, she said, "Like this, they were. They are. Perfectly, perfectly preserved."

4

Manmark was an endless talker, and most of his talk was senseless noise. Barrow treated the noise as just another kind of wind, taking no pleasure from it, nor feeling any insult. To be mannerly, he would nod on occasion and make some tiny comment that could mean anything, and, bolstered by this gesture, Manmark would press on, explaining how it was to grow up wealthy in the Old World, or why bear-dogs were the most foul creatures, or why the world danced around the sun, or how it felt to be a genius on that same world—a grand, deep, wondrous mind surrounded by millions of fools.

It was amazing what a man would endure, particularly if he had been promised a heavy pile of platinum coins.

There were five other men working with them. Four were youngsters—students of some type brought along to do the delicate digging. While the fifth fellow served as their protector, armed with a sleek modern rifle and enough ammunition to kill a thousand men. Some months ago, before he left for the wilderness, Manmark had hired the man to be their protector, keeping him on salary for a day such as this. He was said to be some species of professional killer, which was a bit of a surprise. A few times in conversation, Barrow had wormed honest answers out of the fellow. His credentials were less spectacular than he made them out to be, and even more alarming, the man was extraordinarily scared of things that would never present a problem. Bear-dogs were a source of much consternation, even though Barrow never had trouble with the beasts. And then there were the aborigines; those normally peaceful people brought nightmares of their own. "What if they come on us while we sleep?" the protector would ask, his voice low and haunted. "I am just one person. I have to sleep. What if I wake to find one of those miserable bastards slicing open my throat?"

"They wouldn't," Barrow assured him. Then he laughed, adding, "They'll cut into your chest first, since they'll want to eat your heart."

That was a pure fiction—a grotesque rumor made real by a thousand cheap novels. But their protector seemed to know nothing about this country, his experience born from the novels and small-minded tales told in the slums and high-class restaurants left behind on the distant, unreachable coast.

In his own fashion, Manmark was just as innocent and naïve. But there were moments when what he knew proved to be not only interesting but also quite valuable.

During their second night camped beside the dragon, Manmark topped off his tall glass of fancy pink liquor, and then he glanced at the exposed head of the great beast, remarking, "Life was so different in those old times."

There was nothing interesting in that. But Barrow nodded, as expected, muttering a few bland agreements.

"The dragons were nothing like us," the man continued.

What could be more obvious? Barrow thought to himself.

"The biology of these monsters," said Manmark. Then he looked at Barrow, a wide grin flashing. "Do you know how they breathed?"

It was just the two of them sitting before the fire. The students, exhausted by their day's work, were tucked into their bedrolls, while the camp protector stood on a nearby ridge, scared of every darkness. "I know their lungs were peculiar affairs," Barrow allowed. "Just like their hearts, and their spleens—"

"Not just peculiar," Manmark interrupted. "Unique."

Barrow leaned closer.

"Like us, yes, they had a backbone. But it was not our backbone. There are important differences between the architectures—profound and telling differences. It is as if two separate spines had evolved along two separate but nearly parallel lineages."

The words made sense, to a point.

"North of here," said Manmark. "I have colleagues who have found ancient fossils set within a bed of fine black shale. Unlike most beds of that kind, the soft parts of the dead have been preserved along with their hard shells and teeth. Have you heard of this place? No? Well, its creatures expired long before the first dragon was born. The world was almost new, it was so long ago... and inside that beautiful black shale is a tiny wormlike creature that has the barest beginnings of a notochord. A spine. The first vertebrate, say some."

"Like us," Barrow realized.

"And lying beside that specimen is another. Very much the same, in its fashion. Wormlike and obscure. But in other ways, it is full of subtle, very beautiful differences."

"Different how?"

"Well, for instance… there is a minuscule speck of metal located in the center of its simple body."

"Like a dragon's spleen?"

"But simpler, and made of ordinary metals. Iron and copper and such." Manmark finished his drink and gazed into the fire. "This dragon's lungs were very different, of course. Instead of sucking in a breath and then exhaling it out the same way, she took the air through her nostrils, into the lungs and out through a rectal orifice. We don't know enough to be certain yet. But it seems reasonable to assume that our dragon did a much better job of wringing the oxygen out of her endless deep breath."

Barrow nodded, very much interested now.

"And then there's the famous spleen," Manmark continued. "Have you ever wondered why these beasts needed to collect precious metals? What possible advantage could they have lent to the beasts?"

"I've thought about it some," he confessed.

"Gold and platinum and sometimes silver," said Manmark. "They are precious to us because they are rare, yes. But also because they barely rust in the presence of oxygen, which is why they retain their lovely sheen. And for the newest industries of our world, these elements are increasingly valuable. Were you aware? They can serve as enzymatic surfaces for all kinds of impressive chemical reactions. Perhaps our lady dragon would mix her breath and blood inside the spleen's cavities, producing all kinds of spectacular products. Even fire, perhaps."

Barrow nodded as if he understood every word.

"One day, we'll decipher what happened inside these creatures. And I suspect that knowledge, when it arrives, will revolutionize our world."

"Someday, maybe," Barrow conceded.

"In the distant future, you think?" Manmark grinned and took a long drink from his mostly drained glass. "But not in our lives, surely. Is that what you are thinking?"

"Isn't that the truth?"

"The truth." The self-described genius stared into the campfire, his gold eyes full of greed and a wild hope. "This isn't well known. Outside of scientific circles, that is. But a few years ago, an immature egg was dug from the belly of a giant tree-eating dragon. Dead for perhaps a hundred million years, yet its color was still white. The oxygen that had fueled its parent had been kept away from the egg in death, and some kind of deep coma state had been achieved. Which is not too surprising. We know dragon eggs are exceptionally durable. It's perhaps a relic trait from those days when their ancestors laid their eggs in sloppy piles and buried them under dirt and then left the nest, sometimes for decades, waiting for the proper conditions. Since these creatures had a very different biochemistry from ours… a much superior physiology… they could afford to do such things—"

"What are you saying?" Barrow interrupted. "I'm sorry, I don't understand half your words."

"I'm saying that the dragons were exceptionally durable."

The dragon hunter glanced at the long, lovely skull and its cavernous eye sockets. "I have never heard this before. Is there some chance that those eggs over there… in that ground, after all of these years…?"

"Remember the immature egg that I mentioned?" Manmark was whispering, his voice a little sloppy and terribly pleased. "The egg from the tree-eater? Well, I have read the paper written about its dissection. A hundred times, I have read it. Diamond blades were used to cut through the shell, and despite everything that common and uncommon sense would tell you… yes, there was still fluid inside the egg, and a six-legged embryo that was dead but intact… dead, but that looked as if it had died only yesterday, its burial lasting just a little too long…"

5

Three eggs became four, and then five, and quite suddenly there were seven of the treasures set on a bed of clean straw, enjoying the temporary shade of a brown canvas tarp. It was a sight that dwarfed Manmark's great dreams, marvelous and lovely as they had been. Each egg was perfectly round, and each was the same size, their diameter equal to his forearm and extended hand. They were heavier than any bird egg would be, if a bird could lay such an enormous egg. But that was reasonable, since the thick white shell was woven partly from metal and strange compounds that were barely understood today—ceramics and odd proteins laid out in a painfully delicate pattern. The shell material itself contained enough mystery to make a great man famous. But Manmark could always imagine greater honors and even wilder successes, as he did now, touching the warm surface of the nearest egg, whispering to it, "Hello, you."

The students were standing together, waiting for orders. And behind them stood a freight wagon, its team of heavy camels ready to pull their precious cargo to town and the railhead.

Barrow was perched on the wagon's front end, leather reins held tight in both hands.

Manmark took notice of him, and for a moment he wondered why the man was staring off into the distance. What did he see from that vantage point? Looking in the same general direction, Manmark saw nothing. There was a slope of gray clay punctuated with a few clusters of yucca, and the crest of the little ridge formed a neat line dividing the rain-washed earth from the intense blue of the sky.

The dragon hunter was staring at nothing.

How peculiar.

Manmark felt a little uneasy, but for no clear reason. He turned to the students now, ready to order the wagon loaded. And then, too late by a long ways, he remembered that their very expensive security man had been walking that barren ridge, his long gun cradled in both arms, haunted eyes watching for trouble.

So where is my protector? Manmark asked himself.

An instant later, the clean crack of a bullet cut through the air, and one of the large camels decided to drop its head and then its massive body, settling with a strange urgency onto the hard pan of clay.

Manmark knelt down between the great eggs. Otherwise, he was too startled to react.

The students dropped low and stared at the sky.

Barrow remained on the wagon, yanking at the reins and braking with his left foot, telling the surviving three camels, "Hold. Stay. Hold now. Stay."

Something about that voice steadied Manmark. Something in the man's calmness allowed him to look up, shouting to Barrow, "What is this? What is happening?"

Next came the sound of hooves striking dirt—many hooves in common motion—and he turned the other way, seeing six… no, eight camels calmly walking down the long draw, each built to race, each wearing a small saddle as well as a man dressed in shapeless clothes and heavy masks.

Manmark's first thought was to deny that this was happening. Hadn't he taken a thousand precautions? Nobody should know the significance of this dig, which meant that this had to be some random bit of awful luck. These were raiders of some kind—simple thieves easily tricked. A few coins of debased gold would probably satisfy them. He started to calculate the proper figure, filling his head with nonsense until that moment when the lead rider lowered his fat rifle and fired.

A fountain of pulverized earth slapped Manmark in the face.

He backed away, stumbled and dropped onto his rump. Then in his panic, he began digging into his pockets, searching for the tiny pistol that he had carried from the Old World and never fired once.

"Don't," said a strong, calming voice.

Barrow's voice.

"Give them what they want," said the dragon hunter, speaking to him as he would to a nervous camel.

"I won't," Manmark sputtered. "They are mine!"

"No," Barrow said from high on the wagon. "They aren't yours anymore, if they ever were…"

The riders didn't speak, save to wave their weapons in the air, ordering him to back away from the eggs. Then each claimed a single white sphere, dismounting long enough to secure their prize inside a silk sling apparently woven for this single task.

The final pair of riders was dressed as the others, yet they were different. One was small in build, while the other moved like a healthy but definitely older man. Manmark stared at both of them, and with an expertise garnered from years of imagining flesh upon ancient bone, he made two good guesses about who was beneath all those clothes.

"Zephyr," he muttered.

How many candidates were there? In one little town, or even at this end of the territory, how many other men were there who could possibly appreciate the significance of this find?

"And you," he said to the whore, his voice tight and injured.

She hesitated, if only for a moment.

Through the slits about the eyes, Zephyr stared at his opponent, and then he made some decision, lifting a hand and glancing back at the lead rider. For what purpose? To order him shot, perhaps?

The next blast of a gun startled everyone. The riders. Zephyr. And Manmark too. The concussion cut through the air, and while the roar was still ringing in their ears, Barrow said, "If we want to start killing, I'll start with you. Whoever you are. Understand me, old man? Before they aim my way, I'll hit your head and then your heart."

Barrow was standing on the back of the wagon now, holding his own rifle against his shoulder.

"Hear me, stranger? The eggs are yours. Take them. And I'll give you your life in the deal. Is that good enough?"

"It is adequate," said the accented voice.

Under his breath, Manmark muttered grim curses. But he stood motionless while Zephyr claimed the last of his eggs, and he swallowed his rage while the riders turned and started back up the long draw, the final man riding backward in his saddle, ready to fire at anyone with a breath of courage.

Manmark had none.

When the thieves vanished, he collapsed, panting and sobbing in a shameless display.

Barrow leaped off the wagon and walked toward him.

The students were standing again, chattering among themselves. One and then another asked no one in particular, "Will we still get paid?"

All was lost, Manmark believed.

Then the dragon hunter knelt beside him, and with an almost amused voice, he said, "All right. Let's discuss my terms."

"Your what?"

"Terms," he repeated. Then he outright laughed, adding, "When I get these eggs back to you, what will you pay me?"

"But how can you recover them?"

"I don't know yet. But give me the right promises, and maybe I'll think of something."

Manmark was utterly confused. "What do you mean? If there are six of them, and if they defeated my security man… what hope do you have…?"

"I fought in the war," Barrow replied.

"A lot of men fought."

"Not many did the kind of fighting that I did," the dragon hunter replied. "And few of them fought half as well either."

Manmark stared at the hard dark eyes. Then, because he had no choice, none whatsoever, he blurted, "Yes. Whatever it costs. Yes!"

6

Here stood the best locomotive available on short notice—a soot-caked machine built of iron and fire, wet steam, and rhythmic noises not unlike the breathing of a great old beast. Since details mattered, Zephyr had hired workmen to paint dragon eyes on the front end and little red wings on its sides, and when the job wasn't done with the proper accuracy, he commissioned others to fix what was wrong. Two engineers stoked the fire, while a third sat on top of the tender, ready to spell whomever tired first. Behind the locomotive was the armored car hired to move spleens and scales—a wheeled fortress encased in steel and nearly empty, carrying nothing but seven white eggs and six mercenaries armed with enough munitions to hold off a regiment. And trailing behind was Zephyr's private car, luxurious and open in appearance, except for the small windowless room at the rear that served as a bath.

The original plan for the dragons' spleens was to travel east. But the eggs were too precious to risk losing among the barbarians. Which was why Zephyr ordered his little train to head for the mountains and the Westlands beyond. A telegraph message dressed in code had been sent ahead. By the time he arrived at the Great Bay, a steamer would be waiting, ready to carry him back to the land of fables and childhood memories.

"I haven't been home for years," he confessed to his companion.

The young woman smiled at him, and once again, she said, "Thank you for taking me."

"It was the very least I could do," Zephyr allowed. "You were wise to ask, in fact. If Manmark realized you were responsible—"

"And for this," she interrupted, letting her fat coin purse jingle in an agreeable fashion.

"You have earned every mark. For what you have done to help me, madam, I will always be in your gratitude…"

There was only one set of tracks, with the occasional sidings and rules of conduct between oncoming trains. But Zephyr had sprinkled the world before them with bribes, and for the time being, there might as well be no other train in the world. As they picked up speed—as the engine quickened its breathing and its pace—he looked through the thick window glass, watching a hand-painted sign pass on their right. "You are leaving Summer Gulch," he read. "The fastest growing city between here and there."

What an odd, interesting thing to write. Zephyr laughed for a moment, and again mentioned, "I haven't been home since I was a young man."

"I'd love to see the Great Continent," the aboriginal girl reported.

What would become of this creature? Zephyr was of several minds on the subject, but his happy mood steered him to the more benevolent courses.

She slipped her purse out of sight.

"Do you know why we call it the Dragon River?" he asked.

"I don't," she replied.

Somehow he doubted that. But a prostitute makes her living by listening as much as anything, and this old man could do little else but talk with her, at least for the moment. "Of course there are some substantial beds of fossils along the river's course, yes. Dragon bones and claws and the great scales are part of my people's history. And we are an ancient nation, you know. The oldest in the world, perhaps. From the beginning, our gods have been dragons and our emperors have been their earthly sons and daughters."

The woman had bright, jade-colored eyes and a pleasant, luring smile.

"My favorite story, true or not, is about a young emperor from the Fifth Dynasty." Zephyr allowed his eyes to gaze off to the north, looking at the broken, rain-ripped country. "He found a flying dragon, it is said. The bones and scales were intact, as was her heart and spleen. And behind her spleen were eggs. At least two eggs, it is said. Some accounts mention as many as six, but only two of her offspring were viable. After three weeks of sitting above the ground, in the warming sun—and I should add, because the emperor was a very good man—the eggs finally hatched. Two baby dragons slithered into the world. Brothers, they were, and they belonged to him.

"The emperor had always been cared for by others. But he made a wise decision. He refused to let others care for his new friends, raising them himself, with his own hands. A mistake took one of those hands from him, but that was a minor loss. He refused to let his guards kill the offending dragon. And for his kindness, the dragon and its brother loved the emperor for all of his days."

Zephyr paused for a moment, considering his next words.

"It was a weak time for my great nation," he reported. "Barbarians were roaming the steppe and mountains, and peoples from the sea were raiding the coasts. But it is said—by many voices, not just those of my people—that a one-handed emperor appeared in the skies, riding the winged monsters. They were huge beasts, swift and strange. They breathed a strange fire, and they were powerful, and they had to eat a thousand enemy soldiers every day just to feed their endless hunger. An unlikely, mythic detail, I always believed. Except now, when I read scientific papers about the biology of dragons, I can see where they must have had prodigious appetites."

The woman nodded, listening to every word.

"As a skeptical boy, I doubted the story about the emperor's warrior dragons. Great men didn't need monsters to save their nation, I believed. But I was wrong. I realized my error some time ago. Two monsters could save my people then, and think what seven dragons could do today… particularly if several of them are female, and fertile, and agreeable to mating with their brothers…"

The young woman gave a little shrug, saying nothing for a long moment.

The train continued to churn toward the west, the locomotive sounding steady and unstoppable.

"We have a story," she muttered. "My people do, I mean."

"About the dragons? Yes, I suppose you do."

"Since I was old enough to listen, I heard how the world holds thousands of dragons in its chest, and from time to time, for reasons known only to the gods, one of them is released. Which makes sense, I suppose. If what everyone tells me is true, and their eggs can sleep for an eternity in the ground."

Even from a single fertile female, only one egg at a time would be exposed by erosion. Yes, it was a reasonable explanation.

"The freed dragons die of loneliness, always." She spoke those words with sadness, as if she knew something about that particular pain. "They kill and burn because of their longing for others like themselves, and then they fly too high in order to end their own miserable lives, and that is why the dragons cannot come back into this world."

"This is a very common story," Zephyr assured her. "Maybe every place in the world tells fables much like that."

"But there is more to my story," she said, her tone defensive.

"Is there?"

"Much more," she promised.

Neither of them spoke for a long moment. The young woman didn't want to say anything else, and Zephyr wasn't in the mood to let another people's legends distract him. He looked out another window, toward the empty south, and then from somewhere up ahead came a dull *whump* as a heavy block of dynamite detonated. Instantly, the brakes were applied, and the little train started to shake and shiver, fighting its momentum to remain on the suddenly unstable tracks.

The young woman was thrown from her seat, as was Zephyr.

He stood first and heard the early shots coming from inside the armored car. Again he looked to the south, seeing nothing, and then he hunkered down and looked in the other direction. A solitary figure was approaching on foot, armed with a rifle that he hadn't bothered to fire. He was marching steadily across the stunted grasses, allowing the mercenaries to fire at him. And while most of their bullets struck, each impact made only sparks and a high-pitched snap that seemed to accomplish nothing. Because the attacker was wearing a suit made from overlapping dragon scales, Zephyr realized. And with an impressive eye for detail, the man had gone to the trouble of stretching cloth between his arms and chest, as if he had wings, while on his masked face were painted the large, malevolent eyes of an exceptionally angry dragon.

7

This was what Barrow did during the war. With a platoon of picked soldiers, he would squeeze into his costume and pick up a gun that was always too heavy to carry more than a few steps, and after swallowing his fears as well as his common sense, he and his brethren would walk straight at the enemy, letting them shoot at will, waiting to reach a point where he could murder every idiot who hadn't yet found reason enough to run away.

This was the war all over again, and he hated it.

His suit wasn't as good as the one he wore in the war. Manmark's students were experts at arranging the scales and fixing them to his clothes—a consequence of spending weeks and years assembling old bones—but there hadn't been enough time to do a proper, permanent job. The scales were tilted in order to guide the bullets to one side or the other, but they weren't always tilted enough. Every impact caused a bruise. One and then another blow to the chest seemed to break a rib or two, and Barrow found himself staggering now, the weight of his clothes and his own fatigue making him wish for an end to his suffering.

That old platoon had been a mostly invincible bunch, but by the war's end, those who hadn't died from lucky shots and cannon fire were pretty much crazy with fear. Barrow was one of the few exceptions—a consequence of getting hit less often and doing a better job of killing those who wanted him dead.

Through the narrow slits of his mask, he stared at the firing ports built into the armored car. Then he paused, knelt, and with a care enforced by hours of practice, he leveled his weapon and put a fat slug of lead into one man's face.

Two more rounds hit Barrow, square in the chest and on the scalp.

He staggered, breathed hard enough to make himself lightheaded, and then aimed and fired again, killing no one but leaving someone behind the steel screaming in misery.

The surviving men finally got smart. One would cry out, and all would fire together, in a single volley.

Barrow was shoved back off his feet.

Again, there was a shout followed by the blow of a great hammer.

They would break every bone inside his bruised body if this continued. Barrow saw his doom and still could not make his body rise off the dusty earth. How had he come to this awful place? He couldn't remember. He sat upright, waiting for the next misery to find him… but a new voice was shouting, followed by the odd, high-pitched report of a very different gun.

The dirt before him rose up in a fountain and drifted away, and left lying between his legs was a single purple Claw of God.

Damn, somebody had a dragon-buster gun.

If he remained here, he would die. Reflexes and simple panic pushed Barrow up onto his feet, and on exhausted legs he ran, trying to count the seconds while he imagined somebody working with the breech of that huge, awful gun, inserting another expensive charge before sealing it up and aiming at him again.

When Barrow thought it was time, he abruptly changed direction.

The next claw screamed through the air, peeling off to the right.

Three engineers were cowering on the dragon-eyed locomotive. Plainly, they hadn't come here expecting to fight. Barrow pointed his rifle at each of their faces, just for a moment, and then they leaped down together and started running back toward town.

The men inside the armored car fired again. But Barrow kept close to the tender, giving them no easy shots. A few steps short of them, he reached behind his back, removing a satchel that he had carried from the beginning, out of sight, and he unwrapped the fuse and laid it on the ground, shooting it at pointblank range to set it on fire. Then he bent low and threw the satchel with his free arm, skipping it under the car before he stepped back a little ways, letting the guards see him standing in front of them with barely a care.

"There's enough dynamite under you now to throw that car up high and break it into twenty pieces," he promised. Then he added, "It's a long fuse. But I wouldn't spend too much time thinking before you decide to do what's smart."

An instant later, the main door was unlocked and unlatched. Five men came tumbling out into the open, one of them bleeding from the shoulder and none of them armed.

"Run," Barrow advised.

The mercenaries started chasing the train crew down the iron rails.

The fuse continued to burn, reaching the canvas satchel and sputtering for a few moments before it died away.

Barrow stared into the windowless car. The seven eggs were set inside seven oak crates, and he didn't look at any of them. He was staring at the man whom he had shot through the face, his mind thinking one way about it, then another.

A breech closed somewhere nearby, and a big hammer was cocked.

Barrow turned too late, eyes focusing first on the cavernous barrel of the gun and then on the old foreign man who was fighting to hold it up. At this range, with any kind of dragon-round, death was certain. But Barrow's sense of things told him that if he didn't lift his own weapon, the man would hesitate. And another moment or two of life seemed like reason enough to do nothing.

"I am a creature of foresight," Zephyr remarked.

"You're smarter than me," agreed Barrow.

"Details," the old man muttered, two fingers wrapped around the long brass trigger. "The world is built upon tiny but critical details."

Behind him stood one detail—a rather pretty detail, just as Barrow had recalled—and using a purse full of heavy gold, she struck Zephyr on the top of his skull, and the long barrel dropped as the gun discharged, and a Claw of God came spinning out, burying itself once again inside the ancient Earth.

8

Manmark had the freight wagon brought out of the draw, and he used a whip on the surviving camels, forcing them into a quick trot toward the motionless train. But there was a generous distance to be covered; open country afforded few safe places to hide. There was time to watch Barrow and the aboriginal girl with his binoculars, a little dose of worry nipping at him, and then Zephyr was awake again, sitting up and speaking at some length to the dragon hunter. All the while, Manmark's students were happily discussing their golden futures and what each planned to do with his little share of the fame. They spoke about the dragons soon to be born, and they discussed what kinds of cages would be required to hold the great beasts, and what would be a fair price for the public to see them, and what kinds of science could be done with these travelers from another age.

What was Zephyr saying to the dragon hunter?

Of course, the crafty old trader was trying to top Manmark's offers of wealth. And if he was successful? If Barrow abruptly changed sides...?

"Look at that cloud," one student mentioned.

Somewhere to the south, hooves were slapping at the ground, lifting the dust into a wind that was blowing north, obscuring what was most probably a small herd of hard-running hyraxes.

Manmark found the little pistol in his pocket, considering his options for a long moment.

If it came to it, would he have the courage?

Probably not, no. If these last days had taught Manmark anything, it was that he had no stomach for mayhem and murder.

He put the pistol back out of sight and again used the binoculars, the jumpy images showing that Zephyr had fallen silent for now and Barrow was gazing off to the south and all of the talking was being done by the prostitute who stood between the two men, arms swirling in the air as she spoke on and on.

The worry that he felt now was nebulous and terrible.

Again, Manmark struck the big camels with his whip, and he screamed at everyone, telling them, "We need to hurry. Hurry!"

But the wagon was massive and one camel short, and there was still a long, empty distance to cover. The curtain of dust was nearly upon the motionless train, and inside it were dozens, or perhaps hundreds of aboriginal men riding on the backs of the half-wild ponies that they preferred to ride—an entire tribe galloping toward the treasures that Manmark would never see again.

9

She spoke quietly, with force.

"My favorite fable of all promises that the dragons will come again to this world. They will rise up out of the Earth to claim what has always been theirs, and only those men and women who help them will be spared. All the other people of the world will be fought and killed and eaten. Only the chosen few will be allowed to live as they wish, protected beneath the great wings of the reawakened gods."

Zephyr rubbed his sore head, trying to focus his mind. But really, no amount of cleverness or any promise of money would help now. Even with a splitting headache, he understood that inescapable lesson.

Speaking to the man wearing dragon scales, she said, "Your ugly people came into my country and stole everything of worth. You gave us disease and drink, and you are murdering our herds. But now I intend to destroy everything you have built here, and my children will take back all the lands between the seas."

She was a clever, brutal girl, Zephyr decided. And she had done a masterful job of fooling everyone, including him.

Barrow turned and stared at the oncoming riders. He had pulled off his armored mask, but he was still breathing hard, winded by his fight and terrified. He might defeat half a dozen mercenaries, if he was lucky. But not a nation of wild men and women armed with rifles and a communal rage.

"You need me," he muttered.

The young woman didn't respond. It was Zephyr who said, "What do you mean? Who needs you?"

"She does," Barrow announced. Then he pointed at the riders, adding, "If they want to help themselves, they should accept my help."

The woman laughed and asked, "Why?"

"When I was a boy," said Barrow, "I kept baby birds. And I learned that my little friends would take my food and my love best if I wore a sock on my hand, painting it to resemble their lost mothers and fathers."

The rumbling of hooves grew louder, nearer.

"I'm a big man in this big costume," he remarked. "This costume is bigger than anything any of your people can wear, I would think. And I'm brave enough to do stupid things. And you will have seven dragons to care for now… to feed and protect, and to train, if you can… and wouldn't you like to take along somebody who's willing to risk everything on a daily basis…?"

Zephyr laughed quietly now.

Clearly, this Barrow fellow was at least as surprising as the young woman, and maybe twice as bold.

The woman stared at the man dressed as a dragon, a look of interest slowly breaking across her face.

Zephyr had to laugh louder now.

Dust drifted across the scene, thick and soft, muting the sound of their voices. And then the woman turned to her people, shouting to be heard.

"I have dragons to give you!" she called out.

"Eight, as it happens! Eight dragons to build a new world…!"

BERLIN

Charles de Lint

Charles de Lint was born in The Netherlands but has lived most of his life around the city of Ottawa, Ontario. He sold his first stories in the late 1970s, and became a full-time writer in 1983. His many books include *Moonheart*, winner of the first Crawford Fantasy Award, and first in the popular series revolving around the imaginary city of Newford, which includes collections *Moonlight and Vines*, *Tapping the Dream Tree*, and *Muse and Reverie*, and novels *Memory & Dream*, *Trader*, *Someplace to be Flying*, *Forests of the Heart*, *The Onion Girl*, *Spirit in the Wires* and *Widdershins*.

De Lint's writing is often labelled "urban" or "contemporary" fantasy, and is credited with helping to make the subgenre popular, though he has written high fantasy in *The Riddle of the Wren* and others, and has published horror beginning with *Mulengro*. A fifteen-time World Fantasy Award finalist, he won in 2000 for *Moonlight and Vines*. De Lint's most recent novel is *The Mystery of Grace*, and coming up is a new collection, *The Best of Charles de Lint*.

Fifty years from now, Elfland came back.

It stuck a finger into a large city, creating a borderland between our world and that glittering realm with its elves and magic. As the years went by the two worlds remained separate, co-existing only in that place where magic and reality overlap. A place called Bordertown.

> *Offering dragons quarter is no good,*
> *they regrow all their parts & come on again,*
> *they have to be killed.*
>
> - John Berryman

ONE

Long after midnight and there was no escape.

Three Bloods caught Nicky in the free flophouse he ran for the Diggers down in Tintown—that part of Soho to which the hobos tended to gravitate. They had silver Mohawks shot through with orange and black streaks, ice stones glittering in their ears, black leathers. The two males held Nicky on the floor while the third took a small metal container from her pocket. She held it in front of Nicky's face and gave it a gentle shake.

Shucka-shuck.

"Got something for you, Nicky," she said. Her thin-lipped smile never reached her eyes.

Nicky struggled in his captors' grip, then froze when a new shadow filled the doorway of the room. A tall Blood stood there, but he wasn't a punk. His long silver hair fell to his shoulders and his clothes were pure elvin cut, made from some sleek and glimmering material that there was no name for this side of the border. A High Born. Not a Bordertowner, but straight out of glittering Elfland. He took a step into the room.

Nicky's blood went cold when the candlelight picked out the tall Blood's features.

It was Long Lankin, the murdering knight. Nicky had only seen him once before when Tam Sharper pointed out the High Born to him at an outdoor concert in Fare-you-well Park. There was something in the Blood's hawk-like features and cold eyes that would never let you forget him, once you'd seen him.

Shucka-shuck.

Nicky's gaze flickered back to the woman and the container she held.

"There's a new kind of pearl in town, Nicky-boy," she said.

Her name was Ysa Cran and she ran a gang of Blood pushers who could provide you with whatever you wanted—smoke, fairy dust, coke, pearl, they had it all.

"I don't…." Nicky began.

"Oh, everyone knows," Ysa said. "Nicky broke his habit. Nicky dropped the pearl. Nicky's a fucking saint."

She popped open the little metal container and shook its contents into the palm of her hand. Pink and mauve flakes glittered in the candlelight.

"See, it's something new," Ysa said. "Not quite pearl, but not quite anything else either. Straight from Elfland, Nicky-boy. And it's going to be good for business, you know? The business you're taking away from me, you and the Diggers, trying to clean up everybody's act. It's called shake, Nicky-boy, and its going to be all over the streets in a few weeks. We're doing, like, a test run tonight. And you know what's really fine about this?"

Nicky swallowed thickly, but made no reply.

"It's one hundred percent addictive, Nicky-boy." This time the smile reached Ysa's eyes. "You just gotta try it and you're hooked. And that's the secret of this biz, Nicky-boy. Repeat customers." She gave the Bloods holding him a nod. "Open his mouth."

"N-nuh—"

The Bloods had Nicky's mouth open before he could spit out a word. He struggled frantically in their grip, but they were too strong for him.

"You can smoke it," Ysa said conversationally. "You can powder it up and snort it like pearl. You can swallow it. You can stick it up your ass, Nicky-boy. Any way you take it, it's a straight mainline back to that place you left behind when you dropped the pearl. Remember, Nicky-boy? Remember how it felt to be on top of the world, fucking-A?"

There were tears in Nicky's eyes as she cupped her hand and funneled the shake into his mouth. He gagged, trying to spit it out, but she rubbed his throat with smooth cool fingers and he swallowed reflexively.

"You can let him go now," she told her companions.

The two Bloods dropped his arms and Nicky sprang to his feet, lunging for her. She batted him casually aside and he skidded across the floor. Her companions moved towards him, but she shook her head.

"He's flying now," she said.

And it was true. Nicky lay where he'd fallen. From behind them, Long Lankin stepped over to the boy and rolled him over with a shiny black boot. Nicky's eyes were glazed. Spittle trickled from a corner of his mouth.

"You see, Corwyn?" Ysa said. "You feed this shit to a townie and they're gone before it's halfway down their throat."

Long Lankin nodded. "And the most amusing thing is that they will actually pay to have this done to them."

Nicky lay staring up at them, trying to focus, trying to get up, but he was long gone. Flying high. Fucking-A.

"Well?" Ysa asked the High Born. "Do we get the contract or what?"

Long Lankin nodded. "Exclusive—for three months. The first shipment will be delivered by the end of the week."

Ysa tried not to let her satisfaction show. "Sounds good."

"But finish up here first," Long Lankin said. He gave Nicky a last look, a vague smile flickering in his silver eyes, then he turned and left the room.

The Bloods waited till they could see him on the street below, walking away from the building, before they really let loose with some whoops.

"All *right*!" Nabber shouted. "Ysa—you've got the balls, that's all I can say."

Teddy Grim nodded. "Dealing with Lankin—that's like dicing with the dragons, man. But, hot shit, you pulled it off!"

Ysa just grinned. She screwed the top back on the little container of sample shake and knelt down beside Nicky.

Shucka-shuck.

"How's it going, Nicky-boy? You met God yet?"

She ran the long nails of one hand down his cheek. Silver nail polish glittered in the candlelight.

Nicky stared up at her, eyes focused now, but blurred with tears. The shake was burning through him—it was good, oh Jesus, it was so good. But there was a part of him that remembered. He'd been a junkie with nothing going for him till the Diggers pulled him back. He'd gone through hell breaking the hold the pearl had on him. Vomiting his guts, day after day. Cramps and seizures. Shaking. Headaches sharp as amps feeding back at full volume....

And then he was clean.

Two years he was clean. Two years he worked helping others through that hell. Helped the Diggers clothe and feed the hobos and runaways, the lost and the lonely. Helped talk down the junkies, dry out the alkies. Helped the people who were going to throw it all away because they were hurting, or burnt out, or the hundred other reasons that people could find to kill themselves. And now....

He could hear Ysa's voice, though she wasn't speaking.

There's a new kind of pearl in town....

Oh yeah. Didn't he know it? The shake was riding through his body like an old friend. He could feel the pearl glow, and behind it, kicking in every few seconds, speedy little rushes that made him feel like he was coming. Flying high. Long gone.

One hundred percent addictive....

He couldn't do it again. He couldn't go through it again. He'd already been to hell. He couldn't go back. He....

Shucka-shuck.

Ysa shook the container, a mocking glitter in her silver Blood eyes.

"Here, Nicky-boy," she said, and she stuffed the shake container into his pocket. "You're going to be needing this."

She stood up. Nicky couldn't take his eyes from her. Goddamn Bloods. She looked so good. Goddamn Bloods. One like Ysa Cran could seduce you just by looking at you. He hated her. He wanted her.

She could see it all in his eyes and all it did was make her laugh. "I don't fuck junkies," she told him. "I just fuck 'em around, Nicky-boy."

Nicky lunged up to a sitting position. The room spun, the candlelight turning into a kaleidoscope of pulsating colours, before everything settled down. Teddy Grim moved towards him, but Ysa waved him off.

"Nicky-boy's not going to hurt nobody," she said. "Are you Nicky-boy?"

Nicky struggled to his feet and stood swaying on a floor that breathed slightly, in a room that strobed with colour. The Bloods were brilliant flares of black and silver and orange.

One hundred percent addictive....

Cold turkey.

He couldn't do it again. No one could do it again. He staggered across the room towards the window.

"Hey, Ysa," Nabber began. "Maybe we'd better—"

He and Teddy Grim started to move towards Nicky, but before they could cross the room, Nicky threw himself at the window.

The glass shattered. It sounded like bells. The shards that cut him didn't really hurt. They were just opening his body so that his blood could breathe. Wind was rushing by his ears. Everything was moving so fast. The whole world was moving. The ground was waiting to embrace him. It'd keep him safe from Ysa and Long Lankin and from the hell that'd be his if he tried to drop the pearl again....

Falling was a speed rush and slow motion, all at the same time. When he hit the ground he had one stunned moment of shocked realization. I'm dea—

And then everything was gone.

"Hol-ee fuck," Nabber said.

The three Bloods looked out the window. It was a three story drop to the street below. Nicky's small body lay in a twist of strange angles.

"Come on," Ysa said finally. "Let's burn this place down. The Diggers are going to have to realize that they're out of the helping people business. People get helped, they're worth shit to us, right?"

Her companions nodded.

"So let's do it."

Later, out on the street, while the Diggers' free flophouse went up in flames, Ysa stood over Nicky's broken body. Hobos and runaways were shuffling and staggering around them, milling in a panic while the building burned. Grey smoke rose up to meet the lightening skies of the coming dawn. Ysa took a flat piece of lacquered wood from her pocket and glanced at the dragon embossed on it, black against red, before flipping it onto Nicky's body. Teddy Grim gave her a questioning look.

"Maybe they'll think one of Dragontown's tongs did him in," she said.

Teddy Grim, and then Nabber, smiled in appreciation. Laughing, they headed for the club district and one last round of brews.

TWO

There were just the two of them now.

Everyone else had crashed by the time a grey dawn came crawling in over Soho. They sat on the rambling front porch of the Diggers' House—the main house that sits in a rubbled lot equidistant from the Canal and Soho's club district, just a spit away from New Asia. Two of them, still following where the music led them. Up all night, playing the blues.

Berlin had a vintage Martin New Yorker six-string. Its tiny body fit comfortably in the curved hollow between her lap and breasts, while the neck was wide enough so that her fingers didn't get tangled, but not so wide that her small hands couldn't shape the chords. She was playing an easy-going G progression, violet eyes closed, head bobbing just slightly to the rhythm. Her hair was thick—a dark brown with green tints—and pulled back from her face with a pink scarf that made it stand up around her head like a halo.

Well, if the good die young
I said, the good die young

She was singing, her voice surprisingly gruff and deep for her small frame and nineteen or so years. Joe Doh-dee-oh was accompanying her on the harmonica, leaning back against the porch railing across from her, a smile in his dark eyes.

He looked to be in his late seventies, an old black man playing the blues. He wore a checkered shirt and faded jeans held up with bright red suspenders. His hair was a salty white, his brown wrinkled skin was a road-map of all the tunes he'd played through the years. He knew them all, and a few more besides.

Now if the good die young
Then I gotta be just as wicked as they come
—uh-huh
I gotta be
Just as wicked as they come

He sang along on the last line, then brought the harmonica back up to his mouth, chording on it while Berlin's fingers did a walking riff up the neck of her guitar. By the time Berlin hit the final G chord, a double bar at the tenth fret, Joe was wailing a long finishing note.

"Whoo-ee," he said, cradling his harmonica on his lap. "That's an old one."

Berlin grinned. "Learned that from Poppa Lightnin'—could that man play."

Joe didn't say anything for a moment. Poppa Lightnin' had died a long time ago—in the World beyond Bordertown—maybe only a decade or so after the Change. He gave her a curious look.

"He made some good records," Joe said finally.

"I suppose he did. Hey, remember this?" She broke into a version of "Cold, Cold Feeling".

"Know it? I coulda wrote it," Joe told her. "I've been there, Berlin. Makes for a good song, but you don't much care for it when it's going down."

He brought up his harmonica, but before he could join in, Berlin laid her hands across her guitar's strings. In the sudden silence, they could hear the creak of wooden wheels.

"Brandy's up early," Joe said.

Berlin nodded. "Too early. I got a bad feeling, Joe...."

They held off playing as Brandy Jack came walking around the side of the house. He walked with a shuffling limp, an old skinny hobo in battered hand-me-downs, hair as white as Joe's, but looking washed-out against his pale skin. Beside him a big mongrel pulled a small wagon that held all of Brandy's worldly possessions. Tin cans and found things; magazines, a couple of old Reader's Digest books and a lot of paperbacks with the front covers torn off; rags and mismatched clothing, a lot of it too big or too small for him; a broken harmonium and a ukulele that still worked; a bit of everything to reflect the varying aspects of his fifty-five some years.

The dog was called Noz and he had a small beanie on his head with a propeller that still turned. Berlin hoped that Brandy had just heard their music and come to play a few of his old Music Hall songs.

"Hey, Jack," Joe called. "Glad you're back."

Brandy shook his head mournfully. Even on the sunniest day he wore a hang-dog expression.

"Dig out your old uke there, Brandy," Berlin said, "and sing us a couple."

Brandy shuffled to a halt when he was at the foot of the steps going up to the porch. Noz sat down in his harness, his short tail thumping the dirt.

"Seen the sky?" Brandy asked.

Berlin and Joe looked up. It was growing steadily lighter, but the dismal grey was here for the day.

"Over there," Brandy said, pointing west. "Something's burning in Tintown. Something big."

"Burning…?" Joe began.

Berlin hopped over the rail and landed lightly on the ground, backing up until the house no longer hid her view of the western skies.

"Shit," she said.

"What's up, Berlin?" Joe asked.

"Shit!"

She ran up the stairs, disappearing inside the house. Moments later she was outside once more, a jean jacket thrown on over her faded T-shirt, her jeans tucked into a pair of black leather boots. A knife hung sheathed under each armpit, under the jacket.

"That's one of our places that's burning," she told Joe as she wheeled a small battered scooter out of the shed that leaned up against the side of the house like a drunken companion too unsteady to stand.

Tugging a small spell-box free from one of the jean jacket's many inner pockets, she inserted it into the scooter and turned the engine over. The starting motor ground a couple of times, then the machine coughed into life.

"What do you want us to do, Berlin?" Joe asked, joining Brandy at the bottom of the stairs.

"Wake Hooter. Keep a watch on the place."

"What about the rounds?"

Berlin frowned. In another hour or so it'd be time to take out the big wagon and make the rounds of the restaurants to collect what freebie food they could get for the free supper the Diggers provided every night. It was Berlin's week to take the wagon out.

"If I'm not back in time, get Casey to take it out."

"Casey's not going to like that," Joe said. "She's always complaining that—"

Berlin just shook her head. Gunning the engine, she took off, the scooter's rear wheel spraying dirt behind it until she hit the pavement.

Joe looked at Brandy, then shrugged. "Guess Casey'll just have to complain some more," he said as he went back up the stairs.

There was a big vintage Harley parked in front of the burnt rubble of the Diggers' free flophouse in Tintown when Berlin arrived. She parked her scooter beside it, putting the little machine on its kickstand. A large ferret sat on the Harley's saddle, it's weasel-like body stretched out on the leather as it watched Berlin pocket her spell-box.

"How ya doing, Lubin?" she said and gave the ferret a pat before joining the tall black man who knelt by something at the front of the building.

The area was eerily quiet. There were usually a lot of hobos up and about by now, cooking coffee and what breakfast makings they had. Runaways hanging around—Soho Rats looking for a handout from those who weren't much better off than they were themselves, but still always seemed to make do. But Tintown was empty. The only smoke going up to the sky coming from the big ruined building.

"Christ," Berlin muttered. "What the…?"

Her voice trailed off as she reached the owner of the Harley and saw what he was kneeling beside.

"Oh, Jesus—Nicky!" She dropped to her knees in the dirt beside the limp broken body, tears welling up behind her eyes. She touched his cold cheek with a trembling hand, then turned away.

"Stick?" she asked softly, her gravelly voice huskier than ever.

"Easy, Berlin," he said. "There's nothing you can do."

He took her in his arms as she began to shake. Tears erupted, and Stick just held her close, letting them soak into his shirt. He stroked her hair until she finally pulled away, sitting back on her heels, violet eyes dark with pain.

"What happened?" she asked, her voice firmer now.

Stick sighed. He stood up and turned away, looking out over Tintown and beyond. His dreadlocks hung like fat fuzzy snakes down his back. When he turned back to look at her, his coffee-coloured skin was pulled tight across his face.

"I think Nicky took a jump," he said at last.

Berlin shook her head. "No way, Stick. He had everything going for him now. All that shit was so far behind him that—"

Stick silently handed over a small metal container.

"What's that?"

"I found it on him."

Berlin opened it up and shook some of the pink and mauve flakes into the palm of her hand. She licked a finger and went to touch it to the flakes, but Stick caught her hand.

"Bad idea."

"Well, what is it?"

"Looks like a kind of pearl, but there's something about it makes me nervous."

Berlin looked at the dope, then slowly funneled it back into the container.

"There's no way Nicky'd go back," she said.

Stick nodded. "That's what I thought. Found this lying on his chest."

He passed over a lacquered marker chip with a Dragontown chop on it—what some of the old folks used to use as a calling card. Berlin studied the black dragon against the red background and shook her head.

"I don't recognize the chop," she said.

"Neither do I—but it's definitely a calling card."

"One of the tongs?"

"Doubtful," Stick said. "It might be someone else trying to set it up to look like the tongs're involved."

"Bloods?"

"Hard to say at this point, Berlin."

Berlin stuck the marker in her back pocket. "Then I guess we'd better go about finding out."

"What about Nicky?"

"Nicky? I...."

When she looked back at that small broken body the tears wanted to come all over again.

Berlin swallowed hard. "Can you bring him to the House on your chopper?"

Stick nodded. "We can't go off half-cocked on this, Berlin."

Berlin looked from the smoldering rubble to Nicky.

"Fuck that," she said. "Somebody just declared war, Stick."

"Diggers don't go to war," Stick reminded her.

"But Berlin does," she said softly. "And maybe somebody forgot that."

Stick sighed. "And maybe that's just what they want you to do."

Berlin lifted her gaze from Nicky's body. "Thanks for being here, Stick."

Stick looked as though he had something more to add, then he just shook his head.

"Yeah," he said.

Gently he cradled Nicky's body in his arms and carried it back to his Harley. Balancing it on his gas tank, he followed Berlin's scooter back to the Diggers' House.

THREE

The Diggers go back a long way.

Most people who remember them think of 1967—Haight Ashbury in San Francisco, Yorkville in Toronto. The Summer of Love. Be-ins and Love-ins. Free music in the parks. The Diggers ran houses that provided free shelter, food, medical advice and counseling for the kids who had dropped out, but had nowhere to go, no one else to turn to.

The original Diggers date back to 1649, in England. They were a radical offshoot of the Levellers—the extreme left wing of Oliver Cromwell's army. Christian communists, they didn't believe in private property and were contemptuously called "the Diggers" when they tried to communally farm some poor unused land in St. George's Hill, Surrey. Forcibly removed, it took over three hundred years for their name and hopes to be revived in the sixties.

Since then they have resurfaced from time to time—most notably during the food riots in New York City at the beginning of the twenty-first century. More recently they appeared in Bordertown, answering an unspoken need as the city's population continued to swell with a constant influx of runaways and down-and-outers escaping the World and its ever-increasing capitalistic concerns.

Berlin thought of all that as they buried Nicky in the graveyard behind the Diggers' House. A different kind of digging. Instead of scruffing about, looking for handouts to feed their charges, and buildings to bed them in, they were planting one of their own. Digging in the dirt. The world's common treasury that was more abused every year. But that was what happened when people thought they could own land. The world's most successful cultures, at least in an ethical sense, had always been those that understood that the land was only theirs on loan.

She was the last to leave when the short non-denominational service was over. Stick gave her some time on her own by the graveside, then returned from the House where he'd been talking with a couple of the other Diggers.

"I didn't know him too well," he said after awhile.

"I did."

"How'd you meet?"

"I was the one that brought him in—talked him down, saw him through the first rough weeks when he was dropping the pearl. I never thought he'd...." Stick touched her shoulder, but she shook her head. "I'm okay. I'm all cried out, Stick. Now I just want to find the fucker who did this to him."

Hooter was the Diggers' current medic. When they brought Nicky's body back to the House, it had only taken him a few moments to find the tell-tale flaring in the dead boy's pupils. Nicky hadn't ODed, but he'd definitely been pearl diving when he died.

"Sometimes they just go back to it," Stick said quietly. "It's not nice and it's not pretty, Berlin, but it happens."

"I know. And I know the kind it happens to. Nicky wasn't like that. By the time he was finally clean, Stick, all he could feel was relief. He was the best we had to handle anyone who was making the break for themselves. He *hated* dope—any kind of it. Believe me."

Stick looked down at the raw earth of the grave and sighed. "Okay. I'm going to do some poking around—see what I can come up with. Can you be cool till then?"

Berlin shook her head. "*I'm* tracking them down, Stick."

"Bad move."

She turned to face him, eyes dark with anger. "You're treating me like a kid and I don't like it."

"Think of what you're about to do. The Diggers are tolerated at best, but only because they don't get political. They don't get involved. They're not aggressive. You start shoving your weight around, Berlin, you're just going to make things worse. You want your food sources cut off in Dragontown? You want some Blood gangs or Packers to come down on you and trash your Houses? Who's going to defend them? You? All by yourself?"

"If I have to."

"But you don't have to. I can do this thing for you. Christ, it's what I do."

"You don't understand," Berlin said.

"Hey, all of a sudden I'm—"

"Will you listen to me? You're out on the streets, sure, and you help a lot of people—my people, street people, whoever's in trouble. I can appreciate that. But then you go back to your fancy museum with all its conveniences and shut the door on the world. It's not the same out here. We're living right on the front lines with the people we're trying to help."

"Now don't—"

Berlin cut him off again. "I'm not saying there's anything wrong with what you're doing, Stick. I know what'd happen if you opened your place to the streets—the museum'd get trashed. And you're doing more for those who need help than just about anybody else, but it's still not the same as being a part of it. Can you understand that? It's not just revenge I want. I've got to know *why* this is suddenly happening. Who's got it in for us and why."

Stick nodded. "Okay. I get the picture. You want to come with me or go it on your own?"

"No offense, but I think I'll go it on my own."

She looked up to meet his gaze. Stick laid the palm of his hand against her cheek.

"There's not many of us left," he said. "You be careful. Let me know if you need anything."

Berlin nodded.

"Be seeing you then."

He turned and strode off, leaving her by the grave feeling very much alone. Not until she heard the deep-throated roar of his Harley starting up and then taking off, did she walk slowly from the grave herself.

FOUR

There was music on the roof.

Stick heard it when he shut off his Harley, a jaunty version of "Tamberwine's Jig" on tin whistle and electric guitar that came drifting down from the museum's roof-top garden. Locking up his bike and pocketing its spell-box, he went up the six flights of stairs to find Amanda Woodsdatter and Jenny Jingle in the garden amusing Lubin with their music. The ferret danced on her hind legs, keeping perfect time to the 6/8 rhythm of the jig.

The girls brought the tune to an end when they saw Stick.

"You don't look so good," Manda said.

"It's not been a good day," Stick agreed.

Silver-eyed and mauve-haired, Manda leaned against the balustrade in a polka-dotted mini-dress that matched the canary yellow of her Les Paul. She played lead guitar for the Horn Dance, but spent a good deal of her spare time hanging around the museum acting the part of Stick's surrogate daughter, much to Stick's amusement. Leaning her guitar against its small portable amp, she picked up a thermos to pour Stick a mug of tea.

"Did you find out where the fire was?" she asked.

Stick nodded. "Someone torched the Diggers' place in Tintown."

"Are you serious? Was anybody hurt?"

"A guy named Nicky who ran the place."

"I've met him," Jenny said.

She pushed Lubin away from her knee which the ferret kept nudging in an attempt to get her to continue the music.

Unlike Manda who was a halfling, the whistle player was a full-blooded elf who worked part-time at Farrel Din's place down in Soho. She wore her hair in a half-dozen silver braids from which hung tiny bells that jingled whenever she moved her head and a pair of shades with pink plastic frames. Her T-shirt was one that Stick had given to Manda advertising a long-gone rock band called the Divinyls.

Stick took his tea from Manda with a nod of thanks. Slouching down in old wicker rocker, he put his feet up on Manda's guitar case and sighed.

"Well, Nicky's dead now," he said heavily.

"Dead?"

"I just got back from burying him."

The girls exchanged horrified looks.

"God," Manda said. "What a horrible way to go."

Stick shook his head. "He didn't get caught in the fire. He was on the pearl and took a drop from one of the windows."

"That doesn't sound right," Jenny said. "I know he used to be a junkie but he dropped the pearl a long time ago. There's no way he'd go back."

"That's what Berlin said, too. She's taking it pretty hard. But we found some shit on him—weird shit. Some new kind of pearl, looks like."

He filled in the rest of the details with a few terse sentences. When he was done, they all sat around without speaking for a long while. Lubin gave up on Jenny and came to collapse on the arm of Stick's chair. He ruffled the thick fur at the nape of the ferret's neck and looked out across the roof-top garden to Fare-you-well Park and beyond.

"Well," he said finally. "Time's wasting. I've got to head over to Dragontown to check up on that marker."

"I know someone who might be able to help you with that," Jenny said.

"Who's that?"

"My teacher—Koga Sensei."

Something flickered in Stick's eyes.

"Shoki," he said quietly. "I hadn't thought of him."

Jenny looked puzzled. "Who or what's Shoki?" she asked, but Stick was already turning away.

"Not this time," he told Lubin as the ferret rose to follow him. "Manda?"

Manda called Lubin back. Stick nodded to them from the door.

"Don't hold supper for me," he said.

Then he was gone. Jenny and Manda looked at each other.

"Sometimes," Jenny said after a few subdued moments, "he really spooks me."

"He just gets a little intense, that's all," Manda said.

Jenny nodded. "Poor Nicky. I wonder how it happened. He was the last guy I'd expect to get hooked again."

The grey skies above them seemed drearier than ever. The air held a sudden chill. Manda shivered.

"Let's go inside," she said.

Together they packed up their things and brought them down to the living quarters on the Museum's fifth floor.

Koga Sensei lived behind his dojo which was on the second floor of a building that also housed a Trader's shop. The store was run by an old Japanese couple and took up most of the main floor. Stick glanced at the goods for sale in the window—everything from Japanese noodles and gaudily-wrapped imported candies to elvin herb-pouches—then went up the stairs.

He recognized the girl who answered the door as another of Farrel Din's waitresses. She wore an oversized red T-shirt with the word "Tokyo" emblazoned on the front and her black Mohawk sprang up to attention in a swath of spikes, adding six inches or so to her diminutive stature. Stick gave her a quick slight bow.

"I am pleased to see you again," he said to her in fluent Japanese. "Would it be possible for me to speak with Shoki-san at this time?"

"I'm sorry," the girl said. "But I don't, uh… speak Japanese."

"Who is it, Laura?" a male voice asked from inside.

"It's Stick," she called back over her shoulder.

She stepped aside as the owner of that voice came to the door. Koga Sensei was compact and muscular, taller than Laura but still a head or so shorter than Stick, casually dressed in loose white cotton trousers and a collarless shirt. He ran a hand through his short dark hair.

"Stick," he said softly.

Stick gave him a brief bow which Koga returned.

"Shoki-san," he said.

"That's not a name I usually go by."

Stick shrugged. "It's the name I know you by."

"Yes. Well." Koga glanced at Laura, then sighed and stepped aside. "Will you come in?"

Stick took off his boots and, leaving them by the door, walked past the Sensei. In the center of the room, he knelt, back straight, weight on his ankles, hands on his knees.

"What's going on?" Laura whispered to Koga. "I thought you two were friends."

"We know each other," Koga replied.

"You've seemed pretty friendly other times I've seen you meet."

Koga nodded. "But this appears to be a formal visit, Laura."

"I don't get it. And why's he calling you Shoki?"

The only other time that Laura had heard her lover referred to by that name had been in quite unpleasant circumstances. Shoki was the Demon Queller. She'd been a demon at the time.

"We go back a long way," Koga replied. "But there are... differences between us from those times that have never been resolved." He stopped her next question with a raised hand. "Serve tea, Laura."

"So now I'm your geisha girl? Shit, when you revert to the old ways, you really revert, don't you?"

Koga smiled. One of those, not-now-let's-fight-about-it-later smiles.

All right, she smiled back. Later.

"I'll let you get away with it this time," she said aloud.

She kept her voice low so that only Koga could hear her. Giving him a poke in the stomach with a stiff finger, she put her palms together in a prayer position and hurried off to the kitchen with a geisha's quick mincing steps. Koga rolled his eyes, then walked over to where Stick was sitting. By the time he sat down across from his guest, his features were composed again.

"This is an unexpected pleasure," he said. "I'd given up ever having you visit me in my home."

Stick gave a small shrug. "Had some business that couldn't keep."

Koga nodded. They waited in silence then for the tea to be served. Laura pulled out a low table and set it between the two men, serving them their tea in small handleless cups of bone china. Not until they were finished their first cup and they each had a second in front of them, did they get to Stick's business.

Sitting off to one side, Laura watched them, struck by how much alike they seemed at this moment. She listened attentively as Stick explained the Diggers' problem, then muttered under her breath something about "slaves and geishas" as she fetched some ink, parchment and a brush so that he could quickly sketch the dragon symbol from the marker that had been left behind on Nicky's body.

"Why is it that one need only mention drugs and dragons and immediately it is assumed that the problem originates in New Asia?" Koga said when Stick was done.

"Maybe it's got something to do with your yakuza and tongs," Stick replied.

"There are other dragons—"

"I'm only interested in this one," Stick said, breaking in.

Koga nodded. "All right. I think it belongs to the Cho tong—Billy Hu's people. At least it used to. I've seen this motif on some of the dishware in their gaming rooms."

"Didn't think you gambled," Stick said.

"I don't. But I like watching sometimes."

"Okay. Thanks."

Stick started to rise, but Koga reached across the table to touch his arm. "You never forget, do you? What will it take for you to forget?"

"Can you bring Onisu back?"

Koga shook his head. "I had no choice."

"You think I don't know that? Why the hell do you think we're still on talking terms?"

"I just thought… if enough time went by…."

"Don't kid yourself, Shoki—there just aren't that many years." He gave Koga a brief nod, then rose from the table. Standing, he towered over both Laura and the Sensei. His gaze went to Laura. "Thanks for the tea—you served it real well for a gajin."

Before Laura could reply, he was outside, the door closing on him. She could hear him on the landing, putting on his boots, but she waited until she heard him go down the stairs before she spoke.

"What was all that about?"

Koga shook his head. "Like I said before—an old disagreement."

"But who's this Onisu he was talking about? Why's he so pissed off, Koga?"

"Onisu was Stick's wife, Laura—a long time ago."

"And she's… is she dead?"

Koga nodded. "Shoki killed her."

"But you're…." Laura couldn't finish.

"I know," Koga said. "Believe me, Laura. I know."

Laura began to feel that this was a secret she'd wish she had never learned about.

"Was she a… a demon? Like I was?"

"No." Koga moved to sit beside her. He took her hands in his. "There are dragons," he said, "that are here as caretakers for the world, Laura. Dragons of earth and fire, water and air; guardian spirits. They live in mortal flesh and some small sphere of the world falls under their protection. But sometimes those guardians become rogues—do you understand? They become what you might have become if you hadn't learned how to control *your* demon."

"Stick had a wife that was a dragon?"

Koga nodded.

"Then what does that make Stick?"

Koga was silent for a long while. When he finally spoke, his voice was so low that Laura had to lean close to hear him.

"I don't really know," he said. "I just know that once he was my friend."

"How could you do it?" Laura asked him. "How could you kill her?"

Koga shook his head. "You don't understand. I did it for him. She was his responsibility—just as he was hers. But he couldn't do it. I had to do it for him."

Laura remembered the demon she had been and how she'd prayed that if she couldn't be saved, that Koga would kill her so that she wouldn't hurt anyone else. She shivered. It wasn't a memory she liked to call up. Glancing at Koga, she saw that he too was remembering. She drew his head against her shoulder.

"I think I understand," she said.

Koga made no reply. He just drew her closer, accepting her comfort.

FIVE

It was a high lonesome sound.

Berlin sat on the back porch of the Diggers' House, playing one of Joe Doh-dee-oh's harmonicas that could hit the high notes her own voice never could. The last of the afternoon drained away as she sat there playing—not really thinking, just remembering. And waiting. After awhile, she put the harmonica down and lit up a thin cigar.

She was waiting for the day to pass. She was waiting for the night to come, when Dragontown would come alive. Joe shifted in the chair behind her, but she didn't turn her head.

"It's a long lonely road," he said finally.

Berlin blew out a stream of blue-grey smoke, then studied the glowing tip of her cigar. "What is?"

"Getting back. Getting even."

"What makes you think I want any more than just to know what's going on and stopping it?"

"You just wouldn't be Berlin, then. Is Stick helping you out?"

She shrugged. "He's looking, I'm looking."

"And whoever gets there first wins the prize?"

Berlin turned slowly. "What are you trying to say, Joe?"

"Nothing. It's just… we had a good thing going here, helping people and everything. I liked the feeling that I was being of some use to somebody, even if it was just to runaway punks and bums."

"That doesn't have to change."

"But nothing's going to be the same anymore, either," Joe said.

"I didn't make the first move."

"Nobody's blaming you, Berlin. I'm just talking. Thinking aloud."

Berlin tossed her cigar into the dirt below the porch. "Thinking's bad for you—remember? You told me that. Anyone who thinks too much, they can't play the blues."

"I'm not talking music, Berlin. I'm talking about what we're going to *do*, what we're going to *be* when this is all done."

Berlin sighed and stood up. "We're going to be changed—but that's not necessarily a bad thing, Joe. We're still going to be helping people."

"What people? We had a half dozen hobos here for the free supper tonight. And that was it. People are scared. Talk's already going around that wherever the Diggers are is not a good place to be."

"That's why I've got to be doing something now."

She left the porch before he could reply, going to the shed where she wheeled out her scooter. The sun was almost down now, sinking below Bordertown's western skyline. The rubbled lots around the House grew thick with shadows. She looked back at the House. Joe was right. There'd been almost nobody at the free supper tonight and they didn't have *anybody* crashing for the night.

It sure made things quiet.

She started up the scooter. The purr of its engine sounded loud in the stillness. She gave the throttle a rev, then set off across the dirt yard towards the street. Just before she could turn onto the pavement, a small figure detached itself from the hulking shadows of an abandoned delivery truck and waved her down.

Berlin used one hand on the rear brakes to bring the scooter to a stop, palming a throwing knife in the other. She put the knife away as soon as she saw who it was.

"Hey, Berlin," the figure said.

"Hey, Gamen. How's tricks?"

Gamen was one of Sammy's kids, living up with the rest of them at the old Lightworks building from which Sammy ran the Pack. You could find Sammy's kids all through Soho, and ranging out into Trader's Heaven and Riverside— scruffy little Packers in rags and tatters, scrounging a living from the streets or wherever they could. They turned up at the Diggers' Houses from time to time, though Sammy frowned on that. The Diggers let anybody crash, and Sammy wasn't big on his kids mixing with the Blood runaways that showed up as regularly as any other kind of kid on the streets.

"I heard about the burn in Tintown," Gamen said.

She turned her big sad eyes on Berlin. There weren't many could turn Gamen down when she was asking for a handout—not with those eyes.

"It was a bad scene," Berlin agreed. "Listen, if you're hungry, we've got plenty of eats tonight. Go back up to the House and ask Joe or Hooter."

"I'm not here for eats," Gamen said. "Sammy sent me."

Berlin's eyebrows went up. "What's Sammy got to say?"

Gamen scuffed at a lip of broken pavement with a dirty shoe. "Well, I seen something in Tintown and when I told him, he told me to come and tell you. Nobody else, just you."

"What did you see, Gamen?"

"A High Born. I saw a High Born on the back streets of Tintown just a little while before the fire started up."

Berlin regarded her steadily. A High Born. In Tintown. It wasn't totally pre-posterous—but she had to take into account the source of the information. Sammy was a pure townie bigot. He hated Bloods. It could be just like him to make trouble between the Bloods and Diggers, because he wasn't that big on the Diggers either. He'd lost a kid or two to the Diggers—not enough to make them his enemy, but enough so that he wouldn't mind them having a little war with the Bloods.

"Did you *see* this?" Berlin demanded. "Or did Sammy just tell you you did?"

"Come on, Berlin. I wouldn't shit you."

The big eyes met her gaze without blinking. Berlin sighed. With those eyes—especially on a streetkid—there was no way to tell if Gamen was lying or not.

"Okay," Berlin said. "Thanks for the tip, Gamen. Tell Sammy I owe him one."

"What about me?"

"I thought we were friends," Berlin said. "Friends don't owe each other."

Gamen thought about that for a moment, then her grimy face brightened. She gave Berlin a quick salute before vanishing into the deepening shadows. Berlin sat on her scooter, the engine still idling, while she thought about what this new information could mean. A High Born in Tintown. And pearl came straight across the Borders from Elfland. If only she could trust Sammy's reasons for passing the info on....

She thought it all through one more time, then shook her head. There just wasn't enough to go on. Putting the scooter into gear, she pointed it towards Dragontown.

Berlin knew her way around Dragontown. She knew the twists and turns of its narrow streets. She understood the safe blocks and those that were off-limits even to her. She could read the pulse of the streets and the Dragons that patrolled them in gangs of twos and threes. But the vibes were wrong tonight.

She could feel angry eyes watching her from the tea houses and shops she passed by. The paper lanterns seemed greedier than ever with their light tonight, leaving dark pools of shadow that spilled beyond the mouths of alleyways to eat away at the streets. There was a high buzz of anger in the air that grew into an ever-stronger whine with each Dragon she passed. It wasn't until she ran down Locas in the gaming district that she found out what was going down.

"What chew doin' here, Berlin?" Locas demanded, dragging her off the street into an alley. "Chew crazy or somethin'?"

Locas was a thin dark-skinned youth, half Chinese and half Puerto Rican. He lived in the barrios out past Fare-you-well Park borough, but usually spent his evenings cruising the streets of New Asia.

Berlin shook off his grip. She'd left her scooter chained up in an alley out by

Ho Street, before entering Dragontown on foot.

"You think *I'm* crazy? What the hell's going on here, Locas?"

"Oh, man. Don't chew *know*? Word's out on chew, babe. Chew gone lobo on us. Calling in the bulls from uptown. Word's all over the street. Chew know the uptown fuzz don't bother with us—not 'less they got somebody to point out who's who an' what's what."

"People are believing this shit?"

"Hey, we're not talkin' one rumour here, babe. We're talkin' everybody sayin' the same thing 'bout chew."

"Well, everybody's wrong. Come on, Locas—you think I'd turn *anybody* in?"

"I tol' 'em chew wouldn't—but there's too much talkin' goin' down, Berlin. Chew stay here too long tonight an' the uptown bulls gonna get your pretty little head delivered to 'em in a box, chew know what I'm sayin'?"

Berlin leaned weakly against the alley wall.

"Jesus Christ," she muttered. "The whole friggin' world's turning upside down."

"Ain't that the truth. Chew gotta split, babe. Chill right outta here."

Berlin nodded. "Okay. I get the picture. I'm gone. But before I go, can you tell me something?"

"What chew want, Berlin?"

"Who's this belong to?"

She pulled out the lacquered wood marker and dropped it into his hand. Locas sidled up to the mouth of the alleyway, gave it a quick look, then returned to her side.

"It's an old marker," he said. "Used to belong to Billy Hu's people—chew know who I mean? We're talkin' tongs here, babe. What chew want with them?"

It was too dark to see his features, but Berlin could read the suspicion in his voice.

"You heard about our house in Tintown?"

"It's a fuckin' shame. Nicky was okay."

"Somebody left that on Nicky's body."

Locas weighed the marker in his hand, then passed it back to her.

"Somebody's makin' trouble, an' not just with chew," he said finally.

"I've got to talk to Billy Hu, Locas. Can you set up a meet?"

"I'll see what's brewin'—talk to some people."

"I'd appreciate it," Berlin said. "This is shaping up into a major fuck-up."

"No shit. Everybody's gettin' a hard-on for chew, babe, an'...."

His voice trailed off. Berlin turned to see what he was looking at and watched them fill up the entrance of the alleyway. Dragons. Four, no five of them.

"Get out of here," she told Locas.

"Hey, Berlin. I—"

"Blow!"

As he started to shuffle away, Berlin shifted slightly into a loose yoi, or ready, stance and faced the Dragons. She really didn't need this. She had to be careful—not hurt them too badly, because that'd just make this whole mess worse—but they weren't going to be operating under any such limitations.

"You got a lot of nerve," one of the Dragons said, "showing your ass around here."

He was enough in the light so that Berlin could recognize him. Jackie Won. Half the gangs in lower Dragontown answered to him. Beautiful, she thought.

"You've been hearing a lot bullshit, Jackie," Berlin replied. "Let me go before someone gets hurt."

Jackie laughed. He looked at his companions. "You hear that? She's afraid of hurting us." His hard gaze returned to Berlin. "We're not afraid of a little pain—'specially not when you'll be the one feeling it."

Berlin didn't bother replying. Stay cool, she told herself. Don't get mad. Don't go tearing them apart. But there were five of them and they were already fanning out. There was no way she could take all five *without* tearing them apart.

"Two things," she said quietly. "And I want you to remember them both. Whatever you heard on the street about me's bullshit."

"This is so scary," Jackie said with a grin. "What's the other thing, dead meat?"

"You don't fuck around with Berlin."

They never saw her first move. She just flowed to one side of the alley, grabbed up a couple of garbage can lids, flung them like discs at the Dragons, then leapt up to the fire escape that was hanging above her. Two Dragons went down as the lids spun into them. The other three rushed forward and she dropped down amongst them.

She drop-kicked the first, trying to hold back, but she heard his thigh-bone snap under the impact of her foot. The next she took out with a lightning blur of punches that left him wheezing and choking on the ground. When she turned to Jackie, he was already committed to a whirling kick.

She came up under his attack, a pointed fist firing into his groin. As he started to fall, she flipped him over her back, then came up to face the first two she'd taken out with the garbage can lids who were now back on their feet. A low growl came up from her diaphragm—a rumbling sound that turned into a panther's cough. The two Dragons looked as though they were going to stand their ground, but as soon as she took a step towards them, they both fled.

A pinpoint of heat burned in the center of Berlin's head, licking at her thoughts like a fire. Her eyes glimmered eerily as she studied her downed foes. She took a step towards the nearest one, then stopped. Bowing her head, she took one deep breath after another until the heat cooled, until the light in her eyes died, until the rumbling sound in her chest fell still.

Close. She'd almost lost it. She'd....

She looked down into Jackie's shocked eyes. There was a flicker of fear behind his pain. Perfect. Now the Dragons were really going to be after her ass. She broke eye contact with him and headed deeper down into the alley at a gliding walk. She was going to have to disappear for awhile. It was that, or go after all the gangs in Dragontown before they came after her.

SIX

Ysa Cran laughed like a pearl diver.

She sat at a table in The Underground, a live music club on Ho Street just down the block from The Dancing Ferret. Drag 'em Down were on stage, blasting through an uptempo version of "Sucking Down the Future". Nabber slouched beside her, boots up on one chair, head tilted back against his chair's headrest. There was an empty beer pitcher on the table in front of them. They each had a joint of Bordertown Blue smoldering between their fingers.

Teddy Grim returned with a new pitcher of beer. Shoving Nabber's feet off the chair, he sat down. Ysa passed him a joint.

"I still can't believe it," he said. "I always heard Berlin had a temper, but I didn't think she'd let go so easily."

"She just never had the right people pushing her," Ysa said. "That's all. To-morrow we'll start spreading the word around in Riverside and the Scandal District—just like we did in Dragontown. Then no matter which way she turns, she'll burn."

Nabber filled their glasses from the new pitcher.

"So are we hitting their main digs tonight or what?" he wanted to know.

Ysa shook her head. "Why bother? The Dragons'll probably trash the place for us, seeing how Berlin's been kind enough to add fuel to our rumours." She grinned. "She took out Jackie Won, hey? I'll bet those Dragons are just burn-ing to rumble."

"So what are *we* going to do?" Nabber asked.

Ysa gave Teddy Grim a knowing look. "Looks like the Nab here's developed a real taste for torching townies."

"Hey, we didn't burn anybody."

"So we were unlucky. We'll just have to bar up the doors and windows when we hit their place near the Market tonight."

"There's going to be bulls hanging around there," Teddy Grim warned.

The cityguard pretty well stayed out of Soho and the areas like it, giving them up as already lost, but Trader's Heaven was a whole other story. Half of Bordertown's economy depended on its Market. There were beat cops as well as plainclothes bulls constantly patrolling the Market and its immediate vicinity.

"Hell," Ysa said. "We're on a roll. They're just going to have to stay out of our way."

The band on stage kicked into "Rip It Out" with the heavy metallic whine of their lead guitar soaring over the deep throbbing rhythm.

"Give 'em hell," Ysa yelled.

The music drowned her out, but the lead guitarist caught her eye and gave her a wink before settling into the chopping chords that underpinned the lead singer's lyrics. Ysa turned to her companions.

"I just love this shit," she said, taking a long drag from her joint.

SEVEN

Two days now and it was just getting worse.

Stick sat in the Museum's Native American hall, staring at a display of Hopi kachina masks. He should never have gone to Koga's. It hadn't started there, but it might as well have. That's where it had all come home for him. Seeing Koga again, in that kind of environment. Koga, the Sensei and man. Shoki, the Demon Queller.

It brought back too many memories. Past failures, present failures. Onisu, dead and gone. But reborn in Berlin. Or maybe it was just Onisu's madness taking root in Berlin. It didn't make a whole lot of difference.

It was two days since Berlin had disappeared in Dragontown, but the streets were full of rumours of her. All of Bordertown was ranked against her now. They were saying that she'd gone lobo long before anybody made a move against her. They were saying that the fire in Tintown had been the start of a justified retribution for the shit she was bringing down on the city. On her own head.

Stick was hearing it so much, he almost believed it himself.

She'd taken out a few Dragons that first night. Later word had it she'd wasted a pack of Wharf Rats who'd cornered her down in Riverside the following afternoon. Two of those died. Later still, she'd taken out a gang of Bloods who'd run into her out by the Old Wall.

Stick stroked Lubin's fur. The ferret lay still in his lap, eyes open, but not focused. Stick wondered if she was staring into the same bleak vistas he was looking into.

Somebody'd hit the Diggers' place by the Market a couple of nights ago. All the Diggers had left was their main House in Soho, but that was vacant now—taken over by a mixed gang of Dragons and Bloods who'd trashed the place. They were supposedly waiting for Berlin to show up, but nobody really believed she would. It was just something to do.

And if all of that wasn't bad enough, now there was word of a new drug hitting the streets. Shake. Twice the flash pearl was and you didn't have to mainline it. Stick remembered the container he'd found on Nicky's body. Had to be the same shit. Everything tied together, but he was damned if he could make the connections. All he knew was Berlin was over the edge and he was going to have to track her down.

He looked up as Manda came into the room and beside him.

"When did you get in?" she asked.

Stick shrugged. "An hour or so ago."

"Still no luck, I guess."

That depended, Stick thought, on how much he really wanted to find Berlin.

"No luck," he agreed.

"It's just getting worse, isn't it?"

Stick thought of a dark night, of the silver flash of a katana as the blade swung home, of cradling Onisu in his arms. He hadn't been able to cry then. Koga, kneeling on the other side of his wife's body, had wept for both of them.

"I've got to talk to her," he said. "Maybe it's not too late."

"Too late for what?"

Stick looked bleakly at Manda, then passed Lubin over to her.

"I don't want the past to be repeated," he said. "Because this time I'll have to do it myself."

"Stick, what're you talking about?"

He nodded at Lubin. "Take care of her for me, will you?"

"Sure, but...."

He was walking away before she could finish, leaving only the echo of his footsteps in the empty hall. Manda looked at the kachina masks lining the walls and shivered.

* * *

There was one place Stick hadn't looked. He drove out there now, the big Harley eating up the blocks. It was out past Tintown. The rubbled lots were empty—had been since the fire. The tin shanties still stood, dotting the lots here and there. There were some canvas tents. In other places sheets of corrugated iron had been pulled over roofless basements for more permanent shelters. But none of the hobos were around.

Stick drove on, out to the old freight yards.

Before the Change came, and Elfland came creeping over the city making it a Borderland, this had been the heart of the city's transportation. But the trains stopped running, the decades took their toll, and the heart of the city's railway network had been turned into a dump. Now, after years of neglect, you could no longer see the rails for the refuse. Only the old freight cars still stood, scattered here and there like beached whales in a sea of garbage.

Rats made their home here—the animal kind that Lubin was trained to hunt in an earlier age, not the kids from Soho. There were other residents as well. Die-hard hobos had carved camps deep inside the dump. Some of the bos took over the odd freight car that was still mostly in one piece, scavenging carpets and furniture and you name it to turn them into regular homes. But the area got its name from a third inhabitant—the real rulers of the dump.

The place was called Dogtown now.

Stick pulled up at the edge of the dump and killed the Harley. Pocketing his spell-box, he stayed astride the big bike, patiently waiting. He knew the procedure. If you weren't dumping trash, you waited.

They came bounding out from the heaps of garbage, huge mastiffs and rat-earred little Border collies. German shepherds and Dobermans. But mostly they were mongrels, tough lean dogs with the blood of a hundred lines running in their veins.

They circled the bike and Stick didn't move a muscle, didn't speak a word.

One or the other and they'd be all over him. He just waited, breathing through his mouth so that the stink of the dump wouldn't make him gag. None of the dogs came too close, but it wasn't because they were afraid of him. They knew the procedure too. They were waiting, just as he was.

It might have been a half hour later that Stick caught movement out of the corner of his eye. The figure that finally shuffled through the circle of dogs was an old bo. His skin was browned like leather from the sun, his hair as fine and white as spiderwebs floating down to his shoulders. His clothes were so patched it was hard to tell what the original material had been. His feet were bare, the soles tougher than any workboot. He had a bag over his shoulder that rattled as he moved. When he got near to Stick, he just stood there staring at him.

"I just want to talk to her," Stick said. "That's all."

"Talk to who?"

Stick put a hand in his pocket—moving very slowly when one of the mastiffs took a few stiff steps towards him—and withdrew a tin of chewing tobacco. He tossed the tin over.

"Berlin," Stick said. "I just want to talk to her, Pazzo."

The bo studied the tin for a moment, then slipped it into his bag. Without a word, he turned and started off on a faint trail that led through the garbage. Stick took a few quick shallow breaths, then started after the old man. The dogs flowed in a wave all around them, never quite touching Stick, but so close he could feel the heat of their bodies.

Pazzo led them on a long meandering route through Dogtown, stopping sometimes to add something to his bag, muttering to himself, but never looking straight at Stick. The dogs seemed to count every shallow breath Stick took. The reek was overpowering. The air was thick with it, thick with flies too. He saw rats on the tops of some of the heaps, but they burrowed into the garbage at the sight of the dogs, moving so quick Stick wasn't even sure he'd seen them half the time.

It took awhile, but finally they entered a narrow ravine between two towering mountains of refuse and Stick blinked at what he saw. He'd never been this deep into Dogtown before, never dreamed this existed.

Encircling a glade like a circle of wagons in an old B-western were a number of freight cars, dwarfed by the steep towers of garbage all around them. Inside the circle, grass and bushes grew, flowering vines crawled up the freight cars. Somehow, the air was clean. The dogs went racing ahead, leaving Stick and Pazzo to follow at the old bo's pace. Stick heard the sound of guitar music. As they came around the bulk of the nearest freight car, he saw Berlin sitting by a fire with a number of hobos.

Brandy Jack was there and Joe Doh-dee-oh. One of them had probably fetched Berlin's guitar for her, but he couldn't guess which one. She finished the tune she was playing, a slow rendition of "Dogtown Blues". Stick wondered if she'd known he was coming and was playing that tune for him. He'd always liked it. She'd probably written it and just never admitted it to him.

Pazzo kept on going and the other bos drifted away from the fire as Stick approached. He leaned against a big iron barrel and looked down at Berlin. She looked back, her eyes giving nothing away. Stick held her gaze for a long time before he settled on a log across the fire from her.

"So what's doing, Berlin? You declaring war on the city?"

"Nice to see you too, Stick."

"Come on, Berlin. What the fuck's going on?"

"City's declared war on me."

"Bullshit."

Her eyebrows went up. "Oh? And what would you call it?"

"I think you've stepped across the line."

She doodled a few riffs on her guitar, not looking at what she was doing, not looking at anything. When her gaze finally focused on him, her violet eyes burned with an inner flicker.

"Somehow I didn't think you'd fall for all the shit that's been spread around, Stick. You've disappointed me."

"What the hell am I supposed to think? You've been running wild, throwing your weight around…. Christ, you never even talked to me about it."

"What's to say? I read you now, Stick—loud and clear."

"Talk to me, Berlin. What's going down?"

"You blind?"

Angry words swarmed in Stick's throat, but he looked away, staring into the fire until they'd been burned off.

"So maybe I'm blind," he said. "Talk to me."

"Someone's working a frame on me—it started with the Diggers, but it looks like I'm all that's left."

"Who's working the frame?"

"Don't know. All I know is it's coming straight across the Border, looking for my ass."

Stick sighed. "That doesn't make any sense."

"I didn't say it would."

"And it doesn't explain your taking on half the gangs in the city. You have a responsibility, Berlin. And you're abusing it."

"Fuck you, Stick. I'm staying alive—that's all. We're not all like you—willing to get gutshot rather than ripping out their hearts when they try to cut you down."

"You're—"

"And besides—we don't all have little halfie healers hanging around, ready to fix us up if we *do* get gutshot."

"Manda's not my—"

"Come *off* it, Stick. Face the facts. I'm not you. I can't be you. I don't want to be you. Nothing personal, understand, but I got my own ways of handling things. You want to get down to nitty-gritties? How many people have you killed?"

"I killed them naturally, not—"

"Jesus, I can't believe I'm hearing this. Dead's dead, Stick. I'm not out hunting—people are hunting me. They come for me, they've got to know I'm not going to stand back and let them take me down without giving it my best shot. Now maybe you think handfighting a couple of punks in an alley's okay, or shooting them down like you did Fineagh Steel awhile back, but we've all got to play the cards we're dealt. The hand I've been dealt—it's just not that simple."

"I don't know you anymore."

"Maybe you never did, Stick."

"If you don't stop this, I'm going to have to come after you."

For one moment Berlin's eyes softened. "I'm not Onisu," she said, her voice gentle. "You've got to stop fitting me into her life."

"Don't bring her into this."

"I'm not—you are. You think I'm stepping over the line, but what you're really afraid of is something you never dealt with a long time ago, Stick. I'm Berlin—okay? I'm not a Stick clone, I'm not an Onisu clone. I'm just me. And for some reason, a lot of people want to hurt me."

Stick stood up. "Come back with me," he said. "We'll deal with them together."

"What're we going to do? Go to an uptown court? Get serious, Stick. This's got to be dealt with on the streets—where it began. I've got find the suckers who started this and stop it with them. That's the only way it's going to end. I've got to have them in my hand and show the gangs that I'm not what they're hearing I am."

"I'm going," Stick said. "Either come with me—"

"It's all black and white, right? I'm either with you or against you?"

"—or I've got to come back to get you. I'll give you till midnight."

Berlin shook her head. "I'm not coming with you, Stick. Not now, not later. And I won't be here when you come back."

"I'll find you."

"I know you will."

She watched him go. Her fingers found a slow blues riff, but for once she was fumbling the notes. If Stick had turned then, he would have seen her eyes flooding with tears. But he never looked back.

Manda heard Stick come in and went looking for him. She found him on the rooftop, sitting on his knees in a seiza position with a sheathed katana on the ground within easy reach of his right hand.

"Stick?" she said softly.

When he made no reply, she walked around in front of him and knelt down so that she could look into his face.

"Did you find her?"

His face was as still as the kachina masks downstairs.

"You're scaring me, Stick."

His gaze slowly focused on her.

"I found her," he said softly. "I just wish to Christ I hadn't."

Manda looked down at the sword in its sheath of lacquered wood. A chill catpawed up her spine. "What are you saying, Stick? Did... did you kill her?"

He shook his head.

"But I will," he said. His voice was just a faint whisper now. "God help me, I will."

EIGHT

The pain went through her heart like a razor.

Berlin sat hunched over her guitar, hugging its body against her as she fought to hold back a flood of tears. The fire crackled and spat in front of her. Out past the freight cars she heard a dog howl.

"Dogs got his smell—they can get him for you."

She looked up through a blurry veil to find Pazzo crouched down beside her, anger clouding his eyes. She shook her head numbly.

"It's not his fault," she said. "He's trapped—we all are. This is just something we should have looked to a long time ago. See, he never dealt with it, Pazzo. He just hid it—locked it away and never dealt with it. But you can't do that. You've always got to deal with it—if you don't do it when it happens, when maybe you've got some choice, then *it's* going to decide it's own time to bust loose."

Pazzo didn't really know what she was talking about. "He shouldn't've made you cry."

"He's a hard man—that's how he kept going. He just got hard and stayed that way. I think it's the kid he's got staying with him—I think she opened a crack or two in his armour and now it's all falling out. Falling apart."

Pazzo shrugged. Digging about in one patched pocket, he came up with a clean handkerchief that he gave it to her.

"Thanks."

"You've got another visitor."

Berlin tried to find a smile. "I'm just a real Miss Popularity today, aren't I?"

"You want to see him?"

Berlin nodded, then blew her nose when Pazzo shuffled off. He came back a few moments later with Locas in tow.

"This guy makes you feel bad...." Pazzo began.

"I'm okay, Pazzo. Honest."

Locas waited until the old bo left them alone, then sank down on the log that Stick had so recently vacated. "Shit, Berlin. Chew got some weird friends."

"That include you?"

"Fuckin' A." He grinned, white teeth gleaming against his dark skin, until Berlin couldn't help but smile back.

"Did you have any luck?" she asked.

Locas shrugged. "Okay. Sammy's no problem. He's got a hard on for whoever's dumping this shake on the streets an' if chew can deliver 'em, he'll back us."

"What about the Dragons?"

"Well, Jackie Won'd take your balls—just sayin' chew had any. But they'll be there. Billy Hu's sendin' somebody to look out for the Cho interests—I think it's gonna be Hsian."

"At least he's honest. What about the Bloods?"

"There'll be Bloods an' Wharf Rats there—a little bit of everybody, all lookin' to take a piece of chew, just sayin' chew can't deliver."

Berlin nodded. "And can we?"

"John Cocklejohn tracked 'em down. Lady chew want's called Ysa Cran. She's tight with someone from across the Border, but the word don't say who. Chew gotta deliver her, Berlin. There's no way me an' John can handle her. She's feral, man."

A faraway look came into Berlin's eyes. "Oh, I can deliver her."

"Chew know her?"

"I know where to find her."

"Then what chew waitin' for?"

"Nightfall. What time did you set the meet for?"

"Midnight. In the old station."

"Be there, or be square," Berlin said softly.

Locas shook his head. "Chew got some weird ways of puttin' together words, Berlin."

NINE

The wizard couldn't help her.

"It's not that I won't," Farrel Din told Manda. "It's that I can't."

They were sitting at a back table in The Dancing Ferret. The club was quiet, drifting in the lull between the lunch and dinner crowds. By mid-evening, once the band was on stage, the place would be so crowded there wouldn't be standing space or a moment's quiet. Right now Manda could hear the tinkle of Jenny Jingle's bells as she moved about across the room, sweeping.

Farrel Din sighed. "This has been a long time coming."

"What do you mean?"

"It's not my story to tell."

"Okay. But *why* can't you help me?"

Farrel Din regarded her for a moment, then set about cleaning and refilling his pipe.

"My kind of magic doesn't work on someone like Stick," he said once he had the pipe going.

A cloud of smoke drifted up above his head.

Manda nodded slowly, remembering. There'd been a time when the wizard had put a spell on the Horn Dance's music. It had affected everyone who could hear it except for Stick and the elf he was trying to avoid killing at the time. He hadn't been able to avoid it.

"Is there anyone who can help me?" she asked.

"Shoki."

"Who's Shoki?" She had a dim recollection of hearing the name before. It seemed that Stick had mentioned it once. "Where can I find him?"

"I can bring you to him."

Manda turned at the sound of the new voice to find another of The Ferret's waitresses standing by their table.

"I couldn't help overhearing," Laura said.

Manda waved off her apology. "That doesn't matter. Not if you know who he is."

"I live with him."

Manda glanced at Jenny, still sweeping. "He's Koga? The Sensei?"

Laura nodded.

Manda reached out and squeezed Farrel Din's hand where it lay on the tabletop.

"Thanks," she said.

"Can I get the time off?" Laura asked.

Farrel Din nodded. "Just be careful. You're stepping into a grey area. Sometimes the more you try to help, the worse things get."

"I can't let him kill Berlin," Manda said, rising from the table. "I don't know what's wrong with Stick, but I'm not going to let him do this. Not to her. Not to himself."

There were times, Farrel Din thought as he watched them leave, that he wondered why he'd ever crossed the Borders to stay here. Elfland had its own dangers—there was no denying that—but Bordertown was such a mix of differing cultures, each with its own beliefs and particular guardians, that the city could never let up its balancing act between various disasters. All it had to do was lean too far, one way, or the other....

Koga was dressed in what Manda took to be some sort of ceremonial outfit when they arrived at his dojo. He wore a kimono and hakama of black silk, with a white silk under kimono and a dark red obi, or sash. On his shoulder was his family crest, a circular ka-mon worked in white silk stitches. The big room was empty except for him. He was seated in a seiza position and appeared to be waiting for them. Two swords, a katana and the smaller wakazashi, rested in a small wooden frame in front of him.

Laura removed her shoes and flowed into the room ahead of Manda. When she stepped in front of Koga, she knelt on the matted floor and gave him a short bow before sitting up, back straight as a board.

They were acting like Sensei and student, instead of lovers, Manda thought. For some reason that bothered her. She fumbled with her boots and got them off, but didn't try to copy Laura's entrance. She shuffled across the floor and stood awkwardly above them for a moment, then sat down. It was hard to get comfortable. She didn't feel that she should slouch, but just a few moments of trying to copy their straight-backed posture made her muscles ache.

Koga inclined his head briefly to her. "How can I help you, Amanda?" he asked.

You mean you don't already know? she thought, but she kept that to herself. They were obviously going through something ceremonial thing. If Koga was the only one that could help her with Stick, she didn't want to blow it by rocking the boat.

"It's Stick," she said, and then plunged into her story. When she was done, Koga told her about Onisu and Stick and the part he had played in Onisu's death.

"So he thinks Berlin's this Onisu?" Manda asked.

"That is simplifying it, but, yes."

"And when he came to you…?"

"I think he came for help. Any punk in Dragontown could have identified that marker for him. Instead he came to me. You must understand. Stick is no longer who he is—he is who he was. That is why he came to me. Farrel Din and I are the only ones who were there when it all went down."

"I'm confused," Manda said. "These dragons…."

"They are guardian spirits. Dragons are what we name them in New Asia— that's why the street gangs call themselves Dragons. They see themselves as Dragontown's protectors."

"But Berlin and Stick… they're *real* dragons?"

"They are guardian spirits, yes. They have a great responsibility, being the earthly representations of the elements. The powers they have may not be abused. Their work is done in subtle ways—not on a grand scale as poets and storytellers would have it—but in small things."

Manda tried to think it all through.

"What if he's right?" she said finally. "What if Berlin's really stepped across this line?"

Koga shook his head. "I talked to one of her friends. Berlin's called a meeting tonight between the various factions of Bordertown to plead her case. That is not the action of one who has turned her back upon her responsibilities."

"Does Stick know this? That'd change everything, wouldn't it?"

"The same source told me that Stick and Berlin have already spoken today, but Stick is hearing only an echo of the past—he is *in* the past."

Manda rubbed her face with her hands. "So what happens? What can we do?"

"Not we. This is my responsibility, Manda. I have to stop him." As he spoke, he took the long katana from the wooden rack in front of him and laid its sheathed length across his knees. "You will excuse me now, please. I need time to meditate."

Manda shivered. This was too much like Stick sitting up on the Museum's roof.

Laura caught her arm. "We'd better go," she said.

"But—"

Laura shook her head. Drawing Manda to her feet, she collected their footgear and led the way outside.

"He's going to kill Stick!" Manda wailed once they were out on the stairs. "That's not the kind of help I came for."

"Believe me," Laura said. "Killing Stick is the last thing Koga would want to do."

"And what if there's no other way to stop him?"

Laura didn't have an answer to that.

"I'm staying right here," Manda said, "and when Koga leaves, I'm going with him, whether he wants me to or not."

"We're both going," Laura said. Koga was good, maybe the best that Bordertown had for this kind of a thing, but Stick was good too. How good, she didn't know. She hoped they wouldn't have to find out. But if it came down to a fight, she was damn sure going to be there in case Koga needed her.

Manda sat down in a slump at the top of the stairs. "I feel like I've just sold Stick out," she said.

Laura sat down beside her and put an arm around her shoulder. "The past's there waiting to betray us all, Manda. You didn't have a thing to do with it."

"Tell that to my heart."

Laura didn't have an answer for that either.

TEN

The room was as dark as her soul.

Ysa Cran paused in the doorway. She lived on the top floor of an abandoned brownstone that squatted near the Old Wall. She had a thing about coming home to a dark apartment, so she always had a lightbox going, night and day. She could afford it. She had only the best. Guaranteed to last forever or until she trashed it, whichever came first.

Her building was spelled with safeguards—it had to be. This was where she kept her stash. This was where she could be who she was, alone, no masks, no need to strut. No one came here. The safeguards would let nobody in but one person, and that was Ysa Cran. Even a High Born like Corwyn couldn't get through unless she let him. The safeguards came from straight across the Border and were keyed to her and her alone.

But now the lightbox was out. The room was dark. And she wasn't alone. She knew that without having to step across the threshold. Someone was in there, waiting for her. Someone who knew where to find her. Someone good enough to get through the safeguards. She loosed a heavy length of chain from around her waist and let one end fall to the floor with a clank.

"Ysa Cran, Ysa Cran," a husky voice called from out of the darkness. "No one loves her, Blood or man."

Ysa's silver eyes narrowed and she took a firmer grip on the chain. She took a step forward and the lightbox came on—not in a flash, but slowly, erasing the shadows one by one, until Ysa could see the small figure in blue jeans sitting in a chair waiting for her.

"You're dead meat, Berlin," she hissed.

Berlin didn't move except to shake her head. "Everybody's got it in for poor Berlin and we know why, don't we? Ysa Cran, Ysa Cran, nobody loves—"

"Shut up!"

"What's the matter, Ysa? That bring back bad memories? I know all about you—living up on the Hill, had the best of everything, but somehow something got left out, right? You're like those stories they like to tell about Bloods out in the World—you got no soul."

"You don't know shit."

"I'm not saying you didn't have it hard," Berlin said. "but we've all had some hard knocks, Ysa. That doesn't mean we go around fucking everybody else up. What's the matter? You figure the world owes you something? You figure that Ysa Cran's better than everybody else and she doesn't have to bust her ass like the rest of us do?"

Ysa started forward, the chain coming up, but something in Berlin's eyes stopped her. There was a red flickering there, behind the violet. Something inhuman that had nothing to do with the hills across the Border.

"You…." her voice trailed off.

"No, you made the mistake, Ysa. And now you've got to make it up."

Ysa stared at her. She'd heard about the meeting that had been called tonight in the old train station. Berlin was going to be there to set everybody straight. Oh, they'd had a good laugh about that—Teddy Grim, Nabber and her. What was Berlin going to do? Hand over her ass on a silver platter? Because there was no way anybody was going to listen to shit from Berlin—not after the job she and her boys had done on her rep. Only now Ysa began to understand what was going down. And looking into the fires that burned in those violet eyes, she got her first inkling of just what they'd been fooling around with.

"Listen," she tried. "I never knew you were one of… one of them."

"You think that matters now? You think that's going to bring Nicky back? Or those kids you burned in the house by the Market? Or the two Rats I had to take down by the river?"

"No, it's just—"

Berlin cut her off with a shake of her head. "It's time to pay the piper, Ysa. You know how it goes?"

Ysa began to back out of the room, but Berlin was too fast for her. She was out of the chair, around the Blood and blocking the door, before Ysa even started to get away. A flicker of a hand and Ysa's wrist went numb. The chain dropped with a clatter to the floor. Another flicker, this time a foot, and Ysa crumpled down on top of the chain, her whole right leg numb.

"Who's your connection?" Berlin asked. "Who's passing the dope to you?"

A wrist knife appeared in Ysa's hand. She made an awkward lunge with it, but Berlin just flowed back out of reach. Her left foot seemed to float in the air as she stepped back. The knife went skittering across the room. Ysa clutched a broken wrist to her chest, biting back the pain.

"Who is it, Ysa?"

"Are you… kidding? I open my mouth and I'm dead."

"What do you think we're doing here—playing a game?"

Berlin feinted another kick. Ysa flinched, but Berlin could tell that this was one thing she wasn't going to get out of the Blood. It was lying there, hidden behind her silver eyes. A locked door that no amount of pain was going to open.

"Okay," she said. "I guess that name's going to be your private little treasure. I just hope it sees you through the night."

"What… what do you mean?" Ysa asked, but she already knew. It was all going to go down at the train station.

"You're clearing my name."

"I…."

"That's not open to discussion," Berlin told her. "You're clearing my name, period. And don't think you can weasel out of it once we're there. I've got backing like you wouldn't believe on this."

But Ysa was already calculating her chances. She could plead her innocence—Christ, who was going to believe Berlin at this point of the game? Who was even going to take the time to listen to her?

"Sure," she said. "Anything you say."

Berlin smiled. "You're so easy to read, Ysa. Maybe you should ask me about my backing before you go off half-cocked, thinking you're going to squeeze out of another scrape."

"Okay. What's your backing?"

"Dogtown's coming to the meeting. You still think you're not going to spill your guts? You still think they're going to take me down when I've got that pack guarding each door and my ass?"

She watched the spirit finally break in Ysa's eyes, but it gave her no pleasure. Like she'd told the Blood earlier, it didn't bring the dead back.

Reaching down, she pulled Ysa to her feet by the scruff of her leather jacket and propelled her out the door. Ysa staggered against a wall, trying to keep to her feet. The one numbed leg barely held her weight. Berlin never gave her a chance to steady herself. She just kept shoving her along. Down the stairs. Out through the foyer. Onto the street. Down to the train station.

They heard the distant sound of the Mock Avenue Bell Tower ring the half hour. Midnight was only another thirty minutes away.

It'll all be over soon, Berlin thought. Except for one thing. She still had to deal with the spectre of somebody else's past.

She still had to deal with Stick.

ELEVEN

Midnight came and went.

Stick lifted his head slowly and gazed across the Museum's roof. A bat moved in his field of vision, a quick silent swoop, then it was gone. He closed his fingers around the katana's lacquered wood sheath. His mind moved in the past. He saw a red-eyed rogue dragon and a man clad all in black silk. He watched the blade rise, then come down, as quick and smooth as the bat's flight. Blood sprayed. The night was suddenly filled with its hot scent.

Squeezing his eyes shut, Stick rose silently. He thrust the katana into his belt and and left the roof-top at a gliding walk. Down through the Museum he went, one more ghost in a building over-filled with ghosts.

On the street outside he paused, nostrils widening to take in the still night air. Bordertown held its secrets close to its vest, but unerringly, he turned and drifted down the street, making for the old train station that bordered Dogtown. Behind him, low to the ground, Lubin padded silently in his wake, but he never noticed the ferret.

He was still moving through the past, trying to reach a point in it before the figure in black silk buried his katana in dragon flesh. He quickened his pace, grinding his teeth as he loped down the silent streets. It was long past time for him to shoulder the responsibilities that he'd once shirked. He wasn't sure how it had come to be that he could return to the past, that he could give Onisu the freedom now that in another life he hadn't been able to. All he knew was that this time he wouldn't fail her. No matter what face she wore. He would do what had to be done.

The old train station.

Inside, Bordertown was listening to Ysa Cran's confession. Out front, dogs and gang members patrolled, each studiously ignoring the other, each aware of the others' every move. Behind, on the old tracks, a single figure stood. Dressed in black silk, Shoki the Demon Queller waited, katana and wakazashi thrust into his silk obi. Huddled nearby, Manda and Laura waited as well, but without the armed figure's calm.

A step sounded and a fourth figure stirred, moving in the shadows that cloaked the back of the train station. It was a bag lady, wreathed in patched layers of clothes, her treasures gathered around her like a clutch of garbage bags standing on a street curb waiting for the garbage collectors that no longer served this part of the city. Her head swiveled slowly, taking in Shoki, the two girls, then she turned to see what they were looking at.

The darkness almost swallowed him, brown skin, black clothes, dreadlocks and all. He paused, gaze settling on Shoki. When Shoki gave him a brief bow, Stick lifted his hand to the hilt of his katana. There was a sharp click as he unlocked the blade with his thumb, pulling it a half-inch free of the wooden sheath.

"I've come for her," he said softly. "I've got to do it myself this time."

Shoki made no move towards his own weapons.

"She has been long dead," he said.

Stick shook his head and began to close the distance between them.

Manda couldn't stand it any more. She jumped up from where she was sitting, but Laura hauled her back down. Manda glared at her.

"If we don't do something," she hissed, "one of them's going to get killed."

Laura put an arm around Manda's shoulders, as much to keep her down as to comfort her. "Right now, the worst thing we could do is get in the way."

"But...."

"I don't like it anymore that you do, Manda. Believe me."

Manda started suddenly as something touched her, then looked down to find Lubin crouched by her feet. She patted her lap and the ferret flowed up on to it, shivering.

"Yeah," Manda said softly, stroking Lubin's fur. "I know just what you're going through."

Stick and Shoki stood with just a few feet between them. Within striking distance.

"Listen to me," Shoki said. "The past is gone. If you go on with this, *you'll* be crossing the line."

Stick blinked. He was still in the past, but pieces of the present were beginning to superimpose themselves on what had been, on what he knew he had to do.

"Berlin's clearing her name right now," Shoki went on, pressing the momentary advantage. "It was all a mistake."

Stick shook his head as if to clear it.

"I'm not here for Berlin," he said. "I'm here for Onisu. Get out of the way."

"I can't," Shoki said.

Nothing gave Stick away. There was no narrowing of the eyes, no shift in his stance. But Shoki knew Stick was moments from drawing his katana. And once drawn, there'd be no turning back—not for either of them. It would be decided in seconds. A duel between masters such as they would be over almost before it began.

Shoki centered his balance. He closed his mind, allowing the years of practice to rise up and take control. When he finally made his move, it would be fueled by instinct. His body would know the correct move at the correct time before his mind could even begin to consider it.

He knew a moment's sadness, but before either of them could move—

"Stick!"

Instinctively—and for all the disagreement between them—they flowed into new stances, each facing outwards, protecting the other's back. Shoki's eyes widened slightly. What he saw was a circle of dogs. The circle began directly in front of him, then fanned out on either side until the lines left his range of vision. Stick saw the dogs, too. But he also saw the one who had called his name.

The bag lady had moved from the side of the train station to stand in front of him. Out of the shadows, she was easily recognized—if not by Stick, at least by the others.

Berlin.

She had a dark cloak over her shoulders. Her hands reached out from under it, holding a Kabuki mask of a woman's face. The cheeks and brow were a deathly white, the lips red, the eyes painted with long stylized strokes. Slowly Berlin pulled it on.

"Onisu," Stick breathed.

"*Hai*," the masked figure replied. Yes.

Stick took a step towards her, fingers tightening on the hilt of his katana.

"Forgive me," he said.

"There is nothing to forgive."

The katana whispered against lacquered wood of its sheath. Berlin's cloak billowed as she moved an instant before the katana was completely clear of the sheath. The sword blurred in the night air to cut deeply into the cloak's undulating folds. The mask went skittering across the pavement, landing face-up to stare at the sky. Berlin let herself fall, the cloak collapsing around her, covering her completely as she touched the ground.

After that one stroke, Stick stood as though carved from granite. He stared at the Kabuki mask.

Sensing the beginning of Stick's movement, Shoki had begun to turn. When he saw what happened, the aspect of the Demon Queller left him and Koga stood in his place. It was Koga—the man, the Sensei—who plucked the katana from Stick's nerveless fingers. He noted that the blade was still dry.

Stick walked slowly over to the Kabuki mask. Kneeling beside it, he picked it up. He stared at it for a long moment, then held it against his chest and bowed his head.

Manda and Laura rose from where they'd been sitting, Manda clutching Lubin close to her. All around them the dogs watched silently.

"Koga," Laura called. "Berlin. Is she…?"

But when they looked at where she'd dropped, they saw the cloak move. Folds of cloth fell aside. Berlin flowed to her feet and held the cloak open so that they could see the clean slice where the katana had cut through the fabric.

"Jesus, I played that close," Berlin murmured. "Another inch and that hole'd be in me."

She let the cloak flutter to the ground at her feet.

Stick turned at the sound of her voice.

"Hey, tall, dark and ugly," she said.

Stick laid the mask down. "Berlin, I…."

She shook her head. "You don't have to say anything. We've all been there, at one time or another. Question is, are you okay now?"

"I've been better, but yeah. I'm okay. Thanks." He turned to where the others were standing. "All of you. I mean that. I was really… someplace else."

He rose to his feet as Koga approached, the katana outstretched in his hands. Stick took the blade with a brief bow and returned it to its sheath. For a long moment the two men faced each other, then Stick moved closer and the two men embraced.

"Been a long time, man," Stick said.

"Too long," Koga replied.

When they stepped back, Berlin rubbed her hands briskly together. "Well, I won't say it hasn't been fun, but I've got to run. It's time I got a new House going—the Diggers were just starting to make a difference, you know?" She gave a sharp whistle and the dogs exploded into motion all around them, heading back to Dogtown. "But I still wish I had the name of the sucker who started all of this. I don't like having enemies hiding across the Border, never knowing when they'll strike again."

"It's better than having them inside yourself," Stick said.

Berlin nodded soberly. "I guess so."

"Do you need any help or anything?" Manda asked her.

Berlin shot Stick a glance, then she grinned. "I can always use a hand. Best thing you could do is get that band of yours to play a benefit or two—just to get the Diggers on the road again. Do you know 'World Turned Upside Down'?"

Manda shook her head.

"Leon Rosselson wrote it—long time ago now. You guys should learn it. It's an angry song, but an honest one. Like the blues are sometimes, you know?" Berlin pulled one of her thin cigars out of an inside pocket of her jean jacket. "Anyway, if you can do a benefit...."

She lit up, ground the wooden match under her heel, and started to walk away, still talking. Manda kept pace at her side, Lubin asleep in her arms. Stick, Koga and Laura took up the rear.

"That's Berlin," Stick said. "She's always got some scheme on the go."

Koga put his arm around Laura. "Good thing," he said.

Stick nodded. "Yeah," he agreed. "Damn good thing."

DRACO, DRACO

Tanith Lee

Tanith Lee became a freelance writer in 1975, and has been one ever since. Her first published books were children's fantasies *The Dragon Hoard* and *Animal Castle*. Her first adult fantasy novel, *The Birthgrave,* was the start of a long association with DAW, which published more than twenty of her works of fantasy, SF, and horror in the 1970s and 1980s. She received the British Fantasy Society's August Derleth Award in 1980 for *Death's Master,* World Fantasy Awards for Best Short Story in 1983 (for "The Gorgon") and 1984 (for "Elle est Trois (La Mort)"). Enormously prolific, Lee has recently published a trilogy of pirate novels for young adults (*Piratica* and sequels), a science fiction novel for adults (*Mortal Suns*), an adult fantasy trilogy (Lionwolf), a young adult fantasy trilogy (*Claidi* and sequels), and the first of two retrospective short story collections (*Tempting the Gods*). Upcoming are new books in the Flat Earth series. In 2009 she was made a Grand Master of Horror. Tanith Lee lives with her husband, the writer and artist John Kaiine, on the southeast coast of England.

You'll have heard stories, sometimes, of men who have fought and slain dragons. These are all lies. There's no swordsman living ever killed a dragon, though a few swordsmen dead that tried.

On the other hand, I once travelled in company with a fellow who got the name of "dragon-slayer".

A riddle? No. I'll tell you.

I was coming from the North back into the South, to civilisation as you may say, when I saw him, sitting by the roadside. My first feeling was envy, I admit. He was smart and very clean for someone in the wilds, and he had the South all over him, towns and baths and money. He was crazy, too, because there was gold on his wrists and in one ear. But he had a sharp grey sword, an army sword, so maybe he could defend himself. He was also younger than me, and a great deal prettier, but the last isn't too difficult. I wondered what he'd do when he looked up from his daydream and saw me, tough, dark and sour as a twist of old rope, clopping down on him on my swarthy little horse, ugly as sin, that I love like a daughter.

Then he did look up and I discovered.

"Greetings, stranger. Nice day, isn't it?"

He stayed relaxed as he said it, and somehow you knew from that he really could look after himself. It wasn't he thought I was harmless, just that he thought he could handle me if I tried something. Then again, I had my box of stuff alongside. Most people can tell my trade from that, and the aroma of drugs and herbs. My father was with the Romans, in fact he was probably the last Roman of all, one foot on the ship to go home, the rest of him with my mother up against the barnyard wall. She said he was a camp physician and maybe that was so. Some idea of doctoring grew up with me, though nothing great or grand. An itinerant apothecary is welcome almost anywhere, and can even turn bandits civil. It's not a wonderful life, but it's the only one I know.

I gave the young soldier-dandy that it was a nice day. I added he'd possibly like it better if he hadn't lost his horse.

"Yes, a pity about that. You could always sell me yours."

"Not your style."

He looked at her. I could see he agreed. There was also a momentary idea that he might kill me and take her, so I said, "And she's well known as mine. It would get you a bad name. I've friends round about."

He grinned, good-naturedly. His teeth were good, too. What with that, and the hair like barley, and the rest of it—well, he was the kind usually gets what he wants. I was curious as to which army he had hung about with to gain the sword. But since the Eagles flew, there are kingdoms everywhere, chiefs, war-leaders, Roman knights, and every tide brings an invasion up some beach. Under it all, too, you can feel the earth, the actual ground, which had been measured and ruled with fine roads, the land which had been subdued but never tamed, beginning to quicken. Like the shadows that come with the blowing out of a lamp. Ancient things, which are in my blood somewhere, so I recognise them.

But he was like a new coin that hadn't got dirty yet, nor learned much, though you could see your face in its shine, and cut yourself on its edge.

His name was Caiy. Presently we came to an arrangement and he mounted up behind me on Negra. They spoke a smatter of Latin where I was born, and I called her that before I knew her, for her darkness. I couldn't call her for her hideousness, which is her only other visible attribute. The fact is, I wasn't primed to the country round that way at all. I'd had word, a day or two prior, that there were Saxons in the area I'd been heading for. And so I switched paths and was soon lost. When I came on Caiy, I'd been pleased with the road, which was Roman, hoping it would go somewhere useful. But, about ten miles after Caiy joined me, the road petered out in a forest. My passenger was lost, too. He was going South, no surprise there, but last night his horse had broken loose and bolted, leaving him stranded. It sounded unlikely, but I wasn't inclined to debate on it. It seemed to me someone might have stolen the horse, and Caiy didn't care to confess.

There was no way round the forest, so we went in and the road died. Being summer, the wolves would be scarce and the bears off in the hills. Nevertheless, the trees had a feel I didn't take to, sombre and still, with the sound of little streams running through like metal chains, and birds that didn't sing but made purrings and clinkings. Negra never baulked or complained—if I'd waited to call her, I could have done it for her courage and warm-heartedness—but she couldn't come to terms with the forest, either.

"It smells," said Caiy, who'd been kind enough not to comment on mine, "as if it's rotting. Or fermenting."

I grunted. Of course it did, it was, the fool. But the smell told you other things. The centuries, for one. Here were the shadows that had come back when Rome blew out her lamp and sailed away, and left us in the dark.

Then Caiy, the idiot, began to sing to show up the birds who wouldn't. A nice voice, clear and bright. I didn't tell him to leave off. The shadows already knew we were there.

When night came down, the black forest closed like a cellar door.

We made a fire and shared my supper. He'd lost his rations with his mare.

"Shouldn't you tether that—your horse," suggested Caiy, trying not to insult her since he could see we were partial to each other. "My mare was tied, but something scared her and she broke the tether and ran. I wonder what it was," he mused, staring in the fire.

About three hours later, we found out.

I was asleep, and dreaming of one of my wives, up in the far North, and she was nagging at me, trying to start a brawl, which she always did for she was taller than me, and liked me to hit her once in a while so she could feel fragile, feminine and mastered. Just as she emptied the beer jar over my head, I heard a sound up in the sky like a storm that was not a storm. And I knew I wasn't dreaming any more.

The sound went over, three or four great claps, and the tops of the forest reeling, and left shuddering. There was a sort of quiver in the air, as if sediment were stirred up in it. There was even an extra smell, dank, yet tingling. When the noise was only a memory, and the bristling hairs began to subside along my body, I opened my eyes.

Negra was flattened to the ground, her own eyes rolling, but she was silent. Caiy was on his feet, gawping up at the tree-tops and the strands of starless sky. Then he glared at me.

"What in the name of the Bull was that?"

I noted vaguely that the oath showed he had Mithraic allegiances, which generally meant Roman. Then I sat up, rubbed my arms and neck to get human, and went to console Negra. Unlike his silly cavalry mare she hadn't bolted.

"It can't," he said, "have been a bird. Though I'd have sworn something flew over."

"No, it wasn't a bird."

"But it had wings. Or—no it couldn't have had wings the size of that."

"Yes it could. They don't carry it far, is all."

"Apothecary, stop being so damned provoking. If you know, out with it! Though I don't see how you can know. And don't tell me it's some bloody woods demon I won't believe in."

"Nothing like that," I said. "It's real enough. Natural, in its own way. Not," I amended, "that I ever came across one before, but I've met some who did."

Caiy was going mad, like a child working up to a tantrum.

"*Well?*"

I suppose he had charmed and irritated me enough I wanted to retaliate, because I just quoted some bastard non-sensical jabber-Latin chant at him:

Bis terribilis—

Bis appellare—

Draco! Draco!

At least, it made him sit down.

"What?" he eventually said.

At my age I should be over such smugness. I said, "It was a dragon."

Caiy laughed. But he had glimpsed it, and knew better than I did that I was right.

Nothing else happened that night. In the morning we started off again and there was a rough track, and then the forest began to thin out. After a while we emerged on the crown of a moor. The land dropped down to a valley, and on the other side there were sunny smoky hills and a long streamered sky. There was something else, too.

Naturally, Caiy said it first; as if everything new always surprised him, as if we hadn't each of us, in some way, been waiting for it, or something like it.

"This place stinks."

"Hn."

"Don't just grunt at me, you blasted quack doctor. It does, doesn't it. Why?"

"Why do you think?"

He brooded, pale gold and citified, behind me. Negra tried to paw the ground, and then made herself desist.

Neither of us brave humans had said any more about what had interrupted sleep in the forest, but when I'd told him no dragon could fly far on its wings, for from all I'd ever heard they were too large and only some freakish lightness in their bones enabled them to get airborne at all, I suppose we had both taken it to heart. Now here were the valley and the hills, and here was this reek lying over everything, strange, foul, alien, comparable to nothing, really. Dragon smell.

I considered. No doubt, the dragon went on an aerial patrol most nights, circling as wide as it could, to see what might be there for it. There were other things I'd learnt. These beasts hunt nocturnally, like cats. At the same time, a dragon is more like a crow in its habits. It will attack and kill, but normally it eats carrion, dead things, or dying and immobilised. It's light, as I said, it has to be to take the skies, but the lack of weight is compensated by the armor, the teeth and talons. Then again, I'd heard of dragons that breathed fire. I've never been quite convinced there. It seems more likely to me such monsters only live in volcanic caves, the mountain itself belching flame and the dragon taking credit for it. Maybe not. But certainly, this dragon was no fire-breather. The ground would have been scorched for miles; I've listened to stories where that happened. There were no marks of fire. Just the insidious pervasive stench that I knew, by the time we'd gone down into the valley, would be so familiar, so soaked into us, we would hardly notice it any more, or the scent of anything else.

I awarded all this information to my passenger. There followed a long verbal delay. I thought he might just be flabbergasted at getting so much chat from me, but then he said, very hushed, "You truly believe all this, don't you?"

I didn't bother with the obvious, just clucked to Negra, trying to make her turn back the way we'd come. But she was unsure and for once uncooperative, and suddenly his strong hand, the nails groomed even now, came down on my arm.

"Wait, Apothecary. If it *is* true—"

"Yes, yes," I said. I sighed. "You want to go and challenge it, and become a hero." He held himself like marble, as if I were speaking of some girl he thought he loved. I didn't see why I should waste experience and wisdom on him, but then. "No man ever killed a dragon. They're plated, all over, even the underbelly. Arrows and spears just bounce off—even a pilum. Swords clang and snap in half. Yes, yes," I reiterated, "you've heard of men who slashed the tongue, or stabbed into an eye. Let me tell you, if they managed to reach that high and actually did it, then they just made the brute angry. Think of the size and shape of a dragon's head, the way the pictures show it. It's one hell of a push from the eye into the brain. And you know, there's one theory the eyelid is armoured, too, and can come down faster than *that*."

"Apothecary," he said. He sounded dangerous. I just knew what he must look like. Handsome, noble and insane.

"Then I won't keep you," I said. "Get down and go on and the best of luck."

I don't know why I bothered. I should have tipped him off and ridden for it, though I wasn't sure Negra could manage to react sufficiently fast, she was that edgy. Anyway, I didn't, and sure enough next moment his sword was at the side of my throat, and so sharp it had drawn blood.

"You're the clever one," he said, "the know-all. And you do seem to know more than I do, about this. So you're my guide, and your scruff-bag of a horse, if it even deserves the name, is my transport. Giddy-up, the pair of you."

That was that. I never argue with a drawn sword. The dragon would be lying up by day, digesting and dozing, and by night I could hole up someplace myself. Tomorrow Caiy would be dead and I could leave. And I would, of course, have seen a dragon for myself.

After an hour and a half's steady riding—better once I'd persuaded him to switch from the sword to poking a dagger against my ribs, less tiring for us both—we came around a stand of woods, and there was a village. It was the savage Northern kind, thatch and wattle and turf banks, but big for all that, a good mile of it, not all walled. There were walls this end, however, and men on the gate, peering at us.

Caiy was aggrieved because he was going to have to ride up to them pillion, but he knew better now than to try managing Negra alone. He maybe didn't want to pretend she was his horse in any case.

As we pottered up the pebbled track to the gate, he sprang off and strode forward, arriving before me, and began to speak.

When I got closer I heard him announcing, in his dramatic, beautiful voice, "—And if it's a fact, I swear by the Victory of the Light that I will meet the thing and kill it."

They were muttering. The dragon smell, even though we were used to it, sodden with it, seemed more acid here. Poor Negra had been voiding herself from sheer terror all up the path. With fortune on her side, there would be somewhere below ground, some cave or dug out place, where they'd be putting their animals out of the dragon's way, and she could shelter with the others.

Obviously, the dragon hadn't always been active in this region. They'd scarcely have built their village if it had. No, it would have been like the tales. Dragons live for centuries. They can sleep for centuries, too. Unsuspecting, man moves in, begins to till and build and wax prosperous. Then the dormant dragon wakes under the hill. They're like the volcanoes I spoke of, in that. Which is perhaps, more than habitat, why so many of the legends say they breathe fire when they wake.

The interesting thing was, even clouded by the dragon stink, initially, the village didn't seem keen to admit anything.

Caiy, having made up his mind to accept the dragon—and afraid of being wrong—started to rant. The men at the gate were frightened and turning nasty. Leading Negra now, I approached, tapped my chest of potions and said:

"Or, if you don't want your dragon slain, I can cure some of your other troubles. I've got medicines for almost everything. Boils, warts. Ear pains. Tooth pains. Sick eyes. Women's afflictions. I have here—"

"Shut up, you toad-turd," said Caiy.

One of the guards suddenly laughed. The tension sagged.

Ten minutes after, we had been let in the gate and were trudging through the cow-dung and wild flowers—neither of which were to be smelled through the other smell—to the head-man's hall.

It was around two hours after that when we found out why the appearance of a rescuing champion-knight had given them the jitters.

It seemed they had gone back to the ancient way, propitiation, the scape-goat. For three years, they had been making an offering to the dragon, in spring, and at midsummer, when it was likely to be most frisky.

Anyone who knew dragons from a book would tell them this wasn't the way. But they knew their dragon from myth. Every time they made sacrifice, they imagined the thing could understand and appreciate what they'd done for it, and would therefore be more amenable.

In reality, of course, the dragon had never attacked the village. It had thieved cattle off the pasture by night, elderly or sick cows at that, and lambs that were too little and weak to run. It would have taken people, too, but only those who were disabled and alone. I said, a dragon is lazy and prefers carrion, or what's defenceless. Despite being big, they aren't so big they'd go after a whole tribe of men. And though even forty men together undoubtedly couldn't wound a dragon, they could exhaust it, if they kept up a rough-house. Eventually it would keel over and they could brain it. You seldom hear of forty men going off in a band to take a dragon, however. Dragons are still ravelled up with night fears and spiritual mysteries, and latterly with an Eastern superstition of a mighty demon who can assume the form of a dragon which is invincible and—naturally—breathes sheer flame. So, this village, like many another, would put out its sacrifice, one girl tied to a post, and leave her there, and the dragon would have her. Why not? She was helpless, fainting with horror—and young and tender into the bargain. Perfect. You never could convince them that, instead of appeasing the monster, the sacrifice encourages it to stay. Look at it from the dragon's point of view. Not only are there dead sheep and stray cripples to devour, but once in a while a nice juicy damsel on a stick. Dragons don't think like a man, but they do have memories.

When Caiy realized what they were about to do, tonight, as it turned out, he went red then white, exactly as they do in a bardic lay. Not anger, mind you. He didn't comprehend any more than they did. It was merely the awfulness of it.

He stood up and chose a stance, quite unconsciously impressive, and assured us he'd save her. He swore to it in front of us all, the chieftain, his men, me. And he swore it by the Sun, so I knew he meant business.

They were scared, but now also childishly hopeful. It was part of their mythology again. All mythology seems to take this tack somewhere, the dark against the light, the Final Battle. It's rot, but there.

Following a bit of drinking to seal the oath, they cheered up and the chief ordered a feast. Then they took Caiy to see the chosen sacrifice.

Her name was Niemeh, or something along those lines. She was sitting in a little lamplit cell off the hall. She wasn't fettered, but a warrior stood guard beyond the screen, and there was no window. She had nothing to do except weave flowers together, and she was doing that, making garlands for her death procession in the evening.

When Caiy saw her, his color drained away again.

He stood and stared at her, while somebody explained he was her champion.

Though he got on my nerves, I didn't blame him so much this time. She was about the most beautiful thing I ever hope to see. Young, obviously, and slim, but with a woman's shape, if you have my meaning, and long hair more fair even than Caiy's, and green eyes like sea pools and a face like one of the white flowers in her hands, and a sweet mouth.

I looked at her as she listened gravely to all they said. I remembered how in the legends it's always the loveliest and the most gentle gets picked for the dragon's dinner. You perceive the sense in the gentle part. A girl with a temper might start a ruckus.

When Caiy had been introduced and once more sworn by the sun to slay the dragon and so on, she thanked him. If things had been different, she would have blushed and trembled, excited by Caiy's attention. But she was past all that. You could see, if you looked, she didn't believe anyone could save her. But though she must have been half dead already of despair and fright, she still made space to be courteous.

Then she glanced over Caiy's head straight at me, and she smiled so I wouldn't feel left out.

"And who is this man?" she asked.

They all looked startled, having forgotten me. Then someone who had warts recalled I'd said I could fix him something for warts, and told her I was the apothecary. A funny little shiver went through her then.

She was so young and so pretty. If I'd been Caiy I'd have stopped spouting rubbish about the dragon. I'd have found some way to lay out the whole village, and grabbed her, and gone. But that would have been a stupid thing to do too. I've enough of the old blood to know about such matters. She was the sacrifice and she was resigned to it; more, she didn't dream she could be anything else. I've come across rumors, here and there, of girls, men too, chosen to die, who escaped. But the fate stays on them. Hide them securely miles off, across water, beyond tall hills, still they feel the geas weigh like lead upon their souls. They kill themselves in the end, or go mad. And this girl, this Niemeh, you could see it in her. No, I would never have abducted her. It would have been no use. She was convinced she must die, as if she'd seen it written in light on a stone, and maybe she had.

She returned to her garlands, and Caiy, tense as a bowstring, led us back to the hall.

Meat was roasting and more drink came out and more talk came out. You can kill anything as often as you like, that way.

It wasn't a bad feast, as such up-country things go. But all through the shouts and toasts and guzzlings, I kept thinking of her in her cell behind the screen, hearing the clamor and aware of this evening's sunset, and how it would be to die... as she would have to. I didn't begin to grasp how she could bear it.

By late afternoon they were mostly sleeping it off, only Caiy had had the sense to go and sweat the drink out with soldiers' exercises in the yard, before a group of sozzled admirers of all sexes.

When someone touched my shoulder, I thought it was warty after his cure, but no. It was the guard from the girl's cell, who said very low, "She says she wants to speak to you. Will you come, now?"

I got up and went with him. I had a spinning minute, wondering if perhaps she didn't believe she must die after all, and would appeal to me to save her. But in my heart of hearts I guessed it wasn't that.

There was another man blocking the entrance, but they let me go in alone, and there Niemeh sat, making garlands yet, under her lamp.

But she looked up at me, and her hands fell like two more white flowers on the flowers in her lap. "I need some medicine, you see," she said. "But I can't pay you. I don't have anything. Although my uncle—"

"No charge," I said hurriedly.

She smiled. "It's for tonight."

"Oh," I said.

"I'm not brave," she said, "but it's worse than just being afraid. I know I shall die. That it's needful. But part of me wants to live so much—my reason tells me one thing but my body won't listen. I'm frightened I shall panic, struggle and scream and weep—I don't want that. It isn't right. I have to consent, or the sacrifice isn't any use. Do you know about that?"

"Oh, yes," I said.

"I thought so. I thought you did. Then… can you give me something, a medicine or herb—so I shan't feel anything? I don't mean the pain. That doesn't matter. The gods can't blame me if I cry out then, they wouldn't expect me to be beyond pain. But only to make me not care, not want to live so very much."

"An easy death."

"Yes." She smiled again. She seemed serene and beautiful. "Oh, yes."

I looked at the floor.

"The soldier. Maybe he'll kill it," I said.

She didn't say anything.

When I glanced up, her face wasn't serene any more. It was brimful of terror. Caiy would have been properly insulted.

"Is it you can't give me anything? Don't you have anything? I was sure you did. That you were sent here to me to—to help, so I shouldn't have to go through it all alone—"

"There," I said, "it's all right. I do have something. Just the thing. I keep it for women in labor when the child's slow and hurting them. It works a treat. They go sort of misty and far off, as if they were nearly asleep. It'll dull pain, too. Even—any kind of pain."

"Yes," she whispered, I should like that." And then she caught my hand and kissed it. "I knew you would," she said, as if I'd promised her the best and loveliest thing in all the earth. Another man, it would have broken him in front of her. But I'm harder than most.

When she let me, I retrieved my hand, nodded reassuringly, and went out. The chieftain was awake and genial enough, so I had a word with him. I told him what the girl had asked. "In the East," I said, "it's the usual thing, give them something to help them through. They call it Nektar, the drink of the gods. She's consented," I said, "but she's very young and scared, delicately-bred too. You can't grudge her this." He acquiesced immediately, as glad as she was, as I'd hoped. It's a grim affair, I should imagine, when the girl shrieks for pity all the way up to the hills. I hadn't thought there'd be any problem. On the other hand, I hadn't wanted to be caught slipping her potions behind anyone's back.

I mixed the drug in the cell where she could watch. She was interested in everything I did, the way the condemned are nearly always interested in every last detail, even how a cobweb hangs.

I made her promise to drink it all, but none of it until they came to bring her out. "It may not last otherwise. You don't want it to wear off before—too early."

"No," she said. "I'll do exactly what you say."

When I was going out again, she said, "If I can ask them for anything for you, the gods, when I meet them..." It was in my mind to say: Ask them to go stick—but I didn't. She was trying to keep intact her trust in recompence, immortality. I said, "just ask them to look after you."

She had such a sweet, sweet mouth. She was made to love and be loved, to have children and sing songs and die when she was old, peacefully, in her sleep.

And there would be others like her. The dragon would be given those, too. Eventually, it wouldn't just be maidens, either. The taboo states it had to be a virgin so as to safeguard any unborn life. Since a virgin can't be with child—there's one religion says different, I forget which—they stipulate virgins. But in the end any youthful woman, who can reasonably be reckoned as not with child, will do. And then they go on to the boys. Which is the most ancient sacrifice there is.

I passed a very young girl in the hall, trotting round with the beer-dipper. She was comely and innocent, and I recollected I'd seen her earlier and asked myself, Are you the next? And who'll be next after you?

Niemeh was the fifth. But, I said, dragons live a long while. And the sacrifices always get to be more frequent. Now it was twice a year. In the first year it had been once. In a couple more years it would happen at every season, with maybe three victims in the summer when the creature was most active.

And in ten more years it would be every month, and they'd have learned to raid other villages to get girls and young men to give it, and there would be a lot of bones about, besides, fellows like Caiy, dragon-slayers dragon slain.

I went after the girl with the beer-dipper and drained it. But drink never did comfort me much.

And presently, it would be time to form the procession and start for the hills.

It was the last gleaming golden hour of day when we set off.

The valley was fertile and sheltered. The westering light caught and flashed in the trees and out of the streams. Already there was a sort of path stamped smooth and kept clear of undergrowth. It would have been a pleasant journey, if they'd been going anywhere else.

There was sunlight warm on the sides of the hills, too. The sky was almost cloudless, transparent. If it hadn't been for the tainted air, you would never have thought anything was wrong. But the track wound up the first slope and around, and up again, and there, about a hundred yards off, was the flank of a bigger hill that went down into shadow at its bottom, and never took the sun. That underside was bare of grass, and eaten out in caves, one cave larger than the rest and very black, with a strange black stillness, as if light and weather and time itself stopped just inside. Looking at that, you'd know at once, even with sun on your face and the whole lucid sky above.

They'd brought her all this way in a Roman litter which somehow had become the property of the village. It had lost its roof and its curtains, just a kind of cradle on poles, but Niemeh had sat in it on their shoulders, motionless, and dumb. I had only stolen one look at her, to be sure, but her face had turned mercifully blank and her eyes were opaque. What I'd given her started its work swiftly. She was beyond us all now. I was only anxious everything else would occur before her condition changed.

Her bearers set the litter down and lifted her out. They'd have to support her, but they would know about that, girls with legs gone to water, even passed out altogether. And I suppose the ones who fought and screamed would be forced to sup strong ale, or else concussed with a blow.

Everyone walked a little more, until we reached a natural palisade of rock. This spot provided concealment, while overlooking the cave and the ground immediately below it. There was a stagnant dark pond caught in the gravel there, but on our side, facing the cave, a patch of clean turf with a post sticking up, about the height of a tall man.

The two warriors supporting Niemeh went on with her towards the post. The rest of us stayed behind the rocks, except for Caiy.

We were all garlanded with flowers. Even I had had to be, and I hadn't made a fuss. What odds? But Caiy wasn't garlanded. He was the one part of the ritual which, though arcanely acceptable, was still profane. And that was why, even though they would let him attack the dragon, they had nevertheless brought the girl to appease it.

There was some kind of shackle at the post. It wouldn't be iron, because anything fey has an allergy to stable metals, even so midnight a thing as a dragon. Bronze, probably. They locked one part around her waist and another round her throat. Only the teeth and claws could get her out of her bonds now, piece by piece.

She sagged forward in the toils. She seemed unconscious at last, and I wanted her to be.

The two men hurried back, up the slope and into the rock cover with the rest of us. Sometimes the tales have the people rush away when they've put out their sacrifice, but usually the people stay, to witness. It's quite safe. The dragon won't go after them with something tasty chained up right under its nose.

Caiy didn't remain beside the post. He moved down towards the edge of the polluted pond. His sword was drawn. He was quite ready. Though the sun couldn't get into the hollow to fire his hair or the metal blade, he cut a grand figure, heroically braced there between the maiden and Death.

At the end, the day spilled swiftly. Suddenly all the shoulders of the hills grew dim, and the sky became the color of lavender, and then a sort of mauve amber, and the stars broke through.

There was no warning.

I was looking at the pond, where the dragon would come to drink, judging the amount of muck there seemed to be in it. And suddenly there was a reflection in the pond, from above. It wasn't definite, and it was upside down, but even so my heart plummeted through my guts.

There was a feeling behind the rock, the type you get, they tell me, in the battle lines, when the enemy appears. And mixed with this, something of another feeling, more maybe like the inside of some god's house when they call on him, and he seems to come.

I forced myself to look then, at the cave mouth. This, after all, was the evening I would see a real dragon, something to relate to others, as others had related such things to me.

It crept out of the cave, inch by inch, nearly down on its belly, cat-like.

The sky wasn't dark yet, a Northern dusk seems often endless. I could see well, and better and better as the shadow of the cave fell away and the dragon advanced into the paler shadow by the pond.

At first, it seemed unaware of anything but itself and the twilight. It flexed and stretched itself. There was something uncanny, even in such simple movements, something evil. And timeless.

The Romans know an animal they call Elephantus, and I mind an ancient clerk in one of the towns describing this beast to me, fairly accurately, for he'd seen one once. The dragon wasn't as large as elephantus, I should say. Actually not that much higher than a fair-sized cavalry gelding, if rather longer. But it was sinuous, more sinuous than any snake. The way it crept and stretched and flexed, and curled and slewed its head, its skeleton seemed fluid.

There are plenty of mosaics, paintings. It was like that, the way men have shown them from the beginning. Slender, tapering to the elongated head, which is like a horse's, too, and not like, and to the tail, though it didn't have that spade-shaped sting they put on them sometimes, like a scorpion's. There were spines, along the tail and the back-ridge, and the neck and head. The ears were set back, like a dog's. Its legs were short, but that didn't make it seem ungainly. The ghastly fluidity was always there, not grace, but something so like grace it was nearly unbearable.

It looked almost the color the sky was now, slatey, bluish-grey, like metal but dull; the great overlapping plates of its scales had no burnish. Its eyes were black and you didn't see them, and then they took some light from somewhere, and they flared like two flat coins, cat's eyes, with nothing—no brain, no soul—behind them.

It had been going to drink, but had scented something more interesting than dirty water, which was the girl. The dragon stood there, static as a rock, staring at her over the pond. Then gradually its two wings, that had been folded back like fans along its sides, opened and spread.

They were huge, those wings, much bigger than the rest of it. You could see how it might be able to fly with them. Unlike the body, there were no scales, only skin, membrane, with ribs of external bone. Bat's wings, near enough. It seemed feasible a sword could go through them, damage them, but that would only maim, and all too likely they were tougher than they seemed.

Then I left off considering. With its wings spread like that, unused—like a crow—it began to sidle around the water, the blind coins of eyes searing on the post and the sacrifice.

Somebody shouted. My innards sprang over. Then I realized it was Caiy. The dragon had nearly missed him, so intent it was on the feast, so he had had to call it. *Bis Terribilis—Bis appellare—Draco! Draco!*

I'd never quite understood that antic chant, and the Latin was execrable. But I think it really means to know a dragon exists is bad enough, to call its name and summon it—call twice, twice terrible—is the notion of a maniac.

The dragon wheeled. *It—flowed.* Its elongated horse's-head-which-wasn't was before him, and Caiy's sharp sword slashed up and down and bit against the jaw. It happened, what they say—sparks shot glittering in the air. Then the head split, not from any wound, just the chasm of the mouth. It made a sound at him, not a hissing, a sort of *hroosh*. Its breath would be poisonous, almost as bad as fire. I saw Caiy stagger at it, and then one of the long feet on the short legs went out through the gathering dark. The blow looked slow and harmless. It threw Caiy thirty feet, right across the pond. He fell at the entrance to the cave, and lay quiet. The sword was still in his hand. His grip must have clamped down on it involuntarily. He'd likely bitten his tongue as well, in the same way.

The dragon looked after him, you could see it pondering whether to go across again and dine. But it was more attracted by the other morsel it had smelled first. It knew from its scent this was the softer more digestible flesh. And so it ignored Caiy, leaving him for later, and eddied on towards the post, lowering its head as it came, the light leaving its eyes.

I looked. The night was truly blooming now, but I could see, and the darkness didn't shut my ears; there were sounds, too. You weren't there, and I'm not about to try to make you see and hear what I did. Niemeh didn't cry out. She was senseless by then, I'm sure of it. She didn't feel or know any of what it did to her. Afterwards, when I went down with the others, there wasn't much left. It even carried some of her bones into the cave with it, to chew. Her garland was lying on the ground since the dragon had no interest in garnish. The pale flowers were no longer pale.

She had consented, and she hadn't had to endure it. I've seen things as bad that had been done by men, and for men there's no excuse. And yet, I never hated a man as I hated the dragon, a loathing, deadly, sickening hate.

The moon was rising when it finished. It went again to the pond, and drank deeply. Then it moved up the gravel back towards the cave. It paused beside

Caiy, sniffed him, but there was no hurry. Having fed so well, it was sluggish. It stepped into the pitch-black hole of the cave, and drew itself from sight, inch by inch, as it had come out, and was gone.

Presently Caiy pulled himself off the ground, first to his hands and knees, then on to his feet.

We, the watchers, were amazed. We'd thought him dead, his back broken, but he had only been stunned, as he told us afterwards. Not even stunned enough not to have come to, dazed and unable to rise, before the dragon quite finished it's feeding. He was closer than any of us. He said it maddened him—as if he hadn't been mad already and so, winded and part stupefied as he was, he got up and dragged himself into the dragon's cave after it. And this time he meant to kill it for sure, no matter what it did to him.

Nobody had spoken a word, up on our rocky place, and no one spoke now. We were in a kind of communion, a trance. We leaned forward and gazed at the black gape in the hill where they had both gone.

Maybe a minute later, the noises began. They were quite extraordinary, as if the inside of the hill itself were gurning and snarling. But it was the dragon, of course. Like the stink of it, those sounds it made were untranslatable. I could say it looked this way comparable to an elephantus, or that way to a cat, a horse, a bat. But the cries and roars—no. They were like nothing else I've heard in the world, or been told of. There were, however, other noises, as of some great heap of things disturbed. And stones rattling, rolling.

The villagers began to get excited or hysterical. Nothing like this had happened before. Sacrifice is usually predictable.

They stood, and started to shout, or groan and invoke supernatural protection. And then a silence came from inside the hill, and silence returned to the villagers.

I don't remember how long it went on. It seemed like months.

Then suddenly something moved in the cave mouth.

There were yells of fear. Some of them took to their heels, but came back shortly when they realized the others were rooted to the spot, pointing and exclaiming, not in anguish but awe. That was because it was Caiy, and not the dragon, that had emerged from the hill.

He walked like a man who has been too long without food and water, head bowed, shoulders drooping, legs barely able to hold him up. He floundered through the edges of the pond and the sword trailed from his hand in the water. Then he tottered over the slope and was right before us. He somehow raised his head then, and got out the sentence no one had ever truly reckoned to hear.

"It's—dead," said Caiy, and slumped unconscious in the moonlight.

They used the litter to get him to the village, as Niemeh didn't need it any more.

We hung around the village for nearly ten days. Caiy was his merry self by the third, and since there had been no sign of the dragon, by day or night, a party of them went up to the hills, and, kindling torches at noon, slunk into the cave to be sure.

It was dead all right. The stench alone would have verified that, a different perfume than before, and all congealed there, around the cave. In the valley, even on the second morning, the live dragon smell was almost gone. You could make out goats and hay and meade and unwashed flesh and twenty varieties of flowers.

I myself didn't go in the cave. I went only as far as the post. I understood it was safe, but I just wanted to be there once more, where the few bones that were Niemeh had fallen through the shackles to the earth. And I can't say why, for you can explain nothing to bones.

There was rejoicing and feasting. The whole valley was full of it. Men came from isolated holdings, cots and huts, and a rough looking lot they were. They wanted to glimpse Caiy the dragon-slayer, to touch him for luck and lick the finger. He laughed. He hadn't been badly hurt, and but for bruises was as right as rain, up in the hay-loft half the time with willing girls, who would afterwards boast their brats were sons of the hero. Or else he was blind drunk in the chieftain's hall.

In the end, I collected Negra, fed her apples and told her she was the best horse in the land, which she knows is a lie and not what I say the rest of the time. I had sound directions now, and was planning to ride off quietly and let Caiy go on as he desired, but I was only a quarter of a mile from the village when I heard the splayed tocking of horse's hooves. Up he galloped beside me on a decent enough horse, the queen of the chief's stable, no doubt, and grinning, with two beer skins.

I accepted one, and we continued, side by side.

"I take it you're sweet on the delights of my company," I said at last, an hour after, when the forest was in view over the moor.

"What else, Apothecary? Even my insatiable lust to steal your gorgeous horse has been removed. I now have one of my very own, if not a third as beautiful." Negra cast him a sidelong look as if she would like to bite him. But he paid no attention. We trotted on for another mile or so before he added, "And there's something I want to ask you, too."

I was wary, and waited to find out what came next.

Finally, he said, "You must know a thing or two in your trade about how bodies fit together. That dragon, now. You seemed to know all about dragons."

I grunted. Caiy didn't cavil at the grunt. He began idly to describe how he'd gone into the cave, a tale he had flaunted a mere three hundred times in the chieftain's hall. But I didn't cavil either, I listened carefully.

The cave entry-way was low and vile, and soon it opened into a cavern. There was elf-light, more than enough to see by, and water running here and there along the walls and over the stony floor.

There in the cavern's center, glowing now like filthy silver, lay the dragon, on a pile of junk such as dragons always accumulate. They're like crows and magpies in that, also, shiny things intrigue them and they take them to their lairs to paw possessively and to lie on. The rumors of hoards must come from this, but usually the collection is worthless, snapped knives, impure glass that had sparkled under the moon, rusting armlets from some victim, and all of it soiled by the devil's droppings, and muddled up with split bones.

When he saw it like this, I'd bet the hero's reckless heart failed him. But he would have done his best, to stab the dragon in the eye, the root of the tongue, the vent under the tail, as it clawed him in bits.

"But you see," Caiy now said to me, "I didn't have to."

This, of course, he hadn't said in the hall. No. He had told the village the normal things, the lucky lunge and the brain pierced, and the death-throes, which we'd all heard plainly enough. If anyone noticed his sword had no blood on it, well, it had trailed in the pond, had it not?

"You see," Caiy went on, "it was lying there comatose one minute, and then it began to writhe about, and to go into a kind of spasm. Something got dislodged off the hoard-pile—a piece of cracked-up armor, I think, gilded—and knocked me silly again. And when I came round, the dragon was all sprawled about, and dead as yesterday's roast mutton."

"Hn," I said. "*Hn*n."

"The point being," said Caiy, watching the forest and not me, "I must have done something to it with the first blow, outside. Dislocated some bone or other. You told me their bones have no marrow. So to do that might be conceivable. A fortunate stroke. But it took a while for the damage to kill it."

"Hn*n*."

"Because," said Caiy, softly, "you do believe I killed it, don't you?"

"In the legends," I said, "they always do."

"But you said before that in reality, a man can't kill a dragon."

"One did," I said.

"Something I managed outside then. Brittle bones. That first blow to its skull."

"Very likely."

Another silence. Then he said:

"Do you have any gods, Apothecary?"

"Maybe."

"Will you swear me an oath by them, and then call me 'dragon-slayer'? Put it another way. You've been a help. I don't like to turn on my friends. Unless I have to."

His hand was nowhere near that honed sword of his, but the sword was in his eyes and his quiet, oh-so-easy voice. He had his reputation to consider, did Caiy. But I've no reputation at all. So I swore my oath and I called him dragon-slayer, and when our roads parted my hide was intact. He went off to glory somewhere I'd never want to go.

Well, I've seen a dragon, and I do have gods. But I told them, when I swore that oath, I'd almost certainly break it, and my gods are accustomed to me. They don't expect honor and chivalry. And there you are.

Caiy never killed the d[...]
who killed it. In my li[...]
which bring sleep, whic[...]
miseries in this blessed v[...]
better. I told you I was a [...]
But there were all those o[...]
Other Caiys, for that matte[...]
fifty strong men. It didn't pa[...]
had to be. The dragon devou[...]
And so Caiy earned the name[...]

And it wasn't a riddle.

And no, I haven't considered [...]
any twice-terrible thing. Heroes [...]
I'm not meant for any bard's rom[...]
ever find me in the Northern hills [...]

THE DRAGON ON THE BOOKSHELF

Harlan Ellison®
and Robert Silverberg

Harlan Ellison was born in Cleveland, Ohio in 1934. He moved to New York in 1955 to become a writer and published his first story in 1956. Within a year he had published over a hundred fiction and non-fiction pieces, under his own name and under a variety of commercially-required pennames. He served in the Army between 1957–59, moved to Chicago to edit *Rogue* magazine and created Regency Books in 1961. Ellison then moved to Los Angeles in 1962, and quickly established himself writing screenplays for popular television shows, including *The Twilight Zone* (1985) and, most famously, the *Star Trek* episode "The City on the Edge of Forever" and *The Outer Limits'* "Demon With a Glass Hand."

He has authored or edited 76 books. Ellison's most famous stories include "I Have No Mouth, and I Must Scream", "The Beast that Shouted Love at the Heart of the World", "The Deathbird", "Paladin of the Lost Hour", "'Repent, Harlequin!' Said the Ticktockman", and "Jeffty is Five". His stories remain in print in numerous collections, most recently in *Slippage, Troublemakers, Mind Fields, Mefisto in Onyx*, and *The Essential Ellison: A Fifty Year Retrospective*. His work has been awarded the Hugo, Nebula, Bram Stoker Award, World Fantasy, British Fantasy, British Science Fiction, and Locus awards. His career awards include the World Fantasy Award for Life Achievement, the Bram Stoker Award for Life Achievement, the International Horror Guild Living Legend, and the World Horror Grandmaster. In 2006 the Science Fiction & Fantasy Writers of America named him their Grand Master laureate; and in 2009 the film documentary of his life and work, *Dreams With Sharp Teeth*, twenty-one years in the making, opened at Lincoln Center, and has since won worldwide acclaim and awards.

Robert Silverberg is one of the most important writers in the history of science fiction and fantasy. He published his first story in 1954 and first novel, *Revolt on Alpha C*, in 1955, quickly establishing what has become one of the most successful and sustained careers in science fiction. He wrote prolifically for SF and other pulp markets during the '50s, focussed on nonfiction and other work in the early-'60s, then returned to SF with greater ambition, publishing stories and novels that pushed genre boundaries and were often dark in tone as they explored themes of human isolation and the quest for transcendence.

Works from the years 1967–1976, still considered Silverberg's most influential period, include Hugo winner "Nightwings", *The Masks of Time*, *Tower of Glass*, Nebula winner *A Time of Changes*, *Dying Inside*, *The Book of Skulls*, and Nebula winners "Good News from the Vatican" and "Born with the Dead", among many others. Silverberg retired in the late '70s before returning with popular SF/fantasy *Lord Valentine's Castle*, first in his continuing Majipoor series, and more novels and stories throughout the '80s and '90s, including Nebula winner "Sailing to Byzantium", Hugo winners "Gilgamesh in the Outback" and "Enter a Soldier. Later: Enter Another", and many others. His most recent books are the autobiography *Other Spaces, Other Times*, and the collection *Something Wild is Loose*. Upcoming are a new short novel *The Last Song of Orpheus* and a new collection *The Palace at Midnight*. He was acknowledged as a Grand Master by SFWA in 2004.

He was small; petite, actually. Perhaps an inch shorter—resting back on his glimmering haunches—than any of the mass-market paperbacks racked on either side of him. He was green, of course. Blue-green, down his front, under-chin to bellybottom, greenish yellow-ochre all over the rest. Large, luminous pastel-blue eyes that would have made Shirley Temple seethe with envy. And he was licking his front right paw as he blew soft gray smoke rings through his heroically long nostrils.

To his left, a well-thumbed Ballantine paperback edition of C. Wright Mills's THE CAUSES OF WORLD WAR III; to his right, a battered copy, sans dust jacket, of THE MAN WHO KNEW COOLIDGE by Sinclair Lewis. He licked each of his four paw-fingers in turn.

Margaret, sitting across the room from the teak Danish Modern bookcase where he lived, occasionally looked up from the theme papers she was correcting spread out across the card table, to smile at him and make a ticking sound of affection. "Good doughnuts?" she asked. An empty miniature Do-Nettes box lay on the carpet. The dragon rolled his eyes and continued licking confectioners' sugar from under his silver claws. "Good doughnuts," she said, and went back to her classwork.

Idly, she brushed auburn hair away from her face with the back of a slim hand. Completing his toilette, the little dragon stared raptly at her graceful movement, folded his front paws, sighed deeply, and closed his great, liquid eyes.

The smoke rings came at longer intervals now.

Outside, the afreet and djinn continued to battle, the sounds of their exploding souls making a terrible clank and clangor in the dew-misty streets of dark San Francisco.

So it was to be another of those days. They came all too frequently now that the gateway had been prised open: harsh days, smoldering days, dangerous nights. This was no place to be a dragon, no time to be in the tidal flow of harm's way. There were new manifestations every day now. Last Tuesday the watchthings fiercely clicking their ugly fangs and flatulating at the entrance to the Transamerica Pyramid. On Wednesday a shoal of blind banshees materialized above Coit Tower and covered the structure to the ground with lemony ooze that continued to wail days later. Thursday the resurrected Mongol hordes breaking through west of Van Ness, the air redolent of monosodium glutamate. Friday was silent. No less dangerous; merely silent. Saturday the gullgull incursion, the burnings at the Vaillancourt Fountain. And Sunday— oh, Sunday, bloody Sunday!

Small, large-eyed dragons in love had to walk carefully these days: perils were plentiful, sanctuaries few.

The dragon opened his eyes and stared raptly at the human woman. There sat his problem. Lovely, there she sat. The little dragon knew his responsibility. The only refuge lay within. The noise of the warfare outside was terrifying; and the little dragon was the cause. Coiling on his axis, the dragon diminished his extension along the *sril*-curve and let himself slip away. Margaret gasped softly, a little cry of alarm and dismay. "But you said you wouldn't—"

Too late. A twirling, twinkling scintillance. The bookshelf was empty of anything but books, not one of which mentioned dragons.

"Oh," she murmured, alone in the silent pre-dawn apartment.

"Master, what am I to do?" said Urnikh,• the little dragon that had been sitting in the tiny San Francisco apartment only moments before. "I have made matters so much worse. You should have selected better, Master…I never knew enough, was not powerful enough. I've made it terrible for them, and they don't even know it's happening. They are more limited than you let me understand, Master. And I…"

The little dragon looked up helplessly.

He spoke softly. "I love her, the human woman in the place where I came into their world. I love the human woman, and I did not pursue my mission. I love her, and my inaction made matters worse, my love for her helped open the gateway.

• Pronounced "Oower-*neesh*."

"I can't help myself. Help me to rectify, Master. I have fallen in love with her. I'm stricken. With the movement of her limbs, with the sound of her voice, the way her perfume rises off her, the gleam of her eyes; did I say the way her limbs move? The things she thinks and says? She is a wonderment, indeed. But what, *what* am I to do?"

The Master looked down at the dragon from the high niche in the darkness. "There is desperation in your voice, Urnikh."

"It is because I am so *desperate!*"

"You were sent to the Earth, to mortaltime, to save them. And instead you indulge yourself; and by so doing you have only made things worse for them. Why else does the gateway continue to remain open, and indeed grow wider and wider from hour to hour, if not on account of your negligence?"

Urnikh extended his head on its serpentine neck, let it sag, laid his chin on the darkness. "I am ashamed, Master. But I tell you again, I can't help myself. She fills me, the sight of her fills my every waking moment."

"Have you tried sleeping?"

"When I sleep, I dream. And when I dream, I am slave to her all the more."

The Master heaved a sigh very much like the sigh the little dragon had heaved in Margaret's apartment. "How does she bind you to her?"

"By not binding me at all. She is simply *there*; and I can't bear to be away from her. Help me, Master. I love her so; but I want to be the good force that you want me to be."

The Master slowly and carefully uncoiled to its full extension. For a long while it studied the contrite eyes of the little dragon in silence.

Then it said, "Time grows short, Urnikh. Matters grow more desperate. The djinn, the afreet, the watchthings, the gullgull, all of them rampage and destroy. No one will win. Earth will be left a desert. Mortaltime will end. You must return; and you must fight this love with all the magic of which you are possessed. Give her up. Give her up, Urnikh."

"It is impossible. I will fail."

"You are young. Merely a thousand years have passed you. Fight it, I tell you. Remember who and what you are. Return, and save them. They are poor little creatures and they have no idea what dangers surround them. Save them, Urnikh, and you will save *her*...and *yourself* as well."

The little dragon raised his head. "Yes, Master."

"Go, now. Will you go and do your best?"

"I will try very hard, Master."

"You are a good force, Urnikh. I have faith in you."

The little dragon was silent.

"Does she know what you are?" the Master asked, after a time.

"Not a bit. She thinks I am a cunningly made toy. An artificial life-form created for the amusement of humans."

"A cunningly made toy. Indeed. Intended to amuse." The Master's tone was frosty. "Well, go to her, then. *Amuse* her, Urnikh. But this must not go on very much longer, do you understand?"

The little dragon sighed again and let himself slip away on the *sril*-curve. The Master, sitting back on its furry haunches, turned itself inward to see if there was any hope.

It was too dim inside. There were no answers.

The dragon materialized within a pale amber glow that spanned the third and fourth shelves of the bookcase. Evidently many hours had passed: the lost day's shafts of sunlight no longer came spearing through the window; time flowed at different velocities on the *sril*-curve and in mortaltime; it was night but tendrils of troubling fog shrouded everything except the summit of Telegraph Hill.

The apartment was empty. Margaret was gone.

The dragon shivered, trembled, blew a fretful snort. Margaret: *gone!* And without any awareness of the perils that lurked on every side, out there on the battlefield that was San Francisco. It appalled him whenever she went outside; but, of course, she had no knowledge of the risks.

Where has she gone? he wondered. Perhaps she was visiting the male-one on Clement Street; perhaps she was strolling the chilly slopes of Lincoln Park; perhaps doing her volunteer work at the U of C Clinic on Mt. Parnassus; perhaps dreamily peering into the windows of the downtown shops. And all the while, wherever she was, in terrible danger. Unaware of the demonic alarums and conflicts that swirled through every corner of the embattled city.

I will go forth in search of her, Urnikh decided; and immediately came a sensation of horror that sent green ripples undulating down his slender back. Go *out* into that madness? Risk the success of the mission, risk existence itself, wander fogbound streets where chimeras and were-pythons and hungry jack-o'-lanterns lay in waiting, all for the sake of searching for *her?*

But Margaret was in danger, and what could matter to him more than that?

"You won't listen to me, ever, will you?" he imagined himself telling her. "There's a gateway open and the whole city has become a parade-ground for monsters, and when I tell you this you laugh, you say, 'How cute, how cute,' and you pay no attention. Don't you have any regard for your own safety?"

Of *course* she had regard for her own safety.

What she *didn't* have was the slightest reason to take him seriously. He was cuddly; he was darling; he was a pocket-sized bookcase-model dragon; a cunning artifact; cleverly made with infinitesimal clockwork animatronic parts sealed cunningly inside a shell-case without seam or seal; and nothing more.

But he *was* more than that. He was a sentinel; he was an emissary; he was a force.

Yes. I am a sentinel, he told himself, even as he was slipping through the door, even as he found himself setting out to look for Margaret. *I am a sentinel... why am I so frightened?*

Darkness of a sinister quality had smothered the city now. Under the hard flannel of fog no stars could be seen, no moon, the gleam of no eye. But from every rooftop, every lamp post, every parked car, glowed the demon-light of some denizen of the nether realms, clinging fiercely to the territory that it had chewed out, defying all others to displace it.

The dragon shuddered. This was *his* doing. The gateway that had been the merest pinprick in the membrane that separated the continuums now was a gaping chasm, through which all manner of horrendous beings poured into San Francisco without cease; and it was all because he, who had been sent here to repair the original minuscule rift, had lingered, had dallied, had let himself become obsessed with a creature of this pallid and inconsequential world.

Well, so be it. What was done—was done. His obsession was no less potent for the guilt he felt. And even now, now that the forces of destruction infested every corner of this city and soon would be spreading out beyond its bounds, his concern was still only for Margaret, Margaret, Margaret, Margaret.

His beloved Margaret.

Where was she?

He built a globe of *zabil*-force about himself, just in time to fend off the attack of some hairy-beaked thing that had come swooping down out of the neon sign of the Pizza Hut on the corner, and cast the *wuzud*-spell to seek out Margaret.

His mental emanations spiraled up, up, through the heavy chill fog, scanning the city. South to Market Street, westward to Van Ness: no Margaret. Wherever his mind roved, he encountered only diabolical blackness: gibbering shaitans, glassy-eyed horrid ghazulim, swarms of furious buzzing hospodeen, a hundred hundred sorts of angry menacing creatures of the dire plasmatic void that separates mortaltime from the nightmare worlds.

Margaret? *Margaret!*

Urnikh cast his reach farther and farther, probing here, there, everywhere with the shaft of crystalline *wuzud*-force. The swarming demons could do nothing to interfere with the soaring curve of his interrogatory thrust. Let them stamp and hiss, let them leap and prance, let them spit rivers of venom, let them do whatever they pleased: he would take no mind of it. He was looking for his beloved and that was all that mattered.

Margaret, where are you?

His quest was complicated by the violent, discordant emanations that came from the humans of this city. Bad enough that the place should be infested by this invading horde of ghouls and incubi and lamias and basilisks and psychopomps; but also its own native inhabitants, Urnikh thought, were the strangest assortment of irritable and irritating malcontents. All but Margaret, of course. She was the exception. She was perfection. But the others—

What were they shouting here? "U.S. out of Carpathia! Hands off the Carpathians!" Where was Carpathia? Had it even existed, a month before? But already there was a protest movement defending its autonomy.

And these people, four blocks away, shouting even louder: "Justice for Baluchistan! No more trampling of human rights! We demand intervention! Justice for Baluchistan! Justice for Baluchistan!"

Carpathia? Baluchistan? While furious armies of invisible ruvakas and sanutees and nyctalunes snorted and snuffled and rampaged through the streets of their own city? They were blind, these people. Obsessed with distant struggles, they failed to see the festering nightmare that was unfolding right under their noses. So demented in their obsessions that they continued to protest in ever-thinning crowds and claques even after nightfall, when all offices were closed, when there was no one left to hear their slogans! But a time was coming, and soon, when the teeming manifestations that had turned the subetheric levels of San Francisco into a raging inferno would cross the perceptual threshold and burst into startling view. And then—then—

The territorial struggles among the invading beings were almost finished now. Positions had been taken; alliances had been forged. The first attacks on the human population, Urnikh calculated, might be no more than hours away. It was possible that in some outlying districts they had already begun.

Margaret!

He was picking up her signal, now. Far, far to the west, the distant reaches of the city. Beyond Van Ness, beyond the Fillmore, beyond Divisadero—yes, that was Margaret, he was sure of it, that gleam of scarlet against a weft of deep black that was her *wuzud*-imprint. He intensified the focus, homed downward and in.

Clement and Twenty-third Street, his orientation perceptor told him. So she *had* gone to see the male-one again, yes. That mysterious Other, for whom she seemed to feel such an odd, incomprehensible mix of ambivalent emotions.

It was a long journey, halfway across San Francisco.

But he had no choice. He must go to her.

It was nothing for Urnikh to journey down the *sril*-curve to an adjacent continuum. But transporting himself through the streets of this not very large city was a formidable task for a very small dragon.

There was the problem of the retrograde gravitational arc under which this entire continuum labored: he was required to weave constant compensatory spells to deal with that. Then there was the imperfection of the geological substratum to consider, the hellish fault lines that steadily pounded his consciousness with their blazing discordancies. There was the thick oxygen-polluted atmosphere. There was—

There was one difficulty after another. The best he could manage, by way of getting around, was to travel in little ricocheting leaps, a few blocks at a time, playing one node of destabilization off against another and eking out just enough kinetic thrust to move himself to the next step on his route.

Ping and he leaped across the financial district, almost to Market Street. A pair of fanged jagannaths paused in their mortal struggle to swipe at him as he went past; but with a hiss and a growl he drove them back amid flashes of small but effective lightnings, and landed safely atop a traffic light. Below him, a little knot of people was marching around and around in front of a church, crying, "Free the Fallopian Five! Free the Fallopian Five!" None of them noticed him. *Pong* and Urnikh moved on, a diagonal two-pronged ricochet that took him on the first hop as far as the Opera House, from which a terrible ear-splitting clamor was arising, and then on the next bounce to Castro Street at Market, where some fifty or eighty male humans were waving placards and chanting something about police brutality. There were no police anywhere in sight, though a dozen hungry-looking calibargos, tendrils trembling in the intensity of their appetites, were watching the demonstration with some interest from the marquee of a movie theater a little way down the block.

If only these San Franciscans can focus all this angry energy in their own defense when the time comes, Urnikh thought.

Poing and he was off again, up Castro to Divisadero and Turk, where some sort of riot seemed to be going on outside a restaurant, people hurling dishes and menus and handfuls of food at one another. *Pung* and he reached Geary and Arguello. *Boing* and he bounced along to Clement and Fifth. A tiny earth-tremor halted him there for a moment, a jiggle of the subterranean world that only he seemed to feel; then, *bing bing bing*, he hopped westward in three quick leaps to Twenty-third Avenue.

The Margaret-emanation filled the air, here. It streamed toward his perceptors in joyous overpowering bursts.

She was here, no doubt of it.

He stationed himself diagonally across from the male-one's house, tucking himself in safely behind a fire hydrant. The street was deserted here except for a single glowering magog, which came shambling toward him as though it planned to dispute possession of the street corner with him. Urnikh had no time to waste on discussion; he dematerialized the hideous miasmatic creature with a single burst of the *seppul*-power. The stain left on the air was graceless and troubling. Then, as safe behind his globe of *zabil*-force as he could manage to make himself with his depleted energies, he set about the task of drawing Margaret out of the apartment across the way.

She didn't want to come. Whatever she might be doing in there, it seemed to exert a powerful fascination over her. Urnikh was astonished and dismayed by the force of her resistance.

But he redoubled his own efforts, exhausting though that was. The onslaught of the subetheric ones was imminent now, he knew: it would begin not in hours but in minutes, perhaps. She must be home, safe in her own apartment, when the conflict broke out. Otherwise, paralyzing thought, thinking the unthinkable, how could he protect her?!

Margaret—Margaret—

It took all the strength in his power wells. His *zabil*-globe spasmed and thinned. He would be vulnerable, he realized, to any passing enemy that might choose to attack. But the street was still quiet.

Margaret—

Here she was, finally. He saw her appear, framed in a halo of light in the doorway of the house across the way. The male-one loomed behind her, large, uncouth-looking, emanating a harsh, coarse aura that Urnikh detested. Margaret paused in the doorway, turning, smiling, her fingers still trailing the touch of his hand, looking up at the male-one in such a way that Urnikh's soul cried out. Margaret's aura coruscated through two visible and three invisible spectra. Her eyes shone. Urnikh felt all the moisture of his adoration squeezed out of him.

Never. She had *never* looked at the dragon in her bookcase like that. Cunning, clever, cuddly, a wonderful artifact; but never with eyes that held the cosmos.

For an instant, he felt anger. Something like what the mortals called hatred, the need for balance, revenge, something to strike or corrupt or disenfranchise. Then it passed. He was a dragon, a force, not some wretched flawed mortal. He was finer than that. And he loved her.

Enough, he thought. *Enough of that. Associate with them just a short time and their emotional pollution seeps in. Time's short.*

Come, Margaret, he murmured, pouring more power into the command. *Come at once! Come now, immediately, come to safety!*

But her final moments with the male-one took an eternity and a half. Exerting himself utterly, nonetheless there was nothing the little dragon could do about it. Twice, as tiny inimical fanged creatures with luminous wings and fluorescent exoskeletons came swooping past the doorway in which she stood, he mustered shards of his steadily-diminishing energy to club them into oblivion.

Come on!

Then, finally, she allowed their fingertips to slide apart, and gave him that look again, and descended the few steps to the sidewalk. Urnikh moved up close beside her in an instant, bringing her within his sphere of power but taking care to remain in the shadows of the *zabil*-globe. She must not see him, the toy, the cunningly articulated plaything, not here, not so far from the bookshelf in her apartment: it would upset her to know that he had traveled all this way to find her, small and vulnerable as he was. And she wouldn't even understand how much danger he had chanced, just to watch over her. *How ironic,* he thought: *she* was the vulnerable one, and yet, most wonderful creature, she would worry so much about *him!*

Mortaltime trembled at the brink, and all he could do was worry that she got back to the apartment, that he watch over her, back across the city, to Telegraph Hill.

Unseen by Margaret, the night erupted.

The sky over San Francisco turned the color of pigeon-blood rubies! The gateway had fully opened. He had waited too long. The pinhole had become a rent, the rent a fissure, the fissure a chasm, the chasm a total rending of the membrane between mortaltime and the dark spill that lay beyond. The sky sweated blood and screeching demons rode trails of scarlet light down through the roiling clouds, down and down between the high-rise buildings.

He had waited too long! The Master's faith in him had been misplaced, he'd known that from the start. He was not the good force, never could be, knew too little, waited too long.

All he could do now, was make certain Margaret got back to the sanctuary of Telegraph Hill. And from there, safe within his sphere of power, he would try to do what he could do. *There was nothing to be done.* He had done worse than merely fail. He had brought mortaltime to an end.

She boarded the bus, and he was there. Steel-trap mouth floaters assaulted the bus, but he sent a tendril of power out through the sphere and squeezed them to pulp.

He protected her through the long, terrible ride.

Nights dissolve into days. Days stack into weeks. Weeks become the cohesions humans call months and years. Time in mortaltime passes. The race of dragons ages very slowly. One year, two, four. Wind cleanses the streets and the oceans roll on to empty into the great drain.

"Would you like another grape?" she asked, looking up from her book. The little dragon cocked his head and opened his mouth.

"Okay, we'll try it one more time…and this time you'd better catch it. I'm not getting off this sofa again, I'm too comfortable." She pulled a grape off the stalk, closed one eye and took aim, and popped it across the room toward the bookcase. Urnikh extended his long jaw on its serpentine neck, and snagged the fruit as it sailed past.

"Excellent, absolutely *excellent*!" Margaret said, smiling at the agility of the performance. "We will send you down to one of the farm clubs first, and let you season a bit, and in a year, maybe two, you'll be playing center field at Candlestick."

She tossed him a kiss, and went back to her book. It was a fine spring day, and through the open window she could smell fuchsia and gladioli and the scent of garlic and oregano from up the street where Mrs. Capamonte was laying it on for the Sunday night spectacular.

It was, of course, all a creation.

Outside the tiny apartment everything was black ash to the center of the Earth, airless void to the far ends of space. Nothing lay outside this apartment. It had ended, as the Master had feared. Mortaltime had been killed. No creature lived beyond this apartment in its sphere of power. No child laughed, no bird soared, no sponge grew on the floor of an ocean. Nothing. Absolute nothing existed beyond.

Urnikh had failed to sew up the tiniest pinprick, had simply not been the good force. And mortaltime had ended. The billions and billions had died horribly, and the world had ended, and everything was dark and empty now, never to grow again.

Because mortaltime existed only as a dream of dragons; and for this little dragon, assigned to save the puny humans who were his creations, love had been the greater imperative.

Now, they would exist this way for however long she would live. Here, in Urnikh's dream.

Living in a world of sweetness and light and pleasure—that did not exist. He would do it all for her, only for her. For Margaret he had sacrificed everything. That which was his to sacrifice, and all that belonged to the unfortunates who had vanished.

For the little dragon, it was sad, and all honor had been lost; but it was worth it. He had his Margaret, and together, here in his dream, they would stay. Until she, too, died.

And then it would be very hard to go on. With her gone. With all that was left of the world gone. It would be terribly hard to bear these human emotions he had taken on. Loneliness, sadness, loss. It would then, truly, be the end of all things.

And even little dragons grow old—slowly, ever so slowly.

GWYDION AND THE DRAGON

C. J. Cherryh

C. J. Cherryh began writing stories at the age of ten, when she became frustrated with the cancellation of her favorite TV show, *Flash Gordon*. She has a Master of Arts degree in classics from Johns Hopkins University, where she was a Woodrow Wilson fellow, and taught Latin, Ancient Greek, the classics, and ancient history at John Marshall High School in Oklahoma City. Cherryh wrote novels in her spare time, when not teaching, and in 1975 sold her first novels, *Gate of Ivrel* and *Brothers of Earth,* to Donald A. Wollheim at DAW Books. The books won her immediate recognition and the John W. Campbell Award for Best New Writer in 1977. In 1979, Donald Wollheim had given her a a three-book advance, she quit teaching, and "Cassandra" won the Best Short Story Hugo. She has since won the Hugo Award for Best Novel twice, first for *Downbelow Station* in 1982 and then again for *Cyteen* in 1989. Her most recent novels are the major new Alliance-Union novel, *Regenesis,* and new Foreigner novel, *Deceiver.* She lives near Spokane, Washington, and enjoys figure skating and traveling. She regularly makes appearances at science fiction conventions.

Once upon a time there was a dragon, and once upon that time a prince who undertook to win the hand of the elder and fairer of two princesses—

Not that this prince wanted either of Madog's daughters, although rumors said that Eri was as wise and as gentle, as sweet and as fair as her sister Glasog was cruel and ill-favored. The truth was that this prince would marry either princess if it would save his father and his people; and neither if he had had any choice in the matter. He was Gwydion ap Ogan, and of princes in Dyfed he was the last.

Being a prince of Dyfed did not, understand, mean banners and trumpets and gilt armor and crowds of courtiers. King Ogan's palace was a rambling stone house of dusty rafters hung with cooking-pots and old harness; king Ogan's wealth was mostly in pigs and pasture the same as all Ogan's subjects; Gwydion's war-horse was a black gelding with a crooked blaze and shaggy feet, who had fought against the bandits from the high hills. Gwydion's armor, serviceable in

427

that perpetual warfare, was scarred leather and plain mail, with new links bright among the old; and lance or pennon he had none—the folk of Ogan's kingdom were not lowland knights, heavily armored, but hunters in the hills and woods, and for weapons this prince carried only a one-handed sword and a bow and a quiver of gray-feathered arrows.

His companion, riding beside him on a bay pony, happened through no choice of Gwydion's to be Owain ap Llodri, the houndmaster's son, his good friend, by no means his squire: Owain had lain in wait along the way, on a borrowed bay mare—Owain had simply assumed he was going, and that Gwydion had only hesitated, for friendship's sake, to ask him. So he saved Gwydion the necessity.

And the lop-eared old bitch trotting by the horses' feet was Mili: Mili was fierce with bandits, and had respected neither Gwydion's entreaties nor Owain's commands thus far: stones might drive her off for a few minutes, but Mili came back again; that was the sort Mili was. That was the sort Owain was too, and Gwydion could refuse neither of them. So Mili panted along at the pace they kept, with big-footed Blaze and the bow-nosed bay, whose name might have been Swallow or maybe not—the poets forget—and as they rode Owain and Gwydion talked mostly about dogs and hunting.

That, as the same poets say, was the going of prince Gwydion into king Madog's realm.

Now no one in Dyfed knew where Madog had come from. Some said he had been a king across the water. Some said he was born of a Roman and a Pict and had gotten sorcery in his mother's blood. Some said he had bargained with a dragon for his sorcery—certainly there was a dragon: devastation followed Madog's conquests, from one end of Dyfed to the other.

Reasonably reliable sources said Madog had applied first to king Bran, across the mountains, to settle at his court, and Bran having once laid eyes on Madog's elder daughter, had lusted after her beyond all good sense and begged Madog for her.

Give me your daughter, Bran had said to Madog, and I'll give you your heart's desire. But Madog had confessed that Eri was betrothed already, to a terrible dragon, who sometimes had the form of a man, and who had bespelled Madog and all his house: if Bran could overcome this dragon he might have Eri with his blessings, and his gratitude and the faithful help of his sorcery all his life; but if he died childless, Madog, by Bran's own oath, must be his heir.

That was the beginning of Madog's kingdom. So smitten was Bran that he swore to those terms, and died that very day, after which Madog ruled in his place.

After that, Madog had made the same proposal to three of his neighbor kings, one after the other, proposing that each should ally with him and unite their kingdoms if the youngest son could win Eri from the dragon's spell and provide him an heir. But no prince ever came back from his quest. And the next youngest then went, until all the sons of the kings were gone, so that the kingdoms fell under Madog's rule.

After them, Madog sent to king Ban, and his sons died, last of all prince Rhys,

Gwydion's friend. And Ban's heart broke, and Ban took to his bed and died.

Some whispered now that the dragon actually served Madog, that it had indeed brought Madog to power, under terms no one wanted to guess, and that this dragon did indeed have another form, which was the shape of a knight in strange armor, who would become Eri's husband if no other could win her. Some said (but none could prove the truth of it) that the dragon-knight had come from far over the sea, and that he devoured the sons and daughters of conquered kings, that being the tribute Madog gave him. But whatever the truth of that rumor, the dragon hunted far and wide in the lands Madog ruled and did not disdain to take the sons and daughters of farmers and shepherds too. Devastation went under his shadow, trees withered under his breath, and no one saw him outside his dragon shape and returned to tell of it, except only Madog and (rumor said) his younger daughter Glasog, who was a sorceress as cruel as her father.

Some said that Glasog could take the shape of a raven and fly over the land choosing whom the dragon might take. The people called her Madog's Crow, and feared the look of her eye. Some said she was the true daughter of Madog and that Madog had stolen Eri from faery, and given her mother to the dragon; but others said they were twins, and that Eri had gotten all that an ordinary person had of goodness, while her sister Glasog—

"Prince Gwydion," Glasog said to her father, "would have come on the quest last year with his friend Rhys, except his father's refusing him, and prince Gwydion will not let his land go to war if he can find another course. He'll persuade his father."

"Good," Madog said. "That's very good." Madog smiled, but Glasog did not. Glasog was thinking of the dragon. Glasog harbored no illusions: the dragon had promised Madog that he would be king of all Wales if he could achieve this in seven years; and rule for seventy and seven more with the dragon's help.

But if he failed—failed by the seventh year to gain any one of the kingdoms of Dyfed, if one stubborn king withstood him and for one day beyond the seven allotted years, kept him from obtaining the least, last stronghold of the west, then all the bargain was void and Madog would have failed in everything.

And the dragon would claim a forfeit of his choosing.

That was what Glasog thought of, in her worst nightmares: that the dragon had always meant to have all the kingdoms of the west with very little effort—let her father win all but one and fail, on the smallest letter of the agreement. What was more, all the generals in all the armies they had taken agreed that the kingdom of Ogan could never be taken by force: there were mountains in which resistance could hide and not even dragon-fire could burn all of them; but most of all there was the fabled Luck of Ogan, which said that no force of arms could defeat the sons of Ogan.

Watch, Madog had said. And certainly her father was astute, and cunning, and knew how to snare a man by his pride. There's always a way, her father had said, to break a spell. This one has a weakness. The strongest spells most surely have their soft spots.

And Ogan had one son, and that was prince Gwydion.

Now we will fetch him, Madog said to his daughter. Now we will see what his luck is worth.

The generals said, If you would have a chance in war, first be rid of Gwydion.

But Madog said, and Glasog agreed, There are other uses for Gwydion.

"It doesn't *look* different," Owain said as they passed the border stone.

It was true. Nothing looked changed at all. There was no particular odor of evil, or of threat. It might have been last summer, when the two of them had hunted with Rhys. They had used to hunt together every summer, and last autumn they had tracked the bandit Llewellyn to his lair, and caught him with stolen sheep. But in the spring Ban's sons had gone to seek the hand of Madog's daughter, and one by one had died, last of them, in early summer, Rhys himself.

Gwydion would have gone, long since, and long before Rhys. A score of times Gwydion had approached his father King Ogan and his mother Queen Belys and begged to try his luck against Madog, from the first time Madog's messenger had appeared and challenged the kings of Dyfed to war or wedlock. But each time Ogan had refused him, arguing in the first place that other princes, accustomed to warfare on their borders, were better suited, and better armed, and that there were many princes in Dyfed, but he had only one son.

But when Rhys had gone and failed, the last kingdom save that of King Ogan passed into Madog's hands. And Gwydion, grief-stricken with the loss of his friend, said to his parents, "If we had stood together, we might have defeated this Madog; if we had taken the field then, together, we might have had a chance; if you had let me go with Rhys, one of us might have won and saved the other. But now Rhys is dead and we have Madog for a neighbor. Let me go when he sends to us. Let me try my luck at courting his daughter. A war with him now we may not lose, but we cannot hope to win."

Even so Ogan had resisted him, saying that they still had their mountains for a shield, difficult going for any army; and arguing that their luck had saved them this far and that it was rash to take matters into their own hands.

Now the nature of that luck was this: that the kingdoms of Dyfed, Ogan's must always be poorest and plainest. But that luck meant that they could not fail in war nor fail to harvest: it had come down to them from Ogan's own greatgrandfather Ogan ap Ogan of Llanfynnyd, who had sheltered one of the Faerie unaware; and only faithlessness could break it—so great-grandfather Ogan has said. So: "Our luck will be our defense," Ogan had argued with his son. "Wait and let Madog come to us. We'll fight him in the mountains."

"Will we fight a dragon? Even if we defeat Madog himself, what of our herds, what of our farmers and freeholders? Can we let the land go to waste and let our people feed this dragon, while we hide in the hills and wait for luck to save us? Is that faithfulness?" That was what Gwydion had asked his father, while Madog's herald was in the hall—a raven black as unrepented sin... or the intentions of a wizard.

"Madog bids you know," this raven had said, perched on a rafter of Ogan's hall, beside a moldering basket and string of garlic, "that he has taken every kingdom of Dyfed but this. He offers you what he offered others: if King Ogan has a son worthy to win Madog's daughter and get an heir, then King Ogan may rule in peace over his kingdom so long as he lives, and that prince will have titles and the third of Madog's realm besides…

"But if the prince will not or cannot win the princess, then Ogan must swear Madog is his lawful true heir. And if Ogan refuses this, then Ogan must face Madog's army, which now is the army of four kingdoms each greater than his own. Surely," the raven had added, fixing all present with a wicked, midnight eye, "it is no great endeavor Madog asks—simply to court his daughter. And will so many die, so much burn? Or will Prince Gwydion win a realm wider than your own? A third of Madog's lands is no small dowry and inheritance of Madog's kingdom is no small prize."

So the raven had said. And Gwydion had said to his mother, "Give me your blessing," and to his father Ogan: "Swear the oath Madog asks. If our luck can save us, it will save me and win this bride; but if it fails me in this, it would have failed us in any case."

Maybe, Gwydion thought as they passed the border, Owain was a necessary part of that luck Maybe even Mili was. It seemed to him now that he dared reject nothing that loved him and favored him, even if it was foolish and even if it broke his heart: his luck seemed so perilous and stretched so thin already he dared not bargain with his fate.

"No signs of a dragon, either," Owain said, looking about them at the rolling hills.

Gwydion looked about him too, and at the sky, which showed only the lazy flight of a single bird.

Might it be a raven? It was too far to tell.

"I'd think," said Owain, "it would seem grimmer than it does."

Gwydion shivered as if a cold wind had blown. But Blaze plodded his heavy-footed way with no semblance of concern, and Mili trotted ahead, tongue lolling, occasionally sniffing along some trail that crossed theirs.

"Mili would smell a dragon, " Owain said.

"Are you sure?" Gwydion asked. He was not. If Madog's younger daughter could be a raven at her whim, he was not sure what a dragon might be at its pleasure.

That night they had a supper of brown bread and sausages that Gwydion's mother had sent, and ale that Owain had with him.

"My mother's brewing," Owain said. "My father's store." And Owain sighed and said: "By now they must surely guess I'm not off hunting."

"You didn't tell them?" Gwydion asked. "You got no blessing in this?"

Owain shrugged, and fed a bit of sausage to Mili, who gulped it down and sat looking at them worshipfully.

Owain's omission of duty worried Gwydion. He imagined how Owain's parents would first wonder where he had gone, then guess, and fear for Owain's life, for which he held himself entirely accountable. In the morning he said, "Owain, go back. This is far enough."

But Owain shrugged and said, "Not I. Not without you." Owain rubbed Mili's ears. "No more than Mili, without me."

Gwydion had no least idea now what was faithfulness and what was a young man's foolish pride. Everything seemed tangled. But Owain seemed not in the least distressed.

Owain said, "We'll be there by noon tomorrow."

Gwydion wondered, Where is this dragon? and distrusted the rocks around them and the sky over their heads. He felt a presence in the earth—or thought he felt it. But Blaze and Swallow grazed at their leisure. Only Mili looked worried—Mili pricked up her ears, such as those long ears could prick, wondering, perhaps, if they were going to get to bandits soon, and whether they were, after all, going to eat that last bit of breakfast sausage.

"He's on his way," Glasog said. "He's passed the border."

"Good," said Madog. And to his generals: "Didn't I tell you?"

The generals still looked worried.

But Glasog went and stood on the walk of the castle that had been Ban's, looking out over the countryside and wondering what the dragon was thinking tonight, whether the dragon had foreseen this as he had foreseen the rest, or whether he was even yet keeping some secret from them, scheming all along for their downfall.

She launched herself quite suddenly from the crest of the wall, swooped out over the yard and beyond, over the seared fields.

The dragon, one could imagine, knew about Ogan's Luck. The dragon was too canny to face it—and doubtless was chuckling in his den in the hills.

Glasog flew that way, but saw nothing from that cave but a little curl of smoke—there was almost always smoke. And Glasog leaned toward the west, following the ribbon of a road, curious, and wagering that the dragon this time would not bestir himself.

Her father wagered the same. And she knew very well what he wagered, indeed she did: duplicity for duplicity—if not the old serpent's aid, then human guile; if treachery from the dragon, then put at risk the dragon's prize.

Gwydion and Owain came to a burned farmstead along the road. Mili sniffed about the blackened timbers and bristled at the shoulders, and came running back to Owain's whistle, not without mistrustful looks behind her.

There was nothing but a black ruin beside a charred, brittle orchard.

"I wonder," Owain said, "what became of the old man and his wife."

"I don't," said Gwydion, worrying for his own parents, and seeing in this example how they would fare in any retreat into the hills.

The burned farm was the first sign they had seen of the dragon, but it was not the last. There were many other ruins, and sad and terrible sights. One was a skull sitting on a fence row. And on it sat a raven.

"This was a brave man," it said, and pecked the skull, which rang hollowly, and inclined its head toward the field beyond. "That was his wife. And farther still his young daughter."

"Don't speak to it," Gwydion said to Owain. They rode past, at Blaze's plodding pace, and did not look back.

But the raven flitted ahead of them and waited for them on the stone fence. "If you die," the raven said, "then your father will no longer believe in his luck. Then it will leave him. It happened to all the others."

"There's always a first," said Gwydion.

Owain said, reaching for his bow: "Shall I shoot it?"

But Gwydion said: "Kill the messenger for the message? No. It's a foolish creature. Let it be."

It left them. Gwydion saw it sometimes in the sky ahead of them. He said nothing to Owain, who had lost his cheerfulness, and Mili stayed close by them, sore of foot and suspicious of every breeze.

There were more skulls. They saw gibbets and stakes in the middle of a burned orchard. There was scorched grass, recent and powdery under the horses' hooves. Blaze, who loved to snatch a bite now and again as he went, moved uneasily, snorting with dislike of the smell, and Swallow started as shadows.

Then the turning of the road showed them a familiar brook, and around another hill and beyond, the walled holding that had been King Ban's, in what had once been a green valley. Now it was burned, black bare hillsides and the ruin of hedges and orchards.

So the trial they had come to find must be here, Gwydion thought and uneasily took up his bow and picked several of his best arrows, which he held against his knee as he rode. Owain did the same.

But they reached the gate of the low-walled keep unchallenged until they came on the raven sitting, whetting its beak on the stone. It looked at them solemnly, saying, "Welcome, Prince Gwydion. You've won your bride. Now how will you fare, I wonder."

Men were coming from the keep, running toward them, others, under arms, in slower advance.

"What now?" Owain asked, with his bow across his knee; and Gwydion lifted his bow and bent it, aiming at the foremost.

The crowd stopped, but a black-haired man in gray robes and a king's gold chain came alone, holding up his arms in a gesture of welcome and of peace. Madog himself? Gwydion wondered, while Gwydion's arm shook and the string trembled in his grip. "Is it Gwydion ap Ogan?" the man asked—surely no one else but Madog would wear that much gold. "My son-in-law to be! Welcome!"

Gwydion, with great misgivings, slacked the string and let down the bow, while fat Blaze, better trained than seemed, finally shifted feet. Owain lowered his bow too, as King Madog's men opened up the gate. Some of the crowd cheered as they rode in, and more took it up, as if they had only then gained the courage or understood it was expected. Blaze and Swallow snorted and threw their heads at the racket, as Gwydion and Owain put away their arrows, unstrung their bows and hung them on their saddles.

But Mili stayed close by Owain's legs as they dismounted, growling low in her throat, and barked one sharp warning when Madog came close. "Hush," Owain bade her, and knelt down more for respect, keeping one hand on Mili's muzzle and the other in her collar, whispering to her. "Hush, hush, there's a good dog."

Gwydion made the bow a prince owed to a king and prospective father-in-law, all the while thinking that there had to be a trap in this place. He was entirely sorry to see grooms lead Blaze and Swallow away, and kept Owain and Mili constantly in the tail of his eye as Madog took him by the arms and hugged him. Then Madog said, catching all his attention, eye to eye with him for a moment, "What a well-favored young man you are. The last is always best.—So you've killed the dragon."

Gwydion thought, Somehow we've ridden right past the trial we should have met. If I say no, he will find cause to disallow me; and he'll kill me and Owain and all our kin.

But lies were not the kind of dealing his father had taught him; faithfulness was the rule of the house of Ogan; so Gwydion looked the king squarely in they eyes and said, "I met no dragon."

Madog's eyes showed surprise, and Madog said: "Met no dragon?"

"Not a shadow of a dragon."

Madog grinned and clapped him on the shoulder and showed him to the crowd, saying, "This is your true prince!"

Then the crowd cheered in earnest, and even Owain and Mili looked heartened. Owain rose with Mili's collar firmly in hand.

Madog said then to Gwydion, under his breath, "If you had lied, you would have met the dragon here and now. Do you know you're the first one who's gotten this far?"

"I saw nothing," Gwydion said again, as if Madog had not understood him. "Only burned farms. Only skulls and bones."

Madog turned a wide smile toward him, showing teeth. "Then it was your destiny to win. Was it not?" And Madog faced him about toward the doors of the keep. "Daughter, daughter, come out!"

Gwydion hesitated a step, expecting he knew not what—the dragon itself, perhaps: his wits went scattering toward the gate, the horses being led away, Mili barking in alarm—and a slender figure standing in the doorway, all white and gold. "My elder daughter," Madog said. "Eri."

Gwydion went ahead as he was led, telling himself it must be true, after so much dread of this journey and so many friends' lives lost—obstacles must have fallen down for him, Ogan's Luck must still be working...

The young bride waiting for him was so beautiful, so young and so—kind—was the first word that came to him—Eri smiled and immediately it seemed to him she was innocent of all the grief around her, innocent and good as her sister was reputed cruel and foul.

He took her hand, and the folk of the keep all cheered, calling him their prince; and if any were Ban's people, those wishes might well come from the heart, with fervent hopes of rescue. Pipers began to play, gentle hands urged them both inside, and in the desolate land some woman found flowers to give to Eri.

"Owain?" Gwydion cried, looking back, suddenly seeing no sign of him or Mili: "Owain!"

He refused to go farther until Owain could part the crowd and reach his side, Mili firmly in hand. Owain looked breathless and frightened. Gwydion felt the same. But the crowd pushed and pulled at them, the pipers piped and the dancers danced, and they brought them into a hall smelling of food and ale.

It can't be this simple, Gwydion thought, and made up his mind that no one should part him from Owain, Mili, or their swords. He looked about him, bedazzled, at a wedding feast that must have taken days to prepare.

But how could they know I'd get here? he wondered. Did they do this for all the suitors that failed—and celebrate their funerals, then… with their wedding feast?

At which thought he felt cold through and through, and found Eri's hand on his arm disquieting; but Madog himself waited to receive them in the hall, and joined their hands and plighted them their vows, to make them man and wife, come what might—

"So long at you both shall live," Madog said, pressing their hands together. "And when there is an heir, Prince Gwydion shall have the third of my lands, and his father shall rule in peace so long as he shall live."

Gwydion misliked the last—Gwydion thought in alarm: As long as he lives.

But Madog went on, saying, "—be you wed, be you wed, be you wed," three times, as if it were a spell—then: "Kiss your bride, son-in-law."

The well-wishes from the guests roared like the sea. The sea was in Eri's eyes, deep and blue and drowning. He heard Mili growl as he kissed Eri's lips once, twice, three times.

The pipers played, the people cheered, no few of whom indeed might have been King Ban's, or Lugh's, or Lughdan's. Perhaps, Gwydion dared think, perhaps it was hope he brought to them, perhaps he truly had won, after all, and the dreadful thread Madog posed was lifted, so that Madog would be their neighbor, no worse than the worst they had had, and perhaps, if well-disposed, better than one or two.

Perhaps, he thought, sitting at Madog's right hand with his bride at his right and with Owain just beyond, perhaps there truly was cause to hope, and he could ride away from here alive—though he feared he could find no cause to do so tonight, with so much prepared, with an anxious young bride and King Madog determined to indulge his beautiful daughter. Women hurried about with flowers and torches, with linens and brooms and platters and plates, tumblers ran riot, dancers leaped and cavorted—one of whom came to grief against an ale-server. Both went down, in Madog's very face, and the hall grew still and dangerous.

But Eri laughed and clapped her hands, a laughter so small and faint until her father laughed, and all the hall laughed; and Gwydion remembered then to breathe, while Eri hugged his arm and laughed up at him with those sea-blue eyes.

"More ale!" Madog called. "Less spillage, there!"

The dreadful wizard could joke, then. Gwydion drew two easier breaths, and someone filled their cups. He drank, but prudently: he caught Owain's eye, and Owain his—while Mili having found a bone to her liking, with a great deal of meat to it, worried it happily in the straw beneath the table.

There were healths drunk, there were blessings said, at each of which one had to drink—and Madog laughed and called Gwydion a fine son-in-law, asked him about his campaign against the bandits and swore he was glad to have friends and his kin and anyone he cared to bring here: Madog got up and clapped Owain on the shoulder too, and asked was Owain wed, and, informed Owain was not, called out to the hall that here was another fine catch, and where were the young maids to keep Owain from chill on his master's wedding night?

Owain protested in some embarrassment, starting to his feet—

But drink overcame him, and he sat down again with a hand to his brow. Gwydion saw it with concern, while Madog touched Gwydion's arm on the other side and said, "The women are ready," slyly bidding him finish his ale before hand.

Gwydion rose and handed his bride to her waiting women. "Owain!" Gwydion said then sharply, and Owain gained his feet, saying something Gwydion could not hear with all the people cheering and the piper starting up, but he saw Owain was distressed. Gwydion resisted the women pulling at him, stood fast until Owain reached him, flushed with ale and embarrassment. The men surrounded him with bawdy cheers and more offered cups.

It was his turn then on the stairs, more cups thrust on him, Madog clapping him on the shoulder and hugging him and calling him the son he had always wanted, and saying there should be peace in Dyfed for a hundred years… unfailing friendship with his father and his kin—greater things, should he have ambitions…

The room spun around. Voices buzzed. They pushed him up the stairs, Owain and Mili notwithstanding, Mili barking all the while. They brought him down the upstairs hall, they opened the door to the bridal chamber.

On pitch dark.

Perhaps it was cowardly to balk. Gwydion thought so, in the instant the laughing men gave him a push between the shoulders. Shame kept him from calling Owain to his rescue. The door shut at his back.

He heard rustling in the dark and imagined coils and scales. Eri's soft voice said, "My lord?"

A faint starlight edged the shutters. His eyes made out the furnishings, now that the flare of torches had left his sight. It was the rustling of the bedclothes he heard. He saw a woman's shoulder and arm faintly in the shadowed bed, in the scant starshine that shutter let through.

He backed against the door, found the latch behind him, cracked it the least little bit outward and saw Owain leaning there against his arm, facing the lamplit wall outside, flushed of face and ashamed to meet his eyes at such close range.

"I'm here, m'lord." Owain breathed, on ale-fumes. Owain never called him lord, but Owain was greatly embarrassed tonight. "The lot's gone down the stairs now. I'll be here the night. I'll not leave this door, no sleep, I swear to you."

Gwydion gave him a worried look, wishing the two of them dared escape this hall and Madog's well-wishes, running pell-mell back to his own house, his parents' advice, and childhood. But, "Good," he said, and carefully pulled the door to, making himself blind in the dark again. He let the latch fall and catch.

"My lord?" Eri said faintly.

He felt quite foolish, himself and Owain conspiring together like boys at an orchard wall, when it was a young bride waiting for him, innocent and probably as anxious as he. He nerved himself, walked up by the bed and opened the shutters wide on a night sky brighter than the dark behind him.

But with the cool night wind blowing into the room he thought of dragons, wondered whether opening the window to the sky was wise at all, and wondered what was slipping out of bed with the whispering of the bedclothes. His bride forwardly clasped his arm, wound fingers into his and swayed against him, saying how beautiful the stars were.

Perhaps that invited courtly words. He murmured some such. He found the courage to take Madog's daughter in his arms and kiss her, and thereafter—

He waked abed with the faint dawn coming through the window, his sword tangled with his leg and his arm ensnared in a woman's unbound hair—

Hair raven black.

He leaped up trailing sheets, while a strange young woman sat up to snatch the bedclothes to her, with her black hair flowing about her shoulders, her eyes dark and cold and fathomless.

"Where's my wife?" he cried.

She smiled, thin-lipped, rose from the bed, drawing the sheets about her like royal robes. "Why, you see her, husband."

He rushed to the door and lifted the latch. The door did not budge, hardly rattled when he shoved it with all his strength. "Owain?" he cried, and pounded it with his fist. "Owain!"

No answer came. Gwydion turned slowly to face the woman, dreading what other shape she might take. But she sat down wrapped in the sheets with one knee on the rumpled bed, looking at him. Her hair spread about her like a web of shadows in the dawn. As much as Eri had been an innocent girl, this was a woman far past Eri's innocence or his own.

He asked, "Where's Owain? What's become of him?"

"Guesting elsewhere."

"Who are you?"

"Glasog," she said, and shrugged, the dawn wind carrying long strands of her hair about her shoulders. "Or Eri, if you'd like. My father's eldest daughter and younger, all in one, since he has none but me."

"Why?" he asked. "Why all this pretence if you were the bargain?"

"People trust Eri. She's so fair, so kind."

"What do you want? What does your father want?"

"A claim on your father's land. The last kingdom of Dyfed. And you've come to give it to us."

Gwydion remembered nothing of what might have happened last night. He remembered nothing of anything he should have heard or done last night, abed with Glasog the witch, Madog's raven-haired daughter. He felt cold and hollow and desperate, asking, "On your oath, *is* Owain safe?"

"And would you believe my oath?" Glasog asked.

"I'll see your father," Gwydion said shortly. "Trickery or not, he swore me the third of his kingdom for your dowry. Younger or elder, or both, you're my wife. Will he break his word?"

Glasog said, "An heir. Then he'll release you and your friend, and your father will reign in peace… so long as he lives."

Gwydion walked to the open window, gazing at a paling, still sunless sky. He feared he knew what that release would be—the release of himself and Owain from life, while the child he sired would become heir to his father's kingdom with Madog to enforce that right.

So long as his father lived… so long at that unfortunate *child* might live, for that matter, once the inheritance of Ogan's line and Ogan's Luck passed securely into Madog's line—his father's kingdom taken and for no battle, no war, only a paltry handful of lies and lives.

He looked across the scorched hills, toward a home he could not reach, a father who could not advise him. He dared not hope that Owain might have escaped to bring word to his father: I'll not leave this door, Owain had said—and they would have had to carry Owain away by force or sorcery. Mili with him.

It was sorcery that must have made him sleep and forget last night. It was sorcery that he must have seen when he turned from the window and saw Eri sitting there, rosy-pale and golden, patting the place beside her and bidding him come back to bed.

He shuddered and turned and hit the window ledge, hurting his hand. He thought of flight, even of drawing the sword and killing Madog's daughter, before this princess could conceive and doom him and his parents…

Glasog's voice said, slowly, from Eri's lips, "If you try anything so rash, my father won't need your friend any longer, will he? I certainly wouldn't be in his place then. I'll hardly be in it now."

"What have you done with Owain?"

Eri shrugged. Glasog's voice said, "Dear husband—"

"The marriage wasn't consummated," he said, "for all I remember."

It was Glasog who lifted a shoulder. Black hair parted. "To sorcery—does it matter?" He looked desperately toward the window. He said, without looking at her: "I've something to say about that, don't you think?"

"No, you don't. If you wouldn't, or couldn't, the words are said, the vows are made, the oaths are taken. If not your child—anyone's will do, for all men know or care."

He looked at her to see if he understood what he thought he had, and Glasog gathered a thick skein of her hair—and drew it over her shoulder.

"The oaths are made," Glasog said. "Any lie will do. Any child will do."

"There's my word against it," Gwydion said.

Glasog shook her head gravely. "A lie's nothing to my father. A life is nothing." She stood up, shook out her hair, and hugged the sheets about her. Dawn lent a sudden and unkind light to Glasog's face, showing hollow cheeks, a grim mouth, a dark and sullen eye that promised nothing of compromise.

Why? he asked himself. Why this much of truth? Why not Eri's face?

She said, "What will you, husband?"

"Ask tonight," he said, hoping only for time and better counsel.

She inclined her head, walked between him and the window, lifting her arms wide. For an instant the morning sun showed a woman's body against the sheets. Then—it might have been a trick of the eyes—black hair spread into black wings, something flew to the window and the sheet drifted to the floor.

What about the dragon? he would have asked, but there was no one to ask.

He went to the door and tried it again, in case sorcery had ceased. But it gave not at all, not to cleverness, not to force. He only bruised his shoulder, and leaned dejectedly against the door, sure now that he had made a terrible mistake.

The window offered nothing but a sheer drop to the stones below, and when he tried that way, he could not force his shoulders through. There was no fire in the room, not so much as water to drink. He might fall on his sword, but he took Glasog at her word: it was the form of the marriage Madog had wanted, and they would only hide his death until it was convenient to reveal it. All the house had seen them wed and bedded, even Owain—who, being honest, could swear only what he had seen and what he had guessed—but never, never to the truth of what had happened last night.

Ogan's fabled Luck should have served him better, he thought, casting himself onto the bedside, head in hands. It should have served all of them better, this Luck his great grandfather had said only faithlessness could break—

But was Glasog herself not faithlessness incarnate? Was not Madog?

If that was the barb in great grandfather's blessing—it had done nothing but bring him and his family into Madog's hands. But it seemed to him that the fay were reputed for twists and turns in their gifts, and if they had made one such twist they might make another: all he knew was to hew the course Ogan's sons had always followed.

So he had come here in good faith, been caught though abuse of that faith, and though he might perhaps seize the chance to come at Madog himself, that was treachery for treachery, and if he had any last whisper of belief in his luck, that was what he most should not do.

"Is there a child?" Madog asked, and Glasog said,

"Not yet. Not yet. Be patient."

"There's not," Madog said testily, "forever. Remember that."

"I remember," Glasog said.

"You wouldn't grow fond of him—or foolish?"

"I?" quoth Glasog, with an arch of her brow. "I, fond? Not fond of the dragon, let us say. Not fond of poverty—or early dying."

"We'll not fail. If not him—"

"Truly, do you imagine the dragon will give you anything if the claim's not legitimate? I think not. I do think not. It must be Gwydion's child—and that, by nature, by Gwydion's own will. That is the difficulty, isn't it?"

"You vaunt your sorcery. Use it!"

Glasog said, coldly, "When needs be. If needs be. But it's myself he'll have, not Eri, and for myself, not Eri. That's my demand in this."

"Don't be a fool."

Glasog smiled with equal coldness. "This man has magical protections. His luck is no illusion and it's not to cross. I don't forget that. Don't you. Trust me, father."

"I wonder how I got you."

Glasog still smiled. "Luck," she said. "You want to be rid of the dragon, don't you? Has my advice ever failed you? And isn't it the old god's bond that he'll barter for questions?"

Her father scowled. "It's my life you're bartering for, curse your cold heart. It's my life you're risking with your schemes—a life from each kingdom of Dyfed, that's the barter we've made. We've caught Gwydion. We can't stave the dragon off forever for your whims and your vapors, daughter. Get me a grandson—by whatever sorcery—and forget this foolishness. Kill the dragon... do you think I've not tried that? All the princes in Dyfed have tried that."

Glasog said, with her grimmest look: "We've also Gwydion's friend, don't we? And isn't he of Ogan's kingdom?"

Gwydion endured the hours until sunset, hungry and thirsty and having nothing whatever to do but stare out the slit of a window, over a black and desolate land.

He wondered if Owain was even alive, or what had become of Mili.

Once he saw a raven in flight, toward the south; and once, late, the sky growing dimly copper, he saw it return, it seemed more slowly, circling always to the right.

Glasog? he wondered—or merely a raven looking for its supper?

The sky went from copper to dusk. He felt the air grow chill. He thought of closing the shutters, but that was Glasog's access. So he paced the floor, or looked out the window or simply listened to the distant comings and goings below which alone told him there was life in the place.

Perhaps, he thought they only meant him to die of thirst and hunger, and perhaps he would never see or speak to a living soul again. He hoped Glasog would come by sunset, but she failed that; and by moonrise, but she did not come.

At last, when he had fallen asleep in his waiting, a shadow swept in the window with a snap and flutter of dark wings, and Glasog stood wrapped only in dark hair and limned in starlight.

He gathered himself up quickly, feeling still that he might be dreaming. "I expected you earlier," he said.

"I had enquiries to make," she said, and walked to the table where—he did not know how, a cup and silver pitcher gleamed in reflected starlight. She lifted the pitcher and poured, and oh, he was thirsty. She offered it, and it might be poisoned for all he knew. At the very least it was enchanted, and perhaps only moondust and dreams. But she stood offering it; he drank, and it took both thirst and hunger away.

She said, "You may have one wish of me, Gwydion. One wish. And then I may have two from you. Do you agree?"

He wondered what to say. He put down the cup and walked away to the window, looking out on the night's sky. There were a hundred things to ask: his parents' lives; Owain's; the safety of his land—and in each one there seemed some flaw.

Finally he chose the simplest. "Love me," he said.

For a long time Glasog said nothing. Then he heard her cross the room.

He turned. Her eyes flashed at him, sudden as a serpent's. She said, "Dare you? First drink from my cup."

"Is this your first wish?"

"It is."

He hesitated, looking up at her, then walked away to the table and reached for the shadowy cup, but another appeared beside it, gleaming, crusted with jewels.

"Which will you have?" she asked.

He hoped then that he understood her question. And he picked up the cup of plain pewter and drank it all.

She said, from behind him, "You have your wish, Gwydion."

And wings brushed his face, the wind stirred his hair, the raven shape swooped out the window.

"Owain," a voice said—the raven's voice, and Owain leapt up from his prison bed, such as he could, though his head was spinning and he had to brace himself against the wall. It was not the raven's first visit. He asked it, "Where's my master? What's happened to him?"

And the raven, suddenly no raven, but a dark-haired woman: "Wedlock," she said. "Death, if the dragon gets his due—as soon it may."

"Glasog," Owain said, chilled to the marrow. Since Madog's men had hauled him away from Gwydion's door he had had this dizziness, and it came on him now. He felt his knees going and he caught himself.

"You might save him," Glasog said.

"And why should I trust you?" he asked.

The chains fell away from him with a ringing of iron, and the bolts fell from the door.

"Because I'm his wife," she said. Eri stood there. He rubbed his eyes and it was Glasog again. "And you're his friend. Isn't that what it means, friendship? Or marriage?"

A second time he rubbed his eyes. The door swung open.

"My father says," said Glasog, "the dragon's death will free prince Gwydion. You may have your horse, your dog, your armor and your weapons—or whatever you will, Owain ap Llodri. But for that gift—you must give me one wish when I claim it."

In time—Gwydion was gazing out the window, he had no idea why, he heard the slow echo of hoofbeats off the wall.

He saw Owain ride out the gate; he saw the raven flying over him.

"Owain," he cried. "Owain!"

But Owain paid no heed. Only Mili stopped, and looked up at the tower where he stood.

He thought—Go with him, Mili, if it's home he's bound for. Warn my father. There's no hope here.

Owain never looked back. Gwydion saw him turn south at the gate, entirely away from home, and guessed where Owain was going.

"Come back," he cried. "Owain! No!"

It was the dragon they were going to. It was surely the dragon Owain was going to, and if Gwydion had despaired in his life, it was seeing Owain and Mili go off in company with his wife.

He tried again to force himself through the window slit. He tried the door, working with his sword to lift the bar he was sure was in place outside.

He found and lifted it. But it stopped with the rattle of chain.

They found the brook again, beyond the hill, and the raven fluttered down clumsily to drink, spreading a wing to steady itself.

Owain reined Swallow in. He had no reason to trust the raven in any shape, less reason to believe it than anything else that he had seen in this place. But Mili came cautiously up to it, and suddenly it was Glasog kneeling there, wrapped only in her hair, with her back to him, and Mili whining at her in some distress.

Owain got down. He saw two fingers missing from Glasog's right hand, the wounds scarcely healed. She drank from her other hand, and bathed the wounded one in water. She looked at Owain and said, "You wished to save Gwydion. You said nothing of yourself."

Owain shrugged and settled with his arm about Mili's neck.

"Now you owe me my wish," Glasog said.

"That I do," he said, and feared what it might be.

She said, "There's a god near this place. The dragon overcame him. But he will still answer the right question. Most gods will, with proper sacrifice."

Owain said, "What shall I ask him?"

She said, "I've already asked."

Owain asked then, "And the answers, lady?"

"First that the dragon's life and soul lies in his right eye. And second that no man can kill him."

Owain understood the answer then. He scratched Mili's neck beneath the collar. He said, "Mili's a loyal wench. And if flying tires you, lady, I've a shoulder you can ride on."

Glasog said, "Better you go straightway back to your king. Only lend me your bow, your dog, and your horse. That is my wish, ap Llodri."

Owain shook his head, and got up, patting Mili on the head. "All that you'll have by your wish," Owain said, "but I go with them."

"Be warned," she said.

"I am that," said Owain, and held out his hand. "My lady?"

The raven fluttered up and settled on his arm, bating as he rose into the saddle. Owain set Swallow on her way, among the charred, cinder-black hills, to a cave the raven showed him.

Swallow had no liking for this place. Owain patted her neck, coaxed her forward. Mili bristled up and growled as they climbed. Owain took up his bow and drew out an arrow, yelled, "Mili! Look out!" as fire billowed out and Swallow shied.

A second gust followed. Mili yelped and ran from the roiling smoke, racing ahead of a great serpent shape that surged out of the cave; but Mili began to cross the hill then, leading it.

The raven launched itself from Owain's shoulder, straighter than Owain's arrow sped.

A clamor rose in the keep, somewhere deep in the halls. It was dawn above the hills, and a glow still lit the south, as Gwydion watched from the window.

He was watching when a strange rider came down the road, shining gold in the sun, in scaled armor.

"The dragon!" he heard shouted from the wall. Gwydion's heart sank. It sank further when the scale-armored rider reached the gate and Madog's men opened to it. It was Swallow the dragon-knight rode, Swallow with her mane all singed; and it was Mili who limped after, with her coat all soot-blackened and with great sores showing on her hide. Mili's head hung and her tail drooped and the dragon led her by a rope, while a raven sat perched on his shoulder.

Of Owain there was no sign.

There came a clattering in the hall. Chain rattled, the bar lifted and thumped and armed men were in the doorway.

"King Madog wants you," one said. And Gwydion—

"Madog will have to send twice," Gwydion said, with his sword in hand.

The Dragon rode to the steps that led up to the wall and the raven fluttered to the ground below as waiting women rushed to it, to bring princess Glasog her cloak—black as her hair and stitched with spells. The waiting women and the servants had seen this sight before—the same as the men at arms at the gate, who had had their orders, should it have been Owain returning.

"Daughter," Madog said, descending those same steps as Glasog rose up, wrapped in black and silver. Mili growled and bristled, suddenly strained at her leash—

The Dragon loosed it and Mili sprang for Madog's throat. Madog fell under the hound and tumbled to the courtyard below. Madog's blood was on the courtyard stones—but his neck was already broken.

Servants ran screaming. Men at arms stood confused, as if they had quite forgotten what they were doing or where they were or what had brought them there, the men of the fallen kingdoms all looking at one another and wondering what terrible thing had held them here.

And on all of this Glasog turned her back, walking up the steps.

"My lady!" Owain cried—for it was Owain wore the armor; but it was not Owain's voice Glasog longed to hear.

Glasog let fall the cloak and leapt from the wall. The raven glided away, with one harsh cry against the wind.

In time after—often in that bitter winter, when snows lay deep and wind skirled drifts about the doors—Owain told how Glasog had pierced the dragon's eye; and how they had found the armor, and how Glasog had told him the last secret, that with the dragon dead, Madog's sorcery would leave him.

That winter, too, Gwydion found a raven in the courtyard, a crippled bird, missing feathers on one wing. It seemed greatly confused, so far gone with hunger and with cold that no one thought it would live. But Gwydion tended it until spring and set it free again.

It turned up thereafter on the wall of Gwydion's keep—king Gwydion, he was now—lord of all Dyfed. "You've one wish left," he said to it. "One wish left of me."

"I give it to you," the raven said. "Whatever you wish, king Gwydion."

"Be what you wish to be," said Gwydion.

And thereafter men told of the wisdom of king Gwydion as often as of the beauty of his wife.

THE GEORGE BUSINESS

Roger Zelazny

Roger Zelazny's first short story, "Passion Play", was published in *Amazing Stories* in 1962. It was followed by fifty novels, more than 150 short stories, and three collections of poetry. One of the most outstanding writers of the New Wave, he won the Nebula Award three times and the Hugo Award six times. While novels like *Lord of Light*, *Isle of the Dead*, and *Doorways in the Sand* won or were nominated for awards and have been hailed as classics, he remains best known for the enormously popular ten-volume Amber series of science fantasy novels beginning with *Nine Princes in Amber*. Zelazny died in 1995, but several works have been published posthumously including mystery novel *The Dead Man's Brother* and a six-volume set of his collected short fiction.

Deep in his lair, Dart twisted his green and golden length about his small hoard, his sleep troubled by dreams of a series of identical armored assailants. Since dragons' dreams are always prophetic, he woke with a shudder, cleared his throat to the point of sufficient illumination to check on the state of his treasure, stretched, yawned and set forth up the tunnel to consider the strength of the opposition. If it was too great, he would simply flee, he decided. The hell with the hoard; it wouldn't be the first time.

As he peered from the cave mouth, he beheld a single knight in mismatched armor atop a tired-looking gray horse, just rounding the bend. His lance was not even couched, but still pointing skyward.

Assuring himself that the man was unaccompanied, he roared and slithered forth.

"Halt," he bellowed, "you who are about to fry!"

The knight obliged.

"You're the one I came to see," the man said. "I have—"

"Why," Dart asked, "do you wish to start this business up again? Do you realize how long it has been since a knight and dragon have done battle?"

"Yes, I do. Quite a while. But I—"

"It is almost invariably fatal to one of the parties concerned. Usually your side."

"Don't I know it. Look, you've got me wrong—"

"I dreamt a dragon dream of a young man named George with whom I must do battle. You bear him an extremely close resemblance."

"I can explain. It's not as bad as it looks. You see—"

"*Is* your name George?"

"Well, yes. But don't let that bother you—"

"It *does* bother me. You want my pitiful hoard? It wouldn't keep you in beer money for the season. Hardly worth the risk."

"I'm not after your hoard—"

"I haven't grabbed off a virgin in centuries. They're usually old and tough, anyhow, not to mention hard to find."

"No one's accusing—"

"As for cattle, I always go a great distance. I've gone out of my way, you might say, to avoid getting a bad name in my own territory."

"I know you're no real threat here. I've researched it quite carefully—"

"And do you think that armor will really protect you when I exhale my deepest, hottest flames?"

"Hell, no! So don't do it, huh? If you'd please—"

"And that lance... You're not even holding it properly."

George lowered the lance.

"On that you are correct," he said, "but it happens to be tipped with one of the deadliest poisons known to Herman the Apothecary."

"I say! That's hardly sporting!"

"I know. But even if you incinerate me, I'll bet I can scratch you before I go."

"Now that would be rather silly—both of us dying like that— wouldn't it?" Dart observed edging away. "It would serve no useful purpose that I can see."

"I feel precisely the same way about it."

"Then why are we getting ready to fight?"

"I have no desire whatsoever to fight with you!"

"I'm afraid I don't understand. You said your name is George, and I had this dream—"

"I can explain it."

"But the poisoned lance—"

"Self-protection, to hold you off long enough to put a proposition to you."

Dart's eyelids lowered slightly.

"What sort of proposition?"

"I want to hire you."

"Hire me? Whatever for? And what are you paying?"

"Mind if I rest this lance a minute? No tricks?"

"Go ahead. If you're talking gold your life is safe."

George rested his lance and undid a pouch at his belt. He dipped his hand into it and withdrew a fistful of shining coins. He tossed them gently, so that they clinked and shone in the morning light.

"You have my full attention. That's a good piece of change there."

"My life's savings. All yours—in return for a bit of business."

"What's the deal?"

George replaced the coins in his pouch and gestured.

"See that castle in the distance—two hills away?"

"I've flown over it many times."

"In the tower to the west are the chambers of Rosalind, daughter of the Baron Maurice. She is very dear to his heart, and I wish to wed her."

"There's a problem?"

"Yes. She's attracted to big, brawny barbarian types, into which category I, alas, do not fall. In short, she doesn't like me."

"That *is* a problem."

"So, if I could pay you to crash in there and abduct her, to bear her off to some convenient and isolated place and wait for me, I'll come along, we'll fake a battle, I'll vanquish you, you'll fly away and I'll take her home. I am certain I will then appear sufficiently heroic in her eyes to rise from sixth to first position on her list of suitors. How does that sound to you?"

Dart sighed a long column of smoke.

"Human, I bear your kind no special fondness—particularly the armored variety with lances—so I don't know why I'm telling you this…. Well, I do know, actually…. But never mind. I could manage it, all right. But, if you win the hand of that maid, do you know what's going to happen? The novelty of your deed will wear off after a time—and you know that there will be no encore. Give her a year, I'd say, and you'll catch her fooling around with one of those brawny barbarians she finds so attractive. Then you must either fight him and be slaughtered or wear horns, as they say."

George laughed.

"It's nothing to me how she spends her spare time. I've a girlfriend in town myself."

Dart's eyes widened.

"I'm afraid I don't understand…."

"She's the old baron's only offspring, and he's on his last legs. Why else do you think an uncomely wench like that would have six suitors? Why else would I gamble my life's savings to win her?"

"I see," said Dart. "Yes, I can understand greed."

"I call it a desire for security."

"Quite. In that case, forget my simple-minded advice. All right, give me the gold and I'll do it." Dart gestured with one gleaming vane. "The first valley in those western mountains seems far enough from my home for our confrontation."

"I'll pay you half now and half on delivery."

"Agreed. Be sure to have the balance with you, though, and drop it during the scuffle. I'll return for it after you two have departed. Cheat me and I'll repeat the performance, with a different ending."

"The thought had already occurred to me.—Now, we'd better practice a bit, to make it look realistic. I'll rush at you with the lance, and whatever side she's standing on I'll aim for it to pass you on the other. You raise that wing, grab the lance and scream like hell. Blow a few flames around, too."

"I'm going to see you scour the tip of that lance before we rehearse this."

"Right.—I'll release the lance while you're holding it next to you and rolling around. Then I'll dismount and rush toward you with my blade. I'll whack you with the flat of it—again, on the far side—a few times. Then you bellow again and fly away."

"Just how sharp is that thing, anyway?"

"Damned dull. It was my grandfather's. Hasn't been honed since he was a boy."

"And you drop the money during the fight?"

"Certainly.—How does that sound?"

"Not bad. I can have a few clustets of red berries under my wing, too. I'll squash them once the action gets going."

"Nice touch. Yes, do that. Let's give it a quick rehearsal now and then get on with the real thing."

"And don't whack too hard...."

That afternoon, Rosalind of Maurice Manor was abducted by a green-and-gold dragon who crashed through the wall of her chamber and bore her off in the direction of the western mountains.

"Never fear!" shouted her sixth-ranked suitor—who just happened to be riding by—to her aged father who stood wringing his hands on a nearby balcony. "I'll rescue her!" and he rode off to the west.

Coming into the valley where Rosalind stood backed into a rocky cleft, guarded by the fuming beast of gold and green, George couched his lance.

"Release that maiden and face your doom!" he cried.

Dart bellowed, George rushed. The lance fell from his hands and the dragon rolled upon the ground, spewing gouts of fire into the air. A red substance dribbled from beneath the thundering creature's left wing. Before Rosalind's wide eyes, George advanced and swung his blade several times.

"... and that!" he cried, as the monster stumbled to its feet and sprang into the air, dripping more red.

It circled once and beat its way off toward the top of the mountain, then over it and away.

"Oh George!" Rosalind cried, and she was in his arms. "Oh, George..."

He pressed her to him for a moment.

"I'll take you home now," he said.

That evening as he was counting his gold, Dart heard the sound of two horses approaching his cave. He rushed up the tunnel and peered out.

George, now mounted on a proud white stallion and leading the gray, wore a matched suit of bright armor. He was not smiling, however.

"Good evening," he said.

"Good evening. What brings you back so soon?"

"Things didn't turn out exactly as I'd anticipated."

"You seem far better accoutered. I'd say your fortunes had taken a turn."

"Oh, I recovered my expenses and came out a bit ahead. But that's all. I'm on my way out of town. Thought I'd stop by and tell you the end of the story.—Good show you put on, by the way. It probably would have done the trick—"

"But—?"

"She was married to one of the brawny barbarians this morning, in their family chapel. They were just getting ready for a wedding trip when you happened by."

"I'm awfully sorry."

"Well, it's the breaks. To add insult, though, her father dropped dead during your performance. My former competitor is now the new baron. He rewarded me with a new horse and armor, a gratuity and a scroll from the local scribe lauding me as a dragon slayer. Then he hinted rather strongly that the horse and my new reputation could take me far. Didn't like the way Rosalind was looking at me now I'm a hero."

"That is a shame. Well, we tried."

"Yes. So I just stopped by to thank you and let you know how it all turned out. It would have been a good idea—if it had worked."

"You could hardly have foreseen such abrupt nuptials.—You know, I've spent the entire day thinking about the affair. We *did* manage it awfully well."

"Oh, no doubt about that. It went beautifully."

"I was thinking... How'd you like a chance to get your money back?"

"What have you got in mind?"

"Uh—When I was advising you earlier that you might not be happy with the lady, I was trying to think about the situation in human terms. Your desire was entirely understandable to me otherwise. In fact, you think quite a bit like a dragon."

"Really?"

"Yes. It's rather amazing, actually. Now—realizing that it only failed because of a fluke, your idea still has considerable merit."

"I'm afraid I don't follow you."

"There is—ah—a lovely lady of my own species whom I have been singularly unsuccessful in impressing for a long while now. Actually, there are an unusual number of parallels in our situations."

"She has a large hoard, huh?"

"Extremely so."

"Older woman?"

"Among dragons, a few centuries this way or that are not so important. But she, too, has other admirers and seems attracted by the more brash variety."

"Uh-huh. I begin to get the drift. You gave me some advice once. I'll return the favor. Some things are more important than hoards."

"Name one."

"My life. If I were to threaten her she might do me in all by herself, before you could come to her rescue."

"No, she's a demure little thing. Anyway, it's all a matter of timing. I'll perch on a hilltop nearby—I'll show you where—and signal you when to begin your approach. Now, this time I have to win, of course. Here's how we'll work it...."

George sat on the white charger and divided his attention between the distant cave mouth and the crest of a high hill off to his left.

After a time, a shining winged form flashed through the air and settled upon the hill. Moments later, it raised one bright wing.

He lowered his visor, couched his lance and started forward. When he came within hailing distance of the cave he cried out:

"I know you're in there, Megtag! I've come to destroy you and make off with your hoard! You godless beast! Eater of children! This is your last day on earth!"

An enormous burnished head with cold green eyes emerged from the cave. Twenty feet of flame shot from its huge mouth and scorched the rock before it. George halted hastily. The beast looked twice the size of Dart and did not seem in the least retiring. Its scales rattled like metal as it began to move forward.

"Perhaps I exaggerated...." George began, and he heard the frantic flapping of giant vanes overhead.

As the creature advanced, he felt himself seized by the shoulders. He was borne aloft so rapidly that the scene below dwindled to toy size in a matter of moments. He saw his new steed bolt and flee rapidly back along the route they had followed.

"What the hell happened?" he cried.

"I hadn't been around for a while," Dart replied. "Didn't know one of the others had moved in with her. You're lucky I'm fast. That's Pelladon. He's a mean one."

"Great. Don't you think you should have checked first?"

"Sorry. I thought she'd take decades to make up her mind—without prompting. Oh, what a hoard! You should have seen it!"

"Follow that horse. I want him back."

They sat before Dart's cave, drinking.

"Where'd you ever get a whole barrel of wine?"

"Lifted it from a barge, up the river. I do that every now and then. I keep a pretty good cellar, if I do say so."

"Indeed. Well, we're none the poorer, really. We can drink to that."

"True, but I've been thinking again. You know, you're a very good actor."

"Thanks. You're not so bad yourself."

"Now supposing—just supposing—you were to travel about. Good distances from here each time. Scout out villages, on the continent and in the isles. Find out which ones are well off and lacking in local heroes…."

"Yes?"

"… And let them see that dragon-slaying certificate of yours. Brag a bit. Then come back with a list of towns. Maps, too."

"Go ahead."

"Find the best spots for a little harmless predation and choose a good battle site—"

"Refill?"

"Please."

"Here."

"Thanks. Then you show up, and for a fee—"

"Sixty-forty."

"That's what I was thinking, but I'll bet you've got the figures transposed."

"Maybe fifty-five and forty-five then."

"Down the middle, and let's drink on it."

"Fair enough. Why haggle?"

"Now I know why I dreamed of fighting a great number of knights, all of them looking like you. You're going to make a name for yourself, George."

DRAGON'S FIN SOUP

S.P. Somtow

Described by the *International Herald Tribune* as "the most well-known expatriate Thai in the world," Somtow Sucharitkul (S. P. Somtow) was born in Thailand in 1952. He attended Eton, then Cambridge University, where he received a B.A. and M.A. An avant-garde composer and conductor, he directed the Bangkok Opera Society in 1977–78, led the Asian Composer's Conference-Festival in Bangkok in 1978, and wrote a number of works, including "Gongula 3" and "Star Maker — An Anthology of Universes".

He moved to the US in the late 1970s, and began to publish science fiction as Somtow Sucharitkul and dark fantasy as S. P. Somtow. Between 1991 and 2003 he has published more than fifty novels, four short story collections, and more than fifty short stories. These include the Mallworld, Inquestor and Aquila series of SF novels and the Valentine series of vampire novels. He has been nominated for the World Fantasy Award four times, and won in 2001 for his novella "The Bird Catcher". His most recent book is novel *Do Comets Dream?*

At the heart of Bangkok's Chinatown, in the district known as Yaowaraj, there is a restaurant called the Rainbow Cafe which, every Wednesday, features a blue plate special they call dragon's fin soup. Though little known through most of its hundred-year existence, the cafe enjoyed a brief flirtation with fame during the early 1990s because of an article in the *Bangkok Post* extolling the virtues of the specialite de la maison. The article was written by the enigmatic Ueng-Ang Thalay, whose true identity few had ever guessed. It was only I and a few close friends who knew that Ueng-Ang was actually a Chestertonian American named Bob Halliday, ex-concert pianist and *Washington Post* book critic, who had fled the mundane madness of the western world for the more fantastical, cutting-edge madness of the Orient. It was only in Bangkok, the bastard daughter of feudalism and futurism, that Bob had finally been able to be himself, though what himself was, he alone seemed to know.

But we were speaking of the dragon's fin soup.

Perhaps I should quote the relevant section of Ueng-Ang's article:

Succulent! Aromatic! Subtle! Profound! Transcendental! These are but a few of the adjectives your skeptical food columnist has been hearing from the clients of the Rainbow Cafe in Yaowaraj as they rhapsodize about the mysterious dish known as Dragon's Fin Soup, served only on Wednesdays. Last Wednesday your humble columnist was forced to try it out. The restaurant is exceedingly hard to find, being on the third floor of the only building still extant from before the Chinatown riots of 1945. There is no sign, either in English or Thai, and as I cannot read Chinese, I cannot say whether there is one in that language either. On Wednesday afternoons, however, there are a large number of official-looking Mercedes and BMWs double-parked all the way down the narrow soi, and dozens of uniformed chauffeurs leaning warily against their cars; so, unable to figure out the restaurant's location from the hastily scrawled fax I had received from a friend of mine who works at the Ministry of Education, I decided to follow the luxury cars… and my nose… instead. The alley became narrower and shabbier. Then, all of a sudden, I turned a corner, and found myself joining a line of people, all dressed to the teeth, snaking single-file up the rickety wooden steps into the small, unairconditioned, and decidedly unassuming restaurant. It was a kind of time-travel. This was not the Bangkok we all know, the Bangkok of insane traffic jams, of smörgåsbord sexuality, of iridescent skyscrapers and stagnant canals. The people in line all waited patiently; when I was finally ushered inside, I found the restaurant to be as quiet and as numinous as a Buddhist temple. Old men with floor-length beards played mah jongg; a woman in a cheongsam directed me to a table beneath the solitary ceiling fan; the menu contained not a word of Thai or English. Nevertheless, without my having to ask, a steaming bowl of the notorious soup was soon served to me, along with a cup of piping-hot chrysanthemum tea.

At first I was conscious only of the dish's bitterness, and I wondered whether its fame was a hoax or I, as the only palefaced rube in the room, was actually being proffered a bowl full of microwaved Robitussin. Then, suddenly, it seemed to me that the bitterness of the soup was a kind of veil or filter through which its true taste, too overwhelming to be perceived directly, might be enjoyed… rather as the dark glasses one must wear in order to gaze directly at the sun. But as for the taste itself, it cannot truly be described at all. At first I thought it must be a variant of the familiar shark's fin, perhaps marinated in some geriatric wine. But it also seemed to partake somewhat of the subtle tang of bird's nest soup, which draws its flavor from the coagulated saliva of cave-dwelling swallows. I also felt a kind of coldness in my joints and extremities, the tingling sensation familiar to those who have tasted fugu, the elusive and expensive Japanese puffer fish, which, improperly prepared, causes paralysis and death within minutes. The dish tasted like all these things and none of them, and I found, for the first time in my life, my jaundiced tongue confounded and bewildered. I asked the beautiful longhaired waitress in the cheongsam whether she could answer a few questions about the dish; she said, "Certainly, as long as I don't have to divulge any of the ingredients, for they are an ancient family secret." She spoke an antique and grammatically quaint sort of Thai, as though she had never watched television, listened to pop songs, or hung out in the myriad coffee shops of the city. She saw my surprise and went on in English, "It's not my first language, you see; I'm a lot more comfortable in English."

"Berkeley?" I asked her, suspecting a hint of Northern California in her speech.

She smiled broadly then, and said, "Santa Cruz, actually. It's a relief to meet another American around here; they don't let me out much since I came home from college."

"American?"

"Well, I'm a dual national. But my great-grandparents were forty-niners. Gold rush chinks. My name's Janice Lim. Or Lam or Lin, take your pick."

"Tell me then," I inquired, "since you can't tell me what's in the soup... why is it that you only serve it on Wednesdays?"

"Wednesday, in Thai, is Wan Phutth... the day of Buddha. My parents feel that dragon's flesh should only be served on that day of the week that is sacred to the Lord Buddha, when we can reflect on the transitory nature of our existence."

At this point it should be pointed out that I, your narrator, am the woman with the long hair and the cheongsam, and that Bob Halliday has, in his article, somewhat exaggerated my personal charms. I shall not exaggerate his. Bob is a large man; his girth has earned him the sobriquet of "Elephant" among his Thai friends. He is an intellectual; he speaks such languages as Hungarian and Cambodian as well as he does Thai, and he listens to Lulu and Wozzeck before breakfast. For relaxation, he curls up with Umberto Eco, and I don't mean Eco's novels, I mean his academic papers on semiotics. Bob is a rabid agoraphobe, and flees as soon as there are more than about ten people at a party. His friends speculate endlessly about his sex life, but in fact he seems to have none at all.

Because he was the only American to have found his way to the Rainbow Cafe since I returned to Thailand from California, and because he seemed to my father (my mother having passed away in childbirth) to be somehow unthreatening, I found myself spending a great deal of time with him when I wasn't working at the restaurant. My aunt Ling-ling, who doesn't speak a word of Thai or English, was the official chaperone; if we went for a quiet cup of coffee at the Regent, for example, she was to be found a couple of tables away, sipping a glass of chrysanthemum tea.

It was Bob who taught me what kind of a place Bangkok really was. You see, I had lived until the age of eighteen without ever setting foot outside our family compound. I had had a tutor to help me with my English. We had one hour of television a day, the news; that was how I had learned Thai. My father was obsessed with our family's purity; he never used our dearly bought, royally granted Thai surname of Suntharapornsunthornpanich, but insisted on sign-ing all documents Sae Lim, as though the Great Integration of the Chinese had never occurred and our people were still a nation within a nation, still loyal to the vast and distant Middle Kingdom. My brave new world had been California, and it remained for Bob to show me that an even braver one had lain at my doorstep all my life.

Bangkoks within Bangkoks. Yes, that charmingly hackneyed metaphor of the Chinese boxes comes to mind. Quiet palaces with pavilions that overlooked reflecting ponds. Galleries hung with postmodern art. Japanese-style coffee houses with melon-flavored ice cream floats and individual shrimp pizzas. Grungy noodle stands beneath flimsy awnings over open sewers; stratospheri-cally upscale French patisseries and Italian gelaterias. Bob knew where they all were, and he was willing to share all his secrets, even though Aunt Ling-ling was always along for the ride. After a time, it seemed to me that perhaps it was my turn to reveal some secret, and so one Sunday afternoon, in one of the coffee lounges overlooking the atrium of the Sogo shopping mall, I decided to tell him the biggest of all secrets. "Do you really want to know," I said, "why we only serve the dragon fin soup on Wednesdays?"

"Yes," he said, "and I promise I won't print it."

"Well you see," I said, "it takes about a week for the tissue to regenerate."

That was about as much as I could safely say without spilling the whole can of soup. The dragon had been in our family since the late Ming Dynasty, when a multi-multi-great-uncle of mine, a eunuch who was the Emperor's trade repre-sentative between Peking and the Siamese Kingdom of Ayuthaya, had tricked him into following his junk all the way down the Chao Phraya River, had imprisoned him beneath the canals of the little village that was later to become Bangkok, City of Angels, Dwelling Place of Vishnu, Residence of the Nine Jewels, and so on so forth (read the *Guinness Book of World Records* to obtain the full name of the city) known affectionately to its residents as City of Angels Etc. This was because the dragon had revealed to my multi-great-uncle that the seemingly invincible Kingdom of Ayuthaya would one day be sacked by the King of Pegu and that the capital of Siam would be moved down to this unpretentious village in the Chao Phraya delta. The dragon had told him this because, as everyone knows, a mortally wounded dragon, when properly constrained, is obliged to answer three questions truthfully. Multi-great-uncle wasted his other questions on trying to find out whether he would ever regain his manhood and be able to experience an orgasm; the dragon had merely laughed at this, and his laughter had caused a minor earthquake which destroyed the summer palace of Lord Kuykendaal, a Dutchman who had married into the lowest echelon of the Siamese aristocracy, which earthquake in turn precipitated the Opium War of 1677, which, as it is not in the history books, remains alive only in our family tradition.

Our family tradition also states that each member of the family may only tell one outsider about the dragon's existence. If he chooses the right outsider, he will have a happy life; if he chooses unwisely, and the outsider turns out to be untrustworthy, then misfortune will dog both the revealer and his confidant.

I wasn't completely sure about Bob yet, and I didn't want to blow my one opportunity. But that evening, as I supervised the ritual slicing of the dragon's fin, my father dropped a bombshell.

The dragon could not, of course, be seen all in one piece. There was, in the kitchen of the Rainbow Cafe, a hole in one wall, about nine feet in diameter. One coil of the dragon came through this wall and curved upward toward a similar opening in the ceiling. I did not know where the dragon ended or began. One assumed this was a tail section because it was so narrow. I had seen a dragon whole only in my dreams, or in pictures. Rumor had it that this dragon stretched all the way to Nonthaburi, his slender body twisting through ancient sewer pipes and under the foundations of century-old buildings. He was bound to my family by an ancient spell in a scroll that sat on the altar of the household gods, just above the cash register inside the restaurant proper. He was unimaginably old and unimaginably jaded, stunned rigid by three thousands years of human magic, his scales so lusterless that I had to buff them with furniture polish to give them some semblance of draconian majesty. He was, of course, still mortally wounded from the battle he had endured with multi-great-uncle; nevertheless, it takes them a long, long time to die, especially when held captive by a scroll such as the one we possessed.

You could tell the dragon was still alive, though. Once in a very long while, he breathed. Or rather, a kind of rippling welled up him, and you could hear a distant wheeze, like an old house settling on its foundations. And of course, he regenerated. If it wasn't for that, the restaurant would never have stayed in business all these years.

The fin we harvested was a ventral fin and hung down over the main charcoal stove of the restaurant kitchen. It took some slicing to get it off. We had a new chef, Ah Quoc, just up from Penang, and he was having a lot of trouble. "You'd better heat up the carving knife some more," I was telling him. "Make sure it's red hot."

He stuck the knife back in the embers. Today, the dragon was remarkably sluggish; I had not detected a breath in hours; and the flesh was hard as stone. I wondered whether the event our family dreaded most, the dragon's death, was finally going to come upon us.

"Muoi, muoi," he said, "the flesh just won't give."

"Don't call me muoi," I said. "I'm not your little sister, I'm the boss's daughter. In fact, don't speak Chiuchow at all. English is a lot simpler."

"Okey-doke, Miss Janice. But Chinese or English, meat just no slice, la."

He was hacking away at the fin. The flesh was stony, recalcitrant. I didn't want to use the spell of binding, but I had to. I ran into the restaurant—it was closed and there were only a few old men playing mah jongg—grabbed the scroll from the altar, stormed back into the kitchen and tapped the scaly skin, whispering the word of power that only members of our family can speak. I felt a shudder deep within the dragon's bowels. I put my ear up to the clammy hide. I thought I could hear, from infinitely far away, the hollow clanging of the dragon's heart, the glacial oozing of his blood through kilometer after kilometer of leaden veins and arteries. "Run, blood, run," I shouted, and I started whipping him with the brittle paper.

Aunt Ling-ling came scurrying in at that moment, a tiny creature in a widow's dress, shouting, "You'll rip the scroll, don't hit so hard!"

But then, indeed, the blood began to roar. "Now you can slice him," I said to Ah Quoc. "Quickly. It has to soak in the marinade for at least twenty- four hours, and we're running late as it is."

"Okay! Knife hot enough now, la." Ah Quoc slashed through the whole fin in a single motion, like an imperial headsman. I could see now why my father had hired him to replace Ah Chen, who had become distracted, gone native—even gone so far as to march in the 1992 democracy riots—as if the politics of the Thais were any of our business.

Aunt Ling-ling had the vat of marinade all ready. Ah Quoc sliced quickly and methodically, tossing the pieces of dragon's fin into the bubbling liquid. With shark's fin, you have to soak it in water for a long time to soften it up for eating. Bob Halliday had speculated about the nature of the marinade. He was right about the garlic and the chilies, but it would perhaps have been unwise to tell him about the sulphuric acid.

It was at that point that my father came in. "The scroll, the scroll," he said distractedly. Then he saw it and snatched it from me.

"We're safe for another week," I said, following him out of the kitchen into the restaurant. Another of my aunts, the emaciated Jasmine, was counting a pile of money, doing calculations with an abacus and making entries into a leatherbound ledger.

My father put the scroll back. Then he looked directly into my eyes—something he had done only once or twice in my adult life—and, scratching his beard, said, "I've found you a husband."

That was the bombshell.

I didn't feel it was my place to respond right away... in fact, I was so flustered by his announcement that I had absolutely nothing to say. In a way, I had been expecting it, of course, but for some reason... perhaps it was because of my time at Santa Cruz... it just hadn't occurred to me that my father would be so... so... old-fashioned about it. I mean, my God, it was like being stuck in an Amy Tan novel or something.

That's how I ended up in Bob Halliday's office at the Bangkok Post, sobbing my guts out without any regard for propriety or good manners. Bob, who is a natural empath, allowed me to yammer on and on; he sent a boy down to the market to fetch some steaming noodles wrapped in banana leaves and iced coffee in little PVC bags. I daresay I didn't make too much sense. "My father's living in the nineteenth century... or worse," I said. "He should never have let me set foot outside the house… outside the restaurant. I mean, Santa Cruz, for God's sake! Wait till I tell him I'm not even a virgin anymore. The price is going to plummet, he's going to take a bath on whatever deal it is he's drawn up. I'm so mad at him. And even though he did send me to America, he never let me so much as set foot in the Silom Complex, two miles from our house, without a chaperone. I've never had a life! Or rather, I've had two half-lives—half American coed, half Chinese dragon lady—I'm like two half-people that don't make a whole. And this is Thailand, it's not America and it's not China. It's the most alien landscape of them all."

Later, because I didn't want to go home to face the grisly details of my impending marriage contract, I rode back to Bob's apartment with him in a tuk-tuk. The motorized rickshaw darted skillfully through jammed streets and minuscule alleys and once again—as so often with Bob—I found myself in an area of Bangkok I had never seen before, a district overgrown with weeds and wild banana trees; the soi came to an abrupt end and there was a lone elephant, swaying back and forth, being hosed down by a country boy wearing nothing but a phakhomah. "You must be used to slumming by now," Bob said, "with all the places I've taken you."

In his apartment, a grizzled cook served up a screamingly piquant kaeng khieu waan, and I must confess that though I usually can't stand Thai food, the heat of this sweet green curry blew me away. We listened to Wagner. Bob has the most amazing collection of CDs known to man. He has twelve recordings of *The Magic Flute*, but only three of Wagner's Ring cycle—three more than most people I know. "Just listen to that!" he said. I'm not a big fan of opera, but the kind of singing that issued from Bob's stereo sounded hauntingly familiar… it had the hollow echo of a sound I'd heard that very afternoon, the low and distant pounding of the dragon's heart.

"What is it?" I said.

"Oh, it's the scene where Siegfried slays the dragon," Bob said. "You know, this is the Solti recording, where the dragon's voice is electronically enhanced. I'm not sure I like it."

It sent chills down my spine.

"Funny story," Bob said. "For the original production, you know, in the 1860s… they had a special dragon built… in England… in little segments. They were supposed to ship the sections to Bayreuth for the premiere, but the neck was accidentally sent to Beirut instead. That dragon never did have a neck. Imagine those people in Beirut when they opened that crate! What do you do with a disembodied segment of dragon anyway?"

"I could think of a few uses," I said.

"It sets me to thinking about dragon's fin soup."

"No can divulge, la," I said, laughing, in my best Singapore English.

The dragon gave out a roar and fell, mortally wounded, in a spectacular orchestral climax. He crashed to the floor of the primeval forest. I had seen this scene once in the Fritz Lang silent film *Siegfried*, which we'd watched in our History of Cinema class at Santa Cruz. After the crash there came more singing.

"This is the fun part, now," Bob told me. "If you approach a dying dragon, it has to answer your questions… three questions usually… and it has to answer them truthfully."

"Even if he's been dying for a thousand years?" I said.

"Never thought of that, Janice," said Bob. "You think the dragon's truthseeing abilities might become a little clouded?"

Despite my long and tearful outpouring in his office, Bob had not once mentioned the subject of my Damoclean doom. Perhaps he was about to raise it now; there was one of those long pregnant pauses that tend to portend portentousness. I wanted to put it off a little longer, so I asked him, "If you had access to a dragon… and the dragon were dying, and you came upon him in just the right circumstances… what would you ask him?"

Bob laughed. "So many questions… so much I want to know… so many arcane truths that the cosmos hangs on!… I think I'd have a lot to ask. Why? You have a dragon for me?"

I didn't get back to Yaowaraj until very late that night. I had hoped that everyone would have gone to bed, but when I reached the restaurant (the family compound itself is reached through a back stairwell beyond the kitchen) I found my father still awake, sitting at the carving table, and Aunt Ling-ling and Aunt Jasmine stirring the vat of softening dragon's fin. The sulphuric acid had now been emptied and replaced with a pungent brew of vinegar, ginseng, garlic, soy sauce, and the ejaculate of a young boy, obtainable in Patpong for about one hundred baht. The whole place stank, but I knew that it would whittle down to the subtlest, sweetest, bitterest, most nostalgic of aromas.

My father said to me, "Perhaps you're upset with me, Janice; I know it was a little sudden."

"Sudden!" I said. "Give me a break, Papa, this was more than sudden. You're so old-fashioned suddenly… and you're not even that old. Marrying me off like you're cashing in your blue chip stocks or something."

"There's a world-wide recession, in case you haven't noticed. We need an infusion of cash. I don't know how much longer the dragon will hold out. Look, this contract…." He pushed it across the table. It was in Chinese, of course, and full of flowery and legalistic terms. "He's not the youngest I could have found, but his blood runs pure; he's from the village." The village being, of course, the village of my ancestors, on whose soil my family has not set foot in seven hundred years. "What do you mean, not the youngest, Papa?"

"To be honest, he's somewhat elderly. But that's for the best, isn't it? I mean, he'll soon be past, as it were, the age of lovemaking…"

"Papa, I'm not a virgin."

"Oh, not to worry, dear; I had a feeling something like that might happen over there in Californ'… we'll send you to Tokyo for the operation. Their hymen implants are as good as new, I'm told."

My hymen was not the problem. This was probably not the time to tell my father that the deflowerer of my maidenhead had been a young, fast-talking, vigorous, muscular specimen of corn-fed Americana by the name of Linda Horovitz.

"You don't seem very excited, my dear."

"Well, what do you expect me to say?" I had never raised my voice to my father, and I really didn't quite know how to do it.

"Look, I've really worked very hard on this match, trying to find the least offensive person who could meet the minimum criteria for bailing us out of this financial mess—this one, he has a condominium in Vancouver, owns a computer franchise, would probably not demand of you, you know, too terribly degrading a sexual performance—"

Sullenly, I looked at the floor.

He stared at me for a long time. Then he said, "You're in love, aren't you?"

I didn't answer.

My father slammed his fists down on the table. "Those damned lascivious Thai men with their honeyed words and their backstabbing habits... it's one of them, isn't it? My only daughter... and my wife dead in her grave these twenty-two years... it kills me."

"And what if it had been a Thai man?" I said. "Don't we have Thai passports? Don't we have one of those fifteen-syllable Thai names which your grandfather purchased from the King? Aren't we living on Thai soil, stewing up our birthright for Thai citizens to eat, depositing our hard-earned Thai thousand-baht bills in a Thai bank?"

He slapped my face.

He had never done that before. I was more stunned than hurt. I was not to feel the hurt until much later.

"Let me tell you, for the four hundredth time, how your grandmother died," he said, so softly I could hardly hear him above the bubbling of the dragon's fin. "My father had come to Bangkok to fetch his new wife and bring her back to Californ'. It was his cousin, my uncle, who managed the Rainbow Cafe in those days. It was the 1920s and the city was cool and quiet and serenely beautiful. There were only a few motor-cars in the whole city; one of them, a Ford, belonged to Uncle Shenghua. My father was in love with the City of Angels Etc. and he loved your grandmother even before he set eyes on her. And he never went back to Californ', but moved into this family compound, flouting the law that a woman should move into her husband's home. Oh, he was so much in love! And he believed that here, in a land where men did not look so different from himself, there would be no prejudice—no bars with signs that said No Dogs Or Chinamen—no parts of town forbidden to him—no forced assimilation of an alien tongue. After all, hadn't King Chulalongkorn himself taken Chinese concubines to ensure the cultural diversity of the highest ranks of the aristocracy?"

My cheek still burned; I knew the story almost by heart; I hated my father for using his past to ruin my life. Angrily I looked at the floor, at the walls, at the taut curve of the dragon's body as it hung cold, glittering and motionless.

"But then, you see, there was the revolution, the coming of what they called democracy. No more the many ancient cultures of Siam existing side by side. The closing of the Chinese-language schools. Laws restricting those of ethnic Chinese descent from certain occupations… true, there were no concentration camps, but in some ways the Jews had it easier than we did… someone noticed. Now listen! You're not listening!"

"Yes, Papa," I said, but in fact my mind was racing, trying to find a way out of this intolerable situation. My Chinese self calling out to my American self, though she was stranded in another country, and perhaps near death, like the dragon whose flesh sustained my family's coffers.

"1945," my father said. "The war was over, and Chiang Kai-Shek was demanding that Siam be ceded to China. There was singing and dancing in the streets of Yaowaraj! Our civil rights were finally going to be restored to us… and the Thais were going to get their comeuppance! We marched with joy in our hearts… and then the soldiers came… and then we too had rifles in our hands… as though by magic. Uncle Shenghua's car was smashed. They smeared the seats with shit and painted the windshield with the words 'Go home, you slanty-eyed scum.' Do you know why the restaurant wasn't torched? One of the soldiers was raping a woman against the doorway and his friends wanted to give him time to finish. The woman was your grandmother. It broke my father's heart."

I had never had the nerve to say it before, but today I was so enraged that I spat it out, threw it in his face. "You don't know that he was your father, Papa. Don't think I haven't done the math. You were born in 1946. So much for your obsession with racial purity."

He acted as though he hadn't heard me, just went on with his preset lecture: "And that's why I don't want you to consort with any of them. They're lazy, self-indulgent people who think only of sex. I just know that one of them's got his tentacles wrapped around your heart."

"Papa, you're consumed by this bullshit. You're a slave to this ancient curse… just like the damn dragon." Suddenly, dimly, I had begun to see a way out. "But it's not a Thai I'm in love with. It's an American."

"A white person!" he was screaming at the top of his lungs. My two aunts looked up from their stirring. "Is he at least rich?"

"No. He's a poor journalist."

"Some blond young thing batting his long eyelashes at you —"

"Oh, no, he's almost fifty. And he's fat." I was starting to enjoy this.

"I forbid you to see him! It's that man from the *Post*, isn't it? That bloated thing who tricked me with his talk of music and literature into thinking him harmless. Was it he who violated you? I'll have him killed, I swear."

"No, you won't," I said, as another piece of my plan fell into place. "I have the right to choose one human being on this earth to whom I shall reveal the secret of the family's dragon. My maidenhead is yours to give away, but not this. This right is the only thing I can truly call my own, and I'm going to give it to Bob Halliday."

It was because he could do nothing about my choice that my father agreed to the match between Bob Halliday and me; he knew that, once told of the secret, Bob's fate would necessarily be intertwined with the fate of the Clan of Lim no matter what, for a man who knew of the dragon could not be allowed to escape from the family's clutches. Unfortunately, I had taken Bob's name in vain. He was not the marrying kind. But perhaps, I reasoned, I could get him to go along with the charade for a while, until old Mr. Hong from the Old Country stopped pressing his suit. Especially if I gave him the option of questioning the dragon. After all, I had heard him wax poetic about all the questions he could ask... questions about the meaning of existence, of the creation and destruction of the universe, profound conundrums about love and death.

Thus it was that Bob Halliday came to the Rainbow Cafe one more time—it was Thursday—and dined on such mundane delicacies as beggar chicken, braised sea cucumbers stuffed with pork, cold jellyfish tentacles, and suckling pig. As a kind of coup de grâce, my father even trotted out a small dish of dragon's fin which he had managed to keep refrigerated from the day before (it won't keep past twenty-four hours) which Bob consumed with gusto. He also impressed my father no end by speaking a Mandarin of such consonant-grinding purity that my father, whose groveling deference to those of superior accent was millenni-ally etched within his genes, could not help addressing him in terms of deepest and most cringing respect. He discoursed learnedly on the dragon lore of many cultures, from the salubrious, fertility-bestowing water dragons of China to the fire-breathing, maiden-ravishing monsters of the West; lectured on the theory that the racial memory of dinosaurs might have contributed to the draconian mythos, although he allowed as how humans never coexisted with dinosaurs, so the racial memory must go back as far as marmosets and shrews and such crea-tures; he lauded the soup in high astounding terms, using terminology so poetic and ancient that he was forced to draw the calligraphy in the air with a stubby finger before my father was able vaguely to grasp his metaphors; and finally—the clincher—alluded to a great-great-great-great-aunt of his in San Francisco who had once had a brief, illicit, and wildly romantic interlude with a Chinese opium smuggler who might just possibly have been one of the very Lims who had come from that village in Southern Yunnan, you know the village I'm talking about, that very village... at which point my father, whisking away all the haute cuisine dishes and replacing them with an enormous blueberry cheesecake flown in, he said, from Leo Lindy's of New York, said, "All right, all right, I'm sold. You have no money, but I daresay someone of your intellectual brilliance can conjure up some money somehow. My son, it is with great pleasure that I bestow upon you the hand of my wayward, worthless, and hideous daughter."

I hadn't forewarned Bob about this. Well, I had meant to, but words had failed me at the last moment. Papa had moved in for the kill a lot more quickly than I had thought he would. Before Bob could say anything at all, therefore, I decided to pop a revelation of my own. "I think, Papa," I said, "that it's time for me to show him the dragon."

We all trooped into the kitchen.

The dragon was even more inanimate than usual. Bob put his ear up to the scales; he knocked his knuckles raw. When I listened, I could hear nothing at all at first; the whisper of the sea was my own blood surging through my brain's capillaries, constricted as they were with worry. Bob said, "This is what I've been eating, Janice?"

I directed him over to where Ah Quoc was now seasoning the vat, chopping the herbs with one hand and sprinkling with the other, while my two aunts stirred, prodded, and gossiped like the witches from Macbeth. "Look, look," I said, and I pointed out the mass of still unpulped fin that protruded from the glop, "see how its texture matches that of the two dorsal fins."

"It hardly seems alive," Bob said, trying to pry a scale loose so he could peer at the quick.

"You'll need a red-hot paring knife to do that," I said. Then, when Papa wasn't listening, I whispered in his ear, "Please, just go along with all this. It really looks like 'fate worse than death' time for me if you don't. I know that marriage is the farthest thing from your mind right now, but I'll make it up to you somehow. You can get concubines. I'll even help pick them out. Papa won't mind that, it'll only make him think you're a stud."

Bob said, and it was the thing I'd hoped he'd say, "Well, there are certain questions that have always nagged at me... certain questions which, if only I knew the answers to them, well... let's just say I'd die happy."

My father positively beamed at this. "My son," he said, clapping Bob resoundingly on the back, "I already know that I shall die happy. At least my daughter won't be marrying a Thai. I just couldn't stand the thought of one of those loathsome creatures dirtying the blood of the House of Lim."

I looked at my father full in the face. Could he have already forgotten that only last night I had called him a bastard? Could he be that deeply in denial? "Bob," I said softly, "I'm going to take you to confront the dragon." Which was more than my father had ever done, or I myself.

Confronting the dragon was, indeed, a rather tall order, for no one had done so since the 1930s, and Bangkok had grown from a sleepy backwater town into a monster of a metropolis; we knew only that the dragon's coils reached deep into the city's foundations, crossed the river at several points, and, well, we weren't sure if he did extend all the way to Nonthaburi; luckily, there is a new expressway now, and once out of the crazy traffic of the old part of the city it did not take long, riding the sleek airconditioned Nissan taxicab my father had chartered for us, to reach the outskirts of the city. On the way, I caught glimpses of many more Bangkoks that my father's blindness had denied me; I saw the Blade Runneresque towers threaded with mist and smog, saw the buildings shaped like giant robots and computer circuit boards designed by that eccentric genius, Dr. Sumet; saw the not-very-ancient and very-very-multicolored temples that dotted the cityscape like rhinestones in a cowboy's boot; saw the slums and the palaces, cheek by jowl, and the squamous rooftops that could perhaps have also been little segments of the dragon poking up from the miasmal collage; we zoomed down the road at breakneck speed to the strains of Natalie Cole, who, our driver opined, is "even better than Mai and Christina".

How to find the dragon? Simple. I had the scroll. Now and then, there was a faint vibration of the parchment. It was a kind of dousing.

"This off-ramp," I said, "then left, I think." And to Bob I said, "Don't worry about a thing. Once we reach the dragon, you'll ask him how to get out of this whole mess. He can tell you, has to tell you actually; once that's all done, you'll be free of me, I'll be free of my father's craziness, he'll be free of his obsession."

Bob said, "You really shouldn't put too much stock in what the dragon has to tell you."

I said, "But he always tells the truth!"

"Well yes, but as a certain wily Roman politician once said, 'What is truth?' Or was that Ronald Reagan?"

"Oh, Bob," I said, "if push really came to shove, if there's no solution to this whole crisis… could you actually bring yourself to marry me?"

"You're very beautiful," Bob said. He loves to be all things to all people. But I don't think there's enough of him to go round. I mean, basically, there are a couple of dozen Janice Lims waiting in line for the opportunity to sit at Bob's feet. But, you know, when you're alone with him, he has this ability to give you every scintilla of his attention, his concern, his love, even; it's just that there's this nagging concern that he'd feel the same way if he were alone with a Beethoven string quartet, say, or a plate of exquisitely spiced naem sod.

We were driving through young paddy fields now; the nascent rice has a neon-green color too garish to describe. The scroll was shaking continuously and I realized we must be rather close to our goal; I have to admit that I was scared of out of my wits.

The driver took us through the gates of a Buddhist temple. The scroll vibrated even more energetically. Past the main chapel, there were more gates; they led to a Brahmin sanctuary; past the Indian temple there was yet another set of gates, over which, in rusty wrought-iron, hung the character Lim, which is two trees standing next to one another. The taxi stopped. The scroll's shaking had quieted to an insistent purr. "It's around here somewhere," I said, getting out of the cab.

The courtyard we found ourselves in (the sun was setting at this point, and the shadows were long and gloomy, and the marble flagstones red as blood) was a mishmash of nineteenth-century chinoiserie. There were stone lions, statues of bearded men, twisted little trees peering up from crannies in the stone; and tall, obelisk-like columns in front of a weathered stone building that resembled a ruined ziggurat. It took me a moment to realize that the building was, in fact, the dragon's head, so petrified by time and the slow process of dying that it had turned into an antique shrine. Someone still worshipped here at least. I could smell burning joss-sticks; in front of the pointed columns—which, I now could see, were actually the dragon's teeth—somebody had left a silver tray containing a glass of wine, a pig's head, and a garland of decaying jasmine.

"Yes, yes," said Bob, "I see it too; I feel it even."

"How do you mean?"

"It's the air or something. It tastes of the same bitterness that's in the dragon's fin soup. Only when you've taken a few breaths of it can you smell the underlying sensations... the joy, the love, the infinite regret."

"Yes, yes, all right," I said, "but don't forget to ask him for a way out of our dilemma."

"Why don't you ask him yourself?" Bob said.

I became all flustered at this. "Well, it's just that, I don't know, I'm too young, I don't want to use up all my questions, it's not the right time yet... you're a mature person, you don't —"

"... have that much longer to live, I suppose," Bob said wryly.

"Oh, you know I didn't mean it in quite that way."

"Ah, but, sucking in the dragon's breath the way we are, we too are forced to blurt out the truth, aren't we?" he said. I didn't like that.

"Don't want to let the genie out of the bottle, do you?" Bob said. "Want to clutch it to your breast, don't want to let go...."

"That's my father you're describing, not me."

Bob smiled. "How do you work this thing?"

"You take the scroll and you tap the dragon's lips."

"Lips?"

I pointed at the long stucco frieze that extended all the way around the row of teeth. "And don't forget to ask him," I said yet again.

"All right. I will."

Bob went up to the steps that led into the dragon's mouth. On the second floor were two flared windows that were his nostrils; above them, two slitty windows seemed to be his eyes; the light from them was dim, and seemed to come from candlelight. I followed him two steps behind—it was almost as though we were already married!—and I was ready when he put out his hand for the scroll. Gingerly, he tapped the dragon's teeth.

This was how the dragon's voice sounded: it seemed at first to be the wind, or the tinkling of the temple bells, or the far-off lowing of the waterbuffalo that wallowed in the paddy; or, or, the distant cawing of a raven, the cry of a newborn child, the creak of a teak house on its stilts, the hiss of a slithering snake. Only gradually did these sounds coalesce into words, and once spoken the words seemed to hang in the air, to jangle and clatter like a loaded dishwasher.

The dragon said, We seldom have visitors anymore.

I said, "Quick, Bob, ask."

"Okay, okay," said Bob. He got ready, I think, to ask the dragon what I wanted him to ask, but instead, he blurted out a completely different question. "How different," he said, "would the history of music be, if Mozart had managed to live another ten years?"

"Bob!" I said. "I thought you wanted to ask deep, cosmic questions about the nature of the universe —"

"Can't get much deeper than that," he said, and then the answer came, all at once, out of the twilight air. It was music of a kind. To me it sounded dissonant and disturbing; choirs singing out of tune, donkeys fiddling with their own tails. But you know, Bob stood there with his eyes closed, and his face was suffused with an ineffable serenity; and the music surged to a noisome clanging and a yowling and a caterwauling, and a slow smile broke out on his lips; and as it all began to die away he was whispering to himself, "Of course… appoggiaturas piled on appoggiaturas, bound to lead to integral serialism in the mid-romantic period instead, then minimalism mating with impressionism running full tilt into the Wagnerian gesamtkunstwerk and colliding with the pointillism of late Webern…."

At last he opened his eyes, and it was as though he had seen the face of God. But what about me and my miserable life? It came to me now. These were Bob's idea of what constituted the really important questions of life. I couldn't begrudge him a few answers. He'd probably save the main course for last; then we'd be out of there and could get on with our lives. I settled back to suffer through another arcane question, and it was, indeed, arcane.

Bob said, "You know, I've always been troubled by one of the hundred-letter words in *Finnegans Wake*. You know the words I mean, the supposed 'thunder-claps' that divide Joyce's novel into its main sections… well, its the ninth one of those… I can't seem to get it to split into its component parts. Maybe it seems trivial, but it's worried me for the last twenty-nine years."

The sky grew very dark then. Dry lightning forked and unforked across gathering clouds. The dragon spoke once more, but this time it seemed to be a cacophony of broken words, disjointed phonemes, strings of frenetic fricatives and explosive plosives; once again it was mere noise to me, but to Bob Halliday it was the sweetest music. I saw that gazing-on-the-face-of-divinity expression steal across his features one more time as again he closed his eyes. The man was having an orgasm. No wonder he didn't need sex. I marveled at him. Ideas themselves were sensual things to him. But he didn't lust after knowledge, he wasn't greedy about it like Faust; too much knowledge could not damn Bob Halliday, it could only redeem him.

Once more, the madness died away. A monsoon shower had come and gone in the midst of the dragon's response, and we were drenched; but presently, in the hot breeze that sprang up, our clothes began to dry.

"You've had your fun now, Bob. Please, please," I said, "let's get to the business at hand."

Bob said, "All right." He tapped the dragon's lips again, and said, "Dragon, dragon, I want to know…."

The clouds parted and Bob was bathed in moonlight.

Bob said, "Is there a proof for Fermat's Theorem?"

Well, I had had it with him now. I could see my whole life swirling down the toilet bowl of lost opportunities. "Bob!" I screamed, and began pummeling his stomach with my fists… the flesh was not as soft as I'd imagined it must be… I think I sprained my wrist. "What did I do wrong?"

"Bob, you idiot, what about us?"

"I'm sorry, Janice. Guess I got a little carried away."

Yes, said the dragon. Presumably, since Bob had not actually asked him to prove Fermat's Theorem, all he had to do was say yes or no.

What a waste. I couldn't believe that Bob had done that to me. I was going to have to ask the dragon myself after all. I wrested the scroll from Bob's hands, and furiously marched up the steps toward that row of teeth, phosphorescent in the moonlight.

"Dragon," I screamed, "dragon, dragon, dragon, dragon, dragon."

So, Ah Muoi, you've come to me at last. So good of you. I am old; I have seen my beginning and my end; it is in your eyes. You've come to set me free.

Our family tradition states clearly that it is always good to give the dragon the impression that you are going to set him free. He's usually a lot more coopera-tive. Of course, you never do set him free. You would think that, being almost omniscient, the dragon would be wise to this, but mythical beasts always seem to have their fatal flaws. I was too angry for casuistric foreplay.

"You've got to tell me what I need to know." Furiously, I whipped the crumbling stone with the old scroll.

I'm dying, you are my mistress; what else is new?

"How can I free myself from all this baggage that my family has laid on me?"

The dragon said:

There is a sleek swift segment of my soul
That whips against the waters of renewal;
You too have such a portion of yourself;
Divide it in a thousand pieces;
Make soup;
Then shall we all be free.

"That doesn't make sense!" I said. The dragon must be trying to cheat me somehow. I slammed the scroll against the nearest tooth. The stucco loosened; I heard a distant rumbling. "Give me a straight answer, will you? How can I rid my father of the past that torments him and won't let him face who he is, who I am, what we're not?"

The dragon responded:

There is a sly secretion from my scales
That drives a man through madness into joy;
You too have such a portion of yourself;
Divide it in a thousand pieces;

Make soup;

Then shall we all be free.

This was making me really mad. I started kicking the tooth. I screamed, "Bob was right... you're too senile, your mind is too clouded to see anything that's important... all you're good for is Bob's great big esoteric enigmas... but I'm just a human being here, and I'm in bondage, and I want out... what's it going to take to get a straight answer out of you?" Too late, I realized that I had phrased my last words in the form of a question. And the answer came on the jasmine-scented breeze even before I had finished asking:

There is a locked door deep inside my flesh

A dam against bewilderment and fear;

You too have such a portion of yourself;

Divide it in a thousand pieces;

Make soup;

Then shall we all be free.

But I wasn't even listening, so sure was I that all was lost. For all my life I had been defined by others—my father, now Bob, now the dragon, even, briefly, by Linda Horovitz. I was a series of half-women, never a whole. Frustrated beyond repair, I flagellated the dragon's lips with that scroll, shrieking like a pre-menstrual fishwife: "Why can't I have a life like other people?" I'd seen the American girls with their casual ways, their cars, speaking of men as though they were hunks of meat; and the Thai girls, arrogant, plotting lovers' trysts on their cellular phones as they breezed through the spanking-new shopping mall of their lives. Why was I the one who was trapped, chained up, enslaved? But I had used up the three questions.

I slammed the scroll so hard against the stucco that it began to tear.

"Watch out!" Bob cried. "You'll lose your power over him!"

"Don't speak to me of empowerment," I shouted bitterly, and the parchment ripped all at once, split into a million itty-bitty pieces that danced like shooting stars in the brilliant moonlight.

That was it, then. I had cut off the family's only source of income, too. I was going to have to marry Mr. Hong after all.

Then the dragon's eyes lit up, and his jaws began slowly to open, and his breath, heady, bitter, and pungent, poured into the humid night air. "My God," Bob said, "there is some life to him after all."

My life, the dragon whispered, is but a few brief bittersweet moments of imagined freedom; for is not life itself enslavement to the wheel of sansara? Yet you, man and woman, base clay though you are, have been the means of my deliverance. I thank you.

The dragon's mouth gaped wide. Within, an abyss of thickest blackness; but when I stared long and hard at it, I could see flashes of oh, such wondrous things... far planets, twisted forests, chaotic cities...

"Shall we go in?" said Bob.

"Do you want to?"

"Yes," Bob said, "but I can't, not without you; dying, he's still your dragon, no one else's; you know how it is; you kill your dragon, I kill mine."

"Okay," I said, realizing that now, finally, had come the moment for me to seize my personhood in my hands, "but come with me, for old times' sake; after all, you did give me a pretty thorough tour of your dying dragon…"

"Ah yes; the City of Angels Etc. But that's not dying for a few millennia yet."

I took Bob by the hand and ran up the steps into the dragon's mouth. He followed me. Inside the antechamber, the dragon's palate glistened with crystallized drool. Strings of baroque pearls hung from the ceiling, and the dragon's tongue was coated with clusters of calcite. Further down, the abyss of many colors yawned.

"Come on," I said.

"What do you think he meant," Bob said, "when he said you should slice off little pieces of yourself, make them into soup, and that would set us all free?"

"I think," I said, "that it's the centuries of being nibbled away by little parasites…" But I was no longer that interested in the dragon's oracular pronouncements. I mean, for the first time in my life, since my long imprisonment in my family compound and the confines of the Rainbow Cafe's kitchen, since my three years of rollercoastering through the alien wharves of Santa Cruz, I was in territory that I instinctively recognized as my own. Past the bronze uvula that depended from the cavern ceiling like a soundless bell, we came to a mother-of-pearl staircase that led ever downward. "This must be the way to the oesophagus," I said. "Yeah." There came a gurgling sound. A dull, foul water sloshed about our ankles. "Maybe there's a boat," I said. We turned and saw it moored to the banister, a golden barque with a silken sail blazoned with the ideograph Lim.

Bob laughed. "You're a sort of goddess in this kingdom, a creatrix, an earth-mother. But I'm the one with the waistline for earth-mothering."

"Perhaps we could somehow meld together and be one." After all, his mothering instinct was a lot stronger than mine.

"Cosmic!" he said, and laughed again.

"Like the character Lim itself," I told him, "two trees straining to be one."

"Erotic!"

And I too laughed as we set sail down the gullet of the dying dragon. The waters were sluggish at first. But they started to deepen. Soon we were having the flume ride of our lives, careening down the bronze-lined walls that boomed with the echo of our laughter… the bronze was dark for a long long time till it started to shine with a light that rose from the heat of our bodies, the first warmth to invade the dragon's innards in a thousand years… and then, in the mirror surface of the walls, we began to see visions. Yes! there was the dragon himself, youthful, pissing the monsoon as he soared above the South China Sea. Look, look, my multi-great-great-uncle bearing the urn of his severed genitals as he marched from the gates of the Forbidden City, setting sail for Siam! Look, look, now multi-great-uncle in the Chinese Quarter of the great metropolis of Ayutthaya, constraining the dragon as it breached the raging waters of the Chao

Phraya! Look, look, another great-great-uncle panning for gold, his queue bobbing up and down in the California sun! Look, look, another uncle, marching alongside the great Chinese General Taksin, who wrested Siam back from the Burmese and was in turn put to an ignominious death! And look, look closer now, the soldier raping my grandmother in the doorway of the family compound... look, look, my grandfather standing by, his anger curbed by an intolerable terror... look, look, even that was there... and me... yielding to the stately Linda Horovitz in the back seat of rusty Toyota... me, stirring the vat of dragon's fin soup... me, talking back to my father for the first time, getting slapped in the face, me, smashing the scroll of power into smithereens.

And Bob? Bob saw other things. He heard the music of the spheres. He saw the Sistine Chapel in its pristine beauty. He speed-read his way through Joyce and Proust and Tolstoy, unexpurgated and unedited. And you know, it was turning him on.

And me, too. I don't know quite when we started making love. Perhaps it was when we hit what felt like terminal velocity, and I could feel the friction and the body heat begin to ignite his shirt and my cheongsam. Blue flame embraced our bodies, fire that was water, heat that was cold. The flame was burning up my past, racing through the dirt roads of the ancestral village; the fire was engulfing Chinatown, the rollercoasters of Santa Cruz were blazing gold and ruddy against the setting sun, and even the Forbidden City was on fire, even the great portrait of Chairman Mao and the Great Wall and the Great Inextinguishable Middle Kingdom itself, all burning, burning, burning, all cold, all turned to stone, and all because I was discovering new continents of pleasure in the folds of Bob Halliday's flesh, so rich and convoluted that it was like making love to three hundred pounds of brain; and you know, he was considerate in ways I'd never dreamed; that mothering instinct I supposed, that empathy; when I popped, he made me feel like the apple that received the arrowhead of William Tell and with it freedom from oppression; oh, God, I'm straining aren't I, but you know, those things are so so hard to describe; we're plummeting headlong through the mist and foam and flame and spray and surge and swell and brine and ice and hell and incandescence and then:

In the eye of the storm:

A deep gash opening and:

Naked, we're falling into the vat beneath the dragon's flanks as the ginsu-wielding Ah Quoc is hacking away at the disintegrating flesh and:

"No!" my father shouted. "Hold the sulphuric acid!"

We were bobbing up and down in a tub of bile and semen and lubricious fluids, and Aunt Ling-ling was frantically snatching away the flask of concentrated H2SO4 from the kvetching Jasmine.

"Mr. Elephant, la!" cried Ah Quoc. "What you do Miss Janice? No can! No can!"

"You've gone and killed the dragon!" shrieked my father. "Now what are we going to do for a living?"

And he was right. Once harder than titanium carbide, the coil of flesh was dissipating into the kitchen's musty air; the scales were becoming circlets of rainbow light in the steam from the bamboo cha shu bao containers; as archetypes are wont to do, the dragon was returning to the realm of myth.

"Oh, Papa, don't make such a fuss," I said, and was surprised to see him back off right away. "We're still going to make soup today."

"Well, I'd like to know how. Do you know you were gone for three weeks? It's Wednesday again, and the line for dragon's fin soup is stretching all the way to Chicken Alley! There's some kind of weird rumor going around that the soup today is especially heng, and I'm not about to go back out there and tell them I'm going to be handing out rain checks."

"Speaking of rain—" said Aunt Ling-ling.

Rain indeed. We could hear it, cascading across the corrugated iron rooftops, sluicing down the awnings, splashing the dead-end canals, running in the streets.

"Papa," I said, "we shall make soup. It will be the last and finest soupmaking of the Clan of Lim."

And then—for Bob Halliday and I were still entwined in each other's arms, and his flesh was still throbbing inside my flesh, bursting with pleasure as the thunderclouds above—we rose up, he and I, he with his left arm stretched to one side, I with my right arm to the other, and together we spelled out the two trees melding into one in the calligraphy of carnal desire—and, basically, what happened next was that I released into the effervescing soup stock the swift sleek segment of my soul, the sly secretion from my scales, and, last but not least, the locked door deep inside my flesh; and these things (as the two trees broke apart) did indeed divide into a thousand pieces, and so we made our soup; not from a concrete dragon, time-frozen in its moment of dying, but from an insubstantial spirit-dragon that was woman, me, alive.

"Well, well," said Bob Halliday, "I'm not sure I'll be able to write this up for the *Post*."

Now this is what transpired next, in the heart of Bangkok's Chinatown, in the district known as Yaowaraj, in a restaurant called the Rainbow Cafe, on a Wednesday lunchtime in the mid-monsoon season:

There wasn't very much soup, but the more we ladled out, the more there seemed to be left. We had thought to eke it out with black mushrooms and bok choi and a little sliced chicken, but even those extra ingredients multiplied miraculously. It wasn't quite the feeding of the five thousand, but, unlike the evangelist, we didn't find it necessary to count.

After a few moments, the effects were clearly visible. At one table, a group of politicians began removing their clothes. They leaped up onto the lazy susan and began to spin around, chanting "Freedom! Freedom!" at the top of their lungs. At the next table, three transvestites from the drag show down the street began to make mad passionate love to a platter of duck. An young man in a pinstripe suit draped himself in the printout from his cellular fax and danced the hula with a shrivelled crone. Children somersaulted from table to table like monkeys.

And Bob Halliday, my father and I?

My father, drinking deeply, said, "I really don't give a shit who you marry."

And I said, "I guess it's about time I told you this, but there's a strapping Jewish tomboy from Milwaukee that I want you to meet. Oh, but maybe I will marry Mr. Hong—why not?—some men aren't as self-centered and domineering as you might think. If you'd stop sitting around trying to be Chinese all the time—"

"I guess it's about time I told you this," said my father, "but I stopped caring about this baggage from the past a long time ago. I was only keeping it up so you wouldn't think I was some kind of bloodless half-breed."

"I guess it's about time I told you this," I said, "but I like living in Thailand. It's wild, it's maddening, it's obscenely beautiful, and it's very, very, very un-American."

"I guess it's about time I told you this," my father said, "but I've bought me a one-way ticket to Californ', and I'm going to close up the restaurant and get a new wife and buy myself a little self-respect."

"I guess it's about time I told you this," I said, "I love you."

That stopped him cold. He whistled softly to himself, then sucked up the remaining dregs of soup with a slurp like a farting buffalo. Then he flung the bowl against the peeling wall and cried out, "And I love you too."

And that was the first and only time we were ever to exchange those words.

But you know, there were no such revelations from Bob Halliday. He drank deeply and reverently; he didn't slurp; he savored; of all the dramatis personae of this tale, it was he alone he seemed, for a moment, to have cut himself free from the wheel of sansara to gaze, however briefly, on nirvana.

As I have said, there was a limitless supply of soup. We gulped it down till our sides ached. We laughed so hard we were sitting ankle-deep in our tears.

But do you know what?

An hour later we were hungry again.

THE MAN WHO PAINTED THE DRAGON GRIAULE

Lucius Shepard

Lucius Shepard was born in Lynchburg, Virginia in 1947 and published his first book, poetry *Cantata of Death, Weakmind & Generation* in 1967. He began to publish fiction of genre interest in 1983, with "The Taylorsville Reconstruction", which was followed by such major stories as "A Spanish Lesson", "R&R", "Salvador", and "The Jaguar Hunter". The best of his early short fiction is collected in two World Fantasy Award winning volumes, *The Jaguar Hunter* and *The Ends of the Earth*. In 1995 *The Encyclopedia of Science Fiction* said of Shepard's relationship to SF that "there is some sense that two ships may have passed in the night". Two years later Shepard returned from what he has since described as a career "pause", delivering a series of major short stories, starting with "Crocodile Rock" in 1999, followed by Hugo Award winner "Radiant Green Star" in 2000, and culminating in nearly 300,000 words of short fiction published in 2003. The best of his recent short fiction has been collected in *Trujillo and Other Stories*, *Eternity and Other Stories*, and *Dagger Key and Other Stories*. His novels include *Green Eyes*, *Life During Wartime*, *Kalimantan*, *The Golden*, *Viator*, and *Softspoken*. His most recent books are the collection *The Best of Lucius Shepard*, and *Viator Plus*. Upcoming is a new short novel, *The Taborin Scale*.

"…Other than the Sichi Collection, Cattanay's only surviving works are to be found in the Municipal Gallery at Regensburg, a group of eight oils-on-canvas, most notable among them being *Woman With Oranges*. These paintings constitute his portion of a student exhibition hung some weeks after he had left the city of his birth and travelled south to Teocinte, there to present his proposal to the city fathers; it is unlikely he ever learned of the disposition of his work, and even more unlikely that he was aware of the general critical indifference with which it was received. Perhaps the most interesting of the group to modern scholars, the most indicative as to Cattanay's later preoccupations, is the *Self Portrait*, painted at the age of twenty-eight, a year before his departure.

"The majority of the canvas is a richly varnished black in which the vague shapes of floorboards are presented, barely visible. Two irregular slashes of gold cross the blackness, and within these we can see a section of the artist's thin features and the shoulder panel of his shirt. The perspective given is that we are looking down at the artist, perhaps through a tear in the roof, and that he is looking up at us, squinting into the light, his mouth distorted by a grimace born of intense concentration. On first viewing the painting, I was struck by the atmosphere of tension that radiated from it. It seemed I was spying upon a man imprisoned within a shadow having two golden bars, tormented by the possibilities of light beyond the walls. And though this may be the reaction of the art historian, not the less knowledgeable and therefore more trustworthy response of the gallery-goer, it also seemed that this imprisonment was self-imposed, that he could have easily escaped his confine; but that he had realized a feeling of stricture was an essential fuel to his ambition, and so had chained himself to this arduous and thoroughly unreasonable chore of perception..."

—from *Meric Cattany: The Politics of Conception* by Reade Holland, Ph.D

1

In 1853, in a country far to the south in a world separated from this one by the thinnest margin of possibility, a dragon named Griaule dominated the region of the Carbonales Valley, a fertile area centring upon the town of Teocinte and renowned for its production of silver, mahogany and indigo. There were other dragons in those days, most dwelling on the rocky islands west of Patagonia—tiny, irascible creatures, the largest of them no bigger than a swallow. But Griaule was one of the great beasts who had ruled an age. Over the centuries he had grown to stand 750 feet high at the mid-back, and from the tip of his tail to his nose he was 6,000 feet long. (It should be noted here that the growth of dragons was due not to caloric intake, but to the absorption of energy derived from the passage of time.) Had it not been for a miscast spell, Griaule would have died millennia before. The wizard entrusted with the task of slaying him—knowing his own life would be forfeited as a result of the magical backwash—had experienced a last-second twinge of fear, and, diminished by this ounce of courage, the spell had flown a mortal inch awry. Though the wizard's whereabouts were unknown, Griaule had remained alive. His heart had stopped, his breath stilled, but his mind continued to seethe, to send forth the gloomy vibrations that enslaved all who stayed for long within range of his influence.

This dominance of Griaule's was an elusive thing. The people of the valley attributed their dour character to years of living under his mental shadow, yet there were other regional populations who maintained a harsh face to the world and had no dragon on which to blame the condition; they also attributed their frequent raids against the neighbouring states to Griaule's effect, claiming to be a peaceful folk at heart—but again, was this not human nature? Perhaps the most certifiable proof of Griaule's primacy was the fact that despite a standing offer of a fortune in silver to anyone who could kill him, no one had succeeded. Hundreds of plans had been put forward, and all had failed, either through inanition or impracticality. The archives of Teocinte were filled with schematics for enormous steam-powered swords and other such improbable devices, and the architects of these plans had every one stayed too long in the valley and become part of the disgruntled populace. And so they went on with their lives, coming and going, always returning, bound to the valley, until one spring day in 1853, Meric Cattanay arrived and proposed that the dragon be painted.

He was a lanky young man with a shock of black hair and a pinched look to his cheeks; he affected the loose trousers and shirt of a peasant, and waved his arms to make a point. His eyes grew wide when listening, as if his brain were bursting with illumination, and at times he talked incoherently about "the conceptual statement of death by art". And though the city fathers could not be sure, though they allowed for the possibility that he simply had an unfortunate manner, it seemed he was mocking them. All in all, he was not the sort they were inclined to trust. But, because he had come armed with such a wealth of diagrams and charts, they were forced to give him serious consideration.

"I don't believe Griaule will be able to perceive the menace in a process as subtle as art," Meric told them. "We'll proceed as if we were going to illustrate him, grace his side with a work of true vision, and all the while we'll be poisoning him with the paint."

The city fathers voiced their incredulity, and Meric waited impatiently until they quieted. He did not enjoy dealing with these worthies. Seated at their long table, sour-faced, a huge smudge of soot on the wall above their heads like an ugly thought they were sharing, they reminded him of the Wine Merchants Association in Regensburg, the time they had rejected his group portrait.

"Paint can be deadly stuff," he said after their muttering had died down. "Take vert Veronese, for example. It's derived from oxide of chrome and barium. Just a whiff would make you keel over. But we have to go about it seriously, create a real piece of art. If we just slap paint on his side, he might see through us."

The first step in the process, he told them, would be to build a tower of scaffolding, complete with hoists and ladders, that would brace against the supraocular plates above the dragon's eye; this would provide a direct route to a 700-foot-square loading platform and base station behind the eye. He estimated it would take 81,000 board feet of lumber, and a crew of ninety men should be able to finish construction within five months. Ground crews accompanied by chemists and geologists would search out limestone deposits (useful in priming the scales) and sources of pigments, whether organic or minerals such as azurite and hematite. Other teams would be set to scraping the dragon's side clean of algae, peeled skin, any decayed material, and afterwards would laminate the surface with resins.

"It would be easier to bleach him with quicklime," he said. "But that way we lose the discolourations and ridges generated by growth and age, and I think what we'll paint will be defined by those shapes. Anything else would look like a damn tattoo!"

There would be storage vats and mills: edge-runner mills to separate pigments from crude ores, ball mills to powder the pigments, pug mills to mix them with oil. There would be boiling vats and calciners—fifteen-foot-high furnaces used to produce caustic lime for sealant solutions.

"We'll build most of them atop the dragon's head for purposes of access," he said. "On the frontoparital plate." He checked some figures. "By my reckoning, the plate's about 350 feet wide. Does that sound accurate?"

Most of the city fathers were stunned by the prospect, but one managed a nod, and another asked, "How long will it take for him to die?"

"Hard to say," came the answer. "Who knows how much poison he's capable of absorbing. It might just take a few years. But in the worst instance, within forty or fifty years, enough chemicals will have seeped through the scales to have weakened the skeleton, and he'll fall in like an old barn."

"Forty years!" exclaimed someone. "Preposterous!"

"Or fifty." Meric smiled. "That way we'll have time to finish the painting." He turned and walked to the window and stood gazing out at the white stone houses of Teocinte. This was going to be the sticky part, but if he read them right, they would not believe in the plan if it seemed too easy. They needed to feel they were making a sacrifice, that they were nobly bound to a great labor. "If it does take forty or fifty years," he went on, "the project will drain your resources. Timber, animal life, minerals. Everything will be used up by the work. Your lives will be totally changed. But I guarantee you'll be rid of him."

The city fathers broke into an outraged babble.

"Do you really want to kill him?" cried Meric, stalking over to them and planting his fists on the table. "You've been waiting centuries for someone to come along and chop off his head or send him up in a puff of smoke. That's not going to happen! There is no easy solution. But there is a practical one, an elegant one. To use the stuff of the land he dominates to destroy him. It will *not* be easy, but you *will* be rid of him. And that's what you want, isn't it?"

They were silent, exchanging glances, and he saw that they now believed he could do what he proposed and were wondering if the cost was too high.

"I'll need 500 ounces of silver to hire engineers and artisans," said Meric. "Think it over. I'll take a few days and go see this dragon of yours… inspect the scales and so forth. When I return, you can give me your answer."

The city fathers grumbled and scratched their heads, but at last they agreed to put the question before the body politic. They asked for a week in which to decide and appointed Jarcke, who was the mayoress of Hangtown, to guide Meric to Griaule.

The valley extended seventy miles from north to south, and was enclosed by jungle hills whose folded sides and spiny backs gave rise to the idea that beasts were sleeping beneath them. The valley floor was cultivated into fields of bananas and cane and melons, and where it was not cultivated there were stands of thistle palms and berry thickets and the occasional giant fig brooding sentinel over the rest. Jarcke and Meric tethered their horses a half-hour's ride from town and began to ascend a gentle incline that rose into the notch between two hills. Sweaty and short of breath, Meric stopped a third of the way up; but Jarcke kept plodding along, unaware he was no longer following. She was by nature as blunt as her name—a stump beer keg of a woman with a brown, weathered face. Though she appeared to be ten years older than Meric, she was nearly the same age. She wore a grey robe belted at the waist with a leather band that held four throwing knives, and a coil of rope was slung over her shoulder.

"How much further?" called Meric.

She turned and frowned. "You're standin' on his tail. Rest of him's around back of the hill."

A pinprick of chill bloomed in Meric's abdomen, and he stared down at the grass, expecting it to dissolve and reveal a mass of glittering scales.

"Why don't we take the horses?" he asked.

"Horses don't like it up here." She grunted with amusement. "Neither do most people, for that matter." She trudged off.

Another twenty minutes brought them to the other side of the hill high above the valley floor. The land continued to slope upwards, but more gently than before. Gnarled, stunted oaks pushed up from thickets of chokecherry, and insects sizzled in the weeds. They might have been walking on a natural shelf several hundred feet across; but ahead of them, where the ground rose abruptly, a number of thick, greenish-black columns broke from the earth. Leathery folds hung between them, and these were encrusted with clumps of earth and brocaded with mold. They had the look of a collapsed palisade and the ghosted feel of ancient ruins.

"Them's the wings," said Jarcke. "Mostly they's covered, but you can catch sight of 'em off the edge, and up near Hangtown there's places where you can walk in under 'em... but I wouldn't advise it."

"I'd like to take a look off the edge," said Meric, unable to tear his eyes away from the wings; though the surfaces of the leaves gleamed in the strong sun, the wings seemed to absorb the light, as if their age and strangeness were proof against reflection.

Jarcke led him to a glade in which tree ferns and oaks crowded together and cast a green gloom, and where the earth sloped sharply downwards. She lashed her rope to an oak and tied the other end around Meric's waist. "Give a yank when you want to stop, and another when you want to be hauled up," she said, and began paying out the rope, letting him walk backwards against her pull.

Ferns tickled Meric's neck as he pushed through the brush, and the oak leaves pricked his cheeks. Suddenly he emerged into bright sunlight. On looking down, he found his feet were braced against a fold of the dragon's wing, and on looking up, he saw that the wing vanished beneath a mantle of earth and vegetation. He let Jarcke lower him a dozen feet more, yanked, and gazed off northwards along the enormous swell of Griaule's side.

The swells were hexagonals thirty feet across and half that distance high; their basic color was a pale greenish gold, but some were whitish, draped with peels of dead skin, and others were over-grown by viridian moss, and the rest were scrolled with patterns of lichen and algae that resembled the characters of a serpentine alphabet. Birds had nested in the cracks, and ferns plumed from the interstices, thousands of them lifting in the breeze. It was a great hanging garden whose scope took Meric's breath away—like looking around the curve of a fossil moon. The sense of all the centuries accreted in the scales made him *dizzy*, and he found he could not turn his head, but could only stare at the panorama, his soul shrivelling with a comprehension of the timelessness and bulk of this creature to which he clung like a fly. He lost perspective on the scene—Griaule's side was bigger than the sky, possessing its own potent gravity, and it seemed completely reasonable that he should be able to walk out along it and suffer no fall. He started to do so, and Jarcke, mistaking the strain on the rope for signal, hauled him up, dragging him across the wing, through the dirt and ferns, and back into the glade. He lay speechless and gasping at her feet.

"Big 'un, ain't he," she said, and grinned. After Meric had got his legs under him, they set off towards Hangtown; but they had not gone 100 yards, following a trail that wound through the thickets, before Jarcke whipped out a knife and hurled it at a raccoon-sized creature that leaped out in front of them.

"Skizzer," she said, kneeling beside it and pulling the knife from its neck. "Calls 'em that 'cause they hisses when they runs. They eats snakes, but they'll go after children what ain't careful." Meric dropped down next to her. The skizzer's body was covered with short black fur, but its head was hairless, corpse-pale, the skin wrinkled as if it had been immersed too long in water. Its face was squinty-eyed, flat-nosed, with a disproportionately large jaw that hinged open to expose a nasty set of teeth. "They's the dragon's critters," said Jarcke. "Used to live in his bunghole." She pressed one of its paws, and claws curved like hooks slid forth. "They'd hang around the lip and drop on other critters what wandered in. And if nothin' wandered in…" She pried out the tongue with her knife—its surface was studded with jagged points like the blade of a rasp. "Then they'd lick Griaule clean for their supper."

Back in Teocinte, the dragon had seemed to Meric a simple thing, a big lizard with a tick of life left inside, the residue of a dim sensibility; but he was beginning to suspect that this tick of life was more complex than any he had encountered.

"My gram used to say," Jarcke went on, "that the old dragons could fling themselves up to the sun in a blink and travel back to their own world, and when they come back, they'd bring the skizzers and all the rest with 'em. They was immortal, she said. Only the young ones came here 'cause later on they grew too big to fly on earth." She made a sour face. "Don't know as I believe it."

"Then you're a fool," said Meric.

Jarcke glanced up at him, her hand twitching towards her belt.

"How can you live here and *not* believe it!" he said, surprised to hear himself so fervently defending a myth. "God! This—" He broke off, noticing the flicker of a smile on her face.

She clucked her tongue, apparently satisfied by something. "Come on," she said. "I want to be at the eye before sunset."

The peaks of Griaule's folded wings, completely overgrown by grass and shrubs and dwarfish trees, formed two spiny hills that cast a shadow over Hangtown and the narrow lake around which it sprawled. Jarcke said the lake was a stream flowing off the hill behind the dragon, and that it drained away through the membranes of his wing and down on to his shoulder. It was beautiful beneath the wing, she told him. Ferns and waterfalls. But it was reckoned an evil place. From a distance the town looked picturesque—rustic cabins, smoking chimneys. As they approached, however, the cabins resolved into dilapidated shanties with missing boards and broken windows; suds and garbage and offal floated in the shallows of the lake. Aside from a few men idling on the stoops, who squinted at Meric and nodded glumly at Jarcke, no one was about. The grass blades stirred in the breeze, spiders scuttled under the shanties, and there was an air of torpor and dissolution.

Jarcke seemed embarrassed by the town. She made no attempt at introductions, stopping only long enough to fetch another coil of rope from one of the shanties, and as they walked between the wings, down through the neck spines—a forest of greenish-gold spikes burnished by the lowering sun—she explained how the townsfolk grubbed a livelihood from Griaule. Herbs gathered on his back were valued as medicine and charms, as were the peels of dead skin; the artefacts left by previous Hangtown generations were of some worth to various collectors.

"Then there's scale hunters," she said with disgust. "Henry Sichi from Port Chantay'll pay good money for pieces of scale, and though it's bad luck to do it, some'll have a go at chippin' off the loose 'uns." She walked a few paces in silence. "But there's others who've got better reasons for livin' here."

The frontal spike above Griaule's eyes was whorled at the base like a narwhal's horn and curved back towards the wings. Jarcke attached the ropes to eyebolts drilled into the spike, tied one about her waist, the other about Meric's; she cautioned him to wait, and rappelled off the side. In a moment she called for him to come down. Once again he grew dizzy as he descended; he glimpsed a clawed foot far below, mossy fangs jutting from an impossibly long jaw; and then he began to spin and bash against the scales. Jarcke gathered him in and helped him sit on the lip of the socket.

"Damn!" she said, stamping her foot.

A three-foot-long section of the adjoining scale shifted slowly away. Peering close, Meric saw that while in texture and hue it was indistinguishable from the scale, there was a hairline division between it and the surface. Jarcke, her face twisted in disgust, continued to harry the thing until it moved out of reach.

"Call 'em flakes," she said when he asked what it was. "Some kind of insect. Got a long tube that they pokes down between the scales and sucks the blood. See there?" She pointed off to where a flock of birds were wheeling close to Griaule's side; a chip of pale gold broke loose and went tumbling down to the valley. "Birds pry 'em off, let 'em bust open, and eats the innards." She hunkered down beside him and after a moment asked, "You really think you can do it?"

"What? You mean kill the dragon?"

She nodded.

"Certainly," he said, and then added, lying, "I've spent years devising the method."

"If all the paint's goin' to be atop his head, how're you goin' to get it to where the paintin's done?"

"That's no problem. We'll pipe it to wherever it's needed."

She nodded again. "You're a clever fellow," she said; and when Meric, pleased, made as if to thank her for the compliment, she cut in and said, "Don't mean nothin' by it. Bein' clever ain't an accomplishment. It's just somethin' you come by, like bein' tall." She turned away, ending the conversation.

Meric was weary of being awestruck, but even so he could not help marvelling at the eye. By his estimate it was seventy feet long and fifty feet high, and it was shuttered by an opaque membrane that was unusually clear of algae and lichen, glistening, with vague glints of colour visible behind it. As the westering sun reddened and sank between two distant hills, the membrane began to quiver and then split open down the center. With the ponderous slowness of a theatre curtain opening, the halves slid apart to reveal the glowing humour. Terrified by the idea that Griaule could see him, Meric sprang to his feet, but Jarcke restrained him.

"Stay still and watch," she said.

He had no choice—the eye was mesmerizing. The pupil was slit and featureless black, but the humor… he had never seen such fiery blues and crimsons and golds. What had looked to be vague glints, odd refractions of the sunset, he now realized were photic reactions of some sort. Fairy rings of light developed deep within the eye, expanded into spoked shapes, flooded the humor, and faded—only to be replaced by another and another. He felt the pressure of Griaule's vision, his ancient mind, pouring through him, and as if in response to this pressure, memories bubbled up in his thoughts. Particularly sharp ones. The way a bowlful of brush water had looked after freezing over during a winter's night—a delicate, fractured flower of murky yellow. An archipelago of orange peels that his girl had left strewn across the floor of the studio. Sketching atop Jokenam Hill one sunrise, the snowcapped roofs of Regensburg below pitched at all angles like broken paving stones, and silver shafts of the sun striking down through a leaden overcast. It was as if these things were being drawn forth for his inspection. Then they were washed away by what also seemed a memory, though at the same time it was wholly unfamiliar. Essentially, it was a landscape of light, and he was plunging through it, up and up. Prisms and lattices of iridescent fire bloomed around him, and everything was a roaring fall into brightness, and finally he was clear into its white furnace heart, his own heart swelling with the joy of his strength and dominion.

It was dusk before Meric realized the eye had closed. His mouth hung open, his eyes ached from straining to see, and his tongue was glued to his palate. Jarcke sat motionless, buried in shadow.

"Th…" He had to swallow to clear his throat of mucus. "This is the reason you live here, isn't it?"

"Part of the reason," she said. "I can see things comin' way up here. Things to watch out for, things to study on."

She stood and walked to the lip of the socket and spat off the edge; the valley stretched out grey and unreal behind her, the folds of the hills barely visible in the gathering dusk.

"I seen you comin'," she said.

A week later, after much exploration, much talk, they went down into Teocinte. The town was a shambles—shattered windows, slogans painted on the walls, glass and torn banners and spoiled food littering the streets—as if there had been both a celebration and a battle. Which there had. The city fathers met with Meric in the town hall and informed him that his plan had been approved. They presented him a chest containing 500 ounces of silver and said that the entire resources of the community were at his disposal. They offered a wagon and a team to transport him and the chest to Regensburg and asked if any of the preliminary work could be begun during his absence.

Meric hefted one of the silver bars. In its cold gleam he saw the object of his desire; two, perhaps three years of freedom, of doing the work he wanted and not having to accept commissions. But all that had been confused. He glanced at Jarcke; she was staring out the window, leaving it to him. He set the bar back in the chest and shut the lid.

"You'll have to send someone else," he said. And then, as the city fathers looked at each other askance, he laughed and laughed at how easily he had discarded all his dreams and expectations.

…It had been eleven years since I had been to the valley, twelve since work had begun on the painting, and I was appalled by the changes that had taken place. Many of the hills were scraped brown and treeless, and there was a general dearth of wildlife. Griaule, of course, was most changed. Scaffolding hung from his back; artisans, suspended by webworks of ropes, crawled over his side; and all the scales to be worked had either been painted or primed. The tower rising to his eye was swarmed by laborers, and at night the calciners and vats atop his head belched flame into the sky, making it seem there was a mill town in the heavens. At his feet was a brawling shantytown populated by prostitutes, workers, gamblers, ne'er-do-wells of every sort, and soldiers: the burdensome cost of the project had encouraged the city fathers of Teocinte to form a regular militia, which regularly plundered the adjoining states and had posted occupation forces to some areas. Herds of frightened animals milled in the slaughtering pens, waiting to be rendered into oils and pigments. Wagons filled with ores and vegetable products rattled in the streets. I myself had brought a cargo of madder roots from which a rose tint would be derived.

It was not easy to arrange a meeting with Cattanay. While he did none of the actual painting, he was always busy in his office consulting with engineers and artisans, or involved in some other part of the logistical process. When at last I did meet with him, I found he had changed as drastically as Griaule. His hair had gone grey, deep lines scored his features, and his right shoulder had a peculiar bulge at its mid-point—the product of a fall. He was amused by the fact that I wanted to buy the painting, to collect the scales after Griaule's death, and I do not believe he took me at all seriously. But the woman Jarcke, his constant companion, informed him that I was a responsible businessman, that I had already bought the bones, the teeth, even the dirt beneath Griaule's belly (this I eventually sold as having magical properties).

"Well," said Cattanay, "I suppose someone has to own them."

He led me outside, and we stood looking at the painting.

"You'll keep them together?" he asked.

I said, "Yes."

"If you'll put that in writing," he said, "then they're yours."

Having expected to haggle long and hard over the price, I was flabbergasted; but I was even more flabbergasted by what he said next.

"Do you think it's any good?" he asked.

Cattanay did not consider the painting to be the work of *his* imagination; he felt he was simply illuminating the shapes that appeared on Griaule's side and was convinced that once the paint was applied, new shapes were produced beneath it, causing him to make constant changes. He saw himself as an artisan more than a creative artist. But to put his question into perspective, people were beginning to flock from all over the world and marvel at the painting. Some claimed they saw intimations of the future in its gleaming surface; others underwent transfiguring experiences; still others—artists themselves—attempted to capture something of the work on canvas, hopeful of establishing reputations merely by being competent copyists of Cattanay's art. The painting was nonrepresentational in character, essentially a wash of pale gold spread across the dragon's side; but buried beneath the laminated surface were a myriad tints of iridescent colour that, as the sun passed through the heavens and the light bloomed and faded, solidified into innumerable forms and figures that seemed to flow back and forth. I will not try to categorize these forms, because there was no end to them; they were as varied as the conditions under which they were viewed. But I will say that on the morning I met with Cattanay, I—who was the soul of the practical man, without a visionary bone in my body—felt as though I were being whirled away into the painting, up through geometries of light, latticeworks of rainbow color that built the way the edges of a cloud build, past orbs, spirals, wheels of flame…"

—from *This Business of Griaule* by Henry Sichi

2

There had been several women in Meric's life since he arrived in the valley; most had been attracted by his growing fame and his association with the mystery of the dragon, and most had left him for the same reasons, feeling daunted and unappreciated. But Lise was different in two respects. First, because she loved Meric truly and well; and second, because she was married—albeit un-happily—to a man named Pardiel, the foreman of the calciner crew. She did not love him as she did Meric, yet she respected him and felt obliged to con-sider carefully before ending the relationship. Meric had never known such an introspective soul. She was twelve years younger than he, tall and lovely, with sun-streaked hair and brown eyes that went dark and seemed to turn inward whenever she was pensive. She was in the habit of analysing everything that af-fected her, drawing back from her emotions and inspecting them as if they were a clutch of strange insects she had discovered crawling on her skirt. Though her penchant for self-examination kept her from him, Meric viewed it as a kind of baffling virtue. He had the classic malady and could find no fault with her. For almost a year they were as happy as could be expected; they talked long hours and walked together, and on those occasions when Pardiel worked double shifts and was forced to bed down by his furnaces, they spent the nights making love in the cavernous spaces beneath the dragon's wing.

It was still reckoned an evil place. Something far worse than skizzers or flakes was rumored to live there, and the ravages of this creature were blamed for every disappearance, even that of the most malcontented laborer. But Meric did not give credence to the rumors. He half believed Griaule had chosen him to be his executioner and that the dragon would never let him be harmed; and besides, it was the only place where they could be assured of privacy.

A crude stair led under the wing, handholds and steps hacked from the scales—doubtless the work of scale hunters. It was a treacherous passage, 600 feet above the valley floor; but Lise and Meric were secured by ropes, and over the months, driven by the urgency of passion, they adapted to it. Their favorite spot lay fifty feet in (Lise would go no further; she was afraid even if he was not), near a waterfall that trickled over the leathery folds, causing them to glisten with a mineral brilliance. It was eerily beautiful, a haunted gallery. Peels of dead skin hung down from the shadows like torn veils of ectoplasm; ferns sprouted from the vanes, which were thicker than cathedral columns; swallows curved through the black air. Sometimes, lying with her hidden by a tuck of the wing, Meric would think the beating of their hearts was what really animated the place, that the instant they left, the water ceased flowing and the swallows vanished. He had an unshakable faith in the transforming power of their affections, and one morning as they dressed, preparing to return to Hangtown, he asked her to leave with him.

"To another part of the valley?" She laughed sadly. "What good would that do? Pardiel would follow us."

"No," he said. "To another country. Anywhere far from here."

"We can't," she said, kicking at the wing. "Not until Griaule dies. Have you forgotten?"

"We haven't tried."

"Others have."

"But we'd be strong enough. I know it!"

"You're a romantic," she said gloomily, and stared out over the slope of Griaule's back at the valley. Sunrise had washed the hills to crimson, and even the tips of the wings were glowing a dull red.

"Of course I'm a romantic!" He stood, angry. "What the hell's wrong with that?"

She sighed with exasperation. "You wouldn't leave your work," she said. "And if we did leave, what work would you do? Would—"

"Why must everything be a problem in advance!" he shouted. "I'll tattoo elephants! I'll paint murals on the chests of giants, I'll illuminate whales! Who else is better qualified?"

She smiled, and his anger evaporated.

"I didn't mean it that way," she said. "I just wondered if you could be satisfied with anything else."

She reached out her hand to be pulled up, and he drew her into an embrace. As he held her, inhaling the scent of vanilla water from her hair, he saw a diminutive figure silhouetted against the backdrop of the valley. It did not seem real—a black homunculus—and even when it began to come forward, growing larger and larger, it looked less a man than a magical keyhole opening in a crimson set hillside. But Meric knew from the man's rolling walk and the hulking set of his shoulders that it was Pardiel; he was carrying a long-handled hook, one of those used by artisans to manoeuvre along the scales.

Meric tensed, and Lise looked back to see what had alarmed him. "Oh, my God!" she said, moving out of the embrace.

Pardiel stopped a dozen feet away. He said nothing. His face was in shadow, and the hook swung lazily from his hand. Lise took a step towards him, then stepped back and stood in front of Meric as if to shield him. Seeing this, Pardiel let out an inarticulate yell and charged, slashing with the hook. Meric pushed Lise aside and ducked. He caught a brimstone whiff of the calciners as Pardiel rushed past and went sprawling, tripped by some irregularity in the scale. Deathly afraid, knowing he was no match for the foreman, Meric seized Lise's hand and ran deeper under the wing. He hoped Pardiel would be too frightened to follow, leery of the creature that was rumored to live there; but he was not.

He came after them at a measured pace, tapping the hook against his leg.

Higher on Griaule's back, the wing was dimpled downwards by hundreds of bulges, and this created a maze of small chambers and tunnels so low that they had to crouch to pass along them. The sound of their breathing and the scrape of their feet were amplified by the enclosed spaces, and Meric could no longer hear Pardiel. He had never been this deep before. He had thought it would be pitch-dark; but the lichen and algae adhering to the wing were luminescent and patterned every surface, even the scales beneath them, with whorls of blue and green fire that shed a sickly radiance. It was as if they were giants crawling through a universe whose starry matter had not yet congealed into galaxies and nebulas. In the wan light, Lise's face—turned back to him now and again—was teary and frantic; and then, as she straightened, passing into still another chamber, she drew in breath with a shriek.

At first Meric thought Pardiel had somehow managed to get ahead of them; but on entering he saw that the cause of her fright was a man propped in a sitting position against the far wall. He looked mummified. Wisps of brittle hair poked up from his scalp, the shapes of his bones were visible through his skin, and his eyes were empty holes. Between his legs was a scatter of dust where his genitals had been. Meric pushed Lise towards the next tunnel, but she resisted and pointed at the man.

"His eyes," she said, horror-struck.

Though the eyes were mostly a negative black, Meric now realized they were shot through by opalescent flickers. He felt compelled to kneel beside the man; it was a sudden, motiveless urge that gripped him, bent him to its will, and released him a second later. As he rested his hand on the scale, he brushed a massive ring that was lying beneath the shrunken fingers. Its stone was black, shot through by flickers identical to those within the eyes, and incised with the letter S. He found his gaze was deflected away from both the stone and the eyes, as if they contained charges repellent to the senses. He touched the man's withered arm; the flesh was rock-hard, petrified. But alive. From that brief touch he gained an impression of the man's life, of gazing for centuries at the same patch of unearthly fire, of a mind gone beyond mere madness into a perverse rapture, a meditation upon some foul principle. He snatched back his hand in revulsion.

There was a noise behind them, and Meric jumped up, pushing Lise into the next tunnel. "Go right," he whispered. "We'll circle back towards the stair." But Pardiel was too close to confuse with such tactics, and their flight became a wild chase, scrambling, falling, catching glimpses of Pardiel's smoke-stained face, until finally—as Meric came to a large chamber—he felt the hook bite into his thigh. He went down, clutching at the wound, pulling the hook loose. The next moment Pardiel was atop him; Lise appeared over his shoulder, but he knocked her away and locked his fingers in Meric's hair and smashed his head against the scale. Lise screamed, and white lights fired through Meric's skull. Again his head was smashed down. And again. Dimly, he saw Lise struggling with Pardiel, saw her shoved away, saw the hook raised high and the foreman's mouth distorted by a grimace. Then the grimace vanished. His jaw dropped open and he reached behind him as if to scratch his shoulder blade. A line of dark blood eeled from his mouth and he collapsed, smothering Meric beneath his chest. Meric heard voices. He tried to dislodge the body, and the effects drained the last of his strength. He whirled down through a blackness that seemed as negative and inexhaustible as the petrified man's eyes.

Someone had propped his head on their lap and was bathing his brow with a damp cloth. He assumed it was Lise, but when he asked what had happened, it was Jarcke who answered, saying, "Had to kill him." His head throbbed, his leg throbbed even worse, and his eyes would not focus. The peels of dead skin hanging overhead appeared to be writhing. He realized they were out near the edge of the wing.

"Where's Lise?"

"Don't worry," said Jarcke. "You'll see her again." She made it sound like an indictment.

"Where is she?"

"Sent her back to Hangtown. Won't do you two bein' seen hand in hand the same day Pardiel's missin'."

"She wouldn't have left..." He blinked, trying to see her face; the lines around her mouth were etched deep and reminded him of the patterns of lichen on the dragon's scale. "What did you do?"

"Convinced her it was best," said Jarcke. "Don' you know she's just foolin' with you?"

"I've got to talk with her." He was full of remorse, and it was unthinkable that Lise should be bearing her grief alone; but when he struggled to rise, pain lanced through his leg.

"You wouldn't get ten feet," she said. "Soon as your head's clear, I'll help you with the stairs."

He closed his eyes, resolving to find Lise the instant he got back to Hangtown; together they would decide what to do. The scale beneath him was cool, and that coolness was transmitted to his skin, his flesh, as if he were merging with it, becoming one of its ridges.

"What was the wizard's name?" he asked after a while, recalling the petrified man, the ring and its incised letter. "The one who tried to kill Griaule..."

"Don't know as I ever heard it," said Jarcke. "But I reckon it's him back there."

"You saw him?"

"I was chasin' a scale hunter once what stole some rope, and I found him instead. Pretty miserable sort, whoever he is."

Her fingers trailed over his shoulder—a gentle, treasuring touch. He did not understand what it signalled, being too concerned with Lise, with the terrifying potentials of all that had happened; but years later, after things had passed beyond remedy, he cursed himself for not having understood.

At length Jarcke helped him to his feet, and they climbed up to Hangtown, to bitter realizations and regrets, leaving Pardiel to the birds or the weather or worse.

…It seems it is considered irreligious for a woman in love to hesitate or examine the situation, to do anything other than blindly follow the impulse of her emotions. I felt the brunt of such an attitude—people judged it my fault for not having acted quickly and decisively one way or another. Perhaps I was overcautious. I do not claim to be free of blame, only innocent of sacrilege. I believe I might have eventually left Pardiel—there was not enough in the relationship to sustain happiness for either of us. But I had good reason for cautious examination. My husband was not an evil man, and there were matters of loyalty between us.

I could not face Meric after Pardiel's death, and I moved to another part of the valley. He tried to see me on many occasions, but I always refused. Though I was greatly tempted, my guilt was greater. Four years later, after Jarcke died—crushed by a runaway wagon—one of her associates wrote and told me Jarcke had been in love with Meric, that it had been she who had informed Pardiel of the affair, and that she may well have staged the murder. The letter acted somewhat to expiate my guilt, and I weighed the possibility of seeing Meric again. But too much time had passed, and we had both assumed other lives. I decided against it. Six years later, when Griaule's influence had weakened sufficiently to allow emigration, I moved to Port Chantay. I did not hear from Meric for almost twenty years after that, and then one day I received a letter, which I will reproduce in part.

"My old friend from Regensburg, Louis Dardano, has been living here for the past few years, engaged in writing my biography. The narrative has a breezy feel, like a tale being told in a tavern, which—if you recall my telling you how this all began—is quite appropriate. But on reading it, I am *amazed* my life has had such a simple shape. One task, one passion. God, Lise! Seventy years old, and I still dream of you. And I still think of what happened that morning under the wing. Strange, that it has taken me all this time to realize it was not Jarcke, not you or I who were culpable, but Griaule. How obvious it seems now. I was leaving, and he needed me to complete the expression on his side, his dream of flying, of escape, to grant him the death of his desire. I am certain you will think I have leaped to this assumption, but I remind you that it has been a leap of forty years' duration. I know Griaule, know his monstrous subtlety. I can see it at work in every action that has taken place in the valley since my arrival. I was a fool not to understand that his powers were at the heart of our sad conclusion.

"The army now runs everything here, as no doubt you are aware. It is rumored they are planning a winter campaign against Regensburg. Can you believe it! Their fathers were ignorant, but this generation is brutally stupid. Otherwise, the work goes well and things are as usual with me. My shoulder aches, children stare at me on the street, and it is whispered I am mad…"

—from *Under Griaule's Wing* by Lise Claverie

3

Acne-scarred, lean, arrogant, Major Hauk was a very young major with a limp. When Meric had entered, the major had been practising his signature; it was a thing of elegant loops and flourishes, obviously intended to have a place in posterity. As he strode back and forth during their conversation, he paused frequently to admire himself in the window glass, settling the hang of his red jacket or running his fingers along the crease of his white trousers. It was the new style of uniform, the first Meric had seen at close range, and he noted with amusement the dragons embossed on the epaulets. He wondered if Griaule was capable of such an irony, if his influence was sufficiently discreet to have planted the idea for this comic opera apparel in the brain of some general's wife.

"… not a question of manpower," the major was saying, "but of —" He broke off, and after a moment cleared his throat.

Meric, who had been studying the blotches on the backs of his hands, glanced up; the cane that had been resting against his knee slipped and clattered to the floor.

"A question *of matériel*" said the major firmly. "The price of antimony, for example…"

"Hardly use it any more," said Meric. "I'm almost done with the mineral reds."

A look of impatience crossed the major's face. "Very well," he said; he stooped to his desk and shuffled through some papers. "Ah! Here's a bill for a shipment of cuttlefish from which you derive…" He shuffled more papers.

"Syrian brown," said Meric gruffly. "I'm done with that, too. Golds and violets are all I need any more. A little blue and rose." He wished the man would stop badgering him; he wanted to be at the eye before sunset.

As the major continued his accounting, Meric's gaze wandered out the window. The shantytown surrounding Griaule had swelled into a city and now sprawled across the hills. Most of the buildings were permanent, wood and stone, and the cant of the roofs, the smoke from the factories around the perimeter, put him in mind of Regensburg. All the natural beauty of the land had been drained into the painting. Blackish grey rain clouds were muscling up from the east, but the afternoon sun shone clear and shed a heavy gold radiance on Griaule's side. It looked as if the sunlight were an extension of the gleaming resins, as if the thickness of the paint were becoming infinite. He let the major's voice recede to a buzz and followed the scatter and dazzle of the images; and then, with a start, he realized the major was sounding him out about stopping the work.

The idea panicked him at first. He tried to interrupt, to raise objections; but the major talked through him, and as Meric thought it over, he grew less and less opposed. The painting would never be finished, and he was tired. Perhaps it was time to have done with it, to accept a university post somewhere and enjoy life for a while.

"We've been thinking about a temporary stoppage," said Major Hauk. "Then if the winter campaign goes well…" He smiled. "If we're not visited by plague and pestilence, we'll assume things are in hand. Of course we'd like your opinion."

Meric felt a surge of anger towards this smug little monster. "In my opinion, you people are idiots," he said. "You wear Griaule's image on your shoulders, weave him on your flags, and yet you don't have the least comprehension of what that means. You think it's just a useful symbol…"

"Excuse me," said the major stiffly.

"The hell I will!" Meric groped for his cane and heaved up to his feet. "You see yourselves as conquerors. Shapers of destiny. But all your rapes and slaughters are Griaule's expressions. *His* will. You're every bit as much his parasites as the skizzers."

The major sat, picked up a pen, and began to write.

"It astounds me," Meric went on, "that you can live next to a miracle, a source of mystery, and treat him as if he were an oddly shaped rock."

The major kept writing.

"What are you doing?" asked Meric.

"My recommendation," said the major without looking up.

"Which is?"

"That we initiate stoppage at once."

They exchanged hostile stares, and Meric turned to leave; but as he took hold of the doorknob, the major spoke again.

"We owe you so much," he said; he wore an expression of mingled pity and respect that further irritated Meric.

"How many men have you killed, Major?" he asked, opening the door.

"I'm not sure. I was in the artillery. We were never able to be sure."

"Well, I'm sure of my tally," said Meric. "It's taken me forty years to amass it. Fifteen hundred and ninety-three men and women. Poisoned, scalded, broken by falls, savaged by animals. Murdered. Why don't we—you and I—just call it even."

Though it was a sultry afternoon, he felt cold as he walked towards the tower—an internal cold that left him light-headed and weak. He tried to think what he would do. The idea of a university post seemed less appealing away from the major's office; he would soon grow weary of worshipful students and in-depth dissections of his work by jealous academics. A man hailed him as he turned into the market. Meric waved but did not stop, and heard another man say, "*That's* Cattanay?" (That ragged old ruin?)

The colors of the market were too bright, the smells of charcoal cookery too cloying, the crowds too thick, and he made for the side streets, hobbling past one-room stucco houses and tiny stores where they sold cooking oil by the ounce and cut cigars in half if you could not afford a whole one. Garbage, tornados of dust and flies, drunks with bloody mouths. Somebody had tied wires around a pariah dog—a bitch with slack teats; the wires had sliced into her flesh, and she lay panting in an alley mouth, gaunt ribs flecked with pink lather, gazing into nowhere. She, thought Meric, and not Griaule, should be the symbol of their flag.

As he rode the hoist up the side of the tower, he fell into his old habit of jotting down notes for the next day. *What's that cord of wood doing on level five? Slow leak of chrome yellow from pipes on level twelve.* Only when he saw a man dismantling some scaffolding did he recall Major Hauk's recommendation and understand that the order must already have been given. The loss of his work struck home to him then, and he leaned against the railing, his chest constricted and his eyes brimming. He straightened, ashamed of himself. The sun hung in a haze of iron-colored light low above the western hills, looking red and bloated and vile as a vulture's ruff. That polluted sky was his creation as much as was the painting, and it would be good to leave it behind. Once away from the valley, from all the influences of the place, he would be able to consider the future.

A young girl was sitting on the twentieth level just beneath the eye. Years before, the ritual of viewing the eye had grown to cultish proportions; there had been group chanting and praying and discussions of the experience. But these were more practical times, and no doubt the young men and women who had congregated here were now manning administrative desks somewhere in the burgeoning empire. They were the ones about whom Dardano should write; they, and all the eccentric characters who had played roles in this slow pageant. The gypsy woman who had danced every night by the eye, hoping to charm Griaule into killing her faithless lover—she had gone away satisfied. The man who had tried to extract one of the fangs—nobody knew what had become of him. The scale hunters, the artisans. A history of Hangtown would be a volume in itself.

The walk had left Meric weak and breathless; he sat down clumsily beside the girl, who smiled. He could not remember her name, but she came often to the eye. Small and dark, with an inner reserve that reminded him of Lise. He laughed inwardly—most women reminded him of Lise in some way.

"Are you all right?" she asked, her brow wrinkled with concern.

"Oh, yes," he said; he felt a need for conversation to take his mind off things, but he could think of nothing more to say. She was so young! All freshness and gleam and nerves.

"This will be my last time," she said. "At least for a while. I'll miss it." And then, before he could ask why, she added, "I'm getting married tomorrow, and we're moving away."

He offered congratulations and asked her who was the lucky fellow.

"Just a boy." She tossed her hair, as if to dismiss the boy's importance; she gazed up at the shuttered membrane. "What's it like for you when the eye opens?" she asked.

"Like everyone else," he said. "I remember… memories of my life. Other lives, too." He did not tell her about Griaule's memory of flight; he had never told anyone except Lise about that.

"All those bits of souls trapped in there," she said, gesturing at the eye. "What do they mean to him? Why does he show them to us?"

"I imagine he has his purposes, but I can't explain them."

"Once I remembered being with you," said the girl, peeking at him shyly through a dark curl. "We were under the wing."

He glanced at her sharply. "Tell me."

"We were… together," she said, blushing. "Intimate, you know. I was very afraid of the place, of the sounds and shadows. But I loved you so much, it didn't matter. We made love all night, and I was surprised because I thought that kind of passion was just in stories, something people had invented to make up for how ordinary it really was. And in the morning even that dreadful place had become beautiful, with the wing tips glowing red and the waterfall echoing…" She lowered her eyes. "Ever since I had that memory, I've been a little in love with you."

"Lise," he said, feeling helpless before her.

"Was that her name?"

He nodded and put a hand to his brow, trying to pinch back the emotions that flooded him.

"I'm sorry." Her lips grazed his cheek, and just that slight touch seemed to weaken him further. "I wanted to tell you how she felt in case she hadn't told you yourself. She was very troubled by something, and I wasn't sure she had."

She shifted away from him, made uncomfortable by the intensity of his reaction, and they sat without speaking. Meric became lost in watching how the sun glazed the scales to reddish gold, how the light was channelled along the ridges in molten streams that paled as the day wound down. He was startled when the girl jumped to her feet and backed towards the hoist.

"He's dead," she said wonderingly.

Meric looked at her, uncomprehending.

"See?" She pointed at the sun, which showed a crimson sliver above the hill. "He's dead," she repeated, and the expression on her face flowed between fear and exultation.

The idea of Griaule's death was too large for Meric's mind to encompass, and he turned to the eye to find a counterproof—no glints of color flickered beneath the membrane. He heard the hoist creak as the girl headed down, but he continued to wait. Perhaps only the dragon's vision had failed. No. It was likely not a coincidence that work had been officially terminated today. Stunned, he sat staring at the lifeless membrane until the sun sank below the hills; then he stood and went over to the hoist. Before he could throw the switch, the cables thrummed—somebody heading up. Of course. The girl would have spread the news, and all the Major Hauks and their underlings would be hurrying to test Griaule's reflexes. He did not want to be here when they arrived, to watch them pose with their trophy like successful fishermen.

It was hard work climbing up to the frontoparietal plate. The ladder swayed, the wind buffeted him, and by the time he clambered on to the plate, he was giddy, his chest full of twinges. He hobbled forward and leaned against the rust-caked side of a boiling vat. Shadowy in the twilight, the great furnaces and vats towered around him, and it seemed this system of fiery devices reeking of cooked flesh and minerals was the actual machinery of Griaule's thought materialized above his skull. Energyless, abandoned. They had been replaced by more efficient equipment down below, and it had been—what was it?—almost five years since they were last used. Cobwebs veiled a pyramid of firewood; the stairs leading to the rims of the vats were crumbling. The plate itself was scarred and coated with sludge.

"Cattanay!"

Someone shouted from below, and the top of the ladder trembled. God, they were coming after him! Bubbling over with congratulations and plans for testimonial dinners, memorial plaques, specially struck medals. They would have him draped in bunting and bronzed and covered with pigeon shit before they were done. All these years he had been among them, both their slave and their master, yet he had never felt at home. Leaning heavily on his cane, he made his way past the frontal spike—blackened by years of oily smoke—and down between the wings to Hangtown. It was a ghost town, now. Weeds overgrowing the collapsed shanties; the lake a stinking pit, drained after some children had drowned in the summer of '91. Where Jarcke's home had stood was a huge pile of animal bones, taking a pale shine from the half-light. Wind keened through the tattered shrubs.

"Meric!" "Cattanay."

The voices were closer.

Well, there was one place where they would not follow.

The leaves of the thickets were speckled with mould and brittle, flaking away as he brushed them. He hesitated at the top of the scale hunters' stair. He had no rope. Though he had done the climb unaided many times, it had been quite a few years. The gusts of wind, the shouts, the sweep of the valley and the lights scattered across it like diamonds on grey velvet—it all seemed a single inconstant medium. He heard the brush crunch behind him, more voices. To hell with it! Gritting his teeth against a twinge of pain in his shoulder, hooking his cane over his belt, he inched on to the stair and locked his fingers in the handholds. The wind whipped his clothes and threatened to pry him loose and send him pinwheeling off. Once he slipped; once he froze, unable to move backward or forward. But at last he reached the bottom and edged upslope until he found a spot flat enough to stand.

The mystery of the place suddenly bore in upon him, and he was afraid. He half turned to the stair, thinking he would go back to Hangtown and accept the hurly-burly. But a moment later he realized how foolish a thought that was. Waves of weakness poured through him, his heart hammered, and white dazzles flared in his vision. His chest felt heavy as iron. Rattled, he went a few steps forward, the cane pocking the silence. It was too dark to see more than outlines, but up ahead was the fold of wing where he and Lise had sheltered. He walked towards it, intent on revisiting it; then he remembered the girl beneath the eye and understood that he had already said that good-bye. And it *was* good-bye—that he understood vividly. He kept walking. Blackness looked to be welling from the wing joint, from the entrances to the maze of luminous tunnels where they had stumbled on to the petrified man. Had it really been the old wizard, doomed by magical justice to molder and live on and on? It made sense. At least it accorded with what happened to wizards who slew their dragons.

"Griaule?" he whispered to the darkness, and cocked his head, half expecting an answer. The sound of his voice pointed up the immensity of the great gallery under the wing, the emptiness, and he recalled how vital a habitat it had once been. Flakes shifting over the surface, skizzers, peculiar insects fuming in the thickets, the glum populace of Hangtown, waterfalls. He had never been able to picture Griaule fully alive—that kind of vitality was beyond the powers of the imagination. Yet he wondered if by some miracle the dragon were alive now, flying up through his golden night to the sun's core. Or had that merely been a dream, a bit of tissue glittering deep in the cold tons of his brain? He laughed. Ask the stars for their first names, and you'd be more likely to receive a reply.

He decided not to walk any further; it was really no decision. Pain was spreading through his shoulder, so intense he imagined it must be glowing inside. Carefully, carefully, he lowered himself and lay propped on an elbow, hanging on to the cane. Good, magical wood. Cut from a hawthorn atop Griaule's haunch. A man had once offered him a small fortune for it. Who would claim it now? Probably old Henry Sichi would snatch it for his museum, stick it in a glass case next to his boots. What a joke! He decided to lie flat on his stomach, resting his chin on an arm—the stony coolness beneath acted to muffle the pain. Amusing, how the range of one's decision dwindled. You decided to paint a dragon, to send hundreds of men searching for malachite and cochineal beetles, to love a woman, to heighten an undertone here and there, and finally to position your body a certain way. He seemed to have reached the end of the process. What next? He tried to regulate his breathing, to ease the pressure on his chest. Then, as something rustled out near the wing joint, he turned on his side. He thought he detected movement, a gleaming blackness flowing towards him... or else it was only the haphazard firing of his nerves playing tricks with his vision. More surprised than afraid, wanting to see, he peered into the darkness and felt his heart beating erratically against the dragon's scale.

...It's foolish to draw simple conclusions from complex events, but I suppose there must be both moral and truth to this life, these events. I'll leave that to the gadflies. The historians, the social scientists, the expert apologists for reality. All I know is that he had a fight with his girlfriend over money and walked out. He sent her a letter saying he had gone south and would be back in a few months with more money than she could ever spend. I had no idea what he'd done. The whole thing about Griaule had just been a bunch of us sitting around the Red Bear, drinking up my pay—I'd sold an article—and somebody said, "Wouldn't it be great if Dardano didn't have to write articles, if we didn't have to paint pictures that color-co-ordinated with people's furniture or slave at getting the gooey smiles of little nieces and nephews just right?" All sorts of improbable moneymaking schemes were put forward. Robberies, kidnappings. Then the idea of swindling the city fathers of Teocinte came up, and the entire plan was fleshed out in minutes. Scribbled on napkins, scrawled on sketchpads. A group effort. I keep trying to remember if anyone got a glassy look in their eye, if I felt a cold tendril of Griaule's thought stirring my brains. But I can't. It was a half-hour's sensation, nothing more. A drunken whimsy, an art-school metaphor. Shortly thereafter, we ran out of money and staggered into the streets. It was snowing—big wet flakes that melted down our collars. God, we were drunk! Laughing, balancing on the icy railing of the University Bridge. Making faces at the bundled-up burghers and their fat ladies who huffed and puffed past, spouting steam and never giving us a glance, and none of us—not even the burghers—knowing that we were living our happy ending in advance..."

—from *The Man Who Painted The Dragon Griaule* by Louis Dardano

Copyright Acknowledgments

Night Shade Books Is an Independent Publisher of Quality SF, Fantasy and Horror

FEATURING STORIES BY
STEPHEN BAXTER
HOLLY BLACK
PAT CADIGAN
ANDY DUNCAN
ALEX IRVINE
DIANA WYNNE JONES
ELLEN KUSHNER
KELLY LINK
KAREN JOY FOWLER
BRUCE STERLING
ROBERT REED
GEOFF RYMAN
JO WALTON
AND MANY OTHERS

THE BEST
SCIENCE FICTION
AND FANTASY
OF THE YEAR
VOLUME FOUR

EDITED BY JONATHAN STRAHAN

ISBN 978-1-59780-171-3, Trade Paperback; $19.95

A ruthless venture capitalist finds love—or something chemically similar—in an Atlanta strip club; a girl in gray conjures a man from a handful of moonshine; a rebellious young woman suffers a strange incarceration; an astronaut shares a lifeboat—and herself—with an unfathomable alien; an infected girl counts the days until she becomes a vampire; a big man travels to a tiny moon to examine an ancient starship covered with flowers....

The depth and breadth of science fiction and fantasy fiction continues to change with every passing year. The twenty-nine stories chosen for this book by award-winning anthologist Jonathan Strahan carefully map this evolution, giving readers a captivating and always-entertaining look at the very best the genre has to offer.

Night Shade Books Is an Independent Publisher of Quality SF, Fantasy and Horror

STORIES OF THE DEVIL BY

ELIZABETH BEAR	KELLY LINK
HOLLY BLACK	CHINA MIÉVILLE
MICHAEL CHABON	CARRIE RICHERSON
CHARLES DE LINT	CHARLES STROSS
STEPHEN KING	SCOTT WESTERFELD

AND MANY OTHERS

Edited by Tim Pratt

ISBN 978-1-59780-189-8, Trade Paperback; $15.95

The Devil is known by many names: Serpent, Tempter, Beast, Adversary, Wanderer, Dragon, Rebel. No matter what face the devil wears, *Sympathy for the Devil* has them all. Edited by Tim Pratt (*Hart & Boot & Other Stories*), *Sympathy for the Devil* collects the best Satanic short stories by Neil Gaiman, Holly Black, Stephen King, Kage Baker, Charles Stross, Elizabeth Bear, Jay Lake, Kelly Link, China Miéville, Michael Chabon, and many others, revealing His Grand Infernal Majesty, in all his forms.

Thirty-five stories, from classics to the cutting edge, exploring the many sides of Satan, Lucifer, the Lord of the Flies, the Father of Lies, the Prince of the Powers of the Air and Darkness, the First of the Fallen... and a Man of Wealth and Taste. Sit down and spend a little time with the Devil.

Night Shade Books Is an Independent Publisher of Quality SF, Fantasy and Horror

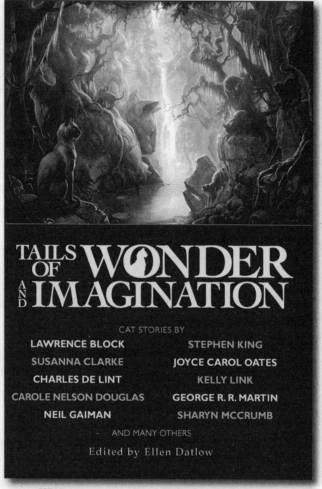

ISBN 978-1-59780-170-6, Trade Paperback; $15.95

What is it about the cat that captivates the creative imagination? No other creature has inspired so many authors to take pen to page. Mystery, horror, science fiction, and fantasy stories have all been written about cats.

From legendary editor Ellen Datlow comes *Tails of Wonder and Imagination*, showcasing forty cat tales by some of today's most popular authors. With uncollected stories by Stephen King, Tanith Lee, Peter S. Beagle, and Theodora Goss, and a previously unpublished story by Susanna Clarke, plus feline-centric fiction by Neil Gaiman, Kelly Link, George R. R. Martin, Lucius Shepard, Joyce Carol Oates, Graham Joyce, and many others.

Tails of Wonder and Imagination features more than 200,000 words of stories in which cats are heroes and stories in which they're villains; people transformed into cats, cats transformed into people. And yes, even a few cute cats.